**Three intriguing love stories
from Harlequin's famed Romance Library
by a favorite author, Catherine Airlie**

One Summer's Day... When Aunt Betsy
returned to Scotland after years abroad she
included the delighted Ailsa in her plans to buy
an island. However, Huntley MacLaren was very
reluctant to sell his five-hundred-year-old family
home, and Ailsa couldn't help but sympathize!
(#1062)

Passing Strangers... Jane Lambert had loved
Felipe, but her sister, Grace, had taken him away.
Now Grace was dead, leaving behind two small
children, and Felipe requested Jane to come to
Teneriffe. After all these years, would their love
be rekindled? (#1081)

Red Lotus... Alone in the world, Felicity
accepted her uncle's summons to the Canary
Islands where he claimed he needed her. But just
before her arrival he died. What was expected of
her now in this household of contentious
strangers who despised the estate manager,
Philip Arnold? (#1170)

**Another collection
of Romance favorites...
by a best-selling Harlequin author!**

In the pages of this specially selected
anthology are three delightfully
absorbing Romances—all by an
author whose vast readership all over
the world has shown her to be an
outstanding favorite.

For those of you who are missing
these love stories from your
Harlequin library shelf, or who wish
to collect great romance fiction by
favorite authors, these Harlequin
Romance anthologies are for you.

We're sure you'll enjoy each of the
engrossing and heartwarming stories
contained within. They're treasures
from our library... and we know
they'll become treasured additions
to yours!

The second anthology of 3 Harlequin Romances by

Catherine Airlie

Harlequin Books

TORONTO • NEW YORK • LONDON
AMSTERDAM • PARIS • SYDNEY • HAMBURG
STOCKHOLM • ATHENS • TOKYO • MILAN

Harlequin Romance anthology 80

Copyright © 1977 by Harlequin Enterprises Limited. Philippine copyright 1984. Australian copyright 1984. All rights reserved. Except for use in any review, the reproduction or utilization of this work in whole or in part in any form by any electronic, mechanical or other means, now known or hereafter invented, including xerography, photocopying and recording, or in any information storage or retrieval system, is forbidden without the permission of the publisher, Harlequin Enterprises Limited, 225 Duncan Mill Road, Don Mills, Ontario, Canada M3B 3K9.

These books by Catherine Airlie were originally published as follows:

ONE SUMMER'S DAY
Copyright © 1961 by Catherine Airlie
First published in 1967 by Mills & Boon Limited
Harlequin edition (#1062) published November 1966

PASSING STRANGERS
Copyright © 1963 by Catherine Airlie
First published in 1963 by Mills & Boon Limited
Harlequin edition (#1081) published February 1967
under the title *Nurse Jane in Teneriffe*

RED LOTUS
Copyright © 1958 by Catherine Airlie
First published in 1958 by Mills & Boon Limited
Harlequin edition (#1170) published January 1968

ISBN 0-373-20080-3

First edition published as Harlequin Omnibus in October 1977
Second printing January 1984

Printed in Canada

Contents

One
Summer's Day

Aunt Betsy arrived from America full of plans that would change Ailsa's quiet life forever.

Her aunt's ambition to buy the Scottish island of Corrae created a conflict of interest when Ailsa fell in love with the island's proud owner, Huntley MacLaren.

Ailsa knew his only chance to save his ancestral home was to marry for money. She also knew that Lucy Fulton was at hand, wealthy and waiting!

CHAPTER ONE

AUNT BETSY BELLINGER came back to Scotland fully determined to strike roots deep into her native soil. She had made up her mind to buy an island.

Ailsa Monro could just remember Aunt Betsy, although she had been Aunt Betsy Nicholson in those days. She had married Russel G. Bellinger after the death of her first husband, Archie Nicholson, and Ailsa's mother had been Rowena Nicholson before she had changed her name to Monro.

So that it was her first husband's roots as well as her own that Betsy Bellinger really sought to restore to their native heath. She had only been married to Russel G. Bellinger for a year before he died, leaving her in undisputed possession of a considerable fortune in dollars, there being no child of his former marriage and none, of course, of his union with the vivacious Betsy.

As she waited at the airport, Ailsa supposed that her aunt must be in her middle forties. Her mother had been forty-six when she had died, just over two months ago, and she and Aunt Betsy had been schoolgirls together. Her mother's untimely death was part of the reason for Aunt Betsy's arrival.

Sudden tears dimmed Ailsa's eyes as she thought how dearly her mother would have loved to have seen Betsy again before the end, but her letters to New York had remained unanswered until a week after the funeral. Betsy had been wintering in the Bahamas and had been on a fishing trip on a friend's yacht when Ailsa's news had finally reached her. Too late then to fly across three thousand intervening miles of ocean to her sister-in-law's side, as she undoubtedly would have done in happier circumstances.

But now she was about to descend on Scotland — literally — from a Comet jet liner, due to land at any moment on the wet stretch of runway.

A very affectionate smile curved Ailsa's lips as her grey eyes searched the sky above the dark ridge of Arran's sleeping hills. Aunt Betsy had always been more than kind, more than just a name in a distant land. Her long, newsy letters had been landmarks in their rather lonely life after Duncan Monro's death at sea, and more than once Betsy had urged them to sell up and join her in America. But that was something Ailsa's mother could never have done. Her roots were too firmly implanted, her memories too rich, for her ever to leave the land of her birth even for the leisurely existence which Betsy had promised them.

And now Betsy herself was coming home. Ailsa could not quite believe it, although she clutched the letter with her aunt's detailed instructions firmly in her hand as she waited.

'Meet me at Prestwick,' Betsy had cabled, 'and we'll go on to Edinburgh from there."

Why Edinburgh? Why not home to the quiet house on the shores of Loch Lomand, where Ailsa had prepared a room for her? She had expected her aunt to want to stay at Achnasheen, at least for a week or two, and had, in a vague sort of way, relied on asking her advice about its disposal. It had been her home for so long that she had not been able to think about parting with it without an overwhelming sense of dismay, and for a moment she had wondered if Aunt Betsy might be prepared to strike her roots into the fertile soil surrounding one of the most romantic lochs in the world.

Within little more than an hour's journey from Glasgow, lovely, smiling Loch Lomand still lay in the heart of its surrounding mountains untouched and unsullied by commercialism, but it appeared that her aunt had made other plans.

Before she could wonder any more about these plans the Comet made its appearance in the sky above her, coming in between a break in the clouds with a bright shaft of sunlight turning it to silver as it circled once and came swiftly in to land.

The steps were wheeled into position and Ailsa's heart began to beat swiftly as the heavy door in the fuselage was opened. As she might have expected, her aunt was first to descend.

Although she had not actually met her for sixteen years, Ailsa would have picked out Aunt Betsy anywhere. The frequent snapshots and studio portraits they had received from the far side of the Atlantic had left few details of her aunt's mode of life to their imagination, but the portraits had done Betsy Bellinger an injustice. They had all been rather formal glimpses of this bright little bird of a woman who came swiftly across the tarmac, followed by a small retinue of the opposite sex, all carrying bits and pieces of Aunt Betsy's luggage. Aunt Betsy herself was quite free from impedimenta when she embraced her niece.

"Well, now — Ailsa!" she exclaimed, standing on tiptoe to kiss Ailsa on both cheeks. "Isn't this nice, meeting at last? Although it could have been in kinder circumstances."

The slightly high-pitched voice was in no way harsh, and there was real warmth behind the wide hazel eyes. Before Ailsa could answer, Aunt Betsy had turned to her waiting cavaliers.

"I'll relieve you of my parcels," she smiled to the nearest one, a tall, portly American with an infectious smile who looked slightly ludicrous standing holding Aunt Betsy's white leather vanity case. "You've been so kind!"

"It was a pleasure, ma'am."

The big man touched his hat and moved away, and Ailsa was quite sure that it had been a pleasure to him to help her aunt. Soon they had rescued another small case, a luxurious-looking mink coat and several magazines, and the attendant males departed in search of their own luggage.

"Oh, my!" Aunt Betsy exclaimed. "My satchel! I must have left it in the plane." She looked back towards the gleaming Comet. "I have such a habit of doing that," she admitted. "I misplace things so easily."

Since all her tickets and a good deal of her money were probably in the missing handbag, Ailsa started towards the plane, but already the air hostess was approaching them with a large lizardskin bag in her hand. She was smiling broadly.

"Here it is, Mrs. Bellinger!" she teased. "I don't really think you want it, you know. You nearly left it behind at Idlewild, didn't you?"

11

"Do forgive me," Aunt Betsy murmured. "I really do need someone to look after me!"

"I thought," Ailsa said, as they made their way to the customs, "that you had a campanion."

Aunt Betsy slipped a hand through her arm. It was a very soft, white hand that had never done a day's work in all Aunt Betsy's life.

"That's why I wired you to meet the plane, honey," she confided. "The wretched woman let me down at the last moment, the day before we were due to leave New York. I guess she took cold feet or something. Anyway, she decided she didn't want to leave America, after all. Maybe I shouldn't blame her too much, because she *was* an American, but she had been with me for three years, ever since I married Russel." Aunt Betsy heaved a small sigh. "I depended on that woman. She went everywhere with me. I always feel kind of lost when I'm on my own."

All the same, Ailsa ventured to think that Betsy Bellinger was no fool. The bright eyes, the swift, darting movements, suggested that this little woman, who looked as neat as a new pin, was quick and shrewd enough to assess people at a glance, and that it was probably companionship she needed more than care. Betsy was small, but she was far from helpless, and in next to no time they had cleared the customs and she was enquiring about the hire of a car to take them to Edinburgh. When she was advised that she could continue her journey to the Scottish capital by air, she said quite firmly that she had had enough of airships and had decided to go by road.

"You won't change your mind and come home with me to Achnasheen?" Ailsa asked, hoping that she would accept.

"I thought of that," Betsy said, "but then I remembered how little room you had to spare and I had Dora Veitel with me and all this baggage."

"But you haven't Dora now," Ailsa pointed out as the taxi drew up.

"No," her aunt agreed, "but I've made an awful lot of plans." She watched her luggage being put in front beside the driver, counting the pieces as they were stacked one on top of the other. "I'd got most of them made before we left

12

New York, and I hadn't time to cancel any of them." She gave Ailsa a long, thoughtful scrutiny. "I hope you haven't any plans," she said as she settled herself in the back seat, "Any immediate plans."

"No," Ailsa confessed, remembering that it was no more than eight weeks since her whole world had been turned upside down by her mother's unexpected death. "I don't think I've had time to make plans. Not very definite ones, anyway."

"That's good," said Aunt Betsy. "Then you can come with me. After all you've been through, a change and a breath of sea air will do you a world of good."

Ailsa repeated rather breathlessly, "Sea air?"

"Yes. Now just relax, honey, and I'll explain as we go along. How long will it take us to get to Edinburgh?" Betsy asked.

"About an hour and forty minutes, I think——"

"Oh, well, that's nice!"

Aunt Betsy settled herself against the leather cushioning and took off the dashing little hat which Ailsa had been admiring silently ever since they had met. It was no more than a froth of tulle and rose petals, but it suited Aunt Betsy Bellinger very well. Underneath the hat her soft white hair was meticulously waved and curled. Not one hair was out of place.

"Maybe I'd better start at the begnning," she conceded as they drove away through the airport gates. "When I had made up my mind to come, my lawyer in New York got into touch with a colleague in Edinburgh who said he would do his best to find what I wanted. Of course," the white hand clasped Ailsa's arm again, "I knew that I wouldn't just be able to walk into an agent's office over here and get the *right* place without waiting, so I decided to go on a sort of inspection tour first." She looked round and nodded. "Yes, the sea trip! Last spring some friends of mine in New York toured Europe and one of the highlights of their trip was a cruise they took round Scotland. I put my name down right there in New York and got a cabin straight away!" she added triumphantly.

Ailsa's heart sank. It was no use pretending that she did not feel disappointed.

"Then—you'll be leaving Edinburgh quite soon?" she suggested.

Aunt Betsy nodded. Her hazel eyes were very bright and she had the look of a conspirator as she said:

"So will you! There's Dora Veitel's cabin. It was all fixed up in New York. She was to travel with me, of course, but now you must come instead!"

Surprised and not quite sure of her reaction to such an amazing suggestion, Ailsa turned in her seat to meet the smiling eyes which were searching her face rather anxiously.

"Don't say you're going to refuse," Betsy pleaded. "I couldn't possibly go by myself!"

"But—all the arrangements," Ailsa protested. "The cabin in Miss Veitel's name?"

"Oh, you mustn't worry about that," her aunt assured her. "I'll see to everything when we reach Edinburgh. I booked both cabins in my name—Mrs. Bellinger and companion— so that it should be easy enough to explain the change to the shipping people, even at the last minute."

Ailsa believed it would be, if Aunt Betsy did the explaining. She was an amazing personality, quick and volatile, never at a loss for an idea or a suggestion, and she took life in her stride. It might be that she would rush in occasionally where angels would fear to tread, but she would rush with an acceptable explanation. She would rarely be rebuffed.

"When do we sail?" Ailsa asked, accepting the incredible situation because, even at this early stage in their acquaintance, she realized that it would be useless to protest once she had assured her aunt that she had no definite plans for the immediate future.

"A week today." Having leapt lightly over the first obstacle, Betsy allowed her enthusiasm to mount with all its accustomed agility. "It's a wonderful schedule—all around these wonderful islands on the west coast after we've done the Shetlands. It's a sort of cultural thing. When you go ashore there are people to explain everything—sort of couriers who know all about the islands and the bird life and all that sort of thing. Naturalists, I suppose you call them. Anyway, they explore the islands and bring back specimens, but you don't *have* to be interested in that sort of thing to enjoy the cruise. It's a real luxury trip, with dancing aboard for the younger people and everything!"

When Aunt Betsy paused for breath Ailsa asked, "Do you think you're going to find the island you want to buy?"

"Oh, I'm hoping so!" The bright hazel eyes were full of enthusiasm. "I'd be mortally disappointed if I didn't. As a matter of fact," Betsy confided, "there's just a chance that one is coming on the market quite soon. My lawyer in New York said I'd get to know for sure when I reached Edinburgh."

So this was why Edinburgh had to come first!

"I didn't think the islands came on the market every day," Ailsa mused.

"Oh, they don't! This will be a wonderful chance of it does happen—almost an omen," Betsy decided thoughtfully. "As if I really *am* meant to settle over here for good and all."

"And you've no idea where this place is?"

"Not a hint!" Betsy smiled. "It could be as far out in the Atlantic as St. Kilda, for all I know, and then it wouldn't be any good to me, of course."

"Most of the outlying islands have already been evacuated," Ailsa remarked. "It would seem as if your island was nearer at hand."

"There you are!" Betsy cried. "You're calling it 'my island' already!"

Ailsa let that pass with a quiet smile. What, in heaven's name, she wondered, would Aunt Betsy do with an island once she had bought it?

They talked about other things; about her mother's illness and how Ailsa had given up her position in a city office to go home to Achnasheen to nurse her.

"Will you look for another job as a stenographer?" Aunt Betsy enquired in a vaguely guarded tone.

"I ought to be doing that now," Ailsa smiled. "But when I knew you were coming I thought I'd put it off for a bit."

"Yes. Yes, indeed," Betsy agreed, still rather vaguely, as if she were preoccupied with quite a different train of

15

thought. And then she shot off at a tangent, in the odd, inconsequential way she had which was so apt to deceive the casual observer. "Aren't the outskirts of a big city ugly? All these dreadful tenements!" She frowned up at the grey wall of buildings rapidly closing in on them as they approached the capital. "Edinburgh hasn't changed a bit since my young days," she declared.

"It's not a particularly good day for seeing it for the first time," Ailsa answered, looking through the little rivulets of rain on the taxi window to the wet pavements beyond. "But we'll soon be in Princes Street, and that could never look drab!"

"It's just occurred to me," Aunt Betsy said without answering the reflection, "that you won't have any luggage if we decide to spend the night here."

Ailsa looked taken aback.

"Did you intend to stay?" she asked.

"Well I couldn't be *sure*," Betsy pointed out. "If there's any hope of seeing this place I suppose we could go along right away. Things move more quickly in America than they do here, of course, so maybe I'm just being too impatient."

"I hope you're not going to be disappointed," Ailsa murmured sympathetically as her aunt tapped on the glass partition to give the lawyer's address to the driver. "It seems the sort of thing one doesn't do in a hurry."

The taxi had turned into Princes Street, and with all the suppressed excitement of someone seeing a beloved and well-remembered scene after many years, Betsy was sitting forward in her seat, her discreetly tinted lips parted a little, her eyes very bright. Here and there she saw and recognized a well-established name above a shop which set off a train of reminiscences until the taxi turned abruptly into a side street where there were only offices.

"How it all comes back!" she mused. "Yes, Ailsa, I think I have made the right decision. Fond as I have become of America, this is my country!"

Ailsa was aware of a sudden lump in her throat, knowing that she was going to be almost as disappointed as her aunt if the island she sought did not materialize in the very near future.

16

They had climbed up into the labyrinth of narrow streets surrounding the old town and the taxi slowed and finally stopped before a narrow entry.

"Wait for us," Mrs. Bellinger commanded as the driver opened the door for them. "We probably won't be much more than half an hour, and then you can drive us to an hotel somewhere for lunch."

The man nodded, shrugging his shoulders in a non-sommital way. He was evidently used to Americans and one hire was as good as another. This one, it would appear, was going to last for the best part of the day.

Aunt Betsy had put on her hat with the aid of the hand mirror from her bag, refreshing herself with a fine dusting of powder from a gold compact.

"I don't think I need any more lip-rouge," she decided after a final, critical glance. "A very little make-up does me."

She sounded like a small, sturdy general getting ready for an important campaign, and possibly that was how she was thinking of her coming interview. She might need all her powers of persuasion to hurry this deal through.

They mounted a rather dark stairway winding round a stone column which supported the ancient roof many feet above them. The solicitor's office was on the third floor and there was no lift. Aunt Betsy was panting a little when they finally reached the landing.

"The age of the elevator hasn't really dawned on Scotland!" she complained. "In New York, stairs have become almost superfluous. Still, here we are! Dobie, Anstruther, Anstruther and Dobie," she quoted, reading from the well-polished brass plate on the wall facing them. "That's the name I want."

Ailsa waited for her in a shabby outer office while she went in to interview the present Mr. Dobie. She had caught a glimpse of a tall, thin old man with a cadaverous face as the clerk had opened the inner door, and it seemed that her aunt had been expected. He shook Betsy very warmly by the hand and closed the door. Her aunt had evidently forgotten Ailsa, but it did not matter. Ailsa had a good deal to think about.

She felt as if she were drawing breath for the first time since she had met her aunt at the airport, yet her eyes were smiling as she thought back over the events of the past two hours. Supposing Aunt Betsy did stay in Scotland? Supposing she was able to buy her island?

Even in the short space of time they had been together it had become apparent to her that no one could come into contact with Betsy Bellinger without being affected in some way by her dynamic personality. If she only saw her aunt once in a while it would be enough to make a great difference to her rather lonely life. It was too soon after her mother's death for Ailsa to assess the full extent of her loss, but at least Aunt Betsy made her feel that she would not be entirely alone. In some ways Betsy seemed almost like a fairy god-mother, popping up out of the blue when she was most needed.

She thought of the suggestion her aunt had made about the Hebridean cruise, wondering if she had really meant it.

Her cheeks flushed at the prospect of such a romantic trip, and already she had learned that Betsy Bellinger generally meant what she said. In fact, it was her habit to make sure of carrying out her impulsive plans almost to the letter, and this was not such a strange excursion for an American to make in the Western Highlands of Scotland. The cruise was largely patronized by visiting Americans, it being about the only way in which they could view the beauty of the Scottish waterways while yet retaining all the comfort and luxury to which the New World had accustomed them.

Her thoughts flew hither and thither to the accompaniment of slow, ponderous typing behind an opaque glass partition which screened off part of the outer office and behind which the clerk had evidently set to work again. Then, alarmingly, stridently, there was the sound of a bell being rung. Ailsa recognized it as the bell they had pressed at the side of the main doorway, and the typing ceased as the clerk went to answer the summons. He came out through the glass-panelled door, but before he had crossed the wating-room floor the outer door had opened.

The man standing in the aperture was not at all the type of person Ailsa had expected to see. He looked very tall and very powerful in his present surroundings and, without stopping to consider why, she knew that he belonged to the sea. He had brought the tang of it into the drab little waiting-room with him, and the look of it was in his eyes. Not only because they were the colour of the sea in deep places, but because the tiny network of lines which surrounded them spoke of long distances and eyes almost perpetually narrowed against bright sunlight and the lash of spray. A sea captain, perhaps?

Suddenly confused, she realized that her own eyes were being held in the stranger's frankly penetrating gaze. She had been guilty of rudeness, she supposed, staring at him like that. His brows were black and drawn a little in a concentrated frown, and he had a hard, lean jaw which tapered towards a relentless-looking mouth and chin.

"I'd like to see Mr. Simpson Dobie," he told the clerk, who had now come forward. "It's rather urgent."

His voice was firmly decisive, as if such wishes on his part were generally attended to with alacrity.

"I'm sorry, sir," the young clerk began nervously, recognizing the note of authority, "but Mr. Dobie is with a client at present."

Ailsa tried not to listen to any more of their conversation. The tall man was still facing her and she saw the frown deepen on his brow as he glanced impatiently at his watch.

"I'll wait," he decided.

The clerk gave a stiff little nervous nod and withdrew, while the newcomer crossed to the window, staring out through the narrow panes, his broad frame seeming to block out all the light.

Ailsa stiffened. It was a very small office and she could almost hear this arrogant young man breathe, but he did not deign to look round. His thoughts appeared to be many miles away as he looked out over the grey slates of the adjoining roof-tops with their jumble of chimney-pots which had long ago earned Edinburgh the sobriquet of 'Auld Reekie'. The smoke hung low today because of the rain, and

19

the unbroken greyness everywhere looked suddenly oppressive.

Ailsa moved uneasily and the man at the window swung round. The same direct blue stare encountered her half-apologetic smile, but he said nothing. His dark brows were still drawn and as if he sought some sort of escape—from his thoughts or merely from her unwelcome presence there at that moment—he turned abruptly on his heels and made for the door.

For no very good reason Ailsa felt angry. If he had wanted to interview Mr. Simpson Dobie he should have made an appointment beforehand, as everyone else had to do!

The outer door closed behind him. He had gone, or was perhaps prepared to wait outside, but unmistakably he had left something of his presence behind him, an aura of freedom, a sense of power, a breath, in fact, of a commanding personality which she could not deny. In many ways it was disturbing, thrust in upon her like this when her thoughts had been hovering pleasantly on the prospect of seven long days spent without conflict, with the smell of the sea in her nostrils and the sound of it in her ears.

But this man carried the suggestion of the sea with him. A sea breaking endlessly against a rugged coast or tossing a ship with its mighty strength, arrogantly aware of its dreadful power. It was not such a sea that she had had in mind while she had been sitting there alone with her day-dreams.

The inner door of Mr. Dobie's room opened and her aunt emerged, followed by the elderly lawyer.

One look at Betsy's tight little mouth and tilted chin convinced her niece that things had not turned out exactly as Mrs. Bellinger had hoped.

"I really am surprised that you find it impossible to give me an answer at once," she was saying, the yellow petals of her gay little hat quivering accusingly as she shook her head at him. "It really is too bad, Mr. Dobie, after I've come all this way."

The implication accused him of negligence. People had been known to take pity on her disappointment before this, but Mr. Dobie said that his hands were tied. He could make

20

no concession, even to such a charming client, because he had not been empowered to do so.

"My client is away from Edinburgh," he explained. "He will not make his final decision about the sale of Corrae for a week."

"Away?" Aunt Betsy echoed incredulously. "When he's trying to sell the place?"

"He has it on the market—yes," the lawyer conceded.

"You seem unsure. What's the matter?" Betsy demanded. Doesn't he *want* to sell?"

"Naturally, he doesn't want to part with Corrae." Mr. Dobie's tone was decidedly dry. "It has been in his family for five hundred years."

Betsy looked nonplussed.

"Yes," she agreed, "I guess that's hard. Still, he must need the money——"

They had reached the door and the old lawyer stooped to open it. Aunt Betsy seemed too preoccupied to introduce Ailsa, but she apologized for her lapse as soon as they were alone.

"I quite forgot, honey!" she exclaimed. "I was a bit upset, I guess. Nothing can be settled, you see, for a week, and it sounds *exactly* what I want."

"Have you had a detailed description?" Ailsa asked as they negotiated the winding stairway to the street.

"Well—I've seen some photographs," her aunt admitted, "and Corrae's on the west coast and it will need a bit of money spent on it, but I was prepared for that. It's not very big, but there's a harbour and a suitable jetty——"

"Is it on a regular steamer route?"

Aunt Betsy halted on the stairs, amazed that anything so delectable as 'her' island might be by-passed by the life-giving mail boat.

"Why, of course, it must be! We're living in the twentieth century, honey!" she pointed out.

Ailsa greeted that with judicious silence.

"Where to now?" she asked. "Since we can't set sail for Corrae right away?"

"I was thinking maybe we could spend a few days at Achnasheen, after all," Aunt Betsy said. "I always loved

21

Loch Lomondside. We could drive back there after we've had some lunch."

It was what Ailsa wanted most. She had hoped that her aunt might have just such a split-second change of mind, and now she was delighted.

They reached the foot of the stairs and where halfway along the close when a tall figure blocked the entrance. It was the man who had refused to wait in the office, and once again, for a fraction of a second, their eyes met, but in the full light of the cold, drab day his were almost grey.

There was recognition in them this time, however, although he did not smile. His quick, decisive tread rang along the stone passageway and he took the stairs two at a time when he had passed them, not even trying to curb his impatience now.

Aunt Betsy pulled up on the edge of the pavement.

"Oh, my satchel!" she exclaimed. "I must have left it behind in Mr. Dobie's office. Yes, I *did* have it there with me! I thought I might have to pay him a cheque or something, if we made a bargain."

"All right, I'll get it." Ailsa turned to retrace her steps. "On you go into the taxi."

She smiled at her aunt's forgetfulness as she re-climbed the awkward staircase. If it had only been to retrieve Mrs. Bellinger's lost property, Dora Veitel's companionship had indeed been vital to her employer! And now it seemed that she had fallen quite naturally into Dora's place. Of course, she couldn't go on travelling around with Aunt Betsy indefinitely, or even settling down on an island with her——

"Oh——!"

She had reached the top of the stairs to come face to face with the tall man who had passed them only a second or two before. He was holding the now familiar lizardskin bag.

"You must be looking for this," he suggested. "Mr. Dobie had just noticed it when I went in."

"Thank you so much."

Ailsa took the bag from him, but he still stood there, as if there was more than this to be said between them. Their eyes met and there was faint amusement in his.

"You look as if you've had quite a shock," he told her. "Did you think you had lost your bag altogether?"

"No—it wasn't that." Ailsa turned back towards the stairs, aware of sudden, inexplicable confusion. "I knew I would find it in Mr. Dobie's office. Thank you," she added rather lamely, and plunged down the stairs.

She thought that he stood there on the landing for several minutes without turning back into the office, but she could not be sure. When she reached the grey world outside she could not remember negotiating the stairs. She seemed to have been on a far journey which had nothing to do with her present surroundings, Edinburgh, or her Aunt Betsy waiting rather anxiously in the taxi for the return of her lost hand-bag.

CHAPTER TWO

ON a morning full of sunshine a week later Ailsa locked the double doors of Achnasheen behind her and her aunt, leaving the heavy key at the police house when they passed through the village on their way to Glasgow. The long silver stretch of Loch Lomond lay placidly in its green cradle of hills, making Aunt Betsy sigh.

"Maybe I should have settled for Loch Lomondside, after all," she mused. "What could be more beautiful than this?"

"Your island!" Ailsa teased.

"What I can't understand is that I haven't heard another thing from that wretched man, Dobie," Betsy frowned. "Would you suppose that he sold it—for more money, for instance?"

"Not without letting you know."

A week with Aunt Betsy had convinced Ailsa that the little lady was quite serious about her island. It was to be that or nothing. She had accepted the fact that her aunt could be singularly determined once she had made up her mind about anything, but she could also be kind and extremely generous.

Her generosity where Ailsa was concerned had bordered on the embarrassing, for they had spent much of the week on what Betsy called 'shopping sprees' to Glasgow, patronizing the most exclusive establishments in Buchanan Street, not for her own benefit but because Betsy liked to spend money on other people!

"Goodness knows, I've got plenty of it!" she declared when Ailsa tried to protest. "When you get to my age you realize that pretty clothes look best on youth. Now, that little blue cocktail frock—I'd have given my eyes for it when I was your age and could wear it, so not another word. Just you wear it for me when we go on this cruise!"

Ailsa knew that she meant what she said, and now they were on their way to join the ship.

It looked as if the weather was going to be kind to them, and Ailsa's heart beat with a strange new excitement as they neared Edinburgh. She had never been on a sea voyage before. It was something she had always wanted to do, and it was May and the Hebrides would be at their loveliest. The magic of places that had been no more than names on a map to her came very near—Skye and Barra and Eriskay and the legend-haunted Minch, together with hundreds of little unknown islands studding the blue of an unbelievably lovely sea. These would be hers quite soon, and although she would never see them afterwards she would have a memory to cherish.

They took a taxi from Edinburgh to the quay at Leith, where their ship was waiting. Ailsa gave a little gasp of surprise when she saw it, for she had not expected anything quite so magnificent.

"Aunt Betsy," she said, "I had no idea it would be anything like this!"

"I meant to show you the brochure," her aunt apologized, "but it must have got mislaid somewhere or other. Yes, she's a nice tidy little ship. Not too big. Just comfortable and friendly. Well," she concluded, "I guess we'd better get ourselves on board."

Lying against the quay, the M.S. *Saturn* was like some graceful bird poised ready for flight. She seemed to have no place in the drab world of coasters and black freighters crowding the berths on either side of her. She was a vivid white bird of the sea. Her trim, clean lines and squat yellow funnel with its two narrow white bands belonged to a world of sunshine and blue water, and Ailsa's heart lifted at the prospect of spending seven whole days aboard her. She was, indeed, a luxury vessel, a thoroughbred of her kind, with sun decks and vast observation lounges and everything that the pampered tourist could desire.

It did not take Ailsa long to realize that most of their fellow-passengers were going to be Americans. The baggage trolleys alone proclaimed the fact. Cases and grips of every shape and size were strewn about the quay adorned with labels from all over the world—Paris and Rome, China and Japan. Her fellow-travellers had been everywhere and the M.S. *Saturn* was waiting to take them on the final, loveliest run of all—a romantic journey into the very heart of the legendary past.

From the moment she stepped aboard Ailsa knew that this journey was going to mean much to her.

Why she should feel so sure she could not explain, but in so many ways her world had changed. She was not foolish enough to believe that it could remain like this for ever—she who had never wished for more than simple happiness—and she had no great desire for wealth. But it was all such a glorious new experience that she would not have been human if she had not stretched out to grasp it with eager hands.

For one week she would be living in a dream world that might never have been hers if an unknown girl called Dora Veitel had not suddenly decided to stay in New York.

"You're on the main deck, by the way," her aunt told her. "Cabin 103. You don't mind having Dora's cabin? I'll put it right with the purser as soon as I remember."

A steward gathered up their baggage. He was a tall, blond young man whose Norse ancestry was obvious at a glance. The *Saturn* was a Bergen Line ship and Norwegian efficiency was evident everywhere. Mrs. Bellinger was shown to her cabin in the fore part of the spacious upper deck and her 'companion' was escorted, no less courteously, to the deck below.

Ailsa's single berth cabin was small, neat and compact, and she unpacked swiftly and went on deck. People were still coming on board, the inevitable stragglers who always seemed incapable of being anywhere on time, but most of the baggage had disappeared from the quayside. A curious sensation of detachment took possession of Ailsa as she leaned on the rail, a feeling of being already cut off from the ordinary world beneath her, and she thought how much her mother would have enjoyed a trip like this, the adventure of it and the utter difference from their prosaic, every day life.

The thought brought regretful tears to her eyes. Her mother had never known luxury of any kind, although happiness and contentment had been granted her in fullest measure at Achnasheen. Suddenly she found herself wondering if Aunt Betsy Bellinger had achieved such happiness in either of her marriages. During their few days together she had sensed a restlessness in the older woman, a lack of fulfilment which was both puzzling and absurd under the circumstances. Surely Betsy had all and more than she had ever wanted from life?

The thought of her mother and the return of the grief which assailed her so suddenly at times took her to the other side of the deck. Here there was comparative privacy, although the docks were still alive with fussy tugs and a ferry chugged importantly across the water to the farther shore, leaving a churned white wake behind it. Riding far out on the Firth the tiny speck of Inchkeith appeared through the morning mist—the first of the islands!

People 'collected' islands, she knew, and there were so many islands round the coast of Scotland waiting to be collected.

Looking along the deck, she saw that she was not the only passenger who had chosen to leave the bustle of departure behind. A tall man in a thick steamer coat stood leaning against the rail, his narrowed eyes searching the distant reaches of the Firth as if he found difficulty in curbing the impatience he felt to be out there with the movement of the waves beneath him and the north-east wind in his face.

Instantly recognition flooded in on her, although she had last encountered him in a lawyer's stuffy little third floor office in an Edinburgh side street. She would have known him anywhere.

And surely he was now in his element, for he had filled his lungs with the breath of the sea. He was part of it.

Before he could look round and perhaps recognize her, she turned away. She felt guilty of trespass, as if she had no real right to witness that absorbed look of belonging which linked him with the far reaches of blue water beyond the distant Isle of May.

He was impatient for their voyage to begin. She knew that about him, at least, but she did not think that he was one of the ship's complement of officers. He was not in uniform, and he was not Norwegian, although he had the slim height and the vivid blue eyes of the Viking breed.

An American then? Quite possibly, although his clothes had a decidedly English cut. Wealthy Americans were known to patronize Savile Row and Forsyth's of Edinburgh as soon as they landed in Britain.

I'm far too fanciful, she thought with a smile, as she went in search of her aunt, but there was a high flush in her cheeks when she reached cabin number 14 and her eyes were very bright.

"You look as if you're enjoying yourself already," Betsy observed, taking her eyes from the passenger list for a split second to look at her. "Is everybody aboard, do you think? It's time we sailed."

"I think most people are." Ailsa hesitated about mentioning the man at the rail for, after all, it might be of little interest to her aunt that someone they had seen for a fleeting second in Mr. Dobie's office was now their fellow-passenger. "All the baggage is on and there are bells ringing every now and then. Would you like to go on deck?"

Betsy shook her head.

"Heaven forbid! Till I've got my sea legs, anyway. Besides," she added happily, "I'm only halfway through the passenger list. There might be someone I know on board."

Ailsa smiled, leaving her to her list. That sort of thing was probably important once you had made a trip or two, she reflected. Once some of the magic had gone.

The magic would never evaporate for her because this was likely to be her one and only luxury cruise. She felt like Cinderella going to the ball. Every minute would be precious, for such luck might not come her way a second time. She knew Aunt Betsy to be slightly quixotic as well as being generous.

Vibrating like some delicate creature to the touch of the sea, the *Saturn* slid smoothly from her berth out towards the open Firth. Ailsa found a position fairly far forward on the upper deck where the wind met her freely, blowing back her hair and loosening the silk scarf about her throat. Another present from Aunt Betsy, she reflected gratefully, rescuing the gaily-printed square from the playful clutches of the wind. Just one other thing she would never be able to say 'thank you' for adequately enough!

"I believe you're Mrs. Bellinger's companion?"

28

Swiftly she spun around at the sound of the voice to find herself face to face with the man who had been standing at the rail less than half an hour ago. His expression was grave.

"Yes. Oh—is there anything wrong?" she asked. "I ought not to have left her——"

"She has had some sort of seizure, I think. She managed to reach her bell and I happened to be in the alleyway when the stewardess came out," he explained.

All the colour drained out of Ailsa's cheeks. This was dreadful. She had no idea that her aunt had even felt ill.

"I must go. I wish I hadn't left her," she repeated. "How selfish of me! It was my duty to stay with her—to look after her——"

He took her arm, steadying her progress along the deck.

"Where you nursing her?" he asked.

"No, but I have nursed sick people," Ailsa told him. "My mother has just recently died."

"This could be only a temporary upset," he consoled, and even in her concern for her aunt she detected a sincerity and strength in his voice which gave her a strange confidence. "Older people often rush about too much and then find that they have overtaxed their strength. Mrs. Bellinger doesn't look as if she rested very often."

"Are you a doctor?" Ailsa asked as they reached the nearest companionway.

He smiled.

"No. But the ship's doctor will be with her now. If there is anything I can do for you," he added quite kindly, "any message I can take to the purser or a cable to be sent off, I can see to it for you."

"I don't think there will be any need for a cable," Ailsa said. "We're alone, you see." She felt suddenly, desperately alone. "But it's very kind of you to offer," she added hastily. "The ship's quite confusing at first." She glanced about her, not quite sure which way she had come, and once again he took her arm in a guiding grip.

"The end cabin on the port side," she directed, releasing her when they had come through the swing doors.

Ailsa ran down the narrow corridor towards a little group gathered outside a cabin door. It was her aunt's cabin.

"Please," she begged breathlessly, "may I come in?"

A nurse in a white starched wrapper made way for her and she saw the ship's surgeon bending over the bed. On it her aunt lay, propped up with extra pillows, rather white, but completely conscious of all that was going on around her. She recognized Ailsa as soon as she came in.

"You're not to worry, honey," she said as the doctor straightened and stood aside. He had a hypodermic syringe in his hand and he kept his fingers on her aunt's pulse. "I have these bouts occasionally. I ought to have warned you, but I haven't had a spasm since I left New York."

Ailsa's eyes went to the doctor's in silent enquiry.

"Asthma," he explained laconically. "She knows how to deal with an attack in the ordinary way, but this one caught her unaware." He glanced about the untidy cabin. "Somewhere she will have a little machine—an electrical gadget to assist her breathing. We must check on the voltage," he added, putting away the syringe. "Otherwise she may fuse our lights! I'm almost certain, though, that she will not need any artificial aid to recovery once we're at sea."

With a certain amount of relief Ailsa realized that he was taking the situation quite lightly. Her aunt was not seriously ill. She had just neglected a few necessary precautions and allowed herself to become excited. Yet she had not seemed unduly excited about the voyage at all. Had something happened in the interval between now and coming on board to disturb her?

There was no immediate way of finding out. The injection which the doctor had given was beginning to have its effect and he handed his patient over to the care of the waiting nurse.

Ailsa stood beside the bed, waiting for her aunt to drop off to sleep. The heavy lids quivered and fell over the hazel eyes and Betsy Bellinger heaved a small, regretful sigh.

"I wouldn't have believed it," she murmured. "I wouldn't really have believed it!"

The nurse smiled and took a chair beside the bed.

"You must not miss your lunch," she told Ailsa. "The bell has just gone. You can't do anything for Mrs. Bellinger at present, and she would only be distressed to know that

30

you had missed a meal on her account. She will be perfectly well when she wakes up."

The serene, slightly-accented voice was encouraging and the tall Norwegian nurse rose as Ailsa reached the door.

"Do not worry, Miss Monro," she added. "It is going to be quite all right. I shall stay here with Mrs. Bellinger till you come back. Did Mr. MacLaren find you without trouble?"

Ailsa hesitated.

"Mr. MacLaren———?"

"He took the message from the steward. We knew Mrs. Bellinger was travelling with a companion and he said he had seen you on deck."

The nurse stood smiling in the doorway and Ailsa said, "Yes, he found me without difficulty."

"That is good. You are sure to meet him again. He is travelling with us this voyage to replace Professor Dickson, who generally leads our tours. Perhaps you know of the Professor," the nurse went on conversationally. "He is a very famous man, a lecturer and ornithologist, and also the author of many books. Huntley MacLaren is an ornithologist too. Not quite so famous as the Professor, of course, and—rather difficult to know."

She smiled over the last few words almost apologetically, but already Ailsa was prepared to agree with her. Huntley MacLaren had been kind in an emergency, but somehow she knew that the Norwegian girl was right in her estimate of him. He would not be easy to know. There was an air of remoteness about him which prohibited too swift an intimacy, and, one kindly action, offered more or less in the way of duty, would not constitute an excuse for closer acquaintance.

There had been that moment, too, when she had stumbled across him at the far side of the deck when his eyes had been on the distant sea and his thoughts had been very far away.

They had been troubled thoughts. She was certain of that with an intuitiveness which surprised her. They were thoughts, perhaps, that he could not share with anyone.

The fact that they had both sought that same sheltered stretch of deck away from the bustle of departure would be

31

no bond between them. This man was the self-sufficient sort, the lone wolf who would tread his destined path without looking about him for sympathy or even understanding.

Why was she thinking so much about him? She tried to shake her mind free of him, finding her way to the dining-saloon on the promenade deck after she had made two wrong turns and finally enlisted the help of a passing steward. Ships were so confusing at first and she felt suddenly shy and a little uncertain without her aunt's cheerful companionship and Betsy's knowledge of ships in general to guide her.

The dining tables were placed on either side of a central dance floor, with a raised orchestra platform at its far end, and she was quickly ushered to a side table for four. The steward pulled out her chair.

"Will you wait for the others to come, ma'am?" he asked.

Ailsa glanced hastily at the other place-names. Her aunt's did not seem to be one of them.

"I'm alone," she explained. "I suppose Mrs. Bellinger has been placed at another table."

"That may be so—if she has already arranged it with the chief steward."

"I don't think she's had time for that. But I shall be quite all right here, thank you." Ailsa smiled. "It's rather confusing on board just at first," she confessed.

"Soon you will feel at home," the steward assured her with a warm, answering smile. "This is a very friendly ship and you are at Mr. MacLaren's table. He has requested it."

Ailsa simply could not believe that a man like Huntley MacLaren would make such a request. Surely the steward had been mistaken? Yet he might have done it out of pity, because he had seen how raw she was, how little she knew about this sort of thing.

She could not change her place now, however, without making an awkward little scene, for already her other table companions were bearing down on her. They were a small thick-set man in his middle forties and a fair-haired girl of about her own age, who looked as if she had come on the cruise much against her will.

The man gave Ailsa a swift, appraising look as he sat down opposite her and the girl slid into the chair facing the orchestra.

"My name's Fulton," the little man said. "Adam Fulton. This is my daughter, Lucy."

The fair girl dragged her glance from the orchestra platform to give Ailsa a half-hearted smile before she let her thoughts wander again to the far end of the room. She was evidently not interested in making new acquaintances of her own sex, and the stubborn expression was even more pronounced when her father added, "I want to show Lucy as much of Scotland as I can. I was born and bred here and a Scot always has a great desire to return to his native land."

"You're over from America?" Ailsa asked, wondering when they were to be favoured by Huntley MacLaren's presence at the table. Already the saloon was filling up and there was still no sign of him.

"From New Orleans," Adam Fulton agreed. "I have business connections there, but our home is really in Florida. That's where we've lived for a number of years now, although Lucy has been away at school for most of 'em." He looked at his daughter with immeasurable pride, although his fondness did not seem to be returned in equal measure. Lucy Fulton continued to gaze abstractedly ahead, and it all seemed rather deliberate to Ailsa, as if she intended to hurt her father with her indifference, to pay him out for dragging her away from America when she didn't want to come. "I think it's nice for a young girl to see a bit of the world before she thinks of settling down," he added tentatively.

Suddenly Ailsa felt sorry for Adam Fulton, although he did not look the sort of man who expected pity. He was small, tough, and quite formidable looking, with keen dark eyes and a jutting jaw which suggested an inflexibility of purpose in most things. Except when he spoke about his daughter, his voice had the ring of authority, the tone of a man long accustomed to command. He was probably very rich and very indulgent as far as Lucy was concerned, Ailsa thought without envy.

"This looks like MacLaren now," he said, glancing up from the menu he held.

Ailsa felt a hot wave of colour rising into her cheeks as Huntley MacLaren took the vacant chair next to hers. She could not account for such foolish confusion and his murmur of apology was lost to her as she caught sight of Lucy's altered face. It had undergone a complete transformation. The expression of boredom had fled and the curiously pale eyes had come to sparkling life. Lucy Fulton was looking at Huntley MacLaren as if he had been sent by the gods to amuse her.

Then, with the effect of a sword-flash, Huntley's eyes came down on hers, steel-blue and questioning, and Lucy's slightly insolent stare was instantly averted. She bit her firm white teeth into her lower lip, as if she were not quite sure about something for the first time in her life.

Huntley MacLaren looked down at Ailsa as she unfolded her table napkin.

"I hope that Mrs. Bellinger has recovered," he said. "It was a most unfortunate start to her trip."

"She's asleep now," Ailsa told him, taking the menu card he offered her. "The doctor assures me she'll be all right by the time we are clear of the coast and out to sea. I had no idea she suffered from asthma. It seems to be a most distressing thing."

"You've only joined her for this trip?" he asked as their steward came up for their order. "You did not come over from America with her?"

"Oh, no." Ailsa shook her head, turning to the waiting steward. "May I have melon, please, to start with?"

Adam Fulton got to his feet.

"I guess we go over and help ourselves to the main course," he said, glancing towards the buffet, where already a small queue was forming. "Shall I take your plate, Lucy?"

"I don't want much," Lucy decided. "Shrimp cocktail, perhaps, and some of that foul-looking Norwegian cheese that tastes so good!" She gave Huntley MacLaren a slow, deliberate smile, hoping to chain him to his chair in order to talk to her. "How many islands are you going to show us, Mr. MacLaren?" she asked. "You are sort of—courier on this trip, aren't you?"

Huntley MacLaren's answering smile was slow and very slightly amused.

"Sort of," he agreed. "I'm hoping to interest you in bird sanctuaries and that sort of thing. It happens to be my life's work."

Ailsa felt uncomfortable, wishing that she had refused the first course and gone to the buffet with Adam Fulton. Lucy had so obviously appropriated Huntley MacLaren for the duration of the voyage that it was embarrassing to sit there between them and feel her deliberate desire to annex him.

What Huntley himself thought about it she could not guess. He had ordered soup and had finished it before Adam returned.

"I hear you're the owner of a place called Corrae, Mr. MacLaren," Adam remarked as he re-seated himself after passing Lucy her shrimp cocktail. "The purser tells me you're the local laird."

Huntley looked up from his plate. There was very little change in his expression, although Ailsa thought that some of the colour had ebbed under his thick coating of tan.

"The term is rather loosely applied these days," he answered dryly. "But I do own Corrae."

"Will we be calling there?" Adam asked.

"Time and weather permitting," Huntley agreed. "And if you have not had a surfeit of islands by then."

The subject was dismissed, but somehow Ailsa knew that Huntley MacLaren would be happier if the passengers from the *Saturn* did not find time to land on the island of Corrae. He did not want them to go there for a reason of his own.

Why should she think, of a sudden, that it was a reason that hurt, a reason that went far deeper than just a superficial desire for privacy or the fact that he might be treading the soil of Corrae for the last time? For Corrae was up for sale. It was the island her Aunt Betsy Bellinger had made up her mind to buy!

A good deal that had been puzzling Ailsa since she had recognized Huntley MacLaren as the man they had met in Edinburgh slipped quickly into place. The sale of Corrae was undoubtedly the reason for his visit to the lawyer's office, but she wondered if he knew who her aunt was, and that they had been in Edinburgh a week ago with a view to making a substantial offer for his island home.

35

There had been Mr. Dobie's reticence, too, about the possibility of their meeting, as if the laird of Corrae had not definitely made up his mind to part with his old home.

She tried to remember exactly what the lawyer had said when her aunt had questioned the apparent lack of decision on the owner's part.

'Naturally he doesn't want to part with Corrae. It has been in his family for five hundred years.'

Five hundred years! Roughly eight generations, stretching back in a long, unbroken line to the days when men fought to the death for their heritage rather than give it up. Back, far back beyond the days of Culloden and the Forty-five to the time when a king sat on the throne of Scotland and the clans warred among themselves. Then the land a man owned was his very life. There was no question of buying and selling in those days and barter was rare. The Chiefs took a fierce pride in their possessions, handing them on, with their titles, from father to son. In those distant days a stranger would have come with money in his hand at the peril of his life.

But now so much was changed. The land still remained, the lovely, breathtaking vistas of loch and mountains were still there to delight the eye and catch at the heartstrings, but many an ancient castle stood in lonely ruin, gazing sadly down upon the estates which had passed into alien hands.

Suddenly Ailsa felt ashamed. Ashamed of her aunt wanting Corrae for no more than a whim, ashamed of their impatience when their journey to Edinburgh had not met with immediate success, and irked beyond reason by Adam Fulton's continuing curiosity.

"Tell me about your island, Mr. MacLaren," Lucy Fulton said when their coffee was served. "It all sounds very romantic. Has it a castle and a village, or is it just one of these terribly remote places where nothing ever happens?"

Huntley's smile was oddly amused.

"Its castle is in ruins," he said, "but there is a village, gradually dying, too, I'm afraid."

36

Over the last few words his voice had grown harsh and constricted, as if he did not want to discuss this thing that meant so much to him.

"Then it *is* off the beaten track?" Lucy suggested. "I find that rather interesting. Everywhere is the same nowadays— so commercialized. There isn't a natural sort of place left."

The affected little speech was meant to impress, and Adam Fulton explained hastily:

"Lucy has been spoiled by too much travel, Mr. Mac-Laren. We've been all around the world now and I reckon she's seen most places."

He said it with a certain amount of pride, as if his great wealth must have given Lucy all she could desire in life, but to Ailsa it seemed that Lucy had only become satiated with gifts.

"I'm looking out for a place where I can settle down now," Adam went on. "I'm ready to retire, you see, and I'm a Scot by birth. Frankly, I've been wondering about Scotland. Maybe I could spend the remainder of my days here," he mused, looking through the porthole at the sunlight dancing on the little choppy waves. "Did you say we went ashore somewhere this afternoon?" he asked.

"On the Isle of May," Huntley answered. "It's your first island of the tour."

"I'm looking forward to it," Adam said, drawing on his cigar while he surveyed his fellow-passengers at the other tables. "Although the worst of coming on this kind of trip is that you meet mostly Americans—and sometimes the folks you already know!"

"You'll be seeing quite a lot of the 'natives' too," Huntley assured him, rising as Lucy got to her feet. "I hope you will enjoy yourselves."

"I'm sure we shall," Lucy said, giving him a dazzling smile. "Everything seems to be so well organized on board this ship. Poppa said it would be a 'coaster' when we booked our berths over in New York, so you can guess I'm more than surprised!"

She gave Ailsa a faint smile, as if she had just remembered her, and Huntley stood aside to let Adam Fulton pass. When they reached the swing doors he was waylaid by a steward, and Adam walked between Ailsa and Lucy towards the lounge.

"You going ashore this afternoon, Miss Monro?" he asked conversationally.

"I don't think so," Ailsa said. "My aunt has had a slight attack of asthma since she came on board, so I'll stay with her until she's able to get about."

"Too bad!" Adam sympathized, blowing a blue smoke ring. "This your first trip too?"

"Yes." Ailsa's eyes were starry with anticpation, her lips parted in a quick smile. "I'm looking forward to it tremendously. I didn't expect to come, you see. It was all arranged very suddenly, when my aunt came over from New York."

"She's an American, is she?" Adam asked, while Lucy gazed out at the gentle rise and fall of the ship's white bow as it breasted the steeper swell of the North Sea.

"She married an American, but really I suppose she still considers herself a Scot," Ailsa said. "I think she wants to settle in Scotland——"

She hesitated, wondering if she might not be abusing her aunt's confidence, and Adam Fulton said,

"Roots are difficult things to tear up, but perhaps your aunt never really got them down into American soil. How long was she out there?"

"About twenty-three years."

"Two years less than me," he reflected. "Twenty-five years is a long time in one country. You get sort of acclimatized to the place by then, I guess." He pulled on the last of his cigar, grinding the stub into the glass ash-tray on the table between them. "This chap MacLaren seems a bit of an enigma," he mused. "Though I dare say he's concerned about that island of his. I wonder if we will go ashore there? It might be interesting to look over the place, seeing it is for sale."

That was the part Huntley MacLaren was finding hardest to bear, Ailsa realized. People going to Corrae out of curiosity, tramping about the island to see what sort of place had come on the market, a living island that its owner could no longer maintain. It was the same sort of feeling as parting with a beloved house, she reflected. It would be the same when she came to sell Achnasheen—people going from room to room looking with cold and perhaps calculating eyes on the treasures of a lifetime—the wrong people to take over the care of the place you had loved and cherished through the years.

"Mr. MacLaren did say the landing would be optional." Lucy had spoken without turning her head. "I think we could persuade him, though."

Adam smiled.

"I think you're going to enjoy this trip, Luce," he said, "after all."

His daughter did not answer him. Her eyes were still fixed on the plunging white bow, but her thoughts were far away.

"I must go and see how my aunt is," Ailsa excused herself after a few minutes. "We'll be meeting again at dinner. No, please don't get up." She smiled at Adam, thinking that she liked him, in spite of Lucy. "You look as if you might be there for the afternoon!"

"Maybe I shall be," he said, his eyes already half closed as he turned towards the door.

She ran swiftly down to the deck below to meet the nurse coming from her aunt's cabin.

"Oh, there you are!" the Norwegian girl exclaimed. "Mrs. Bellinger has had a very nice sleep and she should be able to get up in an hour or two. We must find her a sheltered spot on the sun deck tomorrow—in the veranda, perhaps. She does not want to be considered an invalid."

"I'm sure she doesn't," Ailsa agreed. "Thank you very much for looking after her so well."

"That is my job," Greta Larsen acknowledged cheerfully. "Sometimes on these cruises we get sick people, but not very often, and then I am unemployed! Which is not good."

"There's always the emergency," Ailsa smiled, opening the cabin door.

"Have you had your lunch?" Her aunt greeted her with a perturbed look. "It seems that I've been asleep, helped by that nice kind doctor and his injection! I feel fine now," she declared, easing herself on her pillows. "Come and sit beside me for five minutes and tell me all about everything. Where

39

are you seated and who was at the table with you? Were they nice or just plain dull? If they are too dull, we must get you moved."

"One question at a time!" Ailsa laughed, wondering if she should tell her aunt right away about Huntley Mac-Laren. "You're far too impatient!"

"I hate missing anything," Betsy confessed. "And do you think I could have some lunch? I'm ravenous!"

"I'll ring and find out——unless the doctor put you on a diet?"

"On a diet—me? Good gracious, no!" Scornfully Betsy refuted the idea. "I'm my old self again just as soon as I get over these attacks."

There was a tap on the door and a steward made his appearance with a tray, as if someone had anticipated her desire.

"Everything laid on!" Ailsa murmured. "You've only got to make three wishes!"

"The nurse sent this along for you, ma'am," the steward announced.

"Now that's what I call service," Betsy mused when the door had closed again. She lifted a silver cover to peer underneath. "Mm-m! Chicken Maryland—how nice! They think Americans can't exist without chicken and corn on the cob, I suppose! Now, tell me—who did you sit by and were they nice? Did you have an officer at your table? He'd be Norwegian, but they all speak such excellent English that it wouldn't matter." She took up her knife and fork, surveying the daintily-served meal with deep appreciation. "Just you go on talking while I eat. I'm anxious to hear *everything*!"

Ailsa smiled. It was so rarely necessary to sustain a lengthy conversation with her aunt, but now she had made up her mind to tell her about Huntley MacLaren. It could do no harm, she decided.

"The strange thing is," she began, "that I was placed beside someone you've been wanting to meet."

Betsy looked up, almost in alarm, but her mouth was too full to allow her to make any comment. Her finely arched eyebrows shot up, however, and her hazel eyes were questioning.

"Huntley MacLaren," Ailsa said. "He's the owner of Corrae."

Aunt Betsy blinked rapidly, swallowed, and sat bolt upright.

"*My* island?" she said. "But how did he get here—on a cruise ship, of all things?"

"It seems that there's a system of guides to the islands as we come to them," Ailsa explained. "People who know their history and are able to conduct us round with some authority. Huntley MacLaren is one of them."

"A—sort of courier?" Betsy asked incredulously.

"In a way," Ailsa agreed. "But he is also the laird of Corrae and Miss Larsen—the nurse—told me that he is an ornithologist of some standing."

"Well, did you ever?" Aunt Betsy mused, forgetting her Chicken Maryland and the fact that her coffee was rapidly cooling in its silver pot. "Who would have believed such a thing? I'd call it a golden opportunity, wouldn't you?"

Ailsa flushed.

"I don't think Mr. MacLaren will want to talk business while we are on the cruise," she said awkwardly. "He may have come away like this to give himself time to think."

"But he must have thought it all out pretty thoroughly before he decided to advertise the place," Betsy pointed out, slightly piqued. "You can't have your cake and eat it. Either you want to sell or you don't."

"It could be a case of *having* to sell," Ailsa murmured. "I think I can understand how he feels, Aunt Betsy. Nobody—no one like Huntley MacLaren would part with his heritage unless he had explored every avenue open to him to keep it. Mr. Dobie said it had been in MacLaren hands for five hundred years. It's—a staggering length of time when you come to think of it—all these years reaching so far back into the past and always MacLarens at Corrae. It's like—tearing up a bit of history, destroying something rather precious which can never be replaced by all the good intentions in the world."

Aunt Betsy pushed her chicken aside.

41

"My dear child," she exclaimed, "this Huntley MacLaren certainly seems to have impressed you! What is he like?"

Again Ailsa flushed.

"Oh—tall and sort of spare, with very blue eyes that can look quite grey at times. Very direct eyes. But otherwise he's rather remote. I don't think he'll mix very well, although he'll do the job he's taken on."

"Hm-m!" mused Aunt Betsy, eyeing her more closely, but that was all.

"Who else was there?" she asked after a lengthy pause in which she poured herself more coffee. "I don't suppose you've had a chance to meet anyone other than the people you sat at the table with."

"No," Ailsa agreed. "Just Mr. MacLaren and the Fultons."

Betsy's fingers tightened spasmodically round the handle of the coffee pot. Then she put it down very carefully and very deliberately on the tray, as if it had suddenly become too heavy for her to hold.

"Adam Fulton," she said. "I saw his name on the passenger list when we first came aboard. Is he with his wife?"

"No." Ailsa looked surprised. "His daughter. Do you know them?"

"I'm not sure." Betsy made a little fluttering movement with her hands, as if she were looking for something on the tray which she really didn't expect to find. "I—the name's the same, but Adam Fulton would have his wife with him."

"She might be dead," Ailsa suggested helpfully.

Betsy nodded, a faint colour rising in her cheeks.

"Could be," she agreed. "Of course, it needn't be the same Fulton. It was a long time ago." She looked slightly flustered. "Did you say these people were Americans?"

"Mr. Fulton has lived in America for twenty-five years, but originally he came from Scotland."

The information slid into a lengthy silence. Aunt Betsy's thoughts had obviously gone so far down into the past that Ailsa sat still, not wishing to disturb her until quite suddenly she looked up to ask if she might have some more coffee.

"This has gone quite cold," she complained. "The steward will bring some more. Just press the bell."

42

Even after the coffee had been brought her thoughts were still far away, and by the time Ailsa had poured her a second cup she looked ready to sleep again. Or perhaps she just wanted to be left alone with her thoughts.

"Off you go and see what's going on up on deck," she commanded. "I won't get up today. The nurse thinks the rest will do me good."

It was an altered decision. It was as if Aunt Betsy, who had always been fond of company and strange faces, didn't want to meet her fellow-passengers, after all.

CHAPTER THREE

AILSA went slowly down to her own cabin, wondering why the mention of Adam Fulton's name had masked all the brightness in her aunt's eyes.

The ship was plunging a little now, rolling slightly on the shallow waves of a choppy sea, but she did not mind the unfamiliar motion. She had always loved the sea, and this was going to be a wonderful experience for her.

Eager not to miss one single minute of it, she caught up the cream steamer coat her aunt had bought her and made her way back on deck, tying her scarf over her hair before she went out into the wind. It was quite fresh now, blowing strongly from the north-west, and she had to fight her way against it. That, too, was a delight to her. To breast the wind and feel its power and force, which dwarfed all lesser things.

Most of the passengers had already congregated on the boat deck as the ship began to slacken speed. Ahead of them lay a small, green-clad island riding the waves in utter solitude, and she remembered what Huntley had said about their first landing.

"Are you going ashore?"

Adam Fulton was at her elbow, with Lucy standing behind him in a purple woollen coat and white beret. Lucy looked strikingly beautiful, Ailsa thought, the regal colour of the coat setting off the pale golden colour of her hair and her clear complexion. Lucy knew about clothes. She would not make mistakes. Her feet were encased in neat white shoes, but they were sturdy shoes, laced and secure, so that she might walk across the island without mishap.

"I think I must stay on board this time," Ailsa answered Adam's query. "I wouldn't feel very happy if I left my aunt behind right away."

"It's a pity she's indisposed," Adam agreed. "Still, you can come with us another time. There are plenty of islands to be visited!"

Lucy was obviously looking for someone. Her eyes darted from one group to another, her mouth growing petulant as she failed to discover what she wanted.

"Have you seen Mr. MacLaren?" she asked at last. "Surely he must be taking a party ashore."

Ailsa's heart gave an odd little lurch of disappointment, although it was ridiculous to hope that Huntley MacLaren might remain in the ship while everyone else went ashore. It was his job to go with a party, and the guides were essential to the passengers' enjoyment.

"I haven't seen him, but he's sure to be somewhere around," Adam said, turning up the collar of his coat. "We don't touch land again, by the way, till we get right up nearly to the Shetlands. Fair Isle's our next port of call. Everyone will want to go ashore there, I guess."

Ailsa had been thinking more of the lesser known islands —of Jarlshof with its Viking sound, and Herma, and lone, deserted St. Kilda, far out on the Atlantic tide. But most of all she wondered about Corrae, that unknown island where they might or might not land. Suddenly it seemed to come very near, beckoning to her out of the mists of time.

She turned and saw Huntley MacLaren approaching along the deck, and although he was walking with someone else, they seemed to be standing apart with the winds of distant Corrae blowing in their faces and the scent of bog myrtle all about them.

It was no more than a momentary illusion, a fragment of time stolen out of the past, but it caught her by the throat so that she found difficulty in answering him when he said,

"I hear that Mrs. Bellinger is much better. Can that mean you're coming with us?"

She shook her head.

"I think I ought to stay with her," she decided. "She will be well enough to go ashore tomorrow, I hope."

The other passengers began to crowd round the rail, waiting for the boats to be lowered, and for a moment they were separated from Lucy Fulton and her father.

"Our next landing will be on Fair Isle," Huntley said. "We spend most of the day there, with no very specific task, as far as I'm concerned. It's a sort of get-together with the islanders."

"I'm looking forward to that," she told him, her eyes shining. "I've always wanted to discover the Islands—to see how the people live."

A swift shadow darkened his face and abruptly his eyes left hers, seeking the utmost distances of the sea and taking on some of its greyness as he said:

"Fair Isle is one of the more remote inhabited islands, but they have managed to establish a way of life there that has saved them from extinction. They are supported, too, by the National Trust. Money was essential to keep them going, you see."

She could sense the bitterness in him and wondered if this was the story of Corrae, but she could not ask him about his own island, as Lucy had done. She was far too sensitive for that, too sure that Corrae was the very soul of the man and that something irreplaceable would be torn out of his life when he was forced to part with it.

"I wish money didn't have to matter so much," she said impulsively. "All my life I've never had very much money and I suppose one does learn to do without it. Only sometimes it can bring you the things you could only dream about before—like coming on this cruise for me." She smiled round at him. "It's almost as if I might wake up soon and discover it was just a dream. Only, of course, I don't want to do that—not yet!"

He looked down at her, smiling now, indulgently perhaps, because he had been on this journey before many times, but curiously enough it did not seem to matter. Their eyes met and she felt the contact of the moment like the warmth of sunlight. It had been the same that day in Edinburgh, in Mr. Dobie's office, when she had felt the tang and freedom of the sea in that unlikely place.

"We've met before," she found herself saying. "In Edinburgh, just over a week ago."

"I was coming to that," he smiled. "I'll always remember how you ran back up those dreadful, winding stairs as if the survival of the entire world depended on your finding Mrs. Bellinger's handbag!"

46

He must know, Ailsa thought, that her aunt was in the market for Corrae, yet he had made no mention of the fact. Perhaps he had even come to a decision about the island. There was no reason why he should mention her aunt's business affairs to her, of course, and the whole transaction would likely be settled by letter after they had seen Corrae. For surely Aunt Betsy, impulsive though she undoubtedly was, would not buy an island she had never seen?

"It seems to be quite a habit with her—leaving things behind," she laughed.

"The stewards should be able to cope," he smiled. "The main thing will be to get her on her feet again."

The boats were lowered and the crowd surged between them.

"I'm sorry you're not coming with us," Huntley said when they found themselves side by side again. "I would have liked you to see the birds on May. They are quite a sight."

Impulsively Ailsa wished that she could change her mind and go, but she *did* owe it to Aunt Betsy to stay. It would seem an endless waiting time till the boats came back, riding the blue water like graceful swans.

Standing at the rail, a rather solitary little figure with her coat wrapped tightly round her, she watched Adam Fulton and Lucy take their seats in the second launch and saw Lucy quite unashamedly reserve a place for Huntley between her and her father. It was natural, perhaps, since they had shared the same table at lunch, but suddenly it hurt.

Lucy looked up to where she stood with a small, confident smile on her lips and even waved her white-gloved hand as the launch pulled away, while Adam Fulton levelled his expensive ciné-camera at the ship, taking a series of shots with her standing at the rail.

It was impossible to move away deliberately, and she stood smiling and waving until the launch had reached the shore. The ship seemed curiously empty when she finally turned along the deck, yet not everyone had gone ashore. Small groups had taken up strategic positions round the little tables in the sheltered veranda and in the observation lounge, and heads turned curiously or idly as she pursued her solitary way.

For half an hour she walked briskly round the upper deck because it gave her the greatest scope, and the people walking there smiled at her in the tentative, friendly way of shipboard acquaintances, although they did not speak. They were mostly in groups of twos and threes, and possibly they wondered why she was alone. Certainly all the other young people had gone ashore with the boat party.

Climbing up to the sun deck, she found that she could see the island quite clearly. They were quite close in and the launches were lying against a small landing stage. People were clambering over the rocks, but the main party was out of sight. Somewhere in the heart of the little green isle Huntley and Lucy Fulton would be together.

A step on the deck behind her made her turn to encounter a tall young man in uniform, and for a moment she wondered if someone had come to tell her aunt had been taken ill again. But the ship's first officer smiled pleasantly as he took out a silver case to offer her a cigarette. When she refused he lit one for himself, cradling the match between his hands to shield the flame from the wind.

"You do not like the excursions in the small boats?" he suggested, leaning with his back against the rail to look down at her from his splendid height. "Perhaps you are nervous of the sea?"

"Oh, no!" Ailsa hastened to assure him. "I just couldn't go ashore this time, that was all. My aunt has been ill."

"Ah! the lady with asthma? It was most unfortunate—yes. But we have a good surgeon on board and all is well!"

"A good *Norwegian* surgeon!" Ailsa laughed.

"That is so." He looked down at her, his lean, bronzed face creasing into a thousand laughter lines. "We are very proud of our ship and the way we take care of our passengers! That is why I do not like to see a young lady looking so lonely and perhaps a little sad walking the deck very fast to fill in the time!"

"Is that part of ship's policy too?" Ailsa countered, liking this blond giant of a man instinctively.

48

"To see that everyone is happy? Of course," he said. "Do you come from America?"

"No—sorry!" she laughed. "Only from Scotland!"

"But you love to see your own country—this beautiful land that is so like Norway, and so near to it?"

"Yes, that's quite true," Ailsa agreed. "I've never had a chance to see the Islands before now."

"You will not be disappointed." There was the same assurance in his pleasant voice as there had been in Huntley MacLaren's. "Always I say that people should see their native land before they rush off in search of the world."

"I haven't much chance of searching for the world," Ailsa smiled.

"Then we must make you enjoy this voyage so much that you will want to come again," he suggested, his clear blue eyes openly admiring. "I see you talking much with Mr. Huntley MacLaren. He is with us for the first time on this ship. I do not know much about him, but the captain has just told me that we are to call in at his home. It is the island of Corrae, on the west coast. We have not done this before, but sometimes there is the opportunity of altering out itinerary a little and we do so with pleasure. There may, you see, be some other place where we cannot land because of high seas, so it is best to have something in reserve."

"There's still some doubt about it, though," Ailsa said, remembering how reticent Huntley had been about the landing. "About being able to go ashore there, I mean."

"That may be so, but I think we will try, especially now that we have the owner on board with us."

Of course he did not understand. He probably did not even know that Corrae was for sale. Ailsa bit her lip, turning the conversation to lighter things. She discovered that his name was Erik Larsen and that the nurse was his sister.

"I tell Greta to come on this cruise for a holiday before she settles down to hospital work in Oslo," he explained. "But sometimes I wonder if she will not become engaged to our ship's surgeon before then," he added, smiling down at her. "Love affairs develop swiftly at sea. It is because the ship is a small world on its own and people are thrown so closely together. We are an isolated little community in the most romantic setting of all, and when it is a cruise ship—well, that makes is easier than ever!"

"To fall in love?" Ailsa's gaze went beyond him to the green shoulders of the island where the ship's boats rocked idly in the sun. "Surely," she objected, "it must take longer than a day?"

His smile broadened.

"Sometimes a day is sufficient," he assured her. "And we have seven days!"

Seven days to sail in the sun and get to know the people she had already met. Days to rise to the bait of Erik Larsen's light flirtation and come to know the ship's surgeon and Greta Larsen, who was already half in love with him, according to her brother. Days to take care of Aunt Betsy and sit with Adam Fulton and Lucy at meals. Days to watch Lucy falling in love with Huntley MacLaren!

"This evening when the boat parties return we will dance," Erik told her. "It is the best way to break the ice. You will find yourself much in demand since there are so many ship's officers as well as passengers."

"I've never been so popular!" Ailsa remarked laughingly. "I've met your sister, of course. She was very kind to my aunt when she was taken so suddenly ill."

"Greta is a born nurse," he agreed. "When we were children she used to insist on playing 'hospitals', and I spent a lot of time wrapped up in bandages on that account. Often I was wrapped from head to foot!"

"As tall as you are!" Ailsa smiled.

He laughed outright.

"Everything grows upwards in my country—tall mountains, tall pines, tall people. There is no room to grow sideways!"

"And tall stories!"

He grinned down at her.

"Why not?" he demanded. "They are very amusing!"

They walked together along the deck as the tea bell rang and because he was still off duty she found herself having tea with him at one of the tables in the forward lounge. Soon they were joined by the ship's surgeon and the assis-

50

tant purser, who informed her that her name had now been added to the passenger list.

"You were an unknown quantity at first," he said when they were introduced. "No name. Just Companion to Mrs. Bellinger'. We decided you must be a middle-aged spinster with inhibitions, so you can imagine how relieved we are!"

He was much more polished than Erik Larsen and perhaps for that reason Ailsa did not like him so much, but all these Norsemen were charming in their own way. They seemed to take a delight in their work, lending a happy air of co-operation to the running of the ship which must add to the passengers' comfort and the ultimate pleasure of the cruise.

When it was time to go and change for dinner Ailsa felt that she had made several new friends, although whether she could honestly claim Huntley MacLaren among their number was problematical. He would not make friends easily, and there was the added complication of her aunt wanting to buy Corrae.

Aunt Betsy might decide against the transaction once she had seen the little island, of course. They had no idea what it was really like.

Yet already she had made up her own mind about Corrae. In her imagination she could see Huntley's island home lying off some remote and rocky coast on the western seaboard with its ruined castle looking out across the Atlantic and its tiny harbour facing east towards the mainland. There was a charm and magic about building up her picture of Corrae which was nothing new to her. All her life she had built tiny, glowing castles in the air, peopling them with the children of her fancy, mainly, she supposed, because she had been an only child. And this was the first time she had come anywhere near reality. She was half in love with Corrae long before she saw it.

Looking in at her aunt's cabin on her way to her own, she found Betsy asleep, propped up with extra pillows. It would be best not to disturb her, she decided.

In her own cabin she changed from the woollen suit she had worn under her coat to come aboard into the blue cocktail dress her aunt had admired so much, pausing for a moment to look at her flushed reflection in the mirror behind the door before she made her way along the corridor at the first sound of the dinner bell.

She found her way more easily now, but she was still rather shy about meeting people. In the throng pressing towards the double doors of the dining-saloon she saw Huntley MacLaren's tall figure a little way ahead, and when she reached the table he drew out her chair for her. The Fultons had not come up yet, and suddenly Ailsa's heart increased its beat.

"I wondered if you would come in early," Huntley said. "I made enquiries about Mrs. Bellinger and was told that she was comfortably asleep. She's placed at the captain's table, and he worries about vacancies after the first meal aboard. He likes everyone to enjoy themselves from the word go!"

"Did you enjoy yourself this afternoon?" she asked, glancing at the menu he passed but not really studying it.

"It was an interesting enough excursion," he answered briefly. "I'm sorry you had to miss it."

"I'm looking forward to the others," she told him. "Will you be going ashore with all of them?"

"Only the ones in my own department!" he smiled. "When I am not on duty with the boat parties I shall be busy compiling notes for lectures in the autumn and a possible book."

"Greta Larsen told me you are an ornithologist and—did she say you were an author?" Ailsa asked.

"She flatters me!" When he smiled the lines round his eyes deepened to a fine network of wrinkles, like Erik Larsen's and the doctor's. They were all men who loved the sea and had spent their lives on or near it. Already she could picture this man on Corrae, looking out across the ocean from some rugged headland, as Erik might look from the bridge of his ship. "I've written articles for various journals," he went on to confess, "but never quite got down to a book." His face sobered, the dark brows drawing together at some painful recollection. "Perhaps I shall have time for a longer effort in the near future," he added, and now there was no escaping the edge of bitterness in his strong voice.

"I've got quite a lot of the subject matter tucked away at home, and this voyage will help, of course."

"Will you write it at Corrae?" she asked without thinking.

"No," he said, "I don't think that will be possible."

There was a small, awkward silence, in which so much seemed to be left unsaid between them. Ailsa deeply regretted her impulsive question about Corrae, but somehow she could not tell him so. He seemed to have shut himself away behind that vague barrier of reserve which she had stumbled against at their first meeting, and before she had time to turn the conversation to lighter things, the Fultons had joined them.

Lucy Fulton looked quite different. Once the sullen mask of bored indifference had been cast aside, her whole manner had undergone a change. The excursion of the afternoon seemed to have infused new vitality into her thin body and her eyes sparkled as she sat down opposite Huntley.

"Sorry to be late," she excused herself, "but we *did* linger rather a long time on your first island, didn't we?"

She looked fully at Huntley, ignoring Ailsa as if she did not exist, and Ailsa saw Adam Fulton looking at his daughter several times during the next half hour with an expression that was pitifully fond. Otherwise, he seemed a hard man.

"You going to dance, Luce?" he asked when the first couples took the floor. "Don't mind about me if you want to," he advised. "I'm an old fogey where dancing is concerned, but I can soon find somebody to smoke a cigar with, so off you go!"

Lucy turned to Huntley MacLaren.

"You dance, of course?" she asked, as if there could be only one answer to such a query.

"Not very well." Huntley pushed his coffee cup aside. "I made an effort during my student days, but I haven't kept it up."

"That doesn't matter," Lucy declared charmingly. "You never really forget. It's like driving a car or sailing a boat.

53

Once you know how it comes back quite easily. You really must try," she decided, "just to prove me right!"

Like driving a car or sailing a boat, Ailsa thought. Lucy would know all about these things. There was very little she had not done.

Huntley rose politely to his feet. It was part of his job to see that the *Saturn's* passengers enjoyed themselves.

"I like that young man," Adam Fulton beamed as he led Ailsa on the floor. "He's going to be good for Luce."

It was obvious that he thought his daughter had made a conquest and the idea pleased him.

"She's been running around with an odd sort of crowd in Florida ever since her mother died," he added confidentially. "The arty type who never really produce anything. Hangers-on, most of them, and all of them living more or less on their wits. There was one fellow, Reilley Cregan by name, who thought he had got me all safely tied up and docketed as a father-in-law, but it didn't come off. Interior decorating was supposed to be his line, but he couldn't decorate the inside of a birdcage! Luce talked me into letting him do our place outside Palm Beach, and he made it look like a fifth-rate night club!"

Ailsa could not resist a smile. It was impossible to imagine this dynamic, down-to-earth little man against an 'arty' background, although no doubt he would have tried to accept it for Lucy's sake. If he had rebelled in the end, Reilley Cregan's decor must have been hopelessly extreme.

And now Huntley MacLaren had come on the scene and the little he had discovered about this tall, handsome Scot had pleased him from the beginning, as it undoubtedly pleased Lucy.

Ailsa's heart gave an odd little lurch as she picked them out among the dancers. It was not very difficult, because Huntley stood head and shoulders above most men present, with the possible exception of Erik Larsen, who was well over six feet. He seemed to be dancing well enough, too, under Lucy's expert tuition.

"I've come to claim that dance you promised me," Erik said, standing beside Ailsa's chair.

She rose to her feet, smiling up at him.

54

"Did I promise?" she challenged. "I can't remember."

"You told me you loved to dance but that you hadn't been able to enjoy it for a very long time." Erik swung her out on to the floor. "Why was that?"

"Because my mother was so ill. I nursed her for two years before she died."

"I'm sorry," he apologized instantly. "I did not know. And now you are going to live with your aunt?"

"I've never thought about it," Ailsa confessed. "It will depend very much on where she eventually settles down."

"You would like it to be in Scotland," he guessed.

"I don't know. I haven't thought about it, really—not with any finality."

That was true enough. She hadn't had time to think in definite terms about the future or about Aunt Betsy. Her aunt had come upon the scene so swiftly, so unexpectedly, that her visit still retained some of the nebulous quality of a dream. Ailsa had never been used to people making the impulsive sort of decisions Betsy made simply because she had the money to indulge her every whim. Aunt Betsy's world and her own small, simple world at Achnasheen were poles apart.

"Perhaps your aunt will help you to make up your mind," Erik suggested. "She is a fantastic character, I believe. Already Greta is her willing slave. If there was a cure for asthma I'm sure Greta would be willing to dedicate the next two years of her life to help with it."

"Yes, there's something about Aunt Betsy," Ailsa agreed. "You have to like her. She's so utterly free from pretentiousness, for one thing, and so very, very kind. I don't think I've ever met such an unselfish person."

"Yet I think we're all selfish in at least one respect," Erik declared. "Isn't there something your aunt wants more than anything else which she would set out to get in spite of every obstacle?"

Perplexed by the unexpectedness of the question, Ailsa glanced at her companion rather sharply.

"I don't know," she said. "At least, I'm not definitely sure, but I would say she wants happiness more than anything else and—yes, perhaps that's what she's come in search of."

"Is it not what we are all looking for?" he asked. "In one way or another."

"Yes, I think it is."

"And you are happy at this time?"

"Now you are speaking about superficial happiness," Ailsa pointed out with a disarming smile.

"Superficial?" He considered the word. "On the surface —yes? Are you unhappy, then—underneath?"

Her eyes fell before the frankness of his curiosity.

"I suppose I haven't thought very deeply about ultimate happiness," she confessed.

"You mean love, of course," he said. "The love between a man and a woman."

"Ailsa flushed.

"Perhaps that was what I meant——"

"Then you have never been in love?"

"No."

"What age are you, Ailsa?"

"Twenty. I'll be twenty-one in June."

"And I am twenty-three. An old man by your reckoning!" There was a twinkle at the back of his blue eyes.

"Not so very old," Ailsa allowed. "Have you been all your life at sea?"

"All my life." She noticed again that far look which she had watched in Huntley MacLaren's eyes. "I could not have done anything else. There is Viking blood in me."

And in Huntley, Ailsa thought. They could be men of the same race, for the Viking strain ran strongly in the Celt, and Huntley's forebears had lived on Corrae for generations, far enough back to have taken part in those fierce sea-battles which had ranged all along the western coast. Islands had changed hands many times, captured and recaptured by raiders who had been a fitting match for the proud defenders, but sometimes an island had passed back to its original owner by a dowry. A Norse lady and a Scottish chief. It had happened many times, Ailsa supposed, in those far-off days when life was perhaps more simple than it was now, when

56

a man's physical strength and his iron determination to survive could be pitted against fortune to win.

The music stopped, but Erik did not return her immediately to her own table.

"I've got a lot of people I want you to meet," he explained, escorting her from table to table where members of the ship's complement of officers had already made friends.

It was a gay first night out, and although the deck sloped precariously at times as the *Saturn* met the steeper swell of the open North Sea, the dancing continued. Ailsa found herself circling the highly-polished floor for every number immediately it was announced, but never with Huntley MacLaren.

She saw him from time to time, either dancing with Lucy again or sitting with Adam Fulton, but he did not cross the floor to claim her as a partner.

She was diappointed, of course. It was no use pretending otherwise, but she could not make a deliberate appeal to Erik Larsen to take her back to her own table. He was being amazingly kind and thoughtful, possibly because her aunt had been unable to join her, and she had to admit that he was excellent company. With unflagging energy he had set about the task of making her enjoy herself, and she was more than grateful to him. Her first day on board M.S. *Saturn* had been a memorable one in every respect, and she was aware of a sudden excitement at the thought of tomorrow.

"I think I ought to go down now," she said reluctantly when she noticed how late it was. "I'd like to look in at my aunt's cabin on the way just to make sure she's comfortably settled for the night."

Erik prepared to let her go with equal reluctance.

"Shall I come down with you?" he asked.

She smiled her refusal.

"I'm sure I can find my own way now," she told him.

"Until tomorrow, then!" He stood over her, holding her hand. "Tomorrow and Fair Isle! I may not be able to go ashore right away—I shall be on duty—but it is a whole day trip and I should manage an hour or so in the afternoon."

One swift glance at her own table had proved it to be empty and Ailsa could not see either Lucy or Huntley on the dance floor. Adam Fulton was also missing, but he had probably drifted off to bed, completely happy in the thought that Huntley and Lucy were together.

With her hand on the rail of the companionway leading to the deck below, Ailsa hesitated. The sun had gone down long ago, but there was still a pearly-grey light in the sky which made it possible to see the vast blue-black expanse of water beyond the ship's rail.

Suddenly she wanted to go out there, to stand for a moment in the half-dark, reviewing her day. The sea drew her like a magnet—that and the hidden magic of the warm spring night.

Impulsively she drew her woollen stole more tightly round her shoulders and opened the glass doors. The swish of the sea along the ship's hull met her like a calling voice and she went straight to the rail.

Minutes passed before she was fully aware of the two shadowy figures silhouetted against the skyline, the man's white shirt front gleaming against the darkness, the girl's gay chiffon head-scarf floating like a challenging streamer in the night wind. Then she heard Lucy Fulton's low, spontaneous laughter as the two turned to look down at the sea.

As if she had been dealt some savage, crippling blow, Ailsa groped her way back into the brilliantly-lit hall. The man out there with Lucy was Huntley MacLaren.

Well, what did it matter? What did it matter to her? She could not have fallen in love with him—not in a day!

Blindly she made her way across the hall. What was it Erik Larsen had said only an hour or so ago, out there on the deck? 'Love affairs develop swiftly at sea. It is because the ship is a small world on its own and people are thrown so closely together.'

Ailsa knew that it was far more than that. It was the magic of the sea and the star-filled night; it was the curious sense of isolation from an ordinary, workaday world, and the subtle spell of a romantic journey into the unknown.

It had been all these things for her, and more. Her foolish, receptive heart had been wide open to hurt, and now she had never felt so utterly alone.

Halfway across the hall she was greeted by a familiar voice.

"I'm looking for Lucy," Adam Fulton began conversationally. "I went into the forward lounge to smoke a last cigar and left her dancing, but when I looked in just now she had gone."

Ailsa forced a smile.

"Don't worry," she managed. "She's out on deck with Mr. MacLaren."

Adam beamed at her.

"Oh, well, that's all right," he said. "I guess I'm not going to quibble about them looking at the sea in the moonlight—if there is a moon! I've been making enquiries about MacLaren and he's just the sort of chap I'd like for Lucy— nice and reliable and not too soft with women. He's the regular McCoy, in fact. There's no money attached, of course —that's why there's talk of him having to sell that place of his—but I've money enough to burn. The man who gets Lucy won't go barefooted. No, Sir! I'll take care of that!"

Ailsa felt suddenly cold all over. Was this Huntley's reason for squiring Lucy so assiduously all day? Had he already seen a way to save Corrae, as it had probably been saved long ago by some sea-roving ancestor of his who had married an heiress in his time?

Why did she care? Why did she even think about it? But how could she stop thinking? She made some excuse to Adam, hurrying away to the deck below, but she did not pause at her aunt's door. She had forgotten that she had been going there to say goodnight. All she could think about was the merciful privacy of her own cabin and the pressing need to be alone.

A vast chasm of loneliness seemed to stretch before her, a dark abyss where she was destined to wander eternally because, even before today, even before she had stumbled across him on the deserted deck above her, she had known that Huntley MacLaren could hold her world of happiness in his two strong hands.

She had felt it in Edinburgh at that first moment of their meeting, a brief encounter which had stamped his image on her heart for ever.

CHAPTER FOUR

IN the morning a fresh wind and a choppy sea met them abreast of the Orkneys. They had steamed far out on their course and the rocky, scattered islands were scarcely discernible to port. Through the early morning haze a headland with the sun on it stood out for a moment and then disappeared. Someone said that it was John o' Groats.

"We're farther north than that," Adam Fulton decided, laying his table napkin back on his plate. "The purser told me we were about in line with the last of the mainland an hour ago."

Ailsa and he had breakfasted alone. Lucy had decided to have orange juice, toast and coffee sent to her cabin, and Huntley had obviously been up earlier than anyone else.

During the night Ailsa had tried to come to some sort of terms with her errant heart, and she told herself that she was glad of this. It would give her more time to steel herself to a casual meeting with Huntley somewhere during the morning. Probably when they joined the boats to go ashore. Her aunt had assured her that she would be up and dressed long before then, but she, also, had taken her breakfast in bed.

"Looks as if you and me are the only stayers in this party!" Adam observed as he drew back her chair. "Are you venturing on deck?"

"I'd like to." She would have to return to her cabin for her coat first. "Do we go ashore in special boats?"

"No, we just pile in anywhere there's room, I guess." Adam lit the inevitable cigar, which he seemed to smoke at all times of the day. "Maybe we can look out for each other," he suggested when it was pulling to his satisfaction. "I'd like to meet your aunt."

"I'll watch out for you," Ailsa promised, wondering if Lucy had already made sure of Huntley's company. "I'm sure my aunt would like to meet you, too."

Adam beamed. He was so completely happy because everything was going well for him on this trip. He hadn't

61

wanted to come, really, but he had thought it would be good for Lucy. He ambled off in the direction of the observation lounge while Ailsa went to get her coat. Coming up on deck again, she tapped lightly on her aunt's door.

"Coming!" Betsy replied brightly. "Just let me get a head-scarf."

"There's plenty of time." Ailsa put her head in at the half open door. "What on earth have you been doing?" she gasped as she took in the confusion.

"Looking for something." Betsy sounded evasive.

"Not your handbag? I don't think I can bear that—not again!" Ailsa laughed.

"No—not that."

"What, then?"

"As a matter of fact, I lost my teeth——"

Ailsa sat down on the narrow bunk.

"You couldn't very well go ashore without them, could you?" she remarked, trying to keep a sober face.

"Not very well!"

Ailsa helped to straighten up the disordered cabin. On her aunt's bedside cabinet there was an open form with a brief radioed message pencilled on it.

"I got that this morning," Betsy said. "You'd better read it. It's from Edinburgh. From Simpson Dobie. I asked him to keep in touch with me about the sale."

Ailsa's heart had begun to hammer in her side. She could not read the message from where she stood—she did not want to read it.

"You'll see what he says," Betsy went on. "'My client willing accept offer if island suitable.' As if we didn't already know who his client was!"

Ailsa stood very still, wondering what her aunt would do now.

"Have you—sent any reply?" she asked, at last.

"Not yet. I want you to do that for me," Betsy said. "You'll find a radio office somewhere on one of the upper decks. Ask one of the officers or a steward."

Ailsa bit her lip.

"What message shall I send?" she asked.

"Say: 'Repeat offer subject to island's suitability. Hope to view during present tour.' That will tell Mr. Dobie all he needs to know. It's more or less what one might call a 'gentleman's agreement' at the present moment," she mused, "but if I really like the place when I see it I can go straight across to Edinburgh and sign as soon as we disembark at Oban. In the meantime, I can send off a cheque to seal this part of our bargain."

She was still moving about the cabin, picking up items of clothing which she had scattered in her former search, and Ailsa felt guiltily pleased at the distraction.

"Aunt Betsy," she suggested slowly, "supposing he wanted to back out?"

"Supposing *who* wanted to back out?" Betsy stuffed a bundle of nylon stockings into a drawer.

"Huntley MacLaren."

"He won't—not after sending a message like that. It sounds as if he has been only too thankful to accept."

The issue must have been settled before Huntley left Edinburgh, Ailsa realized. Before he had met Lucy Fulton.

"He could withdraw——"

"Why should he want to withdraw?" Her aunt turned to gaze at her in amazement. "I made him a most generous offer, and I only imposed two conditions. Of course, I had to look at the place before I made my final decision. I couldn't go entirely by touched-up photographs!"

Ailsa didn't stay to ask what her aunt's second condition had been. She went along the alleyway in a daze and bumped into Huntley MacLaren in the main hall.

"The shop's over there," he directed when he saw her with her purse in her hand.

"I wasn't going to the shop." Her heart had given a sickening lurch as she recognized him. "I was looking for the radio office."

He was instantly concerned.

"Has Mrs. Bellinger had a relapse?" he asked.

"No. She's quite well. She's getting ready to go ashore. She—wants me to send off a message for her."

"I'll take you up," he offered. "It's right on top."

"If you're busy——"

How could she tell him that it was a message to Edinburgh—a message about Corrae?

"That's all right. I was going up." He looked down at her in the subdued light of the hallway. "You appeared to enjoy yourself last night," he observed a trifle dryly. "When I came to ask you for a dance you were surrounded by uniforms."

"I didn't know you wanted to dance with me, Mr. Mac-Laren." she told him stiffly, remembering how he had danced most dances with Lucy.

He smiled.

"You surprise me," he said.

They had reached the boat deck and he turned with her along the narrow alleyway leading to the radio officer's cabin. It seemed ludicrous that she was about to send a message off to Edinburgh which she could quite easily have given him on the spot. Yet it could, of course, be by his own mandate that these final details were being conducted in a businesslike way through his solicitor. There was nothing personal about it, after all. It was only by the merest chance that they found themselves shut up together in the small world of a ship cruising among the islands that had always been home for him. He had left the sale of Corrae in Simpson Dobie's hands.

He stooped to open the cabin door for her.

"I half anticipated a queue," he remarked. "It's amazing how many messages people find they must send on a cruise like this, but you are in undisputed possession!"

Ailsa hesitated in the open doorway.

"Thank you very much."

He smiled one-sidedly.

"Can I wait and take you for a drink?" he asked unexpectedly. "There's a bar in the veranda lounge and it's quite warm up there in the sun."

"I—ought to get back——"

"You're very conscientious," he remarked. "I hope Mrs. Bellinger appreciates the fact."

"I think she does." Suddenly she felt that she wanted to share that drink with him up there in the sun. Why not?

"If you'll wait for me in the veranda I won't be very long," she promised.

He smiled crookedly.

"I'll wait," he promised in his turn.

Ailsa let her breath go in a small sigh of relief as he turned away. At least she needn't send off the message under his watchful eye.

The radio officer supplied her with the necessary form and she wrote hastily. If only Huntley would *talk* about Corrae, she thought.

Yet he could not very well tell her in confidence that he wished to withdraw from his bargain with her aunt because he had suddenly met an American girl with a millionaire father.

Was that the truth of the matter? *Was* he cultivating Lucy Fulton because she was one way of saving Corrae?

She paid for the message and turned towards the door. She could not think that of him, she realized, even after what Adam Fulton had said. After all, it was Adam and not Huntley who had suggested that Lucy might bring him a fortune.

He was waiting at the edge of the sun deck when she reached the glassed-in shelter where several couples were already seated out of the wind.

"If you come over here to the rail I'll show you a school of porpoises," he offered, much as a small boy might have done. "They're fascinating to watch, especially when they follow the ship."

He stood behind her, pointing over her shoulder to a line of rapidly-turning black backs on the silver-tinted waves. The whole sea appeared to be heaving with the acrobatic little creatures as they gambolled in the sun, and they seemed to be travelling steadily northwards with the ship. There was rhyme and reason in their steady progress.

"They're fishing for herring," Huntley explained, and suddenly his voice sounded quite young. "They come quite close in to Corrae. My brother and I used to follow them in a sailing dinghy—far too far out for my mother's peace of mind!"

"Is your brother on the island now?" Ailsa asked.

65

He shook his head.

"No. He was lost at sea. At the very end of the war, Hamish was the real laird of Corrae."

"And now there's only you left?"

"Yes. My mother died some years ago. I don't think she really ever got over the shock of that double tragedy." His voice was remote, lost in bitter memory. "My father went into the Navy at the beginning of the war, you see. Hamish and he were both drowned within months of one another. Hamish was nineteen."

Words were poor things when faced with the telling of such a tragedy, Ailsa realized. She could not say that she was sorry, and she knew now why he had hung on to Corrae till the bitter end. She knew, too, that she could not blame him if he married Lucy to keep it his. It was all he had.

"We were a very closely-knit family," he went on reminiscently. "Hamish was five years my senior and he taught me everything I knew about boats and the wild life of the islands. He loved every inch of Corrae."

As you do, Ailsa thought sadly, wondering how her aunt could ever contemplate buying such a place. How could a woman hope to serve Corrae as this man had served it, fighting a losing battle against financial difficulties for years? Corrae was in his blood. It was a part of him, part of a magnificent heritage that no one else had any right to accept.

The double death duties must have crippled the estate. That was really the major part of the story. It had become impossible for Huntley to carry on, and somehow she knew that he was getting out so that Corrae might live.

They were still standing very close together, his arm resting along the rail, and she wished madly that time would stand still, that they might sail on like this for ever with the wind in their faces and the salt tang of spray on their lips. It was a new world to her, but it was his world and she felt content in it.

If it proved to be a hollow contentment, a moment snatched from the heartache of tomorrow, she did not care.

Huntley did not speak again till he was able to point out the tiny island appearing out of the mist ahead of them.

"There it is," he said. "Our next landfall."

Fair Isle lay in the sun, a remote and rocky pinnacle surrounded by a vast waste of sea. As they drew steadily nearer, the white specks of cottages stood out against the hillsides and the whole island looked wonderfully green. There was a quality of mystery about these islands which Ailsa realized would hold her in its spell for the rest of her life. It was difficult to define, but utterly impossible to refute. If the sudden music of fairy pipes had drifted towards them across the restless sea she would not have denied its existence, and the spell was only shattered when Huntley said:

"Time to go, I'm afraid. In half an hour we'll be putting down the boats and I'll be on duty for the rest of the day."

She wondered if he had crashed in on their intimacy deliberately, because she was sure that the spell had been very real for him, too.

When she reached the main hall her aunt was coming up from her cabin.

"Oh, there you are!" Betsy greeted her. "Are you sure you have something warm to wear? We've come an awful long way further north."

Ailsa had not felt cold, even standing up there at the rail with the wind blowing strongly against her. The magic of the islands had entangled her to the exclusion of any physical reaction.

"The boats will soon be going down," she said. "We're going over in a party. Come along and meet the others. I've sent off your message," she added rather breathlessly.

"Good!" Aunt Betsy acknowledged. "Though why I couldn't just have given it to Mr. Huntley MacLaren personally, I just can't see. However, if that's how he wants it to be, we'll deal in a purely businesslike way. But surely he'll condescend to show me over Corrae when we reach there?"

"I don't think he's trying to be difficult," Ailsa excused Huntley. "It all began in Edinburgh, and perhaps there's nothing he can do about it."

"Except decide that he won't sell, after all?" Betsy queried. "That's what you said, wasn't it?"

"I was only making a wild guess," Ailsa reminded her.

They turned towards the lounge, but before they reached the wide double glass doors Aunt Betsy had stopped dead in her tracks. She stared straight in front of her, as if she had seen a ghost, but it was a very substantial human being who came towards her in the shape of Adam Fulton, followed closely by Lucy in her purple coat. They were ready to go ashore.

Ailsa had started to introduce them before she noticed that most of the colour had left her aunt's face. Adam, however, registered his surprise in quite a different way.

"Well, Betsy!" he said, measuring her across twenty-five years of separation. "I'll vow you haven't changed a bit!"

"Get away with you, Adam!" Betsy managed, recovering some of her poise, although her hands were trembling. "It's far too many years ago for you to go talking rubbish like that. I'm an old woman!"

"You can't be more than forty-six—forty-seven at most." He spared her nothing. "You were no more than a spoiled brat of twenty or so when you turned me down and I sailed for America."

"I didn't turn you down, Adam." Betsy had managed to control the emotion in her voice. "I just refused to go to America with you."

"Ay," he mused, "and you followed me there after a bit, with somebody else."

"What is all this?" Lucy demanded. "You appear to be excavating the past in a very thorough way."

"That's about the size of it," her father agreed, still unable to take his eyes from Betsy's surprised face. "Mrs. Bellinger!" he mused as if he had been reading the passenger list. "Who would have believed that it was Betsy MacRae?"

Only two women had counted in Adam Fulton's life—the girl with whom he had first fallen in love and never married, and the daughter who now travelled around the world by his side. He and Betsy had been boy and girl together here in Scotland. He had carried her school books for her and over a silly tiff they had parted. Twenty-six years ago. After twenty-six years and a lifetime of experience they were meeting again like this. Adam's wife had been a brittle, selfish woman who had stood behind him, urging him ever onwards, up the ladder of success to the top. She had strengthened many rungs for him by her overmastering ambition, but why he had married Edie Self was still a matter for conjecture. Out of pique, maybe, but he didn't think so. He had been a desperately lonely man during those first months when he had been trying to find his feet in a new country, and Edie had been sympathetic. He had thought her kind then. Only after their marriage had he known the whole truth, how she had been jilted in her turn and had seized him on the rebound from that unhappy affair. A double sort of rebound, because his own pride had been deeply bruised by Betsy's seeming indifference. He had written to her twice without receiving any reply. She had meant what she had said. America wasn't for her.

And Betsy had regretted her decision too late. Her mother had implored her not to leave Scotland; frail, weak Hester MacRae, the youthful clinging vine who had become the middle-aged parasite. She had survived for only a year after Betsy's marriage to Archie Nicholson. Then Archie, too, had felt the pull of the New World and they had crossed the Atlantic in their turn.

Within two years of refusing Adam Fulton Betsy had been in New York. There had been no child of the union and this, beyond doubt, had been the bitterest disappointment of Betsy's life. She had tried to forget Adam and the poignant fact of their parting, accepting second best with Archie Nicholson, and they had led a prosperous, pleasant existence. Betsy had managed to hide from her husband her deep lack of fulfilment in life. After his death she had known a mounting sense of frustration, rushing here and there without finding any satisfaction in the power her money gave her. Eventually she had married Russel G. Bellinger, but he had died within a year, leaving her richer than ever but still alone.

"Well, this is certainly something!" Adam declared, still managing to look as if he could not quite believe the evidence of his own eyes. "Have we time to celebrate with a drink, do you think?" He turned towards Lucy. "This is my daughter," he introduced her with pride. "We've been taking a look at the world together. My wife died two years ago," he added, "and we've been feeling kind of lost since. Edie was a great manager."

Betsy said "Oh?" but that was all. She looked at Lucy as if she wanted to like her and wasn't quite sure that she could.

Lucy, for her part, dismissed Mrs. Bellinger with a thin smile. Her father was always encountering 'old friends' in this thoroughly disconcerting manner, although she had to admit that they were usually business acquaintances of his own sex.

"We're going ashore," she said rather pointedly. "I suppose you are too? Huntley said last night that the boats would go down as soon as we dropped anchor. We have a whole day on the island."

"Why not let's make it a party?" Adam suggested. "It's not every day I can telescope twenty-six years like this!" His eyes twinkled as he looked at Betsy. "Y'know," he declared, "I think we had to meet again—somewhere."

"Maybe so," Betsy agreed. "I'm ready to go ashore, if you are, Ailsa."

Ailsa was wondering what Huntley had arranged for the Fultons, if he had made some sort of effort to go ashore in their company, even if he did happen to be on duty. She could not refuse to join the boat party, however, and Adam was quick to take up her aunt's remark.

"We'll go up on deck and see what's to do!" he suggested.

An odd sort of boyishness had crept into his manner, banishing the austerity of his former approach. It was, indeed, as if he had turned back the pages of the years and could feel all the old youthful enthusiasms pounding in his blood once more. They were about to set forth on a gay adventure as far as Adam was concerned, and he felt that everyone should share the experience with him.

Lucy, he was sure, was bound to enjoy herself, and that was half his own pleasure already guaranteed. The other half was new and strange to him. If it had to do with this odd, unexpected meeting with Betsy Bellinger—who had never been anything but Betsy MacRae to him—he did not pause to analyse his emotions. He only knew that something warm and half afraid and rather pathetic had stirred in his heart again when, long ago, he had believed it dead.

Huntley was standing beside one of the launches when they appeared on the boat deck and Adam went quickly towards him.

"All set for a good day, Mr. MacLaren?" he asked brightly. "The sea looks fairly choppy to me."

"We haven't far to go," Huntley assured him, looking beyond him to where Aunt Betsy stood.

Ailsa imagined that there was a sudden new stiffness in his manner, but Adam evidently saw nothing wrong.

"I don't suppose you've met Mrs. Bellinger," he said, introducing them. "She's been laid up with asthma since she came on board."

Huntley extended his hand.

"We have met, fleetingly, in Edinburgh," he said. "I managed to rescue Mrs. Bellinger's handbag about a week ago."

"I am a nuisance!" Betsy laughed. "I leave things all over the place." She shook Huntley warmly by the hand. "I'm glad we've met officially, Mr. MacLaren," she added in her forthright way. "I hope we may be able to have a little chat about Corrae before we get on to the west coast. As a matter of fact," she added in a silence which could almost be felt, "I've just been sending off a message to Edinburgh. Ailsa did it for me. I don't know what I should have done without her help," she acknowledged affectionately.

Ailsa's embarrassed gaze was drawn swiftly to Huntley's face, but there was very little change in his expression. The remoteness was there, but there was no sign of anger.

"We must arrange a talk, if you wish," he agreed courteously enough. "If this weather holds we will certainly be able to land on Corrae."

There was little emotion in his voice. It was as if he had steeled it to a determined acceptance of the situation. It was Lucy who said abruptly:

"You always seem to be one jump ahead of me. I thought Corrae was likely to be our very last port of call?"

"It is," Huntley informed her. "But we only have a week, and the weather looks settled enough to make a fair prediction."

"It is rather a pity," Lucy said. "The week, I mean. It won't be nearly long enough for—everything." She looked up at Huntley with a very definite meaning in her eyes. "I guess we can make the most of it, though," she added. "I'm just dying to go ashore! Be a darling, Huntley, and get us places in the first launch."

Huntley turned away with a smile.

"I haven't a lot of influence," he told her, "but I'll do what I can."

"I'm hoping he'll spend most of the day with us," Adam mused. "He's a well of information about the Islands. He's got them right under his skin, I'd say. Pity about that place of his," he added, leaning back against the rail as he took out and lit another cigar. "He seems almost touched about it. Doesn't want to talk much about having to sell it, I guess. Well," he concluded vaguely, "maybe he won't need to. Good Samaritans have come along at the last minute before now!" He inhaled reflectively. "I wonder how big it is?"

"Eleven and a half miles by three."

Betsy's prompt and unequivocal reply made Adam turn to stare at her.

"How do you know?" he enquired, surprised.

"I've been reading about it for the past two or three days," Betsy told him briefly, and then suddenly she seemed to be on her guard. "It interested me and I'll be glad to see it. That's all."

Adam continued to gaze at her in rather an odd manner, but he did not mention Corrae again. The tranquil expression in his eyes altered a fraction, but it would have taken a very keen observer to notice that he also was determined to keep his own counsel.

They went on board the launch and when it was full it sped swiftly towards the island. Huntley had taken the

72

tiller, with one of the ship's officers standing beside him, and Lucy had managed to seat herself not too far away.

Before noon all the hundred and fifty passengers on board the *Saturn* had been safely conveyed to dry land. They spilled over the remote little island in a gay tide, sweeping over the rocks and the rough grass in laughing, chattering groups, buying up, in a day, the islanders' entire yearly output of intricately-patterned jerseys and caps and gloves. Jealously they hugged to their bosoms suit lengths of hand-woven cloth which would be tailored eventually in New York or Chicago or Detroit.

Aunt Betsy bought quite a lot of tweed, which Huntley offered to carry back to the launch for her. She hugged the big parcel to her for a moment in contemplative silence.

"I wouldn't like to lose it," she said.

Smilingly he glanced about him at the little crofts and the gently-grazing sheep and the kirk on the hillside.

"There's not much fear of that here," he pointed out.

"No, I suppose not," Betsy laughed. "How silly of me! Ailsa can go with you and help carry the little parcels," she decided.

Huntley looked enquiringly in Ailsa's direction.

"Why not?" he said. "Then we could be doubly sure!"

Half inclined to look round for Lucy, who had been buying tweed at a cottage door with Adam standing beside her, wallet in hand, Ailsa found herself walking back towards the jetty where they had disembarked.

"Have you seen enough?" Huntley asked. "On land, I mean?"

"Not all I want to see, but I must confess to being a little bit foot-sore!" Ailsa smiled.

"Then I suggest a quick trip right round the island," he said. "All islands take on an entirely different character from the sea."

"That would be lovely!" Her eyes were shining, her cheeks deeply pink from more than the caress of the playful wind that swept up towards them from the rocks. "Today has been wonderful."

"What did you buy?" he asked.

"Oh—not very much. As much as I could afford, of course! I've never seen such wonderful blending of colours worked into knitting before. They are so different."

"They are all natural dyes," he told her, steadying the launch for her to get in. "The islanders have been doing this sort of thing for hundreds of years, and now they have a regular market for their work. A great deal has been done for them to keep them here, of course. Otherwise I'm afraid it would have been another case of St. Kilda."

"Evacuation, you mean?"

He nodded.

"The death of an island is a painful thing to watch," he said.

"Yes, I'm sure it is," Ailsa answered sympathetically. "I suppose the authorities are doing everything that can be done?"

"On the larger islands—yes."

But not on Corrae. It was too small, too unimportant for authority to take action and, of course, it was privately owned. It was Huntley MacLaren's sole responsibility.

He bent his head into the well of the launch and the engine roared into life. The small, trim white craft made a half circle in the calm green water close to the shore and headed northwards along the coast.

To Ailsa it was far more than a wonderful experience. It was a day in a lifetime, snatched out of all the other hours when fate might not be so kind. She was here with Huntley, sitting close beside him with the wind lifting her hair gently back from her forehead and the salt kiss of spray on her lips. It was almost as if his mouth touched her own.

Above them the sky was very blue, with not a cloud to be seen anywhere, and all about them lay the sea, gentle and coloured like a peacock's wing. All along the shore of the craggy little isle the waves broke in a lacy edge of white, and far above them on the grey pinnacles of the cliff face, birds she could not name circled and dived, protesting loudly at their approach.

Huntley throttled back the engine and they went more slowly while he picked out the different species for her.

"The puffins are the clowns of the bird world," he explained. "Just before sunset they hold a sort of general assembly and then they are most interesting to watch. The razorbills, too, do all sorts of acrobatic tricks, like jumping high into the air till it seems they're going to fall down the cliff and come to grief. They never do, of course. It's just a form of exhibitionism, common even in the bird world, I suppose."

"You sound very fond of that world, all the same," Ailsa reflected, trailing her hand idly in the green water. "Will you keep on this sort of work if——"

"If I sell Corrae?" His dark brows shot up in a questioning line. "That is almost decided."

"There's—no other way?"

He looked at her and his eyes were suddenly cold again. "If I could think of one," he said, "I would take it."

But surely he already knew about Lucy? She had made it very plain that she was attracted, and to encourage Lucy, to marry Lucy, would be the 'open sesame' to her father's wealth. Adam Fulton could do for Corrae what Huntley could never do alone.

The thought had such power to hurt her now that her heart seemed to twist with a physical pain and all the wonder and beauty suddenly faded out of her day.

"Isn't there one obvious way?" she pointed out bitterly before she could stop herself. "You could—marry someone who might be able to help."

Instantly the vividly blue eyes came down on hers and for a split second she thought that there was protest in their depths. Then, harshly, Huntley laughed.

"I've thought of that," he confessed. "I've considered it quite carefully. It would be no great hardship—for Corrae."

The words stung her cruelly, cutting deeply across her sensitive heart.

"Of course," she said, "you love Corrae."

He did not answer that. Instead he pulled the tiller hard towards him, sending the launch round the north end of the island in a flurry of white spray. The birds rose higher into the air, screeching their protest——razorbills, kittiwakes, guillemots and hundreds of little sheerwaters, swerving low over the hidden rocks beneath the great dark shadows of the gulls.

The gulls circled and dipped and cried in endless complaint, and Ailsa thought she would never be able to forget the sound as long as she lived. She was to hear it again, many times, in the weeks that followed, and always with an agony in her heart that reminded her of this day.

"Are we nearly round?" she asked when a group of small white crofts came in sight. "The others must be wondering where we are."

"I'm sorry," he said almost harshly. "if I've taken you against your will."

"You know that isn't true!" Before she could check them foolish tears had sprung to her eyes. "I wanted to come. I wanted this trip more than anything else in the world——"

He looked at her and then swiftly away, his eyes resting on the rock-bound shore with the little white houses above it. From them all came the thin spiral of blue peat smoke which told of warmth and a family secure and at peace beneath the humble thatch.

"I hope you have not been disappointed," was all he said.

Deliberately he bent to urge their craft to greater speed, and soon their white wake was flying away behind them like a broad streamer waving in the sun.

When they reached the landing stage Erik Larsen and his sister were standing there. The tall Norwegian girl gave Ailsa a friendly smile.

"Mrs. Bellinger has been searching everywhere for you," she said. "I believe she thinks you have been spirited away! All sorts of things are liable to happen on these islands, you know!" she added with a twinkle.

"Such as launches going adrift," Erik complained dryly, taking over from Huntley. "I've got to go back to the ship," he explained. "There's been a signal from the old man. He may just be wanting to come ashore for a walk, of course. By the way," he added as if it had been an afterthought, "Mrs. Bellinger isn't the only one who has been agitated over your absence. The Fultons have been trying to track you down all over the place. Miss Fulton says you promised to have lunch with them."

Packed lunches had been sent over from the *Saturn* so that they need not deplete the islanders' precious store of food, but in almost every croft a table had already been set. The hospitable islanders would not allow their guests to go away unwelcomed in the traditional manner and so the food was almost equally divided. The passengers from the ship tucked in to homely island fare while their hosts ate chicken in aspic fruit salad and cream.

Aunt Betsy greeted them from the open door of a cottage.

"We're in here," she called gaily. "Adam's gone to have a look at the livestock. He's had his meal. We thought you were never coming back! Lucy wants to see the other side of the island and Mr. Larsen says we've just got time. The launch will be taking us back at five o'clock."

Lucy was sitting inside the cottage, crumbling an oatcake into meal on her plate. She could not keep the look of anger out of her eyes.

"Where have you two been?" she demanded. "I thought you had a lecture?"

She was looking directly at Huntley, openly accusing him of desertion.

"I have," he said evenly. "For most of the afternoon."

"Which means you can't take us over the island?"

"On the contrary," he answered, "that is exactly what I have to do."

Lucy looked angrier still.

"Which means everybody has to go!" she exclaimed. "I loathe this sort of thing—gangs of people wandering about, open-mouthed, while you talk! I've had it all over Europe." She jumped to her feet. "I thought this might be different!"

Huntley stood between her and the door.

"This *is* going to be different," he said. "I think it would be better if you waited for your father and me. It's not so very difficult to get lost or into trouble. We don't want to be picking up the bits out of a remote gully, you know."

He had set out to humour Lucy, aware of the vixen streak in her that would have sent her running from the cottage in a fit of uncontrollable temper, and after the barest hesitation she relaxed and came back to sit in the ingle-nook seat beside the peat fire.

They had bought cloth and travelling rugs and woollen pullovers from the household earlier in the day, and now she watched sulkily as the grandmother, an old crone of ninety, demonstrated the working of the loom. She was a wizened old woman with bent shoulders and sunken cheeks whose skin was like lined parchment, but she had eyes as blue and far-seeing as Huntley's.

Coming out of the gloom at the back of the kitchen, she looked long and earnestly at Ailsa when Betsy brought her forward to be introduced.

"Ay," she said without preliminary, "you have tears to shed, my lassie! Bitter tears. A man of the Viking breed will take your heart and crush it in his hand." Suddenly the blue eyes went beyond Ailsa's confused young face to the man standing behind her. A man who cannot help himself." she added quietly as Huntley turned away. "Fate holds the spindle and the threads are drawn out, one by one! For you they are woven into a strange pattern. I can see an island with great birds flying over it—the Arctic skua and the black Peregrine falcon——"

The cracked old voice dropped into a silence that could almost be felt.

"What nonsense!" Lucy's brittle voice broke the spell. "You're not going to tell me that you believe this sort of thing?"

Scornfully she looked in Ailsa's direction and then she turned towards Huntley.

"You, at least, Huntley?" she said.

He had strode to the window, blocking out a good deal of the light which filtered through the spotless muslin curtains on to the floor at his feet.

"I have lived with it all my life," he said. "They call it 'the second sight' in the Isles. I have often seen such predictions borne out, almost to the letter. You can, of course, call it coincidence, if you like."

Ailsa could not see his face, but she thought that most of the colour had left it. She would not have called him a

78

superstitious man. He was too strong, too down-to-earth for that.

"Aw, shucks!" Aunt Betsy exclaimed. "Don't let's have any more of this. It's spoiling my day!"

She tried to press a coin into the old lady's gnarled fist, but the crooked fingers refused to close on it. The old woman would not take payment for a warning.

Ailsa tried to eat the meal they had prepared for her, but she was glad that the girl who served it was young and shy and did not press her. She was not at all like her grandmother. She was no more than fifteen and she smiled shyly, gently, when Betsy admired the long braids of fair hair on either side of her face which fell well below her slim young waist.

"She's right out of one of the Norse sagas!" Betsy said.

Ailsa was glad to get out into the open air again, although she had been greatly interested in the spotless interior of the little house. It was a wonderfully simple mode of life, lonely but full of an all-pervading peace. The same sort of peace which she had experienced as she had walked down to the launch with Huntley little more than an hour ago.

And now that peace had been shattered, broken by the harsh words they had exchanged and the old woman's strange, dark prophecy.

The sun still shone and the little waves lapped gently against the rocks, but somehow it was different. A shadow had passed between her and the sun.

All afternoon, as they wandered freely over the island, she was aware of Huntley. Of Huntley and Lucy everywhere together, and Lucy's father smiling on them both.

Huntley was a competent guide. He knew all the history of the island and all about the wild bird life along its rocky coast. He was soon popular with the other passengers, although he still managed to remain slightly aloof.

When they returned to the *Saturn* he was in the other launch. Ailsa did not see him again until they went in to dinner.

Since her aunt was to sit at the captain's table, nothing had been changed. They discussed their experiences and their purchases throughout the first part of the meal, Lucy with some reserve and her father with mock horror at the prices he had paid.

'I suppose you could call all the stuff we've got souvenirs," he reflected. "When we get back to the States you'll be able to show them around, Luce."

Lucy treated him to an oddly preoccupied stare.

"When are we going back?" she asked.

"Just whenever you say," he told her. "I thought you wanted another week or two in Paris?"

"We'll see." Lucy turned from him to look at Huntley. "Have you another cruise to do after this one?" she asked.

He shook his head.

"No. I'm filling in for someone else, just for this one trip. When we get to Oban I'm through."

"And then?" she persisted, propping her elbows on the table and resting her chin on her hands to study him. "What then, Huntley?"

He shrugged.

"Corrae, I dare say, for a week or two."

Lucy seemed satisfied with that, turning to let the steward fill her coffee cup.

"Are we dancing tonight?" she asked.

"Every night," he said.

The doctor came over to ask Lucy for the first waltz and she could not refuse him. He had a compelling way which rejected a rebuff even before it was thought up, and he kept Lucy at a far table for the next three numbers.

Huntley glanced down at his watch. He had not attempted to ask Ailsa to dance.

"If you'll excuse me," he said, "I'll say goodnight. I have quite a bit of work to get through before we go ashore tomorrow."

Adam lumbered to his feet, looking across to the captain's table, where Betsy was apparently enjoying herself.

"I'm going to have a smoke," he announced agressively. "Would you like to come through to the lounge or would you rather stay and dance, Miss Monro?"

"I don't feel like dancing tonight," Ailsa said. "I think I'll turn in—catch up with some beauty sleep!"

"I think you're wise," Adam agreed with another swift look in Betsy's direction. "Lucy ought to come too, but she appears to flourish on late nights."

They followed Huntley out, but instead of going down to the deck below he turned up his collar against the wind and went out through the swing doors. He could have gone up on to the boat deck by several different ways, but perhaps he wanted to let them see that he preferred to go alone.

Ailsa went down to her cabin, but it was not really late. Just ten o'clock. She would not be able to sleep if she went to bed, and probably she should have waited for Aunt Betsy. At least she supposed she should have wished her goodnight or asked if there was anything she could do for her.

Slipping into her coat, she went back along the alleyway, wondering why she should try to delude herself in this way. She had every intention of going on deck, and she was going in the hope of meeting Huntley MacLaren!

Why pretend? She wanted to see him, she *had* to see him again before this day was over. In case there was anything left unsaid between them? Anything left undone?

The door of her aunt's cabin was closed when she reached the upper deck and she did not think Betsy had come down yet. She was having too much fun.

In the main hall she stood a little uncertainly, listening to the muted strains of the violins from behind the closed glass doors of the dining-saloon. Then she went on, up and out on to the wide expanse of the boat deck where deep shadows lay in the recesses and there was no sound but the steady swish of the sea against the ship's hull.

For several minutes she believed herself to be in complete and undisputed possession of the deserted deck, and then a long shadow detached itself from the other shadows and Huntley stood waiting for her. She went towards him without hesitation.

"Why have you come?" he demanded without looking round at her.

"To say how sorry I am." Her voice was far from steady. "To try to un-say some of the things I've said to you——"

"Such as?"

"Saying that you—might marry for money."

81

She could feel the tension between them, building up like some tangible thing.

"Was that all?" There was an edge of steel to his voice, the tension all but snapped. "You knew me capable of it, I suppose."

"For Corrae——"

"Yes," he repeated bitterly. "For Corrae. The surest way out."

"I wish there was some other way——"

In the dark silence there was no movement. The ship scarcely seemed to be in motion and the wind had died long ago. In the northern sky there was a pale, unfurled banner of light, but it was very far away.

Ailsa put her hand on the rail, as if for support, and instantly she was in Huntley's arms.

He kissed her with savage intensity which brooked no refusal, and she lay in his arms without protest. In that moment she was his and his alone. She let the fierce tide of his kisses pass over her, kissing him passionately in return until her breath ran out in a little gasp and her hands pressed defensively against his chest.

"Huntley——!" she whispered.

Deliberately he put her from him.

"I'll take you in," he said, and his voice sounded like breaking ice. "I don't know why you came."

Turning, she fled from him in an agony of shame, not stopping in her humiliated, headlong effort at escape until she had reached her cabin door. It seemed that she had to beat against it before it would open, but at last she was alone.

Alone and shaken by harsh, dry sobs which seemed to be driven up from the very depths of her being.

Unutterable despair seized her so that she could only stand staring at her dishevelled image in the mirror behind the door for a long while. It reflected a face she hardly recognized as her own, the pinched in corners of the mouth the outward sign of the twisting pain within her which seemed to consume her more and more with every passing second.

She had shown Huntley so clearly that she loved him, and he had kissed her lightly and sent her away!

CHAPTER FIVE

THE following morning they awoke to a peculiar motion of the ship, a deep, long roll which suggested that they might be in treacherous cross-currents, but the sun was already shining in through the cabin windows and the weather appeared still to be fine.

Ailsa went on deck to find the long neck of the Shetlands lying ahead of them with the ancient settlement of Jarlshof huddled at its southernmost point, a little Viking town poised on the edge of the sea.

All morning, while they went ashore and wandered among the old houses and along the narrow streets, she tried not to think of the events of the night before, but even when they were aboard again and steaming towards the Out Skerries and Herma Ness, she could not rid herself of the memory of Huntley's kisses.

They burned her mouth and her cheeks, while the humiliation of his curt dismissal scorched her soul.

He had made a mistake. The night and the silence and the close, deep pulse of the sea had betrayed him into a sudden foolishness. He had no intention of falling in love.

Not that he had spoken one word of love! It had been she who had shown him that she was ready for his caresses. Fool! Fool that she was!

Quick, passionate tears blinded her. He had told her so plainly that Corrae meant more to him than love ever could. And she had helped him to tell her. Then she had gone back and said that she was sorry—and crawled into his arms.

It was no use. She could not convince herself that she did not care, that she despised him or wanted never to see him again. She would see him, many times. Now—today, before the sun had set.

At Foula there was difficulty in getting ashore and she was almost relieved when they steamed southwards, although every mile brought them steadily nearer to Corrae.

The seas were higher now because they were out in the North Atlantic, but they were in the path of the Gulf Stream and it was warm. People came out to sit on deck, and the glassed-in veranda was not so crowded. Aunt Betsy had a steamer chair put close beside the rail, but when Ailsa went to find her it appeared that she was asleep. She moved quietly away, but almost instantly the penetrating voice called her back.

"Come and sit down beside me, Ailsa. I want to talk to you."

Ailsa retraced her steps.

"Yes, Aunt Betsy?"

"What had you intended to do once this cruise is over?"

"I shall have to sell Achnasheen."

"You don't want to sell?"

"I have no other choice."

"It hasn't always been your home," Betsy pointed out reasonably enough. "Only during the last few years. Still, I suppose one does get attached to a place. I would suggest that you come and live with me. Permanently, I mean."

All the colour fled from Ailsa's cheeks. That might mean living on Corrae, moving in as Huntley MacLaren moved out. Provided, of course, that he kept his 'gentleman's agreement' to sell the island. She did not know what to say.

"It would mean giving up all thought of city life," Aunt Betsy warned. "The idea of finding work in Glasgow or Edinburgh or even London."

"I've never wanted that," Ailsa confessed, unable to think beyond this amazing proposition her aunt had just suggested. "I had thought of Achnasheen as a small holiday hotel—a sort of guest house. Loch Lomondside is the right sort of place, but it would take quite a bit of capital to adapt it and I don't want to run into debt."

Aunt Betsy, who had a great deal of money and was generally known for her impulsive decisions, did not suggest that she might help with Achnasheen. Instead, she said,

"I'm being very selfish about this, I suppose, and I must be getting old when I'm prepared to admit that I need companionship. If you decide to keep Achnasheen and run it as a guest house—which may or may not pay, remember!

—I shall have to look for someone else to live with me—a stranger."

She said this so pathetically that Ailsa felt ashamed. She also felt sorry for her aunt with no one to care for her, as she was undoubtedly meant to do.

"Will you give me time to think it over?" she asked. "You see, if you don't buy Corrae it would mean going back to America, wouldn't it?"

Aunt Betsy considered the point, apparently for the first time.

"I haven't thought of going back," she said. "Of course, America grows on one, but—no, I've quite made up my mind to settle down in Scotland. Ah!" She looked up brightly as a man's long shadow fell across the deck. "Mr. MacLaren! We were just talking about you. Or, at least, we were talking about Corrae!"

Ailsa would have given a great deal to have been able to get up and run, but Huntley stood before them, blocking the way to escape. He looked very tall and very aloof, but he accepted the chair her aunt indicated and sat down by her side.

"Don't go, Ailsa," Betsy said peremptorily. "This may affect you too." She turned back to Huntley with her most disarming smile. "I've been trying to persuade Ailsa to join me permanently, Mr. MacLaren," she explained, "and I'm hoping that will mean that we'll be going to Corrae."

This was awful for Huntley! Ailsa dared not look in his direction, but all her sympathy went out to him in a silent wave of understanding. Only a moment ago she had been discussing with Aunt Betsy the disposal of her own home and although she had only lived at Achnasheen for a very short time, as her aunt had pointed out, the thought of selling up everything that had once been dear to her had been like the turning of a sharp knife in a raw wound.

"I believe we have an agreement," Huntley said stiffly. "One of the conditions is that you see Corrae first, which, of course, is quite reasonable."

Betsy considered him for a moment in silence.

"And you find the other condition intolerable, Mr. MacLaren?" she asked, at last.

85

"Difficult, but not intolerable." His mouth was grim. "I agree with you that it might be necessary—for Corrae's sake. But perhaps we can discuss that part of our bargain once you have seen the island?"

"Then you *do* think a landing might be possible?" Betsy asked, her whole face brightening at the prospect.

Huntley's gaze went beyond her to the soaring peaks of a small island set like a solitary crag in a waste of sea.

"It doesn't look as if we're going to get ashore at North Rona," he said. "It's a difficult landing at the best of times, and in a sea like this, almost impossible. A great many people are going to be disappointed, I'm afraid."

Betsy, at least, was not particularly disappointed.

"You mean our 'island collectors'?" she smiled. "Well, they can always come back, can't they? So you think if we save half a day here and some more time at St. Kilda, perhaps, we will definitely make Corrae?"

"I think you can count on it," he said briefly.

Betsy looked completely satisfied. It was Sunday and they had been cruising for four days. She was a little tired of islands by now.

"I must go down and tidy myself up before lunch," she announced. "Don't bother to come with me, Ailsa," she added as Ailsa rose to her feet. "I can manage quite well by myself. Stay and get all the fresh air you can. If we do manage to make a landing here, I don't think I'll go ashore this time. It looks much the same as Foula, doesn't it?"

She gave the dark pinnacles of North Rona a hurried glance as Huntley and Ailsa picked up all the paraphernalia with which she surrounded herself when on deck — books and chocolates, scarves, rugs and magazines and, of all things, a foot-muff.

"I'll carry these down for you," Huntley offered with the faintest of smiles.

"Not at all," the valiant little lady protested. "Here comes a steward. He'll see to everything for me. You stay and look after Ailsa." She gave him another charming smile. "I'm quite sure we are going to get on well together, Mr. MacLaren," she added.

Huntley's smile deepened. You could not really help liking Aunt Betsy, Ailsa thought.

When the stout little figure had disappeared from sight and the deck steward had relieved them of the foot-muff and the last of the magazines, she stood a little uncertainly by Huntley's side.

"What are you going to do about Corrae?" he asked. "About staying on permanently with Mrs. Bellinger?"

"I haven't really had time to think about it," Ailsa told him. "You see, there's my home. I'd have to give that up——"

She broke off, confused by the thought that they were very much in the same position.

"It's a difficult decision to make," he acknowledged. "The final break."

"I wish you didn't have to make it with Corrae," she said impulsively. "I know this may sound disloyal of me, but do you really think a woman could manage the island's affairs successfully on her own?"

He smiled rather grimly.

"Two women have done it most successfully in the past," he said, "and Mrs. Bellinger isn't going to take any risks. She has made ample provision for her own lack of experience if she does decide to take up her option on Corrae."

The other condition, Ailsa thought with an odd, sinking little feeling at the pit of her stomach.

"She has asked me to stay on as her agent for six months."

His voice had sounded hard and almost without emotion, but this must have been the most difficult decision of all for him to make.

"And you intend to do it?" she said, "for Corrae?"

"What else can I do?" He stared across the intervening strip of water to the craggy shore where it was obvious now, even to her inexperienced eyes, that they would not land. "An island like Corrae could not survive for long without a resident landlord or an efficient factor who has its interests at heart. Mrs. Bellinger has asked me to be that factor for six months. Indeed, she has made it a provision of the sale."

"Oh," Ailsa said, "I'm sorry——"

"Why should you be" he demanded. "A good many people would consider it a stroke of luck as far as I am concerned. Corrae is not likely to survive for long under an absentee landlord and at least for the first six months I'd be keeping my eyes on things."

"And after that?" she was forced to ask.

He shrugged. It was evident that he had not allowed himself to think too far ahead.

"I can only hope that I shall not have to see my home change hands again and again," he admitted. "That, in itself, would be gradual death to an island community. The islanders have a deep sense of allegiance to an ancient name and they don't take kindly to change. Constant changes would make them think that the island was no longer the same."

Ailsa wanted him to go on talking about Corrae, but what he had just told her had shaken her. If her aunt bought Corrae he would be compelled to stay there, and if she accepted Betsy's suggestion about her own future she, too, would be on the island for the next six months, seeing Huntley, meeting him every day.

Her heart raced madly at the thought, yet it was a bitter-sweet prospect which she viewed. Forced to sell Corrae, he might still intend to marry Lucy, with the hope that, one day, he might buy the island back. Somehow she felt that he did not expect Aunt Betsy to stay there very long.

"We both appear to be in the same boat," he observed when she did not speak for a moment. "We both have to sell our home and we are both going to be very much dependent on an American lady's whim."

Ailsa flushed.

"Don't judge her too unkindly," she pleaded. "I don't think this is a whim altogether. It's—something she's wanted very much for some time. For her it's putting down roots in a country she has always loved—her own country, as a matter of fact. She was married here in Scotland the first time. She emigrated to America twenty-three years ago, to be exact. I feel quite sure she'll leave you a fairly free hand on Corrae. Fundamentally she's very easy to get on with."

He smiled thinly, turning away from the rail.

"You make it sound almost bearable," he told her. "Perhaps I will be able to think of it in that way, in time."

"I hope you will," she answered sincerely. "And I hope we can all work together for the good of Corrae."

She was not very sure how he took that. He had not asked her help, only if she intended to go on living with her aunt after the cruise was over, which, of course, brought them round to Corrae. So much depended on Aunt Betsy, she mused, as they walked slowly back along the deck.

When they reached the spot where he had held her in his arms in the cool darkness, she tried not to remember how determinedly Huntley had thrust her from him.

"Since there's been no landing this morning it means a film after dinner," he told her. "I shall be illustrating my lecture with slides too. If you would like to see something of Corrae——"

"Oh, I'd love that!" Ailsa interrupted warmly. "I know it's going to be the loveliest island I've ever seen."

His smile was wry when he looked down at her.

"I've a feeling," he said, "that you're not going to be too disappointed."

All afternoon they played deck games while Huntley prepared his lecture for the evening. The Flannen Isles—Aunt Betsy called them the Flannel Isles—passed, dreaming in sunlight, and soon they were within sight and sound of St. Kilda, that far outpost on the Atlantic tide where now only the bird life held sway.

It was an easy landing, but somehow, as she walked between the rows of ruined houses which had once been a village, Ailsa wished that she had stayed on board the ship.

Huntley had not come with them. He had made his lecture notes the excuse for remaining on board, but it could have been that St. Kilda presented too poignant an example of a deserted island for him to bear.

Lucy, who had expected him to be in the launch when she joined it, tramped over the island's lost roads with a dejected air.

"There's absolutely nothing here," she complained. "Nothing to see!"

Except the life had gone out of what had once been a happy island community. Lucy would not see that, and perhaps she would not be able to understand about Corrae either.

Adam Fulton plodded on gallantly in Betsy's wake. She had made up her mind to walk off a heavy lunch and a too generous tea.

"I've read all about this place," she declared, "so I have to see as much of it as I can."

"Do you have to climb all over these boulders?" Adam complained. "There's a road of sorts and we could sit down at the top and see all there is to see."

"It just wouldn't be the same," Betsy told him firmly. "You've got to really get in among the houses to understand what it was like. You've got to walk in what was once someone's garden or their kail yard, or whatever it was, before you can feel about all this." She looked down between the rows of roofless cottages towards the sea. "Land's sakes!" she exclaimed, "it must have been a lonely place to live, and no mistake."

Adam gave her a swift, sidelong glance.

"And yet you want to end out your days on an island that can't be all that much different," he pointed out. "I've told you before, Betsy, the whole idea is just plain daft!"

"Don't you call me daft, Adam Fulton!" Betsy exploded, mainly because she was already having second thoughts about Corrae. "I know what I'm doing. I've wanted to buy a place in Scotland for years."

"You don't know the first thing about it," he told her placidly. "You've been softened in New York. I'll give you six months on your island, and that's being generous!"

"And I'll prove you wrong!" Betsy retorted. "If I like this place I mean to stay on it, and I'll have expert help to administer it, which is something you *didn't* know!"

"No," Adam was forced to admit, "that's true. But I still think you won't stay. You'll be an absentee landlord, and that'll be the start of your troubles. Who did you say was going to manage the place for you?"

"I didn't." There was the hint of a twinkle in Betsy's hazel eyes. "But right this minute I'll tell you that it's Hunltey MacLaren. He has made me a promise."

"Huntley?" Lucy stood quite still on the grass-grown roadway. "But that's impossible! He just couldn't! Besides, he might want to get away." Her mouth looked very hard. "Right away, I mean. He might even come to America."

Had Huntley discussed it with Lucy? Had he planned to emigrate after those six difficult months in her aunt's service were over? Ailsa drew in a deep breath. He could have told Lucy so. He could have made quite definite plans for the future without having to share them with his prospective employer or her niece.

"Nobody knows what MacLaren's likely to do," Adam said, climbing after Betsy to a new vantage-point. "It's my guess he'll stick by the place out of a sense of duty just so long as it's owned by a woman. He won't want to see it going to pigs and whistles quicker than he could have done it himself."

Betsy drew herself up.

"It's my opinion, Adam Fulton," she declared with sudden insight, "that you wouldn't mind owning Corrae yourself. You've got a lot to say about it and you've tried to talk me out of buying it ever since I told you I'd all but signed on the dotted line!"

"Shucks!" Adam snorted, "I've far more sense than to waste my money on that sort of play! It will cost you a fortune to set it on its feet and then it'll take another fortune to keep it there. If you asked me, somebody saw you coming! And as like as not, it was your fancy Edinburgh lawyer. All this coy talk about selling and not selling. Why, Betsy, it was nothing more than bait!"

"Don't you go calling me a poor fish, Adam Fulton!" Betsy looked angry, although underneath it all she was probably enjoying herself. "There's a flavour of sour grapes about your remarks, although why you should want to own Corrae, I can't imagine!"

"Nobody said I wanted to own it." Suddenly Adam was looking at Lucy. "I just said a woman wasn't the right

91

person to do it. But there's no use us getting all steamed up about it. You haven't seen the place yet."

They tramped back towards the landing-stage where the launches were waiting, and when Adam helped her aunt in, Ailsa saw that all their anger had evaporated.

Lucy took the seat next to her.

"I suppose you're doing your best to convince Mrs. Bellinger that she ought to settle for Corrae," she observed.

Ailsa flushed.

"Not really. It will be entirely my aunt's own decision if she buys the island."

"And if she doesn't?"

"It will be for sale to the next bidder——"

How Huntley would hate that, having to show people over the island, again and again!

"He could, of course, struggle on," Lucy mused.

"I think he's come to the point where he realizes that to struggle on isn't going to do any good." Ailsa's voice was deeply distressed. "He has to sell now, for Corrae's sake. Another year might make too great a difference. There are crofts on the island that need subsidizing and even rebuilding in some cases."

"In fact it all boils down to financial assistance," Lucy reasoned. "If Huntley could—borrow the money or pay his debts in some other way, it could all turn out differently for him. Except," she added deliberately, "for this unfortunate bargain he has made with your aunt."

Ailsa's mouth hardened.

"I'm afraid I don't know enough about it to answer that," she said. "And I don't think Huntley would be exactly pleased if he knew we were discussing his private affairs quite so openly. The option on Corrae was quite a fair proposition though. Huntley need not have signed it if he had not wanted to sell."

Once again the fact that the option had been signed before he had met Lucy nagged at Ailsa's mind, and she tried not to remember his bitter reflection about 'marrying money'.

They reached the ship to find him standing on deck with Erik Larsen, waiting for their return. Lucy immediately claimed his attention, while Erik walked beside Ailsa to the observation lounge.

"Huntley's going to blind us with science this evening," Erik laughed as he ordered drinks. "He's got a whole wad of notes up his sleeve and an hour's cinema programme into the bargain! If you don't want to go, Ailsa, you can come out on deck with me. I hear there's a new moon to-night and we're going in close to the Long Island. It's quite a sight."

They were standing watching one of the most wonderful sunsets Ailsa had ever seen. The sun had disappeared into a cradle of flamingo-coloured cloud and long shafts of living gold shot upwards across the sky. They seemed to quiver and stand there for a moment, as if reluctant to give way to the silver presence of the night, and then, gradually, the colour faded through saffron and yellow to a delicate violet. Then dramatically the whole sky was re-lit with a steadily increasing flame. It painted the contours of the higher clouds and stained the sea until it looked like liquid fire. The bright turquoise heavens were everywhere veiled in it, and the tops of the distant, shadowy hills. It caught the ship, holding it in a noose of light, and sent its reflection back into their watching eyes.

Almost as suddenly as it had come it died away, drawing the turquoise out of the sky with it to leave it grey and cold. Only here and there, on the fringe of a cloud, some of the glory lingered, but after a while that, too, faded.

"Well, that was certainly something!" Erik remarked, drawing in a deeply appreciative breath. "We get these sunsets in Norway too; brilliant affairs that turn everything red."

But the colour was not red, Ailsa thought. It was the colour to be found in the heart of a fire, flaring and dying swiftly even as they watched.

Huntley had contributed nothing to the conversation. He had watched the sunset with them and it was probably not new to him, although she felt that he would never consider it commonplace.

"I'm going down to change," Lucy announced, putting down her empty glass. "I expect your aunt is still arguing with Poppa, Ailsa. Will you tell him I've gone to my cabin, if he asks?"

Ailsa nodded as Erik escorted Lucy to the door, but when she turned back to the table it was to find Huntley frowning across its polished surface.

"Your *aunt?*" he repeated.

Ailsa flushed.

"Yes. I thought you knew——"

"How could I know?" Any warmth that had been there had already died in his eyes. "You were at no great pains to enlighten me, not even when we discussed my prospective employer and Corrae."

"Does it — make any difference?" she asked unsteadily. "I can't see that it should, Huntley."

"I thought you were employed by Mrs. Bellinger," he said stiffly.

"In a way, I *am* employed by my aunt," Ailsa argued. "And if I stay with her I shall be more or less working for my living."

He looked down at her as if he would like to shake her.

"Forgive me if I consider that slightly ludicrous," he said with every intention to hurt. "You can't possibly mean me to take it seriously."

Erik came striding back, still with his glass in his hand, but Huntley made some excuse not to join them in another drink, something about getting a wash before the dinner bell rang.

"What's gotten into him?" Erik asked.

Quite unable to conceal her distress, Ailsa found herself looking up into the far-seeing blue eyes.

"I — suppose he feels that I've lied to him," she confessed unsteadily.

"I think he's in love with you," he said with his engaging grin. "Although he knows, now, that you've got far too much money!"

"Erik, that's nonsense!" Ailsa protested. "I *told* Huntley I hadn't any money — that I had to work for my living — and that's still quite true. He didn't know about me and Aunt Betsy, but I didn't *try* to hide our relationship. It was just a stupid mistake — something that could happen easily enough to anyone. You see, I was down on the passenger list at first just as 'companion to Mrs. Bellinger', but that shouldn't have made any difference."

"I think it would to Huntley MacLaren," Erik reflected. "He might also think that you were acting as a sort of under-cover agent for your aunt."

"But how could he? He had already made a bargain with Aunt Betsy in Edinburgh — with his lawyer."

"Well, of course, he might just not be the type who would run after money."

"Yet he needs it, Erik — he needs it!" Ailsa cried. "And — I once gave him that advice."

"You did what?" He looked at her incredulously.

"I — told him it would be an easy solution to all his prob-lems," she confessed unhappily.

"You addle-brain!" Erik put a comforting arm through hers. "Come and have another drink," he advised, "and if you are very good I'll marry you myself, even with all your money!"

"But, Erik, I haven't *got* any money!" Ailsa protested. "I haven't got a bean. It all belongs to my aunt."

"Maybe Huntley considers that's one and the same thing. It would be like marrying Lucy, as far as he was concerned. One day Lucy's going to have all 'Poppa's' dollars." Erik gave the idea considerable thought. "That's what's wrong with this ship," he concluded. "Too many heiresses!"

"I wish you could be serious," Ailsa sighed. "But you can't! And I wish I could find some reasonable solution to all this muddle!" she cried defiantly.

"It looks easy enough to me," he said. "You could marry Huntley before Lucy does!"

"I knew you wouldn't be any help," she told him impatiently.

"I've been trying," he pointed out laconically. "Do you want me to explain things to Huntley——?"

"No! Erik, please!" Her eyes were suddenly lifted to his amused face so that he could not fail to see how serious she was and how unhappy. "I'm asking you to keep my confidence."

"All right," he agreed reluctantly, "you win. I'll not even drop the faintest hint."

"You must never tell Huntley," she pleaded desperately. "Never! Promise me, Erik. You've got to promise!"

"I promise," he agreed, although not at all willingly, for he thought it a great pity that Lucy should win. He did not like Lucy. In fact, he thought her positively dangerous.

CHAPTER SIX

THE following day the *Saturn* rounded the south end of the Long Island, calling in at Mingulay and Eriskay.

'Eriskay of the Love Lilt', her fellow-passengers called it, and the name drove like a knife into Ailsa's heart.

Lucy was following Huntley everywhere now, quite unashamedly. She had practically sat at his feet during his lecture of the evening before, passing him slides as he talked, and afterwards they had danced together.

There was a new hardness about Huntley as he reserved a place for Lucy next to himself in the launch. And Adam, the fond father, beamed upon them both. After the second day out most of the passengers had formed themselves into small, friendly groups or paired off, at least for the duration of the voyage, and it seemed quite natural that Adam should find himself conducting Aunt Betsy everywhere. They sparred continuously, but it was mostly in a friendly way. Betsy's complete independence irked Adam occasionally, a fact which he did not hesitate to show, but otherwise they were good companions. When he was not thinking about Lucy, Adam allowed himself to think quite deeply about Betsy Bellinger.

Of course, this island idea of hers was nonsense! He did not think too deliberately about putting a spoke in her wheel, but he did consider that something more satisfactory all round could be arranged for Corrae.

The more he came into contact with Huntley, the more he was convinced of this, and when the ship turned southwards and the jagged ridge of the Cuillins stabbed the sky ahead of them he sought Huntley out to ask about his immediate plans.

"We've only a couple of more days to go, MacLaren," he observed as he settled himself beside Huntley at the rail. "I thought I would just like to thank you for the way you've looked after Lucy on this trip. These last two days she's been in her element. I've never seen her so happy."

He paused, but Huntley made no comment. He may have been taken aback by this utterly unexpected tribute, but he did not show it.

"I was wondering," Adam continued, "if you had any special plans for the next few weeks. I'd like to get in a fishing trip — somewhere in the Highlands — but Lucy's going to be darned unsettled if I don't make sure of some young company for her. She doesn't fish. Loathes the 'monotony', as she calls it! Maybe that's natural enough at her age," he smiled. "Fishing's something you come to later in life, as a rule, when you've a lot more patience. Well now, what would you say to a couple of weeks somewhere in the north if I can fix up a house where there's a good trout stream or a handy loch?"

Huntley moved his position on the rail. For a second or two he did not answer, and it was almost as if he were considering Adams proposition with his eyes on the more distant future.

"It's the sort of thing I would like to do very much," he admitted at last, "in the ordinary way, but just now I'm afraid it would be impossible. I've put my home on the market, you see, and the sooner the sale goes through the better."

His lips had firmed into a hard, uncompromising line, but otherwise he did not show emotion.

Adam moved uncomfortably.

"Aw, now, that's a great pity," he said, "if you'll forgive me for saying so, I think just giving the place up for good and all is wrong. Isn't there something else that could be done? Like raising a loan? Now, I've got plenty of money to invest——"

Huntley turned to look at him.

"It wouldn't be a good investment, Mr. Fulton," he said. "Not in the way you mean."

"But it's bound to give me some return for my money!"

Huntley smiled faintly.

"It would depend on what return you expected," he said. "No, Mr. Fulton, I can't go back on my word now. I've entered into a bargain over Corrae, and if a woman wasn't exactly the owner I would have chosen for the island, it can't be helped. I have promised to stand by for six months and I'll do that. It all depends, of course, on what Mrs. Bellinger finally decides once she has seen Corrae."

"And we're nearly there now," Adam mused thoughtfully. "There's no knowing what Betsy will do."

"You've known her for a long time, I understand?" Huntley seemed glad of the opportunity to turn the conversation away from himself.

"We were boy and girl together. Childhood sweethearts, you might say!" Adam savoured the thought for a second or two. "It's a sentimental reflection, especially when you've come right back to where it all happened! I let Betsy go over a damned silly misunderstanding and we've spent half our lives apart in consequence. There's nothing quite like the first time you fall in love, m'boy," he added benevolently. "We ought to hold on to that with both hands, because nothing like it is going to happen to us again. Pride, or money, or anything else shouldn't be allowed to come into it."

"Perhaps it's easier to be wise after the event," Huntley suggested in a clipped, steely voice. "Or maybe we all just look at these things differently. I would certainly find it impossible, for instance, to ask any girl to share my life with me at the present moment."

"Because you consider you have nothing to offer her?" Adam queried. "That's nonsense, man! A woman doesn't think about a man's possessions when she makes up her mind to marry him. Not at first, anyway," he amended. "That may come later. It's the fact of finding happiness that counts, of meeting someone she can live out her life with and never feel stale or frustrated. Someone who is the answer to everything — for her!"

"I believe I know about that," Huntley said briefly, "but it just wouldn't work in my case."

"Because you're too darned proud to marry an heiress?" Adam blurted out.

Huntley took a full minute to answer.

"That may be it," he agreed.

"Well, I think you'll change your mind," Adam predicted. "I'll leave my invitation open, anyway," he added. "I'm taking Lucy to Paris for a couple of weeks right after this trip is finished, and if I can hire a house up north in the meantime, we should be back in Scotland early in June. I'll get into touch with you, and if your affairs are settled then I still hope you can come.

"If I have sold Corrae to Mrs. Bellinger," Huntley pointed out, "I shall be fully employed as her factor for the next six months."

"Aw, Betsy!" Adam said. "You leave Betsy to me! Come to think of it," he chuckled, "we could even ask Betsy to come on the fishing trip. She would keep us in order, and her niece would be good company for Lucy. A nice girl, that!" he allowed generously. "No parents, I understand, but she'll be all right with Betsy. The Bellinger fortune, she tells me, runs into several million dollars and Ailsa is her only relative. Another heiress, eh, MacLaren! The boat's full of 'em!"

He laughed heartily, but Huntley did not seem to appreciate the little joke. He turned abruptly away, excusing himself on the pretext of duty, since they were nearing yet another group of islands and he had to see the captain before they went ashore.

"Which is Corrae?" Lucy asked, coming up behind her father. "I saw you talking with Huntley just now. Did he point it out to you?"

"No," Adam answered absently, "we were discussing something else. How would you like me to take a house in the Highlands for a couple of months, Luce?"

"So that you can fish?" Lucy looked disdainful. "Don't think I'm going to cart gaffs and things all over the Highlands for you, because I'm not! I loathe fish, even on a plate!"

"Would you change your mind if you had the right sort of company?" he asked.

"It would depend on what you mean by 'the right company'," Lucy answered, turning back to the rail, her lovely eyes narrowed a little. "Poppa, you haven't asked Huntley MacLaren to come, have you?" she demanded.

"I have, right this very minute!"

Lucy flushed to the roots of her hair.

"What did he say?"

"He thought he might be too busy," Adam had to admit. "But we — sort of left it open."

"Who else did you ask?" Lucy demanded.

"I — wondered about asking Mrs. Bellinger."

"And Ailsa Monro?"

"Why, yes, Luce, I did think about it——"

"You fool!" Lucy said. "You doddering, stupid old fool!"

She marched away along the deck, leaving Adam to look after her with a pain in his heart which he had felt often in the past but would not acknowledge for what it was. Lucy was the apple of his eye. She was all he had had during those painful years of living with Edie and her overbearing domination.

Sadly he shook his head, and in that moment he looked old.

Ailsa noticed him standing beside the rail as she came on deck and something about the stoop of his shoulders and the hurt expression in his eyes made her feel sorry for him.

"Lucy says we're coming up to Corrae," he volunteered when she stopped beside him. "It must be one of these islands over there between us and the coast."

"I think we have a stop at Staffa first," Ailsa said. "You know — Fingal's Cave. I've always wanted to go there, to stand and listen to the sea."

They leaned against the rail, watching the islands coming closer, with the giant shoulders of Mull standing, green and clear, against the eastern sky. It was a magnificent sight, and Ailsa was lost in the wonder of it until Huntley came to stand beside them.

"It will take about an hour to go ashore at Staffa," he said, "and after that we've decided on the Corrae landing."

The steely inflection in his voice made her heart turn over, and she wondered if he intended to go ashore at Staffa with them or wait till he took charge at Corrae.

"I saw Fingal's Cave a long while ago, on an excursion from Oban," Adam said. "I don't think I'll bother to go ashore. I can safely leave Lucy in your hands, MacLaren," he smiled.

No doubt it had all been arranged, Ailsa thought. Why didn't Huntley tell Aunt Betsy that he didn't have to sell Corrae now?

The bitterness of her own reflection surprised her, but when the launches went down into the water yet again Lucy was with Huntley and it seemed a foregone conclusion that he would take her to the cave. Adam Fulton's satisfaction was so obvious. He was even forgoing the trip ashore in order that Huntley would feel doubly responsible for Lucy.

Aunt Betsy decided that the cave would depress her.

"I just can't stand all that mass of rock up there above my head," she declared. "Why, it might fall down at any minute, and where would we be? I haven't the stomach for caves!"

"It's been there for thousands of years!" Ailsa teased. "But I'll stay behind with you if you like."

"Indeed you won't!" Betsy had cast a quick glance in Lucy's direction. You're on a vacation. Off you go and enjoy yourself with the other young people, honey. I'm not an invalid, you know."

Ailsa would have stayed behind willingly enough, since Lucy was going with Huntley, but it was impossible to run contrary to Aunt Betsy's wishes once she had made up her mind.

Within half an hour the *Saturn* lay between Staffa and the shore and the launches had made the short distance to the difficult little landing-stage. It was no more than a wide slab of rock in a naturally convenient spot among the surrounding boulders, with a little cove running in behind it where the water was dark and deep. Ailsa watched the saffron weed rising and falling on the tide. The motion was like the slow, regular breathing of a sleeping giant, and suddenly the world of ordinary things seemed very far away. She looked up at the mammoth pinnacles of rock and at the great shoulder of the cave itself.

"It's breathtaking," she said aloud, "and rather frightening!"

"Staffa has always been awe-inspiring," Huntley said, standing by her side. "I can't imagine anyone coming here and going away without being impressed."

"Even if we all can't write a Hebridean Overture afterwards?" Ailsa smiled. "How far have we to go to the entrance?"

"Not very far. There's the path over there." He pointed towards the south end of the island. "A bit hazardous, but it's protected in the necessary places."

They were the end of a little column of people making their way along the shore, climbing gradually on a narrow cliff path where the foothold was not always easy.

"Like flies clinging to a wall!" Ailsa mused.

Huntley smiled.

"I can imagine you on Corrae," he said unexpectedly.

Ailsa could not answer that. Lucy had gone on ahead with Erik Larsen, who had seemed determined to escort her once they had left the launches behind. Her purple steamer coat and white headscarf were conspicuous against the muted greys and green of the cliff face, and once or twice she turned to look back, probably in search of Huntley, but Erik urged her on. There was very little room to pass on the narrow pathway and the continuous queue had to be kept moving.

"I'm going to hold you up for five minutes," Huntley said. "I want you to see the cave as it should be seen. Not with a crowd milling around."

"What about — Lucy and Erik?" Ailsa's cheeks were suddenly pink.

"They can arrange it that way if they like. It's easy enough to use a little strategy to hold up a queue. Nobody should go into a place like Fingal's Cave with a horde of other people." Huntley took her arm to help her up a difficult stretch of path. "You're sure to hear somebody saying that there's one exactly like it at San Diego, California, called La Jolla!"

When they reached the great domed entrance with its fluted columns of living stone rising hundreds of feet into the darkness above their heads, like the pipes of a mighty organ that only the ocean might play, they were alone. The cave was still and quiet for a moment, and then the great waves came pulsing in, forcing their way through the narrow neck of the entrance to mount and swell within the shadowed walls. It was an unforgettable, haunted place with its refracted light moving among the pillars and the flaming red and yellow stalactites suspended from its roof. Sea birds flew out at their approach, their wings flashing white against the amazing colours of the cave, their cries of protest echoing and re-echoing hollowly in the sudden silences.

Lonely and unappeased, the soul of Ossian must be destined to wander here for ever, Ailsa thought. She stood very still in the half-light, hearing the distant thunder of the ocean rising in a great swell against the rock-girt bastion of the island's western shore, and neither she nor Huntley spoke for several minutes. It seemed that they had come to the edge of a world which they both understood and loved. Then, very simply, he took her hand to help her back along the way they had come.

Still hand-in-hand, they reached the entrance to the cave where the flooding sunlight turned the seagulls' wings to gold and cast olive shadows into the clear blue water at their feet.

How deep that water was, Ailsa thought suddenly, a little shiver running through her as she remembered the words of the old woman in the island croft. 'A man of the Viking breed will take your heart and crush it in his hand . . .'

Was there any truth in premonition, in what Huntley had called 'the second sight'? With her hand in his she could have walked to the other end of the world, happy and unafraid.

Lucy and Erik were waiting for them when they finally came to the landing stage.

"Did you make your three wishes in Fingal's Chair?" Erik asked with a deep twinkle in his blue eyes.

"We didn't have time," Huntley answered for them both. "I had forgotten about the Chair."

He was not superstitious to that extent, yet Ailsa knew that the old woman's premonition had disturbed him that first day ashore on lovely, lonely Fair Isle.

Within half an hour they were aboard and steaming towards Corrae. The *Saturn* seemed to have gone back on her tracks a little, heading north-east, and Huntley's whole body grew taut as they approached his island home.

Suddenly, there it lay on that unbelievably blue sea, with white birds circling above it and the sunshine lying like a benediction on the bright green cap it wore on its old grey head. It looked sheltered and serene lying almost in the shadow of the great mountains of Mull, a beckoning island of tiny coves where the white sands curved in crescents between dark promontories and sheep grazed placidly high above the sea.

There was the usual stir about going ashore. Both launches were used and the small bay where they landed was soon alive with people.

Adam Fulton had come ashore with Aunt Betsy and Huntley conducted them over the island.

It was not big. They climbed a little way up the steep path leading from the shore, and from a mound of tufted grass and heather they were able to see most of Huntley's domain.

The island was hilly on the east side, but in the west it sloped gently down to the Atlantic, to little bays where the sand was almost pure white, the result of the ceaseless action of the sea on millions and millions of tiny shells. To the north a single, conical peak reared its grey head high above the grazing land, and beyond it a dark buttress of rock fell steeply to the shore. On it stood the remains of an ancient castle, and beyond it the dazzling white column of a light-house stood silhouetted across the sky, sole guardian of the treacherous rocks below.

Walking across the heather they could see a small harbour far beneath them, a cluster of white houses huddled close to the water's edge. Here and there on the hillsides a lone croft nestled in a more sheltered spot, but mostly the inhabitants of Corrae had gathered for protection round the tiny harbour.

Ailsa looked back towards the grim and ruined splendour of the grey castle facing the westering sun. Generations of MacLarens had been born and had died up there in that harsh old fortress, and Huntley was the last of them.

Turning, she saw his tall, tweed-clad figure silhouetted against the rough crags of his island home and was instantly aware that Aunt Betsy, with the best will in the world,

105

could never be a substitute for this man. He *was* Corrae.

By the time they had reached the harbour, their fellow-passengers had laid seige to the little township. There was only one main thoroughfare and it was already thronged with them. The inhabitants had come to the cottage doors at the first signs of invasion, but already they were offering shy hospitality to the strangers. They were slow of speech because loquaciousness had no part in their way of life, but there was no doubt that the advent of the launches from the *Saturn* had made this a red-letter day as far as they were concerned.

The *Saturn* and Huntley! For wherever he went the smiles on old rugged faces deepened. He was their own, the rightful laird. Their ancestry probably went as far back as his and they were universally loyal.

Ailsa's throat felt tight with emotion. She knew now what parting with Corrae would mean to him when it came to the final decision, and she was quite certain that he must have explored every other possibility of saving the island before he had decided to sell. It was years since his brother's death, and she could imagine these years as bitter milestones on the way to his final defeat.

He was talking to her aunt and, presently, Betsy beckoned her to join them. One look at her flushed cheeks and brightly eager eyes convinced Ailsa that she was delighted with Corrae. The island had enchanted her from the moment she had set foot on it, and two hours was going to be far too short a time to cover all she wanted to see.

"Mr. MacLaren suggests we should go over the house," she said. "It's not very far away, and he feels that I really ought to see it."

Ailsa could not refuse to go, even although she knew that every moment was going to be an agony for Huntley. He had made up his mind to go through with this thing. It had to be done, and he had even included Adam Fulton and Lucy in his invitation.

Corrae house was a complete surprise to her. She had expected it to be almost as bleak as the grim old castle on its distant headland, but instead it was a lovely, mellowed old place of weathered stone enclosed by a high, lichen-covered wall. It stood on a grassy height affording superb views from all its rooms; views of the sea and the tiny harbour, and the towering peak of Scuirival rising in the north, and the tall white column of the lighthouse looking down on the treacherous skerries at its foot.

Enclosed by the wall, too, was the loveliest natural garden Ailsa had ever seen. A mountain burn hurried, deep in rock and fern, towards the sea. It was spanned at intervals by little rustic bridges which carried a maze of pathways through rockeries and shrub gardens and rose pergolas to the house. The main avenue, she fancied, must be somewhere at the back, leading from the road by which they had crossed the island, but this must have been the way by which Huntley had always come home. She could imagine him as a small boy climbing up from the harbour after a day's sailing, or rushing through the open doorway in the high wall with a string of fish to be offered proudly at the kitchen door.

That was long before he had come back as the new laird with the bleak knowledge in his heart that he had also inherited a crushing burden of debt.

He conducted them over the house with a silent courtesy which tore at her own heart, and she was glad that, for once, Aunt Betsy seemed to have little to say.

When they came again to the garden door they sat down on a mound of grass and heather, waiting for the last of the stragglers to come up from the harbour.

Huntley left them as they approached the bay where the launches were waiting, and Adam and Lucy became involved in conversation with a couple from Amsterdam who were visiting Scotland for the first time.

Her heart beating suffocatingly close to her throat, Ailsa waited for her aunt to say what she thought about Corrae. Instead, Betsy clutched her arm, while a look of mingled apology and alarm spread quickly over her small, flushed face.

"I've done it again!" she exclaimed. "I've left my satchel back at the house. I'm afraid I'm a very great trouble to you, honey, but I laid it down when we were sitting just outside the garden wall. You remember? While

107

we were waiting for the others to come up from the harbour?"

Ailsa glanced hastily at the small groups gathered beneath them on the shore and at the waiting launches rocking gently by the jetty steps. It was no use getting annoyed with Aunt Betsy. She did these things, and all that could be done was to try to put them right with as little fuss as possible.

"I'll go back," she said. "Don't worry. On you go down to the boats. I won't be able to get my place beside you in the first one, but I should just make it in time for the second launch. There's half an hour between them."

"Really, this *is* too bad of me," Betsy sighed. "But I was thinking about something quite different, and these things do happen——"

Ailsa could not afford to waste any time. Swiftly she retraced her steps over the uneven moorland road, running now and then to cover the distance back to the house as quickly as possible. It would cut off about quarter of a mile to go back through the gardens, and here she was able to run all the way.

Breathless, she arrived at the great wooden door and tugged it open, to be met by a strong gust of wind from the sea. The wind seemed to have risen as they had crossed the island and there was a vague greyness in the sky which had not been there before.

The handbag was lying where her aunt had left it, and she lifted it with a small, indulgent smile. Aunt Betsy really did need someone to look after her!

Back across the garden and over the first of the bridges she ran, going faster than ever now because there was no time to waste. The house was empty, so there was no need for explanations, and she was glad of that.

Hurrying down the drive, where the fallen pine needles made a thick carpet under her feet, she reached the gates and decided to take a narrow path which went up over the moor and appeared to be the more direct way back to the bay.

Almost instantly, however, she regretted her choice. The path was rough and uneven and in some places black with bog water, but there was no time to go back now. Already the first launch would be on its way to the ship and the other would soon be filling up. She did not want to give unnecessary trouble, although she knew that they would wait for her once her aunt had explained the situation.

Her breath was coming in small, quick gasps now, but she could not slacken her pace. She ran on, stumbling a little until, with utter suddenness, she felt her feet go from under her and she had fallen heavily on the rutted path.

Her leg twisted beneath her, and for a split second she could do nothing but lie there without thought — without movement. Then, gradually, the realization came to her that any movement — any at all — meant searing, excruciating pain.

* * *

How long she lay there she was never quite sure. The sky seemed to go dark, and then she rolled over and tried to get to her feet. The effort drove a sharp little gasp of pain between her clenched teeth and it was minutes before she was able to take stock of the situation.

Dragging herself to a boulder by the side of the path, she leaned against it for support, feeling her ankle for the root of the trouble. Already it was evident. Foot and ankle were swelling rapidly and every movement had become agony.

Momentarily dazed, she stared down at the spot where she had fallen, seeing the deep rut as a sure trap for unwary feet, and gradually the full significance of her accident flooded in upon her. She was a mile, at least, from the west side of the island, a mile from the boats on an unfrequented path where nobody would dream of looking for her unless Huntley came back with the search party.

Coming over to the island Huntley had been in the first of the launches, which would automatically be the first to return to the waiting *Saturn*. The thought made her gasp with dismay. There was nothing for it but to try to reach the road by her own volition.

Clenching her teeth, she eased herself to her feet. She could stand, which was encouraging and seemed to prove that there was nothing broken.

Gingerly she moved forward, each step making her gasp with pain, and after she had gone a few paces she was forced to sit down again. She noticed, too, that the narrow ditch which skirted the path was black and deep, a sure indication that there was bog land not very far away. She had seen the little white tufts of cotton grass fluttering in the wind, like tiny, warning flags, as she had climbed up from the road and now they seemed to be everywhere about her. It would be worse than madness to attempt to leave the path.

She could not see the road from where she sat. It had disappeared in a hollow between the hills, and the rising wind caught up her cry of distress, whipping it away towards Scuirival with a demon laugh.

It was a wind that had strengthened and grown cold in the past half hour, and the grey pall which had come in from the east looked like rain. The bright face of the island had changed with alarming rapidity. Corrae was no longer smiling, and suddenly the dark, jagged buttress of Scuirival seemed to come very close.

The first rain drove down from the corries on its grey, riven sides. She could imagine the scene on the beach as the thinly-clad passengers scurried for accommodation in the boats, and for the first time she realized that she might not be missed in the general confusion.

There had been several empty places in the two launches coming over, and if her aunt had not been absolutely explicit about her errand she might not be missed for some time.

The thought made her shiver, because even now she was beginning to feel cold. The first shock of her accident was passing and the aftermath held her in its grip. Her teeth began to chatter, and even when she buttoned her woollen cardigan right to her throat it did not offer her the extra warmth she needed.

I've got to go on, she thought. I've got to get off the moor somehow!

But the wild, bleak expanse of heather and bracken stretched for miles on every side. As far as she could see there was no sign of human habitation whichever way she looked.

Where were the little white crofts that had been tucked into the hillsides when they had looked up from the road? Surely, oh, surely, there must be at least one of them close at hand?

Near enough to walk to. She tried again, biting her teeth into her lower lip as the pain wrenched at her foot but limping on in the hope that, over the next rise, a croft might come into sight.

Trying to remember the whereabouts of the little houses was a difficult task. There had been several, but, of course, she had not paid exact attention. Then she thought about the smoke coming from their chimneys, blue peat smoke rising in a thin spiral into the clear air. She had seen it so often on the other islands they had visited and Huntley had said that it was the warmest sight to a Highlander's eyes.

"I'd give all I possessed, and more," he had confessed, "to see the blue peat smoke rising from every croft on Corrae!"

Which meant that not every croft had an inhabitant. The thought mocked at her as she hobbled along, her hair wet now from the falling rain. It was the fine, thin rain of the west, which clung like mist, and she did not really mind it at first. It had a softness about it which lay like a caress on her cheek and dewed the fine tendrils of hair on her brow. It was the sort of rain you could walk through for miles and feel exhilarated by it if you knew that there was a sheltering roof and a fire at journey's end.

She could almost smell the peat smoke in her nostrils and see the imagined croft long before she came to it.

The little house nestled in the fold of a hill, but a narrow sheep track was all that went up to it. The road — if there had been a road in the full meaning of the word — had long since been swallowed up by the moor.

Before she reached it she knew that there was no one in the croft. The last tenant had left it long ago.

Almost weeping, she tried the door, as if there still might be some hope in the fact that it was securely closed. The handle turned reluctantly, but the room she entered was empty.

Her unexpected presence disturbed a feathered bundle roosting on the ancient black hob of the chimneypiece, and an owl flew clumsily towards a broken pane in the low window.

Her heart jumped, but there were no other occupants of the tiny kitchen. The starlings and the swifts had not yet come home to roost.

The half of the door which she had opened gave sufficient light for her to see an inner room and a narrow, enclosed stair leading to the floor above. Two rooms up there too, no doubt, tucked closely under the thatch. The little house was still habitable and, but for the broken window pane, could have been used again immediately.

But the people had gone. An old couple had died, perhaps, and their offspring, long since migrated to the mainland, had returned only to sell their few humble belongings and sail away.

In that moment Huntley's problem came very close to her. She stood inside the croft much longer than she might have done, realizing that most of the islanders now lived in the cottages surrounding the harbour, and even there blank windows had gazed back at her with a vaguely hopeless stare.

There was nowhere inside the croft to sit down and, in any case, she did not want to stay there.

Painfully she hobbled to the door, drawing the half she had opened shut behind her.

Where now? A terrible feeling of desperation assailed her as she thought of the time and it was almost more than she could do to look at her watch.

Ten minutes to six! The *Saturn* had been due to sail again at six o'clock.

What would they say? What would Huntley think of her, getting lost like this? It might be ages before a search party located her. If they searched at all.

Why did she always have to come back to that supposition? Of course they would search! Of course they would send someone to look for her.

112

Huntley? She could imagine her humiliation when he found her, but she would have given a great deal to have seen his tall, broad-shouldered figure striding along the path towards her at that moment. Of course he would tell her that she had been a fool ever to leave the road, and she knew that now—when it was too late. Perhaps she wasn't the type of person who should ever have been let loose on Corrae. He might tell her that, too.

She knew that she was thinking about him to keep up her courage because the grey pall over the hills had gradually become black and the wind whispered with a sinister voice. It blew strongly among the reeds of the little lochan she stumbled on further along the path, stirring the yellow waterlilies till they trembled at its passing, and then it rushed with the force of an angry bull back across the moor to hurl itself against Scuirival and the gaunt column of the lighthouse on its distant rock.

Suddenly she turned, aware that the wisest thing to do would be to go back by the way she had come. To go back would be easier than attempting to climb right up over the moor.

Undecided whether she had come halfway to the bay or not, she hobbled back down the path. The pain in her ankle had become almost unendurable and her one desire was to curl up among the heather and weep.

Which would get her nowhere, she told herself sternly, struggling on against the rising wind. It made her ordeal more difficult. The light was fading too, and there were dense, shadowy patches on the way ahead where a sparse clump of trees came down to the path's edge or a great boulder reared up against the darkening sky.

It seemed miles before she reached the turning leading down on to the road, and she was limping badly by the time she felt the hard, metalled surface under her feet.

The gates of Corrae House were little more than a hundred yards ahead and the shortest way to the harbour was through the deserted grounds.

Without asking herself if it was wise to leave the road for a second time, she went through the gates and began the long, difficult journey up the drive. There was a small

113

entrance lodge, an odd little house like an inverted bowl with tall chimney-breasts on either side, but it, too, was uninhabited. Huntley had obviously dispensed with the lodge-keeper's services long ago, perhaps when an old family retainer had died.

At a bend in the drive she cut down over the mossy grass. She was covering the ground automatically now, in little spurts of pain, and her brain had almost become numbed by it. Halfway across the garden she felt that she could not go on. She could not take another step. Her final effort had been made. Her ankle was so painful and so swollen that she clung to the rustic handrail of the first bridge across the burn and found herself slipping slowly to her knees among the rain-drenched ferns.

The sky above her seemed to go black and she clung to the support of the little bridge, telling herself that she just couldn't faint, no matter how bad the pain was. Not here, at this stage. She had to go on. She had to reach the harbour where she could seek help . . .

"I thought I would find you here. I thought you would come this way."

Strong arms lifted her, steadying her against the bridge. In her dazed condition she could not believe that Huntley had come at last.

"I tried to get back — across the moor——" Her voice sounded very far away, even in her own ears, and then all control seemed to slip from her and she clung to him as a child might have done. A lost child. "Oh, Huntley——!" she gasped. "I thought I might be left here——"

"To die?" His voice was light, forcing her to make a final effort at control, but for a moment of utter weakness she refused to let him go, holding on to both his arms as if there was nothing else to support her in all the world. And Huntley held her, tenderly, protectively, telling her that everything was all right, now that he had found her. "We'll have to get you to the house," he decided. "It's the only way, the only cover there is for over a mile. How bad is the ankle? Don't try to tell me how you did it — just try to relax a bit. It doesn't look as if there's anything broken if you've come all this way down off the moor."

114

His arms remained strongly about her, his lips close above her hair. Madly she did not want to go on. She wanted to stay here in the warm circle of his arms for ever, feeling no pain.

"It's only when I move," she murmured. "My ankle — it twisted under me. I came back this way because I knew I could never make the bay alone."

He made no reply to that. He seemed to be considering the present situation, not hesitating but reviewing some former plan in the light of her accident.

"We've still got to get you up to the house," he decided. "To shelter. It's a goodish way yet."

He glanced down at her, and then, without another word of explanation, he lifted her bodily into his arms and strode across the bridge.

Carrying her without effort, as if she had indeed been a child, he covered the distance to the house in what seemed a very short time, putting her down carefully in the wide stone porch at the front door.

Doors on the island were never locked. He turned the handle and helped her into the big, open-raftered hall.

"I'll get a fire going," he said, drawing forward a leather armchair for her to sit in. "Then we'll see what we can do about your foot."

"Huntley," she protested weakly, "what about the others? About getting back to the ship?"

He dismissed her distress as he stooped to thrust paper and sticks under the wide chimney.

"We'll come to that presently," he said. "The first consideration is that foot of yours."

The fire sparked up, sending a comforting flare of warmth across the stone hearth, and Ailsa lay back in the big chair, allowing herself the momentary luxury of closing her mind to all thought except the fact that she was here, safe with Huntley.

When he had built up the peats he had taken from an ancient iron-bound chest beside her chair, he stooped to attend to her injury.

"It's going to hurt like the dickens to take this off," he told her, unfastening her shoe. "I'll be as gentle as I can."

115

His movements were quick and dexterous, as he had promised. And gentle too. She was amazed at the lightness of his touch, at the way his strong fingers moved her foot and ankle with a sureness which did nothing to increase the agony she had already endured.

"You've had experience of this sort of thing," she guessed involuntarily.

He smiled at the question.

"On an island like Corrae, where we are often isolated by storms for many days, it pays to know something of first-aid," he said.

That wasn't all, she thought. He had the touch that would have made him a good surgeon and the patience of the man who has dwelt long in remote places dealing mostly with natural things. Now, when she was here alone with him in his own environment, she saw the quality which she had first thought to be indifference as something entirely natural. He was not concerned with the little things of life.

"I'm so desperately sorry about this," she tried to apologize. "Everybody is going to think me such a fool, coming back on a simple errand and — falling down on the job — literally falling down on it! The awful thing for me is the thought of holding everything up — of the *Saturn* not being able to keep to her original schedule and everyone being upset. I know how Captain Lindstrom feels about timetables, and he is due in Oban tomorrow morning."

"He'll be there," Huntley said, quite calmly and without looking up from his task. "The *Saturn* sailed on time."

She gazed at him incredulously.

"You mean — it got away at six?"

He raised his head and their eyes met with an impact which had all the force of shock about it.

"Exactly that," he agreed.

"Then——?"

"How did I get here?" He got to his feet, moving towards a door at the back of the hall which led to a small cloak cupboard where there was a wash-basin and, evidently a first-aid outfit. "Like the others," he explained when he had returned with the box, "I believed you to be safely on board when we weighed anchor. You were not missed till you didn't make an appearance at dinner, and by that time we had reached Iona."

Her searching scrutiny went beyond his dark head to the long windows above the staircase.

"What time is it now?" she asked.

"Almost nine o'clock."

She could not believe it.

"But——"

"You must have been lying out there in the garden for quite a while," he observed. "As soon as I've tied up your foot we'll get those wet clothes off and see about something warm to drink. There's bound to be cocoa or something left in the pantry."

"Huntley," she worried, "if the *Saturn* went on — if it's at Iona by now and they haven't really lost time on their schedule — how did you get back here?"

He unwound a roll of bandage for several inches, examining it carefully before he made reply.

"It was easy enough to borrow a launch. I have several friends down there, and there was someone I knew with a yacht lying in Loch Scridain. They were all very helpful, I must admit."

"And Aunt Betsy?" she asked. "I expect she was in a dreadful state?"

"Not really." His reply was even, almost amused. "She appears to take this sort of thing in her stride. It has, apparently, all happened before."

"But you," she argued. "It must have been terribly inconvenient for you and — very irritating."

Again the blue eyes met hers.

"To come back to Corrae?" he queried.

"To come back—like this," she pointed out.

He did not answer that. Instead he proceeded to bandage her foot, so expertly that she was immediately freed from pain.

"That ought to do the trick till we can get you to the mainland for an X-ray," he decided. "My guess still is that there's nothing broken, though you've certainly wrenched it pretty badly. There could, of course, be a small fracture and that would have to be dealt with professionally."

Ailsa looked at her watch in the light from the fire.

"It must have stopped," she said. "It still says ten minutes to six." Vigorously she shook her wrist. "I looked at it up on the moor——"

"Nearly three hours ago," he said. "What made you take the moor road?"

There was no sign of anger or even of irritation in his deep voice, as she had half expected there would be. Gently and systematically he began to strip off her wet coat and untied the dripping head scarf from her hair.

"I thought it might be quicker that way," she tried to explain.

"It could have been the end of you," he said without looking up. "There is no clearly defined path after you pass the MacPhersons' croft — or what used to be their croft."

"I went in there, I think," she told him. "I felt I had to find shelter and look for help."

"And you found it empty." His voice was bitter once more. "That is the way of it all over the island. It could have cost you your life."

"Something made me turn back," Ailsa explained. "Probably it was the terrible force of the wind and the fact that it was growing dark so quickly. Something else too. I thought I had more than halfway to go to the bay and I knew I wouldn't be able to make it — not in time. I knew I would be safer here——"

She hadn't meant to say that. She hadn't really thought about it until now.

Huntley said, "We guessed as much," taking her coat and putting it over the back of one of the smaller chairs.

"My aunt won't know what's happened," Ailsa said after a moment or two.

"No," he agreed. He appeared to be withholding something, and then he said: "We're pretty well shut in here till tomorrow morning, at least. You won't have heard the wind so much in the garden, but it's blowing a full gale outside. It whipped up pretty quickly, and we're getting everything that can blow from the north-west. I just managed to make the harbour with the launch, and in this wind it would be next to impossible to get out again. That, I'm afraid, is Corrae's chief handicap. An inadequate harbour at the mercy of certain winds."

Ailsa felt tremendously guilty.

"I wish I hadn't got you into all this trouble," she sighed, "but it was so easily done. One minute I was runnning along the path and the next I was doubled up in the ditch!"

"It could have happened to anyone." He straightened, pulling up a footstool from the far side of the hearth. "While I forage around in the kitchen you can amuse yourself by flinging the odd peat on the fire." He was doing his best to make the situation easier for her. "I won't be very long. I can't promise you milk in your coffee or cocoa, or whatever I find, but at least I can see that it will be warm."

"It will taste like ambrosia!" she smiled.

He looked back at her from the open doorway.

"Don't be too sure. The food of the gods wasn't brewed on a paraffin stove!" he warned.

While he was away Ailsa leaned her head back against the smooth leather of the armchair, allowing her gaze to wander over the lovely old room. It looked strangely different now that she was not viewing it with her aunt as the prospective buyer of Corrae.

It had undoubtedly been the family gathering-place in those not-to-distant days when Huntley had lived here happily with his brother and their parents. The lovely old Persian rugs on the floor were well worn without being shabby and the soft cushioning of the chairs sagged a little from use. Someone—Huntley's mother, she guessed—had worked the tapesty backs on the tall chairs, and beside the fire, in the shadows, stood a gay sampler in a dark oak frame. It was impossible to read the neatly-stitched signature at the bottom, but some other MacLaren bride had probably added it with a little flourish of pride, sitting before a glowing peat fire, as she was sitting now.

The thought burned a sudden colour into her pale cheeks, and when Huntley came back she was bending forward to replenish the fire. She was not able to look at him in that moment.

He set a tray down on the low table he pulled in front of the fire.

"It's a bit rough and ready," he apologized, "but at least it might help you to feel better."

The pungent aroma of coffee floated across to her from the two yellow beakers on the tray, making her realize how cold and hungry she really was.

"Nothing much to eat, I'm afraid," he told her. "Only a digestive biscuit or two, and even they are slightly substandard! When I get down to the village I should be able to produce something more substantial."

For the first time Ailsa allowed herself to think beyond the fact that she was no longer alone in a dreadful predicament and that it had been Huntley who had come to her rescue. He had told her that they were likely to be stormbound until the morning, and that meant, she supposed, that the *Saturn* would continue her voyage to Oban without them. Aunt Betsy would certainly begin to be worried when they did not put in an appearance at Iona as expected, because her aunt would have been sure that Huntley would find her waiting on the beach.

"I suppose the storm will have hit the *Saturn* too?" she remarked between sips of coffee.

"It wouldn't do much harm to a ship of her size," Huntley answered without concern. "She'll ride it out quite easily. The trouble for us is getting in and out of the harbour here. Once the *Saturn* is safely through the Torrin Rocks she has nothing more to worry about on her way up the Firth. They wouldn't be able to wait for us, though. She has a quick turn-round at Oban, and most of her passengers are booked to go on elsewhere."

"Yes, of course."

Vaguely Ailsa wondered about the Fultons and about Erik Larsen, whom she was not likely to see again. She felt sorry about not being able to say goodbye to Erik, but not too worried about Lucy Fulton. Lucy hadn't liked her very much.

"Drink it up!" Huntley commanded. "It will do you a power of good." He poured her more coffee, but he did not sit down or even attempt to take off his jacket, which was very wet. He stood over her, with his back to the fire, while she gulped down the hot liquid, and then he lifted the other beaker with an odd sort of smile curving his lips. "To our speedy rescue!" he said. "With this wind blowing, we *could* be trapped on Corrae for days."

"Oh——!" She gazed up at him incredulously. "It seems impossible, so near to—to——"

"Civilization?"

"No," she denied, "I didn't really mean that. I suppose I meant so near to the mainland. We're not so very far off, are we?"

"Six hours' sailing in a small boat, whichever way you like to look at it!" he explained. "That's why the air age has come so swiftly to the Hebrides. An hour would take us to Glasgow in a plane if Corrae had a suitable landing strip."

"What about the bay?" she asked, immediately interested.

"It would need to be extended to make a safe enough runway and there aren't enough people left on the island to justify it."

That was the great regret, the bitter point of return for all his thoughts.

"Do you really expect us to be marooned for days?" she asked.

He shrugged.

"We could be, quite easily. On the other hand, I've seen a gale like this blow itself out in an hour or so." He put down his empty beaker, standing for a moment to look at her in the bright orange glow from the peats. "We haven't a great deal of choice, you see. When you're dealing with the elements you have to bide their time, as my mother used to say. Nothing ever irked her. Even a storm had its own fierce, wild beauty in her eyes. It was all part of Corrae. You're not afraid of being left, are you?"

It was hardly a question. He did not expect her to be afraid; not here, on Corrae.

"No." Her eyes met his. "Why should I be?"

"I was thinking of Lucy," he said.

"Lucy——?" The name struck Ailsa as if he had aimed a deadly blow at her heart.

"I left Lucy down at the lodge," he said, turning away from the fire. "We weren't sure, of course, that you would

121

be here, in the garden, and she was getting wet. She had oilskins, but the rain had run down and got into her shoes. I advised her to shelter in the lodge rather than come all the way up here on what might have been a wild goose chase."

Lucy, Ailsa was thinking. He had brought Lucy back with him! Something that had been lovely and frail and shining seemed to shrivel up and die in her heart.

"I—didn't know," she said foolishly.

Huntley came to stand behind her chair. For a moment it seemed as if he would touch her, laying a kindly, friendly hand on her shoulder, perhaps, and then he said quite harshly:

"It may have solved a problem. I can safely leave you with Lucy if I can't get anyone to come up from the village."

He was depending on Lucy. She had already become necessary to him, if only to help him out of this present fix!

"How foolish you must think me," she said dully, so near to tears that she had to defeat them with anger. "I was a fool to rush around like that, not looking where I was going, leaving the road when I knew nothing about the moor."

He may have heard the tears in her voice and some of the anger too, because he turned rather abruptly towards the door, halting only when his fingers were securely round the latch.

"Don't blame yourself," he said. "I won't be any longer than I can help."

He went out, closing the door firmly behind him. A great rush of wind and rain had come in when he had opened it, leaving dark flecks on the polished pine floor.

Ailsa continued to stare at them long after he had gone. They were like tears. She could not wrench her mind away from the thought, and the sound of the wind in the dark trees outside was like a low, persistent sobbing.

She could hear the wind clearly now that Huntley was no longer with her and she was alone in the house. It seemed to strike belligerently against the long panes of the windows above her on the half-landing, shaking them in impotent rage because the old house could still resist it, because it still remained a stout fortress against any marauder.

It could remain like that, Ailsa thought, for Huntley—and Lucy. If only her aunt refused to complete the bargain over Corrae.

Strange little sounds creaked and echoed about the room. 'You're not afraid. You're not afraid, Ailsa!' Huntley's voice came back to mock at her. She had no fear of little things, of the rattle of a window in a storm or the groan of old timbers shaken by the wind. Yet she was suddenly, desperately afraid of the emptiness which seemed to stretch before her, the lonely, endless years trudging on until Huntley's name would sound like a distant cry in her heart, echoing in an empty place.

I've not got to think like that, she tried to tell herself. There was never anything between Huntley and me. A kiss that meant nothing that was all. If it kindled this flame in my heart, Huntley was not to blame!

Perhaps she had shown him that she had been all too ready for his kisses.

Her cheeks burned and she was glad of the dark, although there was no one to see. The peats had settled down into a subdued glow and long shadows moved stealthily across the ceiling. The latch clicked and she turned towards the door. There were no tears in her eyes now. Only in her heart.

Lucy came in, thrusting the door shut against the wind. She was wearing a long, yellow oilskin coat reaching well down to her ankles, and she had a transparent hood over her hair. When she took it off a little shower of rain fell to the polished floor at her feet.

"Huntley has gone down to the village," she said in an aggressive voice. "He thought it best, under the circumstances." She unbuttoned the oilskin, laying it over one of the chairs. "You've got yourself into a nice mess, haven't you?" she observed dryly. "Huntley didn't have time to go into details, but I gather you've wrenched your ankle pretty badly."

She had not said that she was sorry. She seemed to be thinking about something else.

"I'm putting everyone to a great deal of trouble," Ailsa murmured unhappily. "Especially Huntley——"

"Wasn't that part of the idea?" In the uncertain light Lucy's mouth seemed to be twisted in a sneer. "Wasn't that what you wanted?"

The innuendo was too obvious to miss.

"Nobody could deliberately wrench an ankle," Ailsa cried. "And I hadn't the faintest idea who would come back for me! I could have been found by someone from the village."

"That wasn't at all likely, was it?" Lucy crossed to the hearth, thrusting thin hands out to the warmth. They were like claws. "You knew Huntley would come, if anyone did."

"No—that isn't true!"

"Then shall we say you *hoped* he would come?" Lucy did not turn from the fire. "You're in love with him, aren't you?"

"I——"

"Don't bother to lie!" Lucy cried. "I know you are. I've seen it almost since that first day we all sat down at the same table."

"Lucy—don't say any more," Ailsa begged. "You'll hate it—afterwards, and it won't do any good."

"Won't it?" Lucy turned to stare at her with naked hatred in her eyes. "I think it will," she declared stubbornly. "I believe in clearing the air, you see."

"There isn't anything to clear," Ailsa said desperately. "Huntley isn't in love with me——"

Lucy drew out a cigarette and lit it.

"So long as you realize that," she said deliberately, "I suppose there isn't. It's rather amusing, though, because the fact of the matter is that he's going to marry me. Poor Huntley!" She smiled a little. "He's so desperately in need of money to pay Corrae's debts!"

A small gasp of protest escaped Ailsa's lips, but Lucy either did not hear it or was determined not to notice.

"It's not exactly flattering to know that a man first took an interest in you because your father had more dollars than he knew what to do with," she went on almost dispassionately. "But Huntley and I are beginning to understand one another."

It was hardly light enough to catch the fleeting changes of emotion on her face, but there was certainly a note of subdued triumph in her voice. And there was the fact that

Huntley had brought her to Corrae with him. He could so easily have brought someone else—Adam Fulton or Aunt Betsy, although Aunt Betsy was always nervous in a small boat if there was anything like a sea running.

No, even if Lucy had only been speaking half-truths, it seemed obvious that Huntley had wanted her to come.

Lucy glanced about her with a preoccupied smile.

"Of course, nothing's settled yet about Corrae," she observed after a minute or two. "Huntley still thinks that he owes your aunt first refusal."

"I don't know anything about that," Ailsa returned frigidly. "She was to make her final decision after she saw Corrae."

"And your present little adventure put that right into the back of her mind," Lucy mused. "Huntley won't get his answer now until he can get you off the island."

It may not have been cruelly meant—Lucy did not choose her words very carefully—but Huntley's apparent desire to be rid of her seared deeply across Ailsa's sensitive heart.

"I don't want to stay on Huntley's wretched island!" she cried tempestuously as the door opened for a second time. "I'm here entirely against my will——"

She knew that Huntley was standing in the doorway, that he had put something down on the table just inside the door, but she did not care what she said. He had told Lucy that he wanted her off Corrae as quickly as possible!

"Nobody planned this," he said sternly, coming forward into the fitful glow of the fire. "And we're not in danger of getting in each other's way. Someone is coming up from the village to look after you, Ailsa. It's my old nurse, as a matter of fact. She served my mother for thirty years and she knows her way about the house. You'll be in good hands. I think she would appreciate it if you allowed her to fuss a bit," he added dryly. "She believes that she owes it to me to look after my guests."

Ailsa could have wept. With a dignity which neither she nor Lucy could have matched, he had offered his hospitality, quietly and courteously, as it had been offered at Corrae for years. They were the strangers within his gates, and no matter how unwelcome she might be he would see to her comfort in every way he possibly could.

"I'm sorry," she apologized. "I shouldn't have said what I did."

Without answering he turned to the table where he had put down a bag of provisions.

"There should be enough here to provide a meal for tonight and tomorrow morning," he said briefly. "I won't be able to start up the motor to give you electric light—not at the moment, but there are lamps in the gun-room. I'll trim them for you before Helen arrives."

"Huntley," Lucy said, speaking for the first time, "you're not going to leave us here on our own, are you? I couldn't stand it!" she added before he could answer. "I just couldn't! All that moor stretching around everywhere and the odd noises. I'd go mad!"

"That's nonsense, Lucy," Huntley said lightly enough. "People don't go mad quite so easily. I'll not be far away. I'm going over to the lighthouse. I've stayed there with Malcolm in an emergency many a time."

"But what about us?" Lucy protested. She had even included Ailsa this time. "We can't stay here alone."

"Of course you can." His voice was almost soothing, as if he were attempting to placate a frightened child. "Helen will be in the house, and Rory."

"That old man!" Lucy exclaimed with disgust. "The one that helped to tie up the launch?"

"The same!" he agreed. "Don't underestimate Rory, though. He will make sure that your slightest wish is gratified."

"For your sake?" Lucy's smile was thin. "It must be wonderful to command so much respect—to have such faithful retainers. When must we expect Helen—and Rory?"

"I'll wait till they come," Huntley promised as he left them to go in search of the lamps.

Lucy came back to the hearth, staring moodily into the orange heart of the fire.

"I suppose we could have got back to Iona if it hadn't been for this storm," she observed at last. "Huntley said it would be no more than a two hours job, even if we had to look for you. Poppa will be having a fit! He just can't stand things getting out of hand. He likes everything to go according to plan. *His* plan!"

Ailsa wondered if it had been according to Adam's plan that Lucy was here now, but somehow she didn't think so. It hardly seemed to matter, however, since Huntley had brought Lucy, anyway.

When he came back into the room he was carrying two oil lamps which he had already lit. Their yellow glow cast long shadows across his face, accentuating the lean, finely drawn line of the jaw and mouth and the straight dark brows above the deeply-set eyes. He looked at Ailsa as he put one of the lamps on the high mantelpiece above her head.

"Helen has come in," he said. "She's fussing about airing beds. Nobody has slept here for a couple of months and she says they're bound to be damp. The storm is still pretty much as it was." For the first time he looked at Lucy. "I'm sorry if this is going to worry your father," he said. "We've sent a radio message through to the *Saturn* from the village, but that's the best we can do. There's absolutely no hope of them getting help over here till they reach Oban."

"Poppa'll be livid!" Lucy said with an indifferent shrug. "But it can't be helped. After all, we didn't set out in bad weather." She shivered, drawing her woollen jacket a little closer about her throat. "It's desperately cold, isn't it? We Yankees are utterly spoiled by steam heating!"

"You're quite a long way from that here," Huntley agreed, turning abruptly back to Ailsa. "What about the foot now?" he asked. "Any more pain?"

"None to speak of." She forced a smile. "The bandage did the trick, I think."

"You look tired," he said. "When you've had something to eat I'm going to send you straight to bed."

Before Ailsa had time to answer, someone came from the shadows behind them. She was a tall, slim woman in her late fifties whose hair still retained much of its former gold and whose blue eyes were the same deep, rich colour as Huntley's. Ailsa was beginning to think of them as Island eyes. She had seen that same clear blue so often in the past few days. It was a colour which never seemed to fade, even in extreme old age.

"This is Mrs. MacMillan—Helen," Huntley said. Lucy had turned from the fire, but it was Ailsa he introduced

127

first. "Miss Monro — and Miss Lucy Fulton from New York."

Helen MacMillan gave Lucy a quick scrutiny before she turned back towards Ailsa.

"And this is the invalid!" she exclaimed with a smile which illumined her whole face. "We must see what we can do to make you comfortable. Is that skirt you're wearing wet?" she added practically. "If it is, we'll have it off. Huntley has put on the kitchen fire. We can dry everything in there when Rory comes back with some more peats."

Huntley went back to the kitchen, but Lucy made no effort to follow him. She stood by the fire and shivered. Even when Helen went to prepare their rooms she did not offer to help. She just did not seem to think about it. She sat huddled over the fire, complaining about the cold until Huntley came back with a large tray which he set down beside Ailsa.

"Broth and cold mutton and scones," he intimated. "And after that you can have bannocks and honey."

"Bannocks?" Lucy queried, coming to examine the tray. "Not *oatcakes* again!"

"You'll have to get used to them—on Corrae," Huntley told her. "They're part of our staple diet."

Which meant, perhaps, that he hoped Lucy was going to stay on Corrae. But she was so wrong for Corrae, Ailsa thought, pulling one of the bowls of thick, hot soup towards her. She might even try to persuade Huntley to live away from the island, in time. And that would be one way of destroying him utterly. Even for Lucy, Huntley should not abandon Corrae. They were part of the same thing. He belonged here in this lovely, mellowed old house where he had been born.

As she forced herself to eat she saw Huntley watching her. He had brewed coffee and when he passed her her cup he said:

"Everything's ready upstairs now. Helen's been rushing round with sheets and hot-water bottles for an hour, so even she should be satisfied about the beds! I'll take you up when you've had your coffee, Ailsa. You really must be tired."

She was tired. Tired of the struggle to keep the tears out of her eyes so that Huntley, at least, might not see the pain of her longing. Lucy had guessed, but that had been an instinctive sort of thing, because Lucy, too, was in love with Huntley.

"I'll be glad to go," she admitted. "I'm beginning to feel the strain a little bit now."

"I'm sure you are," Lucy said almost eagerly, and then Helen came down the stairs and Huntley moved to help Ailsa to her feet.

Now that she had rested it the ankle had stiffened up a little and she was more than glad of his support and of Helen's on her other side. Between them she walked slowly the full length of the hall, drawing in a deep breath when she finally reached the foot of the staircase. This would be the crucial test.

Before she could make it, however, Huntley had picked her up into his arms, as he had done in the garden, and had begun the ascent of the shallow oak stairs.

Involuntarily Ailsa looked back to where Lucy stood. She was still beside the fire, but now her pale face was quite convulsed with rage. She stared up at them for a moment with open malice in her eyes before she began to search in her handbag for the inevitable cigarette.

When they reached the wide gallery above the hall Huntley put Ailsa on to her feet again.

"Thank you," she whispered shakily. "Thank you very much."

He stood back without a word and she walked the remaining distance to the room that had been prepared for her with only Helen to support her.

The heavy cretonne curtains had been drawn over the windows to shut out the storm, but she fancied that this room must overlook the front of the house and the garden. Perhaps, too, there would be a distant glimpse of the sea. She could not remember coming in here when Huntley had shown them over the house earlier in the day.

"It was his mother's room," Helen informed her. "The mistress used to love to sit at the window on a summer's evening, watching the sun go down. Sometimes she would say that all the colour came in here, lingering even after it had left the bay. She was not a superstitious woman, or even a very fanciful one, but she always thought that something would turn up to keep Mr. Huntley on the island. She wanted to see him married," Helen added, "but that was not to be."

"Perhaps she—hoped that his marriage might be the solution for Corrae," Ailsa suggested huskily.

"No, she wouldn't think that." Helen was quietly emphatic. "She'd know Mr. Huntley would have too much sense to marry where his heart wasn't given."

How well did Helen really know Huntley? Ailsa wondered, thinking that his old nurse could quite conceivably be prejudiced in his favour. She had taken care of him as a small boy, and that was the person she knew, but did she know the man Huntley had become?

"How long has he known that American girl?" Helen asked in her blunt, forthright way.

"Only since he came on the cruise. We all met at the same time."

It seemed an eternity ago to Ailsa, but Helen looked relieved.

"She's doing her best to catch him," she decided. "But don't you let her! She's not the type for Mr. Huntley at all!"

"I—won't have anything to do with it, Mrs. MacMillan," Ailsa said. "He may already be in love with Lucy."

"T-sh!" said Helen. "Not him! He would have far more sense. He would never know a day's peace if he married a girl like that. He would never know what happiness meant."

But he might be content with less than happiness for Corrae, Ailsa thought.

When Helen had helped her to undress she slipped thankfully between the sheets, too exhausted to reason any more, yet for a long time she could not sleep. Helen had said that Lucy would be in the room next door, but it was long after midnight before footsteps sounded on the corridor and the door banged behind Lucy. Then other, heavier footsteps sounded on the stairs and another door opened and closed again gently. Huntley had evidently been persuaded by Helen or Lucy not to spend the night at the lighthouse, after all.

They were all under one roof, an uneasy trio, loving and hoping and despairing, while the storm which had trapped them there beat ruthlessly against the island, as if it would never cease.

IN the morning, as if the whole thing had been no more than an unpleasant nightmare, the sun was shining. It came slanting through the clouds in a bright shaft of gold to touch the high shoulder of Scuirival and the long white column of the lighthouse and the restless sea itself. The wind had not abated. Giant waves raced in to throw themselves in glad abandonment against the harbour wall and out beyond the headland white horses tossed their manes as they charged towards the land.

"There'll be no Iona for you this day," Helen remarked when she drew back Ailsa's curtains to let in the sun. "Or Oban either! There isn't a boat on the island big enough or strong enough to go out with a sea running like that."

The remark was full of a quiet sort of satisfaction, because Helen was in her element now that she was back at Corrae House and virtually in charge. It was like old times, she confided, setting Ailsa's breakfast tray across her knees after she had forbidden her to get out of bed.

"It was Mr. Huntley's order," she said, as if that settled the matter. "He's up and away to the post-office to get another message through to the ship when she reaches Oban. He hadn't a lot of sleep," she added with a shake of her head. "I heard him moving about early this morning, as if he couldn't settle in his own home! But maybe that's natural enough seeing he has to give it up so soon," she sighed. "Nothing will be the same on this island if he goes," she lamented, crossing to the window. "Even the old people won't stay under a new landlord. They'd have no real ties, nothing to help their memories. New brooms aye sweep far too clean. A stranger might want to change too many things. They're telling me it's a woman who's thinking of buying him out, too."

"Yes," Ailsa said, looking down at the tray. "It's—my aunt."

Helen stood stock still in the centre of the room.

"Your aunt?" she repeated. "But why is she doing it if she hasn't a man behind her? Maybe she has a family, though?" The pleasant old voice hardened. "A son, perhaps, whom she can see as the new laird?"

"No," Ailsa assured her, "it isn't that. My aunt has no family. There would be no one to inherit Corrae."

Helen gave her a deeply penetrating look.

"That seems to me to be the strangest part of all," she remarked as she marched from the room. "What could a woman without an heir want with a place like Corrae?"

Ailsa could hardly have told her that Aunt Betsy was in the market for Corrae just to satisfy a whim.

I mustn't let her do it, she thought. I must stop Aunt Betsy somehow! But it was one thing to make such a resolution and quite another to carry it out in the face of her aunt's amazing determination.

For even in the teeth of a gale Betsy Bellinger made her way back to Corrae.

Lucy had finished a belated breakfast before Ailsa managed to hobble downstairs with Helen's assistance, and they were standing in the hall when Huntley came in. There was a dark frown of concentration between his brows and he glanced down at his watch, making some quick calculation before he turned to Ailsa to explain:

"The *Saturn* got in to Oban shortly after ten o'clock this morning and it would appear that your aunt then left there in a hired M.T.B. Apparently it was a conversion lying in the bay. They were used extensively round here during the war, and it's about the only thing that might make the harbour."

Both Lucy and Ailsa gazed at him in utter surprise.

"But Aunt Betsy's terrified of small boats," Ailsa protested at last. "She'll never get here——"

"I think she will," Huntley answered with a faint smile. "If she has made up her mind to come."

"I can't understand Poppa allowing her to do it," Lucy exclaimed. "She must be quite mad."

"Perhaps," Huntley pointed out, "he had very little choice."

Determinedly Ailsa hobbled the distance to the harbour to watch for the boat. Her ankle was still swollen and painful, but Huntley had decided it was best to use it and not allow it to stiffen up too much. She clung to his arm while

133

Lucy walked on his other side, her fair hair blown back by the wind, her eyes scanning the sea for the first sign of the approaching craft.

"Can that be it?" she asked at last, pointing to where a small black speck struggled among the waves. "Over there —where the light's striking the water!"

Huntley's keen eyes had already picked out the approaching boat and it was evident from his expression that he was assessing its chances of reaching the harbour in safety. His narrowed gaze remained on it as it cut its way through the angry water, but he made no direct comment until it had reached the bar. One final great wave carried it right in and, once it had reached more sheltered water, it came on rapidly.

Above the jetty steps a dozen eager hands were waiting to catch the mooring ropes. The approach of the strange boat had been watched from every cottage window and now the entire population of Corrae was down on the foreshore.

Huntley and Ailsa and Lucy went down the slope leading to the quay, but halfway there Lucy pulled up in amazement.

"It's Poppa!" she exclaimed as Adam Fulton came ashore in Aunt Betsy Bellinger's wake. "Now the sparks are going to fly, and no mistake!"

Ailsa's heart was beaitng very fast. Had Lucy come to the island without her father knowing, she wondered, or was there some other reason for Adam Fulton's journey to Corrae?

Aunt Betsy was not quite steady on her feet when she reached the top of the jetty steps. She staggered a little and her face was an unbecoming green colour, but she was far from being speechless. A trifle out of breath, it took her exactly six seconds to assess the possible damage done by Ailsa's accident, and then she exclaimed:

"Well, I got here! I made it. A good many people thought I wouldn't, but that's by the way!" She gave Adam a glance that was slightly belligerent. "I thought the best thing to do was to come and see for myself what exactly had happened. These wretched beam telephones, or whatever they are, don't seem to be a lot of good. All that crackling and popping so that you don't hear *half* that's said! We'll have to get something more reliable installed, Mr. MacLaren, before I come over here for good."

Ailsa drew in her breath. So Aunt Betsy had made her decision! She was going to buy Corrae. Her rather off-hand way of intimating the fact to Huntley had been anything but business-like, but all that would likely come later.

And what of Huntley? What was he thinking now that Corrae was finally lost to him?

Ailsa found it impossible to look round at him, but she could see the angry flush on Adam Fulton's face, as if he had been cheated in some way. If he had come to get his oar in first, he had come on a wild goose chase, for the bargain Aunt Betsy had made in Edinburgh now gave her first claim on the island. Even if Huntley did marry Lucy now he could no longer save his home. And if ever he had a son of his own, Aunt Betsy Bellinger and her niece would be firmly installed at Corrae House in final and irrefutable possession of his heritage!

How he must hate us, Ailsa thought. How he must wish that he had met Lucy long ago!

"Well," said Aunt Betsy, "we can't just stand here. Where did you three spend the night? At Corrae House?"

Lucy nodded. Her eyes were fixed on her father, as if he had betrayed her in some way. Perhaps she considered that he could have talked Aunt Betsy out of buying Corrae. Perhaps he had tried to do just that. But no one had ever succeeded in talking Betsy Bellinger out of anything.

"I told you they'd be safe enough," he grumbled as he took Lucy's arm in a firm grip. "Though Lucy should have told me she was coming back here."

"I couldn't find you at the time," his daughter retorted. "Someone had to go with Huntley."

Adam's look said that he did not see why that was necessary, but he chose not to argue the point. He was thankful that Lucy was none the worse for her adventure and he had never been able to argue against her, anyway, even when she had been a child.

"I think we ought to go up to the house," Huntley suggested stiffly. It was the first time he had spoken and most of the old coldness was back in his voice. "I'll just have a

135

word with the skipper before we go. He's had a rough crossing and he might like to join us."

"I won't be able to face a trip like that on the way back," Betsy complained. "We'll just have to stay put till this wind blows itself out. It was a pretty bad crossing, the skipper said," she added with a trace of importance in her voice. "Even hardened sailors wouldn't have been too fond of it. Yes," she mused, "maybe I won't mind at all coming over in half a gale once I get used to it!"

"You're mad!" Adam informed her. "You'll never settle down in a place like this. You'll be wanting to be back in New York after you've had one spell of bad weather."

"Oh, no, I won't!" Betsy declared. "You're just saying that because you're sore about not being able to buy the place yourself. You went behind my back and made a higher offer, didn't you?"

"I should never have told you!" Adam groaned.

"There's not much that doesn't come out into the light of day, sooner or later," Betsy reflected. "Probably I'd have found out about it, anyway. But the island's mine now! All I need is Mr. MacLaren's signature. He won't go back on his given word."

"No, I guess not," Adam agreed. "Not that you gave him much of a chance!"

"He wouldn't have taken it if I had done." Betsy seemed to be quite sure of that, at least. "He knew I fell in love with Corrae House as soon as I saw it."

She had put an end to the argument in her own decisive way.

Huntley caught up with them before they reached the house.

"The skipper wants to get back to Oban," he explained. "He has a charter for the week-end and he wants to get provisioned up for the trip. I told him you might not want to make the double journey in one day, Mrs. Bellinger," he added briefly. "I can accommodate you quite well at the house, if you care to stay."

"We couldn't, Huntley!" Ailsa protested. "We can't turn you out of your home."

"That will have to come," he said. "You can hardly call it turning me out when I have already agreed to sell Corrae."

They walked on in silence, through the garden and into the hall, which was now full of sunshine.

Helen MacMillan met them there. She stood frigidly beside the door leading to the kitchen premises, her keen blue eyes searching Betsy's face for some indication of her character, and what she saw there made her smile in quick relief.

"I'm pleased to welcome you, ma'am," she said in her quiet, dignified way. "You would be worried about your niece."

"Indeed I was!" Aunt Betsy agreed. "And now I'm equally worried about us all coming over here and inflicting ourselves on poor Mr. MacLaren like this. If there was an inn somewhere——"

She broke off tentatively, looking round the little group.

"The hotel has been closed for many years," Helen told her. "At one time Corrae got its share of fishermen, but that seems to have fallen off too. There isn't much need for an inn now, and the landlord wasn't an island man, in the first place. He soon got tired when there was little trade about."

Aunt Betsy warmed her hands at the fire. Already she was feeling at home on the island.

"Mrs. Bellinger could have the main bedroom, Helen," Huntley suggested, "and you can put Mr. Fulton in my room."

"Now, wait a minute!" Adam protested. "I'm not going to put anyone out of their room. If there aren't enough beds for all of us you can get me fixed somewhere in the village."

"I'd rather these were the arrangements," Huntley said. "I intended to go to the lighthouse last night, as a matter of fact, but Lucy felt nervous about being here alone. There's always a bed available up there when I need one."

He wanted to go, and he had Ailsa's deepest sympathy. She even wished that there was some way of getting off the island, but already the M.T.B. was on its hazardous journey back to the mainland.

137

All of this was her fault, she reflected miserably. If she had not chosen to return across the moor they would all be safely in Oban by now. Although her accident had nothing to do with the real cause of Huntley's hurt, it had aggravated it, bringing the realization of all he was about to lose much closer.

When he left them they stood in a small group about the fire, gazing rather disconsolately into the heart of the glowing peats.

"Well," Adam asked, "what do we do now?"

"Wait for the gale to blow itself out," Lucy informed him sarcastically. "What did you expect? Dancing girls?"

She marched out of the hall in Huntley's wake and Betsy remarked vigorously:

"What that young madam needs is a real good spanking, and you'll never have any peace, Adam, till you've administered it."

Adam gazed at her, horrified.

"You don't know Lucy!" he protested. "She's capable of anything when she's angry—or frustrated."

"Young people have no right to feel 'frustrated', as you call it," Betsy snorted. "She's no more than a spoiled brat."

"Maybe you're right." Adam heaved a deep sigh. "But it's too late for me to do anything about it now."

Aunt Betsy opened her mouth to reply, thought better of it, and turned instead to her niece.

"Now that I've made up my mind about Corrae," she said, "this will be your home. We'll go across to Edinburgh as soon as we reach the mainland and get everything signed, sealed and delivered. After that I'll help you to sell up at Achnasheen. I don't think there's any point in keeping the cottage when we will be living here most of the time. There's a great deal to be done in the next few weeks, and of course I can't settle any of these points till Mr. MacLaren and I have had a little talk."

She had her 'little talk' with Huntley during the afternoon. He came back from his visit to the lighthouse-keeper saying that he had arranged to sleep there and he and Aunt Betsy remained in the study for over an hour. When they came out he looked pale and drawn, and Ailsa turned abruptly away, not wanting to add to his hurt.

138

Excusing himself almost immediately, he left them in possession of the silent house. Lucy and her father had gone for a walk through the grounds after an excellent lunch which Helen had served to them ceremoniously in the big dining-room.

"I must say Huntley MacLaren is a man of his word," Betsy mused, crossing the room to join Ailsa at the fire. "He fully intends to carry out his part of the bargain."

"And—the condition you made that he should stay on the island?" Ailsa asked.

"He'll honour that too." For a moment Betsy was strangely silent. "I'll make it as easy for him as I can," she added.

"But—how *can* it be easy?" Ailsa blurted out. "It was a cruel condition, Aunt Betsy. It's only prolonging the agony of parting for Huntley——"

"He didn't seem to consider it that way," her aunt said promptly. "It's the best plan for the island, and that's all that matters, as far as he's concerned."

"But it's tying him down to a way of life he would never have chosen for himself," Ailsa protested. "Don't you see that?"

Betsy stooped to throw another peat on the fire.

"Maybe I'm not so blind as you think, honey," she answered slowly. "I've not come to Corrae to destroy the island. I want to see new, vigorous life here—a new beginning, if you like—and then I might be able to feel that I've done something with my life. Some people would call me a selfish woman, but I don't really think I am. I've never had any children, so I haven't that to offer to posterity. Only my money, and, goodness knows, I've got plenty of that! Far too much for one solitary woman ever to need. If I can give new life to Corrae then I might begin to feel satisfied," she concluded.

This was something Ailsa had not expected. It gave her a new insight into her aunt's character and made her feel suddenly humble. There was nothing more she could say about Corrae. The deal was completed. Huntley had lost the island now. The details of conveyance were only a formality to be gone through in the lawyer's office as soon as they all reached Edinburgh.

In the morning, when the gale had blown itself out and there was no more than a steady wind coming in from the sea, Huntley brought the launch round to the little bay below the garden and took them all back to the mainland. To the end he remained the perfect host.

"If you will let me know when you will be coming back," he offered as he bade Aunt Betsy goodbye, "I'll arrange with Helen to have fires lit and the house thoroughly aired."

That was all. There was nothing really personal about it. He shook each of them by the hand in turn before he walked away, a tall, legendary figure silhouetted against the vivid blue water of the bay and the distant hills of Mull.

Ailsa stood watching until he disappeared from view down the jetty steps. His leave-taking of Lucy had been no more intimate than the one brief handshake, but perhaps he considered that he had nothing to offer Lucy until he had completed his six months on Corrae.

He would keep that part of the bargain too, remaining on the island as her aunt's agent, and after that he would ask Lucy to marry him. Lucy herself had hinted as much, although whether or not she had been aware of the six months' servitude he had to endure was difficult to say.

It was an uneasy journey to Glasgow. Betsy and Adam chatted pleasantly enough, but Lucy sat glumly silent, frowning as she stared out of the carriage window at the passing scenery.

"I don't mean this to be goodbye," Adam said when they parted. "I'd like to meet you again, Betsy, before we go back to the States."

Betsy took a full minute to answer him.

"Maybe that could be arranged too," she said. "By the time you've had your Paris jaunt I should be more or less settled on Corrae. If you're still of the same mind by then we'll be pleased to see you—before you go back."

It was anything but a firm invitation, but somehow Ailsa knew that Adam Fulton would take advantage of it. Lucy would see to that.

CHAPTER EIGHT

THREE weeks later Ailsa and Aunt Betsy were making their way back to the island.

"Come to think about it," Betsy mused as the hired launch slid through comparatively calm water, "it doesn't take long to change the established order of things. Here I am, the new owner of Corrae, with the rightful owner waiting over there somewhere to meet me. There won't be any ceremony to mark our arrival—I told Mr. MacLaren in my last letter that I didn't want any—but it is an event. I wonder what the islanders think about it."

"Huntley will probably have talked them over," Ailsa said. Her throat felt dry as they came nearer to the island and her heart began to beat feverishly fast. During these past three weeks she had longed for this day, yet dreaded it too. "It's the sort of thing he would do."

"Yes, I think he would," her aunt agreed. "I have felt badly about asking him to stay on, but it was the only way. For the good of the island," she added, as if it had been an afterthought.

Corrae was coming very near. Ailsa picked out the distant shape of Scuirival, veiled in mist, and the long, low line of the shore. It was like coming home.

And this was how Huntley must have felt for as long as he could remember. As a boy he had returned this way from school in Edinburgh, his eagerness covering the distance to the shore long before the launch had reached the jetty steps.

And he was on the jetty to meet them. The ancient kilt and well-worn jacket gave him a subtle, added dignity, accenting the look of belonging which even Aunt Betsy was bound to recognize. They would never acquire that look, Ailsa realized, no matter how long they stayed. The tall, kilted figure leaning on the high shepherd's crook was part and parcel of Corrae. It went hand-in-hand with tradition and five hundred years of belonging on this tiny, sea-girt isle.

Formally he bade them welcome, stepping down to help with the launch, and for the first time Ailsa realized that he was alone.

He did not attempt to explain the lack of enthusiasm on the islanders' part.

"I've arranged for your luggage to be brought up to the house," he told Betsy. "It may take some time, so if you have anything you particularly want I'll carry it up for you."

"There's a grip somewhere—that tartan one over there —and a case." Betsy indicated two of the smaller items of baggage which the boatman was stacking on the quay. "We've brought most of our stuff over with us, but there's a trunk and some household effects to follow by cargo boat. That's something else we must get altered," she ran on as Huntley helped her up the steps. "Nobody seems to know for sure when things can be delivered around here. 'Maybe this week, maybe next'! There ought to be some sort of system."

Huntley repressed a smile.

"We're not a big enough community for that," he explained. "We can't demand a regular service."

Betsy looked taken aback.

"What," she asked, "do we do in a case of sickness?"

"We use the air ambulance service from Tiree."

"And between here and Tiree?"

'The nearest available launch. In extreme emergency we can, of course, call on the services of the lifeboat."

Betsy cast an apprehensive glance behind her.

"I see," she said rather faintly. "I think it would be much better if we had a landing strip of our own."

Huntley's smile deepened.

"I don't think you need to worry," he said. "It isn't really far to Tiree."

They walked in procession towards the house.

"I think you will find everything in order," he observed as they reached the door. "I've withheld a few personal items for my own use, but otherwise the house is much as you saw it before you left. Helen has put on fires." He turned, facing them in the bright sunlight which suddenly streamed through a break in the veil of mist. "I hope you will both be happy here," he added. "As happy as I have been."

"Now that's real nice of you, Mr. MacLaren!" Betsy said, but Ailsa could not answer him.

"You won't come in?" Betsy turned at the open door. "You're more than welcome, you know."

"I'm quite sure of that," he said, "but I have a great deal to do, if you will excuse me?"

"Mr. MacLaren!" Betsy put an impulsive hand on his arm. "There's no need for us to stand on ceremony, is there? This has always been your home. The fact that you are acting as my agent needn't make any difference. As I've just said, you are more than welcome to come and go as freely as you wish."

"Thank you." His voice was stiffly formal. "You're very kind."

Let him go, Ailsa thought. Oh, Aunt Betsy, please let him go! Every instant of this is an agony to him! The set jaw, the rigid formality, the tight and bitter mouth were all indications that each second he was forced to remain standing there only served to underline the fact of his irretrievable loss. Aunt Betsy heaved a small, disappointed sigh as she turned into the hall.

"Just as you say," she agreed. "We'll get together to-morrow and see what can be done about these empty crofts. I've got a scheme that I talked over with Mr. Dobie and he seemed to think it might work. Then I think we ought to encourage the drifters to use the harbour again. We might even invest in one or two ourselves——"

Aunt Betsy wanted to do everything at once. Her enthusiasms were boundless. When Huntley had left them she glanced about the hall, her bright expression clouding over as she sensed the change which Ailsa had noticed as soon as she had stepped across the threshold.

"It's different, somehow," she said. "What's gone wrong? The whole place looks dead."

"Perhaps it's—the fire," Ailsa suggested in an unsteady voice. "The peats look sullen. Shall I stir them up?"

Betsy shivered.

"Yes, do. I feel chilled to the bone."

143

Even the glow of the stirred peats did nothing to warm the room, however. They had come back to a house that had lost its heart. The few things Huntley had taken away had been the things that had given it character. They had all been personal belongings of his mother. None of them had been particularly valuable, for the furniture which had been part of Corrae House for years had all been included in the sale of the island and was now theirs. It had been easier to do that than bring new stuff over from the mainland at a prohibitive cost, but the warm, personal touch had gone. The kindly presence Ailsa had felt in the house when they had first visited it had turned sadly away.

"There was that old spinning-wheel," Betsy mused, thinking much the same thing. "It stood there beside the hearth, as if someone had used it only yesterday. And the velvet chair. It was worn a bit, but it had a sort of character. And the little bureau in the corner——" Her sigh was regretful. "Maybe Mr. MacLaren needed them, though. Maybe he's not so different for all his brusque ways. Maybe he needs his memories, like the rest of us."

"Aunt Betsy," Ailsa asked, "do you think you're going to be happy here?"

"Happy?" Betsy gave the question her earnest consideration for a second or two. "Well now, why shouldn't I be happy?" she asked. "It's what I've always wanted. I've got so many plans that it will take me a year at least to set them all going. It'll be a full life, Ailsa, and that's what everyone needs. You can be a great help to me. There's a library there, for instance, that needs cataloguing. There's a lot of fine books in there. Huntley MacLaren can help you with it if he can find the time."

It seemed, however, that Huntley had no time at all to spare. In the days that followed he appeared to be avoiding them with a calculated determination which nothing could deflect from its purpose. He worked from early morning till late at night, dealing with the endless problems which presented themselves as soon as one of Aunt Betsy's schemes went into operation, but even at this early stage there was some indication that the island might come gradually back to life.

"Money," Aunt Betsy observed, "makes a lot of difference. It's no use pretending it doesn't, although I'm not foolish enough to imagine it can get you *all* you want. Huntley, for instance, has been able to pay off all the death duties on the estate and still has enough left to think about drifters."

A swift wave of colour mounted to Ailsa's cheeks.

"Do you mean he's going to buy one?" she asked.

"He's going to invest in two." Betsy looked immensely satisfied. "It will mean more work on the island and work means people. Then, when all the crofts are repaired, we'll get stock over and that will mean more people! I've got to put my money to work, and this is the best way of doing it."

Ailsa thought a good deal about the drifters. Huntley would base them on Corrae, but he could not go on living as he was doing at the present moment. He had opened the tiny, upturned bowl of the lodge house for himself, but it was little more than an office in which he slept, convenient for running estate affairs but in no way suitable as a home. When the time came and he wanted to marry Lucy he would not be able to take her there. Yet there was no other habitable accommodation on the island, apart from the crofts, and Ailsa could not imagine Lucy in a croft.

When she passed the lodge on her frequent afternoon walks she often saw Huntley at his desk, but he did no more than acknowledge her and go on working. At other times the bare little room would be empty and she would catch a glimpse of him on a headland surveying a croft, or down at the harbour supervising the repairs which her aunt was having done in order to accommodate larger boats.

Work progressed slowly. Time was the one thing which the islanders had in abundance, and she came to realize that, without Huntley's assistance, the work would not have been done at all. The islanders were making their effort for the laird because he asked it of them. The 'ladies at the big house' were newcomers—strangers. It would be like that for a very long time.

Quite frequently, on her longer walks of exploration, Ailsa went across the headland to where the old ruined stronghold of the MacLarens stood facing out to sea, and here she was aware of a curious sense of peace.

Inside the ruined walls the grass was very green and wild flowers had sprung up in a profusion of colour, making a rich carpet for her feet. When she ate her sandwiches in the shelter of the gaunt old tower she never felt alone. There were so many birds on the rocks beneath her, and once or twice she had glimpsed the dark heads of seals in the water far below.

Gradually she felt drawn to that ancient place and here, at last, she met Huntley face to face.

She had come out after a morning's work in the library where she had made a beginning on the books, and she was unpacking her picnic meal when a shadow fell across the grass at her feet. Without looking up she said:

"I like to come here, but if I'm trespassing in any way, Huntley, I'll go."

He sat down on the grass beside her.

"You have every right to come," he told her. "It's part of your aunt's property."

"Somehow," she said slowly, "I can't quite think of it in that way." She raised her eyes to the stout old walls with the blue canopy of sky above them. "It belongs to the past, to far-off things that have nothing to do with today."

"One is bound to think about the past in a place like this," he said briefly. "But the fact remains, the castle goes with the island. They belong together." He paused, following her gaze to the high ramparts where wind-blown seed had blossomed in a gay riot of purple in the deep crevices and the shadows of wheeling gulls were inked in against the sun warmed stone. "Why do you come so often?" he asked abruptly.

"I'm not sure." Ailsa had scarcely expected such a show of interest on his part. "Perhaps it's because I'm one step away from reality up here."

"Meaning——?"

"I—seem to get nearer Corrae as it was."

He lay back, cradling his head on his clasped hands, his eyes still fixed on the patch of blue sky which served them as a roof, and she allowed herself to turn and look at him. He was completely relaxed, as if all his problems had suddenly been resolved and he could look on the future with confidence and trust.

"I find that quite easy to believe," he said. "I used to come here a lot when I was very young—sometimes with Hamish and sometimes alone—and always there was that sense of getting right away, of slipping back over the years to the more exciting past. I've been a Viking imprisoned here, and a fugitive in a ragged kilt fleeing across the heather after Culloden. I've even been a wicked chief imprisoning a lovely lady in a dark dungeon so that Hamish could rescue her when he came charging up the rocks!" He rolled over on his side, looking up into her amazed eyes. "You find it difficult to believe?" he challenged.

"Not the Viking part," Ailsa confessed, her heart lifting on a sudden wave of excitement. "I always saw you as partly Norse. And I think I can understand the fugitive from Culloden."

"But not the unscrupulous chief imprisoning the fair lady in the dark dungeon?" he queried.

"Not entirely! Besides, I don't suppose there was a dungeon."

"That's where you're wrong!" He held out his hand to her. "Let me show you."

He pulled her to her feet, leading her across the grass to the broken wall of the tower, her fingers still imprisoned in his. The whole enclosed space of what had once been the banqueting hall was full of sunlight. Only the tower was in shadow.

Ailsa's heartbeats quickened and a deeper colour ran up into her cheeks. It seemed that they were in some enchanted place where nothing in the bleak, outside world could possibly harm them.

"Now look!"

Huntley had drawn her close to the wall, to where the thick outside stonework plunged eighty feet or more straight down into the sea. The boom of waves far beneath them had a hollow ring and she could see the white flash as a leaping cascade of spray fell back to the rocks below. It was here that the tower jutted out from the main edifice, the shattered arches of its broken windows framing only the sky.

Huntley pulled her up with him on to the grass-grown parapet to a precarious foothold in one of the arches. It was a heady experience and she clung rather desperately to his

147

supporting hand, gazing down into a deep enclosure within the walls.

"No one—not even a wicked chieftain—would put a defenceless woman down there!" she protested breathlessly.

"You'd be surprised," he smiled. "The MacLarens have always had a ruthless streak when they wanted something badly enough. One, Ruari MacLaren, kept his wife down there for fourteen years, so the story goes, for no greater fault than failing to please him as a cook! Then there was Ronald Dhu—Black Ronald—who stole a bride and let her die there of a broken heart."

Ailsa shuddered.

"I'm glad I didn't live in those desperate days," she said. "They seemed to thrive on cruelty."

"Their tortures were less refined than ours," he admitted sardonically. "Yet probably they stemmed from the same basic emotions—greed, jealousy, the desire for possession—even love."

"Why did you leave love till the last?" she asked unsteadily. "Does it count least?"

They were very close in the tiny niche of the broken archway and she could almost feel the steady pounding of his heart.

"Not least," he said, "but sometimes it has to come last in our reckoning, if we are wise."

Protestingly she turned on him.

"And you are always wise—calculating—knowing what's best in every way!" she cried to her own utter dismay. "Love hasn't got to count with you. You've got it all worked out, all neatly docketed and in order! Love will come a long way second when you think about Corrae."

She was trembling from head to foot, showing him all too plainly how much she cared, perhaps, and felt his body stiffen and grow taut as he sought for the right answer to her impassioned outburst.

"Love is for a summer's day," he said in a voice which seemed curiously without emotion. "I had to think about Corrae first. I had to make sure the island would survive. That's why I promised to serve your aunt for the next six months. After that——"

148

She looked up at him, but his eyes were remote now, his steely gaze passing beyond her to something desirable which he seemed to find reflected in the golden haze of distance. She could not prompt him to speak of it nor could she ask what he intended to do when the six months of his servitude were over. She supposed that he had made up his mind about that too.

Then suddenly it didn't seem to matter very much. They were here, in this enchanted spot high above the sea, with the sunlight trapped behind them and the shadows deep and out of sight in the ancient dungeon at their feet. Huntley drew her to the very edge of the ruined parapet and they sat down with their backs to the sun-warmed stone.

"If you wait a bit till the birds have become used to us," he promised, "I'll show you something quite unique." Her fingers were still laced in his and he kept them there. "You can only see it from this height, on a day like this when there are few clouds and little shadow on the water."

He leaned back against the wall, his keen blue eyes searching the sky, prepared to wait in silence for the moment he sought. And Ailsa found it easy to wait with him, with the whole world suspended on a breath and her fingers warmly clasped in his.

Above them, almost blotting out the sun, a great fulmer hovered in perfect flight and the swift 'dive-bombing' gannets swooped down almost to their feet, quarrelling over a captured fish.

Suddenly Huntley's fingers tightened and he pointed towards the sea.

In a clear pool surrounded by rocks which the saffron weed had turned to gold, three dark shapes were just visible beneath the surface. Growing bolder, the seals swam upwards and dived and surfaced again, frolicking in the green water until, finally, they slithered out through the seaweed to lie full length on the warm, bare rock, rolling blissfully from side to side in the sun.

There was such a look of contentment on their round, be-whiskered faces that Ailsa wanted to laugh out loud, but the pressure of Huntley's fingers forbade her.

"You would have seen hundreds of them on North Rona if we had been able to land there," he said beneath his breath. "They are gathering for the breeding season. If you come up here in a few weeks you should be able to see the first pups. Nobody disturbs them here. They're pure white and completely helpless until they can be taken into the water."

"I hope I'll be here," Ailsa said dreamily. "Aunt Betsy has asked me to stay——"

He looked down at her, obviously surprised by the remark.

"I understood that your aunt had adopted you," he said.

"Oh, no, there isn't anything like that," Ailsa said quickly. "Aunt Betsy helped me to sell up my home, but when that money comes to an end I shall have to look for a job." With her free hand she pushed back the hair from her forehead. "I've never lived in this sort of environment before," she confessed. "That's why it's all so very wonderful for me, but I suppose my Cinderella story will have to come to an end some time. I'm not going to be sorry," she added swiftly. "I've loved every minute of it—the cruise and the sunshine, and being here on Corrae, but I know it can't last. I know I've got to come down to earth and sweep the hearth again!"

Her confession had obviously surprised him, but he made no further comment. When they retraced their steps along the ruined parapet and he jumped down ahead of her into the main enclosure he turned to help her with a smile.

Ailsa slid into his outstretched arms to find herself closely imprisoned there.

"Huntley——!"

He did not let her feet touch the ground, carrying her instead to the spot where they had sat at first in the sunshine and where she had left her cardigan and the packet of sandwiches she had brought with her from the house.

"I'm reasonably hungry!" he hinted shamelessly as he let her slip down to the grass.

Ailsa's heart was beating a mad tattoo in her breast and her cheeks were flushed a deep pink as she fumbled with the wrapping paper. She could not trust herself to speak, and Huntley lay back on the flower-starred grass as he had done an hour earlier, clasping his hands idly behind his head. His narrowed gaze searched the strip of sky above them where there was still no sign of cloud, and then, almost without movement, he had pulled her towards him, kissing her with a passionate disregard of time or place or circumstance.

She lay quite still in his arms, allowing his hungry kisses to obliterate all the agony that had been in her heart for many weeks, feeling only his nearness, the warmth of his powerful body close to her own and the firm, possessive pressure of his lips.

Her response, when it came, was no less passionate and deeply revealing. If she had cried, 'Huntley, I love you. I will go on loving you no matter what happens, till the end of my life!' she could not have told him more plainly what this moment meant to her and how completely she had surrendered.

The world around them, even the grim old castle walls which seemed to have trapped all the sunlight in this enchanted place, was obliterated in one long, final kiss before Huntley drew deliberately away.

"This is madness," he said, not looking at her. "I must have been out of my mind——"

She pressed her hands over her face, willing herself not to cry.

"I thought it meant something to you!" she whispered. "I thought——"

He did not answer, and all the world seemed to be standing still, waiting to hear what he had to say.

"Try to forget about it," he said harshly. "I can't ask you to forgive me. Try to think of it as—the madness of a summer's day."

His voice was like ice, yet underlying it was a rough edge of honesty. They had been foolish but, after all, it was no more than an interlude, a moment when they had both felt the heady magic of youth and togetherness. Nothing more than that. He was sorry now that it had happened—sorry for her, too, because he could not have helped seeing the intensity of her response to his kisses, but it was to be forgotten—forgiven, if she could—thrust to the back of her mind as of no account. Huntley demanded that of her and her pride forced her to take up the challenge with a little, flinty smile.

151

"Why shouldn't I be able to forgive you?" she asked in a voice she just managed to keep steady. "It was nothing to you. Why should you think it mattered so much to me?"

A dark, angry-looking colour ran up under his tan.

"Because I thought you were that sort of person," he said briefly, rising to his feet. "Shall we eat our sandwiches elsewhere? The sun has deserted us."

The grey shadow of the tower had spread to their feet. It was cold where they stood now—cold without the sun.

In silence they walked away from the castle, crushing the heads of the flowers under their feet, careless because they no longer saw them. Huntley had picked up her cardigan and the sandwiches and they sat down on the rocks to eat them. To Ailsa they were tasteless. The sea looked cold now, even with the sun on it, and from this height they could no longer see the mating seals.

She shivered, and Huntley put the cardigan about her shoulders with a brief thoughtfulness which brought foolish tears to her eyes. He didn't really mean it. He was only being courteous and kind. Perhaps he was even sorry for her.

As soon as she could trust her voice she got up from the rocks.

"I ought to get back," she said. "My aunt will begin to wonder what has happened to me."

Huntley got to his feet. For a moment he seemed about to say something important, and then he turned on his heel without a word and led the way up on to the moor.

"I'll see you safely back," he offered. "I want to have a word with your aunt about the new tenancies of the crofts."

"Are they ready to be occupied?" she asked automatically.

"Three of them. There wasn't a great deal to do. Just to put the starlings out and patch a section of roof here and there." His voice was deliberately light. "The others will be ready within the next few weeks."

"Have you prospective tenants for all of them?"

"I hope to have when the time comes. We got quite a good response to our advertisement in the *Scotsman* and the *Glasgow Herald*."

They spoke of the future all the way back to the house, deliberately ignoring the present, pretending that the bitter-sweet interlude in the sunshine had never been. Aunt Betsy smiled when she saw them approaching.

"I've spent the entire afternoon gardening," she announced, laying aside her trowel on a convenient stone. "I'm just crazy about all these flowers you have here, Mr. MacLaren, and I don't mind telling you they were the very last thing I expected. Heather, I thought, and a few blue-bells and things; but not roses like these! Look at the colours! I've grown Skylon and Ena Harkness in America, but they've never had that deep, true colour. It's the air, they tell me in the village, and the fact that they're fed on sea-weed!"

She had been going often to the village and had made friends there on her own account, especially among the fishermen, whom she had promised to help. There had been a certain amount of reserve to overcome at first, but gradually she was breaking it down.

"Of course, I couldn't have done a thing without your help, Mr. MacLaren," she acknowledged. "And now you say that we can soon get people into the crofts?"

"I'm hoping so." When he spoke about Corrae these days there was a new look in Huntley's eyes. "I've sorted through the replies from the newspapers and I think we can consider at least six of them. If you could interview them some time next week——"

"I wouldn't know the first thing to ask them!" Betsy confessed. "No, Mr. MacLaren, I'll leave that to you. You know the type that will do best on the island. All I want is a contented community willing to make the most of any privileges they may receive."

"There are certainly plenty of these," Huntley conceded without bitterness. "Three of the applicants are former natives of Corrae who want to return now that they can get away to a fresh start."

"Excellent!" Aunt Betsy smiled. "Excellent! We're forging ahead much faster than I had hoped." She picked up her gardening basket and gloves. "And now, Mr. MacLaren, you'll come up to the house for something to eat, I hope? Helen will have something ready for us, I'm sure. You'd never believe it," she added confidentially, "but I've gained fifteen pounds in weight since I came here. If things go on like this I'll simply bounce!"

Huntley had stood his ground.

"Can I beg to be excused?" he asked. "I have a great deal of work to get through. I'm afraid I've been guilty of wasting time this afternoon."

"You don't need to worry about that with me," Betsy assured him. "I'm certain you don't waste time, and if you take the odd afternoon off I'm sure you make up for it later by a lot of hard work at your desk in the evening."

He returned her generous smile, but his refusal was still firm.

"Perhaps some other time," he suggested. "I would like to get these letters away by tomorrow's post."

The postal launch went out to meet the steamer three times a week and it was essential that the mail bags were sealed and ready early in the morning. His excuse was valid enough, Ailsa thought, if only he had not added that other bitter little bit about wasting time during the afternoon.

"Where did you go?" Betsy asked when he had left them. "With Mr. MacLaren, I mean."

"I didn't *go* anywhere with him." Ailsa had just managed to control the tremor in her voice. "We met by accident, up at the castle."

"He said you were there all afternoon," she reflected after a while. "He couldn't have called that wasting time, now, could he?"

Ailsa bit her lip, trying hard to control the wave of vivid colour that swept up to her brow.

"That's how he must have thought of it," she tried to say defiantly. "I suppose I—trapped him into showing me the seals from the dungeon wall. Did you know there was a dungeon up there in the castle, Aunt Betsy?" she rushed on now that she was on safer ground. "Huntley's ancestors kept their wives down there, apparently, as soon as they showed any signs of using their wits!"

"Maybe it wasn't such a bad idea at that!" Betsy grinned. "Maybe they needed chastening now and then. Or they may have been just plain stupid. Why did Huntley MacLaren

154

have to take you right up on to the parapet to look at some seals?"

"Because when you are high up you can see right down into the depths of the water at that point, it's so clear. It was as green as an emerald today. But you must have seen us up there when you knew we had gone on to the parapet!"

"My eyes are sharp enough," Betsy agreed with a chuckle. "The pair of you looked as if you owned the world—or Corrae, at least!"

Ailsa turned hastily away.

"Supposing," Betsy said, "I gave you a birthday? You're twenty-one in about two weeks' time, aren't you? This is the sort of place to have a birthday party—a real celebration. I meant to give a house-warming, but this is a better idea. You know — a coming-of-age. Fireworks and dancing and all that sort of thing. We might even have a bonfire. Helen tells me the family always had a bonfire lit on Scuirival when any of the sons came of age."

"Aunt Betsy — no!" Ailsa protested. "Please, no! I couldn't let you do it. I couldn't bear you to——"

"Well, why ever not?" Betsy looked chagrined. Never before had her generosity boomeranged back on her like this, yet she felt instinctively that Ailsa was not ungrateful. "People *do* these things."

"Not for a girl, and not for someone who isn't the heir." Ailsa's voice was not quite steady. "Don't you see what it would mean for Huntley? He must have come of age in that way five years ago, and now—there's nothing left. It would be opening the wound again, hurting him needlessly. I don't qualify for that sort of birthday, Aunt Betsy, so you see I couldn't accept it. I couldn't let you do it. Please don't think I'm ungrateful for all you've already done for me," she begged. "I'm not. I realize that I'd never have had such a wonderful month if it hadn't been for your kindness, and sometimes I don't quite know how to say 'thank you' adequately enough, but please don't ask me to come of age in that way. I know you will understand."

"Well, if you say so," Betsy agreed forlornly. "I had hoped to do something big for you, to really brighten Corrae up!"

155

"You're doing wonders for Corrae," Ailsa acknowledged. "It's next door to miraculous!"

"You think so?" Betsy blinked through her disappointment. She was also well ahead with a new plan. "How would it do if we had a barbecue instead—you know, something in the open? Dancing in the hall, perhaps, but sausages and chicken and things on sticks out of doors. I think the island's just made for that sort of thing on a fine summer's night. We could ask some of your friends over from Glasgow. I've been thinking you need more young company, and I still like to dance. Yes, we could do that, couldn't we, without making it awkward for anyone?"

"It's very, very kind of you——"

"Now, don't say 'but'!" Betsy held up an admonitory finger. "You've scuttled my first plan, and rightly so, now I come to think of it, but I mean to go ahead with this one! I owe it to your mother's memory to see that you come of age properly. Besides," she almost blushed at some sudden recollection, "I did mean to have a visitor or two once I got sort of settled in. You know—folks I met on board ship, like that nice Mrs. Tollerton and her husband——"

"And Mr. Fulton?" Ailsa supplied. "And—Lucy?"

Her aunt went on ahead of her into the hall and for several minutes it seemed that her question was going to remain unanswered. Then, slowly and carefully, Betsy said:

"I had a letter yesterday. It was from Adam Fulton. They want to come back to the island. Adam has asked me to marry him."

Ailsa stood gazing at Aunt Betsy, wondering why all this should seem so difficult to believe.

"I think I've known from the beginning that he was still in love with you," she said automatically. "I think he always has been."

Betsy blushed like a schoolgirl.

"Oh—I don't know," she demurred. "He married somebody else."

Ailsa's heart gave an odd little twist of pain.

"I don't think that matters," she said. "I think there's one love—and that's all. It's the one that counts most all through life, whether you marry the person or not. With

156

you it was first love, wasn't it? It was only—a silly mistake that you didn't marry Adam in the beginning."

"Our own mistake," Betsy said reflectively. "We should have talked things over sensibly and I should have taken a firmer stand with my mother. I should have let him help me to work it all out, but I didn't. I thought it best just to make a clean break in a dumb sort of way that didn't give him a chance. He thought it was America—that I didn't like the idea of going there, so far away from my family." She gave a small, shaky laugh. "I would have gone with him to the end of the world if things had been different!"

Ailsa put a comforting arm about her plump shoulders.

"It isn't too late, even yet," she pointed out. "You can marry Adam now. You can gather up all your dreams and mend them together."

"I wish it was as easy as that," Betsy sighed, "but it isn't. There's Lucy."

"Why should she interfere?" Ailsa's voice was suddenly hard.

"You know she would," Betsy said. "Adam has lived with her for so long and he loves her so much that I couldn't marry him without Lucy agreeing. Then, too, there's Corrae. Adam wouldn't want to live on an island. He'd want to go back to the States."

"Yes," Ailsa agreed, "I suppose he would."

"That isn't an insurmountable obstacle, though," Betsy decided cheerfully. "We could sort things out."

For a moment Ailsa felt that she could shake Aunt Betsy. In her usual impulsive way she was probably already planning to dispose of Corrae when it suited her to do so, to sell it to the highest bidder, or even to accept a financial loss on it in order to marry Adam. It would not really matter to her. Her bargain with Huntley would automatically be cancelled out and his six months' servitude on the island would no longer be necessary. But once again he would be forced to see his beloved home change hands, and this time he would have no say in the matter. He would not be able to protect Corrae or hope that his services would be sought a second time to guide its fortunes over the critical transitory period.

"It would solve a great many problems if Huntley Mac-Laren would marry and settle down here," Betsy mused, turning from the fire. "I can't think of anything better for Corrae."

She paused, as if waiting for Ailsa's reaction to the suggestion, but Ailsa could not speak. Of course, it would solve everything for Aunt Betsy if Huntley married Lucy.

The whole thing had come round full cycle. If Huntley had married Lucy and Aunt Betsy hadn't rushed in and bought Corrae it would have been his without changing hands at all. Adam Fulton would have seen to that. And now Adam and Aunt Betsy could work it all out between them. When Lucy and Huntley married they could make them a present of Corrae.

It all seemed quite straightforward and she could not grudge Huntley such a wonderful answer to all his problems. It was the ideal solution for everybody. With Lucy and Huntley safely installed in Corrae House, Adam could marry his Betsy and take her off to Florida with him. They could come back every now and then, on a visit, and everybody would be happy.

"Anyway, there's plenty of time to thrash all these things out when Adam gets here," Betsy decided. "I'll write and ask them to come over for your birthday celebrations, in any case, and then we can have a little talk. If there's anyone else you would like included, from Loch Lomondside, for instance, we can jot down their names and write to them too. This is going to be quite an event for Helen. She was saying only this morning that the island seemed to be coming back to life already, and that made her very pleased. She loves this place, I guess. She'd hate to see it just die."

Aunt Betsy rarely lost time. Although Ailsa protested that a quiet little family party would suit her best, the birthday preparations went forward with alarming rapidity, taking on an impetus and a magnitude which carried Ailsa and everyone else with it as before a flood. Adam's letter was replied to and an invitation was sent to Connie Tollerton and her husband and daughter, who were staying with friends in Edinburgh and had exchanged addresses with Aunt Betsy before they had parted company so dramatically at Oban. There was, too, a suggestion that Erik Larsen and his sister from the *Saturn* might be able to come, if only for a couple of days.

"Huntley MacLaren would know about that," Betsy suggested. "I'll ask him what he thinks. He could check to see if the ship comes in to Oban again after her final cruise."

It would be nice to see Erik and Greta again, Ailsa acknowledged, since she had been unable to say goodbye to them properly. She began to hope that Erik would come, and Greta too.

Strangely enough, it was Helen who received the news of their swollen guest list with the greatest amount of reserve. When she heard that the Fulton's were coming she looked tight-lipped and went about her task of preparing their rooms with mute disapproval in her eyes.

By the tenth of June Aunt Betsy had received eight acceptances. The three Tollertons were more than eager to come, Mrs. Tollerton wrote, and after a long conversation with Huntley, Betsy said that she thought Greta Larsen and her brother and also the ship's surgeon would be able to avail themselves of their hospitality over the week-end. The *Saturn* was due to berth at Oban on the Friday and would not sail again until the following Wednesday. It would, Betsy decided, be a nice little break for them. The final letter was from Adam Fulton.

Ailsa hardly needed to ask if Lucy and her father were coming. She knew they would come.

In the past two weeks she had only seen Huntley twice, and on both occasions it had been from a distance. Then, on the day Adam Fulton's letter arrived, she met the postman coming up from the harbour and offered to take the mail for him. Huntley generally picked up their letters direct from the launch as it came in from the mail steamer, but today old Nicol Jarvis had come up the hill a little earlier than usual with the worn red mail bag over his shoulder and a triumphant smile on his face. Ailsa thought that he was secretly glad not to be cheated out of the job he had done for over forty years, even though the hill was becoming something of an obstacle for him.

He touched his cap when he saw her, producing two separate bundles from his bag.

"These are for the House, miss," he said, "and the others are for the office. They're all business documents," he added importantly. "Mostly from Edinburgh."

Ailsa had to smile at such detailed knowledge of their correspondence as she put the 'House letters' into her pocket.

"I'll take the others too," she offered. "I shall be passing the lodge and it will save you the journey, Nicol."

The old man looked positively reluctant about passing them over.

"The young master—begging your pardon," he amended, "Mr. MacLaren won't be up there, I'm thinking, or he would have seen the steamer come in. It was a bit early this afternoon, but she always gives us a blow when she's in the bay, so he would have heard that."

"I won't lose anything, Nicol," Ailsa assured him. "If Mr. MacLaren isn't in his office I can leave them on his desk. He's sure to be back before tea time."

"Maybe," Nicol agreed. "Oh, well, I'll be leaving his mail with you, since you insist, miss, although it's not strictly according to regulations. I'm supposed to see that they get to their destination."

"I think you can trust me," Ailsa smiled. "I'll see that Mr. MacLaren gets them quite safely."

Deliberately she waited for Huntley, going slowly up the winding road and lingering at the gates when he did not appear to be in the lodge. She sorted through her own mail and found a letter from Greta Larson, posted in Greenock, which said how pleased both she and Erik would be to come to Corrae.

'We have four days,' she wrote. *'It will be a lovely holiday and so exciting to be at your birthday party. Erik says it is a birthday, by the way! He also says it is your twenty-first, and that is more exciting than ever! Your aunt is very kind to ask us.*

Harald Borgsen (the ship's surgeon) would also like to accept. He is a very lonely man. His wife has just died.'

When she had folded Greta's letter back into its envelope she glanced at the others. Lucy always addressed her father's envelopes for him when he was in a hurry and it was in Lucy's firm, rounded hand that her aunt's name and address was written, although Ailsa had little doubt that the contents had been penned by Adam himself. He had already accepted Betsy's invitation, and this would no doubt contain a detailed itinerary of their journey from London, including the exact time of their arrival in Oban. Her aunt had hired a stout little launch for use between Corrae and the mainland until she decided what sort of craft to buy as a more permanent asset, and it would be sent across to pick up her guests.

No doubt Huntley would take it over. Her thoughts spun across the intervening water with him until she could almost see his meeting with Lucy and her father off the London train. They could, of course, come by plane. They could come from London to Renfrew and then on to Tiree, where, once again, Huntley would have to pick them up. It was inevitable, this meeting of Huntley and Lucy, whichever way she tried to argue.

Idly she began to sort through the office mail. They were all business communications, as Nicol had predicted, with the exception of one. She felt her gaze riveted on the envelope without really taking in what she saw for a moment, but it was the same writing on the envelope addressed to her aunt. This time, however, Lucy would also be the author of its contents. Adam Fulton would not write direct to Huntley.

This was a love letter. She tortured herself with the thought, caught up in an almost overmastering wave of jealousy as she stared down at the familiar capitals and the characteristic little flourish at the end of the address, where Lucy always drew a wavy line. She wanted to crush it in her hand, tear it to shreds, do anything with it rather than hand it over to Huntley, and when she raised her head and saw him walking towards her she felt a sudden panic guilt, as if she had indeed destroyed what was his by right.

"I—brought up your mail," she explained when he came level with her. "Nicol surrendered it most unwillingly, I'm afraid, but I dare say you can assure him that none of it was missing!"

161

How thin he was, she thought. Hollow about the cheeks and drawn at the mouth. His eyes, which had always been deep-set, now looked sunken from overwork or lack of sleep, and she could not help thinking that he was trying to do too much. It was, of course, for Corrae.

A wave of pity engulfed her, yet she could not show him pity. He was not the man to endure it.

Pushing the letters into the inside pocket of his jacket, he said almost brusquely:

"I've been making some final arrangements for your big day, Ailsa. Your aunt asked me to fix up some sort of entertainment for the villagers, but I thought it would be just as well to have them up here to the barbecue."

The few who will come, Ailsa thought. There was still a hard little core of resentment in the village, older people who found it difficult or impossible to accept change, and the fact of a coming-of-age—a stranger's coming-of-age—would not please them.

Did it also distress Huntley? She looked up at him questioningly, but his expression was guarded and withdrawn.

"I've wanted to see you," she told him impulsively. "I wanted to tell you that—I didn't really wish this, Huntley. I didn't want a fuss made of my birthday."

He said indifferently, hardly:

"You're entitled to it. Your aunt is very fond of you."

"I'm sorry she asked you to arrange it, though. I didn't mean her to do that, but I suppose she has come to depend on you for most things connected with Corrae."

Ailsa hesitated. Huntley's mouth had hardened, and his eyes were like flint.

"Why shouldn't she?" he demanded harshly. "She pays me to do just that."

"Huntley," she pleaded, "I'm sorry about all this. I tried to stand out against an elaborate party—people coming over and a great fuss being made. Please believe me when I say so."

He looked down at her, still stony-eyed, his mouth compressed into a harsh, cruel line.

"It's rather difficult to credit you with all that sincerity, Ailsa," he told her harshly. "But you needn't worry about my having to make the arrangements. I can approach the situation entirely without emotion, I assure you."

There was so much she wanted to say, but how could she when he had put up such an impassable barrier between them? It was like iron. She could not reach him through it, and it had been erected gradually since the moment of that impassioned kiss in the shadow of the castle walls.

Deliberately he had avoided her. She knew that now, and he was at no pains about showing her that he was only waiting for her to go. When he had glanced at the bundle of letters she had given him, Lucy's had been on top and no doubt he had recognized the handwriting.

Bleakly she turned away.

"At the moment I can only say thanks for all you've done," she said, not quite steadily. "But I'm sure my aunt has already told you how grateful we are."

He said yes, that was true, and walked away, not turning round once until he had closed the door of the lodge between them.

CHAPTER NINE

"I'M quite determined to go for a swim." Lucy looked about her at the little knot of Aunt Betsy's house guests gathered on the rough grass of the lawn overlooking the bay. "Any takers?"

"Now, Luce!" her father argued, "you mustn't take risks. It's only the beginning of June, after all——"

"And a perfectly baking day!" Lucy looked towards the sea. "I'm going, if no one else is," she decided with slow deliberation. "I should have thought Norwegians were inveterate swimmers," she added with the faintest suspicion of a sneer in her voice as she glanced at Erik Larsen's long legs stretched full length in the sun.

Greta Larsen got up from the deck chair where she had been sitting since lunch, knitting.

"I suppose we ought to go," she admitted. "But it's so heavenly here! I could sit all day in the sun just doing nothing!"

Lucy turned restlessly towards the house.

"What about you, Ailsa?" Greta asked. "Do you swim?"

"A little." Ailsa go up from her own chair to stretch her legs. "I'm not a powerful swimmer, though, and I must admit I've felt nervous of going in off the rocks by myself. However, if we're all going——"

"That makes it sound as if we are!" Erik got to his feet, stretching lazily. "Come on, Doc Borgsen! You're for it with the rest of us, I expect. Lucy wants to swim."

Harald Borgsen groaned.

"Couldn't she—by herself?" he asked, yawning.

"Don't be a complete wet blanket!" Ailsa laughed. "I think Lucy's quite right. We're all getting much too lazy."

"There's always tomorrow," Erik pointed out.

"I'm going for my swim-suit!" Ailsa said, ruffling his fair hair as she passed him.

Lucy had gone on ahead to the house. Since she had returned to the island she had made no secret of her animosity towards Ailsa. They just did not get on, and Ailsa felt that she would be a complete hypocrite to pretend other-wise, even for Aunt Betsy's sake.

Huntley had picked up her aunt's guests in Oban the day before, and to Lucy's obvious chagrin the Tollertons had arrived by the same train and come over on the launch with them. Erik, Greta and Harald Borgsen had travelled with the mail steamer and had been picked up outside the harbour with the mail.

So short a time ago! Ailsa couldn't quite believe that it was only twenty-four hours since Corrae House had come to noisy, active life again, with laughter echoing among the rafters and quick feet on the stairs. Peggy Tollerton was a girl who laughed a lot, thoroughly enjoying life. She was touchingly pleased to have met Erik again and far more excited about the coming birthday celebrations than Ailsa herself.

"There ought to be a bonfire!" she had declared. "Like you read about in books. It would look terrific lit up there on that high mountain near the lighthouse, wouldn't it?"

Ailsa could only be glad that Huntley had not been there to hear. Studiously avoiding their company, he looked a rather lonely figure when they saw him returning to the lodge from a distance, but she had not the courage to go and seek him out.

Courage for the things she wanted, however, was not lacking where Lucy was concerned.

"I'm going to root out Huntley for the afternoon," she announced when they set off down the drive. "I rather promised Poppa I would just now. Huntley knows all the pitfalls in and around Corrae, and I suppose there *are* spots where the tide could be difficult."

"I hope MacLaren can come," Doctor Borgsen said. "I haven't seen him since he left the ship so suddenly at Iona that afternoon." He turned to Ailsa. "He was very worried about you, I think."

"He may have been angry," Ailsa said uncomfortably as she caught Lucy staring at her. "I was holding everything up."

"Maybe," Harald agreed, "but I don't think it was about the ship he was worried. Only about you."

Lucy swung her nautical beach bag over her shoulder and stamped on ahead. At the lodge she went straight into Huntley's office and they could see her sitting on the edge of his desk in a familiar attitude when they came up.

After a while Huntley came to the door.

"You'll be safe enough if you keep clear of the north end of the island," he advised them. "Unless you're very strong swimmers the tides are treacherous up there. There are several underwater caves where the current runs in like a mill race."

"Look," the doctor grinned, "hadn't you better come with us and save our lives beforehand? We've fixed up some sandwiches and we thought we could spend an hour or two up there. I'd like to see over the castle."

Ailsa drew in a deep breath. How could she go back to the castle in Huntley's company? She could not even look at him as she waited for his answer to Harald's request.

"If you think you might feel safer," he said at last, "I'll come with you—certainly. It's a wonderful experience diving off the rocks up there straight into fifty feet or so of Atlantic!"

"I can hardly wait!" Lucy smiled, linking her arm in his as if she had achieved some sort of personal triumph. "I guess I'm going to love every minute of this. Has the castle been restored?"

"Not recently." Huntley's voice was tight and clipped again. "Not in the past hundred years. There are places now where the walls are none too safe, especially round about the tower."

They fell into line after he had gone back into the lodge to fetch his bathing trunks and a towel—a gay little procession on the narrow Highland road. Lucy walked ahead with Huntley and Erik followed with Peggy Tollerton, who seemed determined to entertain him with a detailed description of her first visit to Scandinavia, and Ailsa brought up the rear with Greta and Doctor Borgsen.

Greta seemed strangely preoccupied. She had served in the same ship with Harald Borgsen for three months now and only in the past few weeks had she really got to know him. Since his wife's death, however, the remoteness with which he had hedged himself round had gradually decreased and he had seemed to grow younger. It was as if a heavy load had suddenly slipped from his thin shoulders, and Greta could not help wondering if his wife's death had been a happy release for him.

In half an hour they had reached the far side of the island, but Huntley insisted that they should go farther along the coast by the narrow sheep-track which took them up along the cliff.

Finally they emerged at a spot high above a small, hidden cove where a great spur of rock reached far out into deep water, making a natural spring-board for the experienced diver.

Lucy slipped out of her beach skirt to stand revealed in a black bathing suit which had the hallmark of the Continent stamped all over it. Lazily she stretched slender arms above her head, waiting for Huntley.

"Anyone else going to swim right out?" she asked when the three men joined them, trim in their workmanlike swimming trunks.

"Better keep as near to Huntley as possible," Harald laughed. "That water looks deep to me!"

"I'm going to disgrace myself and go in down there on the beach," Ailsa smiled. "I'm a hopeless diver. I really do hate to be out of my depth!"

Lucy's lips twisted in a nasty little sneer.

"Surely you aren't afraid?" she challenged.

"Not afraid—just cautious, I think," Ailsa returned. "I know my limitations, you see."

"Mine are about the same as yours, Ailsa!" Peggy Tollerton laughed. "I'll paddle with you in the shallow water. Come on!"

The others went with Huntley and Lucy.

"I don't like Lucy Fulton," Peggy said as she followed Ailsa down on to the sand. "She's out to catch Huntley MacLaren, and she'll stop at nothing to have her way. You see, she's been given everything she's wanted all her life and she kind of expects to go on getting it. I hope Huntley doesn't let her make a fool of him. He may, of course, put up with a lot because of the money. It would be the sensible sort of thing for him to do, wouldn't it?" she ran on when Ailsa didn't answer. "Marry Poppa's dollars, I mean. Momma says he's as poor as a church mouse—whatever that means! D'you think he'd be right to marry Lucy, Ailsa? For that reason, I mean?"

It was too direct a question for Ailsa to avoid.

"People do these things for all sorts of reasons, Peggy," she said flatly.

"Well, Huntley's a bit hard, isn't he? He might want the money very badly, and then I don't think he'd hesitate one minute. He'd make his decision and stick by it."

"I don't think we can really judge him on that score," Ailsa answered bleakly. "*Can* you swim, Peggy?" she asked, turning the conversation away from the dangers of Huntley and Corrae and Poppa Fulton's dollars. "We might try to get across the bay."

The green, translucent water was far too tempting for them to remain long on the beach and soon they were floating on their backs, lifted gently by the tide. It was a wonderful experience, and almost as exhilarating as being able to dive straight down into these cool green depths, as Lucy and Huntley were doing.

Ailsa turned over on her side to look for them. She could make out the tall figures of Greta and Erik and the doctor silhouetted against the blue of the sky as they stood on the ledge of rock, but Lucy and Huntley were nowhere to be seen.

A sudden wave of panic swept over her, although in the next instant she was telling herself that her fear was pure folly. Both Huntley and Lucy were strong, experienced swimmers, well able to cope with a calm sea and a sunny, windless day. They were evenly matched in that respect, she realized, when she finally caught sight of them. They were far out in the bay, with Lucy's red cap looking like a bobbing marker-buoy against the deeper blue, and after a while it seemed that they were never going to return.

Perhaps they did not want to return. Her heart was full of a throbbing envy as she thought of her own timidity, of the secret fear she had of the sea when she was actually in it. On board ship it was quite different. She loved the sea.

It was only when she felt it lapping against her with that terrible suggestion of unlimited strength, buoying her up, yet capable, too, of dragging her down, that she knew fear. It was almost a premonition of evil, an insistent warning of disaster to come.

Shaking the thought from her mind, she waded ashore to change with Peggy behind some rocks.

"Lucy's a fool!" Peggy said, standing up to shake her wet hair in the sun. "Look at her taking all sorts of risks to impress Huntley!"

Ailsa could not bring herself to look. She knew that Huntley would not be easily impressed by bravado, but she thought that he might admire a girl who had no fear of the sea.

When they climbed back on to the rocky plateau Huntley and Lucy were still in the water. They were like two sleek dolphins, diving and surfacing again with effortless grace, and suddenly Ailsa was reminded of the seals she had watched with Huntley from the castle parapet so short a time ago.

The memory could do nothing but torture her now as she watched Huntley and Lucy, and she turned abruptly away towards the beach. Erik, who had evidently had enough of Lucy's exhibitionism, followed her.

"Ailsa," he said, catching her hand, "I'm not going to have much more time to speak to you alone. Tomorrow you will be the Birthday Girl—belonging to everybody!" His arm went quickly about her waist, growing tight as the others passed from sight beyond the rocks. "I would like you to belong only to me," he said, adding, with a deep sincerity which she could not doubt, "I love you very much. I loved you as soon as I saw you coming on board the *Saturn* that day at Leith. 'This is the girl I want to marry,' I said to myself. 'She is for you, Erik Larsen. The first girl you have ever really loved!' That is what I told myself, quite truly—what I want you to know."

Taken completely by surprise, Ailsa stood quite still in the tight circle of his arms.

"I—wish you hadn't told me that, Erik," she said dismally.

169

"Why do you wish such a foolish thing?" he demanded, tilting up her face so that he could look directly into her distressed eyes. "Is it because you have not got over Huntley MacLaren yet? Soon you will," he predicted quickly. "When he has married Lucy you will need me."

"No!" It was a little cry of sheer despair tinged with protest and refusal. "Why are you so sure that Huntley and Lucy——?"

"Why do I think they will marry?" He smiled. "It is obvious, *vesla*! Lucy has captured him—or nearly so!"

Everyone could see it, Ailsa thought. Everyone but herself, and that was only because she did not want to see, because her foolish, aching heart would go on keeping hope alive until there was no more hope left.

"We could be happy," Erik urged. "You would come back to Norway with me, to my home. It is peaceful there, Ailsa, and my family would be kind to you. They would love you, for my sake."

"I'm sure they would, Erik," Ailsa agreed in a muffled whisper. "But it wouldn't be any use. I couldn't marry you —not without loving you in return."

"That would come." He held her suddenly close. "You could try to love me, Ailsa, and it would all come right in the end."

His mouth came down close to her own and for a moment her senses swam with the sheer unexpectedness of his kiss. Then, swiftly and as kindly as possible, she thrust him aside.

"No, Erik! No—I couldn't. It wouldn't be any use at all. I like you, but I'm not in love with you." Her voice shook as she looked up at him with shadowed, unhappy eyes. "I wish this hadn't happened," she added unsteadily. "I wish we could have remained friends."

"You and I could never be just friends," he argued logically. "Not when I love you so much."

How bitter it was to hear someone else say these words she had longed to hear from Huntley! Ailsa looked up to see Harald Borgsen coming across the rocks towards them. She did not think he had seen her in Erik's arms, but from the bay, where the rocks had not concealed them, they would be plainly seen.

Yet it could not matter at all to Huntley that she had been drawn swiftly into another man's embrace. If he had seen that ardent kiss of Erik's he would no doubt have dismissed it with an indifferent shrug of his broad shoulders, just as indifferently as he had dismissed the incident within the castle's ruined walls.

When he came across the rocks with Lucy they were all seated on the warm shingle, waiting to begin their picnic. He did not look in her direction nor in Erik's, and on the way back he walked with Lucy again. Naturally with Lucy.

They seemed to have paired off so easily. Greta and Harald Borgsen, Erik and Ailsa, Huntley and Lucy. Only Peggy was odd girl out, but Ailsa knew in her heart that it was she who was destined to stand a little way apart all her life, remembering Huntley MacLaren.

The following morning it was Peggy who woke her, coming into her bedroom to draw back the curtains and sing 'Happy Birthday' in her high, cracked soprano while she deposited a large cardboard box on the pink quilted spread.

"Open it!" she cried. "I want to see your surprise!"

"Peggy!" Ailsa said with a little tremor in her voice as she unfolded her first birthday gift, "I've always wanted a glamorous négligée!"

"Straight from Paris!" Peggy acknowledged proudly. "Not very suitable for Corrae, perhaps, but just right for a honeymoon!"

Ailsa tried to smile her pain away, telling herself that she must get used to such remarks from well-meaning people who only wished for her ultimate happiness.

At breakfast the others presented their gifts. Aunt Betsy and Helen had made a special effort with the dining-room so that every polished wood surface reflected a mass of flowers. Most of them had come from the gardens of Corrae House itself, but some had been sent over from the mainland by the mail steamer.

"Many, many happy returns!" Aunt Betsy said, kissing her, and then Ailsa found herself surrounded by good wishes and reams of white tissue paper as gift after gift was unwrapped. She was far too excited, too happy and

171

grateful, to notice that neither her aunt nor Huntley had offered her any material token of their regard.

She had not expected it of Huntley, in any case. And Betsy was already doing all this entertaining on her behalf. It was more than enough, she would have considered, if she had thought about individual gifts at all.

The day slipped past on happy feet, warmly wrapped in friendship. Lunch was a quick affair because no one felt inclined to eat very much after their prolonged breakfast and the glimpses they had of skewered chickens and steaks and sausages all made ready for the barbecue in the evening.

The villagers had been invited to be at Corrae House before the sun went down and, one by one, and in small, curious or diffident groups, they made their appearances through the door in the east wall and along the drive.

The house party gathered in the drawing-room, where Aunt Betsy said she would like to propose a toast.

"I asked Huntley to come up," she remarked a trifle testily as the men helped to light the pink candles Helen had put in the wall sconces. "I thought he would have been here by now."

"He may be in the hall." Ailsa's cheeks had begun to burn at the mention of Huntley's name. He had not been near the house all day. He had not come to wish her luck or to say 'Happy Birthday' with the others. "Shall I go and see?"

Desperately she wanted to escape from the gaiety, if only for a minute or two, to calm the turmoil in her heart. Lucy, too, was looking for Huntley, expecting him to come, no doubt. She had put on a wonderful dress of silver lamé which made her look breathlessly outstanding, but also a little bold. Peggy had said that, although Ailsa considered that Lucy had the confidence to carry it off. She looked down at the soft folds of her own white chiffon dinner dress with a vaguely rueful smile. Perhaps Huntley admired sophistication in a woman. Lucy seemed to glow, as if all the world was suddenly hers.

In the deserted hall Ailsa hesitated, looking around her, and then she saw a tall figure standing in the shadows just inside the main doorway. Huntley had watched her come into the hall, and there was a bitter twist to his lips as he moved to meet her.

"I wondered if you would come," she said simply.

"I could hardly afford to miss this," he answered curtly. "May I wish you continuing good fortune in the future? Another twenty-one prosperous years!"

It was a harsh little speech, cutting straight across her heart.

"Thank you." Her lips were trembling, but the flickering candlelight was on her side. He would not see. "My aunt said she was expecting you."

They stood gazing at each other for a further split second of indecision, and then Huntley fished in the pocket of his dinner jacket and produced a small covered box.

"It's a brooch," he said in a quite different voice. "Something I meant you to have. It belongs here—at Corrae."

Her hands were none too steady as she took the gift.

"Was it—something that belonged to your mother?" she guessed.

"Yes. How did you know?"

A deep colour flooded into her cheeks.

"Intuition, I suppose," she answered huskily. "Thank you, Huntley. Thank you very much!"

"You haven't opened it," he pointed out.

She looked up at him.

"Do you mind if I wait till I'm alone?" she asked.

For a second or two he appeared to be nonplussed, and then he said:

"You must open it whenever you like."

Voices floated out to them from the inner room, coming on a gust of laughter through the half-open door. Then someone came out and stood in the hall.

"Ailsa," Peggy Tollerton cried, "your aunt is waiting to open the champagne!"

Ailsa glanced back at Huntley.

"Will you come?" she asked.

"After you."

His face might have been carved from granite as he followed her through the doorway, and it was Lucy who was quick to see.

"Oh, here you are!" she exclaimed, thrusting her arm through his. "I wondered when you were going to turn up. Don't tell me you've been working *all* day!"

"I've been away from the island for most of it," Ailsa heard Huntley say before her aunt claimed her.

Betsy led her to a table in the centre of the room where a pink-and-white, two-tiered birthday cake stood in a circle of flowers. All the flowers of Corrae, Ailsa thought, seeing them through a sudden mist of tears.

"And now, everybody!" Aunt Betsy cried, holding up her hand for silence, "we're going to drink a toast to my niece's future!" She put a loving arm about Ailsa's shoulders, drawing her close. "I don't know whether she's noticed it or not," she ran on with a fond smile, "and I don't really think she has, but I haven't yet given her my birthday gift." She released Ailsa's shoulders and clasped both her hands, looking affectionately into her surprised grey eyes. "Ailsa," she said dramatically, "I want you to know that you are now the proud possessor of an island! This morning I made over the title deeds of Corrae to you."

Ailsa clung to her aunt's hand, not in gratitude but in utter, devastating dismay. The room seemed to rock about her and she could not speak. How could Aunt Betsy have done such a thing, passing over Corrae, like a bauble, for a birthday gift?

And Huntley? What must Huntley be thinking of all this? She tried to reach him, to seek him out across the crowded room, but there was too much noise, too many people already pressing in on her, shaking her by the hand, kissing her, congratulating her.

"It's the most wonderful birthday gift I've ever heard of!" Peggy Tollerton was crying above the general din. "Ailsa, aren't you thrilled?"

There could be no answer to that. Thrilled was too paltry a word, and somewhere out there on the fringe of the crowd Huntley was standing alone.

Not entirely alone. When her eyes eventually found him Lucy was still clinging to his arm. There was a little satisfied smile on her painted lips and her eyes were very bright.

Aunt Betsy had done for Lucy what Lucy suspected she could never have done for herself.

The cake was cut; champagne corks popped out of bottles with a great deal of noise; more toasts were proposed and drunk amidst much laughter and clever jest.

"There's just one other thing," Adam Fulton bawled above the general mêlée. "I've got a little announcement to make myself, folks!"

A small, cold fear gripped Ailsa by the throat. Adam was going to say that Lucy would marry Huntley. He was going to announce his daughter's engagement to the rightful laird.

Well, now that she owned Corrae, she could sell it back to Huntley when he married Lucy and had all Lucy's money to buy it with. That was the solution, wasn't it? She couldn't keep Corrae. It really *belonged* to Huntley.

"It's about Mrs. Bellinger and me," Adam explained. "This isn't so sudden as you might think, because we knew each other years ago, but now we've decided to get married, folks. We'd like you to wish us luck!"

Connie Tollerton gasped, and Jake dashed forward to pump Adam's hand. Peggy said, "Gosh! As if *one* surprise wasn't enough!" and Greta and Erik and the doctor lined up to offer their smiling congratulations to the happy pair. Above it all Ailsa heard Aunt Betsy's laughter. It was light and free, and happy as a young girl's. Her aunt had come into her lost paradise at last.

She ought to be happy. She ought to be glad for Aunt Betsy's sake, she told herself. She *was* glad, only something seemed to be breaking up in her heart.

Huntley's eyes were on her at last, and slowly he came across the room towards her. Lucy followed him, as if they had every right to do these things together.

"I hope you are going to be very happy on Corrae, Ailsa," he said. "I can't wish you anything more than that."

He took her hand in a grip that hurt, and suddenly she found herself saying:

"How could I know that Aunt Betsy would do a thing like this?"

He gazed back at her for a long moment, his eyes no longer hard.

"You couldn't," he said quite kindly. "It was something that—overtook us all unawares."

He turned then, looking at Lucy.

"I think it's time I went out to see to the fire," he decided. "I promised to have it ready by ten."

In the light of the charcoal fire and the swinging stable lanterns Ailsa watched him dancing with Lucy and then with Peggy, and even with Mrs. Tollerton and her aunt, but he did not come to dance with her. He was avoiding her now without trying to hide the fact, and that being so, how could she approach him about the sale of Corrae?

Yet she was determined to do so. Tomorrow, perhaps, before Lucy and her father left the island.

A madness of urgency seized her. Why not tonight? Why not now?

When she tried to find him he was nowhere to be seen. Someone said that he had already taken leave of her aunt and left the party, and it seemed that Lucy had gone too. Ailsa had seen the flash of her silver gown against the darkness of the shrubbery on the way down to the sea. They were probably together.

Bitterly she made her way back to the house. It was all over now—all the loving and the hoping and despairing. Her heart felt crushed, dead.

She made her way to her own room, turning on the light, and instantly she was aware of Huntley's unopened gift. The small box he had given her earlier in the evening lay where she had put it on her dressing table and she picked it up to look at it with sudden tears in her eyes.

It was covered in blue velvet and had an intricate silver clasp, and with a quick intake of breath she realized that it was shaped like a heart. A strange sort of gift for Huntley to give her.

Inside, glowing against white satin, lay a single ruby. It had been mounted on silver without a setting and it looked like a spot of blood. A red stain of blood seeping from a wounded heart.

176

Hastily she lifted out the brooch, but pinned to her white dress it looked no better than it had done against its own white satin background, and she could not bring herself to wear it in her present state of mind.

Huntley had said that it had belonged to his mother and she would come to cherish it for that reason—in time. But not now when her heart was torn asunder by the thought of him in Lucy's arms.

Then, because it was her duty, because she was the 'Birthday Girl' and it would be expected of her, she went slowly back down the stairs to her aunt's guests.

It was well after midnight before the party finally broke up. Huntley had not come back to the fire where the last remnants of chicken were being toasted over the dying charcoal.

The villagers had enjoyed themselves. The barbecue, which they had looked upon with grave doubt and no small amount of suspicion, had been pronounced an outstanding success. People were leaving, happy and tired, as a small, pale sliver of a moon took possession of the eastern sky.

Soon the grounds were empty. Shadowy figures came and went between the house and the fire—Helen carrying a tray: Peggy with an armful of cushions; Greta and Harald Borgsen smiling into each other's eyes, and Erik with the fire-basket from which he had emptied the last of the charcoal. Finally Adam and Betsy came up the terrace steps arm-in-arm, tired, happy, content.

"Have you seen Lucy?" Adam asked, passing Ailsa in the doorway. "I noticed her going off with MacLaren an hour ago, but I haven't clapped eyes on them since."

He was jovial and happy about the fact that Lucy was with Huntley. And then, suddenly, Huntley was there on the terrace, saying that Lucy had come back to the house over half an hour ago. He looked pale and tense and far from the happy lover as he faced Ailsa from the foot of the terrace steps.

"We were down on the shore," he said, "but she came back to the house. I walked with her as far as the door in the wall."

Within minutes the search was on. Huntley had taken immediate command.

"Don't alarm her father," he ordered when Erik and Harald appeared on the scene. "There may not be any need to search very far. She could be somewhere in the house."

It was Ailsa who went back to the house to search, without result. When she told Huntley that Lucy was not in her room his whole face darkened.

"Get a coat," he commanded, "and come to the edge of the cliff. If she comes back by the harbour path you can signal to us with a torch."

Ailsa stood on the cliff for over an hour. A wind had blown up and rain clouds now obscured the moon, but it was still comparatively warm. The three men had appeared, silhouetted darkly on the opposite cliff for a moment, and then they had gone on, still searching. She began to feel chilly and terribly alone, and she supposed she really ought to go back to the house and raise a general alarm, but probably Aunt Betsy and the others thought that they had all gone for a romantic, moonlit stroll along the beach—she and Lucy and Erik and Harald Borgsen and Huntley. Would it be better, she wondered, to let them go on believing that a little longer?

Where was Lucy? Her heart began to beat with a new insistence. Supposing Lucy never came back? Supposing something serious had happened?

Foolishly she began to pick her way along the clifftop in the direction taken by the three men, thinking that they really should have split up for an organized search. But it was not yet an organized search. Lucy would probably laugh at them when she came back and discovered how anxious they had been. She could almost hear that satirical laughter as she walked along. Almost she could see the gleam of Lucy's pale, tiger eyes in the darkness.

Soon she realized that she had come further than she had intended. She was over the top of the headland now, looking down on the quiet little bay where Huntley moored the launch when it was not in use. Normally it lay in the harbour against the jetty wall, but the jetty was being repaired and they had not needed the launch all day because of her birthday celebrations. She could see its gleaming white hull as it rode at anchor out on the dark water and the dinghy pulled up on the beach far beneath where she stood.

Then, quite clearly, as the crescent moon slid out from behind a cloud, she saw the figure sitting in the dinghy. It was Lucy. She had a dark cloak over her silver dress, but there was no mistaking her fair head and the rather arrogant carriage of her shoulders.

"Lucy!" she called. "Lucy!"

She was almost crying with relief as Lucy rose slowly to her feet. It was minutes before she realized that her cry had not been heard down there on the shore. Lucy was pushing the dinghy slowly and deliberately into the water.

Ailsa did not stop to think what she should do. Without quite knowing why, she felt sure that Lucy intended to make her way out to the launch. With some madcap scheme in her head she was about to embark on what could so easily be a foolish, if not a tragic, adventure.

She was quite alone. The moon assured Ailsa of that. There was little time to lose. No time to look for Huntley or even to run back to the house. Already Lucy had the dinghy at the water's edge.

Plunging downwards over the rough grass which clothed the cliff top, she sought and found the narrow sheep track leading to the beach. It was the way Lucy must have used to reach the bay and it was difficult and precipitous in places and hidden from the top of the cliff, but at last she found herself running across the shingle, calling to Lucy as she went.

The rising wind was blowing off the land from the west and it carried her voice towards the sea. Lucy turned sharply at the sound of her name. When she saw who it was she straightened from her task, her face full of suppressed fury, her fair hair blown in wisps across her cheek.

"What do you want?" she demanded harshly. "Why have you followed me?"

"I came to look for you, Lucy. It's after one o'clock——"

Lucy uttered a brief, mirthless laugh.

"Did you come to tell me that?" She turned, tugging at the dinghy in an effort to get it further into the water. She seemed to be using up her energy as if it had to be expended on some physical task or it would destroy her. "I know what time it is."

"There's a wind getting up," Ailsa pointed out, "and rain coming. Huntley felt that we ought to look for you."

Huntley's name had a peculiar effect on Lucy. She stopped tugging at the boat, turning with a look of the most utter hatred in her pale eyes.

"Huntley!" she echoed. "What right has he to look for me, or to send you to look? I don't want to hear anything about him. We've said all we need to say to each other—an hour ago!" She began to tug the dinghy further out into the water. "I'll please myself what I do. I don't need to ask Huntley or anybody else when I want to take a boat out!"

"Lucy—please!" Ailsa clung to the gunwale of the dinghy, trying to pull it back as Lucy clambered aboard. "You mustn't do this. The wind's too awful, and there's an outgoing tide. There's no point in going over to the launch at this time of night——"

Suddenly she was gripped by a terrible fear, the certainty that Lucy had every intention of reaching the moored launch and of going off in it in a fit of reckless rebellion against Huntley or against something he had said.

Lucy lurched back towards the stern, fumbling for one of the oars.

"Get back!" she shouted. "Leave go of the damned boat, I tell you! I'm going to row out to the launch whatever you say!"

"No, Lucy!" Ailsa shouted back. "You mustn't! Do you hear me? You mustn't! Whatever has happened, you mustn't take such a risk——"

"Do as I say, blast you!"

Her hair whipped across her face, her velvet evening cloak flapping like dark wings about her, Lucy looked like some avenging fury standing there with the oar poised in her hands ready to strike. Ailsa drew back, appalled more by such a naked display of rage than any thought of personal injury. It was something she could not have imagined,

180

even in her wildest dreams. It was more than an ungovernable, childish fit of temper, shaking its victim from head to foot. It was something fiendishly vindictive and almost sinister and it ravaged Lucy's pale face until it was unrecognizable.

Then, in a split second, the tide lifted the dinghy and the keel was free. Lucy lost her balance and fell, grovelling in the bottom of the boat. The oar spun from her grasp, described a half circle in the air and fell into the water, to be carried away with amazing speed. Ailsa clutched the gunwale, aware of a steady pull of water carrying them both out towards the centre of the bay.

Desperately she clung on. There was no movement from Lucy and she dragged herself aboard the heaving dinghy, glad of the security of solid boards beneath her feet.

Security! She smiled grimly at the word. She and Lucy were adrift, at the mercy of wind and tide, with one oar between them and disaster.

There was a movement in the stern and Lucy stirred uncomfortably. Momentarily stunned by her fall, she glared through narrowed lids at her adversary.

"Get out!" she hissed. "I told you to get out. He'll marry you now that you own Corrae!"

The bitter, vitriolic statement made Ailsa's heart lurch sickeningly. There was no mistaking Lucy's meaning, yet this was no time for quarrelling or even for arguing about Huntley. The dinghy was being swept by a ruthless tide race, swiftly and surely, far beyond the moored launch and out to sea.

"Do you know anything about steering, Lucy?" Ailsa asked. "We've only got one oar. The other went over the side when the tide caught us and you fell."

Lucy looked back at her with a first hint of dismay in her eyes.

"You put it out over the stern," she said dully, the full horror of their predicament only beginning to register in her tormented mind. "I've seen native fishermen paddle a boat that way in the Bahamas and in Portugal. Gondolas are steered from the back too, aren't they?" Suddenly she began to laugh, high-pitched cracked laughter that had no real mirth in it. "Wouldn't you give a lot to be drifting by moonlight down the Grand Canal, Ailsa, with a Venetian gondolier singing you a love song? You might even be in Huntley's arms—instead of just drifting out to sea in the same boat as me!"

"Lucy—stop!" Ailsa commanded. "We've got to work together—think together. Whatever you may feel about me, we're both in this and we're in danger. We've been caught in some sort of current which could carry us right out to sea or one to these awful skerries at the north end of the island. We've got to think of something to *do*!"

"You can't expect me to think!" Lucy sat with her head in her hands for several minutes. Then she looked up and said: "We can't drift very far. There's that headland that juts right out into the sea. The current will sweep round there and we can try to steer in towards the land. If we can pull against it the chances are that we might get away from it into the bay where we had our picnic. Then we could try for the shore and a reasonably safe landing."

If she was afraid she did not show it. Ailsa closed her eyes, envisaging the dark rock face of the headland and the cruel little skerries surrounding it where the waves broke in a crumpled line of foam. Beyond them the lighthouse stood, flashing its warning across the silent sea, but the most vivid recollection of all was of a ruined tower rising steeply above the cliff.

The castle! The old MacLaren stronghold looking grimly out across the waves stood up there, high on the headland, its sheer wall of weathered stone dropping steeply to the treacherous rocks below.

Lucy made the first effort with the single oar, and Ailsa lay in the bottom of the dinghy, watching. She could not help but admire the other girl's strength and the calm way in which Lucy seemed to disregard the sea. Yet her effort had very little effect on their crazy progress on the breast of the current and when she took the oar in her turn she could feel the terrible pull of it fighting against her. All they could do was to drift and reserve their energies for the final struggle when they came to the bay.

182

The wind had strengthened and the pale silver wash of moonlight still filtered through the odd gaps in the clouds, revealing the dark coastline ahead of them. Once Ailsa saw the great cone of Scuirival rising starkly against a track of opalescent sky, but almost immediately the mountain hid his face again.

"Look!" Lucy shouted. "Over there!"

She pointed to where, far ahead of them, a scythe of light reaped the dark heavens. It swung up in an arc and disappeared, repeating its quick curve a second time before sea and headland and shore were plunged into greater darkness than before.

"It's the lighthouse!" Ailsa cried in wild relief. "D'you think we'll ever get as far as the light?"

"There are all those dreadful skerries in between," Lucy reminded her harshly.

The lighthouse was beyond the skerries, of course, and the bay lay close beneath the castle wall. They need not go so far as the lighthouse if their original plan succeeded. If they could reach the bay, steering their craft towards the shore at the right moment, there was yet hope.

We've got to do it, Ailsa thought. We've got to!

"We'll let the dinghy go with the current till we get beyond the Point," she suggested. "That will take us level with the bay. We'll have to make a superhuman effort, Lucy. We'll have to pull with everything we've got. We'll have to be ready too. I think we should both come to this end of the boat, here in the stern."

Lucy crawled back beside her. She still looked sullen and antagonistic, but her eyes were free from fear. Ailsa, who had to admit to a paralysing fear which lay like a dead weight at the pit of her stomach as she got ready for action, could not understand Lucy. Her small, intense face with its narrowed eyes exuded hatred and an odd sort of envy, and she had not forgotten about Huntley even in this present emergency when both their lives were at stake.

"I suppose you're hoping that Huntley will come to your rescue?" she suggested fiercely. "He ought to, of course. You must be most valuable to him now."

"Don't let's quarrel over Huntley," Ailsa begged. "He isn't in love with me——"

"Who said anything about love?" Lucy demanded with a small, malicious laugh. "I said he'd ask you to marry him—to get Corrae. There's a difference."

"Yes," Ailsa whispered, "I know, but I don't think there's any sense in discussing it—just now."

"I wanted him to be in love with me," Lucy mused with that awful sneer in her voice which grated on Ailsa's nerves. "Maybe I was a fool, but I thought it was a foregone conclusion that we would get married, even without love. Poppa waved his cheque-book very firmly in Huntley's face, but it wasn't enough. There was always Corrae. Perhaps if your aunt hadn't bought the place in the first instance, it could have been different."

Her words were carried away in the wind and she sat for a long time in silence, staring at the darkness all about them that was the sea.

"If we have to swim for it," she said at last, "we'd better be prepared." She unfastened the neckband of her cape, letting it lie loosely over her shoulders, and then with steady and deliberate fingers she ripped the tight skirt of her dress for hem to knee. "You'd better do something to yours," she advised. "You'll never swim in a long skirt."

Almost imperceptibly their pace had slackened and suddenly Lucy shouted:

"Now! Pull with everything you've got——"

Ailsa could see the dark bulk of the headland and a sudden gleam of white shingle. They were parallel with the bay.

"My God!" Lucy said. "This is awful! I just can't hold on——"

"You must! Lucy, you must——"

The current was too strong for them. It was still carrying them away, and a fierce gust of wind whipped the next few waves into black mountains of water all about them. The dinghy rose and staggered in the trough of a wave and rose again to the angry crest. It won't do it, Ailsa thought. It'll never survived all this—a little boat meant for a quiet bay!

When they capsized she knew that she had been waiting

184

for the impact of the sea. It seemed to snatch at her hungrily as it bore her away.

'Can you swim?' a voice mocked in her ear. 'Can you swim, Ailsa?'

'Not very well——' Her own voice sounded weak and far away. 'Not in a heavy sea.'

Then she saw Lucy striking through the water. She looked like a silver fish, sure and unerring in her movements. No wonder she had little fear of the sea! They were abreast for a moment, and suddenly Ailsa realized that they were out of the current now. There was only the terrible black depth of water beneath them and the mounting, hungry waves.

"Lucy——!" she gasped, but Lucy was swimming away from her towards the shore.

CHAPTER TEN

MINUTES passed in a desperation of effort. Or was it hours? Ailsa's limbs began to feel numb as she went through the automatic movements of the breast stroke, but gradually all movement seemed to be slowing down to a paralysing desire for sleep.

Then something came towards her over the crest of a wave. It was the dinghy. It struck her with a gentle, almost a caressing bump, but that was perhaps because she did not care. Why should she care any more? She would never reach the land——

'Catch hold of the dinghy and make one last effort. Try! Try!'

The voice was softly persuasive, although it seemed to come from some great distance. It was not a voice she knew, but it held an odd insistency. 'Try—you must try! Hold on to the dinghy——'

Her fingers fastened obediently over the rubber fender that went round the gunwale. The dinghy was floating upside down. With a tremendous effort she clung on, easing herself gradually out of the water. There was nothing to see. Only waves, like a never-ending mountain chain. There was no sight of land anywhere.

How long could you go on, she wondered, clinging to an upturned boat in a sea like this? An hour? Two hours— three, perhaps?

The dinghy rose and fell monotonously. She began to feel drugged by the regular movement, which never varied, and once her fingers loosened their grip. For a split second she watched the dinghy float away, and then she made a supreme effort and caught up with it again.

Her hands were beginning to feel numb with cold and a warning sense of security confused her brain. Her thoughts wandered to pleasant things. It can be warm, so warm when you are completely under the waves. You will not feel anything. It will be warm. Remember the seals playing in the sun? They were warm in the sea. Deep down it's very green and the seals love it. Almost as much as basking on the rocks in the sun . . .

It was minutes before she realized that the regular motion beneath her had ceased and seconds later that her feet touched solid rock. There was a boom and smash of waves somewhere near at hand and the little boat that had saved her was being smacked rhythmically against a high, precipitous wall of dark grey stone.

At first she took it to be the cliff and was sure that it would be only minutes before her frail little craft was pounded to matchwood on the jagged edge of some waiting skerry, and then she saw how sheer the stone was, straight and smooth—man built. She was directly below the castle's ruined tower.

Looking straight up at the high column of grey stone, she knew that there was no foothold anywhere below the parapet. This was the dungeon tower, the captive place where MacLarens long ago had kept their prisoners and their unwilling brides.

The shattered battlements were so far above her that they were lost to sight, but just above the dinghy there was an iron ring let into the wall.

With an effort she caught it and held on, dragging herself up to a precarious foothold on the rocks to watch the dinghy shattering itself against the unrelenting wall.

How long she clung there she did not know, but gradually she realized that the dinghy was much further below her. The tide had gone down. Two feet, perhaps. No more, but it was enough to reveal a rectangular opening at the base of the tower guarded by an iron grille. It was a portcullis in miniature, and half of it had been eaten away by time and the action of the sea. Huntley had said that no effort had been made to restore the castle for the past hundred years.

She squeezed her way through into the dank, wet interior of the dungeon. It was a wicked, fearsome place, but until the tide was high again she was safe.

Feeling round the wall, she discovered a short iron ladder which went up a foot or two before it bedded itself mad-

187

deningly, tantalizingly, in the sheer face of the wall. These ancient MacLarens had been expert at torture!

Beating a clenched fist against the unresponsive stone, she clung to the iron rungs and called and called for help. But who would hear? Her voice echoed hollowly in the darkness and she began to cry, slow, difficult tears which reduced her to a new weakness.

"Huntley! Huntley——!" But how was he to hear? He must believe her dead by now—drowned out there in the bay.

Slowly the tears dried on her cheeks. Would there be any light in the dungeon when the dawn came, she wondered, or would it still be dark?

She slid down to the floor, shivering with cold and crouching against the wall. Down here she could hear and smell the sea, and suddenly it seemed lighter, nearer.

Then, far above her, there was another light, a faint beam, like the flicker of a torch.

"Huntley!" she called. "Huntley!"

The light wavered and steadied, coming close to the dungeon rim. She could see the faint outline of a hurricane lamp.

"Huntley!"

Her voice spiralled upwards, drowned by the crash of the sea against the outer wall, but the light remained steady and high above her.

"Ailsa? Ailsa, are you there?"

"Down here! Down here!" There was a desperate surging passion in her voice and she climbed back to the top of the iron ladder, sobbing her relief. "I'm here! I'm on the ladder. Can you get to me?"

Her voice sounded too feeble, too far away to be heard.

"Hang on!" That voice seemed far away too, but the steady light gleamed like a beacon over her head. "Stay where you are. Stay on the ladder. Don't go back. Do you hear me? Don't go back down to the floor."

"Yes, I hear you. I hear you, Huntley!"

The waiting seemed endless. She felt chilled to the bone and her wet clothes clung to her like a shroud. Time hung suspended in the dank atmosphere around her and only the distant light seemed real. Had she imagined Huntley's voice up there beside the light?

Shivering, she sank back against the wall. How long would it be before help came? Once more she called, seeking reassurance, but only the echo of her own voice came back to her now.

She thought of the MacLaren bride waiting interminably for release down here in her silent prison and her own voice seemed to echo as forlornly among the shadows. But she had never been Huntley's bride. She had never been loved by him, even for a moment. What had Lucy said? 'He'll marry you now that you own Corrae . . .'

It wouldn't matter. It wouldn't matter at all! Just to be with him would be all she could desire.

The light swung away from the rim of her prison and she cried out in sharp protest, but almost immediately something swung down to her side. She recognized it as the knotted end of a rope and clutched at it automatically, still holding on to the top rung of the ladder. Then the light went out altogether and the rope was almost wrenched from her hand.

Before she could cry out she was in Huntley's supporting arms.

"Are you all right?" His voice was firm and strong as he sought a momentary foothold on the ladder beside her. "I'm going to tie you on to the rope and then you've got to help me to climb."

"Yes," she whispered. "Yes, I'm all right—— Tell me what to do."

She bit her teeth into her lower lip to keep them from chattering, and inch by perilous inch, they edged their way up the dungeon wall. The light had been moved a little way from the top and it cast a yellow hollow into the darkness, but gradually, as they neared it, a stronger light, diffused and opal-pale, spread across the ruined walls. The dawn had come, breaking softly in the east. She had been down there longer than she thought.

Yet nothing mattered now—time or place or danger. Nothing but Huntley's encircling arms. He held her even after they had reached the top, lifting her as he had done

189

once before to carry her across the flower-starred grass to the shelter of the far wall, and for the first time she was able to see his face clearly.

What she saw shocked her. It look ravaged and old, as if the past few hours had held all the anxiety of a lifetime.

"Lucy?" Her voice stumbled over the name. "I think she managed to reach the shore——"

"Lucy's dead," he said harshly. "She was picked up by the lifeboat on the far side of the skerries over an hour ago."

Stunned into incredulous silence, she could not answer him. It seemed impossible that Lucy could have been drowned. She had been swimming so strongly, straight for the shore. And Huntley? If he loved Lucy——

"I've got to get you back to the house as quickly as possible," he said, stripping off his jacket to wrap it round her. "There's been a commotion, of course, but I took a chance and came here." Suddenly he was looking at her with a different expression in his eyes, all their bleakness gone. "I must have had some sort of—intuition that I would find you here."

"Imprisoned in the family dungeon!" She tried to smile, but it was a poor effort. "Do you remember telling me about the bride?"

"Yes," he said, "I remember."

He helped her up over the wall and they were instantly hailed by a familiar voice. Harald Borgsen and Erik ran towards them from a stationary jeep.

"We followed you up," Erik explained to Huntley as the doctor took charge. "Someone said they had seen you going in this direction."

After that most things were hazy to Ailsa. Harald had given her an injection of some sort and it seemed to plunge her into a dark confusion. Before she woke again she had wandered for a very long time in a strange country.

Once, in an oddly lucid moment, she heard the word 'pneumonia', but she had drifted off again before she really thought about it.

When, finally, she was able to take stock of her immediate surroundings, she found herself in her own bed in the room which had once belonged to Huntley's mother. Aunt Betsy Bellinger was seated by her side. An oddly quiet, chastened-looking Aunt Betsy.

"We've been worried to death about you, honey!" she said when Ailsa assured her that she could talk quite rationally. "You've been like this for five days. It's been awful, not knowing what was going to happen! Huntley got you out of that dreadful dungeon, but you had been soaked to the skin for so long that you just couldn't escape getting pneumonia!"

"Aunt Betsy," Ailsa asked after many minutes, "what happened to Lucy?"

She felt sure that she must have been dreaming when Huntley had told her that Lucy was dead.

Aunt Betsy shivered.

"She took cramp. It was awful! The lifeboatman found her body washed up on one of those dreadful skerries. Her father was beside himself with grief. Poor man, he's gone to Edinburgh. He just couldn't bear to be on the island a moment longer than was necessary. That's understandable, of course. Lucy was everything to him." Aunt Betsy sighed. "She was an unhappy girl—spoiled, maybe, but that was natural for Adam to do, I guess. She was the apple of his eye. Maybe she had too much and was too impetuous, but that's not for me to say now. I'm going to marry Adam when this has blown over, and I'll try to make up to him for this dreadful loss he's had. We could never live on the island now." She got up, moving restlessly round the bed. "Anyway, it's yours now, Ailsa. I made it over to you and I'll help you to run it, honey. You could be happy here."

She seemed quite sure of that, and somehow Ailsa knew it was what her aunt had planned. But she herself was not so sure. She felt remote and terribly alone. She needed Huntley, yet she could not ask him to go on managing Corrae for her, and now he would never be able to buy it back, however anxious she was to sell it to him.

Before she saw him again another week had passed. The Tollertons and Erik and Greta Larsen, accompanied by the doctor, who was now Greta's fiancé, had all returned to the mainland. The *Saturn* had sailed again from Oban and she had not been able to bid Erik and Greta goodbye nor to thank Harald Borgsen for his professional attention.

Huntley came towards her as she was sitting in the garden for the first time. It was a warm day in early July and the sun was shining strongly. She sat in the shade of a group of alders on the rough lawn at the side of the house and he came over the bridge from the main drive.

"Your aunt tells me you're well enough to have visitors," he said.

She held out her hand to him. It looked thin and pale, and he clasped it warmly in his strong brown fingers.

"I'm glad you came," she said. "I want to thank you for what you did—for saving my life."

"The dungeon lured you in!" he said with an odd, one-sided smile. "It thrives on imprisoned maidens!"

He did not want to be serious, but she had to say something about Lucy.

"Huntley—I'm sorry about Lucy—about what happened." She looked up. The expression on his face had changed and there was a hard, withdrawn look in his eyes. "I know how awful this must be for you," she stumbled on. "Having to be here all the time—remembering."

"Remembering about Lucy?" He stooped and turned her face up to his again, so that she was looking directly into those vividly blue eyes which always had the power to disconcert her. "What are you trying to say, Ailsa? Did you think I was in love with Lucy?"

"I—thought you might marry her," she was forced to confess with truth.

"And that was a different thing!" His voice had a bitter edge. "You thought I was likely to marry the Fulton millions in a bid to keep Corrae? Well, perhaps I deserve that. Perhaps I did think about it in the beginning. Remember," he went on ruthlessly, "you advised me to do something of the kind?"

"That was before I knew Aunt Betsy had bought the island," she defended quickly.

"You saw it as a likely way out for me, all the same," he persisted. "But when I discovered I loved you I just couldn't take it."

192

Ailsa drew in a swift breath and all the colour which had fled from her cheeks at his coming rushed back again.

"Yes, it's true," he said, not waiting for her to speak and thrusting his hands deeply into his pockets. "I wanted to ask you to marry me from the very beginning. That day on Fair Isle I was sure. But how could I while I lived on Corrae? I had promised to serve those six months for my home. Your aunt would have done all the wrong things with the best possible motives. I had given her my word to stay, and I had nothing to offer you at the end of these six months."

"Except your love," she reminded him unevenly.

"Would that have been enough?" His mouth was hard. "Even when I imagined you were only Mrs. Bellinger's paid companion I couldn't have taken that for granted."

His voice was rough with suppressed emotion, but he still stood a little way apart, staring down towards the bay and the tranquil blue sea.

"And so, when Aunt Betsy made me an heiress, you just couldn't ask me at all?" Ailsa guessed softly. "Oh, Huntley! How foolish can pride be? I love you. I've always loved you, right from the beginning. You could serve Corrae, but you couldn't *marry* it. That's what you've been trying to say, isn't it? Well, perhaps I think the same way. Perhaps I don't want you to marry Corrae. Let me give it to you— as a wedding present."

He stiffened as if she had struck him a physical blow, but she struggled to her feet and stood between him and the sea.

"Do you want me to beg for your love?" she asked gently. "Are you going to condemn us both to a life without each other?"

At last he met her eyes.

"No," he said. "No."

All the barriers were down at last. He swept her into his arms, kissing her passionately, all the flood of his longing pouring out to sweep them away on a full, deep tide. And, kiss for kiss, Ailsa returned it all.

"When we are very old," she said after a while, "we'll sit here in the shade of the trees wondering how we could ever have been so foolish as to doubt each other. But by then we will have done so much for Corrae that it won't matter. We'll see it grow and we'll work for it all our lives, Huntley. Our island!"

Very gently he gathered her back into his arms.

"You were made for Corrae and made for loving, Ailsa," he said. "This is our heritage."

PASSING STRANGERS

Passing
Strangers

"It's foolish to run away from the truth," Felipe said, telling Jane about his deceased wife's infidelity. But the woman he was talking about had also been Jane's sister.

True, Jane had been a victim of Grace's selfish appropriation of Felipe; yet she couldn't believe Andrew Ballantyne capable of the additional betrayal outlined in Felipe's accusation.

Losing Felipe had been temporarily painful, but to lose Andrew would be unbearable!

CHAPTER ONE

THE passenger accommodation on the Lisbon-bound plane was fully taken up, with the exception of one place towards the rear. It was an aisle seat, and the girl sitting alone in the single armchair next to it was immeasurably thankful for the comparative isolation of her position.

It gave her time for thought without the distraction of a garrulous new acquaintance, time to draw a little nearer to the problem which she had thrust from her assiduously ever since she had made the decision to leave England.

The promise she had given her mother to seek out her sister's children in an alien land had meant more to Jane Lambert than just an interruption of her nursing career. It had been strong enough and sacred enough to keep any personal feelings at bay while she prepared for her journey, but now that she was airborne, now that she was on her way and the Gordian knot had been cut, she took time to think.

The vision of Felipe rose clearly before her eyes, Felipe as he had been seven years ago. Don Felipe then; Señor Don Felipe, Marqués de Pardo y Cabor now. Seven years was a long time in which to forget, but most of the loving and some of the bitterness still remained.

She had done her best to forget, embracing the career she had just begun with a new fervour, trying to pretend that she had always been a dedicated nurse, only to come again and again to the realization that she would have counted everything well lost if Felipe had asked her to be his wife.

Instead he had asked Grace, carrying her off as a bride to his island home within a month of their meeting. Grace had always been sure of what she wanted from life, and she had wanted Felipe on sight. She had always been the one to take, while Jane had found it easy to give. Easy until Felipe came along.

She clenched her teeth. It was no use going over it all, remembering how she had met Felipe while he was a patient at the Clinic and met him again, several times, before she had taken him home and he had seen Grace. Jane had known, even in that first moment of their meeting, that she had gone out with Felipe for the last time. The chill in her heart as she had watched them together was like the chill of death. She had never been in love before; she had never really loved since. That first bitter-sweet experience had numbed her, taking away something she could never hope to replace. Oh, there had been other affairs — friendships in plenty — but she had never allowed them to take possession of her heart.

Perhaps it had been the fact that it had been Grace who had married Felipe that had made it all so difficult, the sister whom she had loved so wholeheartedly all her life. At seventeen she had seen in Grace the perfection she could never hope to achieve. They were dissimilar in every way; height and features and temperament, Grace taking after their volatile father, while Jane was quite certainly a MacLean. Her Scottish mother had bequeathed her her dark, Celtic good looks and much of her own native shrewdness, but Jane could never forget the golden beauty that had been Grace, the tall, slender goddess who had stolen her early love.

With her hands clasped tightly in her lap, she gazed unseeingly down at the cloud-carpet beneath the plane.

The past was all so far away, so deeply hidden, yet before the day was over she would meet Felipe again.

Something akin to panic seized her so that she almost struggled to her feet in an effort at escape. Why had she come? Why had she given her promise? Grace was dead, but her children were well cared for. "I can't think of them as Spanish children, Janey," her mother had said when the news of her sister's death had reached London. "Go out and see what you can do."

They had never been able to visit Grace to see her home. Twice since her marriage she had spent a holiday in London, but neither John nor Mary Lambert had managed a return visit. Ill-health had intervened, and Jane had never quite been able to bring herself to accept her sister's pressing invitations to the Casa del Sol. Even after she was fully trained as a nurse she had deliberately gone elsewhere, and during the past two years there had been no question of a holiday. She had nursed her father through his last fatal illness and, later, her mother. Grace had not offered to come home for her father's funeral.

Perhaps she couldn't, Jane decided hastily. She had the children to consider, but Chris wasn't exactly a baby any more, and Rozanne was six years old. . . .

The plane sank into the layer of cloud and through it. A wide stretch of sea and a jagged coastline lay beneath them. Lisbon was five minutes away.

Again that odd sense of panic gripped her by the throat, although she had covered only about a third of her journey. Something kept repeating deep inside her that there was still time to turn back. Still time to change her mind.

But it wasn't an impulse that had brought her. It was a promise, and one didn't change one's mind about promises. She would have to try to hide her love, if it

201

still really existed after all those years. She had changed, and no doubt Felipe had, too. She had changed in so many little ways, becoming independent and hardened, perhaps, but secretly she knew herself still vulnerable where love was concerned. Her sensitive spirit yearned for the fulfilment of belonging to one man she could respect and cherish for the remainder of her life, but she knew that the feeling would have to be mutual. And Felipe had chosen Grace.

Her death must have left him heartbroken, although he had said little about his personal feelings in his letters. He had regretted the fact that his children were left motherless at such a tender age, and that, above all else, had finally sealed Jane's decision.

"Fasten your seat-belts, please!" The air hostess came quickly along the aisle.

"How long do we have at Lisbon?" someone asked.

"Only an hour, I'm afraid." The hostess smiled down at Jane. "You should be able to get a cup of tea in the passenger lounge. I'm sorry it's raining," she added.

It ought not to be raining, Jane thought abstractedly. One only expects rain in England!

With the others she walked towards the passenger lounge. The rain came down in a thin drizzle, leaving them little to look at, but she had no desire for food. The average Briton's capacity for tea drove most of her fellow-travellers to the service counter, but she did not join them.

Only one man appeared to dissociate an enforced idleness with the ubiquitous tea-cup. He stood gazing fixedly before him through the plate-glass window which formed one end of the long room, a tall, loose-limbed figure with an air of purpose about him which would have singled him out in any crowd. Jane felt sure that she had not seen him on the plane when they had left London.

When he turned their eyes met. The contact was momentary, fleeting, yet it left her with an odd uneasiness. It was as if he had recognized her, but she had never seen him before in all her life.

She walked away, and he went back to his contemplation of the wet stretch of tarmac outside the window.

When their flight number was finally announced through the loud-hailers she found him walking just ahead of her towards the plane. He was on his way to the Islands.

Curiosity made her consider him more closely until the thought of Felipe thrust all other thoughts from her mind. This was the final lap of her journey. When the plane touched down once more they would be in Teneriffe and Felipe would be waiting for her.

The heart which she had considered stilled long ago began to throb with a full, insistent beat, although she had never consciously wished to fill her dead sister's place in Felipe's affections. She knew that she never could. Felipe had known her before he had known Grace. There had been affection between them, but no love on Felipe's part. The situation was not likely to change now.

The man in the loose grey travelling coat halted at the foot of the gangway to check his reservation and she passed him, going on into the plane where the other passengers were settling down for the remainder of the flight. Most of them had crossed with her from London, and they nodded their recognition as she passed.

"Not long now before we get rid of this dreadful weather," the woman in the seat ahead of her observed.

203

"I'm just longing to sit in the sun and do nothing! February in England always gets me down."

She was going out to the Islands for her annual holiday with her daughter, she had informed Jane at London Airport. Teneriffe was her particular Shangri-la. Jane returned her smile and passed on, aware that she had been blocking the aisle.

Without turning her head, she was aware that the man in the grey coat was close behind her, waiting for her to take her seat. When she had settled herself he took off his coat and sat down beside her.

It was inevitable, Jane supposed. The privacy she had enjoyed since London was no longer hers.

Taking up a magazine, she tried to concentrate on its contents, but she was wholly aware of her companion. He sat with a leather brief-case across his knees, but he did not open it immediately, although it probably contained sufficient reading material to keep him interested for the duration of the flight.

Glancing sideways at the thin, tanned face, she decided that he travelled a great deal and would not now be feeling the intense, stirring excitement which ran in her own veins. She had always longed to take such a journey as this to faraway places, to bridge the gap of distance and discover for herself the beauty and strangeness of the wider world. Her opportunity could have come about in happier circumstances, of course, but she was still young enough and eager enough to accept the joy of change.

"Will you fasten your seat-belts, please?"

They completed the precaution together, Jane still rather clumsily because she wasn't used to it, her companion swiftly and efficiently, as if air travel was an everyday occurrence where he was concerned.

By the time they were through the low strata of rain cloud clinging to the earth she had forgotten everything but the wonder of the blue world into which they had emerged. The sun shone brilliantly and the heavens were a vast azure canopy surrounding them like a cupola. Distance and light were incredible in their immensity and she could only gasp at what she saw.

"Your first flight?"

She looked round at her companion, supposing him to be amused.

"There's always got to be a first time," she said without resentment. "I wouldn't have missed this for the world!"

"I envy you," he confessed.

She turned her head to look at him more fully.

"Surely you're not trying to tell me that it can ever grow stale?"

He smiled quite openly at that, the sudden amusement chasing the darker shadows from his eyes. Now they were neither grey nor blue, but a strange, undeterminable colour between the two which she had seen often in the sea.

"You're right about the beauty," he admitted. "But travelling can often be a great waste of time."

"You're flying on business, I suppose," she suggested.

"I've been in Madrid for a couple of days," he acknowledged. "At a conference. A medical conference," he added for her further enlightenment, and she noticed that the admission had chased the amusement from his eyes.

His face, in repose, looked grim, with a tightness about the finely moulded lips which could have been bitterness.

"You're a doctor?" she asked.

He nodded.

"I take it you're on holiday," he said, changing the subject.

Jane hesitated.

"Not entirely."

He waited for her to continue if she wished, bored perhaps by the casualness of their conversation. He didn't look the sort of person who would waste time on trivialities.

"I haven't been to the Islands before," she offered. "But I should have made this journey long ago. My sister married and went to live on Teneriffe seven years ago."

She paused, conscious once more of the overwhelming pain of loss which assailed her whenever she remembered that Grace was dead, that her sister would not be waiting with Felipe to greet her when she reached her destination.

"You'll like Teneriffe," her companion said. "It's quite unique. Like no other island."

"Even the islands of the Hebrides?" she teased impulsively, detecting in the intonation of a word here and there the unmistakable hint of his Scottish origin.

Her unexpected rejoinder drew his dark brows together.

"I've not been home for six years," he confessed in the tone of a man who had made the nostalgic journey many times in the secret places of his heart. "I haven't had the opportunity. I've worked mostly abroad."

Six years, Jane thought. It was a long time for a man to stay away from the country of his birth, even though he did work abroad.

"I left Scotland as soon as I graduated," he offered. "I haven't been back since."

She hesitated about asking any more questions because he looked as if his answers might be limited to the briefest of explanations. Speaking about the past, his mouth had tightened to a thin line and his whole face had hardened. His jaw was firmly set and there was a tautness about it which suggested that his strong white teeth might be firmly clamped down on further confidences.

All the same, they couldn't just sit there in a stony silence until they reached the Islands. Not when they had begun to talk.

"Do you know Teneriffe?" she asked.

"I live there," he told her.

Jane could not hide her surprise.

"The English doctor," he introduced himself drily. "Invaluable to the tourist trade in cases of Canary fever and similar gastric disorders. Guaranteed to give assurance and confidence to my fellow-countrymen far from their native land."

There was no humour in the observation, yet she could not quite accuse him of bitterness. Perhaps he had passed beyond such an emotion so that it only lingered in the hard set of his jaw and round a mouth which had once been kind.

As he had done, she waited for him to continue.

"I came out to Teneriffe four years ago," he explained. "Before that I did a post-graduate course in Germany. That was where I first met my present partner. He needed help and offered me the job."

A job in a backwater. The thought flashed vividly across Jane's mind, and she flushed at its implication. Everything about this man suggested brilliance, yet he had chosen to come to an island that was more or less off the beaten track in order to practise when surely he could have done much better for himself in London.

There were the missing years, of course. Post-graduate studies couldn't have lasted much more than a year, and he had said that he had been away from Scotland for six.

"You're settled in the Canaries, then?" she suggested, not quite knowing what to say and uncomfortably aware of the silence between them.

He shrugged.

"Yes, I suppose I am — settled."

"I trained to be a nurse," she told him with a proud note of confidence in her voice. "It doesn't really matter where one practises."

He gave her a quick, searching scrutiny.

"You're not looking for a job, are you?" he asked.

She shook her head.

"Not at present. You see, I've come out here to meet my sister's children for the first time." Her mouth curved in a tender smile. "I had to do it. I'd never seen them, and when Grace died I promised my mother I would come — just as soon as I could. Their father is Spanish." She met his surprised gaze. "They live near Orotava. Felipe is the Marqués de Pardo. He inherited the title from an uncle. Perhaps you know him?"

Her question dropped into an odd, tense silence.

"I'm employed by him," her companion said at last.

"By Felipe?" She gazed at him uncomprehendingly. "But you said——"

"I was in partnership with Hans Baer? That's true, but I'm also more gainfully employed looking after the workers on your brother-in-law's estate. The Marqués de Pardo y Cabor is a very wealthy man."

Jane stiffened at the slight dryness of his tone.

"You don't approve of wealth?" she suggested. "You speak as if you have a great contempt for money."

"On the contrary," he corrected her, "I'm only too fully aware of its tremendous power."

It was difficult to understand him, to be quite sure why he had spoken so scathingly. Was there some personal dislike between him and Felipe? She could not believe that he was merely jealous of another man's position and covetous of his worldly goods.

"Money can have a power for good as well as evil," she reminded him rather coldly. "I believe my brother-in-law is reasonably generous."

"Forgive me," he said. "I wouldn't imply otherwise. The art of the island owes much to the Marqués de Pardo y Cabor and he has an immense collection of pictures which, I'm told, are worth a fortune. He also collects precious stones."

Jane was quite frankly bewildered. The inflection in his quiet voice baffled her because it suggested anger rather than envy. This man would want nothing for himself.

But how could she be so sure? She had met him less than an hour ago. They were complete strangers, ships that might have passed in the night but for the amazing fact that he was in Felipe's employment.

"Can you tell me about the children?" she asked, deliberately steering the conversation away from Felipe. "How are they? Is Rozanne very upset by her mother's death?"

He hesitated before he answered her final question.

"Rozanne isn't the type of child who would show her grief to all and sundry," he said.

"But you must know about her," she protested. "Surely you were there when Grace died?"

His face darkened.

209

"Yes, I was there," he admitted.

"Then——?"

"Rozanne was shocked and bewildered," he said.

"She would have Felipe," Jane said.

His eyes left her flushed face to look steadily beyond her through the window.

"Your brother-in-law did what he could," he agreed. "He is not a demonstrative man."

"He was passionately fond of Grace." She bit her lower lip to hold back the spate of sudden anger which rushed through her. "His world must have been completely shattered when she died. After all, a man left with two young children to bring up without a woman's help is bound to feel stunned and a little lost just at first."

Swiftly the grey eyes came round to meet hers. There was no suggestion of blue in them now. They were as hard and cold as steel. The English doctor looked utterly ruthless in that moment.

"Was that why he sent for you?" he asked thinly.

Jane flushed scarlet.

"I came without having to be sent for," she returned frigidly. "My mother was very uneasy about the children before she died."

"And you promised her to look after them," he suggested. "Did you make the same promise to your brother-in-law?"

"We haven't discussed it," she said coldly. "I haven't seen Felipe for nearly seven years."

The reminder set her heart throbbing again and stole the angry colour from her cheeks, but she refused to look away from his calculating gaze.

"It's quite possible that you might find him changed," he remarked. "He wasn't the Marqués de Pardo when you knew him."

"People don't change as easily as that," Jane flashed. "I — knew Felipe rather well."

Deliberately he changed the subject.

"If you've never been to the Canaries before you'll be delighted with the Islands, and you've chosen the right time of year to come," he said.

"When everything is dull and drab in England, you mean," she smiled. "But February is so close to spring. I think November is the dreariest month, but even then there's fallen leaves and Christmas just around the corner. Why do people complain?"

"You're young and starry-eyed," he told her with an odd half-smile which softened his mouth a little and stole some of the hardness from his face. "I could almost envy you."

"I'm twenty-four," she said. "But why shouldn't I be starry-eyed?"

"No reason at all. Life may have been kind to you."

"Or passed me by altogether up till now, do you mean?" she challenged, still a little angry with him for being so autocratic.

"I'm sorry," he apologized unexpectedly. "I didn't mean that. You've just lost your mother, and Grace often spoke about you. She called you 'the little 'un'. I gathered that you were very close."

How much more did he know? she wondered. How deeply had he been in her sister's confidence? If he had been Grace's doctor it was extremely likely that he knew far more about her sister's way of life during those past few years than she did. There had been an odd undercurrent of restraint in Grace's letters home which had puzzled them for a long time, and lately the thought of it had begun to worry Jane.

It was impossible to ask her companion for his confidence, however. Medical etiquette apart, they were no

211

more than casual acquaintances, passing strangers who might not meet so very often in the future.

The doctor's manner seemed to suggest that he was not on the best of terms with his employer and she might remain under Felipe's roof for months without encountering him if he only went there in his professional capacity.

"Why are you called 'the English doctor' when you are really a Scot?" she demanded lightly to cover the confusion of her thoughts.

He shrugged.

"It's the usual label, isn't it? British means 'English' out here. They don't appreciate the difference."

She laughed.

"That's just about the most autocratic statement I've ever heard," she declared. "I suppose your name begins with Mac!"

Once more he looked amused.

"I'm sorry to disappoint you," he said. "It's Ballantyne. Andrew Ballantyne. I'm a Lowlander."

"But still a Scot!"

She studied his profile, aware of the dark, magnetic charm of the man even at this first encounter. His native reserve gave him an air of aloofness which she could easily understand. He would not reveal his emotions at the slighest provocation and he would be clear-headed in an emergency. Ruthless, too, perhaps, because of that square set of the jaw and the mouth which experience must have hardened.

The hostess brought their lunch trays and a bottle of Madeira wine.

"We should be passing near the island now," Andrew Ballantyne mused, reading the label. "You ought to have travelled by sea and then you could have landed on

Madeira and drunk this in its proper setting. All wines taste better in their country of origin."

Jane looked out across the blue world of sky and sea.

"Over there," he said, pointing to a grey smudge on the horizon. "It's too small to see in detail from this distance and it hasn't the stark contour of Teneriffe to recommend it."

"You're very fond of Teneriffe," she guessed.

"There's an odd saying in the Islands that once you've been there it always calls you back," he said without actually answering her question.

When the trays were cleared away he drew her attention to the distant horizon.

"It's well worth waiting for," he promised.

Jane strained her eyes towards the south-east where a tiny dark speck had appeared, like a distant ship riding the waves. It grew and took form in the sun, a conical peak outlined darkly against the sky with a white snow-cap glistening on its head.

"El Teide," Andrew Ballantyne said. "The benign giant, the monarch of the Islands."

"You make him sound mysterious." Her eyes were still on the distant peak.

"All mountains have their reservations and they wield a tremendous influence. At Orotava El Teide is everywhere one looks. The entire island is dominated by its resident giant. Tempers change with his changing moods. You will come to see what I mean and love him or hate him, as the case may be."

It was the most revealing reflection he had made, yet she could not imagine him being influenced by his surroundings to any great extent. If he had a job to do he would do it well, she thought, whatever the environment. Snap decisions were dangerous, of course. One couldn't sum up a man like this in five minutes on an air journey to the unknown.

Her nerves grew taut again, thinking of her destination and the coming meeting with Felipe.

"Is the Casa del Sol very far from Orotava?" she asked.

"About eight miles. The plantations come down to the sea in places, but the house itself stands high — an essential at certain times of the year. It can be unbearably hot in summer on the coast."

She was tempted to ask him where he lived, but decided against the impulse, looking out of the window instead to the rapidly materializing island ahead of them.

The sharp, conical mass of El Teide had taken shape and form, merging into the broad shoulders of the island, but it was still the mountain peak which dominated the view. It seemed to rush towards them out of the haze of distance, and Jane closed her eyes for a moment with an odd premonition of impending disaster.

When she opened them again her hands were clenched over the arm-rests of her chair and her companion was studying her closely.

"It's all right," he said. "We're almost there."

They were gliding in on a wide arc over the northern end of the island. The scarred and rugged face of Teneriffe lay far beneath them, full of dark gullies and haunting shadows. In that first moment Jane was aware of a bitter disappointment. Andrew Ballantyne had promised her so much, and this dark coastline with its jagged promontories and deep defiles of sullen black rock was not what she had expected. It looked harsh and unwelcoming and curiously empty. There was no sign of human habitation as far as she could see; only a sentinel lighthouse on a headland sending out its constant warning and a snarl of white-crested waves breaking endlessly against the shore.

Then, suddenly, it was all changed. A large port with a long mole reaching its white arm far into the sea came into view, and beyond it endless white villas basked lazily in the sun.

"Santa Cruz," her companion informed her, dismissing the lovely white town as the plane slipped down wind and turned towards the interior. "We have only a few minutes more."

And only these same few minutes before she would come face to face with Felipe for the first time in seven years, Jane thought. The moment was here, the moment she had longed for and yet dreaded for the past six months. Would he be changed? Seven years were bound to have made some difference in a man, but in the fundamental things he would be the same — kind, considerate, charming and a little remote. She had loved him for these qualities and knew that she still loved him.

Her heartbeats quickened until they were like a pain in her breast, and suddenly she wanted more time. Time to adjust her thoughts, to calm herself — the time which had been snatched from her when Andrew Ballantyne had followed her aboard the plane at Lisbon. Since then their conversation had excluded too intimate thoughts of Felipe or the future, and even now he would remain as a witness of their meeting.

Resentment flooded over her, yet she could not very well dismiss the doctor with a word on sight of her brother-in-law.

"Do you expect to be met?" he asked, as if there might be some doubt about it.

"Surely," Jane said. "I haven't the vaguest idea what to do once I reach Laguna."

They were circling the broad plateau where the airport lay on the edge of the deciduous forest and she could see the white roads radiating from it to east and west, leaving the rugged central spine with its dark *barrancos* and tormented rock formations unchallenged. El Teide looked back at them from another angle now, smiling and benign in the afternoon sunshine, and then they were dropping down beneath him and turning in to land.

Jane had forgotten her companion now. Nothing seemed to matter but this moment of meeting with Felipe. Would he have the children with him? A new excitement stirred in her as she wondered about Rozanne and Chris.

The plane touched down and taxied across the sunscorched apron towards the airport buildings. Her companion was collecting his few belongings, not looking at her now.

She unfastened her seat-belt, groping round for her hand luggage, hoping that she looked calm. Andrew Ballantyne was scanning the car park beyond the gates.

"You appear to be met," he announced.

Jane's heart lifted. Of course Felipe had come. Why not?

"I expected my brother-in-law to be here," she said.

The doctor followed her from the plane, guiding her towards the barricade. Jane looked about her, blinking in the blinding white light. Several cars were parked in an uneven line outside the railings and it seemed that most of her travelling companions were being met. Whole families appeared to have gathered to welcome a son or father. Few women travelled alone. She stood a little way apart, half eager, half afraid, but no tall figure answering Felipe's description came towards her.

Suddenly the blood seemed to run like ice through her veins. Had he forgotten, after all?

"Your car's waiting." She felt a hand under her arm. "I'll take you across. Miguel must have thought you had other instructions."

She wanted to assure Andrew Ballantyne that she had not been neglected, that Felipe must be here, but she could not. The hand on her arm forced her gently but compellingly forward.

"I'm quite sure I ought to wait, Doctor Ballantyne," she protested, casting an almost frantic glance towards the far end of the airstrip, only to be convinced that assurance could not possibly come from that direction. There was only El Teide in the distance, smiling down at her.

"Felipe will have other commitments," Andrew Ballantyne observed. "He takes a very active interest in the estate."

"But surely, today——"

Her protest was cut short by his grim smile.

"Felipe will tender his apologies in the proper manner when you meet," he assured her. "Meanwhile, let me introduce you to Miguel."

A large, shining Mercedes-Benz stood at the end of the row of cars, a little way apart from the others, and he led her towards it. A chauffeur in an immaculate uniform got out from behind the wheel as soon as he saw them and saluted.

"I've brought your passenger, Miguel," Andrew said. "This is Miss Lambert. You will drive her carefully back to the Casa."

"Si! Si, Doctor!" Miguel regarded him with brown, adoring eyes. "I will go most carefully. I have my instructions from the *dueño* to drive slowly."

He grinned, and Jane found herself smiling into the friendly brown eyes. Grace had often mentioned Miguel in her letters with the suggestion that he had been a tower of strength to her. His grasp of English was excellent and she felt that he might be a great help to her in the weeks to come.

"It appears that Felipe has been too busy to meet me, after all," she turned to say to Andrew Ballantyne, trying to hide the immensity of her disappointment. "Can we offer you a lift to Orotava?"

"It would be out of your way." He deliberately avoided Miguel's direct look. "The road forks some considerable distance from Orotava and your brother-in-law would see the plane coming over. He'll expect you to be punctual."

"It would only take five minutes or so," she asserted.

He smiled down at her.

"Half an hour, to be exact. You mustn't keep the Marqués waiting that long. Besides, I'm already met."

His gaze went beyond her, and Jane turned to see a bulky figure hurrying towards them.

"Ach, my friend, so you are back!" The newcomer embraced the young doctor warmly. "It did not take you too long to complete your business in Madrid, but why is it that you have not taken a holiday? I could have managed on my own behalf till your return."

"All the same, you expected me, you old war-horse!" Andrew pointed out. "Otherwise you wouldn't have taken time off to meet the plane." He turned to Jane. "This is my partner, Doctor Baer. Hans didn't really mean me to take that holiday. He's up to his eyes in work." He put an arm affectionately around the older man's shoulders. "Miss Lambert is on her way to the Casa del Sol. She hopes to stay there."

The odd phraseology of the last remark made Jane look up at him with a quick frown, but he was looking steadily at his colleague and did not seem to notice her annoyance. The squat little German doctor took her hand, bowing over it with an elaborate Latin gesture which seemed utterly foreign in him.

"I am pleased to make the acquaintance of Miss Lambert," he acknowledged. "I hear you are come to look after the children."

Janet hesitated, slightly nonplussed by this unexpected announcement.

"I — haven't made up my mind yet," she said. "I did want to come out right away, when Grace died, but my mother was seriously ill at the time. I had to wait."

"Of course," Hans Baer agreed hastily. "I am so stupid, not understanding so well the English language." He gave her a friendly smile. "But I have an English garden," he added eagerly. I grow roses and many English flowers."

His voice had swelled with pride as he offered her the information and his square, deeply-lined face was wreathed in smiles.

"I'd like to see your garden," Jane told him to his obvious delight. "Perhaps I can pay you a visit quite soon?".

Andrew Ballantyne turned away.

"I would be happy to show you my flowers," the German doctor said. "Our clinic is a very small one. It is down in the *puerto* — very poor, but very busy." Again that swelling note of something was surely more than pride deepened the friendly voice. "Yes, you must indeed come and see!"

219

He moved towards the shabbiest car on the parking lot. Andrew Ballantyne had already opened the near-side door.

"Miguel is impatient to be off," he observed, nodding towards the immaculate Mercedes. "We'll let you go on ahead. It will save you passing us on the road."

It almost seemed to Jane as if he sought to emphasize the difference in their respective conveyances, pointing out to her that their worlds lay very far apart.

Miguel ushered her into the Mercedes, spreading a fur-lined rug across her knees. Up here on the plateau the wind was chilly, blowing down from the waste of rugged mountains between them and El Teide.

"Cool!" Miguel suggested, hunching his thin shoulders. "I turn on the heater for you?"

"Oh, no!" Jane protested, disappointing him. "It isn't as cold as all that, thanks. It's very much like an English summer."

He smiled, not fully understanding her meaning, as he got back behind the wheel. They passed the two doctors just inside the gates. Andrew Ballantyne was driving. The ancient car seemed to be a joint possession and looked thoroughly unreliable.

"Hasn't Doctor Ballantyne got a car of his own?" she asked Miguel from the back seat of the Mercedes.

The young Spaniard shrugged expressively, half turning his head to flash her a smile.

"Too poor," he said. "All his money is spent in the clinic. When he works on the estate my master gives him a car."

"But not always," Jane mused. "How inconvenient for a doctor."

"If he is wanted I fetch him," Miguel said with pride. "I am excellent chauffeur."

"I'm sure you are," Jane murmured, not too fully convinced as they began to negotiate a series of hairpin bends at an incredible speed. "Aren't you afraid of meeting another car on one of these awful corners, Miguel?"

He laughed uproariously.

"No— not afraid," he assured her. "There is much visibility everywhere."

He nodded towards the vast panorama of open country all about them, to the bleak, scarred hills and the winding road dropping down through the terraces to a blue and distant sea. The deciduous forest, now behind them, had given place to cultivated land thickly planted with gnarled old fig trees and the spreading almond. The rich red volcanic soil had been terraced all the way to the coast to conserve the water when the rains came, and every now and then they passed lofty, barn-like sorting sheds where the ripening tomatoes were being crated on the first stage of their journey to Europe.

Great gourds and pomegranates lay stacked by the roadside, adding their vivid quota to the colourful scene, and shy, dark-skinned peasant women saluted them as they passed. The women appeared to be the workers, carrying the heaviest loads on their heads or their backs. The men were the supervisors or merely the loungers.

These small, thick-set peasants were new to her, and she found herself contrasting them with Felipe's arrogant slimness. He was the true Spaniard, of course, and justly proud of his lineage. Her heart began to beat a little faster at the thought of him.

Soon the banana plantations of the lower slopes lay before them like a green, billowing sea, mile after undulating mile, stretching as far as the eye could penetrate. Grace had said that much of Felipe's wealth came from bananas.

Miguel negotiated yet another perilous bend, pointing downwards as he turned to speak to her.

"La Orotava — and the *puerto*!" he announced.

Far beneath them a row of dazzling white buildings stood at the water's edge with a tiny pink-washed chapel clinging to the rock above them.

"The new hotels," Miguel explained proudly. "Very smart!"

But Jane's gaze had passed beyond the vast white palaces of modern tourism to the tiny harbour enclosed within its rock wall where the native fishing boats bobbed idly in the sunshine. From her vantage point high on the winding road the tiny craft looked like toys resting on a sea of glass and the palm-fringed *plaza* was no more than a pocket handkerchief of space between the pastel-washed houses straggling up the hill. It was like all the lovely paintings she had ever seen and now it was here, in reality.

"We do not go down," Miguel informed her, gathering speed once more. "We go on."

A signpost said "Orotava" and they turned away from it. Jane looked behind them for the doctors' car, but could see nothing beyond their own cloud of dust spreading out behind them in the still air. The wind which had made the plateau cool had died at the tree line, leaving the heavy banana fronds to hang limply in the dry air.

So many bananas, she thought. Can they really all be marketable?

The road they followed was narrower than the main highway and deeply rutted in places, although it appeared to be well used. They passed lorries heavily laden with crated fruit or the vivid green foliage of the banana.

"All from the Casa," Miguel informed her. "On their way to Santa Cruz!"

The magnitude of Felipe's inheritance was only just beginning to manifest itself, Jane realized. Grace had been far too modest about her husband's possessions when she had written that they were "comfortably off", and once more the suggestion of restraint which had seeped through to them at home in London disconcerted Jane. It was as if Grace had stumbled upon something she could not quite understand, and now it would be something that Jane would have to work out for herself. Grace had never offered her any confidences to guide her now. Jane drew a deep breath and looked straight ahead.

The sun was slanting towards the western horizon when Miguel slowed the car at the arched entrance to a large estate. For several miles back the road had wound in the shadow of a high wall with a single file of giant eucalyptus trees on its other side. Trees and wall had made a cool avenue of shade right up to the archway where two stout wooden gates were flung open at their approach. A peasant woman bowed in feudal salutation as the car swept through.

It irked Jane to see the old woman bent almost double as they passed, but the incident was almost instantly forgotten as she looked about her at the terraced gardens of the Casa del Sol. Their beauty was breathtaking. They dropped like an enchanted staircase to a distant valley fringed on two sides by the native Canary palm and they were ablaze with flowers, red and yellow and white and blue, tumbling over walls, spilling out of urns, climbing and cascading over trellises in such a profusion of bloom that it looked like a rambling sea of colour running down to the incredible blue of the ocean hundreds of feet below.

Jane's breath caught in her throat. So this had been Grace's home! How happy she must have been; how reluctantly she must have parted with it all!

Tears blurred her eyes for a moment as she took in the scene. How cruel death could be when he came to claim the young!

Miguel brought the car to a halt in the paved courtyard at the side of the house. They had approached the house from the back, and she suddenly realized that all the windows above the *patio* looked out towards El Teide, that aloof, reproving mountain peak whose august presence dominated the entire island.

Storms would rage around El Teide and sunshine flatter him, and somehow she knew that their lives would take their tempo from the moods of their resident giant.

"Here is Sisa to show you to your room," Miguel said. "Her English is not yet so good as mine, but she is quick to learn. I teach her," he added with some satisfaction, "when I have time."

Sisa dropped Jane a neat curtsey while her dark eyes remained admiringly on Miguel's handsome face.

"Come," she said. "I take you to your room."

Jane got out of the car feeling suddenly chilled and cold. Why wasn't Felipe there to greet her? And where were the children?

From somewhere in the interior of the house came a sudden burst of childish laughter — a boy's laughter, she imagined — followed by the prim chiding of a young girl. Impulsively she moved across the tiled floor of the *patio*.

"I'd like to meet my niece and nephew straight away," she said, turning back to Sisa.

224

"They are not to be disturbed." Sisa looked apologetic.

"You may go on ahead, Sisa."

Startled by the unexpected remark, Jane turned to find herself face to face with a tall, dark young woman who bore a striking resemblance to the younger Felipe. Her mouth felt curiously parched as she met the quizzical brown eyes. Felipe's sister? Or a cousin, perhaps, with close demands on the Casa del Sol?

"I'm Jane Lambert," she announced unnecessarily. "I — expected Felipe to meet me."

The tall woman's smile was hardly mirthful.

"You must not expect too much, Miss Lambert," she said quietly. "We are busy people at the Casa del Sol. My brother has not yet recovered from his — grief at your sister's death. You could hardly expect him, in the circumstances, to rush to meet you with open arms."

Jane stood back, aghast.

"But he *asked* me to come!" she protested.

"Indeed, yes. Felipe has a reason for all he does and a tremendous sense of family responsibility." The dark eyes under their finely-pencilled brows held a smouldering hostility. "He sent for me when it seemed that you could not come immediately. I am his sister, Teresa Lucientas de Pardo."

Teresa! How often Grace had mentioned her beautiful sister-in-law and her brilliant wedding in Madrid. Her first letters home had been full of it, and then, six months later, had come the news of Teresa's widowhood. Her husband had died in a car crash and Teresa had gone back home.

And now she was here, sent for by Felipe, running his household, no doubt, far more efficiently than Jane

could ever have done in those first tragic months of his
bereavement.

"I couldn't leave England when Grace died," she
tried to explain. "I knew Felipe needed someone, but
my mother was dangerously ill. She died six weeks
ago."

There was no reflection of sympathy in the brown
eyes gazing relentlessly back at her.

"Didn't it occur to you then," Teresa said coldly,
"that you would hardly be needed now?"

Jane looked nonplussed.

"It didn't," she confessed, her own voice hardening
a little. "When I wrote to say I could come Felipe put
no obstacles in my way."

Teresa smiled almost pityingly as she turned away.

"As a Spaniard and a gentleman," she asked, "how
could he? He had invited you once. He could not very
well refuse you when you eventually decided to come.
Besides" — the brown eyes narrowed — "you were
left rather dependent, weren't you?"

A wave of angry colour ran up into Jane's cheeks.

"Not really," she answered. "I could have got a job
in my own profession anywhere."

"Ah, yes," Teresa remembered. "You are a nurse.
Such an exacting profession, isn't it?"

"But not unrewarding." Jane glanced towards the
staircase where Sisa was still hovering. "Perhaps I
should go up and change before Felipe comes in," she
suggested.

Teresa arched her dark brows in amusement.

"You have plenty of time," she announced. "Felipe
will not return before tomorrow. He has flown across to
Las Palmas on business."

Jane halted on her way across the hall. Her back was
turned towards Teresa now, but she was still aware of

that dark, hostile stare and the red lips twisted into a tormenting smile. Teresa did not want her here at the Casa del Sol, and Felipe had made it easy for his sister by absenting himself on business.

Was it true, then, that he had acted only out of courtesy when she had written to him and asked if she might come?

She walked slowly towards the stairs. They were cool and broad and uncarpeted, their marbled spiral stretching up to a railed gallery overlooking the hall. When she gripped the iron handrail it felt as cold as ice, and some of its chill drove deeply into her heart.

She was probably over-sensitive, but she could not help herself. "I wish you were more like Grace," her mother had said often enough, but their two natures had been poles apart. Grace had known what she wanted from life and had seized it with both hands, irrespective of any other consideration.

"I'm not blaming her, Jane thought. I'm not really blaming her. She had it for so short a time.

Sisa was waiting at the head of the stairs. She led the way along the gallery and up a short flight of steps to a group of rooms which appeared to be quite apart from the rest of the house.

"The nursery wing," the Spanish girl informed her with a broad smile. "You have your accommodation here."

She opened the nearest door to reveal a sunny apartment facing the mountains and the snow-capped grandeur of El Teide. It was late afternoon and the venetian blinds had been pulled up to reveal the peak and the vast panorama of the banana fields sweeping down to the sea. Nearer at hand, the shadows were already stealing across the garden, throwing the dark silhouette of palms across the pale mosaic of the *patio*.

Eagerly Jane crossed to one of the long windows leading on to a narrow, railed balcony, allowing the beauty of her new surroundings to sweep aside all other impressions.

Beneath her lay a fairyland of flowers, and the clear, clean mountain air met her like a caress. Pale lilies gleamed in the shelter of a hibiscus hedge and roses and geraniums and star-clusters of stephanotis offered up their scent to her on a sudden, truant breeze. If there had been no warmth of welcome in the hall below, Felipe's lovely garden gave her welcome enough. It was the most restful-looking place she had ever seen with its cool fountains and flower-filled *arriates* edging the many pathways leading to its high surrounding wall. Archways and marble urns stood in the half-light festooned by trailing bougainvillea, and over it all lay a contented silence.

Grace had helped to plan the garden in the first few years of her marriage, and suddenly Jane's eyes filled with tears. Grace must have known peace in this lovely place, in spite of their uncertainty. The whole garden breathed of it.

Miguel brought up her luggage, depositing it just inside the door.

"Sisa will unpack," he announced.

Jane moved away from the window.

"There's no need," she began. "I haven't a lot of luggage."

"No more to come?" Miguel looked surprised.

"No."

Both Sisa and Miguel looked at her in some perplexity.

"I left most of my belongings in London," Jane explained. "What I was allowed to bring by air will do me for the time I'm here."

"But you were to stay," Miguel protested. "You were to make this your home."

"*Si! Si!*" Sisa faltered. "To stay!"

Rather abruptly Jane turned her back on the distressed servants.

"At least I shall be here for a few weeks," she said.

Miguel withdrew, and Sisa gave her attention to the two suitcases, which she unpacked with a natural dexterity. Jane's dresses were slipped on to hangers and shut away in the big, heavily-carved wardrobe which occupied most of the space along one wall, and her underwear was folded, layered in tissue-paper, in a drawer of the brass-bound chest between the windows.

The room was furnished in the heavy old Spanish style of a century ago, with a big canopied bed and scattered rugs on a bare parquet floor. The walls were washed white and hung with gilt-framed paintings, mostly of the peak and the surrounding countryside. There was one between the windows entitled *Las Cañadas*, which looked like an artist's impression of Dante's Inferno, all red rock pinnacles and molten lava-flows, bleak and soulless and forlorn.

Jane turned from her contemplation of it with the same feeling of chill as she had experienced in the hallway.

"Las Cañadas!" Sisa smiled. "Up there." She pointed towards the distant peak. "Señor Travers — he painted it one — two years ago."

" 'Travers'?" Jane repeated. "Is he English?"

"*Si!*" Sisa's eyes met hers with an amused twinkle in their dark depths. "He live with the English lady down at Orotava. He gives painting lessons to the *señorita*."

"To Rozanne?"

"*Si!*"

Jane moved away from the picture to look out of the window again.

"Sisa, when do the children come up here?" she asked. "Do they have afternoon tea in the English manner?"

Sisa's eyes lit up with delight.

"Si! Si! I go prepare tea — in the English manner," she offered.

Before Jane could stay her she rushed off, obviously delighted to be given such a congenial task, and Jane was left to wonder if Teresa would join them over the conventional English meal.

Probably not, but at least the children would be there. She could hardly wait to meet Rozanne and the younger Chris, whose uninhibited laughter she was sure she had heard in another part of the house.

Trying to keep her thoughts from drifting to Felipe, she waited for the children to come to her. It was Sisa, however, who appeared first. Struggling under the weight of a huge mahogany tea-tray, she pushed open the door with one broad shoulder.

"I take the tea to the little parlour," she announced. "You come there?"

Jane followed obediently out along a wide stone corridor where heavy chests stood sentinel between the dark carved doors to the last door of all, where Sisa paused. She nodded to Jane to precede her.

The room they entered was an English sitting-room — Grace's room — something her sister had brought from England to remind her of home. It tugged at Jane's heart-strings as nothing else could have done, and she stood for a moment looking at the apple-green walls and the rose chintz covers on the chairs without speaking. There was even a fire, newly lit, in the open grate.

"Sisa, you shouldn't have done this——" she began.

The Spanish girl placed the tray on a table pulled up to the hearth.

"I like to please you," she smiled. "It was this way when the Marquesa was alive."

She turned expectantly as the door opened behind them, and Jane swung round to meet her niece and nephew for the first time.

Only one child stood attentively in the doorway, however. Christopher was small for his age, with his mother's clear white skin and blue eyes. He had Grace's fair hair, too, and her frank, uninhibited smile, but his manner was his father's. He came forward with the same half-languid arrogance which Jane remembered in Felipe, offering her a small, carefully-scrubbed hand in greeting.

"You are my aunt from England," he said in the clear, precise manner of one speaking in a foreign language. "My father said to welcome you to your new home."

Jane could not help smiling at the stiff little speech, convinced that he was far too young to be so conventional.

"Chris!" She held out both hands. "I hope you have a kiss for me as well as a pretty speech."

The child regarded her uncertainly for a moment before the solemnity evaporated and the blue eyes crinkled in laughter. It was her hand, however, that he kissed, making a pretty little ceremony of it, as his father would have done.

Jane sat down on the chintz-covered settee.

"When Rozanne comes we'll have some tea," she suggested with a quick glance towards the door.

Her small nephew sat down beside her.

"Rozanne will not come," he announced. "She doesn't like strange people."

Jane felt taken aback.

"But, Chris," she pointed out, I'm not a stranger. I'm your Aunt Jane. I've come all the way from England to see you."

He regarded her pensively for a moment.

"You didn't come when you were needed," he said in the odd, blunt manner of a very young child repeating something he has overheard.

"No," Jane agreed to avoid argument. "But I'm here now, Chris, and I would like us all to be friends. Where is Rozanne?"

He shrugged his thin shoulders in a gesture so typical of Felipe that Jane's susceptible heart was instantly flooded in a tide of bitter-sweet memories.

"She went to her own room," he said indifferently.

"Then perhaps we ought to let her know that tea is ready," Jane suggested firmly.

Chris sat where he was, eyeing the tea-tray.

"Send Sisa," he said, but Sisa had gone.

They had reached some sort of impasse, Jane realized, wondering why her small niece had chosen to snub her in this way.

"If you tell me where her room is," she suggested, I'll go along and fetch her."

Her nephew looked surprised. Instead of answering her, he rose reluctantly to his feet to tug at an ancient bell-pull by the side of the fireplace. When Sisa reappeared in answer to his summons he spoke to her in rapid Spanish with a haughty inflection in his voice which was almost ludicrous in one so young. Sisa vanished with an indignant swish of her petticoats.

They waited in silence, staring into the fire. It was difficult to make contact with a sophisticated four-year-

232

old who issued autocratic orders to his father's servants in two languages and dismissed his sister's moods with an impatient shrug of the shoulders. His mannerisms were Felipe's, in a way, and it was a sobering thought for Jane that Felipe also might have dismissed his daughter's moods with the same indifference.

Her heart beating a little faster, she wondered what Rozanne was really like. Chris could be endured, but she wanted to love Rozanne.

Then minutes went by, and Chris, grown restless, lay full length on the hearthrug, kicking his heels, his adult dignity abandoned in the face of hunger and impatience.

"Why doesn't she come?" he demanded. "Why don't we begin without her?"

This Jane could deal with. He was a little boy again.

"We'll give her one more minute, Chris," she decided. "Then we shall begin."

Chris turned his head sharply.

"She is here," he said.

Jane swung round on the settee, looking over its high back at the small figure in the open doorway.

Everything about Rozanne was dark, from the severe grey flannel dress she wore to the black frown pencilled between her finely-shaped brows. Her sleek black hair was held in place by a wide bandeau which drew it severely back from her small, heart-shaped face, and the red mouth was sullen. The child's hands were clasped in a defiant attitude behind her back which seemed to say: "Well, here I am. You sent for me. What do you want?"

Jane said: "We're having tea, Rozanne. Please join us. I've had a very thirsty journey!"

"Sisa should have brought you wine." Rozanne's

voice was edged with nervousness. "We don't drink tea any more in the afternoon."

Chris turned over, hiding his face in the soft fur rug. Jane bit her lip. She had made a mistake, ordering an English tea, reminding them vividly of their mother.

"I'm sorry," she apologized. "I didn't know. Sisa should have told me."

Rozanne watched her from the doorway as she crossed towards the tray.

"But there's no need to waste all this lovely food," Jane decided firmly. "We'll have it together, just this once, shall we? Then I can take it alone afterwards, if I really want it."

Chris sat up, examining the cakes, but Rozanne turned her back.

"I don't want any tea. I don't like it," she cried in a surprising falsetto which only served to accentuate her uncertainty. "I hated it! I always hated it — when *she* was here!"

Turning, she fled from the room. Chris's lower lip trembled.

"Chris, would you mind closing the door?" Jane said, giving him something to do. "Shall I pour you some very weak tea?"

He nodded, swallowing his tears. Felipe was trying to make a man of him too quickly, Jane decided.

Chris had a quicksilver temperament, however, and under the mellowing influence of milky tea and chocolate eclairs he was soon himself again. His smile, when he was relaxed, released two dancing elves in his eyes and a dimple in each cheek.

"Tell me about the Casa, Chris," Jane was saying when the door opened for a second time.

"I hear you have ordered tea, Miss Lambert." Teresa's voice, sternly reprimanding, sounded close behind her. "It isn't our custom here to take a meal at this time of day. The children aren't used to it. It was an inconvenience to the servants in your sister's time, so I do not think we will repeat it now."

Remembering Sisa's eagerness to produce the tea-tray, Jane was about to protest when she thought how obvious it was that she would get the young Spanish girl into trouble.

"I'm sorry," she apologized once more. "I asked for the tea, of course. I won't do it again, although——"

"Although, Miss Lambert?" Teresa questioned.

"I was going to say, although my sister must have established the custom fairly definitely, in her time."

"My brother never approved of it," Teresa informed her stiffly. "His household is a truly Spanish one, Miss Lambert."

"Please, couldn't you call me Jane? I didn't mean to start off on the wrong foot, you know. It just seemed natural to ask for tea." Jane forced a smile, already regretting the swiftness of her own retort. "While in Rome', I suppose! I must cultivate a taste for wine. I believe your local wine is delicious."

"Malmsey may be an acquired taste," Teresa said discouragingly. "Your sister never cared for it, I understand."

And Grace wouldn't conform, Jane thought, wondering if there had been a sort of undeclared war between Felipe's sister and his wife.

Chris moved restlessly towards the far end of the room.

"You will have difficulty with the children," Teresa mentioned in a subdued undertone. "Neither of them takes too kindly to strangers." She seemed to use the word deliberately.

235

"I felt I was doing quite well with Chris," Jane said, meeting the dark eyes fully. "It was Rozanne who seemed — difficult."

Teresa shrugged.

"Nobody troubles about Rozanne," she answered. "Her moods are unpredictable. We have long since learned to disregard them. It is unimportant in a girl."

"A child of Rozanne's age shouldn't have moods," Jane countered, a little too quickly. "She's not quite six, is she?"

"If you mean that she should have been scolded out of them long ago, I entirely agree with you," Teresa said. "But the fact is that Rozanne has been left very much to her own devices. My brother was greatly disappointed at her birth. Naturally, he hoped for a son. Your sister must have been equally distressed. She probably felt herself inadequate, failing in her duty to an ancient name."

"But isn't that ridiculous?" Jane protested. "Grace loved her children."

"She worshipped her son," Teresa corrected her softly. "Christopher's birth put everything right for her. She came to consider Rozanne no more than an unfortunate mistake on nature's part."

"I — just refuse to believe that," Jane declared. "I know how fond Felipe and Grace were of each other. They were deeply in love when they married. Nothing could have altered that."

Teresa lit a cigarette, offering her case to Jane almost as an afterthought.

"How long does love really last?" she asked. "The kind of love you mean. Your sister got what she wanted, and Felipe felt that she ought to be contented with her bargain."

"Bargain surely isn't the right word to use," Jane cried, angered by the underlying innuendo. "Marriage is a partnership. My sister would put all she had into it."

Teresa tapped the ash from her cigarette into the jade bowl on the tea-table.

"Grace was a cold person," she said. "Utterly unsuited to my brother's needs. One would hardly label her a gold-digger, but she was extremely selfish in all her demands, excepting, perhaps, where Christopher was concerned. For her son nothing was too good, no sacrifice too great to make. That was how she died, you know," she added. "She was expecting another child and she took Christopher and Rozanne to the *playa* one afternoon, with Sisa to help look after them, of course. It was a comparatively safe beach, but somehow the children got out of their depths. Rozanne was supposed to be watching Christopher, but she allowed him to swim wherever he pleased."

Theresa paused, as if she had reached the crucial point in her narrative, and Jane waited for her to continue with an odd numbness in her heart.

"Grace saw them when Christopher was about to be swept out beyond the breakers," Teresa continued almost languidly. "And Rozanne seemed to be doing nothing about saving him."

"She was only a child!" Jane protested in defence of Rozanne.

"Nevertheless, she was a strong swimmer. She could have gone to her brother's assistance," Teresa insisted, "at least till someone got there."

"She probably lost her nerve," Jane suggested, feeling suddenly cold in spite of the log fire. "She must have been terrified."

"She swam away," Teresa said distantly. "The doctor believed she panicked."

"Doctor Ballantyne?"

Teresa's eyes sharpened.

"You know him?"

"We travelled over on the same plane."

"But Andrew went to Madrid — on business."

"He joined the plane at Lisbon."

"Were you seated together?"

"Yes." Jane felt as if she were undergoing some sort of inquisition. "He was met at La Laguna by Doctor Baer."

"Andrew is a fool," Teresa declared, scowling. "He could have done much better for himself than a back-water practice in partnership with a German fanatic."

"I rather liked what I saw of Doctor Baer," Jane said defensively. "He appears to be absorbed in his clinical work."

"Women have had babies for centuries without the pampering Hans Baer wants to give them," Teresa sneered. "He says they don't die so often in childbed nowadays, but these are just statistics. Andrew and he are obsessed by the Rhesus factor at the moment. They consider more ought to be done about it in the Islands as a whole and it would be nice to start in their own clinic. They appear to think of very little else."

"Was — Doctor Ballantyne there at the time of my sister's accident?" Jane asked, as if she had been compelled to put the question by some force stronger than curiosity.

"He came on the scene after Grace had swum out to the children," Teresa said. "I think they had some sort of rendezvous. Andrew often went to the *playa* when your sister was there," she added pointedly. "The

238

children were fond of him and, of course, he and Grace were both English."

"I see."

Jane turned her back. She did not want to hear any more. Somehow, she did not want to hear about her sister's death from this harsh, enigmatical woman whom she knew would hate as deeply and fanatically as she would love.

Teresa, however, seemed determined to pursue her narrative to its conclusion.

"Grace struck herself against a submerged rock when she had almost reached the shore. She clung on to Christopher, however, and brought him safely on to the beach, where she collapsed. Sisa had gone back to the car for the picnic basket and when she returned Rozanne was lying beside her mother, screaming. I don't think Grace ever forgave her for swimming away. Andrew must have come on the scene then," she added, "for he got them all back here within half an hour. But the damage was already done. There was extensive hæmorrhage, and Grace lost the child—another son. Andrew could do nothing about it. He struggled for forty-eight hours, night and day, without respite, but pneumonia eventually set in and that was the end."

If Teresa had shrugged her indifference Jane would have felt like killing her. The whole tragic incident had been retailed without emotion. It almost seemed as if Teresa was glad that Grace had died.

"Nothing could have been done, I suppose," she murmured in a shaken voice. "Another opinion?"

Teresa stubbed out her cigarette.

"Andrew was more than acceptable to Grace," she said. "And to Felipe, too, at that time."

Slowly, deliberately she had underlined the last three words, her voice dropping at the end of the sentence until it was almost inaudible. Jane drew in a deep breath.

"I can't imagine what you're trying to suggest," she said, "but if it's anything detrimental to my sister's memory I must tell you quite plainly that I resent it. Grace wasn't the kind of person to have illicit love affairs once she was married to your brother."

Teresa crossed to the door.

"You didn't know her very well, did you?" she said. "And she did manage to whisk Felipe from under your nose seven years ago."

Jane stood aghast, staring at the heavily-panelled door which her tormentor had closed softly behind her. How did Teresa know all this? Who had told her about events which had happened in England so long ago? Somehow, Jane did not believe that it could have been Grace.

Felipe, then? Had Felipe realized that she was in love with him all these long years ago, and had he told his sister so now?

It was something Jane could not believe, even though she knew the ties of Spanish family life to be so strong.

It could, of course, have been a shot in the dark on Teresa's part. But what did Teresa mean to do with the knowledge now that it was in her possession?

Her cheeks burning with mortification, Jane glanced across the room to where her small nephew lay on his side contemplating the shaky edifice he had built from a heap af garishly-coloured plastic blocks. Chris lay gazing at his handiwork for a moment longer, and then he swept the uncertain castle to the floor with one petulantly directed blow. The blocks scattered and rolled to Jane's feet as he turned over on to his back.

"I want a pony!" he declared, battering his heels against the parquet floor. "They said I could! They said so!"

Jane began to pick up the discarded blocks.

"If it was a promise—if your father said you could have one—I'm sure you shall," she assured him. "You must be patient, Chris."

He looked up at her with wide blue eyes.

"*She* said I could have it. *She* promised." The great eyes filled with tears. "Why did she go away? Doctor Ballantyne took her away!"

"No, Chris!" Jane caught him to her, cradling his fair head against her shoulder while her throat felt hard and taut with unshed tears. "She had to go. Someone else wanted her——"

Behind them the door opened. She knew that Rozanne was standing there.

"She's dead," Rozanne said. "She's never coming back. You've lost her for ever!"

"Come away, you hateful child!" It was Teresa's voice from the corridor outside. "Your father shall hear of this, I promise you, just as soon as he returns!"

"No—please!" Jane got to her feet to confront the two angry figures silhouetted in the doorway as Chris wriggled from her embrace. "It was my fault. I—must have upset Chris."

"That can be an unforgivable sin." Teresa's tone was scathing. "Go to your rooms, children," she commanded. "Sisa is waiting for you."

Chris hung back.

"Your father will not return tonight," Teresa told him with a hint of satisfaction in her strong voice. "Do as I say, Christopher!"

He passed her with a quick, defiant look.

"And you, my young madam, will go to bed without your supper," Teresa added to the waiting Rozanne. "Remember that I am in charge here while your father is away."

The voice of authority brought a dark scowl to Rozanne's brow and sent a high, resentful flush into her cheeks, but she turned without apparent protest, rushing silently away. Teresa closed the door between herself and Jane for the second time without speaking.

CHAPTER TWO

HER first evening at the Casa del Sol was the longest Jane could remember.

When the swift tropical darkness fell across the banana fields and the last opalescent gleam had faded from the western horizon the house and garden seemed to be surrounded by a dense barrier of silence. They were completely isolated, of course, shut away from the outside world by the high terracotta wall and the undulating sea of the plantations.

After the children had gone to bed her supper was brought to her on a tray. Teresa didn't seem to want her company. In a way, Jane was glad. Teresa was difficult to understand. She made no effort at friendliness and even with the children she was the complete autocrat. Jane did not want to think too deeply about Teresa or her position at the Casa del Sol.

When the tray had been cleared away she ran herself a bath in the pink-tiled bathroom adjoining her bedroom. She had heard Rozanne using it earlier in the evening and supposed that she had to share it with the children. Sisa came with a nightcap of hot wine, but hurried away almost immediately, probably on Teresa's instructions.

Eventually Jane went to bed, having unpacked the remainder of her clothes and tried to write a letter home to the theatre sister at St. Ursula's, where she had trained. Her nursing days seemed so far away now as to seem almost unreal, yet she had been entirely happy in her work and missed it a great deal.

She slept because she was tired, but her oblivion was punctuated by strange, nightmarish impressions of flight, of running endlessly towards some distant, unattainable goal; of stumbling in dark places with the hot breath of her pursuer on the nape of her neck; of ecstasy turned to grief; of disaster and, finally, of death.

Once, vividly, she saw the face of her pursuer, and it was Felipe, but Felipe as she had never known him —ruthless, strange and coldly intent on some strange purpose which she could not understand. When she attempted to question him he turned from her, running in the opposite direction. Then, stumbling beside her, she recognized Andrew Ballantyne with his hands covered in blood.

Shaken and drenched in sweat, she woke to find that her hands were moist with fear. It was a relief to know that it was no more than a dream, a fantastic dream built up out of the impressions of the day before. Her first flight; her disappointment at the airport; her meeting with Doctor Ballantyne and her final encounter with Teresa were all enmeshed in the nightmare of her subconscious thoughts; but dreams passed, and bad ones were no more indicative of the future than the good ones.

Eagerly she rose and ran to the windows, looking out towards the mountains. El Teide, drowsing under his cap of snow, looked gentle and benign. She flung the windows wide open, crossing her balcony to look down into the garden.

Beneath her, in the open *patio,* there was a murmur of voices, but the language was Spanish, spoken largely in the local idiom, so that she could make nothing of what was being said.

The children were having their breakfast when she finally went down. They were seated round a small table at the edge of the *patio,* and some of the argument Jane had first heard was still in progress. There were three servants in attendance—Miguel, Sisa and a darker-skinned elderly woman who kept clasping her hands over her ample bosom and appealing to the Holy Virgin for some boon or other.

"I mean to go!" Rozanne said in English, catching sight of Jane out of the corner of her eye. "I can easily go alone."

"You mustn't go alone," Sisa contradicted her. "I shall have to suffer toothache all day and go with you. You know you are not permitted to go by yourself."

"What is this, Sisa?" Jane asked.

The young Spanish girl turned a woebegone face in her direction.

"It is the *senorita's* painting lesson," she explained, "and I am up all night with a swollen tooth! If I do not go this morning to have it out I must wait one week, and by so long a time I will *die* of pain!"

"What does Dona Teresa say?" Jane was shrewd enough to ask.

"I am to have the tooth out immediately." Sisa's voice quivered.

"Then you must go," Jane decided, "and I must take you for your painting lesson, Rozanne."

The dark eyes on the far side of the table were raised to hers in some surprise. Patently Rozanne did not want her as an escort, but her company was the lesser of two evils. She slid from her chair as Jane took her place at the table.

"I'll go and wash my hands," she suggested.

Chris gazed at Jane with his sober, abstracted stare. His eyes were so blue this morning that they looked like a bright reflection of the cloudless heavens beyond El Teide. Halfway through a plateful of juicy papaya, he had little time for argument, and he seemed resigned to the fact that he would not accompany them to Orotava. He appeared to be waiting eagerly for his father's return. Perhaps there had been a half-promise of the desired pony before Felipe took his leave of him the day before.

Rozanne came back to the *patio* clutching her paint-box.

"We must hurry," she said primly. "It is not good manners to keep Mr. Travers waiting."

The car which had brought Jane from La Laguna was standing on the gravel drive beneath the terrace when they went back through the cool cavern of the hall. There was much more to the house than Jane had already seen, but she supposed her tour of inspection was being reserved for Felipe's return.

She had been terribly disappointed by his absence. She had expected him to be there when she arrived, but it was evidently expecting too much. Business came first with Felipe. She had no real right to assume that he would put it aside in order to meet her, and even less right to hope that he might think of their former friendship with warmth.

"You must tell me about Mr. Travers," she suggested when she had found a hat and taken her place beside Rozanne in the back of the car.

Rozanne stared fixedly at Miguel's broad shoulders for a long time without answering. Her small, rather arrogant face was still sullen and her stubborn chin was thrust out.

"He's an artist," she conceded at last.

"Yes, I know. But what does he teach you? Is it to paint in water-colour, or are you more advanced than that?"

Rozanne gazed straight ahead.

"I am not at all advanced," she said, "but I can learn."

It had been the wrong approach. Jane decided to try again as Miguel steered the car through the main gateway and turned towards the sea.

"You'll have to tell me where we are as we go along," she suggested. "Teneriffe is the loveliest island I've ever seen, Rozanne, and the sea is so full of colour — all these wonderful blues and greens far down there, and the white tops of the waves breaking against the shore. Can I see another island out there — quite a big one?"

"La Palma," Rozanne informed her cryptically.

"I see. Do you ever go there?"

"Once I have been."

There was going to be very little apart from question and answer, Jane realized, and perhaps she was stirring up too many heart-rending memories of Grace.

"Rozanne," she tried once more, "I hope we can become friends."

The child turned slowly round in her seat, fixing her with a wide stare.

246

"No," she said. "I have no friends. I don't need any friends."

"Oh, my dear! Rozanne, we all need friends." Impulsively Jane bent towards the stiff little figure in the expensive blue shantung frock. "We need other people to — share things with. We need them all the time — not only when we are happy and we can be gay together, but when we are unhappy, too."

The dark eyes hardened and the full red mouth grew tight, reminding her of Teresa. Rozanne looked years older than her age in that moment.

"I am happy to paint," she declared. "Sometimes we go to Icod or Garachico, and the Señora Prescott brings a picnic hamper and we have an English tea at the Punta Buenavista."

"It sounds very nice," Jane agreed. "Who is Mrs. Prescott?"

Rozanne considered the question.

"The — person Señor Travers lives with."

Jane smiled.

"Will we meet her this morning?" she asked.

"Yes. She is always there."

Rozanne lost interest in their conversation, and Jane turned her own attention to the scenery as they wound down between the banana plantations. The road still clung high above the shore and the view was superb. The blueness which she was already associating with this paradise among islands stretched for miles and there was no wind to stir the broad, round-topped Canary pines standing sentinel against the sky. Sound came up to them, magnified in the still, clear air, and laden mules plodded conscientiously upwards, passing them on the winding road on their way into the hills. Old men doffed their battered felt hats in salute, pausing in the heat to look after the car as it passed.

Soon they were driving under an avenue of giant eucalyptus trees into Orotava, where Rozanne was to have her painting lesson. The houses straggling down the hillside towards the *puerto* were all brightly colour-washed and festooned with vines, red and blue and white and pink, splashed dramatically against the distant aquamarine of the ocean. At this early hour most of them appeared to be deserted. They had a profoundly withdrawn look, as if they were shrouded in inviolable privacy. Shuttered windows, guarded in iron, gave on to carved wooden balconies clinging high on the warm stucco walls and stout doors put up a barrier against the world. It was a town full of unexpected courtyards and sudden, surprising vistas of lovely, half-hidden gardens, a town of contrasts, of fountains and happy affluence and abject poverty walking side by side.

The car circled the *plaza* and began to climb again. Soon they had left the cobbled streets of the little seaport behind and the alleys and courtyards and back streets were replaced by spacious villas each in its separate garden. Flowers bloomed everywhere in cultivated profusion and the walls surrounding the houses were lower.

Miguel slowed the car, and Rozanne jumped out almost before he had brought it to a halt before a pair of magnificently wrought iron gates. It was the first time Jane had seen the child show any enthusiasm or eagerness.

The drive leading to the villa itself was quite short. It wound through a small orange grove to a wide sweep of terrace where a broad flight of stone steps led up to the main door.

At the head of the steps a tall, lean man in a vividly-printed silk shirt stood waiting for them.

"I saw you coming up the hill," Vincent Travers told Rozanne as she rushed towards him. "You are always on time, *belleza!*"

Rozanne flushed painfully at his praise. The child seemed unable to speak or return the courtesy of this man's charming smile. Mutely she held out one small, white-gloved hand which he carried gallantly to his lips while his amused blue eyes questioned Jane's above the smooth, dark head.

Rozanne had forgotten Jane. There seemed to be nobody on her horizon now but the artist who had given her a secret world of beauty to enjoy.

"It looks as though we'll have to introduce ourselves," he said. "Rozanne is always so eager to begin work that she sometimes forgets her manners. You must be Grace's sister from England. We were expecting you."

It was almost the first welcoming word Jane had heard in the past twenty-four hours, but she was conscious of a sudden reserve as she looked back into Vincent Travers' smiling eyes. They were so full of worldly wisdom, she recognized, but they were also curiously empty.

"I came with Rozanne because Sisa was ill," she explained, getting out of the car to shake hands. "She had a toothache and can only get it out this morning, apparently. Doña Teresa thought she ought to go and have it seen to."

"And Doña Teresa is invariably right." His tone was cynical in the extreme as he gave Teresa her full title. "I'm quite surprised she allowed you to come at all."

Jane glanced towards Rozanne, who was already restless at the delay their conversation was causing.

"There was no need for Rozanne to miss her painting lesson," she answered quickly. "It's apparently the thing she most looks forward to."

"Oh, Rozanne and I understand each other!" The artist's smile was slightly forced.

"Can we begin now?" Rozanne begged, tugging at his hand.

"Don't you think we ought to introduce your Aunt Jane to Mrs. Prescott and the cats first?" Travers suggested lazily. "It won't take a minute."

"If we must." Rozanne was impatient.

Wondering at the artist's easy use of her own Christian name, Jane followed them across the terrace in to the house.

It was an untidy place. The hall was large enough, but it was cluttered with canvases in various stages of completion and overcrowded with furniture. Most of it appeared to be valuable Regency stuff which would have shown to greater advantage without the addition of the canvases, but they were apparently the main preoccupation of the villa's owner. An easel stood on its side near an archway leading to an inner room, and Rozanne eyed it speculatively.

"Are you going to paint, too?" she asked Travers.

The artist shook his head.

"I haven't done a thing for over a week," he confessed. "Not since we painted the little donkey down at the well. I have been very lazy, I'm afraid. Have you brought your water-colours with you?"

Rozanne held out an expensive-looking paint box.

"I'm to have it," she remarked almost aggressively.

Travers gave Jane a quick look.

"It belonged to her mother," he explained. "I also taught your sister to paint."

For a fraction of a second he appeared uncomfortable, but he was soon smiling again. His handsome face under the shock of fair hair falling carelessly across his forehead seemed vaguely familiar to Jane, yet she was quite sure that they had never met until now.

"I feel I must have seen your photograph somewhere," she found herself confessing. "A portrait, perhaps——?"

"I think not," he said a little too quickly. "I haven't been in England for years. I do mean to go back, of course," he added with an odd sort of determination. "What I need at the present moment is a show of my work in one of the London galleries. But that, of course, takes money, and I have no money." He made a small grimace of discontent. "Talent and the hard cash to promote it seldom go together, do they?"

"It would be rather nice if they did," Jane agreed. "But perhaps if life was too easy — if everything came our way just for the asking — some talents might never mature."

"Don't you believe it!" His handsome mouth curved downwards. "All that bilge about starving in an attic being good for the artistic soul is just plain rot. Dozens of competent artists have come out of the Slade and haven't starved at all. They've had to work damned hard, though, trying to make their name. That's the galling part — all this grubbing for money and maybe having to go commercial in order to get it."

Glancing about her at the luxury of his surroundings, Jane felt irritated by the remark. He did not appear to be "grubbing" for anything in his present situation. He seemed to read her thoughts.

"I've been lucky," he acknowledged. "I met a patron of the arts three years ago in London and I've been her guest out here ever since."

"I see." Jane's tone was dry, but it failed to disconcert him. "Do you have many pupils, Mr. Travers?" she asked as he led the way through the arch to a wide *patio* at the rear of the house.

"About half a dozen. Sometimes more, sometimes less. It's easy with the children." He shrugged. "There are fewer complications. The *damiselas* tend to fall in love!"

"You sound hopelessly conceited!" she accused him lightly.

"I speak the truth!"

"Always?"

"To the best of my ability. I don't like flattery."

"You are — very blunt."

"Why not? It leads to understanding. Enigmas irritate me."

"You're part of the English colony, of course?"

He laughed outright.

"Heaven forbid! Even here — here more than anywhere else, I should say — there are outcasts. Most of us are reasonably content to remain on the wrong side of the social fence," he added caustically. "It's often the more interesting side."

"And — Mrs. Prescott?" Jane felt compelled to ask.

"Oh — Daisy? Come and see for yourself," he suggested. "She'll love having you for an hour. She's an inveterate gossip!"

He led the way into the garden where, at this early hour, the trees shed their shade across the pathways and the flowers held their heads up straight. Out here there was none of the confusion which existed inside the villa. All was neat and orderly. Carefully tended rose-beds led to a pergola heavy with Dorothy Perkins, and beyond it the white plume of a fountain rose into the cool, perfumed air. They trod on grass as green and soft as any in England.

"Daisy takes a tremendous pride in her lawns," Travers informed her. "It's her 'little bit of England', although she wouldn't go back to live in 'the dear old country' for all the tea in China. She has more money than she knows what to do with, of course, so she can afford her whims."

They walked a little way in silence because Jane was not quite sure what to say to that.

"Here we are, Daisy!" Travers called out at last. "I've brought you a visitor."

"Oh? Tell Sisa to wait in the *patio*." The voice was light and slightly terse.

"It isn't Sisa," Travers called back into the thick growth of trees at the end of the pergola. "It's Miss Lambert — from England."

"Miss who?"

"Lambert. Grace's sister."

"Oh——! Oh, dear! I'm coming. I'll be with you in a minute."

Before the minute had elapsed an odd figure emerged from the tangle of tropical undergrowth, carrying a large gardening-basket on her arm. Daisy Prescott was a woman in her early fifties who had allowed her body to run to seed without regret or bothering very much about the result. In some ways she looked grotesque, with her rolls of excessive fat and her protruding blue eyes staring at the world from behind their thick spectacles, but there was a kindliness and eagerness in her manner which made Jane warm towards her instantly.

"Daisy! for heaven's sake, what have you been doing?" Travers exclaimed. "You're covered in fungi!"

"I've been gathering figs for your dinner." Daisy thrust her basketful of the luscious red fruit under his

253

nose. "You know you like them gathered first thing in the morning while I'm cutting my flowers." She peered at Jane, gathering up the folds of her outrageous kimono in her free hand. "You're not at all like her," she decided. "Your sister, I mean. Grace was as fair as a lily. All strawberries and cream! Soft, too — soft where that husband of hers was concerned!"

Jane glanced apprehensively to where Rozanne waited at the far end of the pergola.

"She won't hear us," Daisy assured her, following her gaze. "She's a dreamer, that child. Odd! Decidedly odd. Never properly treated, I suppose." Another sharp glance darted in Jane's direction. "Have you come from England to take care of the children?"

"I'm not quite sure," Jane was forced to admit. "I came to see them, of course."

"You should have come in the beginning before Doña Teresa seized her chance," Daisy said bluntly. "Well, off with you, Vincent, and try to earn an honest penny, for once!" She turned to the artist. "Bring the child to the *patio* when her lesson is over," she added. "Miss Lambert and I will have a nice talk till you join us for coffee. Or would Rozanne rather have strawberries and cream?"

"I expect we'd all rather have strawberries and cream," Travers said, half amused, as he walked away.

"He's a rascal, that one!" Daisy remarked in a curiously gentle tone. "But an artist to his fingertips. He'll succeed and make a big name for himself eventually, if he doesn't go and do something rash in the meantime." She led the way back along the grass walk. "Do you know Doctor Ballantyne?"

The question shook Jane because it had been least expected.

"I've met him," she acknowledged. "We flew out from Lisbon on the same plane."

"He's another fool, but in a different way." Daisy was emphatic. "Money doesn't mean anything to him except for that precious clinic of his. Hans and he would willingly starve themselves to death to see it prosper. Did he tell you about it?"

"Not very much," Jane hesitated. "He didn't seem inclined to give me his confidence once he knew where I was going."

"No, of course not!" Daisy agreed. "Felipe employs him and lets him know it. If it wasn't for the Casa del Sol appointment Andrew Ballantyne would be very poor indeed. He wouldn't have a penny to spare for Hans Baer's mad schemes at the clinic, for one thing, but I don't think it would make him return to England. If you ask me," she guessed vaguely, "he was in some sort of trouble at home. He was a clever surgeon, I understand, and men like that just don't throw in the towel for a whim. There isn't the work for him here, for one thing. The Canaries aren't exactly the hub of the universe."

"No," Jane admitted, because she had been wondering about Andrew Ballantyne ever since she had met him. "He'll have his reasons for living here, I'm quite sure."

Daisy said: "Most people have," dismissing the subject because she preferred to gossip about Felipe and the Casa de Sol.

"Tell me about your brother-in-law and that sister of his," she demanded. "You must really look out for Teresa. A vixen couldn't be more sly. You take my word for it! Teresa hated her brother's marriage to Grace, and Felipe's own attitude didn't help."

Jane stiffened. She had no intention of discussing her family affairs with a stranger.

"Felipe has always puzzled me," Daisy ran on, undeterred by her silence. "There's a certain amount of rivalry between us, of course. We both collect like mad — pictures and what-have-you, though Felipe is more interested in precious stones. He has a selection of emeralds up there at the Casa which must be worth a fortune. They would make anyone's mouth water. I used to wonder at first why Grace didn't have them mounted to wear, but afterwards I realized how much she hated them. They were an obsession with Felipe, and I suppose she felt that they had claimed him, body and soul."

Jane drew back, unwilling to hear any more. They had reached the *patio,* and her hostess sank gratefully into one of the long wicker reclining chairs grouped round a low marble-topped table.

"Sit down," she invited, kicking off her shoes, "and tell me all about yourself."

Jane did her best. It was impossible to dislike Daisy Prescott, even though she was such a gossip, and while they spoke of London there could be no harm done. An hour passed almost without Jane noticing.

"Time for our strawberries," Daisy announced, reaching for the large handbell which lay close to her chair. "I toll this when I need any of the servants, and it's handy for recalling Vincent from his daydreams. I'm a lonely person, Miss Lambert," she added almost wistfully, "in spite of my money."

Jane was spared an answer to this by the arrival of a young Spaniard in a white jacket bearing coffee on a silver tray.

"Strawberries, Anselmo," Daisy commanded, ringing her bell again.

This second summons brought Travers and a reluctant Rozanne to the *patio*. Rozanne carried her own canvas, and for the first time since their meeting Jane saw animation in the small, heart-shaped face. Gone was the habitual sullenness with which her niece regarded the world in general, and in it's place was a soft glow of warmth which completely transfigured her. Rozanne looked lovely. She adored Travers, and the artist had brought out the best in her with patience and understanding.

Jane's heart contracted in instant pity, yet she knew that it would be foolish to offer Rozanne her sympathy all at once. The child would shy away like a sensitive colt if she was approached without reserve, but the next few weeks would surely afford her the opportunity she needed.

And Felipe must help her. She was determined about that. However wrapped up in sorrow he might be, he had a duty to his children which he must not be allowed to forget.

When the strawberries and most of the cream were disposed of they took their leave of Daisy. She did not rise from her chair, and Travers was left to accompany them through the villa to the car. Rozanne clung tightly to his hand.

"Will you really, really come to see my picture tomorrow if I work hard and finish it?" she implored. "I'll work all day."

"You do that," Travers encouraged her. "I shall be coming, anyway, to meet your aunt officially."

Jane swung round at the remark.

"What do you mean?" she asked. "Officially?"

"If Felipe has returned in your absence you might find yourself on the mat when you get back to the Casa del Sol," he explained with an underlying harshness in his voice which belied the amused look in his eyes. "Your average Spaniard is a stickler for etiquette, and Felipe only inherited his grand position recently. He'll be — put out, to say the least, when he discovers that you've been acting nursemaid to Rozanne and visiting without his permission."

"But Teresa——"

"Yes," he interrupted quietly, "Teresa told you to come. I know." He held open the door of the car. "I'm sorry for you, Jane," he said, "but I'll come to your reception party tomorrow evening just the same."

Jane continued to look at him, not quite knowing what to say.

"You — knew Grace very well?" she faltered.

"Reasonably well." It was as if a door had closed in his eyes, shutting out the laughter. "I taught her to paint, with her husband's permission."

Jane scarcely remembered Rozanne on the drive back to the Casa. The impressions of the past two hours lay heavily on her mind and her heart seemed to be beating twice as fast as it normally did. Why should two utterly different people seek to warn her about her position at the Casa del Sol? And why had Andrew Ballantyne withdrawn his friendship as soon as he realized who she was?

Suddenly she wondered if Andrew would be at Felipe's "official" reception the following evening. He was the estate doctor and he was English, so there was no reason why he shouldn't be invited. No reason at all, excepting Felipe's unequivocal dislike.

She felt it instinctively, wondering what Andrew had done in the past to invoke it. It could, of course, be mutual.

She was all the more surprised, then, to see them standing side by side on the terrace steps when Miguel turned the car in under the archway and drew up on the gravelled drive in front of the house.

"Felipe!"

The word drifted away from her across the silent garden. He was changed, of course, subtly changed. Grief and the years had etched lines on his face which tore at her heart as she looked at him, but the eyes and the firm handsome mouth were the same. There was the same half-arrogant lift of the head, too, as he came towards her down the few steps which separated them.

"I'm sorry I wasn't here to meet you yesterday, Jane," he apologized in a constrained undertone. "I had business to attend to at Las Palmas which could not be neglected."

"It doesn't matter." Her heart was beating so erratically that she felt sure he must notice her agitation. "You're here now."

The foolishly revealing statement fell into a short silence before Felipe turned to acknowledge Rozanne, and Jane found herself looking up into Andrew Ballantyne's direct grey eyes. They seemed to see so much — too much, she thought uncomfortably — probing deeply into the reason for her being here. The real reason. And suddenly she wanted to assure this man that she had made her journey solely to meet her sister's children, but the doctor's half-mocking regard disarmed her completely.

A dark flush spread slowly across her cheeks. Why should he make her feel like this? Why should he be here at all, at this moment? He had stolen her reunion with Felipe from her, taking away something of its excitement and wonder, and now he stood looking at her as if he had every right to come between them.

She longed to say something which would disconcert him, but could not think of anything strong enough.

I shall always hate him, she thought, for spoiling this meeting for me. It was almost a vow.

Andrew came down the steps to stand beside them. He spoke to Rozanne, but the child darted away with the briefest of answers, clutching her precious water-colour to her breast like a shield.

The doctor made no comment, but Felipe frowned, observingly angrily:

"My daughter has no good manners, I'm afraid. She has been too much alone since her mother's death."

There had been no hint of emotion in his voice, no softening in the dark face turned to watch Rozanne's departure along the terrace. The child had displeased him and probably disappointed him in many ways.

"Give her time," Jane urged impulsively. "She's so very young."

Felipe turned to look at her.

"You were always far too generous, Jane," he said. "I remember how easy it was to win your sympathy when things went wrong."

The dark brown eyes were looking fully into hers at last, and everything else was forgotten. Andrew Ballantyne might never have been there, nor all the years between. Jane was back in that moment when she had first met Felipe and known herself captivated. She had forgotten about Grace and their marriage; she had pushed the memory of wayward Christopher and sullen Rozanne into the background. Even time and convention ceased to matter.

But Felipe was essentially conventional.

"I understand that you have already met Doctor Ballantyne." His quick glance travelled to Andrew and back again to her eager upturned face. "What sort of report has he given you about the Casa del Sol?"

The question had been tinged with suspicion, but Andrew laughed it aside.

"We hadn't much time for reports," he said. "Jane — Miss Lambert was too busy acquiring a general knowledge of the Islands, and I didn't suspect who she was till we were nearing Laguna."

"And then he turned down a lift in your luxurious car in favour of Doctor Baer's battered old convertible!" Jane smiled, realizing almost immediately that she had said the wrong thing.

"Our English doctor has always been fiercely independent," Felipe said, turning back to the terrace. "He rarely comes here, except on business. You must not encourage him to desert his work, Jane, whatever you do."

Once more Jane detected a suggestion of warning in a perfectly ordinary remark. It seemed that Felipe did not expect Andrew Ballantyne to visit them socially.

With a brief salute the doctor moved along the terrace to where he had parked his car.

"I'll make out my report on these fever cases and send it up to you in the morning," he informed Felipe from the driver's seat as he drove past them. "I don't think it's at all serious."

Felipe let him go without answering. He was still frowning when he looked down at Jane.

"You must keep Doctor Ballantyne at arm's length," he said. "I distrust him."

"Oh — surely!" Jane did not know whether to laugh or protest. It all sounded so feudal. "I don't think Andrew Ballantyne's the type who would get over friendly, any way," she added.

Felipe stood rigidly on the top step.

"He was encouraged here once before," he said harshly. "The English doctor had the run of my house. We respected him, accepting him as a friend. My son loved him. I was on the point of pouring money into this ridiculous scheme of his down at the clinic shortly before your sister's death." He paused, his narrowed eyes looking closely into hers. "And then I withdrew my support," he added. "My wife had a lover, Jane. The child she was expecting was not mine, and Andrew Ballantyne was with her when she died. She wanted him with her. I saw them together. He was there that day of the accident, too, at the *playa,* but he was too late to go into the water first. Grace did that, and lost her child and her life. *His* child."

"No!" The word had been driven from between Jane's lips, a dry, strangled sound which did not appear to reach him.

"That sort of retribution isn't enough," he continued slowly. "I am not the man to forget easily. I shall pursue Doctor Ballantyne and punish him for what he did."

"You can't take the law into your own hands!" Jane cried. "It will destroy you, Felipe. You mustn't even try it!"

His eyes looked suddenly remote.

"I shall consider his punishment carefully enough," he decided. "I don't mean to kill Andrew Ballantyne. I shall destroy him in some other way, in my own time."

She stood speechless, gazing at him in the blinding noonday light.

"You can't make me believe it," she said. "Not about Grace. Maybe she was vain and selfish; but she wasn't — like that. She had too much to lose."

262

"When a woman believes herself hopelessly in love," he returned coldly, "she counts everything well lost for the achievement of her desire."

"That's not true!" She faced him squarely. "You know Grace didn't think that way. She loved her children too much. She loved you, Felipe——"

"After her fashion," he agreed, "until the great passion of her life came along."

She put a hand to her forehead, scarcely able to credit that such a scene could be taking place between them so soon after their meeting.

"Are you sure of this?" she beseeched him. "You *must* be sure."

He flung his long length down on one of the cane chairs at the far end of the terrace and rang for drinks.

"Sure? I've lived with it for years — ever since Chris was born," he declared. "I knew then she couldn't stand me, although she would go on living with me 'because of the children'. She told me so, my good, kind little Jane, in so many words. 'Because of the children'. Do you think a man wants that sort of sacrifice from a woman? It was an insult."

"Oh, Felipe — no!" Grace was doing her best — what she considered to be right," Jane protested. "Surely you can see that? She always had an easy time, but it wouldn't be easy for her to live without love. If you wouldn't divorce her — no, I know you couldn't," she rushed on when his eyes flashed their disdain of the word, "and she probably didn't ask. I think Grace would try to keep her part of the bargain as long as she could."

He smiled, catching her by the hand to pull her down into an adjoining chair.

"You don't know the first thing about a person like Grace," he declared. "She may have been your sister, but you were poles apart. I realized that a little too late, didn't I?"

"No, Felipe!" Desperately she tried to release her hand. "You and Grace were so sure. I didn't matter to you in the least, once you had met her. There was nothing between you and me — ever."

"No," he mused quietly. "Nothing."

Miguel came with the drinks, cooling guava juice laced with lime and ice. It was too early for wine.

"You'll stay here, Jane?" Felipe said when they were alone again. "You'll help to look after Chris?"

"If I can," she answered, vaguely surprised because he had not mentioned Rozanne. "They're both in need of love and affection."

He looked across the table at her.

"Rozanne? Yes, you will have difficulty with Rozanne," he said.

CHAPTER THREE

JANE saw nothing of Felipe all the next day. He had shown her over the house the afternoon before, and she had marvelled at its beauty, from the long, cool stretch of the dining-room panelled in Canary pine to the salon with its deep lounges and priceless paintings inset in the many alcoves along the walls.

Chris had taken her hand on a personally conducted tour of the nurseries, laying aside his absurd adult dignity to supervise the working of a mechanical cow which could be realistically milked when a suitable liquid was introduced through a hole in its back.

There were a great many toys in the day nursery, all of which appeared to belong to Chris. Even the dolls, which were a motley collection from the comic strips, were his.

"Rozanne doesn't keep her toys here," he volunteered, " 'cos I break things. She has them in her own room. Not much. Just silly girl dolls and pictures."

Poor, hidden Rozanne, Jane thought. I must ask to see her pictures.

Rozanne, however, seemed to be avoiding her. Breakfast was taken on the *patio* each morning, but the children were up and about almost before the sun had topped El Teide, and the *patio* was deserted by the time Jane came down.

Sisa informed her that Doña Teresa had gone to market and the *señoria* was about his business on the estate.

"And Rozanne?" Jane asked.

"She must learn to read and write. The *duenna* comes each morning from Orotava except when the *señorita* is having her painting lesson."

Left to amuse herself, Jane spent the entire morning in the garden, glad of this short time alone in which to adjust her bewildering thoughts. Her meeting with Felipe was something she could not have conjured up in her wildest dreams and the memory of it was like the aftermath of a nightmare.

Even now, after twenty-four hours, it seemed curiously unreal, something she might have imagined. She had gone through all the emotions during a wakeful night — anger, fear, pity, distrust and envy — thinking of the full life which Grace might have led out here on this loveliest of islands, surrounded by every luxury and the love of her husband and family. Why had Grace jeopardised it all for an illicit love affair?

265

The question brought her face to face with the thought of Andrew Ballantyne. The English doctor had looked so square and solid, so utterly reliable, yet love had trapped him, too. If it was out of character for Grace to turn her back on wealth and position, surely someone like Doctor Ballantyne would think twice before he became involved with the wife of his employer?

Yet she really knew nothing about him. Meeting as they had done, they might have been no more than passing strangers. It was an odd, tangled sort of fate which had brought them closer together like this.

Restlessly she paced the shaded pathways, thinking of Grace and her unhappy love. It was all over now — for Grace — but Felipe had confessed to such a thirst for vengeance that it turned her blood cold even to think about it.

The children joined her for lunch and she supervised their *siesta*. There was no sign of either Felipe or Teresa.

At four o'clock the car returned. There was a slamming of doors and Teresa's voice, sharply querulous, as she crossed the terrace and mounted the stairs. For a short time there was silence, except for the parrot-chatter of the servants going about their tasks in the kitchen premises below. Still there was no sign of Felipe's return.

Jane stood at her window, waiting. Now that the sun had travelled over the house the garden beneath her looked cold and full of lurking shadows. The brilliant colours of trailing vines and flamboyant shrubs were suddenly subdued and only the cool white gleam of the lilies stood out clearly, still and flaxen, like death.

Involuntarily she shivered, thrusting the thought aside as she closed the long casement between her and the swiftly approaching night. The sky above the Casa

266

del Sol was still blue and clear, the sun still shone over the banana fields and the sea, but here, in her sister's deserted garden, darkness had come very close. Soon it would descend with the swiftness of a knife-thrust and the warmth of the sun would be gone from the whole landscape.

A peremptory knock on her door made her stiffen involuntarily.

"I didn't invite you to come to Santa Cruz with me," Teresa began, glancing about her critically as she entered the room. "I thought you might want the morning to yourself while the governess was here, and I had quite a lot of shopping to attend to. Felipe believes that we are entirely self-supporting on the estate, but that is not true. Men are completely naïve about housekeeping, I find, although Felipe does appreciate that it is a full-time job. That was the trouble with Grace," she added with a satisfied smile. "She was never able to grasp the intricacies of Spanish household management. I think she disliked it very much."

Jane's lips tightened.

"Lots of people loathe housekeeping but manage fairly well," she pointed out. "My sister was quite intelligent."

Teresa favoured her with a slow smile.

"Was that why Felipe sent for you?" she demanded.

"I don't know what you mean," Jane said, trying to keep her anger in check.

"I mean that quite possibly Felipe wanted a housekeeper and made the initial error of appealing to you," Teresa explained. "When you didn't come right away, he recognized his mistake and sent for me." She came closer, catching Jane by the arm. "I gave up a great deal to come out here," she declared, "and I won't be flung aside like a discarded cloak. Felipe has offered me a home, and I mean to stay."

Jane freed her arm from the thin fingers.

"You and Felipe must make your own arrangements," she said uncomfortably. "It has nothing to do with me."

Teresa was standing between her and the window, with her back towards the light.

"If you expect to marry Felipe you are mistaken," she said. "He will never marry again."

"I didn't come with that idea in mind at all," Jane declared furiously. "Surely you know that, Teresa?"

"I know you were in love with him years ago, before your sister married him," Teresa said. "I know you are still in love with him."

She crossed to the door, closing it gently behind her. Jane stood where she was in the centre of the room, shaken and angry, listening in the stillness to the sound of Felipe's return.

She heard the clatter of his horse's hoofs on the cobbles of the stableyard beyond the garden wall and the bark of a quick order as a groom came running, and then there was the sound of his heavy tread on the terrace beneath her window. He seemed to pause there, but she could not cross the floor to look down. Some of her love seemed to shrivel within her, poisoned by what Teresa had said.

Was she to believe Teresa, who was so obviously bent on preserving her own position at the Casa and safeguarding her future? Her early widowhood had left her without security and she had come back into the family circle. Jane knew sufficient about the Spanish way of life to realize that Teresa would be made welcome, but what she obviously wanted was power. Teresa had seen herself established as the *ama de casa*,

268

the unquestionable mistress of the household and complete arbiter of the fate of its many servants. And now she found Jane standing in her way.

However ludicrous it might seem, Teresa was firmly convinced that Jane was her enemy, and she would use every means in her power to defeat her. There was no room for them both in the Casa del Sol.

I won't be frightened away, Jane thought, but the scene in her room left her nervous and unsettled, so that Felipe had to send for her when the first of his guests arrived.

Sisa brought the message.

"Please to come down to the salon, *señorita*. The master is waiting."

Jane allowed herself one hasty glance in the long cheval-glass and fled towards the staircase. Beneath her in the hall, Felipe's guests were gathering. They were a mixture of Spanish and English, already clustered into chattering groups among which Felipe moved with the grave concern of the perfect host. He paused at the foot of the staircase as Jane came down.

"I want you to meet these people," he said. "They will give you the introductions you will need. It is quite important here. You will, of course, wish to belong to the English Club. Grace was a member. Mrs. Prescott will see that you are proposed."

He sounded aloof, almost disinterested, so that it was hard for Jane to remember his passionate outburst of the day before. He had mentioned Grace quite naturally, as if he had never bared his soul to her.

Felipe! she wanted to cry. *Time will heal everything;* but he turned away, leaving her with Daisy Prescott.

"This *is* a surprise," Daisy acknowledged. "Felipe throwing a party. An unconventional one, too! Vince and I used to drop in quite often when your sister was

269

alive," she added, "and then, suddenly, it stopped. Felipe was suspicious of everything Grace did at one time, and then, quite abruptly, he seemed to change. Don't ask me why! I gave up trying to understand the machinations of the male brain years ago!" Daisy laughed, examining the huge sapphire on the middle finger of her left hand. "I can afford to disregard their whims, you see. I happen to have sufficient money to please myself."

Jane felt embarrassed, but was saved an answer by the appearance of Daisy's protégé.

"What's new?" Travers asked flippantly "Felipe never invites us in for drinks unless he has something to crow about."

"Or something he wants to find out," Daisy suggested. "Our charming host never acts without a reason."

"The reason for this particular party is to introduce me, I believe," Jane said rather stiffly. "Felipe thinks I ought to know one or two people of my own age and not spend all my time with the children."

Daisy and the artist exchanged glances.

"That means an introduction to the Club," Daisy acknowledged. "I'm perfectly willing. Grace should have come more often, but she decided to find her—amusements elsewhere."

Vincent Travers turned away, as if the reference to Grace had annoyed him. There were times when he looked as if he hated Daisy and all she stood for. The stout little patron of the arts pretended not to notice his anger, passing him with a playful tap on the arm.

"Remember, we mustn't stay too long, Vince," she smiled. "We're dining with the Machados at nine."

"I'll remember," Travers muttered. "You've told me often enough," he added churlishly.

Jane glanced round for a quick way of escape, but she was wedged in a corner between the main door and the telephone alcove, and Travers didn't step aside.

"I'm sorry," he apologized, "but it overpowers me at times."

"What does?"

He smiled at her ruefully.

"My parasitic existence."

"Then why go on with it?"

He shrugged.

"For a number of reasons. One of them being that I still continue to believe in myself."

"In your pictures?"

"Yes, I suppose that's what I meant." He offered her a cigarette and lit one for himself. "This is the sort of life I like, the life I've always wanted and never had until three years ago. Good heavens!" he ejaculated, "have I really been Daisy's 'guest' for three whole years? She's not a bad old trout, really," he added remorsefully, "and I'm just another collector's piece, as far as she's concerned. I came here on a holiday and she pressed me to stay for six months—and paint. Well, I stayed. I saw it as a godsend, at first, the opportunity I had always lacked to give everything to my art without actually starving in the process, but now——" He turned, his face sobered and all the amusement gone out of his eyes. "Now," he admitted, "I'd give everything I possess to get away, to break the shackles, to live free."

Amazed by the unexpected confidence, Jane could not think what to say to him.

"Surely you can walk out whenever you like?" she suggested.

"It isn't so easy." He tapped the ash from his cigarette into one of Felipe's priceless Venetian glasses. "I need money. I haven't a bean. I've been promising myself a one-man exhibition in London or Paris for years and I've been working to that end, but the money I earn selling my pretty pictures to the tourists just isn't sufficient. If I stay here long enough, Daisy will come up with the necessary cash, but *can* I stay? It gets worse every day and she's becoming possessive. She could finance the exhibition tomorrow, but there's always some reason why we should wait — always some excuse."

"I'm sorry," Jane said, because she had no other advice to offer him. "Don't your pupils help a little?"

He shrugged again.

"They keep me in cigarettes."

Jane glanced across the hall to where Felipe was leading his guests down the circular stone stairway to the wine cellars. The vaulted basement had recently been furnished with comfortable lounges and a bar, and was his newest showpiece. When she looked up at her companion Travers' mouth was grim and there was a green glint of envy in his eyes. It was gone almost before she could be sure that she had surprised it there, however, and he said lightly:

"For what your worthy brother-in-law spends on one emerald I could hold a dozen exhibitions, even in London."

They followed the others slowly downstairs. In the vaults beneath the Casa candles flared along the walls in wrought-iron sconces and small tables were set out with sweetmeals and glasses. Sisa and the other servants poured the wine, while Felipe moved easily among his guests, with Teresa, in severest black, to assist him with the few who spoke only Spanish.

Jane was presented to group after group, always with Felipe's hand securely beneath her elbow. The names confused her, but he supplied the details as they passed from one table to the next. A solicitor from La Laguna; a Government official; a judge on circuit; an Air Force officer home on leave from Madrid. The wives were mostly reticent, dark-haired beauties who spoke little English but smiled at her in a friendly way, and Jane liked them.

"You'll meet most of them any afternoon at the Club," Felipe assured her. "They play tennis or croquet there until their husbands pick them up. They even drink tea," he added lightly, "so you shouldn't feel too homesick."

Jane was picturing Grace in their present surroundings, seeing her sister taking her place by Felipe's side. It was her natural environment, the sort of life she must have loved. What had happened to destroy it, to burst the golden bubble of Grace's fondest dreams? Surely not just an ordinary love affair.

No, not ordinary. Suddenly Jane knew that the love of a man like Andrew Ballantyne would be no commonplace thing. It would be the strongly enduring, forceful passion of a lifetime, in no way to be denied. It would supercede all other loves, crushing down every barrier.

The knowledge swept over her like a great tide. She could not deny it. It shook her as it must have shaken Grace, yet she had no respect for the man, only a dawning pity for her dead sister. No wonder Felipe had forbidden him the house!

People began to take their leave in ones and twos, shaking hands with their host at the foot of the staircase. Soon there were only Daisy and Vincent Travers left. Daisy had drunk as much wine as was good for her, and laughed a lot. She held Felipe tightly by the arm.

273

"My dear Felipe, you must!" she protested. "You know how envious I am! But this time it isn't a picture, is it? So I shall find it just bearable to look at your emerald."

Jane, who was standing beside Travers, heard him catch his breath.

"I'll get her home," he said. "We're supposed to be going to the Machados' for dinner."

"Not till I've seen Felipe's emerald," Daisy declared, overhearing him. "He owes me a private view!"

"If you'll come upstairs," Felipe said politely, including them all in his rather thin smile. "Come, too, Jane," he added deliberately. "It may interest you."

They followed him up the winding stone stairs with Teresa hurrying on ahead to open the salon doors. The lights were full on when they got there.

Felipe moved directly to a cabinet in a corner and unlocked the painted wooden doors with a minute key which he kept in his waistcoat pocket.

The cabinet had been especially constructed for its present purpose and consisted of several rows of glass-fronted drawers lined with velvet and individually locked. Felipe opened one of them.

Jane had never seen a collection of gems before, and the beauty of it took her breath away. The drawer Felipe had pulled out for their inspection contained emeralds. Uncut gems of every hue and size winked up at them in the strong artificial light, far more brilliant than the candelabra which illumined them.

There was a little hushed silence before anyone spoke.

"That's it, isn't it?" Daisy said at last. "La Estrella!"

Felipe lifted a large, uncut stone from the centre of the tray. He was standing very near Jane, and he looked down at her as he explained:

"One can almost feel its fire. I was lucky to get the chance of it, but luck occasionally does come my way."

He looked round the silent group, and Vincent Travers let out his breath in a quick sort of gasp.

"It must be worth a small fortune," he said.

"Twenty thousand—in English pounds, to be exact. It is unique," Felipe assured him. He did not seem to be unduly interested in the monetary value of his treasure, although his eyes glinted with an answering fire as he looked at it. "Quite a possession, is it not?" He turned to take Jane's hand. "Hold it," he commanded, pressing the emerald into her reluctant palm.

They stood looking at it, the green fire winking back at them, and all the while it seemed to Jane to be burning its way through her flesh. She wanted to throw it from her, to be rid of it, yet all she could do was to go on holding it there under the light while Daisy Prescott coveted it and Vincent Travers drew in his breath again with that little sucking sound and Teresa said in a strange, harsh undertone that the money could have been better spent.

Felipe looked at his sister as if he couldn't quite understand her remark, and Sisa came to the archway leading into the hall to announce another visitor.

"Doctor Ballantyne."

Jane's fingers tightened spasmodically over the emerald. She had been thinking about Andrew Ballantyne all day, blaming him for her sister's death.

"Show the doctor in, Sisa."

Felipe's eyes still burned with that brilliant, glittering light, but it was at Andrew he was looking now, not at the emerald. He stepped forward as the doctor reached the archway. Andrew hesitated when he saw the group at the far side of the room.

"I thought your guests had gone," he said. "I wanted a word with you."

Felipe glanced round at the curiously tense little group beside the cabinet.

"We've been emerald-worshipping!" he said lightly. "Jane's making up her mind whether to run off with the Estrella or return it safely to its drawer."

Jane thrust the emerald towards him. Nobody seemed to be greatly amused.

"I wish you would put it back, Felipe," she said. "It doesn't seem to me to be real. It's much too big!"

"I can assure you it is quite real—the genuine article, in fact." He took the stone from her, holding it up between finger and thumb towards the light. Every facet, every groove leapt with hidden fire. "It's an odd woman who can say quite truthfully that she doesn't appreciate a precious stone."

Andrew was looking at him fixedly. It was as if he was completing some previous diagnosis which had not quite been rounded off until that moment. Abruptly he turned away.

"I'll wait in the hall," he said.

Jane handed over the emerald with relief, watching as Felipe re-locked the cabinet and slipped the slender key back into his pocket.

She saw Rozanne then, standing in the archway where Andrew had stood a moment ago. Wrapped in a pink, flower-sprigged dressing-gown, with her bare feet thrust into a pair of white silk mules, the child accused Vincent Travers across the width of the room.

"You promised to come and see my picture!"

Lo siento mucho!" he apologized. "It slipped right out of my mind." He crossed the intervening space to hoist her on to his shoulder. "May I come another day instead?"

His charm was lost on Rozanne, and she struggled to free herself.

"I don't want you to carry me," she said, her brow darkening. "You've broken your word!"

"Rozanne! How dare you speak in such a way?" Teresa swooped across the polished floor. "Go back to your room. Go back immediately!"

Rozanne drew herself up with unconscious dignity.

"I am going," she said, struggling with the sob in her voice. "I'm going to tear up the picture. I'll never finish it. I don't want to paint it now!"

She rushed towards the inner hall and the servants' staircase.

"Go with her, Jane," Felipe said, ignoring his irate sister. "See what you can do. I certainly think she ought to be punished for such revolting manners."

His voice had been quite cold, and Jane did his bidding wishing that it had been shaken with suppressed anger instead, which would have been far more natural in the circumstances.

"Go away!" Rozanne cried when she reached her room, where she had locked herself in. "Go away! I hate you. I hate everybody!"

"It is of little use," Sisa advised close behind her. "She will not let anyone go in. By the morning she will be better, perhaps."

Frustration and pity tore at Jane's heart as she retreated along the corridor. There seemed to be nothing she could do for Rozanne.

I've got to go on trying, all the same, she decided, for as long as I remain here.

But how long could she remain? Down there in the salon she had been painfully aware of Teresa's hatred. It had come blazing out at her in the look Teresa had given her when Felipe had ordered her to go with

Rozanne. He had taken authority out of his sister's hands and given it to her as if she had the better right to it. Teresa would never forgive him for such a slight, but Jane did not think she would wage open war. She would bide her time and seek a scapegoat for her brother's wrath.

Desperately Jane looked about her for someone to turn to, and could not think of anyone but Andrew Ballantyne. He was a doctor. He might understand about Rozanne.

But Felipe hated him—with just cause. She could not appeal to Andrew nor to ányone else. Somehow, she must work out this thing alone.

CHAPTER FOUR

IT had rained during the night, but by the time Jane came down to breakfast the sky was devoid of cloud and washed an even clearer blue. El Teide's snow-cap had been renewed and it sparkled brightly in the sun, white against azure and so remote and high as to seem almost unreal. She thought of the mountain as a benign giant this morning, smiling down on her and on the lovely valley at his feet.

To her surprise, Felipe was still seated at the breakfast table, his long legs stretched out in leisurely fashion, as if he had all day to sun himself on the *patio* and little else to think about.

She sought to make the most of these few minutes alone with him, for she knew that he would soon be riding off to the other side of the plantation where some banana cutting was still in progress.

"I love your island, Felipe," she declared, stretching out her arms as if to embrace the whole broad landscape from the lofty shoulders of El Teide to the blue ocean breaking in a white foam of waves far beneath them. "Life could be quite perfect here."

He made no immediate reply, watching her instead through half-closed lids as she stood gazing up at the mountain, her lips parted a little, her cheeks flushed and her eyes bright with her enthusiasm.

"I must take you to El Teide," he offered. "But it is a whole day's journey and I cannot afford the time just now. There will be ample opportunity for that sort of thing later."

He seemed to take it for granted that she would stay for some considerable time, and she felt the colour in her cheeks deepen.

"I'd like to see as much as I can while I'm here," she agreed. "Can one really climb to the top of El Teide?"

"Quite easily." He sounded unimpressed by their resident giant. "He's comparatively harmless, you know. We haven't had a volcanic eruption on Teneriffe for almost a hundred years. Not one worth mentioning, anyway."

"It was a pretty devastating one then, wasn't it?"

"Yes, that is so. Teide poured out his wrath sublimely." He flung back his head to consider the great snow-capped peak in silence for a moment. "The fires of hell are slumbering up there, Jane, and perhaps we should hope never to see them provoked into action again."

Jane shivered, wondering if she had really detected a half note of regret in his pleasant voice. It almost seemed as if he might have enjoyed such a terrible spectacle.

"It's —horrible to think about," she said. "All this prolific beauty and then—destruction and death."

He opened his eyes a fraction wider to look at her.

"Don't let me frighten you with the prospect," he said. "El Teide is a lazy old warrior. He likes to sit and dream in the sun."

"Like so many of us," Jane smiled uncertainly. "But, Felipe, if I am to stay here for any length of time I must have something to do."

"I have already thought of that." He eased his position in the long chair, watching her as she spread the rich yellow country butter on her *pan casero*. "I want you to teach Chris English."

"I'd enjoy that," she agreed instantly. "You mean Rozanne, too, of course."

"Rozanne is not so important," he answered. "I'm not so much concerned about her. She will learn the idiom in time. She speaks well in Spanish and she is starting to learn French. That is quite sufficient for a girl. It is Chris who must have the solid grounding, and you can see that he has it in English, at least. It was something Grace began. You could quite easily finish it."

He paused, as if waiting for her immediate agreement, but she could not respond so quickly this time. She could not look up into his demanding eyes and promise to stay at the Casa del Sol just to teach Chris and Rozanne, to continue their education where Grace had left off. She wanted more than that.

Her heart twisted painfully as he pushed back his chair and came to stand beside her.

"Had you any commitments in England?" he asked. "Serious ones, I mean."

"No—none."

He put his hands on her shoulders, standing behind her, and she felt the magnetism of his forceful personality penetrating through her until her whole body was sharply aware of him, every pulse stirring like a delicate

280

instrument under the master's touch. Yet, perversely, she wanted to rush away from him, to hide her love so that it might not be bruised a second time.

Felipe drew her gently to her feet.

"I'm depending on you, Jane," he said. "The children need you."

"Tears gathered swiftly to her eyes. She could see El Teide through a veil of tears, but instantly she was fighting them back, telling herself that this was no way to behave, even though she could hardly bear Felipe's nearness and the unexpected gentleness of his tone which tore her heart to pieces.

"I can try," she promised, turning to face him. "I can always try."

It was then that she became aware of Teresa for the first time. She was standing in the shadow of the house, in the entrance to the hall, and she had seen them like this.

It would appear to Teresa that they had been in each other's arms. Her face was a mask of angry frustration as she came forward into the brilliant morning sunlight.

Felipe swung round on his heel, releasing Jane with an impatient movement.

"Ah, Teresa!" he said coldly. "What is it you want?"

Teresa was still looking at Jane with a sort of tormented fury in her eyes, and her face was distorted with suppressed passion.

"I thought we might have gone over the household accounts together if you had an hour to spare this morning," she said in a harsh, disjointed voice. "But I see you are otherwise employed."

Felipe chose to ignore the innuendo.

"The accounts must wait," he decided crisply. "There are plenty of hours of darkness in which to deal with them, Teresa. Daylight is too precious a commodity

281

to waste at this time of year. I thought you realized that," he added brusquely. "The last of the banana crop is my main concern at the moment."

Snubbed, Teresa turned quickly away, her face twisted and ugly, her hands tightly clenched to disguise their trembling.

She hates me, Jane thought. She believes that I will take away her authority by remaining here.

Felipe looked after his sister's retreating figure for several minutes before he spoke.

"Teresa is becoming possessive," he observed. "We must nip it in the bud. She led her husband a pretty dance during the short time they were married, but it must not happen here. Otherwise she must go."

He had spoken completely without emotion and with a ruthlessness Jane had never noticed in him in the past. However dependent upon him Teresa might be, he would not allow her to disrupt his household with her possessiveness, nor would he shrink from casting her adrift if she attempted to defy him.

"I expect it's difficult for you to understand the Spanish way of life," he mused. "Teresa is now my responsibility. We have a tremendous sense of family, particularly here in the Islands. It is my duty to provide a home for her since her widowhood. It need not, however, be my own home, although I dare say Teresa would prefer it that way. When Grace died she came out here immediately I asked her. I cannot forget that, of course."

The remark renewed the odd feeling of personal failure which she had tried to cope with before without success. Surely he understood that she couldn't have left England immediately after her mother's death. Or was he selfish enough to believe that his own interests came first?

Chilled by the suggestion, she strove to shake off her misgivings, to accept things as they were. After all, she had no desire to deprive Teresa of her new-found authority. Only Felipe's wife could do that.

He stood back and she preceded him across the hall and out to the terrace overlooking the distant sea. The Atlantic was a stretch of unruffled blue this morning, with hardly a wave breaking on the shore.

"You ride, of course?" Felipe said.

Jane shook her head.

"I never had the opportunity," she said. "I was too busy training to be a nurse."

"Ah, yes," he acknowledged, frowning. "You have that profession at your fingertips."

"I'm very proud of it," she felt impelled to say.

"Indeed." He seemed preoccupied by some other train of thought. "I must teach you to ride. It is a very pleasant way of getting about the estate. In fact," he added, "there's no reason why we shouldn't begin right away. I'm going to Santo Domingo this morning. It's a beautiful ride along the cliff. You can be ready in an hour." His dark eyes appraised her slim figure. "Sisa will provide you with breeches and a shirt. You will also need a hat, or a scarf for your head. We will not return before mid-day."

He pulled the massive bell which hung at the end of the terrace and a boy came running from the direction of the stables.

"I've bought Chris a pony, by the way," he said to Jane. "It will be delivered this afternoon. He can't go riding round on a donkey much longer."

He turned to give his instructions to the boy in rapid Spanish and Jane stood quite still, staring down across the sun-drenched terraces to the white ribbon of the cliff road far below. With a snap of his fingers Felipe could command anything. Or so he believed. She glanced up at the proud, half-averted face of the man who had first captured her girlish heart, and experienced an odd sensation of foreboding.

She had meant to say that Grace would have been glad about the pony, but she could not. Felipe was not making good a promise already made by his dead wife He merely considered that it was time his son had a suitable mount to ride.

"Don't keep me waiting too long, Jane," he said as he strode purposefully along the terrace after the groom. "I shall be ready to start by ten o'clock."

Sisa produced a pair of white jodhpurs and a tangerine-coloured shirt, her eyes dulled by tears as she laid them almost reverently on Jane's bed. They had belonged to Grace. There could be no other explanation.

Jane drew back.

"I can't wear them," she said stiltedly. "I—just couldn't——"

Sisa looked incredulous.

"But it is the master's order," she faltered, as if that were enough to silence all argument. "There is nothing else for you to wear."

"I can have something tailored for me in a day or two," Jane said. "You told me yourself that there were good tailors in the *puerto,* Sisa."

"Yes, very good," the Spanish girl acknowledged, "but today you must wear these. It is the master's instruction," she repeated.

"I can't—hurt him like this," Jane said involuntarily, looking into Sisa's wise young eyes.

"He will not be hurt," Sisa answered with amazing conviction.

There seemed nothing for it but to struggle in to the jodhpurs, although Jane decided to wear a shirt of her own. She found a white one, part of a tennis two-piece which she had worn in her hospital training days, and substituted a printed headsquare for a hat. Sisa watched her admiringly as she walked away.

When she reached the terrace Jane was subtly aware of another watcher. In the shadows along the pink stucco garden wall a darker shadow loomed for an instant before it was swallowed up by the tangle of bougainvillea which festooned a little-used archway. A flight of fancy? A figment of the imagination, perhaps? Jane could not quite make up her mind as she rounded the end of the stable buildings, to find Felipe already there, waiting for her.

If it had been Teresa in the garden why had she concealed herself so deliberately, drawing back through the archway instead of coming forward to meet her face to face?

The thought disturbed her, although it could not completely dull the pleasure of the next two hours. Soon she had forgotten about Teresa and her obvious enmity. To be with Felipe was ecstasy enough, she told herself, but to ride with him through the estate and out on to the high coastal road hundreds of feet above the sea was magic. A fresh breeze blew against her cheeks and the sense of unlimited space all about her made her exclaim delightedly at everything she saw.

The estate was far larger than she had imagined, even when she had first driven through it towards the Casa. Banana and lime and orange groves gave way to coffee and maize, with almond and fig trees lining the sides of the rugged little *barrancos* which cut like dark scars across the landscape.

Every now and then Felipe would halt his mount at a large, square warehouse where the packers sang at their work and patient mules stood twitching their ears in the shade of the walls.

Lorry after lorry, with Felipe's name on their sides, passed them on the dusty road, making their way to the *puerto* or across country to Santa Cruz. It seemed to give Felipe a great deal of pleasure just to look at them and to return the respectful salutes of his workers.

The women appeared grossly overburdened to Jane, toiling in the strengthening sun with their young children at their feet, the men lazy and imperturbable. It was the women who carried the loads of banana fronds on their heads and the men who walked idly behind the mules with their panniers of tomatoes going up to the packing sheds.

Felipe answered her eager questions with an indulgent smile. When he was in conversation with his foreman he seemed to forget her, but when they were alone again she received his undivided attention. He always gave the impression of being the perfect host.

Going down out of one of the *barrancos* they saw a car parked ahead of them at the side of the road. It was Doctor's Baer's battered old convertible and it was covered in dust with the long battle into the ravine.

"The old fool's broken down," Felipe said with some asperity. "He ought not to be allowed out on the roads with that thing. It isn't safe."

But it was Andrew Ballantyne who raised his head from the open bonnet when they reined in beside the stranded car. He looked surprised when he saw Jane, his eyes screwed up in a kind of scowl as he scrutinised her against the sun. Then he appeared to recover himself and said "Good morning," but his face looked peculiarly grey beneath its thick coating of tan, as if he had received an unpleasant shock.

"Buenos dias," Felipe responded. "Are you in trouble?" His manner was distantly polite.

"No — I've managed to iron it out." Andrew wiped his soiled hands on a piece of waste rag which he stuffed back into the tool-box before he slammed down the bonnet. "Thanks all the same." He looked up at Jane for the first time without frowning. "I'm in rather a hurry," he excused himself. "We've got something like an epidemic on our hands."

"Oh?" She was instantly interested. "What's the trouble?"

"Enteric, I think. Anyway, it's going through the *barrancos* like wildfire. The most outlandish places seem to be infected as well as the villages." He glanced up to a huddle of tiny dwellings clinging to the mountainside. "We're short-staffed at the clinic into the bargain, so you'll forgive me, won't you, if I don't waste any more time? I have a couple of nurses reporting from Santa Cruz this afternoon, though we could do with half a dozen."

Jane hesitated.

"I don't suppose I could help?" she suggested.

Andrew was standing on the roadway just beside her horse's head. He allowed his eyes to travel slowly over her, from the bright orange headsquare with its dramatic design of silhouetted palms to Grace's fine kid riding-boots.

"No," he said, "I don't think you could."

Her face flamed scarlet.

"I'm a nurse," she pointed out. "I'm quite capable of helping in an emergency."

"It isn't quite an emergency yet," Andrew said. "If I have to come for you, I will. And now I must push on." He got into the car, pressing the starter. "I've sent up the latest report about the estate workers," he added for Felipe's benefit. "You're reasonably free of trouble at the moment because you're a self-contained unit, but I can make no definite promise for the next week or so."

"I pay you to be sure." Felipe's tone was ice-cold, his narrowed eyes trained on the doctor with marked hostility. "It is your duty to see that my employees are safeguarded from the local epidemics. If there is the slightest danger of this thing spreading I want inoculations done immediately. This may be the end of the season, but I still have an extensive tomato crop to harvest. I can't afford to lose it. Please see that I don't."

Jane gasped inwardly at the sheer arrogance of Felipe's tone, and the doctor gritted his teeth.

"Your tomatoes can go to hell," he said. "I know my duty. Your employees are in perfect health at the present moment. My job, as I see it, lies elsewhere."

Without waiting for a reply, he thrust in his clutch and drove away, leaving them in a cloud of dust.

There was a small, uneasy silence before Felipe said:

"The fellow is intolerable. He knows his livelihood depends on me. If he hadn't the estate job behind him he wouldn't be able to waste so much time on that clinic of Baer's. They expect to work miracles down there, but they will always be up against a primitive lack of response. Old men die, children are born and, unfortunately, some of the children die, also. It is accepted."

"But it's so wrong!" Jane exclaimed. "I'm sure you feel that, in spite of what you say, Felipe. Doctor Ballantyne was rude, I admit, but we have to understand how he feels when an epidemic seems to be getting the upper hand. There's little time for fine speeches. One is just up to one's neck in it, working twenty-four hours a day to win in the end."

He gave her a faint smile.

"The English doctor has bemused you," he said. "But don't let him fool you completely. He thinks of nothing but his clinic."

"That's as it should be," Jane said stonily. "And if he asks for my help I'm bound to give it."

His hand tightened on the rein.

"Professional etiquette has nothing to do with this situation," he said frigidly. "I prefer you to keep away from Doctor Ballantyne and his clinic until this epidemic blows over. I understand it can be carrier-borne. You are here to look after my son, not to hire yourself out as a nurse to the children of the *puerto*."

"Felipe, you can't mean that!" Jane gasped. "You're angry — you have every right to be — but I just couldn't stand aside if I were needed. I just *couldn't!*"

"Let's hope, then, that you will not be needed," he suggested, dismissing the subject with his most charming smile. "I should hate to *forbid* you to go, Jane, but you know my feelings in the matter. There are plenty of other nurses on the Island."

"That seems to be the whole point, doesn't it?" Jane persisted. "There aren't. It would be criminal of me to stand aside if I were really needed. I wouldn't want to do it, anyway," she concluded with some emphasis. "I hope I still remember the nursing code."

"You are no longer a nurse," he said. "You are Grace's sister — one of my family — and you are proposing to work for the man who betrayed me."

"I — can't believe it," Jane faltered. "I just can't imagine Andrew Ballantyne doing such a thing."

He rode on for several yards before he turned to look at her.

"Whether you believe it or not," he said, "the fact remains. I have no intention of justifying my statements to you, Jane. You must allow me to guide you in your choice of friends."

"That's not quite the issue, is it?" she pointed out. 'This isn't a choice of friendship. It's a professional matter, an S.O.S. for qualified assistance, if you like. That was all Doctor Ballantyne wanted."

He dug his heels into his horse's flank.

"At the moment," he returned harshly. "With time his demands would grow. You are not at the Casa del Sol in your professional capacity, Jane. I would advise you to forget Doctor Ballantyne."

But Jane knew that she could no more forget her calling than she could fly to the moon. The swift, utterly unexpected brush with Felipe had spoiled her perfect day. She had seen him for the first time as the autocratic employer, the harsh and unrelenting overlord juggling with the lives and futures of the people who depended upon him for their daily bread, and she did not like it.

Of course, Andrew Ballantyne had been brusque in his odd, straightforward Scots way, but most of what he had said was the truth. They just couldn't turn their backs on the possibility of trouble. Neither of them.

"I'm sorry, Felipe," she apologized. "I ought to understand how you feel. About Grace," she added in a small, choked whisper.

As he pulled in his horse their eyes met and held.

"I feel nothing," he said. "Grace and I ceased to be lovers long before she died."

Jane felt as if she had been struck.

"I don't know what you mean," she faltered.

"Come now!" He gave a short, harsh laugh. "You're not exactly a child. Grace chose to belittle me. She left my house for another man, secretly but nevertheless effectively. I shall punish that man, but not out of any sense of heartbreak. I am free of Grace. I want you to understand that. No doubt I made the wrong choice, but we were reasonably happy during the first years of our marriage, and she gave me a son."

"Please — don't say any more," Jane cried. "I can't go on listening to this. Not about Grace. It's so — so cold-blooded, so brutal!"

"All truth is brutal on occasion," he answered. "You forced me to tell you, Jane."

"No! Oh, no——"

Foolishly she spurred her horse in a mad desire to escape, and the startled animal took to his heels and fled down the dusty road. Trees flashed past between glimpses of the distant sea and a flock of tough little mountain goats scattered, bleating their alarm. Her mind could hold on to nothing but the desire to put as great a distance between herself and Felipe as she possibly could. Then, suddenly, the whole landscape was inverted as she slid from the saddle and catapulted to the ground.

The sky righted itself and she lay panting on the side of the road, scratched and bruised. When Felipe caught up with her she felt foolishly near to tears.

"For heaven's sake, Jane!" He was genuinely concerned. "What made you do such a stupid thing? You could have injured yourself severely. As it is, we can't be sure you haven't done some damage until we have professional advice." His mouth hardened. "I shall send for Baer as soon as we get home."

"I'm all right," Jane protested, getting unsteadily to her feet. "Please don't bother calling Doctor Baer. I'm shaken a bit, but it's entirely my own fault. I shouldn't have been such a fool."

He gave her a long, searching scrutiny.

"That is true," he agreed. "It is foolish to run away from the truth."

Quickly she averted her head.

"I don't want to talk about it," she said in a shaken whisper. "I want to go back to the Casa."

Without a word he helped her to re-mount, leading her horse at a very slow pace back through the estate.

At the Casa, despite her protests, he insisted on a medical inspection.

"I've sent for Baer," he told her when he found her lying down in her shaded room. "He's capable enough with this sort of thing."

Jane closed her eyes. She had liked Doctor Baer on sight, but somehow she would have felt better if it had been Andrew Ballantyne who had been summoned.

It should have been Andrew, in the ordinary way. He was the estate doctor. *Still* the estate doctor, in spite of Felipe's determination to harm him in some subtle way.

She lay listening for Hans Baer's car, tensed and still, while Felipe crossed to the window and remained there, looking out. Surely he did not intend to stay while Doctor Baer made his examination?

When Sisa came bursting in she breathed deeply with relief.

"The doctor is here," the Spanish girl announced. "He is coming at once from the clinic."

Jane turned her head on the pillow to smile at Hans, but it was Andrew Ballantyne who strode across the floor.

"What's this?" he demanded, ignoring Felipe completely. Fallen off a horse? Do you feel that you might have broken anything?"

Felipe strode past him to the door. His face was livid.

"Wouldn't it be better if you made your own diagnosis?" he suggested. "Surely you can tell if there has been any serious injury?"

Andrew bent over Jane. She could see a small pulse hammering above his temple and the hardening of his jaw as he set about his examination with gentle hands, but he would not give rein to his anger in spite of Felipe's provocation.

They were a surgeon's hands, Jane noticed, and the grey eyes above them were steady and wise. Could such a man betray his benefactor and break up his home?

"I'm sorry about Doctor Baer," Andrew apologized. "He's at Laguna today. Too far away to be sent for."

"It's all too silly," Jane declared. "It wasn't a bad fall. Only a very foolish action on my part. I—jumped the gun and thought I could gallop before I'd even learned to trot!" She tried to laugh. "It is my first riding lesson."

"Lots of us make a false start at one time or another," he agreed, straightening. "You appear to be sound in wind and limb, although I expect you'll be showing a nice pattern of bruises in the morning. Rest, if you can, but don't overdo it. You'll live to ride another day!"

He hesitated, as if he were about to add something, more advice, perhaps, and then he crossed to the window.

"What a view you have!" he commented instead. "El Teide in residence, in fact!"

"I mean to climb to the crater one day," Jane confided. "Felipe tells me it's comparatively easy, and I'm glad I won't have to go on a stretcher!"

He laughed with her.

"Make sure you have the proper guide," he warned lightly. "And certainly don't attempt it alone."

He took her hand as Sisa came back into the room, the pressure of his strong fingers reassuring and kind.

"If you please, Doctor Ballantyne," the Spanish girl said, "will you wait in the hall? My master wishes to speak with you."

The request was unexpected, and something about Sisa's manner made Jane catch her breath. The girl looked close to tears.

Andrew lifted his stethoscope.

"I wouldn't go out in the heat straight away, if I were you," he warned. "Have something light to eat and rest for an hour. We English could learn a lot from the Spanish *siesta*. Sisa will look after you."

He put a friendly arm about the Spanish girl's shoulders and Sisa rewarded him with an affectionate smile as they went out together.

Jane lay back against her pillows, her thoughts curiously disturbed. Her few meetings with Andrew Ballantyne had only served to accentuate his kindness and a strength of character which it was impossible not to admire. He was hardly the type of man to be browbeaten, and he would not shrink from the consequences of a decision once he had taken it. Felipe certainly wouldn't be able to intimidate him where his work was concerned.

She had meant to ask him about the clinic and the epidemic, but he had not remained long enough. He had appeared only too anxious to get away once he had given her the benefit of his professional skill.

Perhaps she reminded him too poignantly of Grace. That could be it, although he had not given any outward sign. There had been only that one brief, startled glance when they had first come face to face up there

294

in the *barranco*. Suddenly she remembered that she had been wearing Grace's jodhpurs. Had the memory of other meetings been too sharp for him?

Restlessly she got to her feet, opening the shutters which he had closed after that one brief glance at El Teide. What was she to do about Felipe's ultimatum when she felt in her bones that she ought to be helping Andrew Ballantyne?

The minutes ticked away without bringing her any nearer to a solution, and then, suddenly, she became aware of voices raised in the *patio* beneath her balcony. Without going out to look, she was convinced that it was Felipe and Andrew arguing.

Her breath caught sharply against her throat. Tempers ran high in these parts, and if they were quarrelling anything might happen. Swiftly she crossed to the door, but Sisa was already there with her lunch tray.

"This is what the doctor told me to bring." Sisa still looked rather woebegone. "It will make you well and you are to sleep afterwards."

"Was that Doctor Ballantyne's order, too, Sisa?"

The Spanish girl smiled.

"It was his order," she said.

Because he had anticipated some sort of scene with Felipe? Jane watched Sisa setting out the tray on the table near her bed. It was evident that her brother-in-law had kept Andrew waiting, and he had shown a commendable degree of patience. He had certainly not turned on his heel and walked out, as he might have done considering all the work he had to get through.

Once again Jane felt guilty at the thought of resting while there was so much need of a nurse's assistance down at the clinic. I can't stand aside, she thought. I just can't.

When Sisa had carried off her tray she found it impossible to rest. The house lay under the peace of the *siesta* hour, but there was little calmness in her heart. Andrew Ballantyne had gone long ago, but something of him lingered in her quiet room, a suggestion of strength and purpose which she could not brush lightly aside. She had already acknowledged his courage.

Her enforced rest seemed endless. She hadn't yet accustomed herself to sleeping in the middle of the day, and at the first stirring in the hall below she slipped into a cool green shantung dress and made her way downstairs.

Teresa was standing at the foot of the stairs, an oddly watchful figure in the severe black of her widowhood.

"I thought you were advised to keep to your room," she remarked. "Doctor Ballantyne left orders that you were not to go out in the sun. His authority may have dwindled a little since his interview with Felipe, however," she added, looking amused. "Your English doctor is going to find life rather more difficult from now on."

Jane gazed at her without understanding.

"Am I first to break the news?" Teresa asked. "I thought perhaps Felipe might have spoken to you after the interview."

"I was in my room," Jane pointed out frigidly.

"It overlooks the *patio*." Teresa's insolence was very thinly veiled. "There was quite a scene," she added. "Evidently my brother had the temerity to keep Doctor Ballantyne waiting for quarter of an hour."

"A doctor's time is generally precious," Jane reminded her quietly.

Teresa's eyebrows shot up.

"Doctor Ballantyne is going to find himself with plenty of spare time from now on," she predicted. "We

296

no longer have any use for his valuable services at the Casa del Sol."

"Oh — Felipe couldn't!" Jane cried. "He just couldn't dismiss him. Andrew depends so much on his appointment to the estate."

"So one might have imagined," Teresa agreed. "Nevertheless, he has cast his bread on the waters of independence once again. I believe he did it some years ago," she added, "in England."

"Did Felipe tell him to go?" Jane asked slowly.

"He did." Teresa dismissed the subject with a shrug. "Your Doctor Ballantyne is now a completely free agent, able to do exactly what he pleases."

"He's not 'my Doctor Ballantyne'!" Jane cried sharply. "All the same, I can't help wondering what he's going to do now. The estate work was his bread and butter. What he did at the clinic was entirely voluntary, I understand."

"He has still his partnership with dear old Doctor Baer to fall back on," Teresa reminded her. "That ought to give him a great deal of comfort."

"I think it does," Jane said, turning away.

She was quite unable to think what Andrew Ballantyne was going to do now. There could be no doubt about the fact that he had been dealt a crippling blow. Not only had he lost a well-paid job, but he was now deprived of the means of furthering an ideal. Felipe had been able to do that to him with one devastating stroke of authority.

It was too cruel, especially when Hans Baer and he had a thriving epidemic on their hands into the bargain. Overwork, lack of sleep, insufficient supplies and the added strain of a depleted nursing unit had probably frayed Andrew's nerves to the limit of endurance, but Felipe would be unable to appreciate the fact. His intolerance seemed to lash out at her, striking her under the heart.

I can't just sit here, doing nothing, she decided at last. I've got to influence Felipe, if I can. But even as she made the resolution she knew that the battle was already decided. Felipe was not the sort of person to be influenced, especially by the arguments of a woman.

Rather despondently she went out to join the children.

CHAPTER FIVE

IT was two days before Jane saw Andrew Ballantyne again. In the meantime, she supposed she really hadn't had enough courage to approach Felipe about offering her assistance at the clinic. The epidemic was gathering strength, Sisa reported on her return from the *puerto,* where she went twice a week to visit her family, but the two doctors were working very hard and soon they would have everything cleared up.

The Spanish girl's simple faith in the medical profession as a whole and in Andrew Ballantyne in particular was very touching. It made Jane more ashamed than ever of her own enforced idleness, but she also felt that it would be foolish to run completely contrary to Felipe's wishes without discussing the situation with him once more. He was not the man to trifle with, and his authority had been unquestioned until now.

Except, perhaps, for Grace, his English wife, who had rebelled in her own way.

Jane did not want to think too deeply about Grace just now, nor about Andrew Ballantyne's part in her tragedy. If they had loved each other it would not have been lightly on Andrew's part, at least. Somehow, she knew that, even after such a brief acquaintance with him.

She took the children for their daily swimming lesson in the late afternoon, after *siesta*. Their instructor, a volatile young Spaniard, was in residence at one of the palatial new hotels on the sea front, and while he coached his half-dozen pupils in the sparkling blue-tiled pool, Jane wandered idly back into the *puerto* itself.

The picturesque little port encircling its stone-built harbour had remained entirely unspoiled in the face of growing commercialism, and she wandered happily about its cobbled streets, absorbed in the withdrawn tranquillity of its ancient houses with their lattice-work balconies and high, encircling walls. Life went on behind these walls as it had done on the Island for hundreds of years, guarded from the curious by shuttered windows and a remoteness which she had felt even at the Casa del Sol. The Spanish way of life was impregnable, most jealously preserved against outside intrusion.

In the *plaza* she sat beneath the tall plane trees at one of the innumerable small iron tables, drinking a mixture of fruit juices which tasted like nectar. There was scarcely enough wind to stir the fringes of the orange umbrella above her head and the dust lay without stirring in the centre of the square. It was hot for February, but although Sisa had predicted thunder there was no sign of a cloud in the wide blue canopy of the sky.

A cart clattered down a side street and a man with a string of onions over his shoulder came to drink a glass of malmsey at an adjoining table. A group of loafers sitting in the shade began to talk.

Jane paid for her drink and resumed her wanderings. The odd little closed-in shops attracted her, although there were only a few with any window display. Smiling Spanish girls stood in the doorways, inviting her in, but she hadn't really come on a shopping expedition.

At a street intersection she paused, aware that she had lost her sense of direction and climbed to the higher reaches of the town. In front of her was a narrow cul-de-sac ending in one of the tall, aloof-looking houses so common to the *puerto* with their closely shuttered windows and latticed balconies dripping with bougainvillea. It turned a blind and indifferent eye on her perplexity, until suddenly a door in the high adjoining wall burst open and a laughing group of children spilled out on to the pavement. They were followed by a young nun. Lessons at the Convent of the Precious Blood were over for the day.

The teaching Sister smiled as she passed, shepherding her noisy flock towards a low, white-washed building on the other side of the street. It had an air of modernity about it, suggesting that it might have been built quite recently on the site of some crumbling mansion which had outlived its usefulness, and the wall surrounding it was low enough for some of the older boys to leap over.

The garden beyond the wall looked trim and carefully tended, with roses growing in glorious profusion in the wide flower beds and a neat, English-looking lawn stretching on either side of the central driveway.

Surprised, she recognized the word 'Clinic' above the main door. This, then, was where Andrew Ballantyne worked with the German doctor he respected and admired.

At that moment Doctor Baer himself came bustling out into the sunshine to receive the children from the convent. They swarmed round him, vociferous in their

300

affection for this little man who had gained their confidence and surely deserved their love.

"Herr Doktor! Herr Doktor!" they shouted, while the Sister guided them gently in between the glass doors.

Standing alone on the far pavement, Jane experienced a sharp stab of loneliness. Surely she belonged over there where the work of mercy was going on?

Hans Baer looked up and saw her. They met halfway across the sunlit street, their outstretched hands linking in warm greeting.

"You haf come to see our clinic?" The little German seemed to swell with pride. "We are not at our best today, but you are welcome. So many children to inoculate, and so little time!"

He looked desperately tired, but the eyes beneath the shaggy grey brows were full of light. A dedicated man, aware of time as a challenge, something he must conquer together with the appalling lack of skilled assistance which made an emergency out of every epidemic.

"You will come inside," he invited, "and see for yourself?"

Jane accepted eagerly. Not until she had come here, until the sharply astringent smell of disinfectant was in her nostrils again and the white walls of the clinic had enclosed her, did she realize just how much she had thought about her profession in the past few weeks. There was a sudden new lightness in her step as she followed the square-cut figure of the German doctor along the corridor to a side ward where Andrew Ballantyne and two young Spanish nurses were inoculating a straggling line of children between the ages of three and sixteen. After that age they were considered adult in the Islands, and many of them were already married.

"The babies are in another ward," Hans Baer explained. "We have been busy all day, but now we are run out of serum."

Andrew glanced up and saw her. His face clouded and his heavy black brows drew together as he laid aside the final hypodermic and come towards them.

"Surely this is unofficial?" he said. "I'm quite sure Felipe wouldn't approve."

Jane met his look with a gaze as direct as his own.

"I don't have to ask Felipe what I must do with my spare time," she assured him. "Chris and Rozanne are having a swimming lesson. I met Doctor Baer outside and he asked if I would like to see over the clinic. Don't let me stop you if you're busy, though," she added, glancing towards the waiting children. "I just want to look around and soak up some of the atmosphere."

He unbuttoned his surgical coat. Most of its original pristine whiteness had gone by now, evidence of a long and busy day.

"There isn't much more we can do until a fresh supply of serum comes in from Santa Cruz," he said, unaware of the fatigue which edged his voice. "But we can forge ahead with the blood donors. They've been waiting since this morning. It would be bad policy to turn them away in case they get it into their heads that we don't really need their blood regularly. Once they fall off it won't be so easy to get them into the habit of coming again."

"Please let me help." Jane made the offer spontaneously. "I know the drill. You wouldn't have to supervise. You could get some rest."

He looked at her rather oddly, as if her offer had come as a complete surprise to him, but almost immediately he shook his head.

302

"You would find yourself in trouble at the Casa," he reminded her. "Felipe would take a poor view of your offer in the circumstances."

Her mouth firmed rebelliously.

"Doctor Ballantyne, I'm not exactly a child," she said. "I'm quite capable of making up my own mind."

He hesitated for a moment longer.

"If you're wise," he warned, "you'll go back to the Palm Beach and wait for the children."

She took off her coat.

"They will be fully occupied for over an hour," she said. "They're both perfectly safe."

His smile struggled between amusement and relief, dismissing the suggestion of doubt from his eyes. They were still slightly wary, however, when he said:

"I think you ought to know that I'm no longer in Felipe's employment. I ceased to be the estate doctor two days ago."

"When you quarrelled?" The words were out before she could stay them.

"When we quarrelled," he agreed, handing her a sterile white coat.

A strange excitement ran through Jane as she slipped into the familiar uniform, a sense of renewal, of purpose. She had come home.

For an hour she worked by Andrew Ballantyne's side. There were difficulties. The first donor had never given blood before and fainted at sight of the needle, but when Jane brought her round she insisted on going on with the donation.

"She's desperately ashamed of passing out on us like that," Andrew explained, translating the flow of rapid Spanish for her benefit. "These young Guanches are a tough people, but this sort of thing is away beyond their comprehension. You needn't be afraid. She won't black out on you a second time!"

They worked hard, emptying the waiting-room between them with the help of the two Spanish nurses.

When Andrew straightened at last with a sigh of relief, Jane's hair was slightly awry and her coat not quite so fresh, but there was a light of satisfaction and fulfilment in her eyes which lent a new beauty to her pale face.

The English doctor glanced through the surgery door to the row of donors resting on the white hospital beds in the ante-room beyond.

"I'd never have got through that lot alone," he said. "Thank you, Jane."

She gave him a contented smile.

"I ought to thank you, really," she told him. "You've proved to me this afternoon that I could never be happy doing any thing else."

He offered her a cigarette, lighting one for himself before he said:

"What else had you in mind?"

She hesitated.

"Nothing, really. I was — giving myself a holiday."

His eyes held her half-reluctant gaze.

"Are you going to marry him?" he asked bluntly.

"Felipe? No, I didn't come out with that intention. You must believe me."

She felt almost desperate in her desire to convince him, but he shrugged his indifference.

"It's no affair of mine."

"No."

She felt shut out again, all the warm friendliness of the past hour gone, as if it had never been. Why should a passing stranger care what happened to her, one way or another?

"I ought to join your list of blood donors," she said, veering away from the uncomfortable subject of Felipe. "I'm a Rhesus negative."

His eyes sharpened.

"We need you," he said. "Hans is deeply concerned about our high infant mortality rate. The Rhesus problem hasn't really been tackled fully out here, but given time and a new clinic we could change the entire pattern of things. It's being done everywhere. All we need is the money." His mouth twisted in a wry smile. "About as much money as your respected brother-in-law spends on a single emerald," he added.

Jane felt uncomfortable.

"Couldn't you ask Felipe to help?" she suggested.

He shook his head.

"He wouldn't. Quite frankly, Jane, Felipe and I are on very bad terms." He paused, considering something he had been about to say, and then he added firmly: "Probably because Grace and I were friends."

"I see."

She turned from him, wondering if he had deliberately confirmed his treachery.

Andrew glanced at the clock on the ante-room wall.

"You're late," he said. "The children must have finished their swimming lesson over half an hour ago. I'll run you down to the hotel."

"You mustn't," she protested. "I can quite easily find my own way if you direct me. You're tired. You ought to get some rest."

"You walked almost full circle getting here," he explained. "It won't take much more than ten minutes to go back. I mean to come with you," he added, pulling off his soiled coat. "There may just be some explaining to do."

"Explaining?"

"To Felipe. When you didn't turn up on time the hotel would phone him."

"How foolish of them!" Jane protested, aware of a sudden sinking in her heart. "Santiago will amuse the children. He told me theirs was the only lesson this afternoon."

He led her towards the door.

"You've forgotten that you're part of a strict Spanish household," he said. "The female members of Felipe's family don't wander off unaccompanied into the blue without a hue and cry being raised as soon as they're missed."

"But I'm *not* one of Felipe's household," Jane protested crossly. "The whole thing is too ridiculous for words!"

They stepped out into the brilliant sunshine, and it seemed to strike her with a blinding intensity. Andrew took her arm to guide her across the street.

"You have a lot to learn, Jane," he said.

Felipe was already at the hotel when they reached it. He was standing in the entrance lounge with Daisy Prescott and Vincent Travers, surrounded by an agitated hotel staff which included the manager. His anger when he saw Andrew was ill-concealed.

"We could evidently have saved ourselves a great deal of trouble if we had called at the clinic first," he observed, his narrowed eyes fastened relentlessly on Jane's flushed face. "I should have remembered your defiance, my dear Jane, and the doctor's insolence."

Seconds later Andrew let out his breath.

"If you had phoned the clinic Jane would have collected the children right away," he said in the clipped tone of a man holding his temper in check with the utmost difficulty. "She offered her services and we accepted them. We're sorely in need of help."

"You must find your assistants in the proper quarter in future." Felipe's voice was encased in ice. "I thought I made that perfectly clear when I dismissed you from your position on my estate."

The savage remark drew a gasp of astonishment from Daisy Prescott and the colour drained slowly out of Andrew's face.

"We must leave that to Jane, I think," he said. "She is still entitled to make her own decisions."

"Not while I am responsible for her welfare." Felipe turned on his heel. "You will collect the children, Jane," he added. "They are somewhere on the terrace. Possibly with Santiago. The car is waiting."

He was still in breeches and boots, his riding crop swinging at his wrist. With a small, cold shudder, Jane could imagine him using it to effect on the patient animal tethered beyond the line of parked vehicles in the hotel car-park.

Her eyes flew to the reassuring look in Andrew Ballantyne's eyes. He would not provoke a further scene.

"Thank you," she murmured involuntarily as she passed him.

He turned his back on the watching group, striding off without a word or a backward glance.

The Spanish servants melted away.

"Heavens!" exploded Daisy. "What a scene! You'll have to be more careful in future, Jane, not to provoke Felipe. He has a vile temper when he's crossed, my dear."

"Nobody crossed him," Jane snapped impatiently. "He was just being rude."

"Or jealous?" Daisy's eyebrows shot up and she smiled playfully.

"I don't know what you're trying to suggest," Jane said.

"Don't you, my dear?" Daisy's laugh was a trifle forced. "Jealousy doesn't always spring from love, you know."

"I don't," Jane answered. "I only know that it's a horrible emotion—a soul-destroying sort of thing—and I don't want to talk about it."

"You'd be wise to avoid it, then." Daisy ambled after her towards the terrace. "Felipe has his reasons for disliking Andrew, of course."

"I know the story," Jane said sharply. "Please don't repeat it."

"As you wish." Daisy looked crestfallen. "I was only trying to help. Everybody envies Felipe. It's because of his position and his money, I expect, and there's no denying his tremendous charm. Ah, yes," she concluded, her closely-set blue eyes glittering avariciously, "we all wish something of Felipe's in our possession. I, alas! envy his emeralds, while poor Vincent would commit a crime simply for his money. So little of it would enable him to escape me, you see."

Amazed by Daisy's perspicacity, Jane found nothing to say.

"On the other hand," Daisy went on, "Andrew and his German colleague would give their souls for his authority and the power he wields in the community."

"That isn't exactly envy," Jane contended. "It's an ideal."

"Ideals aren't much use without money to back them up in this case," Daisy remarked shrewdly. "Hans Baer would do anything to further that clinic of his, and Doctor Ballantyne would quite cheerfully commit a felony for Hans. He owes him so much, you see."

Jane didn't see, but she wasn't going to ask Daisy any more questions.

"Then there's Teresa," Daisy ruminated. "It isn't envy with Teresa. It's greed. Simple, honest-to-goodness covetousness. She was brought up to expect more than she attained by her marriage, and now she believes that Felipe owes her a position since he inherited all the family wealth along with his uncle's title. Again, he has everything, while she is left with so little. You must look out for Teresa, Jane," she warned. "I know. I'm trying to help you. It was Teresa who betrayed your sister to Felipe. She swore she saw Andrew and Grace together."

Jane's heart gave a great lurch.

"Felipe wouldn't listen to tales," she tried to say stoutly. "There—must have been some other evidence."

"No doubt there was," Daisy agreed. "I wouldn't have thought it of Andrew Ballantyne, but of course, you never know, do you?"

"No." The word stuck in Jane's throat. She had no intention of discussing Andrew with Daisy. "Here come the children," she added with relief. "Thank goodness they've had the sense to get dressed."

"Don't worry too much," Daisy said quite kindly. "Perhaps you'll be able to handle Felipe. You look intelligent enough."

"Thank you," Jane said a little drily. "I hope I shall be able to 'handle' Teresa, too."

"Ah, Teresa!" Daisy shook her head. "I wouldn't be too sure about Teresa, if I were you. Felipe you might be able to manage, but Teresa's a different kettle of fish!"

Exasperated, Jane shepherded the children towards the waiting car. Felipe had disappeared, riding on ahead so that he might reach the Casa before they did or simply going off about the interrupted business of the estate.

She hoped he would not be at the Casa when they finally reached it.

It was Teresa who was standing waiting for them on the terrace steps. Teresa with an oddly triumphant smile on her thin lips.

"So, you have shown yourself typically English and independent!" she observed. "But my brother will know how to deal with your insubordination. The children's meal has been ready for over an hour."

"I have already seen Felipe," Jane answered. "He came to the hotel."

Teresa showed no surprise.

"Naturally, I had to contact him when you did not return," she said. "The hotel manager phoned to say you were missing."

"For less than half an hour," Jane pointed out, tired of the whole business. "There was no reason why I shouldn't look around while Chris and Rozanne were safely at their lesson."

"No reason, if you were suitably accompanied," Teresa agreed. "But that was not so. Perhaps Felipe has yet to appreciate how indiscreet the English can be."

Jane had to crush down a rising wave of anger because of Chris's growing curiosity and Rozanne's sullen watchfulness.

"I'll take the children up to their rooms," she suggested. "They must be hungry."

Teresa remained standing in the hall as they mounted the staircase, her eyes black pools of resentment as she followed their progress along the gallery.

She hates me, Jane thought. She would do anything to injure me or belittle me in Felipe's estimation. Anything within her power.

CHAPTER SIX

IT was long after dark before Felipe returned. The swiftly closing night had become almost sinister, shutting Jane in dramatically. The blazing fire-ball of the sun dropped perpendicularly into the sea. There was no after-glow; just that sudden, abrupt cutting off of light. It made the first greyness practically imperceptible. The night had come with a sense of shock.

When the stars pricked out they were very bright, and far larger than the stars Jane knew. They glittered with a fierce intensity, piercing the heavens in a million pinpoints of brilliant light.

There was no moon and very little shadow in the garden, and the air felt suffocatingly close and still.

From her window she watched Felipe come in. He stood silhouetted for a moment in the archway leading from the stable buildings, a tall, commanding figure still in his riding-breeches and silk shirt, and her heart fluttered as if at some signal which she should have recognized long ago.

Slowly he came forward into the brightness of the *patio*. His movements were coolly deliberate, as if he already knew he was being watched from her vantage-point. Then with a quick upward movement of his dark head, he was looking straight at her.

"Jane?"

She had to moisten her dry lips before she could answer.

"Yes?"

"Will you please come down here?" He came to stand directly beneath her. "I have something to say to you."

It was virtually a command, and she had no reason to refuse his request.

"It's almost supper time," she reminded him.

"We have twenty minutes before supper," he said. "I take it you are already changed?"

He knew her movements so intimately, knew that she invariably dressed early so that she could spend these few moments alone on her balcony looking out across the silent plantation to the magic of El Teide.

Almost reluctantly she stepped back into her room and lifted the woollen stole from her bed. It was cool in the *patio* at this time of night.

The house seemed curiously deserted as she went slowly down the steep curve of the staircase and crossed the hall, her high-heeled sandals sending their echo ahead of her, but Felipe was still at the far side of the *patio* with his back turned towards her when she reached the folding doors. He knew she was there, but he offered her no word of greeting.

"Felipe, I'm sorry about this afternoon," she apologized when the silence became intolerable. "I didn't think there was much harm in going for a walk while the children were at their swimming lesson."

"You could have amused yourself equally well in the hotel." His voice sounded coldly impersonal. "If you were determined to go slumming you should have come to me for an escort."

"Slumming?" The word stung her. "I was at the clinic, Felipe."

"So I understand."

He turned at last, his face fully revealed in the yellow light from the lantern above their heads. It was

312

harsh with reprimand, the thinly compressed lips and narrowed eyes cruel in their intensity. She had never seen him look like this before, and she took a step backwards, as if to avoid him.

Instantly his thin fingers fastened over her wrist.

"I've spoken to you about Ballantyne," he said almost softly. "He has been dismissed from my service. I will not have him using you for his own ends, at the clinic or anywhere else."

Jane's heart was beating like a sledgehammer now. She attempted to release herself, but without result.

"You don't understand," she protested. "They need help down there. They need it badly. They're hopelessly understaffed, and now there's this epidemic to cope with. I felt bound to stay, Felipe. I am a nurse."

"You are no longer a nurse," he said sharply. "I intend to marry you, Jane, and I will not have you rushing around the countryside behaving as you are doing."

Jane gave a little gasp, not quite believing what she had just heard. Felipe was still holding her. They were so near that their lips might have touched, yet there was no tenderness in him. *I intend to marry you* was what he had said. Just that. It was the thing she had wanted more than anything else in the world—to marry Felipe, to be loved by him and cherished—but no word of love had escaped him. He had made up his mind to marry her. That was all.

Something frail and defeated in her fluttered and lay still. She stood facing him in the yellow lanternlight and wanted to die. He didn't love her. This was a proposal of convenience. He needed her to grace his house, to be a second mother to his children, but there was no love left in his heart.

313

Grace had destroyed all that. Grace and Andrew Ballantyne between them.

Sick with disappointment and grief, she turned her head away.

"I'm waiting for your answer," Felipe reminded her.

"How can I answer you in the way you want?" Her voice was choked with sobs. "I loved you once, Felipe —long ago—but so much has changed since then. You and Grace—you were in love with each other. You must know how I feel."

His mouth twisted in a sardonic smile.

"A man can never understand the workings of a woman's mind, my dear Jane," he said. "What made you fall out of love with me?"

She raised her eyes to his, but she could not bring herself to answer him.

"You said just now 'I loved you once'," he prompted. "Why not now? You led me to suppose that love *could* be for ever."

"It could be." Jane's voice was harsh with pain. "Sometimes it is for ever, even when it's quite hopeless."

He took her by the shoulders, his dark gaze holding hers remorselessly.

"We must hope that you have enough love for both of us," he said. "I put no store on love. It is a woman's business."

She shook herself free.

"You've been hurt," she cried. "You're cruel and sardonic because of it, but one day you may need love, Felipe, more than you've ever needed anything before."

"Then I shall come to you for it, my pretty Jane." He was smiling, holding her close again. "One day you may even recompense me for your sister's treachery."

He bent his head, stifling the cry of protest on her lips with his own. It was a fiercely possessive, almost an angry kiss, and it shook her to the depths of her being. Impotently she sought to escape his embrace, only to find his arms tightening the more determinedly about her.

"It's no use, Jane," he said. "Struggling won't help. You came here with marriage on your mind. The children were only a secondary consideration. Why do you now resist so violently against the truth?"

"Because it isn't the truth!" Jane felt as if she had pushed her way out of some dark cavern towards the light. "I loved you," she repeated, "but I never really knew you. You were a — sort of symbol to me, a — a figure of romance. I clothed you in everything I wanted you to have. I envied Grace. I think I even hated her when you had eyes for no one else. I hated my sister!" Her face was white and pinched, but her eyes looked steadily back into his. "You did that for me, and you married Grace and killed her."

"You little fool!" The closed look had come back into his eyes. He was no longer smiling at her. "You have no idea what you are saying. If anyone killed Grace it was Ballantyne, her secret lover."

"I don't believe you!"

His hands tightened on her arms.

"So he has captured you, also? The English doctor with his high ideals!" He laughed mirthlessly. "But I warn you to be careful. I will not be humbled by Andrew Ballantyne a second time."

"Andrew wouldn't want to hurt anyone," Jane declared. "He has no interest beyond his work."

The smile reappeared in his eyes, mocking now.

"Then you must cut your losses, *Guapa,* and settle for the protective arms of your brother-in-law," he suggested blandly. "As you say, the English doctor has no room in his life for anything but work."

"And you will destroy his work?" She gazed back at him incredulously, scarcely daring to believe what she knew to be true. "You'd go to any length to — to disgrace him."

Felipe released her.

"I intend to punish him," he said, "if that is what you mean."

"You're inhuman — savage!" she denounced him, only to see him smile once more.

"I have other qualities, Jane," he told her, indifferent to her rage. "I can be generous and thoughtful, for instance, and, who knows, I may one day be able to love you in the way you wish. In the meantime, we will get on very well together. You will take your sister's place and rear my children as she would have done. In return I will give you a home and protection. What more can you possibly desire?"

"You don't understand," Jane murmured helplessly. "You just don't understand."

He turned towards the shadowy hallway.

"You may be wrong there," he said. "Sometimes it is the woman who does not understand her own need."

He strode off, leaving her in the silent *patio* with her conflicting thoughts. She felt utterly spent with emotion, drained and empty and afraid. He had taken so much for granted — her continuing love, her loyalty to Grace and the children, her desire for a home — and it was all a nightmare of half-truths.

Of course, she wanted a home — what woman didn't? — but not like this. Not surrounded by uncertainty and suspicion and the dawning knowledge that she had made a mistake.

She still wanted to take care of the children, to take up where her dead sister had left off, but the past half-hour had made her continuing stay at the Casa del Sol almost impossible. She couldn't marry Felipe under these circumstances.

And what other circumstances were there? To wait for his dawning love, as he had hinted, hoping that one day he could give her everything he had given Grace?

The suggestion set up a swift recoil in her. It would never be the same. Felipe had hardened and become cruel and cynical. There was this vindictive streak in him, too, which made him avid for revenge. His pride had suffered a shattering blow.

Shivering, she drew the woollen stole about her shoulders. It was all a hopeless, terrible mess, and if she stayed she would be jumping into it with her eyes wide open this time.

"Why do you not go?"

Teresa was close behind her, materializing out of the shadows.

"I heard what Felipe said," she added harshly. "If you marry him you will only be committing your sister's blunder over again."

Jane swung round. There was nothing to be seen of Teresa but her thin neck and gaunt face emerging from the blackness of her velvet housecoat and her claw-like hands folded over the book she carried. Spanish Household Management, Jane thought irrelevantly.

"You were listening," she said. "Eavesdropping!"

"I heard my brother come in." Teresa's voice was weighted with hatred. "It is my duty to discover what his wishes are for the remainder of the evening."

The efficient housekeeper! The willing slave to Spanish male superiority! Oh, don't let me *think* these things! Jane murmured inwardly.

"You can never hope to understand Felipe," Teresa said deliberately. "Your sister never could. She wanted her independence, to be free to please herself what she did, and that is not the Spanish way. She rebelled, to no good purpose in the end. Felipe would be a fool to risk his happiness a second time with you."

"I didn't come out here to marry Felipe," Jane felt bound to insist. "I came to visit the children, to help in any way I could."

"We do not need your help," Teresa snapped. "Felipe knows that he can leave Chris and Rozanne safely in my care."

"You may want to marry again," Jane pointed out.

Teresa gave her a thin smile.

"Not again," she said. "I have had my fill of marriage."

Jane turned away. There was no point in arguing with Teresa.

When Felipe made his appearance they shared their belated meal in an atmosphere so tense as almost to be hostile. Teresa deliberately addressed her remarks to her brother in a manner calculated to exclude Jane from the conversation altogether, discussing family affairs in Madrid and the conditions on the estate, which a stranger could know nothing about, and Felipe seemed too abstracted to notice the discourtesy. He was busy with his own thoughts.

They were thoughts which etched a deep furrow between his brows and tightened his mouth to a thin line, but he did not unburden himself to either of them. Jane found herself playing with her helping of fruit, unable to eat for the sudden choking sensation of fear in her throat. Felipe had something on his mind which concerned them all.

Normally they sat in the *patio* on a still evening like this, listening to the distant strumming of guitars as the men amused themselves down at the stables, but as soon as Miguel appeared with the coffee Felipe rose and crossed to Jane's chair.

"We will take our coffee in the salon." He signalled to Miguel to remove the tray. "The wind has grown cold."

"If you'll excuse me," Jane began, but he cut her short with a charming smile.

"I will not excuse you, Jane," he said. "I have something to show you."

Jane followed him from the room in silence.

The picture stood on an easel in the centre of the salon. It was one she had last seen propped against the wall in Daisy Prescott's untidy hallway.

"One must patronize the arts," Felipe observed as she stood admiring it. "Especially the local artists. Travers is a competent enough draughtsman, but he lacks imagination. There is no movement in his sea, for instance, but his landscape is effective. You recognize it, of course, as part of my estate? Travers delivered it this afternoon before he met you at the Palm Beach."

"I'm sorry I missed him," Jane murmured, looking round for Teresa who had lingered in the dining-room to give some final instructions to the maidservants.

"Mrs. Prescott motored him over, I believe," Felipe said, moving the coffee tray towards her across the inlaid table. "Will you pour out? You may as well perform those little duties and get used to them."

There could be no mistaking his meaning. The colour flew to Jane's cheeks.

"It is Teresa's privilege," she protested.

"Not any more." His gaze came down dominatingly on hers. "Teresa knows that you will take over."

Jane moved uncomfortably.

"Felipe——"

He stooped to take his cup from her.

"When you are ready I want you to chose an emerald from my collection to be made into a ring," he said.

"I couldn't!" She drew back. "I can't marry you, Felipe, under these conditions. I—don't think I could ever marry you now."

He continued to hold her gaze with undiminished purpose in his dark eyes.

"Never is a long time," he said. "Soon you will change your mind."

"No."

"Then I must persuade you."

Smilingly he took her by the elbow, guiding her across the room to the painted cabinet where his jewels were kept.

With a fascination which cut her breath short, she watched him feel in his pocket for the key and insert it in the lock. The shallow drawers inside were also locked, and instinctively she looked towards the lowest one. He had opened it once before to show them the Estrella, that day when they had all been summoned from the wine vault to view his treasure.

She could see their faces now: Daisy Prescott's pinched with envy and Vincent's full of avarice; she could read the contempt in Andrew Ballantyne's eyes and the glitter of achievement in Felipe's, but most of all she remembered Teresa. Teresa coming into the room as she was coming now, with a naked look of hatred on her face and a grim determination about her mouth.

Felipe opened the cabinet drawer.

The Estrella was no longer there.

Felipe stared at the vacant space in the centre of the tray as if he could not quite credit what he saw, and then he swung round on his heel to look at Jane.

"Someone has been very foolish," he said. "The Estrella has gone."

Jane could only continue to gaze at the tray and the other, smaller, glittering emeralds which still adorned it. It was like staring into a dozen or so evil eyes.

"You're quite sure it has been stolen?" she managed at last. "It — couldn't be anywhere else? In one of the other drawers?"

He dismissed her theory with a swift gesture of his hand.

"I am sure," he said. "I have never made that sort of mistake. Each stone has a place of its own, and the Estrella is my most treasured possession."

"It's — very valuable, isn't it?" Jane could think of nothing else to say.

"Reasonably so. Its value to me isn't just a matter of hard cash, however."

"How can you be sure it has been stolen?"

"Because, Jane, I locked it up myself. No one else possesses a key." He was examining the lock. "Nothing has been broken. This is a very clever thief."

Jane's mouth had gone dry.

"Couldn't we make some sort of search?" she suggested. "It may turn up. You may even have mislaid it, Felipe."

"My dear Jane, one doesn't go round 'mislaying' emeralds — just like that. Especially when they are part of a valuable collection." He stood surveying the cabinet, his brows closely drawn. "This has been a carefully planned robbery," he decided, "but I don't think we will have very far to search for the thief."

"You — already suspect someone?"

Very carefully he locked the drawer and closed the painted doors.

"The money could be useful to so many people," he answered almost lightly. "And for a score of reasons, but I have a theory that whoever took the Estrella took it because it was mine. I have so much, you see, in the material sense." He smiled down at her.

"What will you do?" Jane asked. "Report it to the police?"

"Not yet." His eyes were suddenly remote. "I feel that I might derive no small amount of pleasure out of playing my own detective for a day or two."

"But isn't that rather unfair?" Jane protested. "It leaves us all suspect. After all, I could have taken the emerald, couldn't I? I've been in the house all the time, and you don't know so very much about me."

"I know sufficient to believe in your honesty," he smiled. "No, Jane, I don't suspect you, but I think you might attempt to cover up for the thief if you were given half a chance."

"Then you *do* suspect someone?"

"I have a theory," he said.

"It's going to be very uncomfortable for us all until you make your decision, especially if you believe that it was someone in the house."

Felipe did not answer her immediately, and it was then that Jane realized that Teresa had gone. She had been standing in the doorway when her brother had discovered his loss, and she had withdrawn so quietly that neither of them had heard her go.

Felipe took her by the arm.

"If it will make it any easier for you," he said, "I don't think anyone at the Casa del Sol would do such a thing. The emeralds have been in my possession for years, along with a good many other precious stones. Everyone knows they are here. Even the servants. They dust the cabinet every day. These people are poor, but they are not dishonest. What, for instance, would Sisa or Miguel do with the Estrella? They would not be able to get rid of it, however much they needed the money. No, Jane, we must look about us for a more accomplished thief," he decided. "One, perhaps, who has very little to lose even if he should be discovered."

"Is there such a person?" Jane cried. "Half a dozen people have been in this house during the past week, all of them with a great deal to lose and each one of them known to you!"

Deliberately he poured himself a second cup of coffee, raising it to his lips before he said:

"Shall we enumerate them? First, we have Daisy Prescott, who doesn't need the money but might quite conceivably covet the emerald. Then we have her charming protégé, who delivered his latest painting here this afternoon." He stirred the sugar in the bottom of his cup. "Suspect number three could be Doctor Baer."

"But that's ridiculous!" Jane protested. "Hans Baer wasn't one of the party the other night."

"No, but he was here early this morning." Felipe put down his empty cup. "He came for two reasons. First of all to plead for his colleague. He wanted me to give Doctor Ballantyne back his job on the estate. He also wanted me to invest some money in his precious clinic. Failing that, he suggested a memorial hospital." He allowed himself to smile. "A memorial to my deceased wife."

"You can't possibly suspect him," Jane cried. "He hasn't a thought outside his work."

"Exactly," Felipe agreed. "Which brings us to Doctor Ballantyne."

"You're not accusing Andrew?" she exploded.

Felipe turned from her.

"Your trust in the English doctor is very touching," he observed. "But of course, you also are English. You must stick together."

"I just know Andrew wouldn't do it!"

"Which is most illogical reasoning, you will admit."

"Illogical or not, Andrew Ballantyne just isn't that sort of person."

He came back to stand beside her.

"He stole my wife, remember?"

She swung round to face him.

"You'll never be able to forgive him for it, or to forget it, will you?" she said. "You'll hound Andrew to the bitter end. "You'll ruin him, if you can."

He shrugged.

"You're not suggesting that I shouldn't see justice done, are you, Jane?" he asked.

"Justice, yes, but you're intent on pinning this thing on Andrew because — because you have some reason to hate him."

"I am glad you acknowledge that." He turned the slender silver key of the cabinet over and over in his hand. "I wonder what he used to open the drawer?"

"Have you ever thought that it might have been a woman?" Jane asked desperately.

He looked amused.

"Teresa, you mean? Teresa wouldn't dare do such a thing. The Estrella would be useless to her. No," he reasoned, "I would suspect Teresa of a dozen little treacheries, but not of theft."

"Then there's no one else," Jane said listlessly. "Do you intend to question the servants?"

"Surely," he said. "It may afford me some valuable information."

"Tonight?" she asked.

"Tomorrow will do," he said.

CHAPTER SEVEN

JANE spent a restless night. When, eventually, she was able to sleep, her dreams were haunted with the vision of Andrew Ballantyne. Always he was being pursued by one calamity after another while she was forced to stand aside, powerless to help him. Yet he wasn't the sort of person who looked for help. He made his own decisions and stood by them, she suspected. There was nothing small about him.

The fact that he needed money was natural enough in the circumstances. He would gladly give all he possessed to further Hans Baer's dream simply because the stout little German doctor had once had faith in him. Faith against odds, it seemed. Hans had invited him out here when his profession had been closed to him in England.

I wish I knew, she thought. I wish I knew what had really happend.

There was an uneasy atmosphere at the breakfast table the following morning. Felipe rode off early, clattering across the cobbles without so much as a glance at her window, and she heaved a sigh of relief. At least she would have the day to recover from the recriminations of the evening before.

Sisa and Miguel were upset. Obviously they had been questioned by Felipe, perhaps even threatened. Or was it Teresa who had intimidated them?

Teresa was in a black mood. She refused to speak to Jane as they ate together. She had been to Mass early, but had gained nothing from it. A heavy scowl marred her brow and she avoided meeting Jane's eyes.

"Teresa," Jane said at last, "you know about the emerald, of course?"

"Certainly I know about it." Teresa's voice was thin. "The entire household knows. You did not think you could keep it a secret between you and Felipe for ever, did you?"

"You believe I took it!" Jane gasped. "Teresa, *do* you think that — or is it just because you resent me? Because you wish I had never come to Teneriffe?"

"We know nothing about you," Teresa said stonily. "Your sister was not honest."

"Grace? How can you say such a thing?"

"She was dishonest in her marriage."

Jane drew in a deep breath.

"How much did you contribute to that, Teresa?" she asked.

The older woman bridled, sucking in her cheeks so that they looked thinner than ever.

"I did my duty," she declared. "Your sister was making a fool of Felipe."

"I doubt if anyone could do that," Jane said. "But don't try to — injure me, Teresa. I didn't take the emerald. Felipe offered me the Estrella as an engagement ring."

Teresa stared at her.

"He must be mad," she said. "The stone is worth a fortune. It is unique."

"And whoever took it wanted the money rather badly," Jane suggested. "The Estrella could be broken up into several smaller stones."

"Felipe will find out who took it," Teresa said. "Or the police."

"Has he gone to the police?" Jane's voice was not quite steady.

"Not yet."

A respite — for whom? Jane turned from Teresa as the children invaded the table.

"What are we doing today?" she asked as lightly as she could.

"Lessons," Chris informed her, helping himself to a warm croissant which he proceeded to spread lavishly with guava jam. "One, two, three, four, five, six! I can count in English up to twenty!" he announced with pride.

Rozanne's usual crushing rejoinder was not forthcoming, which made Jane glance at her in some surprise. She looked dreamy, almost bemused.

"And you, Rozanne?" Jane asked. "How are you getting on with your reading?"

"What did you say?" Rozanne turned to her almost in alarm. "I wasn't listening."

"I asked how you were enjoying your new book."

"I haven't begun it yet." Rozanne applied herself to her breakfast without looking up. "I was busy finishing something else."

"A painting?"

"Yes."

"But you don't go to Orotava till the beginning of next week," Jane pointed out. "Painting isn't quite as important as learning to translate fluently."

"It is to me!" Rozanne's eyes flashed. "It's the only lesson I really like, because Vincent is kind to me."

"We all try to be kind, Rozanne."

Jane's remark was met by a resentful silence and she did not press the point. Rozanne looked as if she might burst into tears at any moment. Altogether it was a most unauspicious start to their day.

Teresa left her to deal with the children until the *duenna* came on the scene. The Spanish governess shared her time between two households, the Casa del Sol and a magnificent villa on the outskirts of Orotava, where she taught the five daughters of a wealthy fruit exporter all they needed to know about the history of their country and its literature. When she came to the Casa del Sol a grim sort of relentlessness seemed to descend upon her. She never smiled. She had her duty to do. Felipe had impressed upon her in no uncertain manner what was expected of her, and she would have died rather than fail a *Marqués*.

Jane, therefore, was free to please herself for the entire morning.

Her first impulse was to re-visit the *puerto,* but she thought better of it. There was no point in antagonizing Felipe deliberately.

Too restless for *siesta,* she spent the hour after their mid-day meal in the *patio* trying to read, but the sun was hot and the book did not hold her attention for more than a few minutes at a time.

When a car drove up she wondered if it was Felipe, but halfway across the hall she recognized Hans Baer's old convertible. The German doctor was standing at the top of the terrace steps peering in at the open door.

"You must come," he said with an urgency she could not mistake. "If you please, it is very important. Andrew is telling me that you have the blood we need. There is no one else to give it."

Jane went out to meet him.

"What is it?" she asked. "A baby?"

He nodded eagerly.

"You will come? There is no time to waste. Seconds can be precious. You understand?"

Jane had already reached for her headscarf.

"Yes, I'll come," she said. "Just give me a minute to leave a message for Doña Teresa and I'll be with you."

He nodded in agreement, his eyes shining their appreciation as he got back into the ancient car to start it up in readiness for their dash to the *puerto*.

Jane was forced to leave her message with Sisa. Teresa could not be found anywhere.

"Tell Doña Teresa I've gone to the clinic to help with a blood transfusion," she explained hurriedly. "I'll be back within an hour."

"Andrew is sorry to send for you," Hans told her as they drove away, "but it is urgent. This baby has very little chance of life, but we must try. Always there is the miracle. Fifteen — even ten years ago — there was no chance at all. These little ones died. It was inevitable."

"When did it happen?" Jane asked. She had entirely forgotten the Casa del Sol. "I thought Andrew was due for some rest."

Hans shook his head.

"The baby was born shortly after you left the clinic," he explained. "I have had the mother under observation for some time. We suspected it would be a Rhesus case, but the little one arrived prematurely. We were not fully prepared. The epidemic has taken up much of our time." He smiled ruefully. "Andrew does not seem to need sleep," he said.

But Jane could not help remembering how tired Andrew had looked when she had last seen him. The solution to it all, of course, was another doctor, but the partnership could not afford it.

"You've assisted at transfusions before?" Hans asked.

"Many times." Jane had never felt more thankful for her long years of training. "I hope I'll be allowed to help."

"Andrew may consider that donating the blood is enough." Hans negotiated one of the treacherous bends in the winding road with practised skill. "But I shall ask you to stay," he added, "because I think you wish it."

"He won't be obliged to me for anything," Jane mused. "Will he?"

"He knows how Don Felipe will regard it," Hans answered quietly.

"That doesn't matter," Jane said sharply. "I am only related to Felipe, not married to him."

"I can assure you that Andrew needs your help."

The remark had been calmly deliberate. Jane turned in her seat to look at her companion, but Hans's expression was bland.

"You've known him for a long time," she observed with a hint of envy in her voice which the German doctor was quick to detect. "For several years, isn't it?"

"We worked together in Germany," Hans explained. "Then, when I was coming back here, I knew I could not return without him, although I still think he should have gone back to his own country."

Jane hesitated.

"Why didn't he?" she asked at last.

Hans was gazing straight ahead. They were approaching the *puerto* and the clinic where Andrew was waiting.

"It is a long story," he said. "Too long to be related in a hurry. Andrew has a great sense of justice, but he has also an obsession about his obligations. A colleague older than himself made a mistake. They had worked on the case together. There were complaints, and the hospital Board was forced to hold an enquiry. Andrew — how do you say? — carried the bucket for this other doctor."

" 'Carried the can' for him," Jane murmured. "But surely, at a full-scale enquiry the truth must have come out?"

"The other doctor was the husband of his sister," Hans explained. "He had much to lose. There were three children of the marriage. Andrew was young and without a wife, and he thought much of his sister."

Jane sat in thoughtful silence for the remainder of the journey. How could such a man be guilty of theft and treachery? Andrew Ballantyne seemed the last person in the world who would deliberately betray another man, yet Felipe had accused him twice without hesitation.

Why was she so sure of Andrew? Her heart contracted as she recalled the harsh lines about his mouth and the weariness he could not drive from his eyes. He was working himself to a standstill for the poor people of the *puerto,* and within twenty-four hours, perhaps, Felipe would accuse him publicly of theft.

Hans pulled the car up at the clinic gate and they walked quickly up the short drive. There was the usual file of people in the waiting-room, dark-skinned peasants seeking the doctor's advice. They had been sitting there patiently for a long while, accepting the unavoidable delay stoically, as they did with most of life's trials, and they smiled respectfully as Hans greeted them. He had a kindly way with all his patients, young and old, which won their confidence immediately, and he never went abroad without a pocketful of sweets to

331

offer the children. He was often so stooped with tiredness that he could hardly walk, but he never failed to smile. Jane felt very humble as she walked by his side.

In the consulting-room Andrew came to her. He was hollow-eyed with fatigue.

"I'm sorry about this, Jane," he began, "but it was the only way."

"Please don't apologize," she begged. "Surely you knew I would come as soon as you asked?"

He looked down at her, smiling faintly.

"I had an idea," he agreed.

"Tell me what you want me to do." She glanced about her at the confusion in the inadequate little room which spoke so plainly of the help he needed. "Do you want the blood first?"

"It would be best." He ran a hand through his thick dark hair. "We're running short. I've called in all I can, but these people come a long way, and most of them have already given their quota."

"Don't worry about me," Jane said. "I'm long overdue."

He considered her for a moment in silence, smiling a little.

"I needed you, I guess," he said before he went away.

"It's a funny thing," Jane mused as the blood dripped slowly into the bottle beside her arm, "but I've never felt quite so close to an emergency before. Andrew needs this blood almost immediately. I know we're not supposed to know who we give it to, but it does make a difference. To know, I mean." She looked up into Hans Baer's quiet eyes. "You agree with me, don't you?"

"I agree in this case," he said. "But it would not always do. The Powers That Be have decided that blood donors are not necessarily honest men."

332

"I know," Jane said. "But how many of the unscrupulous few would follow up a transfusion and demand payment for a life?"

"One or two would be enough," Hans said. "We have always to beware of the unscrupulous few." He rose from his chair beside the couch. "There! that will be enough. Now you must rest. I shall send a message to the Casa to say you will return soon.

But Jane had no intention of going back immediately the enforced rest period was over. Andrew had confessed his need of her, and she would only writhe in idleness if she did not offer him her help. Sisa and Teresa and half a dozen servants were quite capable of looking after Chris and Rozanne for one afternoon, she decided.

Hans smiled.

"You will come and see the baby?" he asked.

When he had gone Jane lay very still. Something was happening to her. It was as if, with the giving of her blood in this perfectly normal way, all indecision and uncertainty had been drained from her. She knew where her heart lay.

Jerked out of her drowsy inactivity by the admission, she sat up and swung her legs over the edge of the couch. It was more than that. She had always known that she would eventually go back to nursing. She had recognized it as her life's work, but now it was all bound up with Andrew Ballantyne and his need of her. And her need of him.

This love wasn't new. She had felt its earliest stirrings almost as soon as they had met, the sense of belonging together which their profession had suggested right from the start. They were motivated by the same impulses, tuned in to the same ideal of service. They had trained so far along the road in the same way.

Yet love demanded more than just speaking the same language. It looked for faith and trust, and Felipe had said that Andrew was not to be trusted.

Felipe! She thought of Felipe with a dawning awareness. His fascination had never been so clear to her before, the superficial charm which might have captured any young girl's heart. A sudden cold fear took her by the throat. What had she done? She had admitted to Felipe that she had loved him long ago, and he had taken it for granted that she loved him still. He was prepared to marry her in a coldly detached sort of way which admitted second-best, and if he discovered the truth, no matter what he thought, his pride would suffer.

Not that she had any hope of Andrew's love. He had loved Grace.

She sat with her hands tightly clenched before her, fighting back the tears which threatened to blind her. Why had it to be like this for her a second time, loving where no love was given? Her first swift, passionate attachment to Felipe was as nothing compared with what she felt now, and the despair was darkened by hopelessness. Andrew was hardly aware of her, apart from her profession.

The sound of running feet in the corridor outside her door startled her. The tiled floor did nothing to deaden sound, and soon there were other signs of emergency. A trolley was rushed swiftly past and turned into the lift. There were excited Spanish voices.

The baby?

Quickly Jane opened the door to find Andrew striding along from his office. He was without a coat, in his shirt sleeves, as if he had been trying to snatch a few minutes' rest.

The respite had obviously been denied him, for his brows were drawn in a worried frown.

"What's gone wrong?" she asked.

"The Rhesus baby." He gazed at her for a split second as if he did not quite recognize her. "We thought we were over the worst, but you know how it is with these cases. The pulse-rate has gone down."

Jane knew this was a routine business these days in the big hospitals where Andrew had trained, but it was still tricky.

"Jaundice has set in," he explained briefly.

She did not ask permission to hurry by his side. Somehow they both took it for granted that she would help.

The baby had stopped breathing when they reached the bare white cubicle where he lay, and Hans was on his knees beside the narrow cot. He had inserted a tube into the child's throat to suck out the obstructing fluids, and now he was giving a heart stimulant while a nurse stood by ready to apply pressure to the tiny chest.

Andrew went forward without a word and Jane watched while he endeavoured to coax the reluctant spark of life back into the little body.

The baby gasped, and it was like a miracle. He gasped again.

"He's breathing!" the young nurse said, her eyes shining through sudden tears.

The pathologist came in with the blood tests. Andrew stood talking to him for fully a minute before he turned to Jane.

"We're going to need your help. Two more nurses have reported sick," he told her.

"Tell me what to do," she said.

He handed her a theatre coat.

335

"You're going to do the transfusion right away?"

He nodded. The nurse was putting the baby in an oxygen tent.

"Will you come?" Andrew said to Jane.

She followed him back along the corridor and into the only operating theatre the clinic boasted. Hans had said that they needed at least three.

"Will you take over with the stethoscope," Andrew said "and do the pulse count?"

The hammering in Jane's heart had ceased. She was completely calm now.

The Spanish nurse wheeled the baby in and lifted him tenderly on to the table. Jane tested the electric blanket and fixed the oxygen mask before she turned to adjust the blood bottle to the correct height.

Hans came in, homely and comforting in his enveloping theatre gown. They waited for Andrew to scrub up.

He joined them at last, strong and purposeful, the dedicated surgeon fully engrossed in his task. Deftly he inserted the tube, linking it with the blood bottle above the child's head. It was not Jane's blood, but soon hers might be needed.

She took up her stethoscope.

"Ten in, ten out," Andrew advised.

Jane wrote it down, listening to the feeble heartbeats.

"Pulse one hundred — regular," she reported.

Andrew appeared to be relieved, yet he made no visible sign. All she could see of his face was the watchful eyes and his dark brows drawn above them as they waited for the new blood to do its work.

An hour passed.

"Ten in, ten out." It was almost monotonous until, suddenly, Jane couldn't hear the tiny heart at all. Andrew straightened, waiting for the pulse count."

336

"There isn't any——"

"We'll inject coramine. Two c.c." His voice was quite normal.

The nurse filed a glass ampule and filled a syringe. The baby's pulse grew strong again under the influence of the drug.

They were working now on the thinnest thread of life and the theatre was very still. Another hour passed. Jane did not even wonder what time it was. The blood bottle had been replaced by another, still not hers. The minutes ticked away. Andrew touched the baby's cheek, wondering, speculating.

"Ten in, ten out." It seemed never-ending. There was no thought of *siesta* and none of food. Coffee and sandwiches were snatched in an ante-room. The sun fled swiftly down the sky. That morning, an hour after his birth, a priest had come to baptize the baby. He was christened Luis Juan Alvarez. His mother was English.

"Tired?" Andrew asked, standing behind Jane's chair. "You ought to be."

"I don't feel it." She raised questioning eyes to his. "Is he going to live?"

"If we're lucky."

Her heart lurched with renewed hope. The child might almost have been her own. His life belonged to Andrew and, in some small measure, to herself. She heard the tiny heart, strong and steady, beating in her ears.

"He'll do," Andrew decided when another hour had passed. "You can put him in the incubator now."

She straightened her back at last. It was all over. The fight had ended in victory. Andrew had won.

"Jane," he said very gently, "it's time you went home."

She took off her coat and folded it over the chair in his consulting-room, reluctantly. The lights were on. It was quite dark outside.

"What time is it?" she asked.

"Seven o'clock." He was standing with his back towards her, washing his hands. "Does Felipe know about this?" he asked.

"No."

"I'm sorry," he said. "I shouldn't have asked you."

"I wouldn't have — not been here for the world." She was standing quite still, looking at his broad back. "Once you know about this sort of thing, Andrew, you can never stand aside."

"That's true," he agreed without turning. "At one time I considered giving it up, but I couldn't. It was in my blood." He turned, as if he were about to ask her something, but his mouth tightened before the request was uttered. He glanced at the wall clock above her head. "Come along," he said brusquely. "I'll take you back. If you're lucky you'll get in just before Felipe."

It wouldn't matter, Jane mused with a wry smile. There was Teresa to report her every movement to her brother-in-law and the children to ply her with awkward questions.

Yet why should she be afraid of Felipe? He had no hold over her. She could leave the Casa del Sol whenever she liked. She could come here and work for Andrew and Hans Bear. Her pulses stirred at the possibility.

"Andrew, if I needed a job — if I had to get away," she began, "could I come here? You're short-staffed. You need more than one qualified nurse, even when this epidemic is over."

He looked at her for a long time without answering.

"It wouldn't do," he said at last. "Felipe would find

some way of punishing you for your infidelity. His power here is absolute."

It was more or less a rebuff, Jane realized painfully. If she came to the clinic it would only make things harder for him.

In silence she preceded him to the door.

"If you can get me a taxi," she suggested, "I won't drag you all the way to the Casa. You must be exhausted."

"All the same," he said firmly, "I mean to see you safely home."

Hans' car was parked in the driveway. It loomed up sharply against the mysteries of the moonlit night. They crossed the stretch of lawn towards it.

"Andrew," Jane said, "the Estrella emerald has disappeared."

He startled.

"That bauble of Felipe's," he said after a pause. "Do you mean it has been stolen?"

She moistened her lips.

"Felipe thinks so."

There was a brief silence.

"And he suspects me? Or says he does."

"How can he?" She turned to him appealingly. "You weren't anywhere near."

"On the contrary, I've been to the house several times in the past few days, and — I used to work there, remember?"

What she could see of his face looked grim. He strode on ahead of her, deep in his own conflicting thoughts, not protesting his innocence. When she reached the car he held the door open for her.

"I think it would be better if you didn't come to the clinic any more, Jane," he said. "Your help has been invaluable to me, but Grace's children need you more

339

than I do." He looked down into her distressed eyes. "Especially Rozanne," he added as he closed the car door between them.

"I can't make any contact with Rozanne," Jane confessed when he got in behind the wheel and turned into the main highway. "She's so remote. Hidden, almost. Sometimes I think she resents me being at the Casa at all."

"Rozanne resents anyone who seems to be more loved than she is. Unfortunately, Grace contributed to that," he added. "She was obsessed with the thought of a son even before Chris was born. She felt that she had let Felipe down producing Rozanne when he so passionately desired an heir."

"She must have been very much in love with him at first," Jane said unthinkingly.

"She was." Andrew's tone was harsh. "In spite of her selfishness, Felipe was all she wanted when she first came out here."

"And afterwards?"

"Afterwards it all fell away." He drove the ancient car at what seemed a reckless speed towards the hill. "There's nothing so shattering in life than finding you've made an irretrievable mistake."

"No."

Jane stared out into the darkness. They were driving between the banana plantations and the huge fronds cast black patches of shadow on either side of them with the white ribbon of the road between. They were the only travellers at that hour, locked in between the shadowy earth and the sky. The wide arc of the heavens was full of stars, bright, remote worlds far removed from their small personal problems, and Jane drew a deep breath as she looked at them. The whole world seemed suddenly cold.

"I won't come again," she said, "if that's what you wish."

"It would be best," he answered almost with indifference.

She felt shattered, thrust out, but she had no claim on him. They had worked together, achieving victory, and he was grateful to her, but that was all.

What had she expected? Her heart twisted with pain. Twice she had loved where Grace had come first. It wasn't fair!

Bitterly she allowed her mind to dwell on the might-have-beens, sitting so near Andrew that she had only to stretch out her hand a little way to touch him.

The car sped on, swallowing up the miles. Soon they would be at the Casa. So soon he would be gone out of her life.

They could not live in such a small community without meeting, of course. Inevitably they must come face to face, unless Felipe made good his vow to ruin Andrew.

It would be easy enough. There was the emerald. Her blood ran cold at the thought of the missing jewel.

They drove for a mile along the length of the boundary wall to the arched entrance to the estate. The wooden doors were still open and they went in through the orange grove where the ripened fruit glowed against the dark foliage and the heady scent of flowers hung in the air like a snare to the senses. Jane knew that she would always remember this moment of parting with Andrew. When they met again it would be as strangers.

He pulled the car up at the edge of the terrace, getting down to help her out. In the scented darkness she clung too long to his hand, feeling his strong fingers fastening hard over her own.

341

"Take care," he said briefly. "And don't worry too much about the emerald."

"Andrew——"

Gently he disengaged his hand.

"Goodnight," he said. "Goodnight, Jane."

It was as if he had said goodbye.

She watched him drive away, and when she turned a shadow detached itself from the shadows at the far end of the terrace. It was Felipe.

He came towards her, flinging away the cigar he had been smoking. She watched the yellow glory of the tip as it arched across the terrace into the flower-beds executing a fiery parabola of light before it sank to extinction.

"So, we hear from the English doctor again," he said.

"There was an emergency." Jane's voice sounded breathless, as if she had been running. "A baby was born with defective blood. It was a Rhesus case, one of the worst kind. The child would have died if Andrew hadn't acted quickly."

He came a step nearer, measuring her deliberately with coldly quizzical eyes.

"And where did you come in, Jane?" he asked.

"Andrew sent for me. I had offered to donate my blood, as they were running short of the type they needed."

A strange half-smile lifted his lips.

"I thought I warned you about going to the clinic," he said. "I am not in the habit of repeating my wishes a dozen times before they are obeyed."

"This had nothing to do with your orders," Jane burst out. "A child's life was at stake."

"There are plenty of nurses on the Island paid to do that sort of work," he observed icily.

"Not in the *puerto*. I couldn't stand aside idly and refuse to help." Jane was shaking with anger. "If you understood about these things you wouldn't question me."

He caught her by the shoulders, all but shaking her.

"I understand that you are making a fool of me," he said. "Quite deliberately you have disobeyed my orders. I brought you here to look after my children, not to court infection by nursing every needy brat down in the *puerto*. That is Andrew Ballantyne's concern, not ours. He made his choice, or it was made for him when he was hounded out of England."

"That's not true!" Jane cried. "He made a sacrifice— for someone else."

His mocking smile derided her credulity.

"A pretty story," he laughed. "He'll have to do much better than that when he is questioned about the Estrella."

She stared at him speechlessly.

"Yes, Jane, I intend to accuse him," he said. "I have all the proof I need now."

Jane groped her way to the edge of the terrace, staring out into the night. A bird's shrill cry rent the silence on a note of warning.

"What will you do?" she whispered.

"I have decided to call in the police."

She felt as if she had been turned to stone. He had such power and he was ruthless about using it. What *could* Andrew do if Felipe was determined to injure him?

"What proof have you got?" she asked desperately.

"Enough." He lit a fresh cigar. "Ballantyne was alone in the salon for a quarter of an hour after he came to attend to you the other afternoon. He had plenty of opportunity then to take the Estrella."

"You asked him to wait," Jane said. "Perhaps you even set a trap for him."

"My dear Jane," he smiled, "don't let us become melodramatic. This is a straightforward case of theft. If I had wanted to 'trap' your doctor friend I could have gone about it more subtly, don't you think? The real truth of the matter is that you are bemused by Andrew Ballantyne, just as your sister was."

"That's not true!" Her strangled denial lashed out at him. "You would do anything to injure Andrew. Anything in your power."

"And this is in my power." The smile had left his eyes for good. "I can't allow you to make a laughing-stock of me in the *puerto,* Jane. Your sister did that, and I had to bear it until her death released me. With you it is different. I have already learned my lesson. To treat a woman with leniency is foolish, but to accept her as an equal is lunacy. This much-vaunted freedom of the sexes has played itself out. It has never really existed here, never been fully accepted. I have made the *puerto* out of bounds for the children. I must now forbid you to go there without an escort."

Jane gasped incredulously.

"This is nonsense, Felipe!" she protested. "You can't act as if I were in purdah. We're not married, or even engaged. The whole situation is ridiculous."

"Not as I see it," he contradicted. "My edict, as you consider it, is for your own protection. I am responsible for you while you remain under my roof."

He turned and left her. Jane wanted to run after Andrew and beg him to take her away, but the car had gone long ago and he had already refused her sanctuary. He had let her see quite plainly that he did not want to become involved.

But he was involved. The whole pattern of Felipe's revenge was centred upon him, and now her brother-in-law was ready to come out into the open.

What evidence had he found? On what pretext could he accuse Andrew? Her heart missed a beat as she wondered what had transpired in the hours she had been away. Almost a whole day. Anything could have happened.

Instinctively she sought out Teresa.

"What has happened, Teresa?" she asked, coming straight to the point.

"I suppose you mean about the emerald?" Teresa scarcely lifted her eyes from the fine drawn-thread work she was busy with. "Felipe has already discovered the culprit. Doctor Ballantyne never was very good at concealing the evidence against him. Everyone knew that your sister went to his surgery quite unashamedly out of consulting hours."

"We're not discussing Grace." Jane's voice all but failed her. "You seem to bring her frailty up at every conceivable opportunity, Teresa, but it's all in the past now. Whatever Grace did she paid for it — with her life."

"Yes," Teresa agreed. "Retribution was swift in your sister's case. Now it is Doctor Ballantyne's turn." She raised her eyes until they met Jane's. "Of course he took the emerald," she declared. "He was greatly in debt, and yesterday he went to La Laguna and made good all his promissory notes. He also paid off the outstanding money on the medical equipment Doctor Baer ordered for the clinic two years ago. Felipe discovered this without much trouble," she added. "Nothing remains a secret on the Island for every long."

"No," Jane agreed, hardly able to control the flood of disappointment which threatened to overwhelm her.

"Of course, it could be quite a normal thing for Doctor Ballantyne to do."

Teresa treated her to a pitying smile.

"I'm sure he would be touched if he knew you had such faith in him," she observed. "Certainly no one else has."

"Meaning Felipe?" Jane said. "But Felipe could be wrong."

"He isn't often mistaken." Teresa folded away her work with meticulous care. "Felipe couldn't afford to make an accusation of this kind unless he was reasonably sure. He has his position on the island to consider. It's very important," she added, rising to leave the room. "This added scandal is sure to renew all the old gossip about your sister. But Felipe is quite prepared for that to see justice done."

Helplessly Jane watched her go. There was an elation in Teresa's manner which she could not understand, as if she, too, hated Andrew and wished to see him humiliated.

Sisa made her appearance with a tray of coffee and sweetmeats.

"I can't eat anything, Sisa," Jane said. "I'm not hungry. What have the children been doing all afternoon?"

"They have been out riding. Miguel took them to Orotava to have tea with the *señora*."

"Mrs. Prescott?"

Sisa nodded.

"She telephoned to my master to ask for permission."

It seemed an odd sort of thing for Daisy Prescott to do, but she was fond of the children.

"She ask for you to go, also," Sisa ran on, "but you were not yet returned from the *puerto*."

"Then your master came in early?"

"At mid-day, before he set out for La Laguna. He wished to take you with him, but he could not wait till you were returned from the clinic."

Which meant that there had been more than one reason for Felipe's anger. Jane could not think why he had wanted her to make the journey to La Laguna with him, unless it had been to leave her in no doubt about Andrew's perfidy. La Laguna was also the centre of civil justice for the area. He could have gone there to denounce a thief.

Suddenly her blood ran cold. Was Andrew already arrested?

"Sisa," she asked desperately, "have you seen anyone around the house? Anyone suspicious-looking? A stranger, perhaps?"

Sisa shook her head.

"Only the people we know. Doctor Ballantyne and the Señor Travers. And Mrs. Prescott."

"When they came with the painting," Jane mused, "where did they wait, Sisa?"

"In the *patio*. I served them wine there, and then they went all together into the salon where the picture is to hang."

"And your master was with them all the time?"

Sisa looked perplexed, wondering, no doubt, where all these questions were leading.

"All the time, except for ten minutes in the *patio* where they waited."

"And you were there?"

"Except when I went to draw the malmsey. The *señora* is very fond of our local wine."

"Thank you, Sisa."

There had been nothing in their conversation to help Andrew, no opportunity, it seemed, for either Daisy or her protégé to visit the salon without being observed.

347

Nervously she bit her lower lip. What was she trying to do? To fasten the blame on to anyone so that her faith in Andrew might not be shattered? The facts were plain enough. Neither Daisy Prescott nor Travers had been given the opportunity of visiting the salon unnoticed that afternoon and it was unlikely that they would have broken into the house afterwards in order to steal the emerald.

Whoever had done it knew about the key and where it was kept when Felipe didn't carry it about with him.

The conviction struck her with the force of a physical blow. Who? Who?

There only remained Teresa.

How could she prove anything against Teresa?

"Sisa!" She called the girl back. "How long has Doña Teresa been here?"

Sisa considered the question.

"One—two months, perhaps — this time."

"Then she was here before — visiting?"

"Many times, since she was a widow. Once she thought she would marry Doctor Ballantyne."

Andrew? Jane could not believe it.

"It was so foolish," Sisa said, carrying off the rejected tray, "because the doctor did not like her. Nobody does."

She had been determined to deliver that parting thrust because she was still smarting under Teresa's questioning and it was evident that she had been deeply hurt by the suggestion of suspicion falling on herself or her fellow servants. They were loyal to Felipe to a man, Sisa even more so than the others.

Jane watched her go with the odd conviction that Sisa might have produced the clue she needed to Teresa's treachery.

348

Rejected by Andrew, Teresa was quite capable of stooping to any revenge. Whether or not Andrew had taken the emerald, Teresa would be happy to see him accused. She was the woman scorned.

It seemed fantastic that she could ever have imagined Andrew in love with her, but wasn't it possible that this was her reason for hating Grace and doing her best to sully her memory?

Jane caught her breath. What a tangled web it was, and how wrong she could be! She had yet to prove her theories. She had to find out the truth about Teresa.

There was very little time to spare and she had no one to appeal to. Going in search of Andrew was impossible. It would only antagonize Felipe more than ever, and he had already said that he was about to contact the police.

What could she say to Andrew, anyway? I don't believe you're guilty, but we've got to prove it? She could imagine his disdain, his anger, perhaps.

No, she had to do this thing on her own.

Teresa was already in the salon when she went down to dinner. Jane had heard a car drive up and voices raised on the terrace, but there was no immediate sign of a guest.

Almost instinctively her eyes went to the cabinet against the far wall. The painted doors stood open. Teresa allowed her gaze to follow hers, her thin lips parted in a smile.

"We have a visitor," she mentioned, glancing in the direction of her brother's study. "The Chief of Police."

Jane sank on to the nearest chair. Her legs had refused to support her. So soon? Felipe had scarcely waited to be sure before accusing Andrew.

The study door opened and the two men came out. They were sharing a joke. Felipe looked satisfied.

"Ah, Jane!" he said, seeing her seated beside the cabinet. "May I introduce a friend of mine?"

She did not hear the name or the light banter which followed it. A small, dark-moustached man had taken her hand, bowed, and carried it to his lips in formal greeting and two dark brown eyes were searching hers.

"*Señorita*, I am charmed! I hear much about you from the Marqués, and of course I was acquainted with your sister. So lovely. So charming. Such a tragedy when she died!"

There was a small, awkward silence which Teresa hastened to break.

"You will stay with us the night?" she asked, but their guest shook his head.

"Alas, no! I am on my way to Las Aguas. There has been some trouble there — a stabbing with a knife." He smiled in Jane's direction. "Nothing serious, you understand. No one killed, but it is not good to ignore these things. I go personally because I have a sister at San Juan de la Rambla whom I see too seldom!"

He laughed heartily as Felipe poured him a drink.

"You will call on me on your return journey, of course," Felipe suggested. "I may have more to report on the matter we have just discussed."

Jane felt stunned. She had been hoping against hope that Felipe was bluffing when he had threatened to put the evidence he had accumulated in the past few hours immediately into the hands of the police. She had even thought him sadistic enough to want to play a personal cat-and-mouse game with his victim a little longer.

He went with his visitor to the terrace to see him into his car, and Teresa closed the painted doors of the cabinet.

"We shall see now what becomes of your friend Doctor Ballantyne," she observed. "He cannot hope

350

to stay for long on the Island, even if he isn't convicted of theft."

"You know Andrew didn't do it," Jane said in a tense undertone. "Why are you being so vindictive? He is needed here, among your own people. Hans Baer couldn't run the practice without him, and the clinic would have to be closed."

"The clinic is just another of Doctor Baer's pipedreams," Teresa retorted. "There have been many others. The people of the *puerto* have survived without clinics in the past. Felipe has always been willing to help with money when it was absolutely necessary. When one does too much it is not appreciated. One's generosity is eventually taken for granted."

So that was it! The truth of the matter, Jane thought. Felipe wished to remain the supreme protector, delivering his largesse where he considered it to be necessary, not where a mere newcomer knew it to be essential. Quite apart from his personal animosity towards Andrew, a matter of pride and prestige was involved. The two foreign doctors had unconsciously intruded upon the Marqués de Pardo y Cabor's preserves, and Teresa as well as Felipe was determined that they should be punished for their presumption.

If Andrew had encouraged Teresa's romantic overtures it might have been different, but he had spurned her, and this was the result. Even if Teresa had evidence in his favour she would withhold it deliberately to hurt him.

"I don't understand you," Jane said passionately. "Why won't you help Andrew — if you know the truth?"

Teresa met her pleading with a stony stare.

"I know nothing," she said, "except that my brother is right."

It was hopeless, Jane thought. She had appealed to Teresa in vain.

The meal they shared was the most uncomfortable she had ever sat through. Felipe chose to ignore the subject that was on all their minds, questioning them instead about the children.

"It's a pity you didn't find time to ride over to Orotava with them," he said to Jane. "It would have been excellent practice for you. Miguel tells me that Chris is becoming quite proficient. I must begin to take the boy with me on my rounds of the estate. He is quite old enough now."

"Rozanne would love to go with you," Jane said impulsively. "She is a fine little horsewoman for her age, I understand, and she is often lonely."

"Lonely?" He looked across the table at her as if he didn't quite understand her meaning. "Surely there is plenty for the child to do around the house?"

"Yes, indeed," Jane agreed. "But sometimes she would like to be with you, Felipe."

He stiffened.

"I give her all she needs," he declared.

"In a material way," Jane allowed patiently. "But she shouldn't have to go—elsewhere for affection."

His dark brows met in a sudden frown.

"You mean the Prescott woman," he said, "and that protégé of hers? I agree they are odd sort of people to trust one's daughter with, but they seem to understand Rozanne, and she likes painting as much as riding, I believe. That and the languages I wish her to learn should take care of any extra time or energy she may have at her disposal."

"Jane believes that we have neglected Rozanne since her mother died." Teresa's voice was edged with ice. "She sees her as the Cinderella of the family and wants to make sure that she will go to the ball. But Rozanne has always been secretive and hidden. You know that Grace had difficulty with her, too. She has never been an obedient child, and affection doesn't appear to come naturally to her."

Felipe pushed back his chair, a signal for their conversation to end. He was becoming bored with the subject of Rozánne.

"A great deal of nonsense is talked nowadays about children and their impulses," he said. "Rozanne must learn to understand that she is not the most important member of this household. She can ride and have her painting lessons, and swim and mix with the other children at the Club. What more can a girl of six possibly want?"

"Your love," Jane said, wishing immediately that she had remained silent.

Felipe smiled.

"My dear Jane, you are altogether too sentimental in your approach to life," he said. "You will find out your mistake sooner or later, of course. One of these lame ducks of yours will turn and snap at you one day, and you won't like it, I assure you. Either that or they'll let you down so badly you'll be heartbroken."

"I'll have to take a chance on that," Jane said unhappily.

CHAPTER EIGHT

FELIPE decided to drive to Santa Cruz the following morning.

"I would take you with me, Jane," he said, "but this is a rushed trip. I shall be dealing with business matters and won't have time to show you round. Later we can make a social visit, and I shall try to persuade you that Santa Cruz can be as exciting as London."

"I'd like to go," Jane agreed, "some other time."

She had made up her mind to warn Andrew, and this was the opportunity she needed. With a swiftly-beating heart she watched Felipe go. He drove the car himself, leaving Miguel behind. As a trusted watchdog?

When the children trooped off to their lessons she went out through the archway in the wall to the stables. A groom, busy with one of the horses, looked up at her approach. She asked for Miguel.

The boy appeared surprised. It was customary to ring for servants, but the *señorita* was strange to their ways.

Miguel also looked surprised when he saw her, although he did his best to hide it.

"I want you to saddle a horse for me," Jane told him. "The one I had the other day." When he hesitated momentarily she added: "Your master hadn't time to give the order himself. He—thinks I should ride more often." She smiled at him. "I'm not very good, am I?"

"You need practice, that is all," he agreed, still faintly puzzled by his master's oversight. "I will take you wherever you wish."

"To the *puerto*," Jane said far too urgently. "It isn't too far for a start, is it?"

"No, not too far."

She could imagine Felipe questioning Miguel afterwards, but her need was too urgent for her to care. For a moment she thought that he was about to refuse, and then he smiled, showing all his splendid white teeth.

"*Si*, I go with you?"

354

It would have been too much to hope that she could make the journey alone, Jane realized as she sped up to her room to change. As it was, she had still one further hurdle to clear, Teresa.

Coming slowly down the staircase again in her borrowed jodhpurs and silk shirt, she could hear the sound of Teresa's voice coming from the kitchen premises where she went each morning to discuss the menu for the day. Sisa's and the cook's voice were raised in protest, but these were the usual accompaniments to domestic management in a Spanish household and meant nothing. It gave her the opportunity of passing through the *patio* unobserved. One of the stable lads could deliver a message to Teresa when she had gone.

By the time she was finally mounted on the squat little mare she was quite glad that Miguel had insisted on accompanying her. She was no horsewoman. She was, in fact, almost afraid. There was no elation for her in the feel of a horse's flanks between her knees, and she gripped the reins far too hard.

Aware of her discomfort by some sixth animal sense, the mare ambled along placidly, refusing to trot even when urged by Miguel with a gentle prod of the whip.

"She knows how nervous I am," Jane said, conscious of a double meaning in her words which the young Spaniard could not understand. "I'm happy just jogging along like this."

Miguel was also content. The sun was not yet hot and there was a gentle breeze blowing in from the sea. It swept across the banana fields, turning them into an undulating green swell, and tossed the feathery tops of the palms with an insolent abandon which pleased him. It was a morning for riding leisurely without thought.

They rode down into the *puerto* by a path Jane hadn't used before. It was narrow and winding and came out eventually on the south side of the *plaza*. The small tree-shaded square was busier than she had seen it, with people drinking and laughing and queueing at the back.

"Market," Miguel explained cryptically, pointing to the groups already setting out their wares on the shaded pavements beyond the trees.

Jane waited for him to help her down. Already she felt stiff and sore, but she could not take physical discomfort into account.

"Take care of the horses, Miguel," she commanded. "I have an errand to do."

"You will not go far?" he begged, distressed by her suggestion. "Everything you could wish to buy is here — limes, papaya, lemons, eggs, chicken, bright shawls and shoes. There is also fish," he added for ample measure. "The fish of the *puerto* is very good. Very fresh from the sea."

"Perhaps Doña Teresa would like some," Jane agreed hastily. "Buy some, Miguel." She felt in her pocket for the few *pesetas* she had brought with her. "How much?"

He looked affronted.

"Santiago comes for the fish," he declared, making a wry face. "It does not smell good when carried on horseback in the sun."

And it was also undignified, Jane realized. Marketing was a woman's job, or the task allotted to an inferior servant, like the old man, Santiago, whom Felipe had pensioned off after a lifetime on the estate.

"I won't be long," she promised. Then, to reassure him: "I'm going for five minutes to Doctor Baer's clinic. I was there yesterday donating some blood."

"Si! Si!" Everything was all right now. Miguel knew about the campaign for blood donors and had gallantly offered his quota. "You go for check-up?" he decided.

Jane didn't trouble to enlighten him. She knew her way to the clinic from the *plaza*. In five minutes she was there. It looked deceptively quiet and deserted.

Pushing open the swing doors, she went in to confront the receptionist, who recognized her from the day before.

"Doctor Ballantyne, he has just gone out," the girl told her. "Five — ten minutes ago."

Jane could scarcely hide her disappointment.

"Do you know when he will be back? When will he return?" she amended slowly.

The Spanish girl appeared to be uncertain.

"Perhaps two hours. He go on a call to Realejo Bajo, then to Realejo Alto and return by Orotava."

Past the estate, Jane thought. Right on our very doorstep, and I've come all this way to find him!

"And Doctor Baer?"

"Out also!" The receptionist smiled her apology. "He has gone to the bank."

Jane thanked her, turning to the door. What to do now? She could not very well seek out Hans in the crowded bank. Besides, it was Andrew she had come to see. She seemed fated to draw a blank, and suddenly she felt trapped. She had made her difficult journey quite sure that Andrew would be there at the end of it, but now Felipe seemed to be holding all the cards once more. There was very little hope of her meeting Andrew on their return journey, and Miguel would be with her. Felipe's spy.

She brushed the thought aside, retracing her steps through the old part of the town where the cobbled streets were steep and shady and quiet gardens lay beyond every wrought-iron gateway. She was passing the Hotel Mency when she heard her own name.

"Why, Jane! You're the last person I expected to meet. Where are you bound for? Come in and have a drink with me. It's so dusty sitting in the square under one of these silly little coloured umbrellas!"

Garrulous as ever, Daisy Prescott swept her through the open doorway of the hotel into a cool, colonnaded courtyard where a fountain played in a deep stone basin surrounded by tropical plants.

Jane didn't particularly want to speak to Daisy at that moment, but there was no way of avoiding the invitation short of being rude. As they sat down at one of the tables near the fountain she imagined that Daisy looked pale, and her deeply-set blue eyes were red-rimmed and tearful. She did nothing to conceal her distress.

"I'm terribly upset, Jane," she confided. "I've had the most frightful quarrel with Vincent."

"Oh?" Jane felt embarrassed. "I'm sorry."

"So am I, now that it's all over." Daisy dabbed at her eyes with a scrap of blue linen. "We've often argued," she admitted, "but never quite so violently. I fear he's gone for good this time."

"You mean he's left the Island?"

"I don't know." Daisy applied a liberal coating of powder to her already over-made-up face. "I just don't know. He packed a suitcase and left, saying he would arrange for the remainder of his belongings to be collected. Jane, I think he *wanted* to go. I feel he's been trying to get away from me for ages but just hasn't had the courage after all I've done for him."

"You're feeling hurt," Jane said awkwardly. "You'll forget about him in time."

Daisy sighed.

"I suppose so. Maybe I'm nothing but a foolish old woman," she suggested.

Jane thought how pathetic she looked, sitting there in her frilly cotton dress with the rows and rows of pearls circling her chubby neck and her floppy sun hat weighted down with artificial flowers. Her white sandals had been eased off as soon as she had collapsed into a comfortable chair, and her small, beringed fingers played nervously with the clasp of her expensive handbag.

"I've got a great deal of money, Jane," she said, "but I've never had any real happiness. I suppose I've always coveted the things I didn't possess. That's been my trouble. My husband was a very wealthy man, but he had no time for me. Big business was all that mattered to him. He never wanted us to have a family. We travelled about so much. We came here to Orotava, once, and I fell in love with the place. I promised myself I would come back one day, when I was free to do so." She heaved a deep sigh. "I came back, but it wasn't the same. There was nobody who really cared what happened to me. All our acquaintances had been Henry's business colleagues, and they were all too immersed in their own affairs to wonder what became of me." She sipped idly at her drink. "Then I began to take an interest in art," she continued. "It filled the void. I could always manage to persuade some needy artist that I was essential to him. That's how I came to know Vincent. He was flat broke when we met, and he could paint. All he needed was a little time. I gave him that time."

Her eyes clouded and she sat gazing at the fountain, as if she could see in the falling cascade of water all the mistakes of the past.

"Perhaps I was foolish to expect some sort of gratitude," she said after a few minutes. "All artists are selfish. They think of nothing but their work. Any churlishness — almost any crime — is to be excused if it will further their ambitions. It would seem that creative genius has a moral code of its own."

Bitterness had crept into her voice at last and Jane could not comfort her.

"I forgave him so much," she ran on. "Even his defections with other women. He had quite a few." She paused, colouring with embarrassment as she met Jane's eyes. "I shouldn't be talking to you like this," she apologized. "Drink up your lime and try to forget it."

Jane took a long, cooling gulp of iced lime juice and said that she would have to go. Miguel was waiting.

"What brought you to the *puerto* without the children?" Daisy asked, her curiosity getting the better of her heartache. "You must have left the Casa very early."

"I came to see Andrew," Jane admitted. "I—had something to say to him."

"About the emerald?" Daisy asked guardedly. "The Club's simply seething with the news. Felipe thinks Andrew took it."

"Do you?" Jane asked bluntly.

Daisy looked taken aback.

"Well—no." She hesitated. "I don't think Andrew would so such a thing, but Teresa's making no bones about his guilt. She says Felipe is putting everything into the hands of the police."

Jane's even white teeth clamped down on her lower lip.

"She hasn't a scrap of evidence," she declared, rising angrily to her feet. "She's hopelessly prejudiced, that's all."

"Jane," Daisy said, "I think you're in love with Andrew."

Jane stood gazing down into the wide stone basin where the water of the fountain fell like summer rain.

"If I am, it's hopeless, isn't it?" she said. "He was in love with Grace. He's not the type to change." She turned towards the door. "Thank you for the drink, Daisy. I must go."

"Jane——!"

She did not turn back. Whatever Daisy had been about to say couldn't be important.

Miguel was looking anxious by the time she reached the *plaza,* but his face cleared at sight of her.

"You take cool drink?" he asked, indicating one of the little iron tables in the shades of a gaudy umbrella.

Jane shook her head.

"No, thank you, Miguel," she explained. "I've just had one at the Mency. I met a friend."

He nodded, going off to fetch the horses.

Jane glanced about her in the hope of seeing Hans Baer, but without result. The bank was still full of customers, but he had probably been attended to long ago. There was no point in going back to the clinic, however, because the receptionist had not really been sure when he would return. Besides, he probably knew all about Felipe's accusations by this time, since it was already common gossip at the Club.

The ride back was an agony to her. She was stiff and sore by the time they reached the Casa, and not at all prepared for the news which awaited her.

"You had a visitor while you were out," Teresa told her stiffly. "Doctor Ballantyne."

361

"Andrew?" Jane caught her breath. "Did he—say what he wanted?"

"No." Teresa's mouth tightened. "He would nòt leave any message, but by the look of him it appeared to be urgent."

"Did he offer to call back—or phone?"

"No," Teresa said again. "He promised to get in touch with you later. That was all."

She stood rigid beside the little fountain in the *patio*, waiting for Jane to commit herself, but Jane's thoughts were too busy with the events of the past two hours to give her any satisfaction. If only she had stayed where she was instead of rushing off to the clinic in search of Andrew!

The children, released from their morning in the school-room, came running through the hall.

"You've been out riding!" Rozanne said reproachfully.

"I want to go on my pony!" Chris wailed. "You said I could. Papa said I could," he added to frustrate all argument.

"You can't ride in the middle of the day. You know that," Teresa told him severely. "Eat up your lunch and have your *siesta*, and then you can tell Miguel to bring round your pony." She glanced at Rozanne. "You wish to go with your brother, I suppose?"

Rozanne hesitated.

"Where are they going?" she asked, her thoughts obviously occupied elsewhere.

"Not out of the estate," Teresa reminded her. "Your father is away from home."

"Then I shall not go," Rozanne pouted. "Round and round the boundary wall," she mocked, "with nothing to see but bananas!"

"In that case you had better occupy your time with some sewing," her aunt suggested dryly. "You're well behind with your embroidery."

Rozanne's lips tightened rebelliously, but she said nothing.

They ate their meal in silence. Turning the information she had received at the clinic over and over in her mind, Jane wondered if Andrew would seek her out again on his way back from Realejo Bajo. It was possible. He could return to the *puerto* by the shore road high above the sea or by Realejo Alto to La Orotava.

Her heartbeats quickened. What had he to say to her? Teresa had suggested urgency, but Teresa was not to be trusted where Andrew was concerned.

The *siesta* hour had always been difficult for Jane. The house died after mid-day. There was no sound anywhere. Even the birds and the domestic animals went to sleep. She lay on her bed, restless and hot. It would be an offence to run a bath because one of the servants would come running to attend to her.

When she rose she stood at her window looking out across the hushed garden to El Teide. The old giant of the mountains was asleep, too, nodding in the sun. The heat shimmered on her balcony rail and the arum lilies round the pond wilted and drooped their heads. It was still much too hot to move about with comfort, but she knew that Andrew would be motoring back from his errand of mercy by now.

Selecting a headscarf from a drawer of her wardrobe, she made her way to the terrace and the main drive. Nothing stirred, not even a dog. If she walked in the shade of the boundary wall she would come out on to the road nearer Realejo Alto. It was an odd chance, but she might just be able to intercept Andrew on his way to the Casa. Certainly she would be able to hear

363

the car engine on such a windless day when not even a leaf stirred on the tall eucalyptus trees above her head.

Hurrying in their shade, she reached the wooden door in the wall, only to find it locked. Frustrated and suddenly near to tears, she tugged at it without result, and then she knew what she had to do. She had to get over the wall somehow.

A stout vine clambered over the arch of the doorway and she considered it speculatively, quite sure that it would bear her weight. It had been growing there for years. The gnarled old trunk was safer than any ladder. Clusters of fragrant white blossom festooned the branches spreading liberally on either side, and these, too, would afford her a foothold.

Without a second thought she clambered to the top, pulling herself up on to the wall. The scene which met her eyes was breathtakingly beautiful, but when she looked down to the road she realized her mistake. It lay perhaps fourteen feet beneath her, and there was no convenient creeper on this side to aid her descent.

Defeated, she sat there gazing at the empty road. She had been a fool not to think of such a possibility. If she jumped she might break her leg or injure herself in some other way, calling the attention of the whole Casa to her irresponsibility. Felipe would be told, and Teresa. But to climb back into the plantation and go round to the main gates might mean that she would miss Andrew for a second time.

Desperately she strained her eyes along the dusty highway, but it stretched, deserted, as far as she could see on either side.

She told herself that she could not sit on the wall for ever, yet looking back into the plantation she was conscious of a vague nausea. She had no head for heights.

364

Now she could neither climb back nor jump from her high perch on to the road and take a chance. She felt petrified there on the wall, like a moth held by a pin.

It was madness to sit for long in the full glare of the sun, but she could not move. The ignominy of signalling to a passing vehicle seemed less than the terror of the descent behind her.

She waited. When she finally heard the car's engine in the distance, coming from the direction of Realejo Alto, she wondered if she should let it pass without motioning the driver to stop. She could easily remain unobserved if his attention was riveted to the road.

When the car appeared she recognized Hans' old convertible, and her doubts collapsed in relief. Andrew slowed down even before she signalled to him.

"Jane! For heaven's sake, what are you doing up there?" His expression was a mixture of perplexity and amusement as he got out from behind the wheel and stood looking up at her. "You look like a truant schoolboy!"

"I feel more like a fool," she confessed. "Andrew, I can't come down. I just can't move — either way."

He tried not to laugh.

"What took you up there in the first place?" he asked.

"I came to the door and found it locked. I thought it would be easy to get over this way, but there was no creeper on the outside. I suppose I panicked."

He looked at her for a moment without answering.

"Do you want to come down?" he asked at last.

"Yes, I think so. I — heard you had been at the Casa. Teresa told me."

All the laughter went out of his face, the heavy lines returning to etch themselves deeply between his brows.

"I was going to try again," he said. "But perhaps we'd have more privacy out here."

He was standing directly beneath her, holding out his arms.

"Jump!" he commanded.

Jane drew a deep breath, every pulse in her body pounding in unison with her quickened heart.

"If you're going to do it it must be now," Andrew advised, bracing himself on the side of the dusty road.

The steadiness of his voice gave her the courage she needed to jump. Easing herself off the top of the wall, she let go.

She had closed her eyes, and she felt his arms fasten about her with an overwhelming sense of sanctuary. There, on the dusty road, he held her for a moment. Or was it an eternity? She could feel his heart pounding as swiftly as her own and his quickened breath warm against her cheek.

Then, abruptly, he let her go, almost thrusting her from him.

"It was easier than you thought, wasn't it?" he said gruffly.

"I've always been afraid of heights." Her voice sounded far away to her own ears. "I had to see you, Andrew. I went to the clinic this morning, but you'd gone."

He looked at her sharply.

"Why did you do that?" he demanded.

"I — wanted to tell you about Felipe. To warn you that he had gone to the police."

He thrust her towards the car.

"Get in," he commanded. "We can't afford to be seen here together."

She obeyed him without question, and when he had driven a little way he turned the car into a narrow, rutted side track overshadowed by a row of ragged palms. He pulled up facing the sea. For a moment they sat in silence looking out across the blue ocean to the shadowy outline of La Palma on the horizon. It was like the ghost of an old Spanish galleon stealing away into the mists of time.

"I came to see you this morning," Andrew said into the silence, "because I wanted you to do something for me."

She waited, her heart turning over in sudden fear.

"I want you to return this to Felipe."

He felt in his pocket, holding something out towards her. Without looking at it she knew it was the Estrella.

"You can tell him you got it from me," he said. "Ask him to notify the police that it's been found."

"Andrew!"

She stared at him, unable to believe, unable to credit this thing even when she saw the emerald lying in the palm of his hand. It winked up at her in the strong sunlight, green and evil as the treachery which seemed to hedge her round in every direction.

"Where did you get it?" she whispered, still not able to accept him as a thief.

"It was — returned to me." His voice sounded harsh and the stern face was inscrutable. "I can't tell you any more than that. You'll have to trust me. I'm hoping that Felipe will agree to let the matter drop once he's in possession of the stone again. I think that might well happen. He prizes his material possessions greatly."

Jane knew that her brother-in-law wouldn't let the matter drop. Not even if she pleaded with him.

"If you know anything, Andrew, you must tell me," she begged. "If you didn't take it — who did?"

He turned in his seat to look at her for a long moment and then he shrugged.

"It was asking a lot of you, wasn't it?" he said beneath his breath.

To trust him? Jane's hands were tightly clenched, the nails biting into her flesh.

"If you're trying to shield someone——" she began, but he laughed.

"Forget about it, Jane," he said, starting up the car. "I'll go to Felipe myself. I only thought it might be quicker this way."

"He's at Santa Cruz," Jane said dully. "It will be late before he gets back."

"I'll have to come back then," he said almost wearily. "It will be better if he knows tonight."

"Let me take it." Impulsively she held out her hand for the emerald. "I can speak to him the moment he comes in. I can try to explain."

Her heart felt as heavy as lead and she couldn't quite meet his eyes. He shook his head.

"No, Jane," he said. "It was a foolish mistake on my part even to think of involving you. I should never have considered it. I'll do the job myself once I've finished my evening surgery."

"You can't drive back all this way," she protested. "Let me do it, Andrew."

"No," He was adamant. "It was a moment's madness. I'll see Felipe," he repeated. "We might come to some sort of understanding."

It was such a forlorn hope that Jane felt like snatching the emerald from him even against his will, but he put it safely back in his pocket out of reach. Felipe would never forgive him for the emerald or anything else.

He stopped the car at the main gates.

"Can you walk from here, or shall I run you up to the house?" he asked.

"I can walk."

Jane felt shaken and lost, as if she had failed him in some way, but she could not call him back. She watched as he drove away, a tall, lean, rather lonely figure in the battered old car which didn't even belong to him.

Halfway to the house she halted, aware of a clattering of horses' hoofs on the drive ahead of her, coming towards her. It was Rozanne. She trotted her pony briskly, and was about to pass with no more than a smile when she thought better of it and reined in her mount to hear what Jane had to say.

"You've changed your mind about going out," Jane observed. "It is a lovely afternoon for a ride. You won't go out of the grounds, will you?"

Rozanne avoided the direct question, and Jane noticed that she had been crying. Secretly, perhaps, while the others slept.

"It isn't true, is it?" she asked. "What Doña Teresa says?"

Jane's heart missed a beat. Surely Teresa wouldn't discuss Andrew with the children?

"What did she say?" she asked guardedly.

"That Don Vincent has gone." The sensitive mouth quivered. "That I will never see him again."

Jane could scarcely credit that news could travel so quickly. She had only heard it herself that morning from Daisy and now it had reached the Casa.

"He may come back," she comforted. "He may just have gone for a little holiday."

"No," Rozanne contradicted her in her odd, fatalistic way. "He has gone for good, and he didn't even see my painting. I hate him! I hate him!" she cried passionately. "I hate everybody."

"Rozanne, try to understand," Jane pleaded. "Other people love you besides Don Vincent. Your father—"

"He hates me," the child declared without fury. "He loves only Chris."

Her youthful, tragic awareness of the situation stunned Jane.

"If you and I really got to know each other, Rozanne," she suggested, "we could be friends. I'm your aunt," she added gently. "I love you."

Rozanne's stare was resentful.

"I don't want anybody to love me," she said. "I don't need you." She slid forward in the saddle, clinging round the pony's neck. "I've got Pedro. I don't care!"

Before Jane could guess her intentions she had dug her rebellious little heels into the pony's flank and they were off like the wind, streaking straight for the main gates.

"Bother!" Jane exclaimed aloud. "Rozanne, you are a nuisance!"

But she was more than a little troubled by the course events had taken. Apart from everything else, Felipe would be furious when he returned to find that his daughter had deliberately disobeyed his orders and left the plantation without an escort. He would punish Rozanne, and she was in no mood to accept it as a fair reprimand. Felipe's punishments would be harsh, Jane suspected. Discipline was something which he insisted his family should acknowledge at an early age, and even Chris was often afraid of him.

Without troubling to go in search of Teresa, whose advice she felt would be of little help, she ran to the stables, hoping to find that Miguel was still there, but Chris's wheedling had won the day, and Miguel and he had started off as soon as *siesta* was over. They could be miles away by this time.

370

There was only one groom left around the place, and his grasp of English was so poor that she had to communicate with him largely by signs.

"Horse?" she requested, pointing to herself. "Ride. You get saddle — quick."

She was still in her jodhpurs and shirt, and she waited impatiently for him to lead out the mare. He seemed to take ages to saddle the animal. None of Felipe's servants hurried unless he was about, she thought, exasperated by the delay.

If she had taken a little more time to consider the situation she might have acted differently, but the most important thing seemed to be to catch up with Rozanne before she had put too great a distance between herself and the Casa.

Time had ceased to count. There was only the urgency of the moment, the fear that something might happen to turn the events of the afternoon into tragedy. It had touched the Casa del Sol once before. She could not allow it to happen again.

When she reached the gates she turned instinctively towards the sea. It was a chance she had to take, but she remembered that Rozanne had told her that she liked to ride along the cliff.

Choosing the narrow lane Andrew had taken less than an hour ago, she rode on past the spot where they had parked the car. The road began to deteriorate and to descend steeply. Soon she found herself in a narrow *barranco* wedged between two walls of rock with no apparent outlet anywhere.

The sea was still ahead of her, but she had lost sight of it now. She seemed to have stumbled into a lost valley, an arid wilderness of stone and grey lava which had once been the scene of a minor volcanic eruption. The whole face of the Island was deeply scarred by these terrifying gullies where nothing survived but giant cacti and a fearless breed of little brown goats which she supposed were wild.

Surely Rozanne would not ride into this awful place? Yet something told her that it was the sort of thing Rozanne might do. She would be alone here, and it was no great distance from the estate.

In all the narrow valley there was no sign of horse and rider, however. The rugged cliff sides came down closer and closer together, and a large black bird lifted off a crag to wheel against the sun, its broad wing-span casting a sinister shadow on the way ahead.

The path grew difficult. Water had poured down it in the rainy season, leaving it deeply rutted, and cacti infringed on it in places. Tamarisk bushes appeared, shivering in a sudden wind. The place had become a narrow funnel leading to the shore.

Before she could prove her theory she was startled by the first sound she had heard since she had entered this dead valley. To her anxious ears it sounded like a scream, but when it came again she recognized it as a horse's whinney. From somewhere on the hidden floor of the valley they had been seen and recognized. Rozanne's pony had made his presence known to the mare.

Jane's mount pricked up her ears and started forward, and all Jane could do was to hold tightly to the rein and pray that the mare wouldn't stumble or need a great deal of guidance. She was so lacking in experience that she was probably a handicap to the intelligent little animal who picked her way so carefully between the disrupted rocks.

More and more the *barranco* took on the appearance of a scene from Dante's Inferno. The lava stream had narrowed and piled itself up into an arrested river of grey stone, and the path beside it was all but engulfed.

Then abruptly it began to climb again, winding dangerously round protruding bluffs where the ground dropped steeply away for a hundred feet or more.

It was at the head of one of these miniature canyons that Jane found the pony. He was standing with his head lowered, quivering on the brink of a steep drop, his saddle girth broken, the saddle itself empty.

Rozanne!

Jane was never quite sure afterwards whether she uttered the word or not. It was a protest and a hope. It seemed to echo across the silent valley like a cry of despair.

Rozanne lay halfway down the steeply sloping hillside, her light jodhpurs and yellow shirt making a vivid splash of colour against the eternal grey. She was quite motionless. Jane slipped from the mare's back with a prayer on her lips.

There was only one way to go down, and that was straight over the edge. Her heart missed a beat as the loose gravel began to slip under her, but she found hand grips here and there.

"Don't let me fall," she kept repeating. "Dear God, don't let me fall!"

Slowly, foot by difficult foot, she made the descent, her hands torn by the vicious teeth of the cacti blades, her mouth and nostrils full of black lava dust. It was like some dreadful nightmare, with no real hope at the end of it.

Rozanne lay on her side, quite limp, and she almost hesitated to touch her. There were bruises on her face and arms and one of her dark plaits had come loose. The fine hair fell across her brow, veiling a face as pale as death.

"Rozanne!" Jane whispered the name this time. "Rozanne, are you all right?"

The dark lashes fluttered and lifted. Rozanne opened her eyes to look at her.

"Go away——"

Relief flooded over Jane like a great tide, bringing back her courage. She could deal with this.

"We're in a spot," she said, forcing a practical note of assurance into her voice. "You must do as I say, Rozanne. Put your arm round my neck and hold on, if you can. Have you any pain?"

The child shook her head without opening her eyes again.

"He took the emerald," she murmured. "I gave it to him, but he still went away."

An icy hand seemed to grip Jane by the throat, but she could not stop to question Rozanne now.

"I gave it to him because I loved him." Rozanne's eyes were wide open now.

"Vincent?" Jane said.

"I got it when nobody was there. I took the key." Rozanne was only vaguely conscious, but she was bent on confession, and Jane let her talk. "Papa didn't need it. He has so many. Doña Teresa says it is a sin to steal, but I didn't. I only took it because Don Vincent was so poor. He hadn't got an emerald, and he showed me how to paint."

The pathetic little confession of gratitude and love ebbed into the chill silence of the hidden valley as the sun sank abruptly beyond its western wall. It left the hillside dark and cold. The island's sudden nightfall had caught Jane unaware. They would be trapped here by the rapidly approaching darkness with nothing but instinct to guide her back up the treacherous slope.

She gathered the child into her arms.

"Don't fret, Rozanne," she comforted her. "We'll manage somehow."

Above them the horses whinnied in distress. Would anyone come, Jane wondered, or would they be forced to spend the night there in the dark and cold, slipping to their deaths in the treacherous gully which yawned beneath them if they made just one false move in their effort to reach the top?

CHAPTER NINE

BACK at the Casa del Sol, Sisa was lighting the lamps. The task was not really hers, but Miguel had gone off in search of Rozanne and the *señorita*. Neither of them had returned, and it was presumed that they were together somewhere within the bounds of the estate.

A strange nervousness had taken possession of Sisa. A threatening cloud seemed to have hovered over the Casa all day, like a buzzard, bird of ill-omen, that only had to keep you in the shadow of its pinions for less than a minute to bring disaster.

Sisa had sensed tragedy before. There had been the time when her mother had died, and the year of the volcano on La Palma which had left them homeless, and that bright, sunny afternoon at the *playa* when Chris had almost drowned.

She thought of her former mistress and the tragedy of the dead baby with tears in her eyes. Nothing, she prayed, must happen to Rozanne, although she was wilful and sullen at times and was often a great trial to them all.

Hanging up the lantern in the *patio,* she watched the yellow circle of light glowing against the darkening garden.

375

"How often have I to tell you not to moon about at night, Sisa!" Teresa said behind her. "Close the doors and come inside."

"But — the *señoritas*?" Sisa queried "They may come back."

"Miguel has gone in search of them." Teresa sounded impatient. "They can come in by the terrace. You have other work to do."

But Sisa could not concentrate on work, however important it might be. She went again and again to the terrace with its broad view of the plantations, and only when she saw the file of lanterns approaching up the slope did she draw a breath of relief.

A horse snorted in the darkness and Miguel came towards her. His face was grave.

"The *señorita's* pony has come home," he said. "Some accident has happened. The saddle is missing."

In the silence which followed Miguel's statement they heard the car. Felipe had returned from Santa Cruz.

"The *señorio*!" Sisa whispered. "He will punish us all."

Teresa came out to meet her brother as he ran lightly up the terrace steps. He saw the pony almost as quickly as she did.

"What has happened here?" he demanded, turning to Miguel with a dark frown. "Where are the children — and the *señorita*?"

"Chris is safe," Teresa said at his elbow. "He has been out riding with Miguel, but they returned some time ago, before nightfall."

Felipe turned to look at her.

"And Rozanne?" he demanded.

Teresa was foolish enough to shrug her shoulders.

"Do not ask me about Rozanne," she said. "If she has gone out of the plantations, Jane is to blame."

Felipe turned his back on her.

"Where did you find the pony?" he demanded of Miguel.

"At the west gate, ten minutes past."

"Outside the gate?"

Miguel nodded.

"She went alone. I did not know, *dueño*."

Felipe looked as if he might strike him, but thought better of it. He would never have believed that he could feel this way about Rozanne.

"Get as many men as you can, and lanterns and ropes," he commanded. "We've got to search till we find her. Where's Jane?" he asked sharply, turning back to his sister.

"Out, also," Teresa informed him. "We may take it that they are together, I suppose."

Felipe stared at her.

"I hope so," he said.

Another car drew up at the end of the terrace. It was Andrew.

"I'd like a word with you, Felipe," he said. The servants had melted away to do their master's bidding. "I've come to return the emerald."

Felipe swung round to face him.

"So — you took the Estrella, after all?"

"No," Andrew said, meeting his eyes steadily. "I didn't take it, but I'm returning it. I'm asking you to forget about the theft, Felipe, because it wasn't exactly that."

"You confuse me," Felipe said, "but we haven't time for explanations. My daughter is missing. She may be dead. Her pony returned without a saddle."

Andrew drew in a sharp breath.

"Was she alone?" he asked.

"We don't know. Jane may be with her. They are both unaccounted for."

"Chris?" Andrew asked automatically.

"Chris is safe."

Andrew didn't ask if he could join the search. It was taken for granted. He backed his car out of the way and went with Felipe to the stables where the horses were already saddled. A car would be useless in the *barrancos* where they meant to search.

"You knew my daughter better than I did," Felipe said. "Have you any idea where she might have gone?"

"Towards the sea," Andrew decided without hesitation. "We often rode that way, Rozanne and I, when we met by chance. She loved the cliff road."

Felipe rounded up the search party. There was no moon, but the stars were bright and each man carried a lantern. Andrew and Felipe had powerful torches.

"You lead the way," Felipe said to Andrew, a concession which surprised everybody.

The horses were unaccustomed to the darkness, but soon they were able to pick their way by the light of the stars. Andrew led them off the main road, searching the first *barranco* in vain. Miguel had said that the mare was missing from the stables, and they now knew that Jane had taken it.

"She must have gone after Rozanne," Felipe decided when he had questioned the groom. "I wonder why my daughter defied my instructions and left the plantations." Suddenly he was looking sharply at Andrew. "You always pretended to understand her," he said. "Had it anything to do with the emerald? Rozanne could have taken the key. When I changed in the evening I left it in my waistcoat pocket. She knew that, but what would she do with the Estrella? The child couldn't even guess at its worth."

"She knew that you valued it," Andrew said slowly. "Perhaps more than anything else in the world. She took it to give to the one person who had offered her a genuine affection — Vincent Travers."

"The artist!" Felipe was dumbfounded and slightly outraged. They were riding ahead of the others, and he asked thickly: "How did you come by it, may I ask?"

Andrew hesitated, but only for a moment.

"Travers meant to disappear and take the stone with him," he explained. "He knew that wild horses wouldn't drag the truth out of Rozanne once she had given him the emerald. He's always been terribly hard-up and dependent on other people's generosity."

"The fellow's nothing more than a cheap parasite," Felipe declared hotly. "The worst kind of sponger, and Daisy Prescott is a vain old fool. When did he decide that the Estrella might prove too hot for him to handle?"

"On the morning he left."

"And he came to you with it?"

Andrew nodded.

"I didn't mean to tell you all this," he said. "I thought you might have accepted the Estrella's return without question. It was a naïve idea, come to think of it."

"You were shielding my daughter," Felipe said. "But it also clears you. By heaven, Ballantyne, if this isn't the truth I'll put you as far as you can go! If you're trading on the fact that Rozanne may be dead——"

Andrew drove his heels into his horse's flank.

"There's always Travers," he pointed out through clenched teeth. "He can't have got very far in twenty-four hours."

He had kept his temper with difficulty, and Felipe had the grace to recognize the fact.

"I'm sorry," he apologized. "I accept your explanation, but why you should take it upon yourself to act as go-between for a man like Travers is beyond me."

"I had very little to lose," Andrew said drily. "And, quite frankly, Travers wasn't good for Rozanne."

The thought of Grace stood between them for a moment, and Felipe spurred his horse on ahead. He was first to reach the track leading to the second *barranco*.

"We may be wasting our time," he said when Andrew and the servants met up with him. "But we'll try this. There's a bridle path goes down to the sea."

"Listen!" Andrew stood forward on his stirrups.

"The mare!" Felipe said as a thin whinny came back to them out of the darkness. "She's down there."

Andrew was already forging his way along the narrow track, his mouth grim and determined, his hand tightening on the reins as he urged his nervous mount towards the hidden cliff.

Jane had made little headway in her scramble up the precipitous slope from the valley's rock-strewn floor. Twice she had slithered back in the darkness, breaking her fall only by digging her nails into the meagre pockets of volcanic soil which broke up the lava bed. Cacti had torn viciously at her thin shirt, drawing blood, and her hair was wildly dishevelled. Rozanne had begun to cry.

"Don't leave me!" she sobbed. "Don't leave me any more."

After that Jane had to abandon the idea of climbing up the cliff face alone to fetch help. She heard the pony's nervous blowing and the sharp clatter of his hoofs as he galloped away along the hard, sun-baked

380

track and found a gleam of hope in the animal's desertion. He would probably make his way back home and start a search for them.

A wind rose, turning the *barranco* into a freezing wilderness. Rozanne's teeth began to chatter.

"We must keep close together," Jane whispered, wrapping her arms about the child. "We must keep each other warm."

Rozanne did not answer. Her sobs had subsided, and she appeared to be numbed into silence by cold and fear.

'What made you come here, Rozanne?" Jane asked, to keep her mind alert. "Was it a favourite ride?"

"It was a favourite of hers and Don Vincent's," the child answered reluctantly. "It was where they always came to be alone."

"Your mother?" Jane's throat felt stiff.

"She loved him," Rozanne said flatly. "When they painted they often came here. Sometimes they would let me come. It was their secret place."

Their secret place! The words seemed etched in letters of fire against the dark wall of the barren valley as Jane groped blindly for the truth. Grace and Vincent? Could this be the truth? Not Grace and Andrew, but Grace and Vincent Travers, who had so much in common! Both selfish, both in love with life but unable to bear its strains and disappointments, they had met and loved in spite of themselves. And they had kept their secret from everyone except this lonely child who longed for a love of her own.

She could scarcely believe that it was true, but she could not question Rozanne further. She had stumbled upon the truth in this roundabout way, but she could not pursue it. Grace and Vincent. It was their own

381

dark secret, and Grace had taken it with her to her grave.

Had she the moral right to aprpoach Felipe in order to clear Andrew? The question nagged in Jane's mind for over an hour as they lay huddled together on the cold hillside, waiting.

"Don't go to sleep," she whispered with her lips close to Rozanne's cheek. "Try to keep awake. Someone is sure to come."

But soon Rozanne lay limp in her arms. Jane tried not to panic, but they were flimsily clad and they had no protection from the bitter cold. The *barranco* acted like a funnel for the wind as it swept down from the mountains to the sea.

"Jane!" She heard her own name, believing it to be a nightmare. "Jane! Jane!"

"Here!" she called back automatically. "Down here!"

A volley of shale and loose lava hurtled past her down the slope, but Andrew was keeping clear of them. He came level and crawled towards them.

"Jane, are you all right?"

"Yes! Oh, yes," she sobbed. "I'm all right, but Rozanne——"

He took the child from her, his hand searching professionally under the flimsy yellow shirt.

"She's alive," he said after a moment. "Don't fret."

It was such a tender, comforting admonition that she could have wept.

"I thought you would never come," she confessed unsteadily.

He put a reassuring arm about her, drawing her close against him.

"Here, drink this," he commanded. "You've had about as much as you can take."

382

Obediently she drank the brandy he offered, relaxing against him while she found sanctuary for a moment in his arms, but soon there was the thought of Rozanne and the others waiting at the top of the cliff.

She could see the lights now, winking against the darkness as the sound of voices drifted down to her.

"They're going to lower a rope," Andrew explained. "It's safer than someone else coming down in case they loosen any more lava. We're right on the old flow here and it's breaking up." He bent over Rozanne, murmuring a few reassuring words to the child as he lifted her. "I'll climb with Rozanne first and then I'll come back for you, Jane. You'll be all right here if you don't attempt to move."

"Yes, I'll be all right," Jane repeated, but she felt suddenly forlorn when he had gone. These few minutes with his free arm about her had been a glimpse of a paradise she might long for all her life in vain.

An eternity of waiting seemed to pass before she saw his dark bulk lowering itself carefully over the cliff once more. A thin layer of cloud had veiled the starlight and he carried a lantern slung to his belt. When he reached her he put it down on the rough shale at her feet.

Suddenly, uncontrollably, Jane began to shiver. In spite of the brandy she felt chilled and defeated.

"Steady on!" Andrew said quietly. "It's all over, Jane. You're both safe now. Rozanne's up there with her father."

"Yes — yes, I know. I'm being terribly foolish." She covered her face with her hands. "You'll have to forgive me, Andrew——"

He moved nearer, between her and the lantern, drawing her hands gently away from her face.

"Forgive you for what?" he asked tenderly. "For being you? For getting yourself into a mess because you wanted to shield Rozanne? My darling, foolish Jane!" He swept her into his arms. "I'd give anything to hear you say you love me, though I haven't a lot of right to ask. I've nothing much to offer you but a man and an ideal. You'd have to take me complete with Hans and the clinic and all the Guanche babies who'll be needing blood transfusions from now till the day we die. We'd never have enough money; we'd be as poor as church mice, but we'd have our work together and we'd have the sun."

She clung to him, because she couldn't speak for a moment.

"It's all I'd ever want," she said when she got her breath back. "Oh, Andrew, don't let me go! I can't believe it's true. I can't believe you love me."

"There was never anyone else," he said simply. "I worked too hard when I was younger. I wanted a big success, but it didn't materialize in the way I had planned. Now I know that there are other things in life besides Harley Street. I'm happy here, Jane. Hans and I can do big things together, given the time." He turned her face up to look deeply into her eyes. "Grace spoke about you quite a lot," he added. "We were good friends. I knew how she felt about Vincent and how hopeless it all was. She used me as a father confessor, I suppose. I was treating her for nerves, and we found it easy to talk to one another, strangely enough. Perhaps that's why I felt that I knew you long before I actually met you — knew what you would be like. Then, when I thought you were going to marry Felipe, I couldn't understand it. He had made Grace unhappy enough, but perhaps she never let you guess."

Jane shook her head.

"Her letters were mostly cheerful. She wrote a great deal about the children. Andrew, I wonder why Felipe suspected Grace of being in love with you?"

"I don't know." His arms tightened about her. "Perhaps I was a convenient cover-up for Grace and Vince. Felipe never had any real proof of Grace's infidelity. He knew that she was unhappy and had found some sort of consolation, but he would have felt grossly insulted if he had discovered that it was Vincent. A penniless artist! *I* was bad enough."

"He could have ruined you," Jane said with a shiver. "He meant to use the emerald to do — just that."

"So I gathered, but I couldn't refuse to take the Estrella back when Vincent wanted to make his exit," he pointed out.

"You were shielding Rozanne," she said. "You can't really accuse me for doing the same thing."

"No, that's true."

"Does Felipe know?" Jane asked. "About Grace and Vincent?"

"I think he has a fairly shrewd idea. He wouldn't say so in so many words, but — yes, I think he knows."

"Rozanne told me," Jane said. "She loved Grace — I'm sure of that — and so it was perhaps easy for her to see where her mother's affection was given. I suppose she just — transferred that love to Vincent when Grace died."

"I guess so," Andrew agreed. "But it's going to be different for Rozanne from now on. Felipe has had a decided shock. It's taken all this — the fear that Rozanne might be dead — to make him realize what his daughter did mean to him. He overlooked Rozanne. That was all. I had hoped something like this would happen for the child's sake, though not in this way.

She needs love more than anything else. I think she'll go back to a new home atmosphere now."

"With Teresa in charge?"

He hesitated.

"I'm not awfully worried about Teresa," he said. "Felipe will keep her in check. If she stays she will continue to be an efficient housekeeper, but she will have no real power, and you'll be close at hand to keep a loving eye on your niece."

She sighed happily, close in the protective circle of his arms.

"We can forget about the past now, Jane," he said. "The future is ours for the taking."

There, on the cold hillside with the veiled stars far above them, he kissed her tenderly, then passionately.

"Jane!" he said, pressing his lips against her dishevelled hair. "Jane! There's so much we can do — together!"

RED LOTUS

Red Lotus

Felicity had arrived in the Canary Islands to live with her only relatives. But the death of her uncle changed the situation completely.

Her cousins deeply resented Philip Arnold, who now controlled their lives on the estate. They accused him of having been responsible for the tragic death of Felicity's cousin, Maria. And their accusations went unchallenged.

Philip was definitely not the man Felicity should have fallen in love with!

CHAPTER I

SAN LOZARO VALLEY

THE plane circled the islands and dropped low. From where she sat on the port side, Felicity Stanmore looked down on them, her breath held, her grey-green eyes alight with eager interest. This was the moment for which she had been waiting ever since they had left Madrid: the moment of contact; the moment when she could allow herself to believe that she was really here, at last.

They were a compact group; seven main islands riding an incredibly blue sea, with their smaller satellites clinging to their rugged coastlines like attendant stars. Felicity had always felt attracted by the Canary Islands, where her mother's only brother had lived for most of his adventurous life, but she had not expected the abrupt summons which had reached her in England three months ago on her mother's death and was the reason for her present journey.

"We are your only relatives," Robert Hallam had written. "I shall arrange for your passage out here and you will come as soon as possible. It isn't a matter of charity," he had added in a forthright way which had made her smile at the time, aware that it had given her at least some insight into her uncle's character. "There is a job here that you can do for me."

Several letters had passed to and fro in the interval, but even now, as she approached the islands, Felicity realized that she knew very little about her future and the work she was expected to do.

Sitting forward in her seat, her lips parted in a smile, she had forgotten about the man by her side, the tall, distinguished-looking Spaniard who had boarded the plane at Madrid and taken the only available seat for the journey to Las Palmas.

They had spoken, of course; the desultory conversation

391

of strangers thrown into close proximity on a long journey, yet she had been instantly aware of the reticence of the well-bred Spaniard, the courtesy which drew up short of curiosity. He had not asked her about herself or why she was on her way to a remote part of Tenerife, which she did not seem to know.

"You are being met," he asked now, "at Las Palmas?"

Felicity shook her head.

"No. I understood that I only had to change planes there," she said. "My uncle pointed out that it was quite a simple matter and that I would be met at Santa Cruz."

He looked surprised, as if he considered that she should have been met as soon as the plane touched down on the islands. A gesture of courtesy, perhaps, which a Spaniard would have considered necessary.

"My uncle is a very old man," she explained almost hastily, "and he has not been too well lately. I could not expect him to take a long journey to meet me unless it was really necessary."

He nodded in what she supposed was agreement, although there was still a certain amount of reservation in the dark eyes which met her own. From the moment he had come aboard and taken the vacant seat beside her, Felicity realized, she had been vitally aware of this man. His commanding presence, the quick, arrogant turn of the head and the finely-chiselled profile would remain stamped on her memory for a very long time. It was a face not to be easily forgotten, darkly attractive and aristocratically remote, yet in some subtle way she had become aware of his growing interest as the journey had progressed.

She looked down at his fine, beautifully-manicured hands, wondering what he did for a living, if he did anything at all. There was a suggestion of ease about him, of unlimited time to go about the business of gracious living which she was to encounter, again and again, in the weeks ahead as she came to understand the Spanish character and delight in it.

"If you will allow me," he suggested with the utmost courtesy, "when we reach Las Palmas I shall escort you to your plane for Tenerife. I, also, am going there," he added after the briefest hesitation. "It is my home."

"Oh?"

Suddenly she longed to ask him more about his background, about Tenerife itself, of which she knew so little. His own curiosity had been so pointedly curbed, however, that she hesitated. He had left the decision entirely in her hands whether or not they should probe into each other's past or look forward to the future. Then, just as suddenly, she found herself taking the initiative, aware of time running out and nothing definitely established between them.

"I'm rather nervous about all this," she confessed, looking down on the compact little island beneath them, lying green and placid in the brilliant sunshine. "I've never been abroad before and I have more or less decided to spend the next few years of my life here—or, at least, on Tenerife."

He looked surprised.

"Your uncle is established on the island?" he asked.

"Oh, yes. He has lived there for a very long time. Almost forty years." She hesitated. Did he really want to know this, or was he completely indifferent whether she identified herself or not? The question irked her, because if she were really sensible, she should realize that they were ships that pass in the night, chance acquaintances of a voyage above the clouds which did not hold any permanency or give even a reasonable length of time to foster friendships. "His name is Robert Hallam," she added briefly. "He has banana plantations on the west side of the island, I think."

"In the San Lozaro Valley, in fact." His tone was guarded, his eyes suddenly watchful. "We are practically acquainted," he added after a moment, with the slow smile which was faintly cynical yet only seemed to add to the attraction of the lean, dark face. "I know your uncle quite well. We are—neighbours, shall we say?"

"How—strange!" Felicity exclaimed.

Yet she did not think that it was altogether strange. It all seemed far too inevitable, following a pattern which neither of them could have changed, even if they had wished to do so.

"Perhaps it is not surprising when you consider how small the islands really are," he mused. "We are an isolated group, not quite in mid-Atlantic, but almost so for every practical purpose, clinging to the skirts of Africa, but not African; fiercely proud of our Spanish forebears and looking always towards the mother country of Spain."

"Yet—my uncle is English," Felicity pointed out. "He has never forgotten that."

"He married a Spanish girl."

"Yes. His second wife was Spanish." A small, inexplicable fear crept into Felicity's heart. "Does that make a great deal of difference?"

"Not in your uncle's case, I should say," he assured her lightly. "The Spanish and the English live most amicably on the island. Knowing your uncle, however, I can well see why he sent for you."

She glanced up at him, surprised by the personal nature of the observation.

"Why do you say that?" she asked. "He told me that he had a job waiting for me, but his main reason for asking me to come out here was because my mother has just died." Her voice trembled a little at the memory of that swift and unexpected passing which had left her so utterly alone in England. "We lived rather remotely in Devonshire, in a small village where my father had been vicar for seventeen years," she added, "and my uncle is my only close relative."

"It would be most natural for him to send for you then," her companion acknowledged, "but the job he wanted you to do would be important also. You see," he added slowly, "your uncle does not want his family to grow up entirely Spanish. He is, before anything else, an Englishman."

"It's understandable, isn't it?" Felicity said. "He did write and say that he wanted me to come for that reason."

He smiled a little.

"The leavening influence!" he mused. "You may find your task difficult at first, Señorita——"

"My name is Felicity Stanmore," Felicity supplied when he paused expectantly. "My mother and Robert Hallam were brother and sister."

He looked at her for a full minute before he said:

"In a good many ways you are like Señor Hallam."

Felicity turned eagerly towards him.

"Do you know him very well?" she asked.

"Not very well."

There had been the slightest hesitation before he had made reply, the initial reserve raised like an abrupt barrier between them, but already they had come a long way. He had admitted that they were to be neighbours.

"It's rather nice and very helpful meeting someone who knows all about my destination," she said, turning again to the window to look out. "You will know my cousins, I expect?" Her expression softened in a happy smile. "I am looking forward tremendously to meeting them, although it's sad that I shall never meet María now. She was killed in an accident, wasn't she, just over a year ago?"

For a moment there was silence; a moment which gradually took on the essence of time suspended over some dark abyss of indecision and secrecy. Turning in her seat, she looked at her companion, but his expression was already guarded, the dark eyes telling her nothing.

"That is so," he admitted stiltedly. "It remains a tragedy of which no one wishes to speak."

She was quite sure that he could have told her more of the way in which her cousin had died, but she could not press him for the information. She knew that María's death had been a shattering blow to her uncle, and when they had received the news in England her mother had wept for the small baby she had once held in her arms, the only child of Robert's that she had ever seen. He had come with his second wife on that one brief visit to his homeland, when Felicity had been too young to remember him, and then he had gone back to his "Enchanted Islands" to settle down to the life he knew best and loved most.

"It must have been a terrible blow to my uncle," she said unsteadily. "María was his eldest child and he was passionately fond of her. In his letters to my mother, he wrote of María more than of any of the others. She was spirited, I believe, and very beautiful."

"That is true," he acknowledged slowly, almost reluctantly. "She was the most beautiful creature I have ever seen. All Spanish. There was nothing English about María."

"You say 'nothing English' as if that were an advantage!" Felicity objected. "Perhaps you do not like the English?"

"On the contrary!" he protested. "I go often to London on business and I like your countrymen very much. If they have not the spontaneous gaiety of the average Spaniard, that is not to their discredit. Perhaps," he added with a smile, "it is best to put it down to the climate you are forced to endure on your own island and leave it at that!"

Felicity smiled, aware of a lessening of tension now that the conversation had returned to a lighter vein yet still vaguely troubled by what appeared to have been an unfortunate reference to her cousin's death.

"You certainly can't complain about a lack of sunshine here," she observed, looking down on the sun-drenched sea as they circled the Isleta with its lighthouse standing up clear and white beneath them and the serrated coastline edged with the lacy foam of breaking waves. "Everything seems so warm and bright and so utterly, utterly peaceful!"

"The Fortunate Isles!" he acknowledged with the hint of reservation in his tone, a dryness which she had not quite expected in a man who had just confessed that he was coming home. "You will love or hate them in proportion to whether they are generous or unkind to you, but you will never be able to forget them. Of that I am sure."

Just as I will never be able to forget you, Felicity thought, because you have stamped your charm on this, our first, meeting. And surely we will meet again!

The suggestion had the sudden power to quicken her heart-beats, to send the colour into her cheeks and cover her with a momentary confusion. She was not easily impressed by people and certainly not too quickly overwhelmed by a surface charm, but this man's magnetism had held her from the start. He had an air about him that commanded attention, and fate, or circumstances, or whatever ordained these things, had drawn them together even before they would have met in the ordinary way.

She remembered suddenly that she did not know his name, but thrust the idea from her mind that the omission had been deliberate on his part. There was no real reason why he should trouble to introduce himself, except perhaps that her uncle and he were near neighbours. Which meant that they must inevitably meet again.

The plane was coming down to land. Beneath them, rows and rows of mountains encrusted the land, like deep wrinkles on an ancient face, and all along the shore and straggling up the hillsides behind the port gay red, green and saffron rooftops glittered beckoningly in the sun.

It was the sea, however, which still held the greatest fascination for Felicity as she sat back to fasten her seat-belt and wait for the moment of final impact. It was the bluest sea she had ever seen; a tranquil sea, undisturbed by the least hint of tempest, where dolphins played and flying fish skimmed endlessly, a sea over which it seemed a storm could never break.

When they stood up she realized for the first time how tall her companion was. He had to stoop his dark head as they went out to the gangway, and he turned immediately to help her down the steps.

The warmth and brightness of the sun met them like a benediction. It was February, and Felicity had left London shrouded in fog, with not even a suggestion of spring in the air, and at Madrid there had been nothing to be seen for rain. The high ridges of the Guadarrama had been entirely obscured and the plane had been guided out by radar, so that now they seemed to be in a different world.

"This is glorious!" she exclaimed. "I'm ill equipped, I'm afraid, for so much sunshine!"

He glanced down at her warm travelling coat and the neat suit beneath it.

"You will not need these again for a very long time," he smiled.

Their progress across the airstrip towards the dazzlingly-bright administrative buildings began to take on a small retinue of attendant officials, which immediately suggested that her companion might be someone of importance and a well-known traveller on Iberia Airlines. They were escorted beyond the sun into a dim, cool hall where the sunlight filtered through slatted shutters, and for a moment Felicity hesitated, blinking uncertainly in the green light before she could adjust her eyes to the change.

There were other travellers in the hall, but, since there was no customs barrier on the islands, there did not seem to be the same chaos among them as she had noticed at London and Madrid. People met here and chatted leisurely while they waited for their flight numbers to go up, some to hop from island to island on pleasure or business, others to cross the world or return to Spain, which was still the motherland. There was a great deal of talk and ready laughter. Everyone seemed to know everyone else, and it was not long before Felicity's companion was seen and recognized. She saw him frown as a small man in a brown lounge suit and wide-brimmed hat came swiftly towards them.

The man spoke rapidly in Spanish; Felicity had been attempting to master the language ever since she had accepted her uncle's invitation, but she found it difficult to follow the swift flow of the present conversation. She was aware that her companion was far from pleased by the interruption, however, and would have swept the garrulous little man aside if it had not been for an inbred Spanish politeness which demanded patience and at least a show of courtesy. She heard the word "Marquesa" several times, rolled caressingly on the little man's tongue, as if it gave him incredible pleasure each time he uttered it, and she supposed that he must be talking about some titled acquaintance, someone, perhaps, with whom he had done business.

Felicity was quite sure now that he was a business man. His little black eyes shone when he mentioned "a settlement," and he seemed in no way taken aback when her companion suggested that they might continue their discussion in some more convenient place.

He glanced at Felicity for the first time, saw that she was English, and bowed.

"So many pardons!" he murmured awkwardly. "But the Marqués and I have not met for some time——"

"Rafael!" a smooth voice said behind them. "Can I extricate you from your embarrassment?"

A tall, beautifully-groomed girl was standing in the entrance to the hall, the bright glare of sunshine behind her. Everything about her was smooth and cool, from the shining, severely-parted hair beneath the shady hat-brim to the elegant shoes which encased her long, slim feet. Her dark eyes were keenly alert as they met Felicity's and ever so slightly amused.

"You have already done so, Elena." The frown had not yet left her companion's brow as he watched the little man in the brown suit move away to rejoin the noisy group he had left at the far side of the wide hall, and Felicity found herself wondering what had disturbed him so much. He seemed to hesitate, too, before he introduced the tall girl in the doorway. "May I present the Señorita Elena

Cabenza de Navarro?" he said. "Elena, I would like you to meet Miss Felicity Stanmore."

"You are English?" The tall girl turned to Felicity with a frankly interested smile. "You have come perhaps for a holiday on Gran Canaria?" she suggested.

She appeared to have accepted the fact that Felicity and her companion were no more than casual acquaintances of the journey from Spain and looked amused by the situation rather than anything else. Felicity had liked her at first glance, but now she was not so sure. Señorita Elena Cabenza de Navarro suddenly made her think of a very elegant cat about to play with a slightly-uncertain mouse.

"I have come to stay for a while," she heard herself saying guardedly. "I am going on to Tenerife."

The dark eyes opened wide. They were almost black.

"But this is most interesting!" Elena Cabenza exclaimed with a sidelong glance at the frowning man by her side. "Are you taking Miss Stanmore home, Rafael?"

"Miss Stanmore is going to San Lozaro." His mouth was suddenly grim. "She is the niece of Robert Hallam."

A flicker of amazement crossed the dark eyes looking into his, and Elena turned back towards Felicity.

"How strange," she commented, "that you should meet Rafael on your journey to San Lozaro."

"Not at all," Rafael said dryly. "We merely flew out from Madrid on the same plane."

"A coincidence, nevertheless!" Elena favoured him with a strangely-mocking smile as she turned away. "Give my tenderest regards to dear Isabella, won't you, as soon as you get home?" she added.

Felicity felt strangely and inexplicably ill at ease. The encounter in the sunlit doorway had been brief, but in some odd sort of way it had tarnished the brightness of her first contact with the islands. The whole atmosphere of Grand Canary had seemed so happy and free from strife that even an imagined undercurrent of dissension seemed dark by contrast.

"Perhaps I should enquire about my connection for Tenerife," she suggested hurriedly. "I should not like to miss it, especially as I am being met."

"We have plenty of time," her companion told her

399

leisurely. "The plane from La Laguna is not yet in. You will allow me to find you something to eat?"

"I feel that I have taken up too much of your time already," Felicity said. "You may have other friends to meet."

"None that I care greatly about at the moment." The dark eyes were suddenly, intently on hers, willing her not to refuse the invitation. "It would give me great pleasure if you would allow me to help you. We have perhaps an hour to wait. These delays, I'm afraid, happen on the islands, much as they are to be deplored. Time does not mean so much here as it does in Europe."

She felt that he did not deplore this delay and flushed at the revelation, yet there was no reason why she should not accept his generously-offered hospitality.

"It's very kind of you," she said as he led the way across the hall to the glass doors of the restaurant.

"Now, perhaps, I ought to introduce myself," he suggested as they sat down at one of the smaller tables for two, where they would not be disturbed. "Since we are going to be neighbours, almost, that will be quite in order."

She felt that he was laughing at her now, gently, teasingly, aware of her reticence about speaking to a stranger and a Spaniard to boot. She took the card he offered her with a small smile at her own foolishness. Of course, there was nothing odd or secretive about him!

The card announced, in small black letters in a formal, businesslike way, that he was the Marqués de Barrios and that he had an office on the Avenida Alfonso XIII in the central district of Santa Cruz.

More than a little surprised by the revelation, she sat looking down at the card, remembering the little man in the brown suit and his frequent references to the "Marquesa," remembering, too, Elena de Navarro's small, amused smile and her parting request to be remembered to "dear Isabella," who was evidently waiting on Tenerife for Rafael de Barrios' return. A sister, or a mother, or even a wife?

She looked up at the man sitting across the table from her and knew that Rafael de Barrios did not intend to enlighten her about his household at that moment.

"And now you must let me introduce you to Spanish

food," he suggested. "You will be eating quite a lot of it when you reach San Lozaro. Unless," he added quickly, "you mean to make drastic changes in the running of your uncle's household?"

Felicity shook her head.

"I haven't come with the intention of changing anything," she said. "I don't even know what my uncle expects me to do, apart from looking after the younger members of the family and perhaps teaching them something of the English way of life. I certainly don't mean to sweep everything before me, like the proverbial new broom!" she ended with a smile.

He smiled in return as he handed her the menu.

"Perhaps that is just as well," he agreed, "when there are other people, apart from your uncle, to consider."

Felicity looked up from the printed sheet with a frank question in her eyes.

"I'm afraid I know disgracefully little about San Lozaro," she confessed. "Who else is there to consider once I get there, Don Rafael?"

He looked surprised.

"I should have thought you would have heard of Philip Arnold," he said in a voice which could not quite conceal his dislike of the man.

"No," Felicity answered. "Should I have known about him? It is an English name."

"Mr. Arnold is very English. Shall we say almost aggressively so?" His smile was dry and curiously watchful. "I am surprised that you have not heard of him. He has been part of your uncle's establishment for many years."

"Uncle Robert did mention an agent," Felicity agreed. "Someone who has done a great deal of work on the plantations, but I imagined that he was a Spaniard."

Her companion's smile was openly cynical now.

"Who else could there be at San Lozaro but the Admirable Arnold?" he said. "No Spaniard would ever work as he has done—for so little return."

Once again Felicity felt uncomfortable under the direct regard of the dark, smiling eyes which seemed to reveal and yet to conceal so much. Don Rafael, Marqués de Barrios, was at no great pains to hide the fact that he found her a most agreeable companion, but in the course of their conversation since he had discovered her identity and her destination, she had become increasingly aware of secrecy, of a reserve that went deeper than the natural reticence between two strangers meeting casually, as they had done.

Yet surely there could be nothing personal about it, she decided, although she could feel it there, as a background, to everything they said and did. Elena Cabenza de Navarro's smile, half veiled, wholly cynical, had been part of it, and Don Rafael's own disinclination to continue the conversation with the little Guanche in the hall had added a furtiveness to it which she neither liked nor could reasonably understand.

She assured herself that she could have no interest whatsoever in the business pursuits of the Marqués de Barrios, even if she had felt drawn by the fascinating Don Rafael almost from the moment of their first meeting. He had been courteous and kind, doing his best to make a stranger feel welcome on the islands where he made his home, and even now he was carefully selecting a meal for her from the long and puzzling menu which he hoped she would enjoy. She had already forgotten his reference to the difficulties with which she might find herself faced at San Lozaro. Difficulties, she considered, were meant to be faced, and her uncle was surely very much the man in authority in his own house.

The suggestion of a strong, almost a dominating personality, had come through very clearly in his recent letters to her, and she could remember her mother saying that "Robert was always a very determined sort of person who generally got his own way." All of which did not sound as if Philip Arnold could be anything more than an agent or an overseer on the San Lozaro estate.

Well, she would soon find out for herself. Although not too soon! This pleasant, delightful interval in her long journey to the distant valley where her uncle had settled made everything so much easier. She was freed from the embarrassment of asking directions in her inadequate Spanish, and the meal which was finally set before them could never have been achieved by her own choice. She felt grateful and relaxed as Don Rafael poured the native wine he had ordered into her glass and lifted his own to propose a toast to the future.

"We shall meet again," he said, his darkly-luminous

eyes holding hers across the blood-red wine. "That is to be expected. But may it be—quite soon!"

After that Felicity found it easy to be gay in his company. He told her something of the history of the island to which they would travel when their plane eventually arrived, showing no impatience at the fact that it was already an hour late.

"Something will have happened," he shrugged. "It is frequently so, but you will learn not to care about time when you have settled down at San Lozaro. Time will pass you by there and the care of time, provided there are no complications."

She did not want to ask him about possible complications now. She was prepared to wait, already accepting in essence the meaning of the Spanish *mañana*. To-morrow was time enough. To-morrow, when she would awaken to a new day at San Lozaro and a succession of such days under her uncle's roof.

When the plane came in her companion looked up regretfully.

"And now we must go," he said, rising to collect her coat. "Our little interlude is ended. It is no more than a single hop to Tenerife."

Out in the sunshine again, Felicity wished that they had more time to spare. She would have liked to go down into Las Palmas with Don Rafael as her guide, because already she was aware that he could have shown her the true Spanish scene as no one else could have done. He was completely responsive to the sunshine and the laughter and the blue skies of these fortunate islands in spite of the dignity which he seemed to force upon himself at times.

He had shown her, too, that he liked her and wished her to know more of the golden islands of this lost Atlantis where he had made his home.

Suddenly she knew that her own desperate need was to feel welcomed in a strange land, that, ever since her mother's death, she had felt desolate and alone, without roots or ties in a world where such things were wholly essential. She had wanted her uncle to be at Las Palmas to meet her and he had not come, so that she was doubly grateful to this man who thought that she should have been welcomed.

403

Perhaps Don Rafael found difficulty in understanding the English coldness or matter-of-factness which thought that Santa Cruz was far enough. He had said something of the kind and she had half resented it, but now she knew that it was only because he himself would not have considered time or distance any obstacle to such a meeting. The essence of the man was to live for the moment, but perhaps that had its attractive side, too.

"I'm rather worried about my uncle having to wait all this time at the airport," she confessed as they walked with the other travellers across the hot landing-strip to where their plane waited. "He hasn't been very well lately, and the sun is very hot."

"I don't think you need worry," Don Rafael said, the frown reappearing on his brow. "Your uncle will have found something to do in the meantime. He will already know that the plane is late."

She accepted his assurance as he found her a seat and put his brief-case down on the one adjoining.

"If you will excuse me," he said, "I will see how long we are going to be before we get away."

Settled in her seat, Felicity looked out through the port-hole at the little ripples of sunlight dancing along the wings and her heart lifted, as if at an omen of happiness. This was a lovely land! If it were only for the sunshine itself, it had been well worth coming. She felt it on her skin like a caress, and thought that nothing she could find at San Lozaro could posibly dim it.

After all, it would be like coming home in a good many ways. Robert Hallam was her mother's brother and the cousins she had yet to meet were her own flesh and blood.

When the plane climbed into the cloudless blue above the airport a small stirring of excitement was already rising in her heart. This was journey's end. This was the answer to all her hopes and doubts and fears of the past few months, and this, too, was the future.

Her eyes strained ahead for the first glimpse of the island that would be her home, and it was Rafael de Barrios who pointed it out to her.

"However you may come to the islands, it is always El Teide that dominates," he said, pointing downwards to where a great conical peak rose skywards out of a circle of attendant cloud. Its crest was wreathed in snow, flushed pinkly in the rays of the westering sun, and about it there was a remoteness which struck chill into Felicity's heart. "It is there from the sea and from the air, always the one thing, above all others, that first strikes the eye."

Felicity was still looking at The Peak. The great mountain seemed completely separated from all contact with the land beneath, isolated beyond its barrier of cloud, aloof and cold even under the flush of sun on its lofty crest. She could see it, even then, as the spirit of the island, the presence which man looked at and feared.

"It's volcanic, of course," she said.

"Its origin was volcanic," Don Rafael agreed, "but there hasn't been a major eruption for many years. Here and there, apart from the great cone itself, there have been minor rumblings, but nothing serious has come of them. No," he smiled, "El Teide is a benign and quiet giant now, and none of his subordinates are worth mentioning."

Felicity continued to stare at The Peak, fascinated. Its absolute majesty held her speechless, and even when they dropped beneath the level of the clouds which wreathed it, she could still see that remote summit glittering in the sun.

The plane skimmed in over La Laguna and touched down on the airstrip before she spoke again.

"How far is San Lozaro from The Peak, Don Rafael?" she asked.

"Not very far." He looked at her oddly. "But then, El Teide dominates the entire island, as I have said. You must learn to live with him, to accept him in many moods, or he will have his own revenge!"

She smiled involuntarily.

"I don't think he can frighten me away," she said. "Already I am fascinated by your remote giant of a mountain, Don Rafael. Already, I suppose, I am his slave!"

"So!" he murmured. "He will be kind to you. And now," he added more prosaically, "we must look out for your uncle."

He helped her down the steps and Felicity stood on the tarmac blinking in the bright sunlight. The airport was built on a high stretch of the island and a cool little wind blew down from the surrounding mountains. She found herself in need of her coat, and instantly Don Rafael had laid it across her shoulders.

405

"It is always cool up here at this time of year," he said, "but soon we will go down again along the coast."

He was looking beyond her, scanning the small groups of waiting people at the edge of the runway as they walked away from the plane, and once more she saw him frown.

It was then that she remembered that she might not recognize her uncle from the description her mother had given her of him. Living for most of his life out here, might not Robert Hallam look very much like any other planter on the island?

"I ought to have warned Uncle Robert to wear a red carnation!" she smiled. "I haven't seen him since I was three years old."

Don Rafael was still scanning the bronzed faces of the smiling groups ahead. They were nearly all men. Only one woman, dressed in deepest mourning and clutching a small child by the hand, stood out among them, her black draperies etched sharply against the cream linen suits and light-coloured hats of the men.

"Your uncle does not seem to be waiting." Don Rafael's eyes had gone beyond the waiting groups to the line of cars parked on the gravelled sweep leading from the main Laguna–Santa Cruz road, and the frown between his dark brows had deepened. "It is unusual for anyone on the island to fail to meet a plane," he added.

Following his concentrated gaze, Felicity was aware of the first stirrings of anxiety. She had been perfectly sure that her uncle would meet her, had, in fact, been looking forward to just this moment for the past three weeks, and she knew that no trivial thing would have delayed him. Besides, the plane was over an hour late. He should have been at the airport an hour ago, or at least lingering in the nearby town.

Before she could voice her fears, however, a large black car came swiftly along the deserted highway and turned in between the airport gates. She followed its progress eagerly, unaware that the man by her side had stiffened involuntarily at sight of it, the frown black on his face, his lips thinned and cruel-looking as he watched.

"You are met," he said, "after all. Yonder is the car from San Lozaro, but it is not your uncle who brings it."

Felicity was conscious of the keenest disappointment which was instantly tinged with anxiety.

"Can something have happened?" she asked breathlessly. "Can my uncle be ill?"

Don Rafael did not answer her. He stood very stiffly and very silently by her side as the man who had come to take her to San Lozaro got out from behind the steering wheel and came towards them.

He seemed to have no hesitation about her identity, and it was minutes before Felicity remembered that she had been the only woman passenger on the plane.

In these minutes she was aware of a man taller even than her travelling companion, a sparse, almost gaunt-looking man with a lean, brown face and firm jaw, whose piercing blue eyes were the colour of the distant sea. He came purposefully across the hot tarmac, striding towards them in a manner that was unmistakably English and as unmistakably assured. His whole attitude suggested that he had little time to spare for meetings or lingering sociably in the sunshine.

"You are honoured," Don Rafael murmured at her elbow. "But I wonder what has brought the taciturn Mr. Philip Arnold all this way to meet you?"

Felicity could not reply. Her questioning gaze had met Philip Arnold's, aware now that the blue eyes held nothing but anger and distrust.

"Miss Stanmore?" His voice was abrupt, almost impatient, as he put the question. "My name is Arnold," he added. "Philip Arnold. I am the agent on your uncle's estate."

He had not looked in her companion's direction, but Felicity was quite sure that he had recognized Don Rafael and disapproved of him. It was even more than ordinary disapproval, she felt, as the suggestion of an intense and bitter antagonism rose between them, making her feel unsure and curiously at a loss as she sought for something conventional to say with which to bridge the gap.

"It was very kind of you to come to meet me, Mr. Arnold," she acknowledged, holding out her hand. "But— my uncle——"

The expression in the blue eyes changed as Philip Arnold glanced back towards the car he had just left. The engine was still running, accentuating the suggestion of impatience which she had felt so strongly at their first contact, and it seemed that he was eager to drive away.

407

"I'm afraid my news is not good," he said. "Your uncle had a serious relapse during the night and the doctor was still with him when I left San Lozaro just over an hour ago."

"Oh——!"

The colour ran swiftly out of Felicity's cheeks and only the firm pressure of Philip Arnold's strong brown fingers seemed to steady her as she stood there with the cold little wind from the mountains brushing against her. In some way it seemed to have entered her heart, like the chill premonition of disaster, although the sun still shone brilliantly above her and the wide expanse of the heavens was very blue.

"We can talk more easily in the car." Philip Arnold released her hand and turned towards the waiting vehicle. "I should like to get back to San Lozaro as quickly as possible."

For the first time he looked in Don Rafael's direction, and the Marqués bowed and smiled a little mockingly.

"Good day, Philip!" he said briefly. "We have not met for quite a long time. But then, I have been much away from the island and you are not socially inclined. Is it not so?"

"I have little time for the gay whirligig, if that's what you mean," Arnold returned with the briefness of dismissal. "We have been more than busy on the estate."

"Ah! the estate," Don Rafael mused. "Of course, I must not forget that its welfare is very near to your heart!"

Suddenly Felicity felt her nerves on edge. Why were they fencing with words like this? Or wasn't it Don Rafael who was sparring, thrusting with those queer double-edged innuendoes which meant nothing to her who did not really know either of them, but seemed capable of increasing the other man's wrath. Philip Arnold, she realized, was not even trying to hide his dislike now. He possessed none of the Marqués de Barrios's finesse where words were concerned and no desire, perhaps, to hide the fact that they had little in common but their mutual hatred.

The last word sprang out at her with unguarded ferocity. Why should she imagine that such an emotion existed between them after such a short time in their company? Was it because she realized that her uncle's agent was the type of man who would not try to conceal such a thing,

even for convention's sake, and because she felt instinctively that a man of his calibre would not hate easily?

As she got in the car beside him she wondered what
there could possibly be between these two which would
occasion such bitter enmity.

Don Rafael came to stand beside her, holding her hand
and raising it slowly to his lips as they said goodbye.

"You will permit me to see you again," he asked, "even
in the face of opposition?"

The colour ran swiftly into her cheeks and a small hard
core of resentment took root in her heart.

"Why not, Don Rafael?" she returned. "You have been
very kind. I should have found the journey much more
difficult if you had not been so helpful at Las Palmas." She
drew her hand away, trying not to feel embarrassed by his
kiss. "Thank you for my first real Spanish meal," she added
with a smile.

"I hope it will not be the last meal we will enjoy
together," Don Rafael said as her new escort let in his
clutch. "You will pass on my deepest felicitations to your
uncle, I hope, and I sincerely trust that he will soon be
well enough to manage his own affairs again."

He had made the little speech without looking at the
stern man behind the wheel, but Felicity knew that the
sharp barb had been deliberately directed at Philip Arnold.
Now, beyond doubting, she was sure of bad blood between
these two, stirred deliberately by the Marqués for his own
amusement.

Yet, behind the façade of the Spaniard's smile, a strange
sort of caution lurked, the reflection of which was not to
be seen in Philip Arnold's hard blue eyes.

As the car moved away Don Rafael made her a small,
half-mocking bow and she lifted her gloved hand in salute
almost with a feeling of relief.

For several minutes, while the big, open car gathered
speed as it travelled westwards, Philip Arnold did not
speak. The land on either side of the arrow-straight roadway was rough and covered in gorse until it sloped upwards
to the edge of the deciduous forest which clothed the
mountainsides to the north and west, and it was all so
suddenly and so unexpectedly like her native Devonshire
in high summer that Felicity caught her lip sharply between
her teeth as a nostalgic flood of memory swept over her.

The high reaches of Dartmoor made just such a picture, with Ryder's Hill and High Willhays windswept in the distance. She had not expected the sudden change of scene, the familiarity of landscape which rushed her thoughts back to the past, to home and friendship and the memory of the mother she had lost.

"Can you tell me about my uncle, Mr. Arnold?" she asked when she could trust her voice. "You said just now that he was seriously ill."

Her companion kept his eyes fixed steadily ahead, although he could have turned them for a moment from that long, straight road to look at her. She felt that his anger was still perilously near the surface, that it had been curbed only by the utmost effort of will-power, and that he would not trust himself to speak until he had put as much distance as possible between them and the airport.

The thought also occurred to her that he had not offered Rafael de Barrios a lift, although they were going in the same direction, but, of course, he might have seen the Marqués' car waiting for him among the many others at the airport.

"Your uncle is more seriously ill than I care to admit," he said stiltedly. Most of the anger had gone from his voice, but there was still a reserve in him which bordered on distrust. "He has had these seizures at recurring intervals during the past six years, but lately they have been getting more severe. This present one has left him very weak."

Felicity pressed her hands tightly together as the car began to go steadily downhill.

"Are you trying to tell me that my uncle—may not recover?" she asked.

The blue eyes were suddenly narrowed.

"We have to consider that possibility," he said.

"But—his family? The responsibility for the estate and the children's future?"

"I don't think you need to concern yourself about that," he said abruptly. "Your uncle will have made adequate provision for every emergency."

It was not what she had meant. She had suddenly been concerned with loss, with roots being torn up and a home abandoned. The events leading up to her own recent bereavement were too close, too near at hand, for her not

410

to be able to feel for her cousins in similar circumstances. The loss of their only remaining parent would be the chief tragedy, and even if her uncle had already put his house in order, as this man suggested, there would still be the problem of holding a young family together.

"I'm afraid I'm not being very helpful," she admitted. "I'm even rather vague about why my uncle wanted me to come here—apart from the fact that I was alone after my mother died. It was generous of him to send for me because of that, but I do know he had work for me to do here. He said so in his letters, but I wish I knew a little more about the family. It seems so incongruous to be so vague about one's relations."

He smiled at that, neither agreeing nor disagreeing, but he slowed down the car a little as the distant coastline came into view, saying almost conversationally:

"Your uncle sent for you to preserve the *status quo* at San Lozaro, Miss Stanmore. I hope you are going to succeed, of course, but it is no use my pretending at this stage that you are going to have an easy task."

Felicity drew in a deep breath. His reticence and the quite maddening reserve in him was not helpful, but until she knew more about San Lozaro and what her uncle expected her to do there it was impossible for her to approach the situation with any degree of confidence.

"Perhaps if you would suggest where I might fail," she challenged, "it would be helpful. You obviously think that I am not the right person for the job."

"I haven't the vaguest idea about your capabilities, one way or another," he told her with apparent indifference. "I was offering some sort of warning, I suppose, but perhaps it would have been better if I had let you find these things out for yourself."

"Because you think I am the sort of person who won't take advice?" she queried, aware that she had set the seal on their animosity by her previous remark. "You're quite wrong about that," she added half angrily when he made no immediate reply. "I *do* need advice. I am in a strange country. I have no knowledge of Spanish ways, and I feel that I owe it to my uncle to learn."

"That will not be easy," he said, "but I would advise you to approach it by some other way than by accepting tuition from Rafael de Barrios."

The swift colour of angry embarrassment flooded Felicity's cheeks.

"I have known the Marqués for only a few hours," she pointed out stiffly, "and I have no reason to believe that his kindness was anything but kindly meant!"

The line of his jaw hardened aggressively as his hands tightened their grip on the wheel. She saw the knuckles standing out white on them for a moment before he said, with apparent indifference:

"As you will. But it would be just as well to realize that he is not a welcome visitor at San Lozaro."

She could not ask him why, because the dark tension on his face left her no room for doubt about the seriousness of the enmity which existed between him and Rafael de Barrios. She could not probe for the truth because she knew that this man would not be drawn, that what lay deeply in his heart would not be easily exposed.

Looking at the dark, closed face and the stern brows drawn above the narrowed blue eyes, she was suddenly reminded of the barren places of El Teide, the remote giant of a mountain which stood aloofly apart from the ordinary doings of mankind.

"How far have we to go?" she asked, wishing already that their journey were over.

"I'm afraid we have quite a way to go yet," he admitted. "San Lozaro is a remote valley running inland from the coast. It is cut off completely by the Pico de Tiede."

The word "isolated" hung between them for a moment, drumming in Felicity's ears. Don Rafael had warned her to expect loneliness, but she had not really thought about it until now. The fact that San Lozaro was "cut off" seemed to convey even more than ordinary loneliness and isolation, yet it might only have been Philip Arnold's remote approach which suggested a valley beyond contact with the outside world.

The car was going rapidly downhill now, on a road that wound, in a series of hair-raising bends, towards the coast. A wide, fertile valley opened at their feet. Mile upon mile, a green sea of banana fronds undulated in the sunlight in waves of light and shade, sweeping down to the very edge of the Atlantic to be arrested on the dark shore by a band of lacy white. The true waves broke here, gently, caressingly, as if the great ocean itself approached these fortunate isles with respect.

"It's utterly lovely!" Felicity exclaimed involuntarily. "Far more beautiful than I had ever dreamed."

"Orotava is a show-place," he agreed, "but we have other valleys equally picturesque in the south."

He had not said that San Lozaro was beautiful. In fact, Felicity thought, he had said very little about San Lozaro at all.

"Mr. Arnold," she asked abruptly, "what exactly is your position in my uncle's household?"

He negotiated a bend in the treacherous road before replying.

"In his household, none at all," he said, "at the present moment."

"And the plantations?"

"I am your uncle's agent and the estate manager."

"And, in most things, your word is law?"

The compressed lips relaxed a little.

"If you care to put it like that," he agreed.

So, now we know where we stand, Felicity thought. She was still far from feeling at ease in this man's company, and she had the unnerving impression that her arrival in the care of the Marqués de Barrios had more than a little to do with the chilly reception she had received.

They could sort that out later, however. He seemed to be anxious to reach their destination in the shortest possible space of time, and she sat back in the car by his side giving herself up to the wonder of the drive in silence.

Once they had reached the coast road every turn of the way became a new miracle of lavish colour and long, unexpected vistas of deep valleys running far in from the sea. It was spring, and the rains had come, and all the terraces were a living sheet of emerald, with the almond trees above them smothered in pale pink blossom, as if they wore a cap of snow flushed with sun, like El Teide himself.

The shadow of the great mountain was everywhere, sometimes benign, sometimes terrible in its isolation. Broad streams of lava lay greyly arrested in silent *barrancos* that were grimly devoid of life, but in others it seemed that nature had been almost too prolific with her gifts. Masses of bougainvillaea tumbled over garden walls in the villages through which they passed, and she caught intriguing glimpses of creeper-covered *patios* and the soft green of shutters on balcony windows, from behind which the inhabitants peeped at them as they sped on their hurried way.

There were so many flowers that she could not name them with any certainty, and she could not ask her silent escort to enlighten her. Here and there he named a village for her—Realejo Bajo and San Juan de la Rambla, hugging the steep, indented coastline, and Icod with its ancient Dragon tree, reputed to be over a thousand years old. But always there was the sense of tension between them, the desire in him to reach the end of their journey so that he might pass on his responsibility for her to someone else.

Of course, he could be feeling concern about her uncle, she conceded, and her own concern deepened as they neared their destination.

For the past few miles the road had been extremely lonely, although no less lovely in character. It had turned away from the sea and faced The Peak, and here and there Felicity had caught glimpses of silent, devastated valleys whose sheer sides ran blackly down to a narrow plain, dominated always by one of the lesser peaks which skirted El Teide. The great range of ragged red pinnacles all but circled them, and not so long ago, she realized, these smaller peaks had been active. They were the blow-holes leading from the main volcanic mass, the giant mountain's safety-valves, but they were capable of wreaking their own destruction in a minor way. The earth surrounding some of them was burned black and the grey lava lay like a terrible, dark river flooding over the hillside.

"In time," her companion told her, following her shocked gaze, "these valleys will be workable again, and then it is the most fertile land in the world."

"Is San Lozaro volcanic?" she asked.

"We have our resident peak," he smiled, "but it is at the very head of the valley, too far away to cause any real trouble. It hasn't erupted for over a hundred years."

They drove on in silence, still with El Teide rising grandly above them, majestic, aloof, disquieting in so many ways. Then, abruptly, Philip Arnold turned the car off the wider road into a deep green valley.

The whole impression was one of swaying leaves as the

414

deep-green fronds of the banana trees lifted like a slow-moving tide beneath the paler green of the palms. Higher up, on the slopes of the hillsides, the narrow terraces which she had come to expect ran in their neat, parallel lines as far as the eye could see, clothed with vines, and here and there a vivid scarlet splash of colour rose up as if in defiance of the eternal green.

Felicity had noticed these vividly-red blossoms all the way along the road, but never in such profusion as this. They had flared in a field or over the wall of a cottage garden, but here they seemed to dominate the whole valley. She wanted to ask her companion about them, but they were approaching an archway in a high pink stucco wall and she knew that they had reached San Lozaro, at last.

They drove into an enclosed garden full of flowers, and rioting everywhere, over walls and ancient steps and seats and ornamental urns, flared the bright-red blossom which she could not name.

"The native lotus," Philip Arnold said with a shrug. "It grows everywhere and is at its most flamboyant at this time of year. The people in the valley call it the 'flower of love.'"

His voice, hard with sudden cynicism, had thrust love out. He had no use for it, Felicity supposed, no desire to be entangled in its delicate web, as the groping, grey-green fronds of the lotus entangled the valley where he made his home.

She turned away, curiously disappointed, curiously chilled, and they drove steadily towards the house.

It stood on a narrow terrace looking down across the plantations towards the distant sea, its mellow, golden walls almost hidden by hanging vines and creepers. Purple bougainvillaea cascaded from little carved balconies almost to the tiled floor of the central *patio*, where a fountain splashed into a carved basin to keep the air moist and cool, and two white doves rose and circled above the garden at their approach.

It was all so still and beautiful that the raucous voices issuing from the house seemed doubly harsh in Felicity's ears, and she saw her companion frown as he glanced beyond the *patio* into the coolly-shaded interior where, apparently, the arrival of the car had been the signal for the disturbance.

"You will grow used to the noise made by the average female Spanish servant in time," he observed. "They appear to believe that if they rush around and talk a lot it gives the impression of tremendous diligence."

In a second or two the squabbling ceased and a small, rotund woman with anxious, fearful eyes hurried out to the pavement.

She greeted them with a flood of voluble Spanish, and Philip listened, the frown still heavy on his brow. After what seemed to be a moment of indecision, he turned to Felicity.

"I'm afraid the news is not good," he said. "The doctor is still with your uncle. He is very ill."

"I must be able to do something," Felicity cried, peeling off her gloves. "I nursed my mother——"

"We have plenty of help here," he told her. "The house is full of superfluous women. I think they will be best pleased if you leave the menial tasks to them. Most of them have served your uncle all their lives, and they are born nurses."

"But surely I may see him?" Her voice hardened a little. "I have come a very long way for just that reason, Mr. Arnold."

"Of course," he said, "you may see him. But we must bow to the doctor's orders at the moment. It will depend upon what he feels is best for his patient, I should say."

Felicity bit her lip, not wanting to argue with him in the present circumstances, not wanting to feel that he was being dictatorial, even rude, and above all not allowing herself to contrast his brusque behaviour with that of Rafael, Marqués de Barrios. It was hardly a fair comparison, she acknowledged. The two men were of different races.

A servant began to unpack her luggage from the ample boot of the car and Philip turned to direct a word or two to the man. He was small and dark-skinned, with a low forehead and closely-set black eyes, evidence of the strong strain of Guanche blood running through his veins, but his flashing smile was wide and uninhibited and he made her a small, attentive bow as he walked before them into the house.

"You will show the Señorita Stanmore to her rooms, Sabino," Philip ordered.

"*Sí! Sí*, Don Felipe!" The man crossed the *patio*, standing aside for Felicity to pass. "This way, Señorita!"

Felicity hesitated. It seemed incongruous that she should be shown to her rooms by an outside servant, especially when she had just been told that the house was "full of superfluous women," but no doubt most of them were employed in the kitchen at present, preparing the evening meal or whispering together over the fate of their master.

She began to wonder about her cousins, Robert Hallam's children, whom she had expected to meet straight away. None of them appeared to be within hearing distance of the arriving car, however, and it seemed that Philip Arnold guessed her thought, for he said:

"Sisa is with her father. She will not leave him. Julio has not come back yet. He is out somewhere on the plantations. We have no regular hours for working here, as in England," he added. "Our toil is governed by the sun."

He had spoken of her cousins with easy familiarity and still with the note of authority in his voice which had set her wondering about his true position at San Lozaro. Did he live in the house itself, or had he some other place of domicile within the vast garden's encircling walls?

"I am looking forward to meeting them," she confessed. "Julio is the eldest child, isn't he? I mean—after María."

The name hung, quivering between them. It was as if she had shouted it in the sudden, deathly stillness of the *patio*. Sabino's smile faded on his lips and Philip Arnold's face took on a curious greyness. The light, which had been all about them in the garden, dimmed with the sudden coming of the sub-tropical night and even the climbing fountain seemed arrested in the windless air. There was no sound from within the house. It was as if death itself had taken over where once there had been abundant life.

"Yes." The word came, clipped and aggressive, barring the way to further questioning. "Julio is eighteen. Sisa and Conchita are fourteen and seventeen respectively."

"I ought to have remembered their ages," Felicity said, half nervously, as he stood back, waiting for her to pass. "It's—rather difficult to adjust oneself to a new situation right away."

Philip Arnold nodded, whether in agreement with her

417

sentiments or in dismissal she did not know, and she followed Sabino and her suitcases into the cool interior of the house.

The lamps had not yet been lit and the inner courtyard was shadowy in consequence, but she could see a vast tessellated floor stretching into the shadows and a heavily-ornamented staircase leading up from it to a gallery above. The gallery ran round three walls of the inner structure, the fourth being entirely taken up by the head of the branching stair itself.

Sabino turned, beckoning her with an encouraging smile, the shock of María's name apparently forgotten now that they were no longer in "Don Felipe's" presence.

"This way," he repeated. "I show you where you will go."

Felicity mounted the staircase behind him, walking silently in his wake along the gallery, from which doors opened at regular intervals. Behind one of these doors, she supposed, her uncle lay seriously ill, but no sound came from any of the rooms she passed. The doors were thick and heavily carved, old and substantial as the house itself, and the massive pieces of furniture placed against the walls between them only seemed to accentuate the heavy silence which brooded over everything.

At the end of the gallery Sabino paused, looking back once more as he thrust open a door on the end wall. It led into a little passage, and as she walked ahead of the old servant into her own domain, Felicity had the curious sensation of being completely isolated from the rest of the family.

The rooms she entered were spacious and well furnished in the sparse, Canarian style. The sitting-room held a table, a desk, a wooden settle dark with age, and two comfortable chairs, both facing the window and the balcony beyond it. She told herself that she must get used to the idea of not having a fireplace in a room, the focal point of all English living, and passed on to the bedroom, where Sabino was already setting down her suitcases.

He disappeared with a bow and a murmured word of Spanish which she was too preoccupied to catch, and she looked about her at the big, four-poster bed which would surely swamp her and disturb her sleep. It had no canopy, but the corner posts were most ornately carved, and the beautiful drawn-thread work of the counterpane made it a fitting centrepiece for the room. It was native craftsmanship and had probably been worked by her aunt, the lovely Spanish woman whom she could not remember.

Impatient now to meet her cousins and enquire about her uncle, she washed in the old-fashioned basin on the mahogany stand in the far corner of the room, pouring crystal-clear water from the huge ewer with its garlanded flower pattern which she saw, with a small sense of shock, represented the red lotus that grew in such profusion all over the valley.

She stood gazing at it for a moment before she turned and went slowly back along the gallery towards the stairs.

CHAPTER II

DON JULIO

DOWN in the central hall lamps had been hung along the walls, casting little pools of yellow light against the pale cream of the plaster and deepening the shadows outside in the darkened *patio*. The swift, sub-tropical night had come like the beat of a raven's wing and all sound was stilled. There was no wind left even to stir the feathery heads of the island palms. They stood silhouetted against the deep blue of the sky as if they had been etched in with a dark pencil as the moon came up over the shoulder of the jagged ridge above the valley.

Already its light had touched the high cone of The Peak, paling its snow cap and deepening the shadows in the *barrancos* which scarred its sides. They were purple now, scored sharply against the mountain's face, no light touching them even as the moon rose higher and cast a silver wash across the garden's trees.

The hall was deserted. There was no sound anywhere, no movement. Felicity felt chilled and curiously alone. Had she no part to play in this drama of her uncle's household? Was she completely unwanted, apart from Robert Hallam's natural desire to see his sister's only child?

And now, perhaps, he was dying, somewhere up there behind those guarded doors.

She thrust the suggestion from her mind, but she did not move towards the *patio*, where she knew that the Spanish family generally gathered before its evening meal. A shadow had stirred out there among the other shadows and subconsciously she knew that it was Philip Arnold.

He had not gone there to wait for her. Almost as surely she knew that. He wanted to be alone, and the garden had served his purpose. To go out to him now would be a form of trespass, and she had no desire to incur his anger. The servants, too, seemed to be leaving the *patio* alone. Someone had placed a tray with glasses and a bottle of wine on the stone table beside the fountain, but the occupant of the garden had been left to serve himself.

She did not know what to do. Then, from somewhere behind her, within the house, came the sound of an opening door, and high-pitched sobbing echoed shrilly from the gallery above.

Immediately the shadows in the *patio* dissolved and Philip Arnold passed her. His face was grey and drawn, the blue eyes under the dark brows strangely bleak. There was none of the former arrogance in his face as he said:

"It is Sisa. Will you come?"

The appeal—if it was an appeal—had been just what Felicity had been waiting for. She wanted to help. She felt the need for action more than anything else, and the sound of a young girl's anguish had touched her heart. There was a helplessness about the man who mounted the stairs ahead of her, too, which suggested a typical male inability to cope with tears, although the wild sobbing which still reached them could only have been the tears of a child.

"Someone has told her," Philip said through set teeth. "Her father is dead."

He had not sought to soften the blow in her own case, and Felicity swallowed hard, trying to blink aside the sudden tears which had welled to her eyes before they reached her cousin's room. When they halted outside the door her heart was beating fast.

"Sisa!" her companion said in a voice she would never have recognized as his. "It's Philip. Will you let me in?"

There was no answer.

"I have your cousin here. Your cousin from England. She has come to comfort us in our distress."

There was still no sign from behind the closed door, but the violent sobbing had ceased. They waited.

"Is her sister with her?" Felicity whispered.

"Conchita? No." Philip turned to look at her. "Conchita would not take her father's death in this way."

She felt uncertain and at a loss again. Was he trying to tell her that Conchita would not *care?*

There was a small, groping movement within the room

and the handle of the heavy door began to turn, slowly at first and then with an abruptness which suggested final decision. The door opened and a small, forlorn yet wholly dignified figure stood in the aperture.

Sisa was fourteen years of age, but already she seemed to be curiously mature. She had a small, oval face which had been touched lightly by the sun, giving her skin a golden-brown cast which accentuated vividly-blue eyes, red-rimmed now from weeping. Her hair was straight and very black, and it was braided severely in two tight plaits which fell over her shoulders almost to her waist. The ribbon which bound one of them was untied, but otherwise Sisa's appearance was fastidiously neat. It was almost impossible to believe, save for the evidence of the reddened eye-lids, that she had been weeping in unhappy abandonment less than a moment ago.

The strange, incongruous dignity of the child trying to hide her sorrow from a stranger touched Felicity as nothing else could have done, but she knew that she must leave the next step to Philip Arnold. He knew and loved Sisa. Of that she was sure.

"Please come in." Sisa spoke in stilted English, in spite of the fact that Philip's appeal through the closed door had been made in Spanish. She would not inflict a barely-understood language on a guest, although she could probably have expressed herself better in the tongue she had used since earliest childhood. "We knew you were coming."

The room they entered was much like Felicity's bedroom, with the addition of a *prie-Dieu* beside the bed and a desk between the two long windows. There was also a motley collection of dolls set along a low shelf, most of them in the native costumes of the other islands or of Spain itself, presents brought, no doubt, by a returning parent for a waiting child. Some of them were sadly tattered, those, Felicity knew, that were best loved and most often handled. Others had been scarcely touched at all.

Conchita's, she thought, without knowing why. She had noticed the second bed in the far corner of the room. Conchita had never had a great deal of time for dolls.

"Your cousin has not eaten anything since her arrival, Sisa," Phillip said. "Do you think you could order for her while I have a few words with Doctor Cambreleno? He

422

may wish to go away soon because he has a long journey to make."

"And his task here is finished." Sisa gnawed a quivering lip. "I understand that, Philip. There is a baby coming at El Tanque. It is a happy event for these people."

Felicity went forward into the room.

"If you would rather not come downstairs, Sisa," she said, "I shall understand."

"That would not do." Sisa was re-tying her hair ribbon with a new determination in her eyes. "There is no one else to greet you, so I must come—Felicity."

The final word was all that Felicity needed. She put her arm about the younger girl's thin shoulders and they went down the stairs together. A priest in a black cassock met them in the hall. He was old and bent and looked vastly troubled as he laid his hand in blessing on Sisa's dark head.

When he passed Philip Arnold on the stairs he gave him an odd look, half questioning, half perturbed, but Robert Hallam's agent was already escorting the doctor to his car. They were speaking in rapid Spanish with a good deal of native idiom thrown in, so that Felicity could not even begin to understand what was being said.

"To-morrow," Sisa announced at her side, "Señor Pérez will come from La Laguna and we will know what is to happen to us. My father has made a will, but no one knows, of course, what he has put in it. We do not know what he wishes us to do. Whether we are to stay here or go away."

Her voice had faltered on the suggestion of departure and Felicity's arm tightened about her.

"I don't think your father will wish you to leave the home you love, Sisa," she said, not quite knowing why she should have given her cousin the assurance she had so obviously sought. "He loved San Lozaro, too. He has lived here nearly all his life."

"Yes," Sisa agreed, but she did not seem wholly convinced. "If it depended upon Julio or Conchita, we would go away."

The revelation disturbed Felicity, but she was determined not to ask any more questions. Sisa escorted her to the kitchens, where a tearful domestic staff managed to pull themselves together, including, presumably, the person who

423

had broken the harsh news of her father's death to her cousin. The preparations for an evening meal were set in motion, although there was still no sign of the other members of Robert Hallam's family.

Towards ten o'clock, Julio came in from the fields, to be met in the *patio* by his father's agent. Felicity and Sisa were in the drawing-room, a vast place of many mirrors and much solid old furniture which was rarely used in the ordinary way, and so Felicity saw nothing of that first meeting between Philip and Julio after his father's death.

When her cousin came into the drawing-room to meet her he looked sullen and angry, his mouth drawn down in a petulant line, his black eyes smouldering. Julio was all Spanish, from the crown of his black, curly head to the soles of his gaily-shod feet, and he did not seem to relish the idea of her presence.

"You've come too late," he said, "if you wanted to see my father."

Felicity got to her feet.

"Yes, Julio, I know," she said. "That is my loss. But I hope I can be of some small help to you now."

He shrugged indifferently.

"What can you do?"

"I'm not sure. I thought, perhaps, that I could ask Mr. Arnold."

The suggestion had been entirely spontaneous and she could not understand why she had made it. Unless it was because only Philip Arnold and Sisa had shown any real feeling at her uncle's death. Conchita, it would appear, had not yet come in.

Julio turned slowly to look at her. He had gone to the window to gaze out over the moonlit garden, but when he came back across the room his face was convulsed.

"He has no power in this house now!" he cried. "It is broken with my father's death! He must go away." Suddenly he drew himself up to his full height, which was no more than her own. "I shall be in charge at San Lozaro now that my father is dead," he announced. "I shall be the head of the family. I shall give the orders. Philip Arnold must go away."

The smouldering hatred in his eyes could not be ignored, and Felicity found herself recoiling from it with a hopeless sense of her own inadequacy to deal with the situation rising in her heart.

"I don't think we ought to talk about such things just now, Julio," she warned, glancing in Sisa's direction. "Your sister is tired and we must go early to bed. To-morrow will be a heavy day for us all, but we will help each other best by—by trying to forget our prejudices. Everyone has little differences of opinion," she added lamely.

"This is more than just a difference of opinion, Miss Stanmore."

She wheeled round to find Philip standing in the doorway, and Sisa ran to him immediately.

"Please, Philip, do not let us quarrel to-night," Sisa pleaded. "Julio will say he is sorry. He did not really mean that you should go away."

Felicity saw the older man's lips tighten almost cruelly as he looked at Julio.

"I hardly think it is for Julio to say how and when I should go," he answered thinly. "Your father's will is yet to be read, and then we will know just where we all stand."

Julio gave him a look of the most utter hatred as he picked up the *manta* he had discarded on one of the sofas and went out.

"I'll get what I want to eat in the kitchens," he said harshly. "Perhaps that is really my place."

The tension he left behind him in the quiet room could almost be felt.

"Poor Julio!" Sisa sighed. "He cannot love anyone."

Philip's mouth relaxed as he looked at her.

"And you, *querida*," he answered gently, "are in love with the whole world!"

In the moments of his tenderness to Sisa he was a different being, Felicity realized. There was no harshness in him, no guile. Even his habitual arrogance of manner was softened by Sisa's smile; he had made an adoring slave of her cousin.

Their belated meal was brought into the dining-room beyond the pillared archway at the far end of the room where they sat.

"I have ordered *entremeses* because I thought that Felicity would not care for soup on such a warm evening," Sisa informed Philip.

It would seem that Sisa accounted to Philip automatically

425

for all that went on at San Lozaro, and he nodded absently as the food was served, his thoughts obviously busy with something else.

That they were disturbed, even angry, thoughts was not too difficult to imagine. He had followed them through the pillared archway and taken his place in the heavily-carved armchair at the head of the table with only a second's hesitation. It was probably her uncle's chair, Felicity decided, and she supposed that he had hesitated before the choice of occupying it or leaving it tragically empty for the duration of the meal.

Or shouldn't Julio have occupied that chair? Anger flooded her heart for a moment until Sisa said with evident relief:

"You are going to take care of us, Philip. You are not going to leave San Lozaro now that Papa is taken away?"

Philip's face remained inscrutable.

"For the present, *querida*," he said, "I shall remain with you."

Sisa applied herself half-heartedly to her plate of *hors-d'œuvres*, and the two other chairs at the table remained unoccupied for the duration of the meal.

Their coffee was served on a tray in the drawing-room, but although it was now eleven o'clock, neither Julio nor his sister had joined them.

Once or twice Felicity saw Philip glance at his wrist watch, but he made no comment on her cousins' absence.

Sisa began to yawn.

"Had you not better go to bed?" Philip asked. "Carlota will go up to your room with you till Conchita returns."

"Conchita will not return," Sisa said with conviction. "She is afraid of death. She will not come until the morning, until Father Anselmo brings her back."

Philip's mouth hardened.

"We shall see," he said. "Meanwhile, do you wish your cousin to go up with you?"

Felicity wondered if this was dismissal. Philip seemed to have so much power in the house and he used it ruthlessly.

"It is not necessary," Sisa returned with a smile in Felicity's direction which was meant to soften the refusal. "I am in no way afraid."

Unlike Conchita, she was not disturbed by death. After

426

that first heartbreaking abandonment to grief which she had conquered behind the closed door of her room, she had turned her face resolutely from fear, but less than an hour ago she had confessed to an uncertainty about living. With her roots torn up by her father's passing, she had appealed to Philip for help, and he was evidently not the man to fail her, for the present at least.

"I'll follow you upstairs in a minute, Sisa," Felicity said as the stout old woman she had first met came to the drawing-room door in response to Philip's ring. "May I come and say goodnight?"

"Yes, please come," Sisa said solemnly. "I shall not be asleep."

Felicity felt that she had to speak to Philip alone. There was so much that she had to clear up in her mind, and she believed that it could be done best by the direct approach. It was how Philip himself would handle a similar situation, and she expected him to be frank.

"Mr. Arnold," she began as soon as Sisa and Carlota had left the room, "there are a good many things that puzzle me about San Lozaro. I feel that they would have been cleared up by now if my uncle had not died so tragically as soon as I got here, and I think that you might be able to help me to make a few adjustments."

She paused, waiting for his reply, hoping that he would help her over what was, for her, at least, a difficult moment. She did not want to probe into his affairs, but she had to know something about her uncle's family and it seemed that he was quite closely connected with it.

He did not answer her at once, pouring another cup of coffee for himself before he strode with it to the window overlooking the terraces and the district plantations.

"What is it you want to know?" he asked.

He was not going to be particularly helpful, she realized. He would answer her questions and no more.

Once again anger stirred in her, the anger of frustration and uncertainty, but she knew that it would be useless to voice it. Philip Arnold was not the type of man to be browbeaten into a revelation he had no desire to make.

"It—would be helpful if I had some definite idea just what my uncle expected me to do," she confessed. "He said he had work for me. That was how he put it in his

427

letters, and I admit that I found it easier to accept his invitation under these conditions."

She saw him smile.

"An admirable sentiment," he acknowledged. "Independence is one of the few virtues I appreciate, and your question is quite easy to answer. Your uncle wanted you to preserve the English atmosphere in his home so that it would not become entirely Spanish, at least for Sisa's sake."

"And Conchita and Julio?" she asked.

"Julio has become a law unto himself," he admitted, frowning. "His father hoped that he would be able one day to take on the responsibility of the estate where he laid it down, but Julio, I'm afraid, is running true to type."

"You mean," she frowned, "that he is wholly Spanish?"

"Not entirely. Julio has Guanche blood."

"Can you tell me what that means, please? I'm afraid I am very ignorant of your island's history."

"As far as Julio is concerned, it means complete irresponsibility," he explained. "The Guanches were the original inhabitants of these islands, Miss Stanmore. They were a sturdy peasant race, and they fought bravely for their liberty, but since the Conquest they have been more and more thrust into the background of the island's living until they have agreed to take second place. You will see the true types among the cave-dwellers in the troglodyte villages, but there has been gradual intermarriage between certain types of Spanish settlers and these people, and so we have Julio."

"A—throwback?"

"So far, I'm afraid, as character is concerned."

"He is very young." She felt that she had to defend Julio.

"That may be our one hope for the future."

" 'Our,' Mr. Arnold?" she repeated. "Then you have a definite interest in San Lozaro?"

He put his coffee cup back on the table between them and stood looking down at it for several seconds before he answered the direct question.

"A personal interest," he agreed, "as well as the interest I expect to have vested in me when your uncle's will becomes known."

Swiftly her eyes shot up to his, meeting the cold blue

428

gaze which had disconcerted her so much earlier in the afternoon.

"Are you trying to tell me that you have been left in charge here?" she asked incredulously.

"Does it seem so amazing to you?" The hard mouth had not relaxed, although he looked faintly amused by her disbelief. "I have served your uncle for more than ten years—conscientiously, I hope. I was brought up in a neighbouring valley where my mother struggled unsuccessfully with one misfortune after another when my father died. When she, too, died, I was brought to San Lozaro and given a home."

She was silent a moment, wondering why he had confessed so much.

"Your father was English, of course," she said at last.

"Both my parents were. They loved Lozaro Alto—the valley above this one—and they made their home there. My father was a writer of sorts—a dreamer, perhaps—and they grew vines in the valley, but it did not pay. After his death my mother planned to return to England, but she could not tear herself away. She could not leave the sun. Lozaro Alto had become her life."

"And so you want to remain here?"

"I shall remain on the island whatever happens."

"What—power has Julio?" she found herself asking, remembering her cousin's impassioned outburst of little more than an hour ago.

"None at all until he is twenty-one. Your uncle was an Englishman, remember!"

Felicity forced a smile.

"I can imagine him being almost aggressively British," she admitted.

"At least it may pay dividends in Julio's case."

She did not know about that. She could not imagine her cousin submitting to further domination now that his father was dead. The hand that had been on the rein had slackened and an eighteen-year-old Spaniard with a dash of Guanche blood in his veins would be no more amenable to an enforced discipline than an English teenager in similar circumstances.

If Philip Arnold meant to take up the reins again and even to use the curb, might not Julio rush off headlong to some form of distraction while the bit remained temporarily between his strong white teeth?

"Do you—expect trouble?" she asked.

He shrugged.

"I shall try to avoid it where I can, but you heard Julio to-night. Unfortunately he labours under the delusion that he is being unfairly treated. His father took a firm hand with him some time ago, and he has never liked me." He strode back towards the window. "He blames me, you see, for his sister's death."

"María?"

The word had forced itself from between Felicity's lips and she remembered the effect it had had on Sabino when she had first arrived. And also the effect on the man who now stood with his back towards her so that she might not see his face.

"Perhaps I can most safely call it the tragedy of San Lozaro and leave it at that." His voice was harsh and almost cruel in its bitterness. "It is something that we never discuss."

And something which I must not ask about again, Felicity thought with a small, pained intake of breath as she remembered that María had been her uncle's favourite child.

Yet, surely Robert Hallam had not shared Julio's belief that Philip was responsible for the tragedy which had led to his daughter's death? Otherwise, how could he have entrusted his family's entire future to this man?

Baffled and suddenly overwhelmingly tired by the events of a very long day, she felt that she could not attempt to cope with the problem or hope to bring any very clear reasoning to bear upon it until she had come to know her cousins better.

She had still to meet Conchita, and it was almost midnight. Where was she? And quite apart from her fear of death, what had kept her away from San Lozaro at such a time? There was, she felt, some other reason for Conchita's absence.

Curiously enough, she did not want to ask Philip Arnold about Conchita. His tight mouth and drawn brows when he turned back from the window were evidence enough that Conchita should have been safely in the *hacienda* long

430

ago and that he was both anxious and worried about her. He glanced at the clock and then at his watch.

"It is almost midnight," he said on a definite note of dismissal. "You must be tired after your journey. If there is anything you want that has been forgotten you have only to ring for Carlota or Sabino to fetch it—or to ask Sisa."

He stood waiting, and for the first time Felicity was aware of her own incredible tiredness. It seemed as if a weight had been put upon her shoulders which was heavier than she could bear, the weight of running contrary to this man's will if she thought it necessary to do so in defence of her uncle's family.

"Do you mind if I go to see my uncle?" she asked.

He held the heavy door open for her.

"I should have been disappointed if you had not," he said.

Two elderly, black-clad servants were leaving Robert Hallam's bedroom when she approached the door and a third rose from her knees beside the bed when she went in.

Standing there beside the great bed where her uncle lay, in the yellow glow of its flanking candles, she made her silent promise to look after his family. She had not known this man in life, but something of his strong character was still to be seen in the rugged face with its square jaw and black, beetling brows that stood out so plainly beneath the snow-white hair.

In some ways it was the face of El Teide again, the granite countenance crowned by its white cap of snow, beneath which the ancient volcano slumbered. It was years, Philip Arnold had said, since El Teide had been in eruption, yet there was still evidence everywhere of the devastating effects of his wrath.

And Philip himself had all the granite qualities of the sleeping giant of a mountain that guarded their silent valley, the harshness and the domination and the undeniable strength.

Was it that strength, then, that her uncle had recognized and accepted as the only possible salvation for San Lozaro when he had gone?

She did not know, and only the coming days would allow her to find out. She would try not to begin their enforced partnership with any personal prejudices lurking

431

in the offing, although her uncle's agent had been at little pains to conceal his own.

She could not forget that he had said that San Lozaro was already "full of superfluous women."

Walking slowly along the gallery in the direction of her own rooms, she remembered her promise to Sisa. Was her cousin asleep by now, she wondered, and would it merely be awakening Sisa to fresh sorrow to go to her? But she had made a promise, and somehow she knew that Sisa would expect her to keep it.

She tiptoed to the door outside of which she and Philip had waited, and immediately Sisa's voice bade her go in.

Her cousin was in bed, her small figure entirely enveloped in a long nightgown liberally flounced with the island embroidery, her two dark plaits knotted together at her back. She looked small and peculiarly vulnerable sitting up there in the big bed with her hands clasped tightly about her knees and her eyes expectantly upon the door.

"Hasn't Philip come?" she asked, trying to hide her disappointment when he did not appear. "He always comes to wish me goodnight."

"I think he is rather worried about Conchita," Felicity confessed. "She hasn't come in yet. Does she generally stay out so late as this?"

It did not seem at all incongruous to be speaking to Sisa as if she were an adult. She had an adult perception in most things and a quick way of expressing herself that made her seem older than her actual years. Felicity remembered that the Spanish girl matured young, that what would have seemed precocious in an English child of Sisa's age was only natural in the Spaniard, and she found herself waiting for Sisa's answer with the conviction that it would give her her first real insight into Conchita's character.

"She is sometimes very late when she goes to Zamora, but that is because Rafael brings her home in his car. When she is going to stay there overnight, she always sends a message with one of the servants." The fine dark brows were suddenly drawn in a perplexed little frown. "That is what I cannot understand," Sisa added anxiously. "There has not been any message, and Rafael is away in Madrid."

Felicity hesitated, her heart beginning to beat faster than she cared to acknowledge.

"Is—the Rafael you speak of the Marqués de Barrios, Sisa?" she asked slowly.

Sisa's eyes widened as she fixed them on her face.

"Yes," she agreed. "But how did you know? Rafael is the Marqués de Barrios and Isabella is the Marquesa. They live in the valley next to this one and Conchita can ride over there whenever she likes. Isabella says that it is essential that Conchita should have friends of her own age, but, of course, Conchita could not go to Zamora unless she had a chaperone. There is a country club there where tennis can be played and croquet. Conchita adores that sort of life. It is not such a closed-in valley as San Lozaro."

It seemed to Felicity that Sisa's voice was coming to her from some great distance. Names that she had not even heard of twenty-four hours ago crowded in upon her, one after the other, confusingly. Isabella and Rafael and Philip Arnold: Zamora and Lozaro Alto, where Philip's widowed mother had fought her losing battle against circumstances too powerful for her to subdue; and San Lozaro, torn by conflict, where she had promised to make her home.

Isabella and Rafael! A deep colour stained her cheeks as the names recurred, linked inevitably by the title which had rolled off Sisa's garrulous little tongue with the familiarity of long use. The Marqués and Marquesa de Barrios! Don Rafael, Marqués de Barrios, was married, then, and she had made a fool of herself in front of Philip Arnold by being so obviously captivated by his easy charm!

The gall that rose in her heart was out of all proportion to the cause of her humiliation, but she was too tired to think any more, too stunned by the swift progress of events to reason clearly.

"The Marqués came back in the plane with me," she explained to Sisa to still her anxiety. "He came on at Madrid." She rose to her feet. "I must go, Sisa," she added quickly. "Try to sleep, and we will talk again in the morning."

"Don't worry about Conchita too much," Sisa murmured drowsily when she had tucked the sheets securely round her thin little body. "Philip will take care of her."

Walking along the gallery in the direction of her own rooms, Felicity was aware of a movement in the hall beneath her. The lamps still burned in their wrought-iron sconces along the wall, but the shadows seemed to have deepened as she went to the balcony rail and looked down.

Beneath her Philip Arnold was standing in the centre of the tessellated floor, and she saw with some surprise that he had changed into riding-breeches and a thicker jacket. Remembering how cold it had become with the setting of the sun, she supposed that he was preparing to go out, but where could he possibly be going at this hour of night?

Then, almost with a sense of shock, she saw the riding whip in his hand. And Conchita had, according to Sisa, ridden over to Zamora earlier in the day. Was Philip going to meet Conchita? Was he going to bring her home?

Subconsciously she knew that she must not interfere with his decision. She drew back among the shadows of the silent gallery, waiting till he had gone before she crept to her room and tried to sleep.

In spite of her tiredness, however, oblivion would not come. Somewhere in the now quiet house a clock struck the quarter-hours and she began to count them, automatically, aware that she was straining to catch every sound, no matter how small.

It was two o'clock before the clatter of horses' hooves sounded on the cobbles of the courtyard, and she was out of bed before she realized what she had done.

The moon was three-quarters full and the courtyard beneath her windows was almost as bright as day. Only where the high garden wall cast a black shadow was she unable to see clearly, and even there the white clusters of stephanotis cast an iridescent gleam as they hung down from the ornamental urns above the low stone seats in the alcoves or spilled over the archway of a door.

The door which she could see most clearly stood open and the horses had been halted beyond it. There was the sound of voices raised in argument, followed by an ominous silence which lasted for over a minute before a girl began to laugh.

A figure moved along the shadow of the wall and Felicity saw Sabino go quickly through the doorway to take the horses.

Almost immediately a girl made her appearance in the moonlit aperture. She was taller than Sisa, and fairer, and her vividly-red lips were still parted in a mocking smile. She looked far older than seventeen years of age, Felicity

434

thought irrelevantly, but she had no hesitation in deciding that this was Conchita, at last.

Philip Arnold stepped through the archway behind her, his dark face set and grim.

"Philip! why are you always angry with me?" Conchita demanded as they passed beneath the open window. "You know it will do no good. I will go my own way and you are powerless to prevent me!"

"Not quite powerless." Philip had stopped in his tracks and Felicity could see the harsh line of his mouth and the hands gripped tightly by his sides as he strove for control of a temper which was all but frayed. "I have made a promise to your father, Conchita, and I mean to keep it, whether you like it or not."

"But I am almost eighteen! I am already grown up," she protested. And then, her tone changing, she began to wheedle. "Was that the only reason why you came for me to-night?" she demanded, her voice as soft as silk. "Was it, Philip? Why will you not say?"

She was looking up into his eyes, her face and mocking red lips dangerously near his own, an errant, wilful creature playing with sex for her own enjoyment. Philip took her roughly by the arms and for a moment Felicity thought that he was about to crush his mouth against the tantalizing red one, but instead he shook Conchita as he might have done a tiresome, disobedient child.

"You know it is not," he said in a voice hoarse with suppressed feeling which turned Felicity's blood to ice. "But you choose not to understand."

Conchita put her slim hands behind his dark head and drew it down until her lips all but touched his.

"You are hard, Philip!" she murmured. "But in some ways you are soft." She laughed gently, her white teeth gleaming in the moonlight, her dark eyes aglow. *"Te quiero mucho,* Philip!" she sighed before he put her from him and strode before her into the house.

"I love you very much," Conchita had said.

Pale and shaken, Felicity stood at her window above the moonlit courtyard, trying not to believe what she had just heard, trying to pretend that the words did not mean so much, coming from Conchita. Conchita was flippant and gay and she was also a tease. Sisa had said that she loved the gay life at Zamora, but suddenly she was remembering

Sisa and how much older her cousin had seemed for her years. It was as if she had heard Conchita say again, "But I am almost eighteen, Philip. I am already grown up!"

Was Conchita really in love with Philip? And had he repulsed her down there in the court only because he was so angry with her about Zamora?

What could it matter to her, she thought; what could it really matter? Except for the fact that she knew instinctively that Conchita was just one other problem she would have to face at San Lozaro, if Philip decided that she should stay.

CHAPTER III

STERN GUARDIAN

IT was a full week before anyone knew the contents of Robert Hallam's will. In the ordinary way it would have been disclosed immediately after the funeral, which had brought people from far and near to La Orotava, where the service was held in the English Church.

Felicity had been bewildered by the crowds and the new faces and strange names, and it had seemed to her that both Julio and Conchita had done their best to keep out of her way.

She had not seen very much of Philip, either, so that she had been more than glad of Sisa's company. It was Sisa who had shown her over the entire *hacienda* and much of the surrounding estate, explaining how the banana trees went on producing fruit for most of the year and how difficult it would have been for her father to manage without Philip's help.

"Philip is absolutely indispensable," she had said once with the seriousness of a child endorsing an oft-repeated adult opinion, and that, more than anything else, made Felicity realize how much trust her uncle had in this man to whom he had offered a home in boyhood.

When Philip intimated that the family lawyer would be coming from La Laguna on the Wednesday morning, he did so the evening before when they were all gathered in the long, cool dining-room over the final meal of the day. It was the only meal they took together. The men were out in the plantation long before the first heat of the sun, and Conchita slept late, or at least remained confined to her room until she was ready for her morning ride into the hills. She did not appear to do very much about the house, but Felicity excused her because of her father's death. The family could not be expected to adjust itself immediately to such a sudden loss, although neither Conchita nor Julio had shown any signs of deep unhappiness.

Julio looked at Philip with smouldering eyes when he made the announcement about the lawyer.

"Why is it that the reading of my father's will should be so long delayed?" he demanded. "Perhaps you have had it changed, Philip, to suit yourself?"

Philip's mouth tightened, but he managed to keep his temper.

"You must know that that is something I could not do," he answered briefly. "Señor Pérez has had possession of the will for over a month. No doubt he will tell you that when he arrives, if you wish to ask him," he added dryly. "In the meantime, Julio, I think you should try to adjust yourself to the idea that it *is* your father's will you are going to hear, and not any personal dictate of mine."

Julio frowned, his dark brows drawn together in a heavy line above the suspicious black eyes.

"But you know about it, all the same," he persisted with none of Philip's amazing coolness in the heat of argument. "You already know what we are about to hear!"

Philip rose and pushed back his chair. In the yellow light from the wall sconces his face looked grim and determined.

"Your father discussed the future with me—yes," he acknowledged.

Julio jumped to his feet, his eyes blazing, his sullen mouth drawn tight.

"Then I can guess what it is!" he declared passionately. "I shall still be subservient to you. I shall still have to answer to you for everything I do. I shall be treated like a child and you will be the overlord!"

"You will not be treated like a child, Julio," Philip said, "if you do not act like one."

"I am eighteen! I am of age!" Julio protested vigorously. "Some men are already married by this time."

"Not in England," Philip reminded him decisively.

The parallel seemed strangely incongruous to Felicity as she looked away from Julio's dark, angry face. He was all Latin, fiery, impulsive, given to fits of passion or depression and as sudden fits of gaiety. She had heard him play a guitar down in the *patio* by the light of the moon with all the impassioned awareness of beauty throbbing at his

438

finger-tips so that her heart had turned over in her breast as she had listened, but she had also seen him thrash an animal with a vindictive fury which had turned her blood to ice. It had been the fury of the thwarted child, so that it seemed as if Philip might be right, after all, about Julio's coming of age. Eighteen or twenty-one; what did a number or a date matter? Neither of them automatically brought maturity.

Conchita rose from her chair. Philip's intimation had left her silent and thoughtful, her black eyes apparently slumberous, but behind them Felicity detected watchfulness and the glimmer of suspicion.

"If you know, *amigo*," she asked gently, going behind Philip to twine slim brown arms about his neck, "why do you not tell us? Julio does not want you to leave San Lozaro." She shot a warning glance at her silent brother. "Of that I am sure. All he would wish for is a little more freedom."

Philip unclasped the clinging hands from beneath his chin and turned to look at her. His eyes were no longer guarded nor angry. He was smiling.

"You are wasting your wiles, Conchita," he said. "Nothing will be known until to-morrow. Nothing can be known. It is for Señor Pérez to read your father's will."

Conchita flung away from him with an impatient stamp of her foot.

"There is no need for all this mystery!" she declared. "If we are to obey you, Philip, you must tell us now."

"I have told you," Philip repeated with what must have been maddening equanimity to Julio, at least, "that I do not know with any certainty what will be our position in the future."

Suddenly Conchita turned towards Felicity. It was the first time she had appeared to notice her, and Felicity smiled inwardly, knowing that she was about to be enlisted as Conchita's ally.

"What will you do," Conchita demanded, "supposing my father says that you must stay here?"

Felicity hesitated. She hadn't quite expected the question, such a direct challenge to her attitude in the future— to her whole future, in fact.

"Hadn't we better wait and see what Señor Pérez has to

439

say to-morrow?" she suggested. "Everything might turn out quite differently from the way we imagine just now."

She had no idea what Conchita wanted from life—nor Julio either. All she knew was that she seemed to be sitting on top of some personal volcano which had all the destructive power of El Teide in full eruption.

It was an odd feeling to assail her in that quiet atmosphere of moon-filled night, with the stars calm and large, glittering like distant lanterns far above the tufted heads of the island palms. The sigh of the night wind came in from the Atlantic to stir that other green sea that was the banana fields and wander among the terraces, and all nature seemed to reflect only a benign sense of peace.

Then, from somewhere far in the hills, came the cry of a wild animal, sudden and piercing on the still air.

Felicity looked up, arrested and half frightened by the sound, but no one else seemed to be aware of it. Perhaps they were too accustomed to the predatory prowlings of those night creatures to care very much what became of one of them. Nature, in essence, was fundamentally cruel and they accepted the savageries with a shrug of resignation. They themselves often had to fight for what they wanted.

Philip rose, moved towards the door.

"I think we ought to leave our discussion there," he suggested. "Felicity has been most concise." He gave her a dry smile. "With the typical English desire for a peaceful atmosphere, she has advised us to wait and see what to-morrow brings."

There was hostility and disappointment in the eyes Conchita turned towards her cousin.

"Why do you side with Philip so easily?" she demanded. "You do not know him—how ruthless he can be when he so desires—and how cruel!"

Felicity had not wanted to take sides. She had no intention of ranging herself in either camp, if camps there were, and as far as Conchita was concerned she felt that her cousin wanted it both ways. She wanted Philip to stay because she believed herself in love with him, but she also wanted her freedom.

It was natural enough in a young girl to want to spread her wings, but in which direction did Conchita desire to fly?

440

"Shall we let Felicity discover these things about me for herself, if she decides to stay here?" Philip suggested with indifference. "She may not feel inclined to tackle us, you know."

Was there a very definite hope behind the observation, Felicity wondered, or was he really completely indifferent to whether she stayed or went away? That, too, of course, would depend on her uncle's will.

Suddenly she felt tired and drained of all her habitual energy, aware that nothing that any of them could say or do at this eleventh hour could alter the decision of tomorrow.

"I'm going to bed," Conchita announced with amazing alacrity considering that it was not yet midnight. "And I do not wish to see Señor Pérez in the morning."

Philip was standing between her and the archway leading into the hall. He did not appear to block her way, but it seemed that Conchita could not pass him until she had heard what he had to say.

"I'm afraid that will be impossible, Conchita." His tone was clipped and decisive, refuting all argument. "Señor Pérez is coming to see the family, and you are part of it. He will expect you to be there."

"And you?" Conchita challenged.

"I, also, will be there," he agreed.

He followed her out of the room, but not, Felicity decided, to exact any further promise from her. He expected obedience.

Julio made a quick, angry movement towards the *patio*.

"As you see," he observed fiercely, "no Hallam has any real authority in this place!"

Felicity followed him out into the night where the fountain splashed into its deep stone basin and the cicadas chirped stridently beneath the leaves. There was a smell of stephanotis in the air, thick and cloying, almost unbearably sweet, and a green lizard darted erratically across the tiles.

"Julio," she began, "I'm sorry you are so upset, but can't we forget our differences with Philip until we learn what your father really wants us to do at San Lozaro?"

He swung round, staring at her incredulously.

"Forget about them?" he echoed. "What you say is impossible! How can I forget what Philip is? What he has always been. He killed my sister."

441

Felicity recoiled from the words as if they had been a blow.

"No," she whispered, "surely that isn't true? Your father wrote to us in England saying there had been an accident——"

"That is what was said at the time. That was how it seemed to be. An accident!" Julio's face was pale and strained and full of hatred. "It was the verdict which we all heard in the Court at La Laguna, but we all know that it is untrue. We know that Philip was clever enough to avoid the consequence of the mistake he had made, and we know he was no longer in love with María when she died."

"But—to believe that he killed her!" She shivered, suddenly cold in the warm night. "You can't go on believing that, Julio! You must not. If you do, it will spoil your whole life."

"I know it to be true," he said doggedly. "There were lies told about the car, and I know he quarrelled with María soon before."

"But a quarrel is such a little thing, Julio," she protested, although already the seriousness of his knowledge had taken her by the throat. "All lovers quarrel at one time or another."

"Not in the way that Philip and María quarrelled. She did not cry and storm, as Conchita would have done. They were both cold and distant, but Philip was very, very angry. I heard him say that she deserved to be dead."

Felicity turned sharply away.

"People say these things in a moment of anger, Julio," she reminded him, "but they do not always mean them."

"Philip has never said anything he does not mean."

That was the final argument, she supposed.

"It is in the past," she tried to say with decision. "Your father could not have believed that Philip was responsible for María's—accident, otherwise he would never have allowed him to stay here."

"My father had strange ideas," Julio muttered. "And Philip is very clever."

They stood for a moment in silence.

"What do you do on the plantations, Julio?" Felicity asked, at last.

"Whatever Philip wishes me to do."

They could not get away from Philip Arnold or his peculiar domination. The entire life of San Lozaro seemed to revolve around him, the life of the *hacienda* and the plantations and the terraced vineyards, and the strange, hidden life of the upper valley close to the surrounding mountain rim.

"Tell me about Lozaro Alto, Julio," she said. "What is grown up there?"

"Very little." He did not seem inclined to talk about the other valley. "It is Philip's place."

"Do you mean that it was where he used to live?"

He nodded.

"Before he came here," he agreed. "But it is my father's land now, although it is no use for bananas. It is too high. It is only of use for vines and growing a little wheat."

"And Philip cultivates these things up there?"

He shook his head.

"He will not let anyone go there except himself."

"I see."

Their voices drifted out into the night and there seemed to be nothing but the scent of stephanotis between them and the heavier perfume of lilies. She saw a group of them standing, ghostly white on the far side of the fountain, before a movement behind her made her turn.

It was Philip. He came across the *patio* and stood looking down at the falling water as Julio left them with a murmured "goodnight" to Felicity.

"Has Julio told you all his troubles?" he enquired lightly.

"We were speaking about Lozaro Alto," Felicity confessed, half against her will. "The upper valley."

He did not answer her for a moment, and when she turned to look at him more fully he seemed frozen into immobility.

"What did he tell you?" he asked, at last.

"That the valley once belonged to you. That it was your home."

"That is so," he said without any feeling in his voice. "But it does not matter now."

"Surely one never really feels that?" she protested spontaneously. "There's always the thought of belonging."

"Which is largely sentiment," he assured her dryly. "Lozaro Alto no longer 'belongs' to me. My mother sold it before she died. Six months before. It was only by your

443

uncle's continuing kindness that we remained there. In other words, we were his tenants, responsible to him for the cultivation of the land."

There had not been any bitterness in his voice. Not even the lethargic calm of a stoical acceptance. He was stating a sequence of facts, and he did not expect her to attempt to refute them, even for his comfort or to show her sympathy.

She did not think that he wanted sympathy. This man was a law unto himself. He would not allow the past to interfere with the present or the future.

"I had come to ask you if you think Sisa should be present to-morrow morning," he said briefly. "There may be a considerable amount of argument, and, in spite of her precocity in some things, I consider her still a child."

She was surprised that he should have asked her advice in this way, but she did not say so.

"You know the Spanish custom better than I do, Mr. Arnold," she said.

"I should still like to hear your opinion, all the same," he persisted.

"Would it be—kinder to spare Sisa any unpleasantness?" she suggested.

"Undoubtedly," he agreed. "But she is, of course, one of the family."

"I could take her out all morning," she offered tentatively. "Perhaps we could even go somewhere in the car, since you won't be using it."

"I'm afraid Señor Pérez wants you to be here," he said. "Carlota can look after Sisa. She has a music lesson due, I believe, at Orotava. It is practically a whole morning's drive."

The note of finality in his voice was not to be ignored. Her presence was necessary at to-morrow's meeting with the solicitor. If she had wanted to protest she could not, because already the atmosphere was full of dissension and she could not add to it.

"Very well," she agreed, "I shall stay."

He stood aside to let her pass. The decision had been made as he had wanted it. He was, as Conchita had said, quite ruthless in some things.

Julio's impassioned revelation about Philip and María

444

haunted her far into the night, and even when she did sleep, her restless dreams were disturbed by it.

In the morning Sisa was frankly torn between her wish to go to Orotava for the music lesson which she apparently enjoyed and the desire to be at the *hacienda* when Señor Pérez arrived.

"I wish you could come to La Orotava with me," she said to Felicity when Sabino had brought the car round to the terrace steps. "You would love it, and we could pay a visit to Zamora on the way home. Andrea also goes for her music lessons to Señora Herrandez, and sometimes we are there together, because Andrea stays to talk with the old señor. He is quite bedridden," she added seriously, "and he therefore likes people to go to see him." She looked up at her cousin with a sudden smile. "Andrea de Barrios is my friend," she added proudly.

The name seemed to hit Felicity between the eyes, and there was a strange constriction in her throat as she asked: "Is—your friend, Andrea, as old as you are?"

"She is older," Sisa said. "But that makes little difference."

Surely, Felicity thought, this could not be Rafael de Barrios' daughter. A child—a girl older than Sisa—sixteen or seventeen, perhaps.

"She is Rafael's sister," Sisa informed her, as if she had sensed her curiosity about the de Barrios. "He has four sisters altogether, but they do not all live at Zamora. One of them lives at Las Palmas, on Gran Canaria, and another one is married and lives in Barcelona."

the waiting car. It was evident that she enjoyed the dignity

Sabino blew the horn and Sisa turned eagerly towards

of going alone to Orotava, even with Carlota and Sabino in attendance. She sat demurely in the back seat, pulling on her cotton gloves and waving to Felicity as she drove away.

There was no sign of Julio nor Conchita anywhere in or around the *hacienda*, and Felicity wondered nervously if they intended to defy Philip and stay away from the meeting with the family lawyer.

Defiance, however, would gain them nothing. She felt quite sure of that. It would only postpone the knowledge of their father's provision for them in the future and cause unnecessary delay in the settling of their affairs.

She stood uncertainly on the terrace, wondering if she

should wait out there or in the *patio,* deciding eventually on the *patio* because it might seem too much as if she were waiting to receive the lawyer when he came if she remained where she was.

It was Philip who finally brought him into the house. He was an old man, yet his bearing was upright and proud, like so many of the Spaniards she had seen even on her short journey from Las Palmas to the airport at La Laguna. Like Rafael de Barrios, for instance. . . .

But she did not want to think about the Marqués de Barrios, not with Philip Arnold's far-seeing blue eyes upon her and the memory of his angry contempt in her heart.

"This is Señor Pérez, your uncle's lawyer," he introduced them. "Miss Stanmore still has a little difficulty with her Spanish," he explained, "so perhaps we could conduct our business in English?"

"Certainly. Most certainly!" Señor Pérez agreed as they shook hands. "It is a great delight to me to be able to speak your language, Miss Stanmore," he added. "I studied in England for some years when I was a young man and I find it renews my youth to converse in a tongue I grew to understand almost as well as my own."

"I am hoping to be able to speak Spanish fluently before I return to England," Felicity told him. "It will help me in my search for work there."

Señor Pérez gave her a short, quizzical look before he glanced across the room at Philip, and when Felicity turned in the younger man's direction he was frowning. He pulled the ancient bell-rope hanging on the wall and presently the fat, elderly Marta waddled in with a tray of glasses and a flagon of the fine local wine. She returned in a minute or two with a platter of little sweet cakes and some of the coarse biscuits which Felicity had seen her baking the day before. Marta did everything with the unhurried movements of the person to whom time means nothing at all, and indeed time was often discounted altogether in this enchanted valley. Felicity could not believe, for instance, that she had only been here a week. It seemed already that most of her life had run its course at San Lozaro; that this was where she might belong.

Less than twenty-four hours ago Philip Arnold had discounted such a thought as foolish sentiment. He did not agree with belonging. Only with conquest.

Twice he glanced at his watch, comparing it impatiently with the clock in the corner.

"I have to apologize for Conchita and Julio," he said, turning to the lawyer. "Perhaps Miss Stanmore would pour you out some wine and I shall go and see if they are anywhere to be found."

His courtesy left nothing to be desired, Felicity realized, but his anger with her cousins was obvious. He had been forced to act host in Julio's absence, but she knew that he was not trying to impress the lawyer in any way. She could not imagine him acting a part, she mused as she poured the old man a glass of wine, and when he came back to the *patio* with Conchita and Julio at his heels she saw that he was far from being satisfied with the excuses they had offered for their childish behaviour. It had been a definite slight to the old man, and he would have none of it. Señor Pérez was a family friend as well as being the family lawyer.

When they had drunk their wine he led the way into Robert Hallam's study, offering the lawyer the chair behind the desk so that he could spread out his papers on it in comfort. His brief-case was not bulky. It seemed that he had little to tell them.

He read the will in detail, in Spanish, and then he turned to Felicity to explain:

"Your uncle suggests that you should stay here, Miss Stanmore, at least until Sisa is eighteen. Then, if she wishes it, she could return to England with you, to finish her education there. Your uncle has left you a small bequest, and you will be kept here as one of the family. It was his earnest hope that you will stay and help to further the English way of life at San Lozaro. He was very anxious about that," he added simply.

Felicity did not know what to say. The atmosphere was already electric. Julio sat frowning in his chair, his hands clenched on the carved arm-rests, his brows drawn blackly above protesting eyes, and Conchita's red mouth was frankly rebellious.

With her limited knowledge of Spanish, Felicity had only been able to follow the official wording of the will at intervals, but she had heard Philip's name repeated, again and again, throughout the long text and had been aware of Julio scowling at him with increasing hatred in his eyes.

447

"So now," Señor Pérez concluded, "we have the full knowledge of what Señor Hallam wanted at San Lozaro. 'Stability' is the word he uses most often," he pointed out to his silent audience. "A solid background and a guiding hand in the affairs of the estate."

"Not only in the affairs of the estate," Julio burst out, "but in our personal affairs as well! In our lives! My father has made Philip our guardian—the real ruler of San Lozaro! He has taken away my birthright and given it to— a murderer!"

The dreadful word rang through the silent room, followed almost immediately by Conchita's swiftly indrawn cry.

"No, Julio! No!"

Felicity could not believe for a moment that Julio had really uttered the ugly accusation in Philip's presence, and the old lawyer looked dazed and unhappy as he stood fumbling with the document he had just read.

Only Philip remained calm and appeared to be unconcerned. He gave Julio a coldly calculating look before he said, with a brief shrug of dismissal which might have appeared callous in another man:

"Your father did not hold that view, Julio, and now we have to carry out your father's will. You are not disinherited, nor are you deprived of your brithright in any way. San Lozaro is yours. The only condition that your father has imposed is that you are not to come into your full inheritance till you are twenty-one."

"Yes, that is so." Señor Pérez was still a trifle flurried, although evidently relieved that the situation had not taken a more violent turn. He was taking his cue from Philip and ignoring Julio's impassioned outburst. "All that has been done is that your father has appointed a guardian for you till you come of age, and until Sisa is eighteen. Señor Arnold benefits only to the extent that your father has left Lozaro Alto to him as an outright gift."

Felicity drew in a deep breath. How could Julio object to that? How could he grudge Philip the return of his own land after ten years of faithful service to San Lozaro?

Yet she knew that Julio did object. His sullen face and restless eyes suggested that he would never allow himself to be reconciled to his father's will, but the most hurtful thorn in his flesh was not Lozaro Alto so much as the fact

448

that he was to remain answerable to Philip for the next three years.

Was it too harsh a decision? Looking at Philip and then back to Julio, she found herself unable to answer, but she did know that any peace there might have been in this lovely, hidden, sub-tropical valley had been irrevocably shattered by an old man's hope for the future.

Julio sat gnawing at his lower lip for a moment longer, and then he got to his feet and rushed from the room without saying goodbye to the lawyer. Conchita hesitated, her dark eyes full of tears.

"I must go after him," she said. "He may do something of folly——"

Philip let her go. Underlying the anger in his eyes, there was sympathy—for Conchita, no doubt.

"You will wait and take some food with us?" he asked the lawyer, but Señor Pérez shook his head.

"I am to be at Santa Cruz before three o'clock," he informed them as he gathered his papers together and put them carefully into the black brief-case. "I have urgent business there, and so I must just snatch a meal on the way. At San Juan, perhaps, or with my sister at Tacoronte. Although we do not live far apart," he added with a smile, "we see increasingly less of each other as the years go by."

Philip went out to the terrace with him when he had wished Felicity goodbye, and she stood in the dimness of her uncle's study wondering if it were really fair that a dead man should direct other people's lives for them in such a way as this.

"Your uncle knew what was best for San Lozaro."

Philip had come back into the room. He was standing between her and the door, but even when she turned to look at him she could not guess what he was thinking. His face was a mask, made even more obscure by the dimmed light which filtered greenly into the room through the slatted blinds.

"Yes, I suppose so," she conceded uncertainly. "But was he also sure what was best for his children?"

"Julio *is* San Lozaro," he answered without hesitation. "That has not been changed by your uncle's will."

"No, I suppose not. Julio will come to his inheritance—in time."

She did not know why she had said that. It had been almost a question.

"Yes," he said, "in time."

"And what of Conchita?" she heard herself asking.

"Conchita will stay here, of course," he said. "She is under my guardianship. She will not question her father's wisdom in that respect. Certainly not openly. Conchita is Spanish at heart."

How sure he was! Felicity suddenly felt her cheeks burning. Was he sure of her, also?

"I had no idea that I should be mentioned in my uncle's will," she said. "I find it most generous of him."

"He was, on the whole, a generous man, although not an over-indulgent one. He has asked you to stay here. What are you going to do?"

He shot the question at her without any change of expression, and she found herself saying rather nervously:

"I suppose I shall stay. I had meant to stay for at least a year when I first came."

There was the suggestion of calculation in his blue eyes as he continued to look at her.

"Yet if it hadn't been for this dying request of Robert Hallam's you might quite conceivably have changed your mind?" he suggested.

"I don't know. I—if I had felt that I was really needed, I would have stayed in any case."

He accepted her decision with a brief nod.

"I'm sure your uncle expected it," he said. "He had judged you largely by the letters you wrote to him after his sister's death. He told me that your mother and he were very fond of each other as children, and that made him feel that you were very close to him. He believed, too, that you might be the right sort of person to bring up Sisa and have a restraining influence on Conchita."

"I feel that I have come to know Sisa very well, even after one short week," Felicity said.

"But not Conchita?"

He regarded her quizzically for a moment and then he smiled.

"That is not surprising," he said. "I don't think you will ever really understand Conchita."

"I can try," she said with spirit. "I have no intention of

450

turning Conchita into a prim English miss, if that is what you fear!"

"It would be impossible," he said with a deepening smile. "Conchita was born a tigress."

She met his eyes uncertainly, not able to believe that this was the sort of woman he would want. A girl with spirit, perhaps, but not a teenage spitfire who didn't know her own mind and only wanted to play at being in love.

"I shall appeal to you for help," she found herself saying, "if Conchita gets out of hand."

He shrugged almost indifferently.

"I am more concerned with Julio," he confessed unexpectedly. "No one walking about with an outsize chip on his shoulder as Julio does can be really happy."

"He's too young to have such deeply-rooted prejudices," she agreed. "Perhaps he will forget his—resentment in time."

"About San Lozaro? I hope so." He seemed to be thinking about something quite different, and María's name sprang instantly to Felicity's mind. "Julio is too intense," was all he said, however, as Sisa came rushing in through the sun-warmed *patio* to greet them.

"Philip! Philip!" she cried, "I can play right through *Poet and Peasant* without one single mistake! You must hear me," she declared, "because it is your favourite piece!"

Oddly surprised by the revelation, Felicity looked at Philip, but he did not seem to be at all embarrassed by Sisa's enthusiasm.

"We must play it together, then," he suggested, "when I can find the time. You must remind me, *querida!*"

"When you have made a promise you will keep it," Sisa acknowledged briefly. "Now, tell me what is to become of us, Philip. Are we to stay at San Lozaro?"

"Indeed you are!" He smiled down into her small, flushed face with genuine affection in his eyes. "And I am to stay and look after you."

"I am so happy!" Sisa said, swinging on his arm. "Are you to look after Julio and Conchita, too?"

"To the best of my ability," he told her gravely.

"And Felicity?" Sisa swung round to regard her cousin with wide, contemplative eyes. "Are you to be her guardian, Philip?"

Philip's mouth twisted in a wry smile.

451

"I think not. You see," he explained when Sisa would have protested in disappointment, "Felicity is of age. She is already her own mistress."

Felicity could feel the colour rising in her cheeks as he continued to look at her.

"But she will stay here?" Sisa probed.

"Yes," Philip said, "she has promised to stay."

"That makes everything wonderfully simple!" Sisa declared, clasping her hands ecstatically. "It means that none of us need leave San Lozaro, nor the valley, nor Zamora, nor the de Barrios, nor anything!"

Mention of the de Barrios swept all the indulgence from Philip's eyes.

"Did you call at Zamora on your way back?" he asked almost peremptorily.

"Of course! Andrea and I came back together. Don Rafael picked up their car at La Orotava to drive to Santa Cruz for the afternoon and I gave Andrea a lift home. But I generally do stop at Zamora, Philip."

"Yes," he agreed distantly, "so you do."

His thoughts were obviously elsewhere, but Sisa ran on without seeming to notice his preoccupation.

"We are invited to the *fiesta*," she announced. "We must go, Philip. Promise that we may go!"

"There is plenty of time for that." It surprised Felicity to realize that he was avoiding the issue for the present. "It is several weeks ahead yet."

"But if we are to take part in it," Sisa pointed out, "Isabella must know our decision. She will have other guests, Andrea says."

"We will not be staying at Zamora," Philip told her with some decision.

Sisa looked disappointed, but did not argue. Perhaps she thought that she might be able to approach Philip later with better results.

"Felicity ought to see the *fiesta*," she added as a parting shot before she ran off to change her silk suit for a cotton dress.

"There are many *fiestas* on the island," Philip said without looking in Felicity's direction. "We are rarely without one in some town or another during the summer months."

It would appear, then, that it was only the *fiesta* at Zamora which was to be officially banned. Felicity was

452

already half rebellious at the thought. If it was still some weeks away, as Philip himself had just pointed out, her uncle's death and their period of mourning would have nothing to do with it.

No, this was something personal, hinged to the dislike— the enmity even—which she had surprised in this man's eyes when he had first seen her coming off the plane at La Laguna with Rafael de Barrios by her side.

Although it was a full week since her arrival at San Lozaro, there had been no further word from the Marqués. He had come to her uncle's funeral, but he had bowed gravely over her hand when they had met, saying nothing because Philip had been standing by her side at the time, and he had not come back to the *hacienda* afterwards with the other mourners.

His presence had been a neighbourly gesture which even Philip could not resent, but he had paid his respects and gone, a tall, distinguished-looking figure in that motley company of labourers and estate employees and business men, with only Philip matching him for height and proud arrogance of bearing as they stood for the conventional moment together on the terrace steps.

And now it seemed that Philip would have been better pleased if Sisa had not gone to Zamora on her way back from her music lesson. That, of course, was ridiculous! The girl must have her friends, and especially company of her own age.

Wondering if this was to be the first difference of opinion to crop up between them, Felicity tried to adjust herself to her new position at San Lozaro without coming into conflict with anyone.

For several days she saw nothing of Julio and very little of Conchita, a situation which she was forced to accept because Conchita did come in to the evening meal, and Sisa declared that Julio was "safely concealed" in one of the bothies at the far side of the plantation.

He was evidently living among the estate labourers, indulging himself in the belief that he really belonged there since his father had so little faith in his ability to manage San Lozaro. It was a mood, Sisa said, that would pass in time, but the fact did not make it any more acceptable to Felicity at the present moment. She wished

Julio would come home. Wished, too, that he would try to understand Philip a little better.

At such a point in her reasoning she had always to force back the memory of Julio's terrible belief that Philip was responsible for his sister's death. She would not think about it unless she had to, however. She could not bring herself to believe that it was true.

By the end of a fortnight, Sisa and she had explored all the valley and gone twice on horseback down a long, narrow *barranco* leading to the sea. They had picnicked there, although the beach was no more than a narrow black bar of volcanic sand washed by the ceaseless Atlantic swell.

"To-morrow," Sisa said on the way back from the last of these excursions, "we will go to the Playa. There is yellow sand there, and the water is very blue. Philip will take us on his way to Granadilla," she added, taking her guardian's consent for granted in the delightful way she had when she was sure of Philip's kindness.

He appeared to be willing enough to take them to the Playa, and to Felicity's surprise and delight, Conchita decided to accompany them at the last moment.

"It is so hot!" she complained. "At least, the Playa is beside the sea."

She got into the front of the car, as if it were the accepted thing that she alone should sit beside Philip during the journey, and he did not protest, turning round before they set out to see if Felicity and Sisa were comfortable in the back.

"You will see quite well from there," he said. "I won't drive fast."

It was a wonderful experience for Felicity, sitting there in the open car watching the wide panorama of the winding, indented coast opening out before her with every twist of the road, yet somewhere deep within her she was aware of a growing sense of loneliness, a groping blindly in a world apart which had nothing to do with their journey to the Playa nor the prospect of a perfect day spent leisurely in the sun.

It had to do with the questioning, agonizing doubt in her heart when she thought about Philip Arnold and the accident which had cost her cousin her life.

Was it on a road such as this, she wondered, that María

had crashed to her death, and why had Julio cried so passionately that Philip had lied about the car?

On such a golden day these were black thoughts indeed to carry with her, but Julio's continuing absence from home had accentuated them and Philip himself had done nothing to explain them away.

All along the roadside the tamarisk bushes bent their heads before the prevailing wind from the west and the tall island palms festooned the horizon. Birds sang, and Sisa and sometimes Conchita named them for her, but Philip remained silent, his eyes riveted on the difficult way ahead.

Was this the road? Was it a journey so full of memories for him that he dared not trust himself to speak? She closed her eyes against the sunshine, trying to shut out the vision of a car, driven at speed, along the way they were going now, until Sisa asked if she had a headache and she was forced to open them again and see Philip sitting within the reach of her outstretched hand there in the front seat—there beside Conchita.

He left them at the Playa, and almost immediately another car came hurtling down the narrow road behind them, throwing up a cloud of dust because it was travelling so fast.

"It's the Mercedes!" Sisa cried excitedly. "The de Barrios are coming!"

Felicity's heart seemed to stand still at the words. Would Philip think that this had been a planned affair, she wondered for a split second before she realized how ridiculous that was. She could not have planned his visit to Granadilla for him, even if she had wanted to meet Rafael de Barrios a thousand times over.

It was not the Marqués, however, who stepped from behind the wheel of the big, sleek tourer to wave Sisa a friendly welcome. It was a tall, almost incredibly handsome woman in a white linen dress which enhanced the brown of her skin and deepened her eyes and her blue-black hair to the colour of the midnight sky when there are no stars visible. She was, without doubt, the most distinguished-looking woman Felicity had ever seen and she spoke English with no more than the trace of an accent.

"Sisa, *querida!*" she smiled. "It is good to see you once

again! How long is it since you were at Zamora? Two whole weeks, if I am not mistaken, and Andrea threatening to ride over to San Lozaro every day to bring you!"

"Why did she not come?" Sisa asked, lifting her cheek to be kissed. "She could have come with us on our rides. Oh——" She turned hastily to include Felicity in her excited chatter. "This is my cousin from England. I told you about her when we met on the way back from La Orotava."

Felicity held out her hand to the older woman, aware of an impact she had not been expecting and conscious of two dark eyes scrutinizing her closely and frankly and liking what they saw.

"Sisa never finishes an introduction when she is taken by surprise," the Marquesa de Barrios said with a smile. "I'm Isabella de Barrios and you are Felicity Stanmore. You see, already I know quite a lot about you!"

Which was probably true, Felicity thought. These wide, far-seeing eyes were surely rarely mistaken in their swift summing-up. Isabella de Barrios looked thirty and was possibly a little more. Her skin was flawless and her eyes were clear and amused. She wore her hair in a heavy chignon at the nape of her long, shapely neck, giving her bearing an added dignity, Felicity thought. She was tall for a woman—as tall as Philip, perhaps, and certainly as tall as her husband.

Felicity pulled her thoughts up before the memory of Rafael de Barrios, and then she was aware of nothing but anger—an intense, personal anger directed against herself because she had let herself imagine even for a moment that any man could be attracted to her while he was married to a woman like this.

And suddenly she knew how relieved she was that Philip Arnold could not possibly have taken her attraction seriously.

He knew Isabella de Barrios: knew and respected her, and he must surely be only amused that Felicity should have succumbed to the Marqués' charm so readily.

The thought of his amusement hurt, of course, but it was easier to face than the suspicion of his contempt.

"And now you must meet Andrea—and Celeste." Isabella de Barrios drew her sisters-in-law towards her with a gentle movement which was almost tender in its eagerness to

456

acknowledge them. "We are a large family at Zamora, Miss Stanmore, but soon you must come and meet us all."

"I—think I have already met your husband," Felicity said.

"Rafael?" A small, scarcely-discernible smile passed in the dark eyes. "Yes, he has told me. You travelled from Madrid on the same plane, did you not?"

She had not mentioned Robert Hallam's funeral and their second meeting, and Felicity saw her glance in Sisa's direction and knew that she sought to spare her favourite a return of heartache.

It was then that she appeared to notice Conchita for the first time, and in that moment her expression changed from one of smiling pleasure to acute watchfulness. Conchita had lingered at the water's edge as long as she dared, but now she came towards them with a forced smile, and something like pain crossed Isabella de Barrios' eyes as she greeted her.

"Good day, Conchita!"

"Good day, Isabella!" Conchita returned guardedly. "We did not expect to see you here, at the Playa."

"I came because the children longed to feel the warm sand under their feet and the sea on their skins." Isabella turned towards Felicity with a hint of relief in her smile. "A swimming-pool is not quite the same, is it? There is nothing quite like the feel of the surf."

"I wondered if it was safe to bathe," Felicity said.

"Oh, perfectly safe! No one ever comes here, to this part of the Playa, in the middle of the week."

Isabella had misunderstood her, Felicity mused, thinking that she had been worried about their privacy, but really she had answered both questions. She smiled a little at the thought of the Spanish girl's guarded upbringing, realizing that perhaps this had been her uncle's real reason for appointing Philip to his present position at San Lozaro. In over thirty years on the island he must have accepted at least some of the customs and characteristics of his Spanish wife and neighbours.

They undressed in the tent Isabella had brought with her and plunged thankfully into the sea. The surf at this point was not quite so strong as it was further north. Its approach to the Playa was gentle and beguiling, and Felicity thought that she had never seen a sea so blue. She could have

457

lingered there all day, letting the gentle water flow quickly over her skin or basking in the sun afterwards under the palms. It was an exotic enough setting to please anyone, with El Teide in the background hiding his snow-crowned head in a cloud. She knew that she could have stayed there for ever; that she could have lived her life out on this perfect island with nothing but happiness in her heart.

Yet already there was a small cloud forming on her horizon, as small as the cloud that played about the brow of El Teide, and deep down she was aware of a sense of hurt, of inner conflict which she could not understand, a longing and a fear which set her heart beating ponderously whenever she thought about the months to come.

"Soon we will have to go," Andrea said disappointedly when they had folded up the tent.

"Wait till Philip comes," Sisa begged, looking at Isabella. "He is to return for us at five o'clock."

Isabella hesitated. It was no more than a fraction of a second's doubt, but María's name sprang unbidden to Felicity's mind again, almost as if Isabella de Barrios had repeated Julio's ugly accusation of murder there on the quiet beach.

"Of course we will wait," Isabella agreed almost immediately. "It is far too long since we saw Philip. He is generally much too busy to come on picnics."

"He has gone to Granadilla on business," Sisa agreed. "But he has promised to join us for tea."

"And Philip never breaks his promises," Isabella said.

Conchita shot her a veiled glance. She seemed impatient, almost eager to get away from the Playa now, although she knew that they must wait for Philip's return.

"If you do go before Philip comes, Isabella, may I ride back with you?" she asked. "I have not been to Zamora for a very long time."

Isabella suppressed what might have been an expression of the utmost irritation.

"You must come soon, Conchita," she said, "but not to-day. Not when Philip is expecting to find you here on his return."

Conchita pouted, flinging herself face downwards on the hot sand.

"It will not matter," she murmured rebelliously, "and I like to be at Zamora."

458

"You may ask Philip," Isabella returned with a strange constriction in her voice, "for here he comes."

She had been first to notice the car on its tortuous journey down to the beach, and Philip waved to them when he came near enough to see the Mercedes parked in the shade of the palms.

When he got out he came straight towards Isabella, and Felicity saw the Marquesa catch her breath and smile, as if, indeed, it had been far too long since their last meeting.

Philip held both the long, slender hands in his, but he did not bend over them or kiss them as her husband would have done in similar circumstances. He was far too British in everything he did for that. Yet there was an intimacy beyond doubting between them, a pleasure in this meeting which neither of them cared to deny.

"Philip!" Isabella cried. "This is good, seeing you so unexpectedly! We know you have been to Granadilla on business, but now it is past five o'clock, and you must forget about work, in the English fashion!" she teased.

"I had already made up my mind to do that, just for once," he told her, still holding her fingers imprisoned. "How are you, Isabella?" His blue eyes searched the dark ones which were almost level with his. "Are you quite well again?"

"Quite well, Philip." Isabella's thick black lashes came down for a moment over her eyes, veiling them, hiding her expression for a split second before she added: "The loss of the baby is now almost forgotten."

Philip did not think it was. Felicity could see that. He knew that Isabella was putting up a tremendous fight for composure and he tried to help her. There was tenderness between them for a moment before he let the slim brown fingers go, and then he turned to Andrea and Celeste to talk about their swimming and challenge them to a race some other day.

Both girls seemed to be overjoyed at his coming, and Sisa always blossomed when he was near. It was only Conchita who frowned. She lay on the sand, watching him sulkily, her long, silken lashes veiling her eyes, and what was going on behind those eyes baffled Felicity, at least.

Conchita was half child, half woman, she supposed. She was at that awkward stage of growing up where every reprimand is a slight, every harsh word a heartbreak. She

459

could also fall so easily in love. So easily and so tempestuously!

Looking at her sitting there in the sunshine, covering her slim brown legs with the wide folds of her white skirt, Felicity could not make up her mind whether Conchita was already in love or not.

And suddenly Conchita did not seem to matter so much. For her eyes had turned towards Philip where he sat at Isabella de Barrios' feet, contentedly munching brown bread and tomatoes, his blue eyes on the distant sea.

She had never seen him like this before, and somehow she knew that she would never have done so if Isabella had not driven down to the Playa in her black Mercedes to picnic with the children in the sun.

CHAPTER IV

AN ADMISSION OF GUILT?

ON the way back to San Lozaro Philip seemed strangely elated.

"You have had a good day's business," Conchita said. "I know by your face!"

In spite of her laughter, Felicity felt that there was something personal about Conchita's question. Was she about to ask a favour of Philip and felt that this might be the most propitious time, when he had successfully pulled off a business deal to his own advantage? Conchita was capable of any wile when she wanted something passionately, something which she felt that she could not do without.

Philip smiled.

"True, Conchita," he said, "but what is it you want me to do for you?"

He appeared to be in too mellow a mood to sound cynical or annoyed, but evidently he knew Conchita.

"I want you to let me go to Zamora for the *fiesta*."

"I have told you that there is plenty of time to make plans for the *fiesta*." His voice was more stern now. "We may all go," he conceded.

Conchita drew in a deep, resentful breath.

"Because there is no work to be done! Because you will be forced to grant the holiday to the people on the plantation," she accused. "But that is all. One day! You are a slave-driver, Philip. Julio says so, and I am sure he is right!"

"Maybe so," Philip agreed with what, to Conchita in her present mood, must have been maddening equanimity, "but I have to see that the plantations pay. That has always been my job."

"And now you will not let us do as we wish!" Conchita pouted. "You are our guardian and we must obey you!

But I have always gone to Zamora for more than one day in the past," she added stubbornly.

Sitting behind them with Sisa by her side, Felicity saw Philip's jaw harden. She knew then that he had no intention of letting Conchita have her way. There was some reason why he did not wish her to spend the next two weeks at Zamora, a sound reason, she supposed, because everything about Philip was sound.

When they came to a fork in the road the Mercedes was drawn up under the eucalyptus trees which lined a long avenue stretching to the west.

"Will you come in for a drink?" Isabella called. "You said you were not going to work any more to-day, Philip."

In the split second which followed the impulsive invitation, Felicity saw Philip hesitate.

"We are quite alone," Isabella informed him. "I shall even promise you tea!"

Philip turned from the wheel. His face was expressionless.

"Felicity will like that," he decided, "and she really ought to see Zamora."

Instinctively Felicity wanted to protest, but it would have been too foolish in the circumstances. What could she have said? I don't want to come because this is dangerous ground. Philip has already refsued to let Conchita stay at Zamora, but now he will come because Rafael isn't there!

She drew in her breath and said nothing, and the two cars made their way, one after the other, down the avenue, the giant trees on either side shutting them into a green tunnel of rustling leaves. Soon they had passed under an arched gateway in a high stucco wall which surrounded one of the most beautiful gardens Felicity had ever seen. Terrace upon terrace of rich golden-coloured stone tumbled to the sea a hundred feet below, and far beneath them a small, picturesque port knelt by the water's edge. Its narrow streets climbed steeply and its white and golden houses clustered about a palm-shaded square.

"It's lovely!" Felicity murmured. "I don't think I've ever seen so many flowers all together in all my life before!"

"Everything grows here," Philip said as he swung the car into a cobbled courtyard in the Mercedes' wake. "Isabella is very proud of her garden."

462

They could see the house now, through a screen of oleanders. It was large and mellowed and old, a perfect example of Spanish architecture, with its fine stone doorway and carved balconies with their little tiled roofs and soft green shutters at all the windows. Masses of bougainvillaea tumbled from the walls, purple and cream and deep, warm ochre, and vast beds of freesias and pink and scarlet geraniums made the forecourt look like a veritable sea of flowers. All the terraces were awash with colour, and the seats and ornamental stonework lay steeped in the heat of the sun.

Philip got down from the car and held the door open.

"Welcome to Zamora!" Isabella smiled, coming from her own car. "I'm glad you are going to see my garden when it is at its very best."

They walked between walls of plumbago and jacaranda to the broad terrace surrounding the house itself, and Felicity was immediately aware of a subtle aura of luxury which they did not possess at San Lozaro. There was nothing of ostentation about it. It came from age and the long tradition of belonging. The whole place spoke of gracious living, of something handed down from generation to generation, of roots and the abiding sense of time going on for ever.

"This was my home," Isabella said, "before I was married. We live here most of the year now, although Rafael goes often to Madrid—on business."

There had been the vaguest hint of acceptance in her quiet voice and a barely discernible pause before the last two words which only Felicity appeared to have noticed. Whatever had been her way of life in the first few years of her marriage, this present arrangement whereby Isabella spent most of her time in her girlhood home was pleasant and acceptable to her. Surrounded by her husband's family, if not by her own, she could be happy after a fashion.

But not wholly content? Was it only her own too vivid imagination, Felicity wondered, that painted that fleeting shadow in the older woman's eyes and saw the odd nervous little movement of the long, shapely hands as Isabella de Barrios took off her hat in the shade of the verandah and flung it on to one of the deep lounge-chairs beside the fountain?

She rang for tea, which was brought to them by a white-coated servant, very like Sabino. He was old and perfectly trained, and he walked with the gentle tread of a cat. It did not seem to alarm him at all that his mistress had ordered tea for her guests instead of the usual wine, but perhaps he was used to Philip's visit, Philip who looked so uncompromisingly British against this exotic setting of palms and falling water and headily-perfumed flowers.

Conchita prowled restlessly, and presently she went with Andrea and Sisa to the stable to look at the horses. Celeste, who was cosy and plump, stayed behind to eat another cake.

"You will come to the *fiesta*, Philip?" Isabella asked. "It will be expected of you."

"Now that I am in charge at San Lozaro?" His smile in the rapidly waning light was bitter. "I do not expect to be accepted because of that, you know."

Isabella made a small, abrupt movement of dissent.

"You are too sensitive about the past," she said, although her voice held no real conviction.

"Perhaps." Philip's tone was hard. "All the same, I shall come. Conchita wants it, and Felicity ought to see how carefree we can be when we have something to celebrate."

"I'd love to come," Felicity agreed, trying to forget the bitterness she had detected behind his words. "It will be an entirely new experience for me."

"And a happy one, I hope!"

The words were mocking and as light as air. Felicity turned in her chair to see Rafael de Barrios standing in the gathering shadows behind them, his smile amused and faintly cynical as his dark glance swept the circle of his unexpected guests. Philip got stiffly to his feet and Isabella's face was very pale as she said:

"We did not expect you, Rafael. How did you come in?"

His eyes rested on her for a moment, as if he had just seen her.

"From the port, *querida*," he said, and the word was mocking. "I walked up through the terraces to have a look at the vines."

Tension had taken the atmosphere in its strangling grip, as on the occasion of that first meeting between Philip and Rafael at the airport, but the circumstances were different this time. Rafael looked insolently at ease now and Philip

464

at a disadvantage; from which he proceeded to extricate himself without delay.

"It's getting late," he said, glancing at the rapidly-sinking sun. Night would fall with tropical suddenness, Felicity knew, but the car was equipped with powerful headlamps and there was no real reason why they should rush away so quickly. "Celeste," he added, turning to the child, "would you please tell Sisa and Conchita that we are going?"

But Conchita was already with them. She had come through the house on to the verandah, running hot-foot in Rafael's wake.

"We saw you coming up through the terraces," she told him, her dark eyes alight as they looked into his, her firm young breasts rising and falling with her rapid breathing. "We were at the stables."

Had she run to intercept Rafael and failed by a hair's breadth? Felicity found herself looking from the lovely, flushed face and lustrous eyes to the cool acceptance of Rafael, Marqués de Barrios, aware that she wanted to smack Conchita as much for the red lotus blossom which she had fastened into her dark hair as for the way she looked at Rafael with absolute adoration in her eyes.

What must Philip think? She knew that he would be furious, but she could not see his face clearly. The light had nearly gone, leaving the verandah in shadow, although the western sky beyond the terraces was aflame.

When they were ready to go Rafael bent over Felicity's hand. She felt his nearness with repulsion now, his fascination which was evil.

"I knew we would meet again," he said, watching her closely. "But I did not think you would be permitted to come to Zamora."

"Why not?" She met his eyes evenly, challenging his statement as Andrea and Sisa joined them. "You mentioned when we first met that we were near neighbours."

He shrugged and smiled, standing back to watch as Philip led the way out to the car, with Andrea and Sisa at his heels. Isabella hesitated only for a second before she, too, went out to the terrace to speed her departing guests.

Rafael followed Felicity down the steps.

"That is so," he agreed. His eyes were thoughtful as

they lingered on her flushed face. "I am surprised, though, that Philip Arnold should agree to bring you."

"We met your wife and the children at the Playa," she explained hastily, "and the Marquesa very kindly invited us for tea."

His mouth grew curiously thin.

"Isabella would do that," he said. "You see, she believes in Philip Arnold."

Felicity looked up sharply into the mocking eyes.

"I don't know what you mean," she said.

"Rafael means that only Isabella believes Philip's story about the accident which caused my sister's death," Conchita said, moving like a cat from the shadows of the verandah, "but that is not so! I do not believe that Philip killed María. It was, as he has said, an accident. Only unworthy people could believe that he would do such a thing, like the people in the *puerto* who hate Philip because he is successful and will not allow them to drive a dishonest bargain! These are the people who have spread such wicked tales after the court investigation is all over and Philip is exonerated from all blame by the law! No, Rafael, you must not say that no one believes Philip, because it is not true. *I* believe in him, also! It is only that he keeps so silent, not wishing to speak about this awful tragedy which has shadowed all our lives, but I know. *I know!*"

In that moment Conchita was magnificent. All the spitfire quality in her which Felicity had abhorred and which, in some ways, had frightened her when she had considered her own responsibility where her cousins were concerned, had been thrown unexpectedly into her defence of Philip. Her flashing eyes were black with indignation, her full red mouth scornful, yet Rafael de Barrios only smiled at this demonstration of loyalty.

"*Chi tace confessa!*" he murmured. " 'He who keeps silent confesses his guilt', Conchita. That is an old Italian saying which bears repetition in any language."

"It is not so!" Conchita protested almost in tears. "You are unjust—like the others!"

Rafael took her by the arm, smiling down confidently into her eyes.

"And you are too intense, *querida!*" he said. "Come! We must not keep Philip waiting."

In the hall the lamps had been lit, throwing their revealing light out on to the terrace steps, and as they passed through the wide glass doors Felicity was aware of a certain tension about the man walking beside her. Rafael looked paler than she remembered him, and there was a tightness about his mouth which suggested strain.

When they reached the far end of the terrace Philip was already seated behind the wheel, impatient to be off, but Andrea and Sisa were still chattering eagerly about the forthcoming *fiesta*. Isabella stood by Philip's side, her hand resting lightly on the door of the car, and Celeste turned eagerly towards her brother as he came forward with the remainder of their guests.

"Rafael," she said, "you must organize a drive to Las Canadas for us! It is lovely there, and Miss Stanmore has not yet seen The Peak."

"Miss Stanmore must be without the use of her eyesight, then!" Rafael chided teasingly. "El Teide is to be seen everywhere and at every hour of the day!"

"Except when he is hidden in mist," Celeste reminded him, "and then no one can see clearly. You know that I meant *near at hand*—right up on Las Canadas, or even up to the very top. To the crater itself."

"That will be a major operation," Rafael smiled, evading the issue. "It could be undertaken, of course, given the right circumstances." He looked directly at his wife for the first time. "Isabella will be only too pleased to organize such an excursion, I feel sure. She knows The Peak so well."

Now Felicity was sure of the undercurrent which she had only suspected before. It ran strongly between these two, something that could almost be felt, a suggestion of distrust and pain flowing beneath the surface like a dark river with no outlet, a rising tide of discord which even the patient Isabella might not be able to control much longer.

Suddenly she knew that Philip was also aware of it. The knowledge was in his eyes and in the hard set of his jaw as he looked at Rafael, and more than anything else in the silence he maintained as he waited for them to say their final goodbyes.

He let in his clutch as soon as Conchita had seated herself in her original place by his side, and Felicity settled down in the back beside Sisa for the long drive home.

"Goodbye, Felicity," Isabella said. "I hope you will come again—with Sisa."

Her hand was still resting on the car door, and for a fraction of a second Philip's strong fingers closed over it, pressing it tightly.

"I'm sorry," he said, and Felicity knew that only Isabella had been meant to hear.

The blue eyes and the brown met for a moment of complete sympathy and understanding. Felicity tried to persuade herself that it was nothing more.

They drove back to San Lozaro in a thoughtful silence: Conchita preoccupied; Philip giving all his attention to the dangerous, winding road, and only Sisa smiling happily at the prospect of to-morrow.

When they reached the *hacienda* all the lights were lit and the strains of music came streaming out to them on the cool night air. Guitars and maraccas were being played with island abandonment and there was much laughter flowing from the direction of the *patio* and the sound of tinkling glass.

Philip drew up the car in the courtyard beyond the inner wall.

"It's Julio," Sisa said with a nervous hesitation in her voice. "He is holding a party."

Philip looked as if he might have been acquainted with Julio's parties in the past. The noise from the *patio* was almost deafening, and he strode towards it with a brief word of warning.

"Go in by the terrace—if you can get in," he advised. "I think it might be better if you went straight to your rooms."

Conchita stood her ground. Her eyes were half closed and she was already swaying to the music, her movements fluid and graceful as the wild tempo increased and the unseen guitars sobbed out their message of love.

"Why must you always be like this, Philip?" she demanded. "It is a night for dancing. Come! I will show you. Julio's friends will make the music for us!"

She turned towards Philip, lovely and inviting, the red flower in her hair softly caressing her cheek, but Philip took her firmly by the arm.

"Some other time, Conchita," he said sternly. "You can dance at the *fiesta*—as much as you wish."

"At the Country Club, but not in the streets!" Conchita pouted. "You are so English, Philip—and so cold!"

He led her to the edge of the courtyard without answering, escorting them round the wall to the front of the house. Even here the wild music from the *patio* followed them, the sound of ribald laughter beating fiercely on their ears, and Felicity watched Philip's frown deepen as he saw the line of patient, tethered mules beside the terrace steps and the abandoned ox-carts beyond the wall.

"Can I do anything, Philip?" she asked. "Can I help in any way?"

He turned to look at her as if he had just remembered her and the fact that she had come to San Lozaro to help.

"Keep Conchita with you," he said briefly. "That will be enough."

On the lovely veined marble table in the hall an array of bottles had been scattered, some upended, others on their sides, the wine they had contained swiftly consumed. Abandoned glasses lay about everywhere, and it was evident that the cellar had been well and truly raided. None of the servants were in sight, but Philip did not seem surprised at the fact.

He stood at the foot of the stairs, waiting until they had reached the gallery in safety before he turned towards the *patio*, and Felicity quickened her pace with a rapidly-beating heart.

What had Julio done? In the ordinary way a party was quite a natural thing in this sunny land. Everywhere she had gone in the island she had heard music. It was the natural complement to the life of the country people, and surely Philip could not object to that.

"Julio has grieved Philip," Sisa said sadly as they came to the closed door of her room. "There is something he has left undone, surely, when Philip is so angry."

"Philip is angry because it is the plantation labourers that Julio has brought in," Conchita said. "And Julio has done it on purpose to show Philip that he does not care!" She looked half sympathetic towards her brother and half afraid of Philip's obvious anger. "There will be a scene and Julio will go away to the bothy again with the men. He will brood and say that it is where he should be since Philip wishes it. He will say that Philip wants all San Lozaro for himself!"

"Hush, Conchita!" Felicity warned, glancing in Sisa's direction. "We ought to change," she added nervously as the music came to an abrupt stop and there was a grim sort of silence in the rooms beneath them. "We have been out all day and I feel sticky and in need of a bath."

Conchita lingered beside the door, her ears strained for the first sign of revolt from below.

"Please don't go down and cause further trouble, Conchita," Felicity appealed. "It is evident that Philip does not want us to see these people."

"He thinks they have had too much to drink," Conchita laughed. "Well, maybe so, but that makes their music more alive!"

"All the same, you must not go down." There was finality and a new firmness behind Felicity's order. She was as determined on obedience now as Philip had been. "I will let you have first use of the bathroom and Sisa and I will wait here."

Sisa was looking perturbed, but she washed and changed at Felicity's bidding, while Conchita splashed luxuriously in the adjoining bathroom, humming the languorous tune which the guitars had played.

When they were ready to go down for their evening meal Felicity knew that the *patio* had been cleared. She had heard the ox-carts drive away, their wheels churning over the gravel at the side of the house, and she supposed that Philip had been out there, supervising that comparatively silent departure.

It was impossible to feel happy about the little affair, the clash of wills which she knew must have occurred in the *patio* when Philip and Julio had come face to face, and she felt sorry for Julio.

"There will be a scene and Julio will go away to the bothy again with the men," Conchita had said, and for the first time Felicity began to wonder if Philip had not been too harsh in his disapproval.

She wondered if he really understood Julio, the moody, impetuous creature of impulse who had not yet grown to man's estate yet thought that he had every right to adult privileges. They were of different blood, born and bred under different circumstances, and Julio's standards were far removed from Philip's own. His blood was warmer, his emotions far nearer the surface. He had never learned to

470

control them as Philip had done. She felt that there could be no real harm in Julio and decided that it was her task to convince Philip of the fact.

After all, she had come here at her uncle's expressed wish in the hope that she would keep his family together, and this, she was convinced, was no way to do it.

She could not speak to Philip about Julio, however, while Sisa and Conchita were still with them. The atmosphere in the *patio* was now serene and calm and every sign of the evening's carousal had been removed from the hall by a small army of willing hands. Sabino had donned a fresh white coat and only the satisfaction at the back of his dark eyes suggested that he had been more than relieved at Philip's timely return. He brought a fresh bottle of Malmsey and set it with four glasses on the table beside the fountain, but none of them seemed inclined to sample it. They shared Sisa's lime juice instead, drinking only with their meal.

When their coffee was poured Conchita took her cup and strolled with it to the edge of the *patio*. The red lotus which she had fastened in her hair earlier in the evening was withered now and discarded when she had taken her bath, but she picked a fresh spray of the fiery blossoms from the courtyard wall, tucking it through the belt of her dress with a little secret smile as she came back into the light. The scarlet flame of the star-shaped flowers stood out sharply against the white of her bodice as she stood looking at them for a moment before she said:

"Julio has gone. Philip, you are too hard on him!"

Philip's mouth grew thin.

"I don't think we'll discuss Julio," he said. "He knows that he has done wrong."

"Where has he gone?" Conchita demanded. "Back to the plantation?"

"No," Philip said, but that was all. Even Conchita knew that he would not discuss the situation further while Sisa was there and listening.

"I am going to bed," Sisa said after a while. "If you will excuse me? I am very tired." She stood up, looking across at Philip. "Did you mean it when you said that we could go to Las Canadas with Isabella?" she asked.

"Yes," Philip said, "you can go."

He did not seem to be thinking about Las Canadas, or

Isabella either, and when Conchita strolled off in Sisa's wake, Felicity said:

"Please, Philip, could we speak about Julio for a moment? I know that you have just told Conchita that the subject is closed, but I feel that I have some responsibility towards Julio, too."

The light of one of the wall lamps was directly above her head and Philip sat facing her, his long body stretched out in one of the cane reclining-chairs which they used so much in the evenings, but his face was entirely in shadow. In spite of the fact that she could not see his expression at all clearly, however, she was instantly aware of an intense weariness, of patience stretched to the utmost and a temper held in leash only by the firmest effort of will.

"What is it you want to say—or to ask?"

His voice had been harsh in the extreme, but he had not moved and she could not be sure whether he was angry or not.

"I want to understand about Julio," she said.

"There is very little to understand." Again there was the suggestion of weariness, more evident this time, she thought. "Julio, like a good many other people, is prone to bolt when he feels the bit between his teeth. As soon as the rein is slackened they are away. You cannot give them their head too often for your own safety and peace of mind."

"But—supposing the rein were too tight? Supposing the curb had been applied too freely in the past?"

She sat with her heart racing, waiting for his answer, her cheeks flushed, her hands clasped tightly before her. He would hate to be challenged like this, but she had to know what had happened to Julio.

"Sometimes the curb is more than necessary," he said. "You do not know Julio. He is sullen and quite vindictive, and unfortunately he thinks that I consider him inferior."

"And do you, Philip?"

He took a full minute to answer her.

"No," he said, "not fundamentally. Somewhere there is Hallam blood in him. That must surely count for something in the long run."

"But, at the moment, you distrust him?"

Again he hesitated.

"I can't stand it when I see him throwing away something his father has built up over a lifetime," he said at last.

"You mean the plantation, of course?"

He rose, coming to stand beside her chair and looking down at her in the full light, at last.

"What else?" he demanded. "San Lozaro started from nothing. It started from a dead valley, a place that had been neglected for a hundred years." His eyes went beyond her, out into the still night with its star-bright sky and the constant presence of The Peak hovering above the quiet *barrancos*. "When El Teide erupted this valley was almost wholly destroyed. The lava came down and cut it off, and nothing was done about it afterwards. It was too remote, it seemed. Even when the soil was ready to use again and crops could have been planted, nobody wanted to do that work. Then your uncle bought it and toiled with the sweat of his brow to bring it to life. He took off the top soil in small sections and broke up the earth-stone underneath. He put the soil back and terraced the land and watered it. It took him nearly forty years to work his way to the top." His voice dropped, the fierceness going out of it of a sudden. "When a man has done that, when he sees his family reaping the benefit of what he has achieved with his own bare hands, he is proud in the only way that pride is justified. And he does not want to see his son throwing it all away for the proverbial 'mess of pottage'."

Felicity could not answer him. She had never expected to see him revealed in such a way, the harsh intensity of his words underlining the depths of his feelings as nothing else could have done. He, who had lost his own land, could understand how Robert Hallam had felt about San Lozaro, and because of that he was trying to make sure that Julio would not throw away his splendid inheritance.

But was he going the wrong way about it?

"Julio had a job to do this afternoon," he said, as if he had read her thoughts. "There was a consignment of bananas due to be loaded for Puerto de la Cruz before three o'clock. A boat was waiting there. I left him with the instructions and the bill of lading. When I came back the bill and the bananas were still here—untouched. Julio had decided that it was more important to play."

Felicity looked up at him, aghast.

"But—did he understand?"

473

The smile he gave her was pityingly amused.

"My dear Felicity, Julio is eighteen years of age. He believes himself capable of accepting a man's role in life—in other ways."

She bit her lip, realizing how true that was.

"I had no idea about this," she said.

"How could you?" He strode to the edge of the *patio*, staring through the dividing glass screen which sheltered it. "I doubt if you could ever understand Julio."

"I am going to try," she answered firmly. "Will you leave him to me, Philip? At least for a week or two," she pressed when he did not answer at once.

"You cannot work miracles," he warned dryly.

"I could make the effort!"

She waited, and he turned slowly to look at her. His eyes in the artificial light were much darker but still fiercely probing.

"I would not like to see you getting hurt in the process," he said.

She thought the remark cynical and sighed.

"Need I get hurt, Philip?" she asked. "It is something I want to do. It is what I came here to attempt, I suppose."

"Forgive me if I remind you that you had no idea how difficult it would be," he said.

"No," she confessed, "that is true. But I shall expect you to help me, whether you want to or not."

His mouth relaxed a little.

"What makes you so doubtful about my help?" he asked. "But, no! Don't trouble to answer that! I can do it for you, I think." His tone was suddenly dry. "You consider that I have an axe to grind. You would not be surprised, in fact, if I were slowly feathering my own nest here at San Lozaro."

"No!" she protested immediately. "Honestly, I hadn't thought of that, Philip."

"You flatter me." The firm lips twisted bitterly. "Have you asked Rafael de Barrios what he thinks?"

"No," she protested a second time. "I wouldn't do such a thing."

"But he has told you that he does not approve of me, I feel sure!"

"Does it matter?" she appealed. "We have to work together, Philip, for the peace of San Lozaro."

474

He looked at her keenly for a moment longer before he turned back into the shadows and went towards the hall. The whole house was very still, as if the sound of revelry had never disturbed it, and he looked relieved.

"It is because I believe that Julio would do better without the sort of friendships he has been making among the plantation workmen that I have had to insist like this," he said unexpectedly.

He was not trying to excuse himself nor was he going back on a decision once it had been made. He was merely stating a fact which he had decided she should know about.

"These men are riff-raff of the lowest order. It is Julio's misfortune to believe that they could ever be his friends," he added.

"I would like to think that we could offer him something better," Felicity said. "And Conchita, too."

He halted abruptly at the foot of the staircase and she thought that she had made a mistake, mentioning Conchita in the same breath as her brother. The colour seemed to have drained out of Philip's face, leaving it grey and haggard-looking, and his jaw was suddenly hard.

"Conchita is only a child," he said harshly, as he stooped to pick something from the floor at his feet.

Felicity saw what it was by the light of the staircase lamp above their heads. She saw the scarlet flare of the red lotus like blood lying between Philip's hands before he crushed the spray relentlessly and thrust the broken fragments into the pocket of his white coat.

CHAPTER V

LAS CANADAS

SISA was excited.

"It's wonderful of Philip!" she cried, clasping her white-gloved hands in a rapture of expectation. "He has arranged everything. We are going to El Teide to-morrow, and Julio is to come with us because he has been many times before."

She had just returned from early-morning mass at the little sugar-icing chapel on the hillside and she had run in to tell Felicity her news.

"I have never been allowed to go all the way to the summit before," she confided, laying her rosary aside in its velvet box. "But Philip thinks I am old enough now to make the climb. It is because of you, I know," she added. "Philip wishes you to see the beauty of our island so that you will not go away."

Sisa's expression was full of love and Felicity's heart warmed in gratitude. There was the thought, too, of Philip, but she could not share Sisa's belief that he wished her to stay at San Lozaro. Her presence there meant nothing to him, except, perhaps, some sort of added responsibility which he had not expected to shoulder.

Since their talk of a week ago, she had not been able to contact Julio to try to fulfil her promise about getting to know him better and helping in whatever way she could. She still believed that a measure of sympathy and understanding was all that her cousin really needed, and perhaps the journey to The Peak would provide her first opening.

It might even be that Philip had arranged the climb for that very reason, although she could never be absolutely sure about Philip's motives. He worked harder than anyone else at San Lozaro, seeming to require next to no sleep, for he was always up and away to the plantations before the sun flooding in through her shutters had awakened her in the morning. He returned in time for their evening meal, but she knew that he worked when they had all gone to bed. A light burned in the cell-like room he used as a study long after she had turned down her own lamp, and often, before she finally got in between her sheets, she stood at the unshuttered window of her room looking across the courtyard to the one lighted window on its far side, wondering if she couldn't have helped him with all that paper work, at least.

She felt shy about offering her help where the estate was concerned, however. Philip might think her unduly curious about her uncle's affairs, and she did not want that to happen. It might look as if she did not trust him, and she was quite sure that Robert Hallam had chosen an able administrator for the valley that had been his life's work.

The following morning they set out from the *hacienda* shortly after dawn.

"Wrap up well," Philip warned, and to Felicity's complete surprise, it appeared that he was coming with them.

"I take a day off occasionally," he said dryly, guessing her thoughts. "And this might be called a business trip, in a way. I have a call to make on the road up to Las Canadas which would mean half a day's journey, anyway."

Felicity's heart stirred uncertainly, throbbing hard against her breast. She was beginning to feel something of Sisa's sense of adventure, and it was satisfying to know that Philip was coming with them.

The crisp morning air was like a tonic and the sun came up, yellow and bright, over the shoulder of El Teide. It was several hours' journey to Las Canadas. They would climb The Peak during the night and watch the sun rise out of Africa in the morning. Julio had made all the necessary arrangements, and Philip seemed to have granted him the two days' holiday without question.

He came rather sullenly to the terrace when they were ready to leave. He had brought round the car and fumbled a lot with the hood and side-screens as Philip checked petrol and oil and packed their picnic hampers into the boot.

"I'm looking forward to this, Julio, more than I can say," Felicity told him, going round to the far side of the car where he was standing. "It is kind of you to agree to take us."

"There is an official guide," he muttered half resentfully. "Perhaps you would rather have had him?"

"No," Felicity said carefully. "It will be much nicer going on our own, Julio—as a family.'

"Philip wishes that I should take you," he said.

"He feels that you know the way as well as the guide," she explained. "You have been up many times, Sisa says."

He gave her a quick, almost suspicious look.

"I did not think that Philip trusted me," he said.

"He does in this," she answered quickly. "In the things you really know about, Julio. The things you do well."

He laughed harshly.

"Shall I take my guitar, do you think, to play you a love song on El Teide?"

The unexpected cynicism disconcerted her for a moment. Julio could switch so abruptly from one mood to another.

"Why not?" she suggested lightly. "We have an hour or two to spend at the rest hut, haven't we?"

"Yes," he agreed, "at Altavista. Is Isabella de Barrios going with us?"

A small, chill sense of disappointment touched Felicity's heart.

"I don't know," she answered stiltedly. "Would you expect her to be going, Julio?"

He shrugged.

"Philip is going," he said.

They went up through the woods, away from the vine terraces and the sea by a winding road which took Felicity's breath away. It was not very broad, and it clung to the mountainside, with a sheer drop of several hundred feet in some places, going down darkly into the deep ravines which scarred the island's volcanic face.

Great trees stood all about them, giant chestnuts making a green skirt for the towering, conical peak that rose above them, white-crowned with its eternal snow cap against a sky of turquoise and gold. The silences and the stillness of all mountain regions reigned here, and after a while even Sisa became silent.

An eagle soared and a raven passed overhead. A white mist hovered beneath them, drifting across the valley they had just left, and the first cactus appeared at the roadside.

They were still alone in that high, lost world of rock and

478

scree rising gradually above the tree line. No following car had put in its appearance from the direction of Zamora and Julio did not mention Isabella again.

He sat between Felicity and Sisa, a slim-hipped boy today in his immaculately-cut riding breeches and silk shirt with the hand-worked monogram on its pocket, looking so unlike the Julio who slouched about the plantations in a pair of old jeans and a red sweat-shirt that Felicity's heart lifted at the prospect of reform. After all, she thought, glancing sideways at the handsome profile crowned by the mass of curly black hair, there was no need for Julio to consider himself inferior.

Pine woods began to thicken the way, stretching for several miles, and deep and dreadful gorges plunged downwards at their very feet. For the past half-hour she had been conscious of a deepening silence in the car, a reserve about her companions which she could not penetrate. Conchita, seated beside Philip in the front seat, looked uneasy, and Sisa's eyes were sad. Julio looked at Philip and swiftly away again.

They had come to a part of the road where it twisted in a precarious spiral along the edge of a ravine, a dark and terrible place gouged out of the earth by the violent upheaval of volcanic eruption hundreds of years ago. Its precipitous sides would not support vegetation of any kind. Not even a solitary tree clung to them, and the arid basin they formed was as black as a starless night. It looked like some hideous vale torn out of the depths of hell, a barren, dreadful place where no life could ever exist.

The silence in the car had grown oppressive, and suddenly Felicity saw Philip's hands tighten on the wheel, the knuckles standing out white against the bronzed flesh as he slowed the car down at the junction with a narrow road which went off into a ravine. Yet she knew, even before Sisa told her, that it wasn't the effort of driving nor the need for concentration which had forced the colour from his face and made him look oddly grey beneath his coating of tan.

"We are always made sad when we come this way," Sisa whispered at her elbow. "It was very near here that María died."

It was the only road, Felicity realized, the only way

479

Philip could have taken them from San Lozaro in order to reach The Peak.

She turned her head away, unable to look at him again. How often had he come this way since that dreadful day of tragedy when he had lost his love? How often had he been forced to live it all again because he had to pass near to where María had died in the way of duty? Because there was no other way.

She closed her eyes until she was sure that the ravine was far behind them, and when she opened them again the scene had changed.

They were high on a wide plateau now and there were no trees. The sun poured straight down out of a sky so blue that it seemed incredible at first. Julio had opened the side-screens and she could feel the heat of the sun on her skin, warm and caressing, like the touch of a lover.

Ahead of them, old bent tamarisk bushes crouched by the wayside, and far in the distance the white sand of Las Canadas lay shimmering at the feet of El Teide.

It was a scene straight out of Africa, a sight so surprising, so utterly unexpected to Felicity that she drew in a long, quivering breath of delight.

Philip turned from the wheel as he slowed the car.

"Well," he asked, "what do you think of it?"

"I—had no idea!"

It was suddenly as if they were alone in the car, the revelation of beauty and splendour standing between them like a bond. The white sand stretched everywhere, dominated, guarded, silenced by the omnipotent presence of The Peak. El Teide was indeed magnificent. If he was frightening and remote in some moods, he was kind and wise and gentle, too. His hoary old head rose far into the blue, and within an hour or two she would be on her way to the summit with Philip Arnold by her side!

"We get out here," Julio said abruptly. "It is the end of the carriageway."

A spell seemed to have been broken, and coldly a little wind came slipping through between the tamarisks. Was it a place of meeting, too? Felicity wondered. Was it the likely place for Isabella's black Mercedes to be sheltering in the shadow of the grey stone wall ahead of them that surrounded the only human habitation within sight?

Great boulders lay scattered all about the sand, and

beneath one of these Philip spread the rug he had taken from the car. Felicity and Sisa knelt on it to unpack the picnic hampers, while Conchita wandered away in the direction of the house.

Presently a strange old couple came round the end of the wall bearing a brown jug full of goat's milk and a farmhouse cheese, which Philip paid for with a great show of gratitude that evidently pleased their visitors because they backed away with toothless smiles, opening the iron gates in the wall so that he might drive the car through into the courtyard beyond and leave it there for the night.

Still there was no sign of the Mercedes, and almost guiltily Felicity drew a deep breath of relief. Why should she care whether Isabella came or not? If Isabella wanted to climb to the top of El Teide with Philip it was surely no affair of hers, only—only the thought sent her heart hammering wildly in her breast and a mad protest rose stranglingly in her heart.

"We must eat in the shade," Sisa said. "Soon it will be very warm and we will rest until Philip says it is time to go on. I wish," she added eagerly, "that we had time to go and see the goats."

The little brown mountain goats of El Teide had been part of the landscape all the way up, but evidently the ones Sisa wished to see were special ones.

"There are some like them," she confided when Philip had moved away out of earshot to find a cooler spot for the wine, "at Lozaro Alto. María used to send them, and now Philip keeps them in memory of her. They are pure white."

It did not sound like the gesture of a man who had deliberately killed the woman who loved him, Felicity thought, the pain in her heart growing as she imagined Philip alone in his silent valley among the mountains. If he went there often, might it not even be on some sort of pilgrimage?

How much, she wondered, did she really know about him? She had heard what Sisa had to say about him, and Julio's opinion, and Rafael's, but was she ever likely to discover the whole truth?

She saw him as an enigma, as a man whose life had been darkened by a tragedy not long past, but she could not begin to guess what kind of a man he really was.

Conchita came back and they ate their lunch, seated with their backs against the sun-warmed rocks until Sisa, from force of habit, fell asleep. Philip, who did not seem to need sleep, went in search of the horses that were to take them on the first stage of the ascent, and Conchita followed him after a few minutes, slim and dark and lovely in her white jodhpurs and scarlet shirt.

"When we get to the refuge," Julio said, stretching himself lazily on the sand at Felicity's feet, "I shall play for you on my guitar."

She smiled down at him where he lay with his dark head cradled in his arms and his long, supple body taut in the sun. His eyes were slumbrous, black and reflective as he watched the sunlight on her hair.

"You are beautiful, Felicity," he said.

"And you are an abject flatterer!" she responded.

"That is not so!" He rolled over on to his side as she began to re-pack the picnic basket with suddenly nervous hands. "I only speak the truth," he declared with a touch of resentment. "You are the same as the lotus that grows only rarely here—the white lotus. Its petals are tipped with pink."

She thought of the red lotus, the blossom that the natives called the "flower of love," and looked away from Julio's sultry eyes.

"It is because I am English and my skin is so fair," she said. "But soon I shall be almost as brown as Sisa." She thrust out her bare arm towards him where she had rolled up her sleeves. "See, it is covered in freckles already!"

In an instant he had seized her hand and pressed burning lips to her exposed flesh.

"No, Julio—you must not!"

She tried to drag her arm away, but he would not let her go, looking up at her with a flare of swift passion in his eyes.

"Why do you say I must not?" he demanded. "I must love you if I will."

"Julio, be sensible. This is all—rather ridiculous, isn't it?"

" 'Julio, be sensible!' " he mocked. " 'Julio, you must not love me!' Why must I not love you? Because you are my cousin? But cousins can be in love."

"Not cousins who hardly know each other." Felicity

had tried to keep her voice light, but she felt that the situation was getting beyond her. The calmness at which she clutched was no match for Julio's determination. "Besides," she added almost desperately, "the others will soon be here——"

"The others? Do you mean Philip? He is the only one you care about. Is it not so? You are afraid of Philip. You will do only what he says, and soon he will tell you to go away from San Lozaro because he has no use for you there."

"You know that isn't true," she protested. "Philip has asked me to help him."

"To help him?" He sat up, releasing her and hugging his knees as his brows drew together in a quick frown. "In what way could you help Philip?" he demanded.

"By helping you and Sisa and Conchita."

He laughed outright as Philip came towards them.

"That is very funny," he said.

"We'll start in half an hour, Julio," Philip announced. "I'm not quite sure about Sisa," he added, looking down at the small, sleeping figure in the shadow of the rock. "Do you think she can make the summit?"

"Better than Conchita will," Julio decided. "It is Conchita who will fail us more easily than Sisa."

The horses were brought, small, patient creatures so used to the ascent that they could have done it blindfold, and they began to penetrate the vast circus of Las Canadas.

High above the tableland the great peak looked down on their small company as it wound across the sand, as remote and unperturbed by their presence as a giant who watches flies crawling at his feet. With one blow he could smother them all.

But to-day El Teide was smiling. No storm-cloud ruffled his brow. The face of the mountain was serene.

Soon they were on the rocky, pine-bordered path of Loma Tieso, winding and zig-zagging up towards the refuge of Altavista. It was after five o'clock before they reached the refuge and they were all fairly tired by the ride, although the excitement of the final climb kept them awake and curiously alert. Julio strummed on his guitar, seemingly at peace with the world, and, in fact, here in the mountains, he seemed a different being. Sisa was far

483

too excited, but finally she slept again, after Philip had given her his firm promise to waken her at midnight.

Conchita prowled restlessly. She did not really want to climb El Teide, but she had been unwilling to stay behind. Perhaps she had expected to find the de Barrios' Mercedes at Portillo de las Canadas and Rafael there with it.

Felicity thrust the suspicion from her and helped Philip to make coffee over a wood fire which they built in the wide stone grate.

At midnight the guide lanterns were ready and they set out in a ragged little group, Julio and Philip with torches held high above their heads for the first yard or two to give Felicity and Sisa confidence.

The path rose in a series of uneven lengths, rough and precipitous in places where it was hewn out of the volcanic rock itself, and soon Felicity could feel the piercing chill of these upper regions reaching her bones. Sisa, who had kept up a spate of talk and laughter on the first lap of the journey, fell silent, and Conchita's teeth began to chatter. The whole world seemed suddenly very dark and full of discomfort as the cutting air put an end to conversation and they plodded on to the sound of their own laboured breathing.

The sharp, staccato cry of a night creature, disturbed and fleeing before them into the shadowed crevices of the rock, rent the night, shattering its stillness, and great black pinnacles rose on either side of them, dark and forbidding, piercing the sky wherever they looked. Suddenly Conchita gave up.

"I hate this place!" she gasped. "I'm going back. I am dead of cold!"

Philip came back, holding his torch high, looking at them in the flaring light it gave.

"What do you think?" he asked. "Are we to abandon it?"

Felicity's immediate reaction was acute disappointment. In spite of her physical discomfort, she wanted to go on, she wanted to reach the top, but if Conchita had to go back then perhaps they should all return.

"I knew you would not climb to the top!" Julio said scathingly. "You are too soft, Conchita, and too afraid!"

"And you are a devil!" Conchita spat at him. "You do not know how it is to feel cold!" She was very near to tears. "I hate to come here!" she cried. "I hate El Teide

484

and the long climb it is to reach the top, with nothing to see there but a great empty crater all burned up with the fury of a stupid mountain hundreds and hundreds of years ago! I shall go down alone," she decided petulantly. "I shall wait at the refuge till you come. It is warm there."

She could not go alone. Philip would not permit it.

"What would you like to do, Felicity?" he asked. "Would you like to go on?"

"Not if the others feel that they want to turn back."

"It is only Conchita," Sisa pointed out with stark disappointment in her voice. "Julio could go with her back to Altavista and climb up again behind us."

Philip hesitated.

"What do you think, Julio?" he asked.

"I think Conchita is a great nuisance!"

"So!" Conchita said. "And you are a great fool! I shall return alone!"

"No, you won't!" Philip laid an arresting hand on her arm as she flung away. "Wait for Julio."

The lantern and its accompanying torch began to go slowly downhill. Philip stood waiting until they had disappeared round the first bend in the path before he spoke.

"Are you sure you want to go on, Felicity?" he asked. "It's a stiff climb."

"Yes," she said, "if you think I can make it."

She thought that he smiled, but she could not be sure.

It was, indeed, a difficult climb. They passed La Rambletta, hardly exchanging a word because their breaths seemed to be cutting into their throats, and soon they were climbing what appeared to be a sugar loaf of black rock. Philip was helping Sisa now, and once or twice he put out a hand to Felicity. She gripped it strongly and held on until he had to turn to Sisa again.

Somewhere behind them a faint glimmer seemed to quiver, of a sudden, in the sky. It was the first moment of light. Slowly the mountain masses began to take shape, but the path was still dark ahead. The curious half-light was more treacherous than the true darkness, Felicity thought, and then, with a little, despairing cry, she had stumbled and fallen. Her foot twisted beneath her and a wrenching pain shot straight to her heart.

Philip was beside her in an instant.

"All right, *querida*," he said. "I've got you!"

485

He lifted her, holding her close, and in the strengthening light of the new day she looked at him and knew herself in love.

The fiery disc of the sun rose suddenly from out of the east, lighting up a panorama composed only of elements and simple nature. The whole world was of a uniform, reddish-brown colour, which seemed to absorb everything it touched—the sea, the rocks, the still-distant summit of the volcano, the very atmosphere which surrounded them. They were in a place apart, a strange new world which held all the mystery of the beginning of time.

Felicity lay still in Philip's arms, feeling her heart pounding against his in repeated hammer-blows, feeling his nearness and his arms about her as if they had always been there; wanting them to be there for the rest of her life.

Slowly the contours and profiles of the island began to show themselves, and Sisa, who had climbed a little way ahead, ran back with her useless lantern to hold it anxiously near Felicity's ravaged face.

"What has happened?" she cried. "Philip, what has happened to Felicity? She has hurt herself, falling against the rock!"

Felicity tried to smile. It was no physical pain, such as Sisa might have known, that had suddenly shattered her peace of mind. Her heart, after that first moment of ecstasy in Philip's arms, lay still and bruised. How could she have come to love this man, so swiftly, so unpredictably? One touch—the physical contact in a moment of uncertainty— had been the igniting spark, but what did she really know of him? There were the things she had heard, the wild rumours which might bear no resemblance to the truth, and there was her own estimate of him. Steady, reliable, true. That was what, in three weeks, she had come to consider him, but was it not already the promptings of love?

Her mind veered away from reasoning as Philip set her on her feet again.

"We're almost at the top," he said. "If we could make the crater we could shelter up there and you could rest for a while before we attempt to go down. It's too exposed here."

His words were an encouragement, and she had wanted so much to reach the top of their mountain!

She tried to walk and he put his arm about her to steady her while Sisa took both lanterns. They were almost ineffective now except in the shadows of the giant rocks, dimmed into pale imitations of light by the strengthening glory in the east.

She bit her teeth into her lower lip when the pain in her foot became intense and limped on, feeling that it was not quite so bad when Philip was supporting her.

In the strong, unshaded light the contours of the island began to show themselves, the land beneath them lying at first like a colossal slab of grey granite before it gradually turned into a relief map of deeply indented *barrancos* and steep, precipitous mountain peaks. The strong basalt wall of the road from Santa Cruz to San Andrés marched towards them, and far, far on the distant sea a steamer made for the harbour, the column of its white smoke like a gay plume rising against the deepening blue.

Beyond it, where the sun rose, Grand Canary lay in a bath of light, guarded by two enormous serpent islands lying watchfully along the horizon.

"Lanzarote and Fuerteventura," Philip said, pretending not to look at her too closely. "The islands are very clear to-day."

They had halted on a ledge almost at the summit and he knelt down to inspect her foot. Wreaths of smoke and sulphur vapour emerged from the soil all about them, yet the stones which lay across their path appeared to be coated with ice. It was a strange, weird place for the revelation of love, Felicity thought with a small, painful smile which twisted her lips without rising to her eyes.

"There don't appear to be any broken bones," Philip said, "but I'll see what I can do with a bandage and then we'll begin to go down. We ought to meet Julio about half way."

"It isn't very painful," Felicity managed as she tried to stand again. "I feel so badly about it—spoiling your climb like this."

Instantly the blue eyes were full on hers with a strange, almost angry light in them.

"It was your day," he said. "I have climbed to the top many times."

"I can come again, perhaps," she said in swift confusion.

487

"But you may not want to trust me a second time—after this."

Still the blue eyes held hers, gently probing.

"Should it be a question of trust, Felicity?" he asked. When she could not reply he added on a drier note:

"It's the one instinct that goes wrong most often. We trust like fools and are betrayed."

The underlying note of bitterness seemed harsher and stronger than ever in these primitive surroundings. Felicity pressed her hand to a fissure in the frozen rock to find that what she thought would be ice-like was boiling vapour, like the breath of a wild beast. They were nearly four thousand metres above sea level, on a great, snow-crested peak at dawn, yet the earth beneath them boiled in a turmoil of heaving, volcanic fire.

Suddenly she shivered, and as suddenly Philip turned from strapping up her ankle with a bandage from the first-aid kit to lead her gently but firmly away from the crater with its views over all the island she had come to love in so short a space of time.

They went slowly downwards by a little twisting path leading eventually to a cave, at the bottom of which was a small, still pool of ice.

She wanted to run then, to hurry away from this frozen place whose chill seemed to have entered her heart, but Philip decided that they should stay.

"Julio will look for us here," he said. "We can't attempt the journey down to Altavista without him."

Sisa roamed round the cave, touching the stalagmites with wondering fingers, but in spite of her small cries of delight, it seemed to Felicity that she and Philip were alone. They were both intensely aware of each other. Felicity could sense that, but surely Philip could only be finding her a nuisance in this high place where already the stars had paled and the night was gone?

He had withdrawn behind a mask of silence, yet she knew that he was still intently watchful and anxious about her comfort.

When Julio came sliding down to the cave entrance half an hour later he explained the position as tersely as possible.

"Felicity has had an accident. We must get her down as easily as we can without further trouble."

488

"You are hurt, *querida!*" Julio murmured with sudden tenderness, bending over her. "I shall carry you——"

"There's no need for that." Philip's tone was practical and a trifle curt. "Felicity can walk quite well now that her foot is bandaged. She will only need a little support."

Julio scowled at him but evidently decided not to argue.

"There is an easy way," he said. "Come! I will show you."

He took Felicity's hand, leading the way, with Philip and Sisa bringing up the rear. Philip had extinguished the lanterns and carried them now slung across his back, his torch thrust into the wide leather belt he wore over his wind-cheater.

When Felicity looked back at him from time to time, he seemed like some giant of the mountains striding there behind her, a dark-browed Peer Gynt in restless pursuit of an ideal, perhaps, or maybe just a man fleeing from his own tormenting thoughts.

Whatever María had been to him, whatever Isabella de Barrios was to him now, it was no light emotion which had left its mark on Philip Arnold's face. He was not the man to love lightly, nor would she have had it so, but Isabella was Rafael de Barrios' wife and she felt her heart turn over at the inevitability of pain.

Julio, too, it would appear, believed himself in love. When they eventually reached Altavista and were safely in the refuge, he looked at Felicity with longing eyes.

"I shall play for you while you rest," he offered, taking up his guitar when Philip had gone out to saddle the horses for the ride down to Las Cañadas. "The music will make you feel good and help you to forget your pain."

Felicity smiled. Julio's panacea for every ill was the music he made; sweet music, passionate music, sometimes wild music which was a protest straight from his lonely heart, but music which she had tried to understand.

If she had failed at times it was not Julio's fault, she considered. It was something in herself, no doubt, which did not appreciate the true bond between this typical son of a southern race and the music he made so easily.

Conchita had forgotten her sulks and was all kindness. She rushed about the refuge, making coffee, bringing an extra blanket to put behind Felicity's head, watching

489

Philip to see if he were angry or just very anxious because there had been an accident so high up on the perilous sides of El Teide. She said that they should not have gone, that they should have heeded her warning and returned with her, and Philip said that perhaps she was right.

He had come in to announce that the horses were ready, and he looked in Felicity's direction and frowned.

"I'm all right, Philip," she assured him, trying to stand without showing her pain. "It was only a little thing——"

He smiled wryly, taking her arm to help her round the end of the hut.

"Little things can sometimes develop alarmingly," he said. "We're not taking any risks with this."

Lifting her up into the saddle, he steadied her on the small, honey-coloured pony in spite of her protests. For a moment his hands lingered on her waist and their eyes met. His were very dark, although in the next instant he was smiling.

"That should be better," he said. "Don't attempt to do anything. I'll lead Cinders down."

"But the distance, Philip?" she protested. "And the heat?"

He shrugged indifferently.

"It makes no matter," he said. "I am used to riding about the canyons."

Did he come this way alone? Often alone? Did he ride through the canyons thinking about the past, loving María still? And what of Isabella? Felicity could not think of Isabella de Barrios without a desperate pain in her heart, and she turned her head away so that Philip might not see its reflection in her far too candid eyes.

They rode slowly and took a long time in reaching the sandy plain of Las Canadas, where the heat was a fiery breath straight out of Africa. It met them in a stupefying wave, beading Felicity's upper lip with tiny drops of perspiration and causing Philip to mop his brow.

The lethargic, timeless peace that encompasses all southern habitations at the hour of the *siesta* lay on the old house behind its high stone wall and on the surrounding boulders and on the cacti and the still, white sand. Nothing moved. Even the little buff-coloured goats had disappeared behind convenient clumps of tamarisk and the few trees within the shelter of the wall drooped in the heat.

Philip, however, seemed to be determined to get back to San Lozaro in the shortest possible time. With many apologies, he woke the custodian of the gate and brought out the car. The man he had called Santiago came and stood before them with wine and cheese and bread on a wooden platter, while the old woman with the wrinkled-walnut face peered at them from behind a grille in the inner door. It was too hot, Felicity supposed, for her to come out, or perhaps she was merely overcome by shyness at this second visit, remembering Philip's generosity of the day before.

They drank the coarse red wine and were on the point of getting into the car when a great bird rose protestingly from a pinnacle of rock far down the winding road to San Lozaro and circled twice above their heads.

Philip's eyes narrowed as he looked up at it and he turned sharply to where the road appeared out of a sparse belt of fir. A little cloud of dust came creeping up the valley towards them, and Felicity saw Conchita's eager gaze following his as she clasped her hands before her in quick expectation.

"Someone is coming, Philip," she said. "Let us wait and see who it is."

Philip's eyes seemed to snap their disagreement, but he answered reasonably enough.

"It will be tourists from Orotava. Who but the English 'go out in the mid-day sun'?"

Conchita smiled, but she was not entirely convinced, and when the de Barrios's black Mercedes breasted the final rise she threw Philip a quick look of triumph.

"I knew!" she cried. "I knew it would be Rafael. No one drives a car as he does—so fast, so assured!"

Rafael de Barrios had his family with him. Andrea sat in front, prim and sedate in a white panama hat and white cotton dress, while Isabella and Celeste occupied the rear seat.

Rafael's sisters were not at all like him, Felicity thought, as the newcomers spilled out of the car, but that was no doubt due to their upbringing. The closely-guarded life of the young Spanish girl of good family would account for their natural shyness, and they patently adored their brother. An only son, Rafael must have been the darling of the household ever since he had first drawn breath, and now that he had succeeded to the title, his will was absolute. Perhaps that alone accounted for his assurance.

His manners were impeccable, however. He bowed over Felicity's hand, touched Conchita's lightly with his lips, did the same for Sisa, which pleased her immensely, although she glanced swiftly in Philip's direction as she drew her hand away.

"This is surely one of the many advantages of so small an island," Rafael mused, smiling down into Felicity's eyes. "We meet often when perhaps we thought that we would not see each other again till the *fiesta!*"

"We've been climbing The Peak," Felicity explained unnecessarily because he had already glanced at her workmanlike outfit of linen jeans and checked cotton shirt. "It was a wonderful experience."

"But you have been hurt!" he noticed quickly. "You have a bandaged foot."

She drew back. He had probed too deeply, and his felicitations were something she did not want now even in a friendly way, because underlying them she sensed danger.

"I'm sorry," Isabella said, coming forward as if to extricate her from an embarrassing situation. "How did it happen?"

"I was foolish enough to slip going up over a stretch of rough scree." Felicity wished that the limelight of their interest was not quite so fully upon her and the cause of her accident. "It's nothing," she added. "It will soon mend."

"You must see a doctor," Rafael advised. "Allow me to contact Doctor Gondalez for you as soon as we get back to Zamora."

"That won't be necessary," Philip said, coming up behind them. "I shall take Felicity direct to Orotava from here."

"It's too long a journey," Rafael warned, but he shrugged, as if it no longer concerned him, and turned to where Conchita was waiting.

She had been standing behind Felicity, willing Rafael to notice her, one small foot tapping impatiently, her dark

492

eyes star-bright as she watched the Marqués' every movement and hung on his every word. Convention had demanded that he should enquire about Felicity's accident, of course, but there was no need to enlarge upon it, her impatience seemed to say, and certainly no need to consider the necessity for a doctor's attention. That was surely Philip's job!

"We must not delay you if you wish to go to Orotava." Isabella said. One long, understanding look had passed between her and Philip when they had met, but that was all. Now Isabella appeared calm and serene as ever, with only the hint of a shadow in her eyes. "I hope your ankle will not pain you too much, Felicity," she added sincerely. "And, most of all, I hope it will not keep you from coming to our *fiesta*."

"It will be mended long before that," Philip said abruptly. "If there is anything you want us to do for you, Isabella, you will let me know?"

Isabella looked at him again, steadily, affectionately.

"I will let you know," she said. "I have Rafael back with us, of course," she added slowly. "He tells me he will stay, at least till the *fiesta* is over."

There had been no hint of complaint in her pleasant voice, no suggestion that her husband might have spent more of his time in his own home, yet it was not an abject acceptance of her fate that shone in those clear dark eyes. There was acceptance, but it was of a kind that transcended defeat—an inner calm, a rising above the unhappiness and frustrations of life, which set a strange glow upon this woman who had married without knowing the true meaning of love.

"We will need Sisa and Conchita with us the day before," Rafael suggested lazily. "There is a lot to do."

Sisa glanced at Andrea and smiled. They had already made their youthful plans. It was Conchita who took the invitation as a purely personal one.

"I shall come whenever you say, Rafael," she agreed eagerly. "Philip must not be allowed to refuse when it is in so good a cause!"

"Why should Philip wish to refuse?" Rafael de Barrios looked amused. "He is only your guardian."

"Which is most important!" Isabella retorted with a

493

small flash of anger. "Sisa will come, and Conchita, too. I shall promise Philip to look after them both."

Rafael laughed, but there was uneasiness in the atmosphere now and he made a movement towards the resthouse and its acceptable patch of shade.

Philip helped Felicity into the car, in front, this time, where he could watch her as they drove along. Her face looked white and strangely pinched about the mouth, as if she smiled under strain, and when she said goodbye to Isabella she did it hurriedly.

Isabella did not look at Philip again. She stood back between her sisters-in-law, waving as he turned the car in a wide circle on the beaten sand, and when Felicity looked back before they plunged down the mountain road, Isabella was already seated in the shade of the wall unpacking the picnic hamper which Rafael had produced from the Mercedes' capacious boot.

On the way down the trees gave them shade, but there was no wind, and the heat began to affect Felicity—the heat and the increasing pain in her ankle whenever she moved. Over and above all these physical discomforts, too, she could feel the pain in her heart like a deep, dull ache that must remain with her all her life from now on.

She loved Philip. She loved him madly, and he had nothing to offer her in return except, perhaps, his friendship in the end.

"Felicity," Sisa asked anxiously from the back seat, "are you feeling faint? You look so pale."

"No. No—I'm all right!"

The words had been a tremendous effort and Philip slowed down the car to look at her.

"Are you sure?" he asked.

"Quite sure. Please don't stop, Philip! I'm not going to faint or do anything silly like that."

"We are near Lozaro Alto," Conchita pointed out. "Could we not go there, Philip, so that Felicity can rest? The road is only a little way ahead."

Philip's mouth tightened and his jaw had the cut of granite as a fury of indecision struggled in his eyes.

"No!" Felicity decided sharply. "You must not, Philip. There is no need."

He did not want to take her to Lozaro Alto and she did

494

not want to go. She did not want to travel with him over that road where another car had plunged to destruction, bearing his love and his future happiness with it down into some desolate *barranco* where only the stark rocks and the soaring eagle had been dumb witnesses to its fate. It was his own personal tragedy, to be shared by no one. Ever since, he had gone to the valley alone.

"I don't think it would really help," he returned, tight-lipped. "If there was any point in taking you there, I would, but it will only put added time on to our journey to Orotava."

"Need we go to Orotava?" Felicity asked. "If I rest when we get back to San Lozaro it may be all right by the morning."

He shook his head.

"I'm not taking any risks," he said decisively.

They reached Orotava by late afternoon and the little Spanish doctor they consulted there reassured them immediately.

"A severe sprain," he said. "That is all. Nothing broken, but it must be very painful. It has been strapped up so well by Don Philip that it will soon be useful again!" he smiled. "He is a most reliable person, you know!" he added encouragingly.

Felicity bit her lip, aware that it had trembled. Here was someone who evidently knew Philip well, who liked and admired him in spite of all the rumours. She looked at the little doctor and felt the tears stinging behind her eyes. If only there could be nothing but kindness in the world, she thought weakly—no pain, no intrigue, nobody playing at love!

Philip took her arm and led her gently out towards the waiting car. He had ordered tea at the Hotel Taoro, a large, white edifice standing high on the cliff above the waving banana fields and looking down on Puerto de la Cruz. It formed three sides of a great square and they found a table on the sheltered verandah looking towards The Peak, but very soon Philip was looking at the sky beyond the giant mountain, as if he were impatient to be on their homeward way.

There was no cloud to be seen. The sky looked blue and innocent, but above The Peak a faint haziness had appeared and the breathless atmosphere suggested thunder. They were, it seemed, due for a storm, and Philip was impatient about getting back before it broke.

They followed the road by which he had first brought her to San Lozaro, the geranium-bordered highway hanging between El Teide and the sea, and the beauty of it caught at Felicity's throat like a hurt, urging the tears to her eyes again. This land—this happy land which was Philip's home seemed to be holding out eager arms to her, but she could not accept their comfort. Its beauty stirred all that was lonely in her and all that was sublime. She could have stayed here for ever, if for ever could have given her Philip's love.

But how could she stay, loving him without return? Could she remain beside him, seeing him day by day, knowing herself necessary to him, perhaps, in time, but not in the way she wanted to be necessary? He had promised to keep her uncle's home intact and she had made a similar promise, if not in so many words. She could not run away. She was sure of that, even if to stay must mean heartbreak.

Even Sisa was tired by the time they reached San Lozaro and they went early to bed. Julio came home at nights now instead of remaining sulkily attached to the workers' quarters surrounding the packing sheds, and Felicity was genuinely relieved at his return. It did not mean, of course, that he would not go off when the mood took him once more, but at least the family were together and that was what Robert Hallam had wanted.

Unable to sleep because the night was hot and sticky and her foot ached at every movement, she sat for a long time before her window listening to the approach of the storm. It came at first as a barely-perceptible movement among the palms, a stirring frond, a rustle and a stillness which suggested tension, and she found herself straining to catch the ordinary, accepted little sounds of the night. They appeared to be silenced, however, before the stealthy whisperings of the palms. There was no moon and the sky had become rapidly overcast, making the night as black as jet.

Then, suddenly, beyond the palms and the leaning tamarisks which fringed the cliffs, she could hear the sea.

The voice of the waves had risen to a crescendo of angry sound as the wind rose and freshened, and somewhere nearer at hand a neglected shutter slapped endlessly against the stable wall. A horse whinnied twice, a dismayed, anxious protest rising above the others, and she heard the sound of feet walking away towards the stables across the *patio* tiles.

Someone—either Philip or Julio—had been sitting down there in the darkness for a very long time contemplating the storm-racked sky, feeling the impact of what was to come with a sense of the inevitable, perhaps.

She felt the unseen presence of the man as if he had suddenly stepped close on to the balcony by her side, and instinctively she drew back, half afraid, half guilty about being caught out there when she had promised Philip to rest.

The first flash of lightning lit up the sky, showing her the rugged outline of El Teide. The great mountain stood revealed for a moment in all his awful majesty, only to be hidden again more completely as the thunder of his wrath rolled among the lesser peaks and out to sea.

Again and again the shattering peals shook the night, vibrating against space only to return with demoniacal fury in the wake of another piercing shaft of light which seemed to reveal every contour of the dark hillsides and each detail of the garden at her feet.

The paths and the flower-crowded *poyos* were starkly white under the fierce light and there were no shadows. The recurring flashes illuminated everything, so that she was instantly aware of the returning figure of the man who came up from the stables.

He walked straight towards the house, standing in the shelter of the *patio* as the rain broke, and the gleam of his white shirt told her that it was Philip.

There was release in that first surging downpour of rain. It was as if the heavens had opened and let out all their wrath. The pent-up emotion in her own heart surged to meet it, loosening tension, and it was only after a minute or two that she became aware of another, more sinister sound.

At first she thought that it must be the wind, and then she was aware of rushing water, of a cascading avalanche hurtling over the parched earth, leaping exultantly towards the sea. It filled the arid *barrancos* and terrified the night. The palms which had quivered in the wind now trembled and lay down before it, their feathery heads bent almost to the earth, and the chestnuts and the ancient dragon trees sighed in their troubled sleep.

It seemed to Felicity that the whole island would soon be swamped by that relentless, rushing tide, and then, suddenly, the rain ceased. It was like the swift turning off of a tap, and a little rush of cool air came up to find her where she stood.

She seemed to be arrested there. She could not move, and somehow she knew that she was waiting for the man in the *patio* to come to her.

He came slowly, as if he had known for some time that she was standing there.

"You could not sleep?" he guessed. "Was it your foot?"

"No." She held on to the balcony rail, her knuckles showing up white against her flesh. "No, it wasn't that."

"You must not mind the storm," he said, coming to stand beneath her on the wet tiles of the path. "The rain is necessary to us here. It clears the atmosphere and gives us the moisture we need for growth. We gather the rain in reservoirs on the hillsides. What you can hear is the gulley-pipes running down the sides of the *barrancos* to irrigate the valley below."

"I confess to being frightened at first," she said, "but once you know about the water it doesn't seem so bad. If I had been wakened up by the storm I expect I would have been more afraid."

She could just distinguish his dark profile, upturned towards her, and she thought that he smiled.

"I wondered," he said, "when I saw you out here."

How long had he been sitting in the *patio*, then? He had sensed her presence as she had sensed his, because he could not have seen her except in the illuminating flashes of the lightning. She had stood on the balcony long before the storm had broken. Had he been down there as long?

"Go to bed," he said at last, softly, almost tenderly. "There will be no more thunder. Only perhaps a little rain."

The kindness—the pity—in his voice all but unnerved

her. The new-found love in her heart was a stark and lonely thing, stretching out eager hands towards him, but how could he see? How could he ever see when his eyes were fixed so firmly on a distant star?

CHAPTER VI

THE SHADOW OF THE PALM

LAUGHTER rang up through the narrow streets of Zamora to meet the sunshine. It was very warm, and the windows and shaded courtyards and the tiny *plaza* beneath its tall canopy of palms were alive with people in festive mood.

"The very word *fiesta* spells laughter and gaiety and a sort of careless abandonment to happiness!" Felicity smiled as she stood beside Philip watching the milling crowd. "There could be nothing quite like this in England."

"We are a different race," he said. "Zamora is a happy continuation of Andalusia without the hardness that war and religious fanaticism and passionate violence have left in the Andalusian cities. In Zamora the windows are left unbarred and the doors are open. There is no reminder of the cloister here."

"Yet you would not let Conchita come yesterday to stay overnight. I think that was—ungenerous, Philip."

His mouth hardened at her protest, but his decision had, seemed harsh to her and she would not relent. Conchita's wiles and Conchita's tears had availed her nothing.

"I can't permit Conchita to make a fool of herself," he said coldly.

"But surely—an evening in the company of friends of her own age?" She was beginning to feel that he had been obstinate. "It was a well organized affair, I understand. A tennis dance at the Country Club. What could have been more English—or more American, if you like!"

"It was not Conchita's intention to go to the Club."

There was an angry light in his eyes now and his mouth was grim.

"But——" Her voice wavered. "But surely that was impossible, Philip?"

He laughed.

"Nothing is entirely impossible to the Conchitas of this world," he said. "They are wilful and perverse and when they believe themselves in love no power of reasoning or anything else will convince them that love alone is not enough."

She looked up at him, frowning in the bright sunshine.

"It's—almost as if you didn't believe in love, Philip," she said.

He did not turn to look at her.

"I don't believe in Conchita's kind of love," he acknowledged decisively.

"Are there several kinds?" Her voice was not quite steady. "I always thought there was one supreme passion— and nothing more."

"For some people." He was looking down at her, at last, his eyes fiercely blue in the bright sunlight, penetratingly blue. "You are an idealist, Felicity. Unfortunately, I have to think in terms of Conchita."

"Because of the promise you made to her father?" she asked with fuller understanding. "Promises are often difficult things to keep, I agree."

"I mean to keep this one." His jaw was set, making his face in profile look autocratic and hard, the face of a man to whom a woman might appeal in vain. "Conchita is something of an exhibitionist. With a little encouragement she could set Zamora and the entire island by the ears."

She thought that he did not care for gossip, that he had braved what must have been one of the most outstanding topics for surmise the island had ever known, and then she realized that this was different. This was Conchita. This was something which might injure a young girl's reputation for the rest of her life, and he was Conchita's appointed guardian. A stern gaoler he might be, but it was strength that Conchita needed.

"You would have handled the situation differently?" he suggested.

"I don't know, Philip." She turned to face him more fully. "When I—questioned your decision just now I thought you were being hard and adamant for hardness' sake."

"The man of granite, in fact, without a finer feeling to redeem him?" He smiled dryly. "If that were so I should

501

have let Conchita do as she pleased. But neither am I a sentimental fool, Felicity, and I must see that Conchita does as I say."

"Do you feel that I çan help you?" she asked.

"Not in this," he returned bluntly. "Conchita, as I have said, needs firm handling. You could not even begin to understand her in her present frame of mind. She is no longer a child. She is a woman—a tigress with newly-grown claws—a creature of impulse driven by her emotions towards an end she cannot really see."

"You said she was in love." Her voice all but faltered. "Is it—so very wrong to be in love, Philip—sincerely and whole-heartedly?"

"No." He looked beyond her, away from her questioning gaze. "If I thought that Conchita was really in love 'sincerely and whole-heartedly,' as you put it, I would excuse her, I think."

"How can you know?" she asked automatically. "How can you really be sure?"

"I know Conchita," he answered briefly. "The finest fruit is always just beyond her reach; the most desirable always at the top of the tree."

Felicity did not answer him. She felt anxious and deeply disturbed, and she did not want to ask about the object of Conchita's latest passion. Rafael de Barrios and her cousin had been together almost constantly the day before, the preparations for the *fiesta* at Zamora seized upon as a reasonable excuse for jaunts in the fast-moving Mercedes which had taken them all over the little town nestling above the sea and into the surrounding valleys to gather flowers of the special colouring demanded by the carpet makers.

These lovely, living carpets of blossoms with their exquisite design had taken hours to prepare and men had worked on them all during the night so that they might be ready for the procession of the saint in the early morning, with the dew still wet on them and their radiant colours fresh in the sun.

The procession was over. They had watched it winding its way through the network of narrow streets and out across the shaded *plaza* to climb to the pink stucco chapel on the hill. The priests had walked in front, black-robed and sombre against the brilliant natural background and the carpet of flowers beneath their feet, and the banners had been borne reverently to be replaced beside the saint. The tiny cracked bell on the chapel tower had chimed discordantly and the people had returned to *fiesta* and the ending of their day.

Laughter and gaiety were the predominating notes everywhere. This was a joyous people, Felicity thought as she looked about her, a race attuned to happiness and full of life and movement and blissful with content. She tried to meet their mood, tried to forget her heartache for a day, and because Philip had set out to please her it was proving an easy task.

They had come from San Lozaro early in the morning and had watched the procession before going to the de Barrios's villa for their mid-day meal. Isabella had gone with her family to mass, but Philip and Felicity had stood on the hillside after the procession had passed, listening to the bell in the stillness. They had not spoken much. Felicity had been content just to sit beside Philip on a cool stone seat shaded by a spreading dragon tree, watching the sea breaking gently on the distant shore, as if even the mighty Atlantic must approach this magic island of the ancients with respect and gentleness on such a day.

She had looked up at the dragon tree, at its gnarled branches which plunged dramatically back into the earth from which they had sprung to form new roots, and suddenly she was thinking of the ancient Guanche kings who had ruled and dispensed justice beneath its shade hundreds of years ago. She thought, too, of the loves and the hates and the little passions that had been played out there where she and Philip sat.

There had been scarcely any time for the habitual *siesta*, although Isabella had insisted that they sit for an hour in the *patio* where the air was cool and moist round the fountain.

Rafael, who was the perfect host, had amused them with a long description of a *fiesta* in Seville where he had danced far into the night with a charming señorita who had turned out to be no other than his mother's personal maid, whom he knew very well but whom he had failed to recognize in the mask and the fancy costume she had borrowed for the day.

"It was the mask," he shrugged. "The truth is not always to be seen in a woman's eyes."

Isabella had risen from her chair and gone abruptly into the house, as if she were afraid of the truth in her own eyes in that moment, and Philip had pushed back his chair with a sharp, angry movement which had been like a protest in the sudden silence.

He had taken Andrea and Sisa and Felicity to the *plaza*, where they had eaten strawberries and thick, rich cream, and Rafael had followed lazily in their wake with Conchita between him and Julio.

Julio looked the romantic troubadour he really was. His dark hair had been ruffled by the wind and curled thickly about his brow and his eyes shone and sparkled with the light of adventure. *Fiesta* was no new thing to him, but each *fiesta* brought its own delight, its own spice of the unknown, the unexpected. He had slung his guitar across his shoulders and its broad ribbon seared the front of his white silk shirt with a gallant splash of scarlet. The flash of his smile was as gay and as carefree, it would seem, as any there.

Yet, once or twice, when she looked at him, Felicity was aware of a growing watchfulness, of the dark eyes narrowed a fraction so that the sparkle of abandonment was all but lost. It was the mood of an instant, however, the fleeting glimpse of something only half seen and best forgotten.

When the dancers came, weaving their garland of flowers about the watchers in the *plaza*, he took up the refrains of the island songs on his guitar, looking at Felicity as if he would will her to understand the impassioned words he sang. With a little inward tremor she remembered the scene on the way to El Teide. She had tried to forget about Julio's light love-making in the interval, but now it seemed that he did not want her to forget.

Or was it just the mood of the *fiesta*, the quick passion inspired by the warmth of a sub-tropical sun and the gaiety of a naturally-generous people on a day of rejoicing?

She did not know. She told herself that she must not take Julio too seriously when possibly his protestations of love meant little more than affection, and when he asked her to dance with him she got on to her feet quite eagerly.

"Mind the ankle," Philip warned. "You're still taking a risk with it."

Julio's arm tightened about her.

"It will not hurt!" he said, his lips close against her hair. "To dance is as easy as to walk, and soon you will have forgotten all except the music!"

"It isn't a dance I know," Felicity objected, wondering if she had been foolish to obey the impulse which had drawn her with him into the crowd. "I shall make mistakes, Julio. I'll keep the others back——"

"I shall teach you!" he laughed, holding her close. "You have only to learn to listen to the rhythm and hear what the words are really saying! You have only to let yourself go!"

Which is something the English rarely do, Felicity thought with a smile.

"You are happy—yes?" Julio demanded immediately. "I will make you happy, Felicity!" His arms tightened as he pressed his lips against her hair. "Tell me you love me a little bit."

"I can't tell a lie." Her heart was beating wildly, protestingly, against his.

"It would not be a lie!" He was suddenly full of confidence. "You like me a little. It is true." He waited for a fraction of a second, gazing down at her as they danced. "Why do you not say so?" he demanded.

She drew in a deep breath.

"Of course, I like you, Julio," she said, "but——"

"We will not consider 'but' any more!" he decided with true Latin impetuosity. "It is agreed that we like each other, that you will come one day to like me very much."

"No, Julio, I haven't said that!" she protested weakly.

"But you will," he predicted. "When you have forgotten about Philip you will."

She stiffened in his warm embrace.

"We can't discuss Philip like this," she said.

"No? Are you in love with him, then? So very much in love with him that you will not ever have time for me?" His look was darkly fierce and she could no longer consider it lightly. "Because if that is so," he added before she could think of the words to placate him, "I shall kill him."

"Julio—hush!" she whispered, aghast.

" 'Julio, hush!' " he mocked. "But why should not the whole of Zamora hear? They know that I hate Philip Arnold. They know that already I have an unfulfilled desire to punish him."

She felt suddenly afraid because she could not dismiss this admission of hatred as the idle chatter of a boy. Julio meant what he said. In spite of the findings of the court, in spite of the exonerating words which the presiding judge had uttered in Philip's favour, Julio believed him guilty of María's death. María had loved Philip and he, according to Julio, had grown tired of her.

Felicity shivered at the thought. It wasn't true, of course. Philip had loved María right up to the time of her death. She felt certain of that. She had to be certain.

"Don't let's speak about it, Julio," she begged. "Not here. It is too serious a thing. It is something you must not go on thinking."

He drew her on in the stream of dancers without answering, so that she knew he was far from being convinced.

The dance had taken on the nature of a procession winding in and out between the houses, now in full sunlight, now in shade. They had left the *plaza* behind and she was lost. Lost without Philip.

Julio laughed at her distress.

"I am here!" he reminded her. "You can be happy with me."

It would have been difficult not to enjoy herself and be happy in that gay throng. When night fell with the tropical suddenness which she had never become quite used to, they were still apart from Philip and the others and Julio continued to laugh her protests aside.

"You are safe," he assured her, "with me!"

Perhaps that was so, but she was subtly aware of Philip's disapproval, even at that distance. He had been doing his best all day to keep their small party together, to avoid just such a breakaway as this, and now it must seem that she was defying him, especially after their conversation in the *plaza* when they had first come down from the hill. She had accused him of unnecessary harshness in his handling of Conchita. Might he not think now that she was accusing him also on Julio's behalf in this less direct way?

"Julio," she pleaded when all the lanterns were lit along the miniature stone quay and their reflection as bright as stars in the dark water, "you must take me back to Philip."

"I will never take you back to him, *querida!*" he told her

passionately. "You are mine. He has no right to you. Besides, he is already in love!"

"No, Julio——"

He swept her, protesting, into his arms. The dance was over for the moment and they had been sitting on a bench in the shadow of the stone wall surrounding the harbour, with a group of palms behind them and the murmur of the sea in their ears, and suddenly the shadow of the palm fell darkly across them. Julio's lips sought hers, demanding, arrogant, passionate, and her senses swam for a moment before the insistence of his kiss.

"You will love me," he said. "You do love me. I have seen it in your eyes!"

The shadow behind them stirred and lengthened. She knew that someone was standing there. It was Philip. He had moved away from the wall, turning his back on them.

Desperately she struggled to be free, her heart engulfed by humiliation and anger against Julio who could make such light love to her with such seeming passion.

"Philip," she said. "Were you looking for us?"

He did not answer her immediately, but he did not turn in surprise at the sound of her voice so that she knew he had seen her sitting there locked in Julio's arms.

"I came to find you—yes," he said at length, his voice so unlike the resonant, confident voice she knew that she could have mistaken him for a stranger in that deceptive half-light beneath the palms. "It is time that we went back to San Lozaro."

Why had he not said "It is time that we went back home"? So often he had used the word in the past few weeks, making it sound intimate and warm, part of them both, but now she knew that anger or disillusionment or some other fiercely primitive emotion had choked back the word in his throat. He could not bring himself to utter it. He could not believe that they would ever make a home together at San Lozaro after this.

The effort they were making was no longer congenial, no longer bound together by implicit trust.

Somehow she knew that she had had his trust. She had earned it during those four weeks of silent endeavour when they had both held fast to an ideal and sought to bring about an old man's dying wish. The atmosphere at San Lozaro had lightened, but now it would be fraught with danger again. A danger of her own making. She should have been more firm with Julio. Philip would blame her for her cousin's impetuous love-making, and he had turned from her in anger and scarcely-veiled contempt.

She felt that she could not reach him in that moment. The atmosphere between them was volcanic, as explosive as the dark soil under the crust of El Teide. One break and a whole torrent of fury must burst upon her defenceless head.

Anger against Julio crept uppermost. How dared he do a thing like this? She had never encouraged him to make love to her. She had only tried to be kind, to understand him and perhaps to protect him a little from his own swift passions.

Was kindness a thing, then, that he did not appreciate? Did Julio consider that nothing but love was possible between the sexes? If so, she *had* been to blame.

Confused and angry and strangely dispirited, she realized that Philip was not going to do anything to help her. He strode on ahead, leaving her to follow with Julio, who scowled and murmured, complaining that Philip had always interfered.

"He has always wanted everything to go his way," he declared. "Philip is a tyrant, but one day, we shall see!"

Conchita was strangely silent on the way back to San Lozaro. Like Julio, she looked almost sullen when her wishes had been thwarted for a reason she refused to accept, and she had wished to stay at Zamora. The dancing and the festivities would continue far into the night, but Isabella had looked tired after her long, exacting day and Philip had been adamant. They had been there since early morning. It was time that they went home.

Almost before the car had come to rest at the foot of the terrace steps Conchita flung herself out of it and rushed into the house, looking as if she would burst into a flood of angry tears at any moment.

"Go with her, Sisa," Philip advised. "It is late for you, *querida.*"

Sisa, whose long, silken lashes were already drooping over her dark eyes, kissed Felicity and obeyed. Julio had been driving and he whisked the car away in the direction of the stables.

"Goodnight, Felicity!" he called back to her with a laugh. "We will meet again in the morning!"

Felicity bit her lip. She was standing beside Philip on the top step and he made no effort to follow the others into the house. When the car had disappeared he looked down at the luminous dial of his watch.

"It's two o'clock," he said. "Are you very tired?"

"Not very." She felt as if the weariness of the whole world was weighing her down, but she could not tell him so. It was no physical weariness, and that was what he had meant. "Is there something you want me to do?"

"I want to speak to you," he said, "about Julio."

Her heart gave a swift lurch and then seemed to lie still. What could he want to say to her about Julio? She could not imagine anything short of censure as she followed him slowly through the house and out on to the *patio* overlooking the sleeping garden.

In the light of the new moon all the flowers seemed to have lost their flamboyant colouring and even the lotus looked pale. It hung in great fronds above their heads, cascading from the ornamental urns which topped the wall, but suddenly it was the overpowering scent of stephanotis which filled the night.

It was everywhere, in the very air they breathed, a heady, disturbing fragrance which she knew she would never be able to forget as long as she lived. It would remind her of this moment always.

Philip's stern profile was etched sharply against the yellow circle of the one lamp he had lit.

"What is the position between you and Julio?" he asked harshly. "Are you in love with him?"

"No!" Her voice felt strangled deep in her throat. "How could I be?"

"It would not be an unusual thing." His tone had not changed and there was no reaction to her confession to be seen in his hard, set face. "Julio is not without his attraction."

She pressed her hands together, moistening her suddenly dry lips.

"I'm not going to marry Julio," she said.

He moved then, warily, striding to the edge of the *patio* and back again before he spoke.

"Would you consider marriage," he asked, "with me?"

509

She looked up, stunned by the question for a moment. Philip was not looking at her. His eyes were fixed on the distant pale silhouette of El Teide, which they could see even in that uncertain half-light standing up there, tall and remote, above the valley.

"We must have some sort of stability at San Lozaro," he went on when she did not—could not—answer him. "If you are not in love with Julio he must be made to see that straight away or all sorts of complications will arise."

"I have told him that I am not in love with him," she whispered. "I have said that I don't want him to make love to me."

He turned, coming to stand beside her.

"Julio will take more convincing than that," he told her dryly. "He is all Spanish, and a Spaniard believes that a woman exists for love, which may be true or untrue. I do not know. The point is that we can't go on here at San Lozaro with a small volcano brewing beneath our feet all the time. These things explode eventually. It is best that Julio should understand immediately that you are not for him."

"And so you have asked me to marry you?" Her smile was a small hurt thing which he would barely be able to see in the inadequate lamplight. "What sort of marriage would it be, Philip—without love?"

He took a full second to answer, turning away again so that she could not see his face.

"There have been such marriages in the past," he said. "Built on mutual respect and a shared ideal. We have undertaken a task here at San Lozaro. I believe you are as serious about your part as I am about mine. We could live—peaceably enough together, I have no doubt."

"Because neither of us is in love? But I am in love, Philip! I am in love!"

It was a heart-cry, driven from her by the intensity and pain of her longing, and he turned to look at her sharply before he said:

"Are you going to marry this man, then? Is it someone you knew—in England?"

"No," she said unsteadily. "No, I shall never marry him." Her lips were trembling, but she drove the confession out. "He is not in love with me."

His eyes searched her face with a ruthlessness which she found hard to bear.

"You know that for the truth?" he asked.

"Yes. Yes, I know it."

He drew in a deep breath.

"We seem to be very much in the same boat," he acknowledged with surprising bitterness. "Would it be too difficult to suppose that my former suggestion might work out, all the same?"

"That I should marry you and—and chance our being happy?" Her voice shook. "Oh, Philip! if we could only understand each other! I know you can't be in love with me as you were with María, but——"

He stood waiting for her to continue. His face in profile looked like a mask hewn out of granite and his voice was equally hard when he said, at last:

"No, I am not in love with you as I was with María. That is past."

But you can't forget! You will never forget, Felicity thought desperately. And now you are in love with Isabella. That is a different sort of love, but equally lost to you because Isabella's faith will never permit her to consider her freedom. She has married Rafael and she will remain his wife. Your love is impossible and your heart is torn asunder. And now you have offered it to me. But is it really in the hope that it might be healed one day? Oh, Philip! Philip, she thought. If only I knew the answer!

"I'm not asking you to make up your mind immediately," he said. "I couldn't expect that, but we ought to have something concrete to present Julio with. The fact of our engagement, for instance. He will never be convinced otherwise."

She stood quite still, looking out over the silent garden without seeing the flowers now or any of the beauty of the night.

"I can't answer you, Philip," she said. "I have to think—to reason it all out. It has been so unexpected. Less than an hour ago I would not have believed it possible——"

She saw him smile, but he said gravely enough:

"And now that you know it is possible, how long are you going to take to make up your mind?"

She thought for a moment, her lower lip gripped tightly between her strong white teeth.

"Can you give me till to-morrow?"

He looked surprised.

"It is a decision that will affect your whole life, remember," he warned.

"Yes," she said, "that is true. But I shall know, I think, what I want to do—by to-morrow."

He came behind her, putting a hand heavily on either shoulder, and she could feel the magnetism which she had always known he possessed like something tangible between them.

"You know that once your decision is made I shall not let you reverse it," he said.

"I won't want to," she answered steadily. "I have always tried not to go back on a promise."

"I can believe that," he said, releasing her, although the pressure of his strong fingers still seemed to burn through the thin silk of her dress. "That was what kept you here, wasn't it, after your uncle died?"

"In a way," she said.

"What else could there be?" He turned her to face him. "Was it also a way of escape?"

She looked up at him, not understanding what he meant.

"From England," he supplied tersely, "and the man you loved?"

"No," she whispered, her heart twisting painfully because she could not tell him that she had never been in love until she had come to Tenerife. "No, it wasn't a way of escape."

"I don't think you would run away," he said briefly, "even from love."

She stood waiting as he turned to put out the lamp. There were other lights in the hall but here, in the *patio*, they were surrounded by an intimate darkness. The scent of stephanotis was stronger than ever, heady, powerful, well-nigh overwhelming.

"Philip," she said, "can you tell me why I should not marry Julio?"

The lamp flickered and went out. She saw him for a moment, vaguely, in the sudden darkness, his tall figure silhouetted against the paler oblong of the starlit garden and the distant, shining Peak. He moved then and in an instant she was in his arms, lying there submissive to his kiss.

It was a kiss of passion, sullen and fierce as Julio's might have been in similar circumstances, demanding, powerful, strong as the iron-hard pressure of his encircling arms. She felt the garden reel about her, the light of the stars blotted out as she closed her eyes, and only the scent of the stephanotis merging with the blurred image of her dream.

Then, just as suddenly, he had thrust reality between them again.

"I had no right to do that," he said. "Forgive me, if you can." He turned away, facing The Peak. "If it influences your final decision, I have only myself to blame."

She wanted to say so much to him, but words would not come and his kiss had confused her. She felt unnerved and at a loss, wanting him to take her in his arms again but realizing that he would not. A moment's madness had possessed him. That was all. Perhaps he had even confused her with Isabella or with the dead María for that split second when she had lain in his passionate embrace, feeling the warmth of his lips against hers as if they might draw her whole soul from her body with their strength.

"Go to bed now, Felicity," he said, and his voice was kinder, more tender than she had ever heard it. "Don't try to make any more decisions to-night."

She turned from him, disappointed yet glad to go. What sort of pride did she possess when she knew that she could have begged him to kiss her again, even if it were only with the thought of Isabella de Barrios in his heart?

He followed her to the foot of the staircase, but he did not bid her goodnight. He stood watching until she had reached the top, but when she had walked a little way along the gallery and looked over he had gone.

Out into the night? She did not know, but the first pale streamers of dawn were flying across The Peak before she finally slept herself.

CHAPTER VII

THE THING BELOVED

IN the morning she knew that she was going to give Philip her promise. She was going to marry him.

Oh, yes, it was second-best—even third-best if she allowed herself to consider María—but she had made up her mind to accept it. She had so much love to offer, so much to give that the question of an adequate return didn't seem to enter into it. Did you weigh love, or measure it, and ask how much you were receiving so that the two might be equal and nobody cheated? If she could give Philip peace of mind and some sort of sanctuary here at San Lozaro would that not be enough for her, too?

She said that it would, convincing herself in spite of the recurring ache in her heart, reiterating for her own comfort the fact that they had something to build together. And in building the home Robert Hallam had wanted for his children might she not be drawn into Philip's heart in the end?

That was her hope, her prayer, her one desire. Misgivings had haunted her through the hours of darkness, but with the quiet dawn her decision had been made. They could do so much in this sheltered valley—together.

That was what it amounted to. Being with Philip for the remainder of her life, not cast out into some desert place, alone. They could walk together hand in hand, in trust and companionship, so that the past might, in time, be forgotten or at least buried so deeply that it would rarely affect them.

She thought how odd it was that she should have come all that way to find her love; odd, too, that she had not known about Philip in that first moment of their meeting, but in the beginning he had seemed to resent her.

Now there was no resentment left. She was sure of that, at least.

Dressing slowly, she wondered when she would find the

opportunity to tell him what she had decided. He had said there was no hurry, and the memory sent a small stab of pain to her heart. She wanted to rush to him now, in the full flush of morning, and cry: "Philip, I love you. I will marry you whenever you like!" She wanted to hold out her arms to him, as any young girl might who had just found her love, but Philip had said there was plenty of time. He had been in no hurry to hear her decision. He might even have felt that he had made a mistake.

Her heart burned with shame as she thought of that passionate kiss of his and his subsequent withdrawal. Even then was he regretting the impulse which had made him ask her to protect the future for him?

Sick with uncertainty, she turned away from the mirror where she could see her slim young figure in the lovely blue dress she had selected for this special day in her life, and walked to the window.

It was open, and the faintly-cloying scent of stephanotis still lingered in the air, rising from the garden at her feet. Beneath the window a bed of tall arum lilies shone, wax-like in the sun, too bridal-looking for her to contemplate without a pang. The whole world about her was full of flowers, but they were flowers which lasted for so short a time. Once you stretched out eager hands to gather them they withered in a day. Even the lilies grew listless and lost their sheen too quickly.

Suddenly her eyes lifted and she was looking at The Peak. Strong, grey, enduring in the sunlight, El Teide rose above her and above the valley he had guarded since the beginning of time. His granite face was turned to the sky, his smile was inexorable, but beneath the hardness and the mystery and the remoteness there was a sense of peace enduring and the sky behind the snow-capped crest was very blue.

I mustn't have any doubts, she thought. Whatever happens, I must trust Philip.

She had almost forgotten about María's death, about the gossip there had been.

She went down to the terrace where her breakfast was set, only to find that Philip had gone. Julio, too, had left for the plantations and only Sisa was waiting for her.

"Is Conchita spending the morning in bed?" she asked, selecting a pear from the mound of freshly-picked fruit which the smiling Sabino placed before her. "She danced all day yesterday. She must be tired."

Sisa broke a warm crescent of bread and buttered it thoughtfully before she answered. Her dark, finely-shaped brows were drawn together, her eyes troubled by her inward thoughts.

"Conchita has gone back to Zamora," she said.

"Back to Zamora?" Felicity bit her lip. "But why?"

Sisa shrugged her bare shoulders.

"Because she is disobedient and wishes to show Philip that she will do as she pleases, and because he made her come away last night against her will when Rafael had promised to take her to Santa Cruz."

So that was it! Philip had not been mistaken when he had said that Conchita had no intention of dancing at the Country Club, suitably chaperoned by Isabella. She had wanted to spread her wings, to taste life in fuller measure, accompanied by Rafael, and Philip had been well aware of the fact. It was a difficult problem. Conchita was in her eighteenth year, but the fact remained that she had been placed in Philip's care. If she was to live on the island for the rest of her life, he could not afford to let her be seen in a Santa Cruz night club alone with Rafael de Barrios, no matter how friendly the two families might appear to be.

Yes, it was a difficult position, but one which Philip had sought to deal with in the only possible way. He had been firm, but now Conchita had outwitted him and returned to Zamora.

She had gone on the pretence of helping Isabella.

"But really it is Rafael she has gone to see," Sisa said. She sighed a little, as if she, also, had felt the impact of the Marqués' charm. "It is no wonder that everyone is drawn to Rafael. Even María would not have said that Rafael is a philanderer."

"María—knew him very well?"

Felicity's slow, measured tone brought the other's gaze back from the distance.

"Oh, yes," Sisa said. "She was very fond of him." She gave another little shrug, as if these things were inevitable. "But, you see, it was arranged that he should marry Isabella."

"Arranged?"

516

"Their families desired that it should be so."

"But, Sisa," Felicity protested, "these things don't happen nowadays!"

"Oh, yes," her cousin said, not even emphatically. "It is often so. Rafael was willing, and Isabella was in love with him. She had also a very large dowry. Her father had much money made from tin mines in South America."

Felicity pushed her fruit plate aside. She could not eat any more. Was Isabella's pathetic "marriage of convenience" the reason for the shadow in her dark eyes? Was she still in love with Rafael, or, greater tragedy still, had she come to realize the meaning of love too late, meeting Philip, perhaps, after her vows had been given? It was all so complicated, so difficult to understand.

"What must we do?" Sisa asked, jerking her back to the immediate problem of Conchita's return to Zamora in defiance of authority. "If Philip discovers Conchita's disobedience he will be very angry and none of us will be able to go to Zamora for a very long time. Even Philip will stay away, and that will grieve Isabella."

"I don't know what to do." Felicity rose to her feet, carrying her coffee cup to the terrace edge where she sat on the low stone balustrade looking out towards The Peak.

"What am I to do?" she asked aloud. "What would Philip wish me to do?"

"He would wish you to go to Zamora and bring Conchita back."

"How can I do that?" She turned to look at Sisa, thinking that already her cousin had a great deal of wisdom, the sort of knowledge not found in a girl of her age in a more northerly clime. "If I interfere Conchita may be angry and may do something rash, and then Philip's displeasure would fall on me."

"Not if you succeeded in bringing Conchita back to San Lozaro," Sisa pointed out. "Philip does not think that Conchita is really in love with Rafael. She is in love with the sort of life that Rafael leads when he is not at Zamora."

Once again Sisa's maturity surprised Felicity and now she knew that she was going to act on her cousin's advice.

"How can we get to Zamora?" she asked.

"Sabino will take us in the car."

"But supposing Philip should come back and wants to use it?"

"He will not come back before nightfall," Sisa said. "He has gone to Lozaro Alto."

The knowledge stabbed like a knife thrust deep into Felicity's heart. Philip had left the *hacienda* at dawn, probably after sleeping only for an hour or two. He had left before they were astir, before he could meet her again, to go to the valley where all his memories of the past lay buried. If he had wanted to revive those memories, he could not have chosen a better place, she thought bitterly. Remote and high, the hidden valley where tragedy had overtaken his love was forbidden ground to all of them. Only Philip might go there; and always he would go alone.

"He would ride up to the valley," Sisa said.

Felicity picked up her cup and replaced it on the marble-topped table. Her coffee was quite cold now, but she shook her head when Sisa offered to pour her some more.

"We must get away as soon as possible," she said. "Do you know how Conchita went to Zamora?"

"On horseback, across the ridge. There is a mule track that way," Sisa explained. "It is quicker, but it is not wide enough for a car to go. It is a very dangerous path, like the road up to Lozaro Alto."

They could see the winding thread of the pathway twisting up among the olive trees as they drove along the lower road to Zamora. It clung to the side of the mountain in places with barely a foothold, it seemed, the ground sloping steeply away from it to fall almost perpendicularly to the rock-strewn gullies below. It was old volcanic land, lavishly overgrown now, but treacherous underneath all that abundant sub-tropical vegetation, with small craters scarring it here and there, ugly black sores against the new green of maize and vine.

They screwed up their eyes, shading them with their hands for a first glimpse of a horse and rider on the distant path, but the hillside was without life.

"Conchita must have already got there," Sisa said. "She left more than an hour ago, when it was still cool, and she rides very hard."

Very hard and very recklessly? A new fear began to hammer at Felicity's heart.

"Are you sure she has had time to get to Zamora, Sisa?" she questioned anxiously. "It's a long ride——"

"Oh, Conchita would get there!' Sisa evidently did not share her nervousness on her cousin's behalf. "She can make Diablo go like the wind. Philip taught her to ride, you know."

But not for this, Felicity thought. Not recklessly across the canyon to meet Rafael de Barrios in a clandestine way!

For that, surely, was what Conchita intended to do. She had gone without leaving any message, prepared to face their censure on her return but determined not to be stopped by it beforehand.

Well, she must be stopped somehow!

"I can't make a scene, Sisa," Felicity decided as they approached Zamora. "For Isabella's sake we must persuade Conchita to come home quietly."

When they reached the villa, however, Isabella was there alone.

"We've come to say 'thank you' for yesterday." Felicity had tried to keep the note of anxiety out of her voice, but she was immediately aware of Isabella's understanding. "We decided to come over early," she added lamely.

"But you will stay, surely, for something to eat?" Isabella rang a bell for cooling drinks, and a platter of sun-warmed fruit was brought with them and placed on the low table in the *patio*. "Conchita has also been to say 'thank you,' but I persuaded her to ride back again before it became too hot. Sebastián has gone with her."

Felicity smiled her relief. Isabella had packed Conchita off home again with a suitable escort in the shape of an old and trusted family retainer.

But where was Rafael? He did not seem to be anywhere about the grounds or he would undoubtedly have joined them when he heard the car.

"Rafael has not yet returned from Santa Cruz," Isabella said, sensing the unspoken question. "No doubt he has business to do there this morning."

For the first time Felicity recognized the gentleness in Isabella. It was the quality she had sought to put a name to so often, the reason for Isabella's patience and her belief in the future. Because suddenly Felicity realized that the woman sitting facing her across the narrow table had such

519

a belief. This was her life. Somewhere, somehow, and at some time, there would be something to be made of it.

It was hardly an easy philosophy to accept and one that could only be made possible by Isabella's strong religious convictions, but was it also one that would work out in the end? Isabella de Barrios believed so.

Looking into the dark, calm eyes Felicity was humbly aware of her own shortcomings, her own doubt. She had doubted Philip and she had doubted Isabella, but unless she were set free from her marriage by the dispensation of Divine Providence, Isabella de Barrios would continue to honour it until she died.

Such was her way. Such had been her training all through life, and with it had come a tranquillity which was not often disturbed.

It was hardly ruffled now as she waited for her husband to return from the capital and Conchita to reach San Lozaro in safety.

"We won't stay for a meal, Isabella, if you don't mind," Felicity said when they had refreshed themselves. "Philip has gone to Lozaro Alto, but he may return and want the car."

For the first time Isabella frowned and the fleeting shadow which Felicity had seen so often behind the lovely eyes was there again.

"I wish he would not go to Lozaro Alto alone," she said. "He is only reviving a memory which would be best allowed to die."

"You mean María?" Felicity had made sure that Sisa was far enough away not to hear. "You think that he goes there because of María?"

"Yes. He blames himself needlessly for her death."

"The rumours were so cruel," Felicity said sharply. "How can he be expected to live them down—to forget so easily?"

"Philip is not affected by the rumours," Isabella said slowly. "These he can—and does—discount. Rumour is a thing to be treated with contempt when one is innocent. It is the people who feed the rumours who strangle themselves spiritually in the end. No, Philip is not unhappy about what is said of him in some quarters," she continued thoughtfully. "He does not need to care about that. When a man is at peace with his own conscience he has no fear.

520

Philip's whole reaction is one of overwhelming regret, I'm afraid."

Because he had ceased to care for María before she died? Again the bitter question rose in Felicity's mind, and although she sought to thrust it away, it persisted. Neither could she ask Isabella to share Philip's secret regret with her. Somehow she knew that Isabella had given Philip some sort of promise and that it must remain binding. Yet, if Isabella knew that Philip had asked her to marry him——?

No, she could not presume that the woman who looked at her so earnestly across the table would betray Philip's trust on any account. All she wanted was to know the truth, not to be kept shut out from Philip's confidences.

Jealousy had no part in the promptings of her heart now. She wanted to be loved completely, to be trusted and given her full share in the life of the man she loved.

Was that impossible?

"I wish you would come to San Lozaro more often, Isabella," she found herself saying as they shook hands. "I promised my uncle to stay there for a while, and now Philip wants me to stay. He believes that I can help him to make a home for Conchita and Julio."

"They are the difficult ones," Isabella agreed. "You will have no trouble with Sisa. She is too like her father—your uncle. Conchita and Julio are Spanish—and the Guanche strain is noticeable in Julio."

It was a repeated warning, a pointer to the fact that the greatest trouble might come through Julio in the end.

Felicity sat back in the car and allowed Sabino to drive home to San Lozaro much faster than Philip would have liked. There was an urgency about their return for which she could not account, and when they reached the *hacienda* to find that Conchita had not yet arrived, somehow she was not surprised.

Half an hour later the man, Sebastián, who had been sent with Conchita from Zamora, arrived leading Conchita's pony and his own mule. He looked ashamed and apologetic as he tried to give her an explanation.

"The señorita commanded me to return her horse," he said haltingly, and then broke into a flood of rapid Spanish, liberally interspersed with the local idiom, which Felicity was completely unable to understand.

521

"What does he say, Sisa?" she asked, but the sight of Sisa's face was enough.

"He says that Conchita has gone. He says that she met someone who has taken her to Santa Cruz."

"Does he—say who it is?"

The tears were very near Sisa's eyes as she hesitated, thinking perhaps to shield her sister, and then she seemed to decide that prevarication could not possibly help and would only confuse the issue.

"She has gone with the freight—in the plantation lorry with the bananas," she admitted.

"But Conchita wouldn't dare——"

"Oh, yes! If she wanted to go very much," Sisa said, "she would go—even that way."

"But the lorry will go straight to the docks!" Felicity protested. "And how will she get back before Philip comes home?"

"She can't get back. The lorry will not return until to-morrow. But perhaps someone will bring her home," Sisa suggested. "Conchita would not have gone unless she was very sure that Rafael was still in Santa Cruz, or at La Laguna. There is only one way he will come back—only one road. If he has already left Santa Cruz, Conchita will meet him on the way."

"But it's madness!" Felicity cried. "Anything might happen." Then quickly her lips set. "Sisa," she commanded, "tell Sabino not to put away the car. Tell him to wait. We are going to Santa Cruz."

As quickly she gave her orders to Sebastián. He was to return to Zamora and say nothing of his interrupted journey to his mistress. Felicity explained that she would tell the Marquesa herself when next they met. He had fulfilled his task to the best of his ability. He could do no more. Accustomed to receiving orders all his life, he would not even have thought of protesting to Conchita when she had changed them so dramatically half-way to San Lozaro, and now Felicity thanked him and told him to seek some refreshment in the kitchens and return to Zamora before the hour of *siesta* was fully upon them.

For herself and for Sisa there would be no *siesta*.

"Don't leave me behind, Felicity!" Sisa pleaded. "I may be able to help you. Conchita has told me much about her

522

dreams. It is in her heart to dance for a living and she believes that Rafael is the one to help her."

"Not in this way, Sisa," Felicity said, her heart pounding as she mounted the stairs to change swiftly into a cooler dress and find a shady hat for the long drive across the island. "The right way is to approach Philip."

"Conchita fears that Philip would not permit such a thing," Sisa informed her gravely. "It would be against my father's wishes."

That was sufficient for Felicity. She felt that her hurried journey to Santa Cruz was completely justified now, and they were on their way within half an hour.

As the little towns and villages along the coast dropped away behind them she had thoughts for nothing but the road ahead. Fields of asphodels and patches of wild lilies spread prodigiously on either hand, covering the land like snow, but she had no time to pause even at the sight of beauty. Walls clustered thickly with bougainvillaea flashed past unnoticed, and the wild broom flared arrogantly against the stone-crested peaks unseen by her anxious eyes.

Lean, brown-skinned men stood in the fields, reminding her of Julio, and women with crammed flower baskets on their heads stood waiting for the local buses that would carry them and their fragrant burdens to market. Children laughed, tossing bunches of camellias into the roadway, shouting "Peni? Peni!", a cry, she supposed, that they were taught from earliest childhood, and high up on the ledges and crevices of the *barrancos* wild cineraria in every shade of lilac stained the grey face of the rock.

The elements of a patriarchal world still lingered here and poverty was without too harsh a sting. There was always the sun and the blue sky and the ancient, strong, enduring root of peasant life firmly fixed in the good red earth. Yet Conchita was prepared to thrust it all aside, to discount it and change it for a life of gaiety in some city club.

Subconsciously Felicity began to look into all the lorries they passed on the way, but Conchita had had a good start.

"We will see my father's name on the lorry when we come up with it," Sisa reminded her.

A proud name. A good name. A name which Philip was determined to protect. Felicity's anger with Conchita increased with every mile they covered, but she was more angry still with Rafael de Barrios. Angry because of Conchita and because of Isabella, and in some subtle, inexplicable way, angry also because of Philip.

They passed four of the plantation lorries on the way to Santa Cruz, each with Robert Hallam's name painted clearly on the back, but in none of them was there any sign of her cousin. Could Conchita have changed her mind and returned by some other way?

There was no other way, Felicity reminded herself. Short of Rafael de Barrios' Mercedes passing them going in the opposite direction, with Conchita as a passenger, her cousin must by now be in Santa Cruz.

When they climbed on to the high moorland surrounding La Laguna a wind met them, bringing relief from the heat. They began to pass parked lorries by the roadside, their drivers lying beneath them in the shade sleeping through the *siesta* hour in the dust, and Felicity closed her eyes before each one, hoping that she would not read the familiar name of Hallam as she passed.

Conchita, of course, would have the necessary authority to command a plantation driver to press on to Santa Cruz without a rest. She would not want to spend the *siesta* hour perched on a lorry in the sun.

They began to drop down again towards the sea. Santa Cruz lay before them, stretching round the wide curve of its unbelievably blue bay, its yellow-washed houses with their red rooftops clustered thickly together over the arid slopes of the mountain behind it. Out to sea there was unlimited space. It was a town, Felicity thought, that seemed to stretch eager hands towards the sea.

They drove straight to the waterfront, and she bit her lip as she saw the groups of swarthy loafers on the quay. They had gathered in whatever shade they could find, true sons of a southern race, handsome, black-eyed, idle, whiling the time away and working only when it was necessary to earn a few *pesetas* for their daily bread.

Felicity's heart turned over as she looked at them, but there was no sign of the plantation lorry on the quay.

Sabino drove slowly at Sisa's command. They passed sturdy country women loading their donkeys and lines of bullock carts strung out along the cobbles, but still there was no sign of the vehicle they sought. The harbour was full of ships, loading and unloading, and mostly the cargoes were bananas for the lands of the northern hemisphere which knew so little about the sun. Crate upon crate of them stood stacked high in hold or on deck and jostled each other on the quay itself. No wonder, then, that a single lorry might easily disappear!

Sisa leaned forward and spoke to Sabino, who turned the car towards the town.

"I think I know where to go," she said when she sat back beside Felicity. "We have come here before—with Rafael."

Felicity was silent. She did not know what she was going to do if they should meet Rafael de Barrios here in Santa Cruz, but certainly she meant to take Conchita home to San Lozaro with her.

They crossed the wide Plaza de la Constitución with its high cross symbolizing the name of the port and turned into a broad avenue bordered by magnificent trees. Sabino seemed to know his way and very soon they had pulled up before a large, secluded hotel set in a well-laid-out garden.

Sisa was beginning to look nervous.

"Perhaps I am wrong" she said. "But it is here that we have come before."

Felicity did not hesitate.

"We will have something to eat here, anyway," she said. "Show me the way, Sisa."

There was no need. A commissionaire in a white uniform was at her elbow, ushering them into a spacious reception hall, and almost immediately she became aware of Conchita.

Her cousin was seated at a table at the far side of an inner, palm-shaded lounge where the splash of a fountain into a deep green basin was the predominating sound. Everything else was suitably subdued. The sunlight slanted coolly in through green, slatted blinds, the music was soft and the laughter low-pitched. It was an atmosphere of which even Philip might approve, but for the fact that Conchita sat alone at the table with the Marqués de Barrios.

Neither Rafael nor Conchita looked up as Felicity and Sisa crossed the cool, tiled floor towards them. Rafael was smiling and examining his finger-nails with a look of satisfaction in his eyes and Conchita was absorbed by what he was saying.

"But I am only keeping you to your promise, Rafael!" she protested in a hurt undertone as her cousin came within hearing distance. "You said you would get me this chance—to meet this man——"

She broke off, aware that they were no longer alone, aware that Felicity and her sister were standing there confronting her. For the time it took her to draw in her breath she had the look of a small girl caught in an act of disobedience, and then her face flushed scarlet and her eyes flashed their scorn.

"How dare you follow me!" she cried. "How dare you come here to spy! If Philip has sent you, please to tell him that I am not coming back to San Lozaro—ever. I will not go back to that—that prison!"

She spat the word out, but she had kept her voice low, too well-bred to make a scene, it would appear, or too afraid of what her escort might think. Her rage and disappointment were genuine enough, however, and Felicity even felt sorry for her.

"Come home, Conchita," she begged, "and talk it all over with Philip. It will not do any good taking the law into your own hands like this."

She had ignored Rafael, who was now on his feet making a great show of bowing over Sisa's hand before she snatched it away uncertainly and turned to her sister.

"Please do as Felicity says, Conchita," she begged. "She is right about Philip. Nothing will be gained by angering him in this way. He is our guardian."

"I will not listen to Philip!" Conchita cried, growing more excited. "Rafael, tell them I will not listen to Philip any more! Tell them that it is you who will say what I am to do in the future."

The Marqués looked uncomfortable.

"*Querida*—look," he said. "All this has been too sudden, even for me. I can't keep you here in Santa Cruz. I must go back to Zamora myself. We had arranged nothing. You have simply taken the bull by the horns and rushed off at a tangent. Of course I promised to speak to Luis for you, but not at half a day's notice. These things take time. You must have patience, *querida*. You must learn to wait."

The bright light of expectancy flickered and died slowly in Conchita's eyes.

"You mean that you will send me back, that you will not keep your promise?" she asked falteringly.

She had forgotten Sisa and Felicity. There was nobody in the world for her in that moment but Rafael, Marqués de Barrios, but all she could see in his handsome face was impatience.

"Of course I shall keep my promise," he assured her briefly. "But the time is not yet ripe."

"You mean to go away!" Conchita's face was completely colourless now. "You will return to Spain and I shall not see you again for many months. I know how it is, Rafael, when you want to go away!"

"For your comfort," he said arrogantly, "I am not going to Spain for several weeks yet. There is no reason for me to go." His eyes lingered on Felicity's set face and tightly-compressed lips, willing her to return the smile he gave her. "I am perfectly happy here. And now, since we are all in Santa Cruz so unexpectedly," he added, as if it had been, indeed, the most chance of meetings, "let me order you something to eat. First of all, we will have a bottle of wine, though."

"No, thank you," Felicity refused stiffly. "We must get back as quickly as possible."

"But that is ridiculous!" he protested. "You cannot drive back all that way without food. It would also look—un-civilized to walk straight out after you have just come in. Conchita will return with you," he added without giving Conchita a second look, "as soon as we have had our lunch."

It was three o'clock. Felicity glanced at her watch and supposed that he was right. Nothing would be gained by creating a scene in a place like this and to walk out would be stupid, as he had just suggested. There would be the question of finding another suitable restaurant, too, in a town she did not know, and the possibility of losing contact with Conchita.

That was the deciding factor. Conchita was already half convinced that she should return to San Lozaro. It would be madness to leave her now.

The meal was the usual leisurely Spanish one, served elaborately by three waiters in white coats and the majordomo, a large, swarthy man with a wide, welcoming smile which embraced the whole world in general and Rafael de Barrios in particular. He hovered round their table and had obviously an eye for a pretty girl, because he paid Conchita the compliment of bending very low over her hand when they rose to leave.

Felicity had drawn a quick breath of relief when their coffee had arrived. She had refused the accompanying cognac which Rafael had suggested and was foolishly pleased when Conchita also shook her head.

Throughout the meal her cousin had been curiously silent, sitting almost sullenly in her chair and eating very little. It had seemed as if Conchita's temper might erupt again at any minute. The fiery, smouldering embers were not yet extinguished in her eyes and she twisted and re-twisted the small scrap of linen and lace that was her handkerchief as she sat waiting for Rafael to finish his brandy.

Felicity turned to the door. She was more than impatient to be out again in the fresh air, to be rid of Rafael, although she knew that she could not shake him off for ever. He was the type to whom a rebuff came in the nature of a challenge, and although he was probably already tiring of Conchita, he would not let her go until he had made the decision for himself.

Somehow she felt sure of that, and was strangely afraid in consequence.

At the door she turned, waiting for Sisa. Her cousin came out into the full glare of the afternoon sunlight and stopped as if she had suddenly been turned to stone. She was looking beyond Felicity at the car which had drawn up at the kerb and the man who had jumped out from behind the steering-wheel with anger and impatience in his eyes.

"Philip——!"

Felicity swung round with a madly-beating heart to find Philip mounting the three broad steps to the hotel door-way. He was furiously angry. She could see it in his eyes and in the hard set of his jaw, and it was an anger which embraced them all.

"I had a vague idea that I might find you here," he said, keeping his temper in check with an obvious effort. "When you are ready, I will take you back to San Lozaro."

"We were coming home, Philip." The appeal in Felicity's

voice seemed to pass him by. "I—we came to Santa Cruz for the day. I did not think you would mind. Sisa said you had gone to Lozaro Alto——"

Her voice trailed away. He knew that she was lying, that this was no innocent trip thought up on the impulse of the moment. He believed that it had been planned while they had been at Zamora at the *fiesta*. And how could she deny it, other than by telling him the truth?

Conchita appeared on the steps behind them with Rafael by her side.

"Good heavens, Arnold! this is an honour for Santa Cruz!" the Marqués laughed. "It is not often that we see you on this side of the island in search of the bright lights!"

"The bright lights have never attracted me," Philip told him curtly. "They are too artificial." He looked straight at Conchita. "You had better find a wrap for the journey back," he advised.

"I will not come!" Conchita stamped her foot. "You cannot make me do as you wish, Philip. I am old enough to please myself!"

"Not in this way."

Philip took her by the elbow, leading her firmly towards the waiting car, and for a fraction of a second Felicity thought that Conchita was going to create a scene. She pulled against her guardian's arm, but his was the superior strength, and finally she subsided in the back seat in a flood of humiliating tears.

"Querida," Rafael said softly, coming to the side of the big hired car, "you must not act in this way! I shall remember my promise. I shall speak for Luis for you—one day."

Felicity knew that he had no intention of speaking to the elusive Luis or to anyone else on Conchita's behalf. He had made a promise idly and he would lie his way out of it as charmingly as he could, leaving it to Philip to bear the brunt of Conchita's disillusionment and despair.

Philip stood stiffly on the pavement while they piled into the car. He did not attempt to offer Rafael a lift back to the valley.

"There's Sabino," Felicity remembered. "I sent him to get some food——"

"I have already seen Sabino," Philip answered, holding the front door of the car open for her because Sisa had already climbed into the back in an effort to comfort her sister. "I found the car parked in the Cruz Verde. He is now on his way home to San Lozaro."

She knew that he was grudging the time he had been forced to spend in pursuit of them, but more than anything else his anger lay in the fact that they had come to Santa Cruz with Rafael de Barrios. That was what he thought. He had accused her silently. She was as much, if not more to blame than Conchita in his eyes.

Rafael stood back on the pavement, bowing with a small, relieved smile as they drove away.

"I wish you hadn't had to make this long journey, Philip," Felicity began tentatively as the frowning buttress of San Cristobal towered above them and they made their way out of the city. "I—we meant to be back before dark."

"You could scarcely have managed it," he answered curtly. "It is after four now, and you did not appear to be in any great hurry to leave."

"I'm sorry," she apologized, because there was nothing else she could say. A small pulse was hammering in his cheek, which suggested that his anger had in no way abated, and the blue eyes were fixed sternly on the uphill way ahead. "How did you know where we were?" she asked lamely.

"I came back to the *hacienda* unexpectedly," he told her dryly. "Evidently I was not supposed to do that."

"Philip, please listen," she said beneath her breath so that her voice would not carry to the seat behind them. "I didn't come to Santa Cruz to meet Rafael de Barrios. We—met him just over an hour ago at the hotel."

"Please don't lie to me," he said harshly. "I can stand anything but that."

"You've got to listen——"

"I would prefer not to. We can't discuss this thing here. Please leave it till we get back to San Lozaro."

She felt crushed and humiliated, but she could not blame Philip for what he thought. Had she not shown a marked preference for Rafael de Barrios' company in the beginning?

Her heart felt like ice. Did this mean the end of any trust between herself and Philip, the end of companionship? He had asked her to marry him, but what would be his reaction now?

They drove in a stony silence, past the pink and cream-washed villas on the hill with their green shutters and red-tiled roofs and the cascades of purple clematis spilling over their boundary walls almost to the road. The sea far beneath them was green and blue in alternate patches, with little ships dotting the horizon, and the serried ranks of dark mountain peaks before them were flushed by the dying sun.

When it sank abruptly into the western ocean the darkness came like the cut of a knife, and Philip switched on his lights.

Felicity shivered. She had forgotten a coat; she had forgotten everything but the need to get to Santa Cruz in time to intercept Conchita.

Philip drew the car up by the roadside. He took off his jacket and handed it to her.

"Here, put this on," he commanded. "We can't afford to let you catch pneumonia."

Had he some use for her, then—still something he felt that she could do?

"I can't take your coat, Philip," she protested weakly, thrusting it back towards him.

"I think you must do as you are told," he said briskly, although not too unkindly. "The effects of our abrupt nightfall can be severe and we are still fairly high up. Sisa and Conchita can wrap themselves in the car rug."

Sisa had brought a little woollen bolero and Conchita had the protection of her riding-breeches and the jacket she had worn over her silk shirt for her early-morning departure from San Lozaro. He pulled the hood of the car up, fastening it securely on either side before he got in behind the wheel again and drove off.

Felicity drew the proffered jacket about her shoulders. Huddled in its warmth, she felt nearer to Philip than ever before; nearer, yet in some ways, much, much further away. The scent of the tobacco he used stung her nostrils, reviving the nostalgic memory of these moments when she had lain close in the shelter of his arms, feeling the touch of his lips strong against her mouth. It had been a passionate kiss, demanding and fierce, and in some ways it had not been Philip. It had been too destructive, too much laced with anger to give her any lasting satisfaction. There was more than cruelty and arrogance in his make-up.

Somewhere there was kindness and tolerance and the desire to trust, and it was that she wanted.

For a brief moment he had permitted her a glimpse of it, and then he had turned away. Were there to be no more glimpses, no more trust between them?

Far beneath them as they wound along the rambling coastal road the illuminations of little fishing ports pricked out against the velvet backcloth of the sea, and above them a thin chain of lights that looked like stars traced the steep wandering of a village street against the mountainside. It was a magic night, with a cool breeze straying in from the Atlantic to lift the topmost feathers of the palms, and the white snow cap of The Peak held the last radiance of the sun for a long time, as if in eternal wonder.

Yet the night's magic was lost to Felicity because her heart was out of tune.

When they reached San Lozaro there was a short, sharp brush with Conchita. She got down from the car to confront Philip on the terrace steps.

"Whatever you say, whatever you try to do," she told him bitterly, "I shall never agree to stay here! You may be my guardian but you are not my gaoler! I have it in me to sing, and I have always danced better than anyone else. You know that, Philip, for you have danced with me and said so! You cannot keep me here, because, if you do, I shall die! *I shall die!*"

It was the impassioned outburst of an angry child, of the teenager determined to try her wings, but Felicity realized that behind it Philip recognized another danger. It was the danger of Conchita herself, of a tempestuous nature that gave little thought to consequences when she saw herself about to be deprived of the thing she wanted most.

She rushed off, followed by Sisa, who was now in tears.

"So much for our happy home atmosphere," Philip said between his teeth as Sabino appeared to drive the hired car away. "I seem to be handling everything in quite the wrong way."

The unexpected admission surprised Felicity, coming so closely on the heels of his anger and the events of this disastrous day.

"You have had tremendous patience," she acknowledged, "but perhaps Conchita does need another sort of understanding. I believe she is really serious about her singing, and all young people love to dance. It's a form of expression they need."

"I've thought of that," he agreed. "I shall speak to Conchita again in the morning when she has calmed down a little, but I have no intention of allowing her to dance in a cheap café in Santa Cruz."

She put a hand on his arm.

"You won't be too hard on her, Philip, will you?" she begged.

He looked at her fully then, his eyes very faintly amused.

"That would appear to be my rôle in life," he said grimly, "but I think I have told you before that I am not exactly an ogre, Felicity."

"I know you're not," she said, biting her lip. "I know you didn't mean to be so angry this afternoon when you found us in Santa Cruz, but how could you help it?"

Instantly his face changed.

"I hadn't expected to have to rush off to Santa Cruz in pursuit of Conchita," he said, "nor of you."

"No," she admitted, "I should have been here when you came back from Lozaro Alto." She turned to face him in the swaying light from the lantern above their heads. "Yesterday you asked me to marry you, Philip," she reminded him steadily. "Do you still want me to be your wife?"

He stood for a moment as if he had not heard her, and then he said almost guardedly:

"Nothing has changed. I still feel that I need your support here at San Lozaro."

Nothing of love; nothing of wanting her for himself! Her heart sank even while she tried to tell herself that "nothing had changed," as he had just reminded her. She had already accepted his reasons for their marriage. She was prepared to go to him—without love.

"I wondered," she said, gazing unhappily into the night. "I thought that perhaps—after this afternoon—you might have changed your mind."

Her voice had dropped until it was no more than a whisper, but he did not move away, so that he must have heard. Yet he stood silently, the light from the wind-blown lantern moving rhythmically across his face, leaving it now revealed and now in shadow so that she could only guess at his thoughts until he spoke.

"I didn't go to Lozaro Alto this morning, after all," he told her. "I want you to come there with me."

She felt her throat grow tight. It was something that she would never have expected, but she could not ask him if he was sure about the things he did. He always had a reason for them.

"I'd like to come," she said simply as they turned into the lighted hall. "Are you going to cultivate the land up there, Philip? Is it suitable for farming?"

He smiled broadly.

"Wait and see!" he said. "It's not at all like San Lozaro, if that's what you mean."

She did not want it to be like San Lozaro. The lower valley with all its beauty and lush vegetation, with its vineyards and its ragged green banana plantations, had been the lavish source of her uncle's great wealth, but it was also full of conflict. There was no peace in San Lozaro, and somehow she knew that Philip wanted peace.

Was that what he sought at Lozaro Alto? Was there more up there among his high, remorseless mountain peaks than the gnawing reminder of tragedy? She thought that she might find the answer if she went there with Philip—alone.

That was what he had meant. They were to go there together, without Sisa and without Conchita, and try to iron out the way of the future for them all.

She wondered if that also included Julio, for Julio and Philip were still the bitterest of enemies.

CHAPTER VIII

LOZARO ALTO

PHILIP was seated on the terrace over his second cup of coffee when Felicity came down to breakfast the following morning. He had, she discovered, already been out.

"I've been down to the plantations," he told her. "We have a consignment of bananas to get away before the week-end, but the tomato harvest is over. We've nothing to do now but clear the terraces for the next crop." His keen gaze swept the surrounding hillsides. "This is tremendously fertile country, Felicity. It can support crop after crop—maize, corn, vines, bananas, potatoes and all the citrus fruits you can name."

"It's the orange trees I like best," Felicity said with a rush of warmth finding her heart, because here, it seemed, they were on common ground. "When I first saw one it looked like a tree full of little golden suns. It was growing all alone in a garden, but it seemed to light up all the small space, it looked so bright and full of colour."

"Wait till you see an orchard of them!" he smiled. "I want to grow oranges at Lozaro Alto. The valley floor is rich and deep." He paused, with a look in his eyes which took in the future, the look of a man with an ideal. "It was once volcanic and that is the very best soil you can wish for once it becomes friable. There's a lot of work to be put into the valley yet, of course, but I can start to do it, bit by bit."

Felicity wondered if he had made these plans with María long ago, seeing the future up there at Lozaro Alto as something for which they might strive together. She wondered, too, what María had really been like. There was no photograph of her about the *hacienda,* which was strange, since the Spaniards were prone to collect such mementoes of their children from earliest infancy onwards.

"Did you always plan to farm at Lozaro Alto, Philip?" she asked.

His face hardened at her question, the smile fading out of his eyes.

"It has always been an ambition of mine," he said curtly, but that was all.

They sat in a tense little silence till Julio came in. Felicity had not seen him the day before, and now he looked from her to Philip with deep suspicion in his eyes.

"What has happened to Conchita?" he asked. "I saw her riding up into the valley an hour ago."

In a split second Philip was on his feet.

"You're sure of this?" he asked.

"Quite sure." Julio gave him an odd look. "Was she running away from you, Philip?" he asked.

"I doubt it." Philip's lips were tight. "But I can always go and make sure."

Felicity pushed her chair back.

"Philip——?" There was an anxious question in her eyes.

"No," he said, "I won't do anything rash, but neither must Conchita. I told her I wanted to speak to her this morning, but I can do that just as easily at Lozaro Alto as here." He looked at Julio, as if he might be assessing his worth in an emergency. "I must leave you to see that the bananas get off in time, Julio," he added. "Twenty lorry-loads. They must be at Puerto de la Cruz before twelve o'clock. They're crated and ready in B shed. All you have to do is to see that the bills of lading are correctly filled in and that the men set off in time. You needn't go to Puerto with the lorries," he said, as an afterthought—or was it a warning?

He had put Julio in charge of an important consignment of fruit which would be lost profit if it failed to reach the port in time to be loaded on to the banana boat which was waiting there. It was the sort of authority Julio had always wanted, yet he was frowning when Philip turned away.

"It is always the same," he grumbled. "Always Philip would do the job better himself!"

"No," Felicity said, "he trusts you, Julio."

"And I hate him! I hate him because he will not leave us alone," her cousin cried. "He will not permit us to go our own way. He is the guardian, the maker of rules which we must obey, and they are all harsh rules. Look

536

how he will not let Conchita dance and be gay! Philip will not let anyone be happy because he is unhappy himself. He has a black regret in his heart because of María!"

"Julio, he loved María," Felicity said gently.

"That is what he tells you because he hopes to make you stay here for his own purpose!" Julio cried. "Then—when he does not need you any more—when he has ceased to want you—he will get rid of you as he did of María."

"You mustn't say that, Julio!" Her voice was sharp and firm. "Because, you see, I don't believe it. I believe that this—this accident was exactly as Philip said. A car went out of control and went over the cliff. It could happen to anyone. Miraculously, Philip was saved."

"Miraculously!" Julio echoed scathingly. "Yes, it was miraculous. Philip had no scratch, no bruise on his whole body, but María was dead!"

"Please, Julio," Felicity begged, "can we not talk about it? We can't forget about it, of course, but we can let it remain in the past."

"Is that what Philip has told you to do?" He put down his cup when he had drunk the last of his coffee without eating anything. "He is strong enough—ruthless enough —to make you think as he desires." He came to stand close behind her chair. "Has he also made love to you?" he demanded.

"He has asked me to marry him," Felicity said as steadily as she could.

Julio swung her round to face him, his hands rough and hard on her shoulders.

"And what have you said? What answer have you given him?" he demanded.

"I have told him that I will."

"That you will?" He stared at her incredulously, and then all the devils and furies which possessed him at times seemed to break loose in his dark eyes. They burned and glowed with a fierce light as he looked at her. "The Holy Virgin protect you, then!" he said through set teeth. "Philip will kill you, one way or another. You have given your life to him as a hostage."

"Julio," she protested, "you must understand——"

Her entreaty had fallen on deaf ears. Julio shook her as if she were a child.

"You do not belong to him!" he cried. "You are mine! I shall kill him if he tries to take you away from me!"

He strode off along the terrace and down the steps, not looking back nor apparently hearing her cry of recall, the flash of the brilliant scarlet shirt he wore passing swiftly between the trees. She knew that he was going to follow Philip, but there was nothing she could do. Nothing! Nothing!

Desperately she strove for calmness, forcing back the panic in her heart. She must stop Julio at any price. She did not expect for a moment that his murderous threat against Philip would ever be carried out, but Philip had left him a task to do at the plantations and she must see that he did it. It was important to San Lozaro that the bananas should get away in time, but it was doubly important—to Philip and Julio—that Julio should not neglect his duty in a fit of rage.

It would take her five minutes, perhaps, to change into riding-breeches and a shirt. Philip had taken the car, but she knew that Julio would follow on horseback. She would try to catch up with her cousin before he left the plantations and persuade him to come back.

A quick glance at the sky showed her The Peak hazed in a thin veil of cloud, but that was often so in the early morning. It would dissolve when the sun strengthened, even though there were other, darker clouds hanging about the lesser peaks. It was, she realized, insufferably warm for so early in the day and there was a sort of heavy listlessness in the air which she had not experienced before.

Thunder growled its warning somewhere as she came back along the terrace to find Sisa cutting into an avocado pear. Her cousin extracted the stone with expert ease before she looked up.

"Oh," she said disappointedly. "Where are you going?"

"I'm going to meet Philip." Felicity hesitated, and then added, as if it were the most natural thing in the world to ask: "Have you ever made out a bill of lading, Sisa?"

"For the shipping company? Oh, yes," Sisa smiled. "Often I used to help my father with such things when he was very busy. But never at the offices," she added. "Always here."

"If—Julio doesn't come back in time, do you think you could do some to-day?" Felicity moistened dry lips. "Sabino will go to the offices in the bullock cart and bring the papers back here for you to sign. Then you will tell him what to do at Puerto. He has only to hand over the consignment and get the bills signed there. You are quite sure you can do this, Sisa?"

"Quite sure!" Sisa looked slightly puzzled. "But where has Julio gone?" she asked.

"He—has a message for Philip."

"And Philip is on his way to Lozaro Alto? I see," Sisa agreed. "I will do as you say, Felicity, but is it right that you should ride alone, even as far as Lozaro Alto?"

"I shall meet Philip." Felicity's voice had all but trembled, but she was determined not to let her cousin see her distress. "I shall be all right."

She hurried away from the terrace through the open french windows into the dining-room, where the sun had not penetrated. Coming from the blinding light of the garden into the shaded room, she could not see for a moment, and then she was aware of Sabino holding something on a tray. He thrust it towards her.

"For you, *señorita!*" he said. "I am to give it to you only."

A spray of small white flowers lay on the silver salver, flowers which, for a moment, she mistook for orange blossom. They were twisted roughly into the shape of a wreath—a bridal wreath?

She realized almost immediately that it was a spray of stephanotis. The orange blossom was long since past. She could not understand the gift, nor could she imagine who might have sent it, but she lifted the flowers tenderly, aware of the strong, sweet perfume which filled all the room, and hoping in her heart that they had come from Philip.

"Who has sent them, Sabino?" she asked.

"It is Don Julio's gift," the old servant said with an odd little shake of his head. "He has ask me to see that you get them very soon."

Something hard and cold had touched Felicity's hand as she lifted the flowers, and when she looked down at them again she saw a small, exquisitely-carved rosary lying among the white blossoms.

"Julio!" she gasped beneath her breath. "Why have you done this?"

"It is María's rosary!"

Sisa had come through the windows behind her. She was standing gazing down at the flowers and the tiny cross and her eyes were suddenly tragic.

"Who could have done this?" she cried with a hint of Conchita's easily-aroused passion in her young voice. "Who could have been so cruel? María died on her wedding day."

Felicity's heart turned over. What was Julio trying to do? What message did he mean his flowers to convey? Desperately she fought for control of the situation.

"I don't know, Sisa," she lied. "Will you take María's rosary and keep it safely? Do not let anyone take it again."

Sisa put the beads into the front of her dress. She looked sad and disturbed.

"Sabino," Felicity said, turning to the old servant, "you must go to the plantation offices for me. I want you to bring the bills of lading here if Señor Don Julio is not at the office himself. Then you will return with them when they are signed. You will see that the lorries are all away from the packing sheds before twelve o'clock. There must be no *siesta* before the last lorry has gone. Do you understand?"

"*Si, señorita!*" Sabino obviously thought it strange to be taking orders from a woman, especially orders of this nature, but it was not his place to disagree with anything the señorita said. "I will go," he added. "I will do as you have tell me."

"You will wait here, Sisa." Felicity turned to her cousin. Should she, after all, confide in Sisa? She decided against it. "Julio may come back quite soon—or return to the plantation. Then there will be no need for you to sign the bills."

Sisa nodded.

"You, also, will soon return?" she asked anxiously.

"Yes—quite soon."

Impulsively, and without quite knowing why she should do so, Felicity stooped to kiss the younger girl on the cheek.

"I can trust you, Sisa," she said.

Realizing that she should have asked Sabino to saddle

a horse for her, she made her way towards the stables. It was too late now. He was already on his way to the plantation offices. She must manage for herself.

It cost her precious time. She had only learned to ride since she had come to San Lozaro and she had never saddled her own mount. Sabino, or one of the other servants, had always brought the horse round to the terrace steps for her, or Philip himself had mounted her. Now she had to do it for herself, or waste still more time looking for someone to take Sabino's place. The average Spanish serving man could make himself more scarce than water in a drought, she realized, as she struggled with a refractory girth, but the animal Philip had recommended for her use was patient enough. He turned his head quizzically when she fumbled unnecessarily and laid back his ears when the saddle slipped, but he did accept her, and that was the main thing.

"Treasure," she said, laying a persuasive hand on his smooth red flank, "I want you to go like the wind!"

The horse was sensible, however, and did no more than trot, even when they reached the adequate shade of the eucalyptus trees which fringed the road to Lozaro Alto on its first uphill stretch.

Soon, however, the taller trees began to thin out, the eucalyptus giving place to chestnut and the chestnut to pine until they finally reached the arid wastes above the valley. There was no sign of life up here after the last charcoal-burner's hut had been passed, and the sun was not so bright, although it was still stiflingly warm.

She rode on for what seemed an eternity, hearing the distant growl of thunder like a roll of drums echoing and re-echoing among the crags and pinnacles of this desert place.

The heat seemed to be choking her and there was a band of fire about her brow. She put up her hand, as if to brush it away. I can't faint now, she thought. I can't give in!

The road wound on, interminably, she fancied, but she knew that she had come all this way before. She could not see The Peak now. It was somewhere above her, hidden behind the grey haze which had thickened considerably since she had left the valley behind.

Then, suddenly, she knew that she had missed the way

541

to Lozaro Alto. She had come too far. Somewhere back along the winding, dusty road behind her the scarcely discernible path which Conchita had pointed out on their way back from Las Canadas went deep into Philip's secret valley. She had missed her way and lost precious time.

She was conscious now of time as the main element in her journey and she bit her lip with vexation as she turned her horse and rode slowly back downhill again.

The heat was overpowering now and the rumble of the thunder seemed to come from beneath her feet rather than from the brazen sky above her head. There was a strong smell of sulphur in the air and a tense, deathly stillness. It was some time, she realized, since she had noticed a bird in flight.

Her patient mount trudged on, but there was a nervousness about him now for which she could not account. He appeared to be relieved that they were on their way back to San Lozaro.

When they eventually came to the narrow entrance to the upper valley, half hidden by a screen of stunted sage, he refused to go on. Nervously he sniffed the air, his sensitive nostrils quivering as he pawed the ground before him.

"Treasure, you must!" Felicity besought him. "You must take me there. I may be needed."

Her voice faltered on the final words. She could hardly breathe for the heat, and a desperate unnamed fear rose in her heart.

How long had she taken? How much time had she lost by missing the path and riding those extra miles along the ridge? She had left her watch behind her in her haste to get away, but time seemed scarcely measurable in the ordinary way up here.

She glanced up at where the sun should have been, to see only a molten ball of fire glaring at her through the haze. I've got to go on, she thought. I've got to go on!

The narrow road to Lozaro Alto went down into a steep *barranco* whose sides looked almost precipitous. Great jagged pinnacles of rock towered heavenwards, red and fantastic-looking in the peculiar light of the veiled sun, yet she could see far beneath her a valley of great beauty.

Cradled between these savage mountain crests, Lozaro Alto was a valley to be dreamed about, deep and narrow and green, with trees already growing on its steep sides and a stream running clearly down its entire length.

Life-giving water! No wonder Philip saw it as his future home. Here toil would be abundantly rewarded. Here the vine would grow on the terraced hillsides again and the valley itself would be white with orange blossom covering a thousand trees. There would be maize in the hollows in the spring, and the emerald of corn. They would plant figs and limes and a red camellia tree——

She tore her thoughts away from her smiling vision of the future to attend to the present. Treasure had come to an abrupt halt on the narrow road, quivering in every limb, and the sun had hidden its face again. Even as she watched, the whole world seemed to grow dark. She felt the thunder beneath her feet again and the valley rocked gently as she looked.

The sun, she thought. I've been too long in the sun!

Carefully, steadily, she got down from the saddle, thinking to find some shade for a moment, and almost immediately she felt the earth tremble again. With a final, desperate whinny of terror, Treasure took to his heels and fled.

"Treasure! Treasure——!"

Her voice seemed to echo mockingly through space. He would neither heed nor obey. She watched the cloud of dust which obscured him rise and disappear in the distance. She was alone.

Despair settled on her like the haze that was steadily creeping towards her down the mountainsides. What could she do? What could she possibly do to reach the valley now that Treasure had deserted her?

For a moment her anger with the horse was uppermost, but very soon she recognized the true implication of his flight. Roll upon roll of what she had taken for thunder shook the crags on every side of her, and suddenly the guardian peak which looked down over Philip's hidden valley began to belch smoke from its rugged side.

A blow-hole, she thought in horror. A miniature crater torn in the solid rock by the molten inferno within!

Fear seized her, and a terrifying sense of her desperate vulnerability. She was alone, so alone that the very crags seemed to threaten her and the sight of even a bird of prey would have been welcome. There was no movement anywhere now. The whole valley seemed to be lying still, crouched in expectancy before the coming fury of volanic wrath.

I'm trapped, she thought. Trapped up here by my own stupidity. I should never have got down, never let Treasure go!

Once more panic seized her, and then she was conscious of the calm of acceptance. Philip was somewhere down there in the valley. Somehow she must reach him.

The road she followed wound slowly uphill, however, nearer and nearer to the crater's edge, and the air she was breathing was full of sulphur. It was a difficult, narrow road, with a sharp drop of hundreds of feet on one side down into the valley below. She wondered despairingly if she had come the wrong way, only to remember that Conchita had said that there was only one road into the valley. This road; the way she must go. The way by which she and Philip, Conchita and Julio must come out.

It was so dark now that she could hardly see. A dull, molten cloud had effaced the sun and it seemed to be pressing down close against the sides of the peaks ahead of her. Then, with a terrifying sound which shook the whole *barranco* from top to bottom, the side of a hill caved in and a great fountain of smoking rock and stone leapt into the windless air. Cinders and sparks showered down to cover the whole road ahead of her, and she drew back in terror.

For an endless second she stood watching, her eyes dilated, her heart thumping heavily against her ribs, but the trembling of the earth had ceased. All sound had suddenly fled, leaving a dreadful, awful calm.

There was nothing left in Felicity's mind but the desire to reach Philip. She began to run forward along the path, gasping for breath as she went, stumbling in the darkness and subtly aware of a silent, moving thing somewhere on the steep hillside above her. It was fear, she thought, fear of the unknown. There was nothing there—no tangible thing.

Her breath came in agonized gasps, but the road seemed to be going downwards now, into the valley. Suddenly a flare of angry light seared the sky above her and she saw the whole narrow *barranco* lying at her feet. It looked cold and completely deserted.

For the first time she faced the possibility that Philip might not be there. If he had heard these terrible warnings inside the mountain, wouldn't he already be well on his way back to San Lozaro? Philip, and Conchita, and Julio?

Her heart stood still and a frenzy of loneliness caught her by the throat. The grim, Dante-esque columns of rock on all sides seemed to be pressing closer, slowly, relentlessly, before she began to run.

She ran back along the way she had come in the semi-darkness of the veiled day, stumbling, choking, almost unable to breathe, until gradually a peculiar, diffused light spread across the distant pinnacles of rock until it reached her feet. It lit up the surrounding hillsides and the way ahead.

Then, with a small, inarticulate cry, she had drawn back. It was as if the thing which had moved unseen in the darkness had touched her.

Above her, belching out of the mountainside, a slow stream of boiling lava came steadily down towards the road.

She stood, frozen in horror, watching it, fascinated by the slow-motion destruction of it, a red and black avalanche sweeping everything before it. There was the hot smell of sulphur and a rain of ash as it burned its way forward, and she could see the red core of it, the angry, semi-fluid heart of the lava itself, and the mass of slate-grey rock and stones above. It hurtled down towards her, with the plant life withering and crumbling yards in front of it, and involuntarily she stepped back.

Hours later, when she found herself trapped in the valley, she wondered why she had not run for her life in that terrible moment of indecision, but in that moment, too, she had become aware of the subtle power of instinct which told her that Philip was still at Lozaro Alto.

She fled back along the path, pausing to look only when she was sure that she was out of range of that dark river of death.

The flow seemed to have speeded up, travelling faster. She watched it reach the road and cross it, a dark, molten barrier four feet high, spreading out in width with every second that passed.

When it reached the far side of the road it plunged in an angry red waterfall over the cliff face to the valley below. It filled the little ravine like the waves of a heavy, ponderous sea, piling up slowly and forever rolling on.

She began to run again. She ran till her heart seemed ready to burst, down and down, with that burning smell in her nostrils and utter despair in her heart. Small, incandescent rocks were thrown out of the new crater at intervals to burst in the cooler air above it like a gigantic firework display, and their fragments fell behind and before her. She did not know how she escaped injury, but presently she realized that she was beyond the hail of ash, running over a smoother road, with green grass, not yet scorched, on either side of her.

A herd of small white goats huddled for protection beneath a group of young almond trees. They were bigger than the goats of El Teide, a finer breed, and pure white. She realized that there were dozens of them scattered about the valley, and they began to bleat piteously as she approached. Somewhere, she thought, there must be shelter.

It was then that she saw the house, perched high on a terrace ledge above the valley floor. It was not very big, but it had a comforting red roof and smoke— ordinary smoke—rising in a steady white column from its single wide chimney.

"Philip!" she sobbed. "Philip!" and ran towards it.

The house was empty. She went in through the doorway and called again and again. There was no reply. The house was small, built in the usual style of the Spanish *hacienda* round an enclosed court, where a fountain had once played. It was silent now, and the garden beyond the shaded *patio* was overgrown and neglected.

Yet someone had been there quite recently. A fire of roughly-hewn logs smouldered beneath the huge open chimney in the stone-flagged kitchen and there was evidence of a recent meal on the heavily-carved table.

She searched from room to room. The house had

evidently been lived in up to a few hours ago. There were two bedrooms and a central living-room, with windows overlooking the valley, and on one of the beds she found the jacket Philip had worn when he had set out from San Lozaro in pursuit of Conchita. Beneath it lay a revolver.

She stood staring at the weapon for several minutes before she could think again clearly. Philip would never have left the valley without his coat and his gun. He was here, somewhere.

The deathly stillness of the house drove her outside, but the garden was almost as still. An ominous, waiting silence hovered in the air, a sense of inevitable doom. Even the goats were quiet now, huddled in a pathetic little group on the bare outcrop of rock above her.

A choking sensation of panic rose into her throat, but she tried to crush it down in the need for action. If Philip were here, somewhere, he might be lying hurt in one of the many deep ravines running down to the valley itself. If he were here at all, he must surely need her help.

Standing on the tiny, overgrown terrace, she scanned the hillsides, trying not to look too often towards the thick pall of vapour which marked the stealthy progress of the lava stream, trying not to think of the road which had been closed behind her.

It was then that she noticed the peculiar behavior of a small group of the white goats standing on a pinnacle far above the house. They appeared to be agitated, bleating and scrambling up and down over the rough scree, sure-footed in their native element but not so sure in purpose. The encroaching stream of lava was behind them, and suddenly they began to run.

They came down in a thin white line towards the little plateau where the house stood, leaping and clambering from rock to rock, bleating piteously, but every now and then they would pause to look back at the sharp pinnacles they had just abandoned.

Below the jagged peaks of rock there was a small escarpment running out in a ledge for a hundred yards or so before it fell precipitously to an arid *barranco* far beneath. The goats, she supposed, would graze up there, although there did not appear to be any foothold.

Then, somehow, she knew that she must go there. Instinct warned her of danger, and she tried to thrust the memory of Julio from her mind. She did not think that either Julio or Conchita was still in the valley. Only Philip.

Fear lent wings to her feet. She ran, stumbled, tripped and ran again. Before she had reached the escarpment her shirt was torn and her hands bleeding, but she had no time to notice these superficial things. She passed the herd of goats, noting subconsciously how long and silky their hair was and how piteously they looked at her, but she could not stop. Soon the others had joined the herd, but she passed them, too.

She went up in their tracks, climbing, holding on to the rock with her bare hands, digging her nails into whatever soil she could find when there was no other way of helping herself up.

On the level stretches she ran again, half-sobbing, wondering how near the lava was. It did not seem to matter now. All that mattered was Philip and the thought, driven into her mind with each advancing step, that he needed her. She would not allow herself to believe him dead.

She reached the ledge and lay panting in the fierce heat of the sun. It had broken through the brazen cloud of volcanic smoke and stood scorchingly above the distant peaks, pitiless, beating down upon the rapidly dying valley with no promise of respite in the blue surrounding sky. It was a sun to be hated in that moment, sapping her strength, making the way more difficult for her, clouding her vision as her eyes struggled against it.

Moving to the edge of the escarpment, she looked cautiously down. The deep ravine appeared to be empty. She turned away, a despairing sob racking her from head to foot. What now? What now, Philip?

It was then that she saw the fragment of silk caught on a branch of a stunted tamarisk. It hung limply, but it was still too vividly scarlet to have been there very long. The sun would have bleached it if it had been there for more than a day, or the goats would have eaten it. And Julio had been wearing a scarlet silk shirt when he had left San Lozaro!

Her hands trembling visibly, she caught at the limp

548

scrap of material. It was the pocket of a shirt and it bore the initials J. H. embroidered within each other.

Julio!

There was no sign of struggle anywhere, but as she looked about her she was sure that Julio had been there. And so had Philip. She was as certain as if she had seen them together, seen them locked in a deathly struggle, perhaps, or in bitter argument.

There could have been some sort of accident——

In the breathless air she crawled back to the edge of the escarpment and within minutes she saw a movement far down in the ravine. Shading her eyes and focusing them intently on that one spot, she saw the first evidence of the accident she had feared. The vegetation was thick down there and it had been recently broken, crushed by the fall of a heavy body from a considerable height.

Without thought, without waiting to consider any personal danger, she was making her way down.

Somehow she found the necessary footholds and the grips she needed for her hands. In places the rock itself burned her where the full heat of the sun had been on it, but she was far beyond the consideration of discomfort now.

She reached Philip in under an hour.

He stirred as she dropped to her knees beside him, but she knew that he was not conscious and she gathered him into her arms for an endless moment while her lips moved stiffly in prayer.

"Dear God!" she whispered. "Dear God——" but no more would come. Slowly, carefully, she ran her hands over his crumpled body, but she had no real knowledge of broken bones. All she knew with any certainty was that his heart was still beating, although he seemed to be breathing with difficulty.

What was she to do? She looked about her at the almost impenetrable vegetation on every side and up to the arid waste of rock and scree where only the cactus had taken root. To go back by the way she had come was impossible if she had to support Philip, and to leave him here——

She pushed the suggestion aside. She could not, dared not leave him, even to try to find another way back to the house.

549

Her eyes fastened on a hovering bird of prey far above the highest rock pinnacles and she shivered. Somehow, and in some way, they must reach shelter.

"Felicity——?"

She had not been looking at him and in that moment his eyes had opened. Endlessly, it seemed, they gazed at each other, minds probing, heart searching heart.

"How did you get here?" he asked at last.

"I rode up. I had Treasure——"

She remembered how the horse had gone, fleeing before the terror that slid down from the mountain peak, but she would not let her thoughts dwell on the road, the trap that had closed behind her.

"You followed me up here?"

"Yes, Philip." She knelt down beside him again. "We must get away, back to the house," she urged. "You've been hurt. I must get you out of the sun."

He passed a hand uncertainly across his eyes and slowly the colour began to come back into his face. With it, too, came a dawning realization of their present predicament. He turned his eyes to the serried mountain peaks above them, his brows drawn in a dark line.

"We've got to get out of here," he said tautly. "We haven't a lot of time to lose."

She did not tell him that time was already lost. There was only one road and that had been eaten up by the lava.

"Do you think you can stand—even walk a little way?" she asked, keeping her voice as level as she could. "We ought to get into the shade."

She kept reiterating that, as if it was the most important thing, but each minute held its own importance. Philip rolled over on his side, stifling a groan as he slowly tried muscles that were wrenched and sore from his broken fall. But he could sit up; he could, after a moment, stand.

She stood beside him with a prayer of thankfulness in her heart as he shook the effects of oblivion from him.

"Where is Julio?" he asked curtly.

"He has gone." She was sure of that.

"I told him to take Conchita back to San Lozaro." Once more he drew his hand across his eyes, forcing his scattered thoughts into coherence "There were all the signs of an eruption——"

His eyes went swiftly to the smoking mountainside above them and suddenly his jaw tightened.

"How long have I been here?" he demanded. "That damned fall—the boulder coming away just as I had reached the ledge——"

"I don't know, Philip."

Her voice was suddenly shaken, all her courage gone, and he put an arm about her, comforting and close.

"All right," he said, "we won't think about it. I came down to get the rest of the goats. I wanted to herd them out of the valley before the trouble really started."

She looked up from the shelter of his arms to discover that his face and eyes were grimmer than his tone. He was trying not to frighten her, but she already knew. They were trapped up here in his silent valley, prisoners of the fierce wrath of the mountains, cut off on every side from any hope of rescue. There was no way of escape.

Swiftly his eyes searched the face of the rock.

"We can make it," he said, "if we reach the escarpment."

No, she thought desperately, there's the road. The road cut off now by a black, seething wall with a heart of fire.

"Are you sure you're not hurt?" she asked quickly. "Are you sure there's no other way we can go—back to the house?"

He looked round at the vegetation spreading on all sides, at the spears of cacti quivering in the heat.

"There isn't a chance that way," he said. "We've got to climb."

Slowly, laboriously, they began the journey back up the cliff face. It seemed impossible to Felicity that she had ever come down that way unaided, and Philip's jaw hardened when she spoke of it.

"What made you come?" he demanded almost roughly.

"I had to get to you. I followed Julio up into the valley, but I missed the road. I was well on my way to Las Canadas when I realized that I had come too far. By the time I got back to the top of the valley, Julio and Conchita must have gone."

His mouth tightened, his blue eyes narrowing as he said: "What made you follow Julio?"

"I—he had used threats." She could not tell him anything but the truth now. "I thought I might be in time to stop him doing—anything rash."

The narrowed eyes went beyond her to the twisted tamarisk clinging precariously to the edge of the escarpment.

"I see," he said, but that was all.

He turned, helping her up the final, steeper stretch until they lay, exhausted by their long effort, on the ledge.

From there Philip could see the mountain road for the first time. Felicity watched his face as the blue eyes took in the details of that twisted landscape, the wreaths of smoke and the black, tortuous stream moving silently, ruthlessly towards them.

His hand fastened on her arm.

"We haven't a moment to spare," he said.

"Philip!" She turned to face him. "The road's closed. The lava is over the road."

He stared at her as if he couldn't believe her, as if what she had just told him must be impossible.

"It can't be," he said. "It can't have got that far—not so quickly."

"It's three hours——"

He continued to look at her for a moment in silence, and then he gripped her by the hand.

"Come on," he said. "Run!"

They ran towards the house, with the herd of white goats following at their heels.

"How did you get down?" he asked when they were out of the glare of the sun. "Where were you when the first eruption occurred?"

"I had just come into the valley. I thought it was thunder at first, and then—then I couldn't really be mistaken. The whole side of the mountain seemed to go up in the air. I was terrified," she confesed. "I think I must have stood for a long time not knowing what to do." She shivered at the memory. "It was fascinating, Philip, in a ghastly sort of way."

"Were you cut off?" he demanded.

"Not at first."

"Then——" He caught her by the shoulders, searching her face. "My God! why did you come on?" he demanded. "Didn't you *know* you would be cut off? Didn't you know how quickly the lava would move once it got started. You fool!" His voice was shaken, angry, defeated. "You amazing fool! Why didn't you go back? Why, in heaven's name, didn't you go *back?*"

"I knew you were here. I had to get to you, Philip."

It sounded quite simple, put like that. She had to come to him. For a moment longer he stood staring at her, and then he plunged into the shadowed house.

"I've got to go up to the road and see what chance there is," he decided. "There's no other way out."

She could have told him how slim their chances were, but she knew that he would not be satisfied by anything short of personal endeavour.

"I can't leave you behind and come back for you," he said after a moment's thought. "There wouldn't be time. We've got to make it together."

"Yes, Philip."

She watched him put his jacket on over his thin shirt. The skin beneath it was torn and lacerated, but there was no time for first aid. He took the discarded revolver and slipped it into his belt. Subconsciously she wondered if it were loaded and what Philip used it for. Probably to shoot crows. The great carrion crows were often black over a spot on the hillside between the clumps of cacti where a mountain goat had died or fallen, injured, from a rock.

When they began to climb they cut out as many bends in the road as they could, scrambling over the rough scree and between the red boulders, but long before they had reached the top Philip was aware that their fate was sealed.

Felicity saw his jaw grow taut and a pulse begin to hammer above his temple as his eyes scanned the ring of mountains which closed Lozaro Alto in. On three sides they frowned down, cold, black, formidable, the fierce guardians of a grim landscape which might have been torn from Dante's Inferno. On the fourth side was the narrow entrance to the valley where the road had been. Now there was only the slow, relentless stream of the lava.

It had broadened and deepened even in the short space of time occuppied by their journey to the house and back, sealing them in, confronting them with a burning, impassable sea of molten rock and stone.

Philip turned.

"We must go back," he said. "We must try some other way."

CHAPTER IX

TOWARDS THE DAWN

BEFORE they reached the house again, the second warning of eruption deafened their ears. It appeared to come from under their very feet this time, but the new crater, when it opened, was smaller than the first and only half a mile away. There was less out-throw, but it seemed more violent because one half of the valley was already in shade. The sun, sinking towards the west, had deserted it.

Philip pushed Felicity towards the doorway.

"Go in and see what you can do about something hot to drink," he commanded. "I want to have a look round."

She knew that he was giving her something definite to do so that her mind might be taken off their predicament, if only for a short while. She would rather have gone with him, but she sensed that he wanted to go alone. He knew the valley from end to end. If there was any way of escape other than the road, he would already know it.

Looking up at the great, jagged peaks which surrounded them and back to his tense, controlled face, she felt that she already knew the answer.

She brewed coffee over the fire, listening with a fast-beating heart to the distant rumblings which she could no longer mistake for thunder. The whole earth seemed to be in terrible upheaval, and the final eruption shook the house visibly.

She stood in the centre of the room and watched the four walls cave in. They bulged and quivered and bulged a second time, while beyond them the whole valley trembled.

Felicity put her hands over her eyes, waiting for the final crash, waiting to be smothered by the falling roof and the dust of crumbling masonry, but when she opened them again the house was still intact. The roof was still above her head. Plaster had fallen and every pane of glass lay shattered in a million fragments on the tessellated floor, but the house itself was still standing.

Reaction set in as a tense, breathless silence filled the valley, and in that moment Philip reached the open doorway. He strode across the room towards her, holding her close.

"It's all right, *querida*," he said. "It's over now. There will be no more shocks."

Helplessly she clung to him, aware of how alone she had felt there in the house by herself while he had been away, and his arms remained about her, comforting, consoling, although he did not promise her any way of escape.

After a while they walked to the shattered window. Outside, the valley was very still, the sub-tropic night close and dark except for the fiery little craters on the mountain's face with their plumes of sulphurous smoke rising into the still, warm air.

There was no light in the room behind them. Both lamps had been shattered by that final, violent shock, and only when he moved nearer to the window and stood between her and the strange, orange-yellow glow from the craters could she see Philip's face at all clearly. Silhouetted sharply against the night, his profile was still hard, but there was a pity and a regret in his eyes which she had never seen there before.

"Philip," she said, "I think I want to know the truth. There's no way out, is there?"

Her voice had been quite steady. The fear that had been in her heart up till now had gone.

"We can do nothing," he said, "until the morning."

And somewhere, out there in the night, the stream of lava was creeping stealthily towards them.

"The mountains?" she asked, looking towards the savage, serrated summits above them. "We could not climb them?"

"It would be almost impossible, even in daylight."

She turned towards him.

"If you were alone, Philip," she suggested, "you would take that risk."

"No," he said decisively, but she knew that he was not telling her the truth.

He would not wait here in the valley like some trapped animal until the lava reached him. He would climb high and risk whatever perils the treacherous crags presented, but he knew that she could not climb so far.

"How long could we—stay here, Philip, if we escaped the lava stream?" she asked slowly.

He shrugged, turning towards her with nothing but the truth in his eyes.

"It would eventually force us up on to the peaks," he admitted. "We might be able to live there for a day or two."

"There's—Julio," she whispered, dry-lipped. "Julio and Conchita must have got back to San Lozaro by now."

"Yes," he agreed stonily, "there's Julio."

"He wouldn't let us remain up here—trapped like this!" she said urgently.

"Julio," he answered, "may do nothing until the morning."

He had no faith in the events of the night. She understood that now and felt sick and afraid again, but she would not let him see how weak she was.

"Your back," she said instead. "You've been hurt, Philip, when you fell. You must let me see to it."

His smile was dry.

"It's nothing," he said. "A graze or two."

"All the same," she persisted, "you must let me wash away the blood."

He turned towards the fire that had been scattered on the stone hearth by the final eruption.

"I suppose we can spare the water," he said. "I brought in a supply this morning for the goats."

"Tell me about the valley," she said as he raked the wood embers together and refilled the kettle which had been spilled.

Crouching before the hearth while he nursed the fire into a blaze, he said whimsically:

"Can there be anything you don't already know? It's cruel and savage, yet it can also be quiet and kind. It was my home," he added simply.

"And you wanted to come back to it," she said.

He nodded.

"I have always wanted to come back."

And now the volcano was swallowing it up! The black stream of the lava would obliterate it, in time. All that he had hoped for, all that he had dreamed of achieving, would be lost. She saw the granite set of his jaw and knew how fiercely he was resenting this ill-timed stroke of nature which had torn the future out of his grasp.

"What did you mean to do, Philip?" she asked as she poured water into the basin he had brought and began to bathe the lacerated skin on his back.

The blue eyes narrowed as he put the kettle on to boil for the second time and righted the overturned coffee jug.

"I had planned to restore the valley with the help of the woman I loved."

"María?" she said, not holding back from the name as she had once done, because there could be no reserve between them now.

His face, in the glow from the fire, looked drawn and heavily shadowed, with a new weariness about the mouth, but his eyes remained blue and alert on hers.

"María—at first," he said. "She loved the valley. She used to come here to attend to the goats. It was a small herd at first, but I have built it up steadily since she died."

Somehow, that was all that she needed to know.

"I kept the herd as a—sort of memorial to her," he said quietly. "She was simple and sweet—easily impressed, perhaps, but that was to be expected. She had never been away from San Lozaro in all her life. She had never been deeply in love, I suppose, until the end."

It was an odd thing for him to say, Felicity thought, but she could not go on questioning him. They had come very close in that moment and the hours ahead of them were her own. Whatever happened, they were together now, in the fullness of understanding, at last.

She leaned her head against his arm.

"I love you, Philip," she said. "There has never been anyone but you."

He turned, pulling her towards him.

"You mean that?" he asked.

"Yes. Yes, I mean it, Philip!"

She closed her eyes as his lips found hers. It was no

longer a demanding kiss, fiercely possessive, with the flare of passion behind it as on that other occasion when he had found her in Julio's arms. It was gentle, protective, kind, the kiss that Philip might have given to María up here among the mountains they had both loved.

He had seen María as his gentle, simple shepherdess, and he had come here often to perpetuate her memory.

Vaguely she wondered about death as she lay in his arms. It was all about them, but her fear had gone. The strange calmness of unknowable things seemed to stretch away and away, through the sealed valley and the island to the sea—on, on into a vast infinity where there were no tears, no regrets, no sorrow.

Suspended above it, she felt it in the comfort of Philip's arms.

"Try to sleep," he encouraged after a while. "It won't be dark for very long."

Her hands clung to him.

"Don't leave me, Philip."

"No," he said, "I won't leave you."

She closed her eyes, thinking that she would not sleep. The fire was warm and comforting, with a kindly yellow glow. It wrapped her round, laying the fingers of drowsiness across her brows. The coffee, she remembered, had been sweet and warm. . . .

An hour later—two—three—she opened her eyes to the awareness of light. She had no idea what time it was, but the light she saw was surely not the dawn. It filtered in from the room beyond where she lay, through a faint grey oblong which had once been a window. She had been in that room, but now she was lying in the adjacent bedroom. Philip must have carried her there while she slept.

Strange that she had not felt any movement, the strengthening grip of his arms, the increased beating of his heart as he had borne her through the communicating door. Had the coffee he had given her to drink been slightly drugged?

He had laid her on the bed and drawn a blanket over her and she had slept, mercifully unconscious of the passing hours.

The light she watched was faint, a pale, pearly grey against the encircling darkness. Was Philip, too, asleep?

She put the blanket aside, trying to stifle the sudden fear in her heart, and sat up. There was no sound from the other room, no sound in all the quiet house. No sound in the valley but the occasional sharp snap of a tree falling unobserved in the darkness. The heat, she realized, was stifling. It was probably that and the strengthening light which had wakened her, yet it was no more than the false dawn which quivered above the shattered mountain peaks.

Silently she got to her feet and as silently crossed the room. If Philip were asleep she would not disturb him, although she longed for the comfort of his arms, for the security which his steady gaze could bring her in this moment of fear.

Beads of perspiration stood out along the line of her upper lip and on her brow, and the oppressive heat caught at her throat. The lava was nearer now. It had crept down, inch by inch, during the night, and the whole air was full of the heavy, sulphurous smell of it. She could feel it advancing on the house like a cautious beast of prey, waiting to spring, but she would not let herself think of the moment when it would be upon them.

Reaching the open doorway, she looked into the room beyond.

Philip had allowed the fire to die, but there was still a glowing ember or two on the wide stone hearth which could be blown quickly into a flame. There was no need for a fire's comforting warmth now; the scorching breath of the volcano had come too near.

She looked at the fragments of charred wood, fascinated for a moment, and then she was aware of Philip standing beside the desk in the corner. He was half turned from her, but the slow, deliberate movements of his hands could not be mistaken. She heard the little click of metal on metal as he dropped the bullets into place and the snap of the safety-catch against the barrel as he drove it home. Then, slowly and deliberately, he opened the shallow centre drawer of the desk and laid the revolver in it, ready.

He stood looking down at it for several seconds, his profile etched against the strengthening light, and then he closed the drawer and turned to find her watching him

For a split second Felicity thought that the stern jaw was set in anger, and then he held out his arms to her and she ran to their shelter

He held her without speaking, closely, protectingly, his free hand caressing her hair, her head pressed down against the taut hardness of his chest.

"Say—'All right, *querida!*'" she whispered shakily.

He turned her face up, kissing the tears from her eyes.

"All right, *querida!*" he repeated. "All right!"

He held her as the light grew and strengthened behind them, and then, very gently, he put her from him and went to the window.

When he came back his mouth was grim and his eyes were hard, and she did not ask him what their chances were. At least they had survived the night.

"We've got to make a bolt for it," he said briskly. "We've got to try the mountains."

He looked at her searchingly, seeming to be satisfied with what he saw, although he stood quite deliberately between her and the window alcove, blocking her view of the upper valley and the way to the road.

Or what remained of the road, she thought.

"We'll take what we can with us," he said, "but first of all we ought to get something to drink. Something hot. It will be piercingly cold once we begin to climb."

Briefly, almost matter-of-factly he began to check over the store of food still left in the cupboard on the wall. There was coffee and some maize biscuits and a few thin wafers of goat cheese wrapped in a piece of white muslin. He searched for a flask as Felicity knelt down to stir the wood under the kettle to a blaze, and when she had made more coffee he put the things he had collected into a canvas satchel and came to stand beside her. She thought that his eyes looked bitter, but he did not speak.

The water in the kettle steamed its warning and he poured it over the coffee powder he had put into the flask. Then he poured the coffee from the jug into the two cups she had put ready on the table.

"Don't put anything into mine this time, Philip," she said. "I can manage without it."

He turned, his mouth relaxing in a smile.

"I wanted you to get some sleep," he said. "But now I think I want your company more." He took her by the shoulders, looking down long and searchingly into her eyes. "We're getting out, Felicity," he said between his teeth. "Somehow!"

She did not look behind her at the encroaching lava as they left the house. She did not need to look. It was near enough to be felt.

Philip gave it one backward glance, but that was all. She had seen him take the revolver from the desk along with some papers and stuff it into the holster on his belt, but she had not looked at that either. He meant that they should die quickly, if they had to die.

Immediately they had left the house they were forced to climb, with a pathetic little procession of white goats leaping ahead of them, as if bent on showing them the way.

To Felicity the face of the mountain looked inexorable, frowning down at them with a gaunt and forbidding austerity as they toiled upwards. There seemed to be no footholds, yet Philp found them for her, again and again.

It was better, she thought, not to look up at the grey façade of rock which seemed to repulse them with every step they took. There was nothing to be seen but rock, nothing but the jagged pinnacles high above them, silhouetted remotely against the sky.

It was a sky flushed with the pearly-pink streamers of dawn now, a warm, friendly sky, although it looked down upon a valley torn asunder. Huge rocks and scorched trees lay in the path of the lava, overlaid by a deathly stillness. No life that could possibly escape had remained in that stricken place. No bird sang. There was not even a hovering hawk to chill their blood with its suggestion of death.

No sound but the frightened bleating of the white goats as they leaped from crag to crag where no human foot could possibly follow.

After an hour, when they had climbed only a little way, Philip drew Felicity into the shelter of a rock. A penetrating coldness had come down from the mountain-tops with the dawn, chilling them to the bone in spite of the physical effort they had been making, and he unscrewed the flask top and held it out to her.

"Shouldn't we keep it a little longer?" she asked stiffly. "Till we really need it, Philip."

"There's plenty," he said, his eyes scanning the mountainsides. "Plenty for our needs."

Her teeth chattered against the rim of the cup as she drank and she felt ashamed because part of her unsteadiness was fear.

Philip put a protective arm about her shoulders.

"The sun will soon be up," he promised, but she knew that when the sun came they would be exhaustingly exposed to its merciless glare.

Their position seemed hopeless, but Philip would not discuss it in such a light.

"We've got to keep moving," he said. "We've got to put as much distance as we can between us and the valley floor." He glanced at his watch. "The average lava flow moves at about twenty yards a minute. It's a ponderous, slow affair, and we've got to beat it."

She saw the small, quick pulse hammering in his cheek and the determined set of his lips as the blue eyes travelled to the face of the rock above them and on to the distant mountain rim.

"I wish," she said, "that you had gone on alone."

"Don't talk nonsense," he admonished. "I shall never be able to forget that you came here in search of me."

His voice was suddenly humble, unlike the voice she knew so well.

"I had to come," she said. "There was no other way, Philip."

He took her by the hand, helping her to her feet before her limbs had time to stiffen.

"We've got to go on," he repeated. "I'm going to rope us together in a minute, but I think you should be able to reach the next ledge before I need to do that."

It took them more than an hour to reach the narrow band of rock and loose scree which he had indicated, and when she stumbled on to it she all but confessed herself beaten. She was completely exhausted. They had scarcely exchanged more than half a dozen words during the perilous ascent, and these had been Philip's barked commands uttered in a voice that was sharp with tension.

She had no experience of climbing and the effort she had made on the slopes of The Peak was child's play to this. Her breath sobbed out between her teeth as if it had been cut from her lungs by a sharp knife and her knees had all but given way as Philip had pulled her up the last difficult stretch.

Something in her longed to tell him that she couldn't go on, but she crushed it down. She could not let him see her cowardice. He would despise her for the weakness, turn from her, perhaps, in contempt.

Yet she had found nothing but kindness and compassion in him. The reason for his accident had been that he had gone back to find a straying kid severed from the herd in a moment of panic as the frightened little animals had plunged down from the quivering mountain crest.

"There isn't any shelter here, but we'll rest for a bit," he said. "You're tired."

There was nothing for her to rest against but the bare face of the rock. He put his arm along it and she slid down against it, pillowing her head on his shoulder.

For a long moment he did not move. Then, almost imperceptibly, she felt him stiffen. He appeared to be listening, his ears more attuned to the silence than her own.

Another eruption? Her heart contracted at the prospect, but Philip had thrown back his head and was looking at the sky.

"A plane?" she whispered, wondering why she had never thought of it before.

"Yes," he said. His mouth was still grimly compressed. He would not buoy her up with any false hope of their deliverance. "Do you hear it now?"

She nodded eagerly, her heart surging upwards with that joyous sound as her eyes attempted to follow his.

"Over there!" he said, pointing to the left of the sun which had now topped the highest peaks. "A plane. A helicopter, by the look of it!"

There was sudden, swift elation in his eyes now, the forerunner of hope, but there was caution, too, in his voice as he added:

"It may be on a routine flight, but we've got to make them see us, whatever it is."

He pulled off his shirt and began to wave it as the plane came nearer, a scrap of white silk sending out its signal of distress from an infinitesimal foothold on the bare mountain face. Would it—could it possibly be seen from all that distance away? Would anybody be looking out? The eruption would have been recorded, of course, but this might be no more than an observation flight to assess the damage which had been done by the throw-out of lava or even just to plot the position of the new craters for future geographical research.

It could be anything or nothing. It could be release or the abandonment of hope.

The violently-rotating blades brought the small black object in the sky slowly nearer. The helicopter reached the valley, hovered above it, and moved gradually away. Felicity's heart sank into utter defeat. She knew that she could not go on; she knew that she would never be able to scale these dreadful, precipitous rock faces, even with Philip's help. She was completely exhausted.

She could not look at Philip because she knew that he would not go on without her.

The noise of the helicopter died away, growing fainter and fainter in the distance, and the silence descended on the valley again. More deeply than before, Felicity thought. Neither of them could trust themselves to speak. Philip sat with his head in his hands for a moment, his brows deeply furrowed, and Felicity stared at him without thought. Her brain felt numb. She was beyond reasoning now, frozen into a silence which was part of the heavy, brooding silence all about them.

Then, as if it were a mere echo of the sound they had first heard, thrown back from the steep mountain wall to mock them, the noise of the engine came again, faintly at first and then rising to a great crescendo of sound as the plane came over the ridge of the peaks. It seemed to touch their cruel, jagged edges in its slow, purposeful flight, and it came straight towards them.

"They're searching!" Philip's voice was low and tense. "They've been sent out to look for us." He put his arm about her, drawing her close. "There can be no other possible explanation for such a low flight."

Felicity watched the plane's progress, fascinated into silence by its steady, hovering movement close up there on the ridge. Her heart was beating madly, thankfully, yet she could not see how anything could land in such a place.

"There's a ledge," Philip explained. "A sort of plateau. It's another hundred feet up. They're making for it in the hope that we can reach there or that they can climb down to us." He looked round at her pale face and fear-filled eyes. "We've *got* to make it, *querida!*" he encouraged. "Do you hear me? We've got to make it. The plateau is our only hope."

"Yes," she answered in a dazed voice. "Yes—I'll try."

"You've got to," he repeated relentlessly. "You've got to make it. We can't go out like this now."

He pulled her to her feet, steadying her with gentle hands.

"I'll help you all I can," he promised. "Don't look back, and don't look up too often. Just do as I say."

She nodded as he knotted the rope about her waist. Neither of them was equipped for climbing and more than once Philip's smooth-soled riding-boots slipped on the rock, threatening to hurl them both into oblivion. A kind of numb tenacity crystallized in Felicity's mind, keeping her going, moving her limbs with automatic precision when her brain grew too tired to control them.

They appeared to climb for an eternity, with the hum of the plane above them telling them that it had not yet made a succesful landing. It hovered and swerved and hovered again, and it was minutes before she realized that the powerful engine had cut out.

Nothing seemed to matter now but the desperate, upward toil to reach the ledge. For yards Philip all but carried her, straining on the rope, and she heard his breath driven out in quick, painful gasps as he struggled on.

Properly equipped, it might have been an easy enough ascent for him, but he had nothing but the rope and his two bare hands, and he was further handicapped by her utter lack of knowledge. She could only be a terrible burden to him, Felicity thought.

Once, in a mad moment of despair, she even thought of slipping free from the rope, but Philip had knotted it too securely for that. He allowed her very little slack and no time to fumble with the knot. He drove her on and up, relentlessly, but without a word.

Exhaustion began to cloud her vision. I'll never reach the top, she thought, but I can't let Philip down. I've got to go on trying. I've got to go on!

The rope slackened and she sank back against the rock face, trembling. Philip was above her, but his voice came down to her quite clearly.

"It's now, *querida,* or never! You've got to come up to me."

She closed her eyes, swaying giddily on the narrow foothold he had found for her. She did not want to go on. She did not want to move. She felt sick and giddy because of the height, and she dared not look down or up.

"*Querida,* are you ready?"

The rope tightened and she put her hands round it, but she could not answer him. She felt herself swinging out and back again towards the rock, but this time she caught hold, pulling herself upwards. There was no hold for her feet.

For a moment of panic she felt them swing free, like a pendulum, back and forth across the rock face, with only her hands gripping and the steady pull of the rope from where Philip stood above her. Then she raised them a fraction of an inch and found what was little more than a toe-hold.

Trembling, she waited, closing her eyes.

"Come up slowly, *querida!*" Philip's voice was nearer than she would have believed. "Just one more try!"

When she had made the ledge she lay panting against the loose scree, unable to move for a moment which held neither thankfulness nor relief. There seemed to be no more feeling in her, nothing in the world but distance and height and the merciless glare of the fully-risen sun.

Then, strongly, securely, Philip's arms encircled her, supporting, comforting arms that shut out all the world.

"That was it!" he said. "It's going to be easy now."

She never quite remembered the last stretch, the final effort which took them on to the plateau. It must have been an easier climb, because Philip did not have to use the rope so much. He kept it round her waist, however, and firmly attached about his own.

The navigator of the helicopter pulled them up the last rough incline to the flat green surface where his machine had landed, but she was hardly aware of being placed safely in the cabin, of Philip seated beside her and the engines revving up for the precarious take-off.

Before she realized it they were high above the valley, and in less time than it took her to collect her thoughts they had landed on the firm, dry sand of Las Canadas, where a small fleet of cars stood waiting.

There was an ambulance standing ready, but after one swift look in her direction, Philip waved it aside.

"I shall take her home," he said. "She will be all right. There was no accident."

People surged about them, questioning him volubly in Spanish, but he gave them the barest details, determinedly making his way towards his own car, which he had noticed parked a little way from the others in the shade of the rest hut.

Sabino got down from the driver's seat, inarticulate with relief. In the back Sisa and Conchita were waiting. Sisa was in tears.

"Felicity! Felicity!" she cried. "I thought El Teide had swallowed you up! I thought you and Philip were dead——"

"It was not El Teide that erupted," Philip consoled her. "Only the little mountain above Lozaro Alto."

"But the valley!" Sisa wailed. "It has gone—and you loved it so much!"

"Perhaps it had to go," he said, his eyes suddenly remote. "These things happen to us, Sisa. One day we may be able to make another and easier road to Lozaro Alto. Who knows?"

Felicity was remembering that it was on the high, dangerously winding road to Lozaro Alto that María had lost her life. It was the road to the valley which had held Philip a prisoner to unhappy memory all these months. And now the road had gone, and the valley with it. Years must pass before they would be able to open it again, but they were the years in which he would fulfil a promise.

Philip would continue to make a home for Robert Hallam's children at San Lozaro, and the look he gave Felicity told her that he still expected her help.

Conchita's hands were trembling as she guided Felicity into the car.

"It is all because of me that this has happened," she

568

cried. "I am to blame for it all! Like María, I have been blind to Philip's goodness and his wisdom. Like María I have fallen so easily a victim to Don Rafael's charm!"

Philip turned abruptly towards the driver's seat and got in behind the wheel. He seemed determined to interrupt Conchita's spate of unhappy self-recrimination at all costs.

"Where is Julio?" he asked sternly.

"At La Laguna." Conchita bit her lip, fighting back the tears of humiliation which threatened to flow at any minute now. "We are all most ungrateful, Philip, but Julio, too, is sorry for what he has done."

"He—reported our position immediately, then?"

Philip's tone was dry and Conchita hesitated before she answered his question.

"Almost immediately, Philip."

"Once you had managed to persuade him? I see," Philip said almost indifferently.

"Please do not hold it against him," Conchita begged. "Now that he knows—all the truth about María, too, he is sorry for what he has done."

Philip's mouth hardened as the car plunged downwards towards the tree line. His hands gripped the wheel till the knuckles stood out white against his taut skin, but he said nothing.

Conchita, too, lapsed into silence, and Felicity was left with that last poignant sentence of her cousin's ringing in her ears all the way to San Lozaro. "Now that he knows all the truth about María, too, he is sorry for what he has done"!

What was the truth about María? What had Philip kept hidden about her tragic death for all these months? Conchita had known and never told anyone until she could no longer keep it from her brother, and it had sent Julio to La Laguna in search of the rescue plane which had saved Philip's life.

But before he had heard what Conchita had to say, Julio had deliberately left Philip alone in the doomed valley. He had gone off with Conchita, not caring whether Philip lived or died. Perhaps hoping that he would die.

She shivered at the suggestion that her cousin might even have been witness to Philip's accident, and a fragment of red—the torn pocket of a silk shirt—seemed to flutter mockingly before her eyes.

If he had known, Julio was guilty of murder. As guilty as he had once accused Philip of being. But now Conchita said that Julio knew the truth.

When they reached San Lozaro, Isabella was waiting for them. Her face was pale and drawn, mute evidence of the fact that she had not slept for over twenty-four hours, and she had eyes only for Philip as the car pulled up.

"The Blessed Virgin has answered my prayer!" she breathed, clasping his hand as he got out from behind the wheel. "Philip! you are safe! You have not been too badly hurt?"

"Scarcely scratched!" Blue eyes looked into brown and the blue ones smiled. "You are not to distress yourself on my account, Isabella. Not any more."

Isabella de Barrios looked at him for a moment longer with her whole heart in her eyes. She's in love with him, Felicity thought, completely and irretrievably in love, but this time she acknowledged it without jealousy and without envy. Only with the deepest, truest pity. For Isabella's love was not returned.

Philip looked across at Sabino, who had travelled in the front of the car with him.

"Find Julio," he said. "Tell him to come home. You will say, Sabino, that I sent you. He is at La Laguna. You will know best where to look for him."

He turned to help Felicity out of the car.

"Let me take care of her," Isabella said. "You, too, must rest, Philip. You have a wound on your back. It is necessary for the doctor to see it to make sure that there is nothing seriously wrong. I have sent for him to come here."

"There was a doctor waiting at Las Canadas," he told her, shrugging indifferently. "This is no more than a graze, Isabella. A flesh wound. I have had a fortunate escape, but Felicity is exhausted. Make her go to bed, if you can."

He looked at Felicity and smiled, a strange, detached smile which bade her forget the events of the past twenty-four hours, if she could.

Did it ask her, also, to forget her confession of love for him?

"Come!" Isabella urged. "You are tired. Do not try to tell me what happened until you are rested a little."

But all Felicity's weariness had dropped from her.

Physical exhaustion was something which she felt she could bear a little longer.

"Isabella," she said when they had reached the sanctuary of her own rooms, "can you tell me about María? You see," she added swiftly, "I feel that I have a right to know now."

"Yes," Isabella agreed, "I think you have that right." She drew a deep breath. " 'The truth about María'?" she repeated slowly. "In part, it is what you already know. María was in love with Philip—deeply, fondly in love with him. She had given him her promise to marry him, even as a very young girl, and she meant to keep that promise— until Rafael came along."

"Rafael——?"

Isabella nodded.

"Rafael, Marqués de Barrios," she said with shame in her voice. "The man I married. We had been married for less than a year when I knew him for what he was—a heartless and cynical philanderer. But it was too late then. I was his wife."

"But—María?"

"How can we explain such things?" Isabella sighed. "María was only another sweet and innocent child who fell victim to Rafael's charm. You may not have felt it, Felicity, but he has such charm," she added. "Even though our marriage was more or less one of arrangement between our two families, I, also, felt it. It swept me off my feet. I imagined myself to be the most fortunate girl in the whole world when he came from Spain to court me." Tears dimmed the lovely black eyes. "I was to learn later that love such as Rafael's is as light as air. Always it blows hot and cold and in the end it goes off in another direction. In the direction of the latest pretty face he stumbles across on his travels away from Zamora."

Felicity was very white. She could not hurt Isabella unnecessarily by admitting that she had almost fallen a victim to that fatal charm on her first meeting with Rafael, but no wonder Philip had frowned on her, distrusting her on sight!

"María never meant to fall in love with Rafael, but he swept her off her feet," Isabella continued, crossing to the windows to close the shutters against the sun. "When she tried to run from him, he followed her. I don't quite know

571

whether he meant to break up Philip's marriage or not, but on the eve of her wedding to Philip, María disappeared. She left a note. In it she said that she must go away by herself to sort out her dreadful unhappiness. She was confused and full of despair. Philip guessed that she would go to Lozaro Alto, but he did not follow her at once. He thought that she should be given time to search her own heart for the truth."

"He didn't—really believe that she was in love with Rafael?" Felicity whispered.

"No." Isabella shook her head. "He knew the truth, you see. María was held by no more than a hopeles fascination." She bit her lip. "Philip came to see Rafael. I met him. The Blessed Virgin forgive me! I showed him the letter Rafael had left for me that morning in which he said he was going to take María away. He asked me for his freedom, which I could never have given him. Philip knew that, and he also knew what María would feel, and so he acted to save her. He went to Lozaro Alto and found her dead."

Felicity stared at her, aghast.

"But—the accident?" she protested.

"The accident was to María and Rafael. They were coming back from Lozaro Alto in Philip's car when it went over the cliff. María had taken the car, as she often did when Philip was not using it, to drive to the valley, but Rafael was driving it when it crashed."

"And—Philip accepted the responsibility?"

Isabella nodded.

"It was his car," she pointed out. "That saved the situation as far as Philip saw it. No one would know that Rafael and María had been together. He did it for María, and because of your uncle, Robert Hallam. Philip owed a great deal to María's father, you know, and this was the way in which he sought to repay his debt. He also tried to save me the scandal." Isabella moved slowly back across the room. "Rafael had a slight concussion and a few superficial cuts and scratches from the accident, but that was all. So it was easy, you see, for Philip to send him back to Zamora on the horse he had ridden up to the valley. Rafael's own horse was returned later."

"And nothing—none of all this—came out at the inquest?"

Isabella shook her head.

"No. Philip accepted full responsibility. He was reticent about some points, and that was what led to the gossip. People said that he had been growing tired of María, because they had noticed how unhappy she had looked, and Philip would not stoop to contradict them. He had been exonerated from all blame by the court and that was all he cared about."

"I've been so unjust!" Felicity said in a choked whisper.

"But you love him," Isabella said. "And love and trust must go hand in hand." She halted before she reached the door. "You are still going to marry him?" she asked.

"If he will have me."

She could not tell Isabella that she had been torn by jealousy on her account, also, because she believed that Philip loved and admired her. She felt ashamed of her former emotions and curiously humbled by the knowledge of the trust and friendship which existed between these two. Philip had been so ready to sacrifice himself in defence of Isabella's marriage, as ready as he had been to protect María's name from scandal after her tragic death.

It was all so easy to understand now—so simple.

After Isabella had gone she lay down obediently on the bed in her darkened room, but sleep would not come. The events of the past few hours were too close, too terrible in retrospect to let her slip easily beyond consciousness. She dozed fitfully, waking at every unusual sound, and when a car drew up at the foot of the terrace steps she went out on to her balcony and looked down.

Julio got out from behind the wheel. He appeared strained and tired, with dark smudges beneath his eyes which suggested that he, also, had not slept.

Felicity drew back a little way, but he had already seen her. Before she could speak, before she could even think what he was about to do, he had caught hold of the gnarled old stem of the creeper which grew up the wall and drew himself to the level of the balcony rail.

"*Querida!*" he said. "Are you safe? Are you really safe?"

"Yes, Julio." Her heart was beating madly. "We were taken out by the helicopter you sent from La Laguna."

He swung his legs over the rail and came to stand beside her.

"I didn't mean to send it," he confessed thickly. "I

meant Philip to die. Then I discovered that you were up there with him. I even meant to—leave you with him when I knew that you must love him or you would not have gone there." His words were harsh, but his voice had trembled. "Then Isabella de Barrios came to find me. She told me the truth—the truth about María's death. That was my real reason for hating Philip——"

"I know, Julio," she said gently. "Philip did it for María, and for your father, whom he loved like a son. And now he has promised to look after you and Sisa and Conchita—to keep your home intact. It was what your father wished. It was what he asked me to help Philip to do. You will help us, will you not?"

"I suppose so." He looked down at his feet. "Are you going to stay with us? Are you going to marry him?"

A great flood of longing rose in Felicity's heart. She wanted to marry Philip more than anything else in the world, but suddenly she knew that she wanted all his love in return. Measure for measure. Her loving demanded it. Somehow, the thought of waiting for years until Philip recognized how necessary they were to each other was like putting happiness just beyond her reach.

"I don't know," she said. "I don't know, Julio!"

He backed towards the balcony rail.

"You know what you want," he said. "You ought to let Philip see."

I've already told him that I love him, Felicity thought. He knows. He ought to be sure.

The deep colour of humiliation ran up under her skin. He had shown her pity and tenderness in that moment. Nothing more.

The house was very still when she finally went down in search of the others. Philip had sent up a meal to her on a tray, but she had left much of it untouched. The *siesta* hour had passed and the sun was already well down the western sky. Isabella had gone, and Sisa and Conchita were nowhere to be seen.

"Felicity, will you come out here for half an hour?"

She had not seen Philip standing in the shadow of the palms, but she went to him at once.

"How do you feel?" he asked. "Have you managed to sleep?"

"Not very well." She looked up at him, her eyes suddenly full of tears. "There was so much to think about."

"So much of regret?" he asked.

She shook her head, turning to fumble with a spray of the trailing stephanotis which hung from the wall above them. The little star-shaped flowers sent up their perfume to fill the air between them, and Philip reached out and took her gently by the shoulders, turning her back to face him.

"Of what, then?" he asked. "What has made you sad, *querida?*" His words were gently probing. "If you have no regrets," he said as his hands tightened on her shoulders, "does it mean that you meant what you told me at Lozaro Alto?"

She looked at him, and his eyes seemed to draw her whole soul up to meet his own.

"You said that you loved me." His voice was stronger now, more commanding. In some ways it was the old, arrogant Philip who spoke. "You said it of your own free will, in a moment when nothing else in the world mattered between us, but I want you to say it again, here, in this house, where our loving will mean so much."

"You love me?" she whispered. "You love me, Philip!"

"With all my heart." His hands slipped from her shoulders to her waist, drawing her strongly to him. "I can't tell you when I knew," he said. "You must not ask me. Perhaps it was right from the beginning, when you came here with so little knowledge of this adopted country of mine but with such a brave ideal in your heart. I wanted to protect you—to take you and keep you for my own."

His lips came down on hers, gently and then possessively.

"Yes, I wanted you from the beginning," he said with absolute conviction in his voice.

"And I was foolish enough to be fascinated by—someone else at first," she whispered. "Oh, Philip! Forgive me!"

"What have I to forgive?" he asked, brushing her hair with his lips. "Nothing, *querida*—now that I know you are mine!"

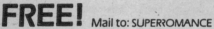